To Karen,
Keep reading!

H. A. Burns

ABSOLUTELY AMAZING eBOOKS

Published by Whiz Bang LLC, 926 Truman Avenue, Key West, Florida 33040, USA.

Cyborg Dreams: Trilogy copyright © 2018 by H.A. Burns. Electronic compilation/ paperback edition copyright © 2017 by Whiz Bang LLC. *Cyborg Dreams: The Mind Is Mine* (Volume 1) copyright © 2017. *Cyborg Dreams: The Buried Past* (Volume 2) copyright © 2017. *Cyborg Dreams: The Awakening* (Volume 3) copyright © 2018

All rights reserved. No part of this book may be reproduced, scanned, or transmitted in any form or by any means, electronic or mechanical, including photocopying, recording, or any information storage and retrieval system, without permission in writing from the publisher. Please do not participate in or encourage piracy of copyrighted materials in violation of the author's rights. Purchase only authorized ebook editions.

This is a work of fiction. Names, characters, places, and incidents either are the product of the author's imagination or are used fictitiously, and any resemblance to actual persons, living or dead, businesses, companies, events, or locales is entirely coincidental. While the author has made every effort to provide accurate information at the time of publication, neither the publisher nor the author assumes any responsibility for errors, or for changes that occur after publication. Further, the publisher does not have any control over and does not assume any responsibility for author or third-party websites or their contents. How the ebook displays on a given reader is beyond the publisher's control.

For information contact:
Publisher@AbsolutelyAmazingEbooks.com

ISBN 13: 978-1949504347
ISBN 10: 1949504344

Included in this volume:

Cyborg Dreams: The Mind Is Mine
(Volume 1)

Cyborg Dreams: The Buried Past
(Volume 2)

Cyborg Dreams: The Awakening
(Volume 3)

H.A. Burns
CYBORG
DREAMS
The Mind
Is Mine

I would like to dedicate this book to my friend Cliff Olmsted, who upon hearing about my crazy dreams told me I needed to write a book.

So, I did.

CYBORG DREAMS: The Mind of Mine

PREFACE

W*as this a dream? Really, it had to be!* Catherine thought as she tried to blink away the lights flashing in a high school hallway full of books and people floating weightless and stunned. Her fellow teacher Elisabeth looked at her in horror and confusion, as if this was her fault! Just because the shadowy man at the end of the hallway was speaking to Catherine didn't mean she knew anything about anything.

The only thing Catherine knew was that even though this somehow wasn't a dream, the man at the end of the hallway was from a dream. A recurrent, bothersome dream that she had been having for months. Every time she awoke, all she could remember was that he had been standing there, staring at her and warning her of something. Now he was just yelling at her, that she hadn't listened and it was too late.

"Why can't this be a dream?" she thought.

Then it was over. The lights were back to normal, the man was gone, and everything (and everyone) fell to the floor with a thud and a few grunts. Elisabeth, the 10th grade geometry teacher who Catherine now knew had a mean scowl, was deadlocked looking at her for an explanation. Her gaze that could kill was interrupted by Jordan, a know-it-all history teacher who seized Catherine by the arm and dragged her to her feet. In an instant they were walking to the principal's office, as if she was in trouble.

"Jordan, did you see what I saw?" she asked.

A quick nod was all the reply she could get. Elisabeth was up and on her feet, marching right behind them, scowl gone and replaced with bewilderment.

"Do you think he will listen?" she said.

Catherine responded with, "I don't know why, he never listened to me before ..."

Jordon interrupted with, "Yes, but that was before the whole world was turned upside down in front of half the school. How can he not believe you? How can anyone?"

CHAPTER 1

Shake and Quake

Catherine Newton was a simple English teacher: mousy, skinny, dull-haired and neatly dressed. She led a simple life with her simple house on a hill overlooking the red rock valley of Desert Grande, Colorado.

Her greatest pleasure was driving the windy road down the hill into the valley to work every day. It was illegal to drive a vehicle in manual mode without an emergency, but the tracker software didn't work well on the hillside, so she got away with it if she remembered to shift to autopilot once she got to the main roads. That little bit of rebelliousness, coupled with the downhill speed, was better than coffee at waking her up and making her feel alive, and she truly needed something to make her feel alive.

It had only been six months since she got assigned to this little town in the middle of nowhere, and things were already starting to feel monotonous. Of course, every town was a little town in the middle of nowhere now. The war of 2020 decimated all the major cities in the US, so everyone was relegated to controlled population towns like Desert Grande, far from the obliterated coastlines and too small to be a target for any large missile strike. She certainly couldn't hope for a better town.

As Catherine drove onto the main road, hit the autopilot button and sat back in her car seat to stare out the window at the passing scenery, she couldn't help but feel out of place. The roads were so different here: all white and smooth. Such a huge contrast to the red rock and dirt of the surrounding desert.

The company, Greggo Sands, which originated in this desert town, was responsible for the invention of the new ceramic roads. The roads harness energy from not only the seasons heating and cooling but the movement and weight of the cars on the road. It was enough to power the high school and other public buildings in the town. The company was proud of the model town and how successful the roads were implemented. Pretty soon the roads would be everywhere, so long as Greggo Sands could mine enough of the minerals they needed from the valley near Desert Grande.

Mining was constant, and small quakes from blasting could be felt in the school on a daily basis. Catherine was already used to the little quakes, and even slept right through a few major ones. She slept right through a lot of things lately, in fact her alarm this morning. She would be late for homeroom for the fourth time this month. Her sleep just wasn't what it used to be, waking dreams and nightmares of things she could not explain.

She arrived to the school, and had to slip in the back so that no one would see her coming in late. Thankfully, everyone was already in class. Her students were all busy on their assigned digital notebooks, the digiStudent Notebook, and they didn't even notice her enter the room. Catherine found her, assigned digital notebook for teachers, the digiTeacher Controller, and did roll call. Only one student absent.

"Has anyone seen Jonny Ricker?" she asked.

Lucy Gamble, a little red-haired, freckled and constantly frazzled girl answered with "He's in the bathroom; I think he is sick." Jonny walked in before she could finish the sentence, waddling and holding his belly.

"Miss Newton, can I go to the nurse?" he asked.

"Of course, Jonny, let me mark your digiStudent so they know you were sent by a teacher."

As he leaned over to grab his notebook, the floor started to shake. Another quake, typical, or so they thought. But it kept going, and jerked both Catherine and Jonny to the ground as a loud ringing "BANG" reverberated throughout the walls and floor.

Jonny hit his head on the desk and was out cold. Catherine asked Lucy to help her get Jonny to his feet. He would need stitches now and was bleeding all over the place. Catherine set the main wall to show current events, News Channel 4, and announced, "I will quiz you on current events tomorrow, so pay attention."

If she left them with nothing, they would have gone wild for sure. It was all she could think of to do and maybe by the time she got back there would be an explanation of the explosion.

Dragging bleeding Jonny, with the help of wincing Lucy, down the hallway she ran into Jordan Muntz. Literally. He almost fell to the ground, but caught himself by clinging onto the lockers. He was a wiry middle-aged man who happened to be the most boring History teacher in the world (according to a few of her students anyway).

"Watch it!" he yelled.

"Excuse me, but you ran into us," Catherine said as she wondered how in the world he could have missed seeing the three of them ambling through the hallway. She had been staring at the gaping wound in Jonny's head and didn't even see Jordan until he was bashed into the lockers.

Un-phased, he proceeded down the hall with what looked like purpose, though he always seemed to have purpose and authority like he owned the place.

Nurse Betty Green was old, kind, and going senile. She looked like something out of a cartoon, with pink hair and horned glasses. Her make-up was so caked it flaked and the red lipstick did nothing for her thin wrinkled lips but accentuate the depth of the wrinkles. Her smile was bright though, and so were her warm brown eyes as she peered over her digital reader to see the motley group enter her office.

Up on her little polka-dot-heeled feet like a rabbit, Betty jumped. She immediately went for the bandages in her drawer to stem the flow of blood coming out of Jonny's forehead. As Jonny sat on the medical bed, he asked in a concerned voice, "You aren't going to make me turn and cough, are you, Nurse Green?"

"Turn and cough? Why would I want you to cough, turn what? OH MY! No, we don't do those kinds of exams here, son. Why in the world would you think I would ask you to do that?!"

"Mr. Foster, my gym teacher did," Jonny alleged, looking down and away from Betty.

"He did what?!?" Betty exclaimed, stepping back at first then clasping little Jonny's hand to comfort him as she searched for what in the world to say next. Jonny giggled, unable to hold the ruse for too long. Then he winced, looked sickeningly green for a second, and then hurled right onto Betty's prize polka-dot shoes.

"He was feeling sick before he fell and hit his head in the quake. The bad jokes have nothing to do with any of it, although he has always had bad jokes," proclaimed Lucy. She looked like she was barely holding it together herself as she was compulsively poking at the blood on her shirt with a small cloth and trying not to look at the puke on the floor.

"Lucy, you can return to homeroom now," announced Catherine. "Thank you for helping out with Jonny today. I will give you a few merits on your digiStudent account when I get back."

Lucy looked relieved, then proud as she scurried away down the hall. Nurse Betty was busy vigorously cleaning up her antique, designer shoes. "No need to stay, Miss Newton," she stated. "He'll need stiches and he is running a pretty high fever. I've already sent the notification with details to the ambulance service."

"Betty, what about his parents? Should I notify them as well?" inquired Catherine.

"No, the system automatically notifies parents when an ambulance is called. Indeed, you can go unless you want to help me clean the nasty puke off of my shoes." With that, Catherine was out the door, opening it quickly just as Jordan walked by. The smack of him hitting the door was so hard it cracked the glass in the pane and left Jordan flat on his butt in the hallway right as the bell for class change rang. Students began milling out of the doors and rushing through the halls as he sat there stunned with Catherine looking over in shock, hands over her mouth, eyes wide.

"I'm so sorry, Jordan. I truly am not trying to beat you up today," declared Catherine, laughing incredulously.

"Why is that hard for me to believe?" he muttered as he pushed Catherine's helpful hands away. He managed to scramble up from the ground while being racked half a dozen times by careless student backpacks. “Good day,” he said as he pushed his way through the crowded hallway.

Twice in one day! What are the odds? Catherine thought as she couldn’t help but notice that Jordon looked atypically disturbed and disoriented. Being hit twice could do that, but maybe it was more than that. It might be the large quake. That was the biggest one Catherine had felt since coming to the desert. They were all from explosions at the mine, but this one felt different. As if something big was released and rumbled out after the initial bang. Maybe the news channel had covered it by now. She hurried down the hall to her classroom to see.

Her new class was settling into their seats, looking up at the north wall where the news was covering mosquitos at the lake, and the hazards of the Quinta virus. This new virus would start with a blackening welt at the site of a mosquito bite, and then move over the skin in small black lines that would leave a permanent scar if not treated immediately. It sounded horrifying but supposedly wasn’t deadly, just ugly. Everyone was warned not to go near the lake until further fumigation efforts could completely eliminate the mosquito threat.

There was nothing on the news about the quake. Odd. She asked the new class if they had heard anything about the big bang. Rick Strand, a second-year senior and popular wisecrack, chimed in with, “Yeah, the big bang started the universe or something. Wait, aren’t you an English teacher? Shouldn’t we be learning how to read and write and stuff?”

As Catherine turned off the news and reached for her digiTeacher Controller, she wondered how in the world she ever ended up a high school English teacher. Dad. It was his fault. So easy to blame Dad. He always believed in her, told he she could be anything. Until he died when she was eleven, leaving her with nothing but a dog and a useless old diary. He had been a teacher too and, on some level, she was just trying to make him proud; to honor or memorialize him in some way. He lived through the great dust war, and managed to provide safety and security even after losing her mom in the initial LA blast. They had been on a fishing trip in Montana vising extended family when everything started. They were never even allowed back in LA to look for her mom. Catherine didn't remember any of it, she was only two at the time. She couldn't even remember her mom. But she remembered her father's pain and loneliness and would do anything to make him happy. Even become a teacher like him. How he did it she didn't know. She had only been a teacher for six months, and man, some of these kids were annoying!

Lunch couldn't come soon enough. Once the bell rang, she headed straight for the teacher's lounge. Elisabeth Gordan, the geometry teacher who she thought might be on drugs because she always seemed so happy, stepped up to her as soon as she walked in. Smirking, she said, "So I hear you knocked Jordan out, he looks pretty beat up. Good job!"

Elisabeth was obviously very entertained. She never liked Jordan; not many of the other teachers did either. He kept to himself and always seemed bored with everyone. Elisabeth was Catherine's only work friend. Actually, she was the only one who ever talked to Catherine. She was bright and bubbly, in her late 50s with graying black hair that had a white streak down the front. Blushing, Catherine said, "It was an accident, both times!"

"Both times?" Elisabeth laughed.

"Oh, so you are laughing about me now, great," interjected Jordan. He was tucked back in the corner next to the window with a bird's-eye view of the whole room. He did look pretty beat up; there was a purple welt on his head that was starting to look like an Easter egg. Catherine took some ice from the refrigerator and a washcloth to bring to Jordan as a goodwill gesture. As she sat at his table and handed him the icy cloth, her mind suddenly went blank. Elisabeth sat down and looked at both Catherine and Jordan and laughed again, saying, "Twice? Please, do tell."

"Jordan was obviously distracted by something, Elisabeth. Else, he wouldn't have run into me and that door in one day if he weren't paying any attention at all. What I want to know, is what was so distracting?" inquired Catherine. Jordon suddenly looked distraught.

"Was it the quake?" Catherine asked.

"What would make you think that?" Jordan replied.

"Just that it seemed bigger than normal. I know I have only been here a little while so I don't know much about the mining, but I don't think it should shake the entire school hard enough to knock people down."

"Who was knocked down?" Jordan responded.

"Me and my student Jonny, the one we were carrying to the nurse's office when you ran into us," Catherine answered.

"I didn't run into you, you ran into me," retorted Jordan.

"Yeah, and I ran the door into your head too. Come on! You were distracted. Why?" said Catherine.

"Look, he is obviously just clumsy and antisocial. Let's leave him alone," said Elisabeth.

"You didn't think the quake was weird, Elisabeth?" Catherine questioned.

"Yes, it did seem a bit stronger, but maybe they just had a big area they needed to collapse today," replied Elisabeth shrugging her shoulders. She smiled and waved at other teachers as they walked into the lounge, and seemed to be getting bored of the conversation. "Anyway, I can't believe the story about the Quinta virus. This is the fifth virus supposedly at the lake in the last few years. Who has ever heard of something that can leave black scars on your body? Now that is sick and twisted!"

"Don't believe everything you hear. Especially if it is about the lake. It has been closed off for over two years now with excuse after excuse and I don't buy any of it. It all seems fishy," said Jordan.

"The lake seems fishy?" Elisabeth couldn't help but smirk at her own joke. "Really, Jordan, the lake seems fishy?" She was trying not to laugh.

"Five viruses in just a few years? If it was a cover up, why wouldn't they just use the same virus? That is peculiar to say the least," pondered Catherine.

"The lake runs straight from the mine and they are just trying to cover up toxic spills," announced Jordan. "There are no viruses from mosquitos. It is a cover up."

"Again, if that was the case, why make up viruses?" replied Catherine.

"So, a conspiracy theorist, is that why no one likes you, Jordan?" asked Elisabeth rhetorically. "I think I have had enough of these fish tacos they keep serving us; hope they didn't get them from the lake," she stated as she got up and dumped the rest of her lunch in the trash. "Hope you don't get knocked out again, Jordan." She looked at Catherine and winked, "Remember, three strikes you're out," she said as she left the lounge with as smug a grin as anyone could manage.

"God, I hate her," Jordan said as she walked away.

"I sincerely am sorry about the lump on your head, Jordan. At least the ice seems to be getting the swelling down," insisted Catherine as she stabbed at her fish tacos with trepidation, wondering if, in fact, the fish had come from the lake. *Would the Quinta virus infect fish too?* she thought. She then held a piece of fish in the air, looking for black streaks.

"Don't worry, the fish come from a farm down in Clarksdale," said Jordan. "Elisabeth knows that and she was just messing with you."

"Are you sure? She is quite the character. Sometimes I wonder if she is on drugs. She sure is in a good mood all the time," replied Catherine. "That can't be normal for a teacher."

"And I am in a bad mood all the time. Do you think I am on drugs too?" said Jordan.

"Yes, of course" she replied quickly and sarcastically. Jordan smiled for the first time, maybe ever, as far as Catherine knew. Despite the lump on his head, he actually seemed handsome. It didn't last long though; he went right back to his vacant brooding.

"Where were you headed when you ran into us the first time today?" asked Catherine.

"You mean when you knocked me into the lockers? I was headed to the principal's office. I just had to ask him a question," stated Jordan. "Thank you for the ice, not so much for the lump." Another brief smile, and with that he was off in his usual hurry.

Maybe it was that smile, but it made her look at him differently. He was probably almost twice her age, early forties? Dark hair, olive skin, an unmistakable Italian nose, and matching attitude. She had never met a patient Italian. It is a wonder he had the fortitude for teaching, much less to high schoolers. He didn't seem like he belonged here. Catherine didn't feel like she belonged here either. *What a pair they would be*, she thought. That was a disturbing thought! Wow, she had a boyfriend! One that was her age and didn't make everyone want to sit on the other side of the room.

Her boyfriend, Anthony Grant, was sweet, kind, handsome, and hard working. They met at an outdoor concert in the park a few months ago when his dog tried to eat the entire contents of her picnic basket. She always liked fluffy puppies and fell in love with the dog immediately: they had the same taste in food, after all. It was Anthony that she wasn't sure about yet.

Anthony's family was assigned to Desert Grande a few years ago from an Ohio city that had become too overcrowded due to the bustling population of Catholics in the area. Three sisters, two parents, an Aunt, and two cousins all came here at once. She envied his big family, and loved his parents who took her in as one of their own. Catherine was starting to realize she liked his family and his dog more than him though, and didn't know how to handle the situation. She was having dinner with him tomorrow night, alone. No dog, no family. She could focus on him and maybe develop her feelings more.

The final bell for the day tolled its blessed release. Catherine got into her car, set the destination to home and set the car to autopilot. One of her favorite activities during the drive home was picking dinner for the night. The sooner she made the selection, the sooner the combinator would have it ready for her when she got to her house. Chicken enchiladas? Lasagna? Tuna casserole? Her go-to favorite was spaghetti and meatballs, which was also her dog's favorite.

Her fluffy white poodle Sass would be waiting for her, and probably was still shaking from the huge quake today. She deserved a treat. *Spaghetti and meatballs, it is!* Catherine thought as she entered the order selection. That would make Sass's day.

As she walked in the door she was greeted with a facial from Sass and the yummy smell of spaghetti in the kitchen. There was a vase shattered on the floor and in the hall way there was a large yellow puddle (courtesy of the poodle) that were likely the result of the scary big bang from the mine. She ordered the Roomba to fix the mess and went straight for the kitchen to pour herself a glass of red wine.

She remembered a time when there were things like refrigerators, ovens or a microwave in a kitchen. Now they were all one item, called a combinator. Basically, you inserted ingredients into the side, entered the bar code for the item and the combinator could offer a selection of meals based on overall contents. It knew cooking times and temperature, self-cleaned and even threw out expired items automatically. All you had to do was grab a utensil and open the door in the front when you were ready to eat your order. Whoever came up with this was living the life somewhere, probably in Oklahoma where all the cleanest land was after the war. It was one of the few places the fall-out dust never reached.

She sat down in her big, downy and comfy couch and offered a few meatballs to the dog. She then leaned back and put her feet up on the coffee table, sighing in comfort as she sipped her wine. She realized her car was automated, her food was automated, and her cleaning was automated. But, one thing that she wished she could automate was checking her student's writing assignments. Sure, spelling and grammar would auto-correct, but not content or proper use of a word. Forty students each class, 6 classes, and with two assignments a week meant her day was just starting when she got home. Spaghetti, and a large glass of red wine would get her through the evening. She snatched up her digiTeacher Controller and began to grade.

Sleep came pretty readily to Catherine. Especially after the tenth paper on how football was the greatest sport ever invented. Rarely did she even make it up to bed before she fell asleep during the school week, and tonight was no exception.

She always had such vivid dreams. Tonight, she was flying. She felt the warm wind in her hair and on her skin. She tasted the dewy tendrils of fog on her lips. The sky was a million colors coalescing into a morning sunrise of oranges faded to dark blue. She smiled as she saw a white-tailed bunny jump in the meadow as her feet landed on the soft, green grass. She turned to her left as she heard the movement of water, with little splashes as it hit the small wooden boat. The splashes and waves were sending up sparkles in the moonlight. She was at the lake in Desert Grande. Suddenly she was worried about the Quinta virus. *Did mosquitos like to bite early in the morning?* she thought. *Wait, this was a dream, mosquitos don't bite in dreams if you're in control!* She knew she was always in control. She walked over to the pier and sat down to watch the water caress the dock as the fog crawled over the lake breaking into little branches, like fingers.

"I thought I would find you here," said a voice that was all too familiar.

Catherine turned to see the man who had been haunting her dreams lately. She had never met him in real life that she could remember and had no idea who he was. His eyes were so different. Where there should have been pupils there was what looked like golden lenses that flashed strange symbols in the low light. Half of the top of his head was shaved and the other half was capped with what looked like a metal plate. He had rusty brown hair in his goatee and for his eyebrows. He wore a black turtleneck, slacks and gloves so that his entire body was covered from the neck down.

He walked straight up to her with almost a rhythmic pulse, as if his legs were mechanical. He put one hand on her arm and said the all too familiar words, "You have to stop the mining."

"Why? Who are you? How?" asked Catherine, as usual.

"You know I can't tell you. You know you can stop it, Catherine," he said, emphatically.

"Why can't you tell me? I don't even think you are real," she retorted.

"I am real, and I want to sleep. Today was close, they have found another lab. This is getting very dangerous for everyone. You do not want to wake me. You irrefutably don't want to wake my brother."

"Your brother?" she queried, standing up and walking towards him. She wanted to reach out and touch him, to see if he was really there.

"I have said too much. Just stop the mining. I have to go," he announced.

There was a bright flash, so bright it hurt her eyes. As she turned away she was jolted awake. Why did she have such weird dreams? Why couldn't she just dream of nice meadows and hopping bunnies and not mechanically enhanced guys trying to tell her what to do? It was 2 a.m. If she went back to sleep now she could get a few more hours before the daily grind. As she climbed the stairs to go to her bed, dog at her feet, she asked, "You don't dream about cyborgs, do you, Sass?" The confused little "woof" reply confirmed it: She was going crazy.

CHAPTER 2

Date of Mine

A*nthony was late. He was never late. Maybe he was breaking up with her?* Catherine thought as she was sitting at the restaurant, staring at her phone band on her left arm, trying to figure out what went wrong. The earlier text to confirm the time/location for their date was pretty straightforward, at least that is what she thought. Her text "Maggiano's, 6?" and his reply "Yes, Babe, CU tonight" couldn't be clearer.

It was 7 p.m. and she had already gone through two glasses of wine and what seemed like a loaf of bread that the waitress just kept filling back up in the center of the table. The tall, young, blonde waitress was well past annoyed and barely hiding it behind a thin smile which made Catherine cringe every time she came by to fill the bread and ask if she wanted more wine.

She had never been stood up before in her life! Should she leave? Wait an hour? Camp out? She had already texted him she was here; she didn't want to be nagging, especially if this was his way of breaking up. She didn't want him to know he upset her; she wanted to be tough!

Anthony walked through the door right as Catherine was getting up and had given up. He waived to her across the restaurant and she sat down with a huge sigh of relief. She didn't know who looked more delighted, her or the waitress. Anthony looked like he had just gotten out of the shower. His hair was slicked back and his skin still looked a little wet. He was dressed nice though, wearing a pressed, white-collared shirt and some pleated grey slacks. He always wore a gold cross on a chain at his neck, a sign of his Catholic heritage which he was more than serious about. Once he had told her the only reason he didn't become a priest was because he wanted a family of his own. He was 6'2", broad shouldered and knew how to turn heads in a room with a smile.

"I am so sorry, Babe," he said with a kiss on her cheek as he sat down across the table from Catherine. "Work kept me late and I was so upset and was rushing to get out of there to get to you that I left my phone band in my locker. I hurried as fast as I could," he said sincerely and then directed to the waitress, "Maim, we'll have an order of calamari for the table and another glass of wine for my beautiful, extra patient girlfriend."

"Coming right up," she replied as she put a thumbs-up behind Anthony, mouthing "Nice catch!"

Catherine couldn't help but blush. She wasn't used to dating handsome men. She wasn't used to dating in general. She had always been a bit of a reclusive bookworm. To have a guy like Anthony notice her was an adventure to say the least, and she was always getting comments from other women about his looks that made her feel a bit uncomfortable.

"I've already had two glasses of wine, Anthony. You know I am a lightweight," Catherine said.

"Oh, you are? Then this will be a cheap date," Anthony said with a smile that lit up his warm brown eyes and made Catherine wonder how she could be mad at him for anything, ever. But, he had stood her up for what felt like all night, so she couldn't just let him slide.

"Cheap date? No, I don't think so, Mr.! I plan to order heavy and make you pay. I will take it back home in a doggy bag for Sass. Those extra hours you worked today should cover it, right?" she asked, playfully.

Anthony laughed, "Well, I knew I would have to pay somehow. I am probably getting off too easy."

"Yes, way too easy, you big meany!" exclaimed Catherine.

"Believe me, I would have rather been here with you than at the mine this afternoon. There was a corridor that collapsed and trapped four guys inside. It took us two hours to clear it and by then, one of the crew was dead from bleeding out. I had to carry him out to medical myself. I've never seen anything like it, and I've worked with all of those guys for years. I actually did a work study stint with the guy who died, Larry Armstrong. He had three kids and even goes to my church."

"Wow, Anthony, I am so sorry to hear that. Has anything like this ever happened before at the mine?" she wondered.

"No, not that I know of, but these corridors where we are mining are very unstable. There are older structures that we keep running into lately. It seems the ancient people who lived here, supposedly a very long time ago, had created tunnels throughout this area right through the bedrock the company is interested in digging up. Ancient Navajo, supposedly. Yesterday I swear it looked like a laboratory though. I mentioned that it didn't look like Native American digs to me but my supervisor said these were Navajo tunnels and that it was impossible that they had labs."

"A lab? What makes you think it was a lab?" she asked, intrigued.

"Well, mind you I didn't get there until an hour after the blast, but there seemed to be broken glass on the ground and what looked like areas cut out of the rock for large rectangular objects. You know, like in the shape of those old refrigerators that they used to use to cool stuff," Anthony replied.

"Were there any electrical outlets or ventilation hoods built into the walls? Navajo's definitely didn't have those," she inquired.

"I don't remember seeing anything like that, no. I didn't think of that. You are so smart," he stated with a smile and clutched her hand from across the table. He had such big, strong hands.

Right then the calamari showed up and the waitress almost put the plate right where their hands had been, they had to quickly release before the plate came down. "What can I get for you two lovebirds?" she asked while looking at Anthony coyly. She was blatantly flirting!

"I'll have the surf and turf and this lovely young lady will have the chicken alfredo, extra parmesan," proclaimed Anthony with confidence as he handed the waitress the menus, not even giving her a glance. The waitress stomped away, a little peeved to be ignored.

"You know my order, do you?" asked Catherine playfully. Deep down she was a little put off though; that wasn't what she wanted. She actually wanted the beef and spinach ravioli tonight but didn't want to embarrass Anthony, and she especially didn't want to call the waitress back.

"Of course I know your order. You always get the cheesiest item on the menu," he responded, jokingly.

She smiled and then looked down at her napkin that she had begun to toy with. It was little things like the wrong order that made her question her relationship. He acted like he knew her so well, but she felt like he didn't know her at all.

"Want to go on an adventure?" he asked, out of the blue.

She must have been showing some brooding on her face, because he obviously wanted to cheer her up. "What kind of adventure?" she said, taking the bait.

"Well, breaking and entering, with intent to take something," he said with a twinkle in his eyes, leaning forward with excitement.

"I would rather not go to jail, thank you very much. What would my students think?" she replied. She knew he would never steal; what was he up to?

"That you are a badass teacher," he said.

"Oh yeah, me a badass!" she retorted.

"Seriously though, I need to get my phone band. They are closing the mine for a few days until after Larry's funeral and I don't think I can survive without it. Want to go with me to the mine to get it?" he asked.

"You are serious?" she replied, curious.

"Yeah, it is not really breaking in though. I have an ID pass. I just said that to get your adrenaline pumping and bring out those rosy cheeks," he said as he slid his finger across her cheek and down her neck, making her blush. "It is not actually stealing either because it is my phone, but it would be an adventure."

"Ok, I am in as long as I don't have to wear a hardhat or anything," she responded.

"You would look extra cute in a hardhat; are you sure?" he asked, lightheartedly.

"Yes, it would mess up my hair," she said while putting her hands through her long brown hair and then flipping it to one side with a sigh.

They laughed and enjoyed the meal, gathering up two large doggie bags for the road when it was done. Anthony left a nice tip for the waitress, who Catherine caught checking out his butt on the way out. He never encouraged her though, which was one thing she liked about him. He was very loyal and never once made her question if he would cheat on her.

As they got to Anthony's car, he grabbed her by the waist and brought her close to him. He was so big and strong and her heart couldn't help but skip a beat or two as he kissed her passionately. Maybe it was the three glasses of wine, but she felt a bit dizzy and almost fell over when he let her go. He quickly gripped her and asked if she was all right.

"You took my breath away," she said wistfully. So, he kissed her again until her knees buckled and he slid her into the car with a laugh.

Catherine had never been to the mine before. She knew it was upstream from the lake, north of the main town and near the east red rock mountains. It was past 9 p.m., and dark, so she didn't see much on the trip up. Not that she would have been able to anyway; Anthony loved to make out in the car with it set to autopilot. By the time they reached the mine the windows were all fogged up and Anthony had to put the wipers on and roll the windows down in order to see to park.

"Let's go to the back entrance. It is closer to the lockers," he whispered as he held her hand and led her towards a path that went up to a cliff face.

"Are you sure this is okay, Anthony?" Catherine asked, looking around at the empty, dimly lit parking lot.

"Yes, don't worry so much. It's an adventure, remember?" he replied.

They went around to a dusky red door with bright yellow reflective tape along the edges that looked like it was built directly into the rocks. Once inside, Anthony turned on a flashlight and seized Catherine by the hand to lead her down an extended, shadowy corridor.

The air was cool but stale and smelt like dust and copper pennies. *It was so quiet!* Catherine thought. The only sound was the shuffle of their feet and what seemed like humming from something far down the passage. When they reached the end, it opened up into a large room with lockers all around and a circular washing station in the center. The humming she had heard earlier was coming from a dim yellow light hanging in the center of the room. There were three more corridors to the right, one had yellow caution tape in the shape of an X covering the entrance.

"Is that the corridor that collapsed today?" asked Catherine.

"You would think that, but no. That caution tape is covering the entrance to the corridor leading to the area I thought was a lab. They closed it off at the end of the day yesterday," stated Anthony. "The area that collapsed today is closed off too, but further down. It is down the first corridor to the right."

Anthony opened his locker and pulled out his phone band, gave it a little kiss and put it back on his left arm. He looked so handsome in the dim light, and the adrenaline from sneaking into the mine was going to Catherine's head.

"You know, wouldn't it be sexy to do it right here, right now?" Catherine whispered as she pushed him against the locker and rubbed her hands down his muscled chest.

"Yes," he said catching his breath between kisses. As her hand caressed his stomach and then began to descend, he grabbed her hand. "But, I am saving myself until marriage; you know how important my faith is to me, Catherine. Please respect that," he pleaded.

"I wasn't serious. I'm sorry if you thought I was," she said and stopped what she was doing immediately. Catherine felt what she always felt when he said those words: frustrated and ashamed. She did not share his faith, but respected his strength in his beliefs. She wasn't a virgin either, and was not used to the reverse situation where the guy was not pressuring her. The way he made out with her all the time left her very flustered to say the least. It was easy for her to forget about his faith in the moment, but he held strong despite her advances. It blew her mind that he was 22 and a virgin still. She had to think of something to change the subject.

"Can we go to your 'lab'? Maybe check for electrical outlets and ventilation shafts?" she inquired.

"Sure, I don't mind breaking some rules every now and then, Babe. Plus, wouldn't it be crazy if there was an electrical outlet in a supposed, 'Navajo tunnel'?"

Catherine wanted to know too. Anthony saying that he found a lab yesterday reminded her of her dream last night. She was curious if it was a lab, maybe her dream was true? The bizarre man in her dream did mention a lab. Up until now, she just thought that the whole time she was dreaming about this cyborg guy telling her to "stop the mining" it had to do with her subconscious not liking all the quakes. That made complete sense to her, and she had a vivid imagination, so he could easily fit into her dark dream world.

"Let's be bad asses, Babe," Anthony decreed as he removed the caution tape and clutched Catherine by the hand. He led her down a dark passage for what felt like a half hour.

"You see this stuff in the side of the rock here," he said as he flashed the light to what looked like grey stone with embedded copper pennies, except they weren't pennies they were just odd shaped circles in the rock that were darker than the adjacent rock. "This is bauxite; it is what we are mostly mining for the ceramic roads we're building. They use that and the gadolinite found in the other mine, of course, to get all the elements they need."

Catherine was not a scientist, and knew nothing about rocks or mining. Science was too cut and dry, no room for creative interpretation or fun. Where was the fantasy in rocks? She could imagine rock giants exchanging money in rock pennies in the wall, and that was far more fun. A good fiction book, to escape her boring life, that is what she was interested in the most. But, she nodded and said, "Pretty neat stuff" because Anthony was obviously fascinated by the rocky walls that his hands were caressing as if they were her body. Further down they finally came to another opening.

"This is it," was all Anthony said as he moved the flashlight around the room. There was still broken glass on the ground.

"Stop. Let me see that," Catherine asserted as she reached for the flashlight. On the ground were lines, exactly two feet apart coming from one of the rectangular holes and leading back down the way they came as if something had been dragged away. Further inspection found a small circular hole in the back of the rectangular cut out.

"There was obviously something here that was drug out and why would the Navajo create a perfectly rectangular indent in the rock with a small hole in the back?" asked Catherine.

"Yeah, something about the cuts in the wall, they look machined. That small hole could be an outlet but, unfortunately, I don't see any electrical wiring. Didn't you say something about a lab needing a ventilation shaft? I don't see one of those either," proclaimed Anthony as he pointed the flashlight to the ceiling and moved it along slowly as if looking for something.

"The ventilation shaft could be anywhere. It doesn't have to be above us. They could have used a fan and moved the air downward, or even sideways. Plus, couldn't it be closed off, full of rubble from the blast?" asked Catherine.

"See, this is why I love you. You're so smart!" Anthony exclaimed with a kiss and a hug that lifted Catherine off of her feet.

Catherine was in shock. He had never said he loved her; this was the first "I love you" between them and she didn't know what to say. She knew one thing: she did not love him, at least not yet. *Maybe it was a figure of speech and not a real "I love you." Maybe she should just ignore it?*

"So, what do you think they drug out of here? A refrigerator?" she asked, quickly trying to distract Anthony.

"I don't know, but whatever it is, it had to be pretty heavy to leave those marks in the rock." He took the flashlight from Catherine and declared, "Look, over here, another one," as he walked across the room towards another rectangular hole in the wall.

"Where does that tunnel go?" she enquired as she moved his hand to point down a long, roughly hewn tunnel to the left.

"I don't know. Honestly, there is a lot I don't know around here. I'm nothing more than a simple miner, after all. We should probably head out. I can ask when I get back to work about the lines on the ground and the small holes in the walls.

Maybe someone will know. It doesn't look like Navajo work to me, but what do I know, right?" he pondered out loud.

"Okay, lead the way, Babe," Catherine said as she took his arm. She was seriously regretting wearing heels to her dinner date at this point. They weren't quite right for the spelunking adventure it had turned into and her feet were killing her.

"So, what if it is a lab, what do you think that means, Anthony?" she queried as they were winding their way through the passageways in the dark.

"I don't know. Honestly, I never thought that far ahead," he replied. He seemed distracted by something.

"What's the matter, Anthony?" she asked.

"I'm sorry, but, I have to say it. I do love you, Catherine. I love how smart you are and how you analyze everything. I love your dimples and doe eyes, and the way you flip your hair when you're nervous. Don't you love me too?" he pleaded as he flashed the flashlight right in her face. She couldn't help but laugh. Then he did too. The sudden spotlight just highlighted how pointed and substantial the question he asked was, and how awkward of a situation to be in when he asked her.

"What I would love is to be out of these heels and back in the car making out some more," she exclaimed as she gave him a kiss on the cheek and moved the flashlight to show her heels on the rocky floor.

They walked in silence though the tunnels in the dark and finally out of the door in the mountainside. When they got in the car, Anthony set the automatic pilot to go back to the restaurant where Catherine's car was waiting. As he rubbed her feet on the drive, he looked up at her with puppy dog eyes and asked, "Will you answer my question now?"

"How could I not love you, you're amazing. Tall, sexy, hardworking and the sweetest man I have ever met," she replied with as big a smile as she could muster. All of it was true, so she wasn't lying. She felt bad though, because she had made it sound like she was saying she loved him without actually saying she loved him. Truthfully, she asked herself the same thing: how could she not love him? But she didn't love him, and it was confusing.

"I am so glad you said that, because there is something else I wanted to ask you, Catherine," he proclaimed.

Right then her heart stopped. *This could not be happening. I mean, she kind of expected it given his faith and the fact that he introduced her to his whole family on the third date. But, it had only been four months! Now?!? She wasn't ready for a proposal!*

"Can you watch Rufus for me this weekend? I have a hunting trip with some of the guys from work and I don't trust my sisters with my dog. Last time Gretchen and Ariana watched him we found him two days later in a landfill eating out of old diapers."

Suddenly Catherine questioned how much she liked Rufus. *Eating WHAT out of a landfill? How many times had he licked her face?*

"Of course, Babe, anything," she replied. "Sass will be happy to have the company."

They arrived at Maggiano's at around 11 p.m. It was another 20 minutes until Catherine would be home. It was another 30 minutes before she was in bed after taking a thorough shower to get rid of all the tunnel dust on her clothes. She couldn't help but focus on the time, she had to be up at 6 to get ready for school. But, she just couldn't sleep. She lay there in bed, staring at the alarm clock wondering how she got to where she was: lying to a man that loved her, unable to love him back.

What was wrong with her? So, he ordered her chicken alfredo instead of ravioli; the chicken alfredo was delicious. Did that mean he didn't know her? No. But, he also didn't ask about her day, in fact he rarely asks her anything about herself. She knew everything about him, and loved all that she knew. He just liked to talk a lot, and joke a lot, which dominated the conversation. He was so charming. Did she need anything more?

Maybe she just needed to talk more? Maybe tell him about herself instead of waiting for him to ask? At least he didn't ask her to marry him tonight! What would she have said? If she had said yes, she would be lying. If she had said no, would he have broken up with her? She didn't want to break up. She loved his parents and his dog Rufus and would miss them dearly.

This whole Catholic thing bothered her a little bit too. *Would she have to convert to Catholicism?* They hadn't even talked about that yet. He probably expected kids right away, and she knew Catholics were against birth control so that meant they would have as many kids as he wanted. She loved kids, and he was handsome, so they would have beautiful children. *But, how many did she want?*

After the war, the vast majority of the population was gone and what was left was encouraged to rebuild. The government had incentives if you wanted kids. She could quit her boring job and just make babies for a living if she married Anthony. The government would pay her to have kids and stay home with them, and Anthony's parents were constantly talking about grand kids. *Would her dad be proud of her if she quit being a teacher?*

The alarm clock was buzzing. It was 6 a.m. already. She hadn't slept a wink. It was going to be a rough day at work!

CHAPTER 3

Merits of Merits

Homeroom went by in a blur. At the bell Lucy asked about her merits for helping with Jonny the other day. Catherine had forgotten to post them to her account with all the commotion of hitting Jordan with the nurse room door and then the news of the Quinta virus at the lake. She gave Lucy 1 extra merit for reminding her and 2 merits for the help with Jonny. When the merits registered into Lucy's digiStudent account, Catherine also had to congratulate Lucy on her silver level merit achievement. Lucy must be quite the teacher's pet to get to that level, maybe that was why she was always in a frazzle.

"Class, please give Lucy a round of applause; she is now a silver level student!" Catherine announced to the class. Lucy blushed as the class gave her a standing ovation. Most of the class was up anyway to leave because the bell had already rung but the sincere ovation still surprised Catherine. This was the first any student she had even came close to silver, so she had no idea how the other students would react to the required announcement. It was amazing how supportive everyone was for Lucy.

"Keep up the good work. You still have time to reach gold before the end of the semester," said Catherine. Lucy gave Catherine a look of determination in a quick smile as she hurried off to her next class.

It took 500 points in one semester to get to silver level; gold was 700. Most students earned less than 200. Academics were rewarded of course, with an A standing for the semester generating 50 points per class, a B 30, C 20, D 10 and F -10. So even with trending straight A's, 100 points are still needed to get to silver. These additional points are achieved through joining extracurricular sports or clubs, volunteer efforts and philanthropy. Each sport is 10 points, so is each club. Presidents and heads of teams and clubs got an additional 5 points. Student body government is 20 for president, and 15 for vice president, and 10 for each member of the board. Helping teachers, running food drives for those less fortunate, bake sales to raise money for band equipment, etc. ... counted as philanthropic endeavors and could generate up to 10 points each semester.

Not only did silver and gold level standing look good on a college resume, but it afforded perks at the school as well. Silver level were able to walk the halls without a teacher endorsement on their digiStudent account and could miss a class for a week without penalty so they could study in the library or work on other philanthropic endeavors. There was also a preferred line at the cafeteria for all silver and gold level students, with extra dessert options.

Catherine knew how the system worked, but couldn't seem to get more students active in earning merits. No one seemed to want to put in efforts past the minimum. The teacher whose homeroom students had the most merits was given a small bonus with a little money to throw a congratulatory party for the students at the end of the semester. Catherine was always a bit competitive and always wanted to win. However, even with Lucy's silver level merit status, her classroom was nowhere near the top performers in the school. Elisabeth probably knew how to motivate students.

When lunch came, Catherine headed straight to the teacher's lounge. Japanese Udon noodles was the special of the day, and the line was long at the faculty combinators. She spent the time in line analyzing the merits of her homeroom class, picking out top performers to hone.

"How do I get my students to want to achieve more merits?" she immediately asked Elisabeth as soon as she was finally able to sit at her table.

Elisabeth had been reading a book while nibbling on what looked like a whole wheat cucumber sandwich that she must have brought from home. From her posture, Elisabeth was deliberately ignoring the two other teachers at the table. The two other teachers looked like they were in a heated discussion, but one of them glanced at Catherine when she sat down and scoffed at Catherine's question before returning to her conversation. Elisabeth laughed at the scoff.

"High school is hard enough without the pressure of merits, Catherine. Why would you want your students to achieve more?" she retorted.

"I like the idea of throwing them a little party, plus I like to win," Catherine responded earnestly.

"Aren't you sweet," replied Elisabeth. "I wouldn't worry about it though. The same teacher has been winning every semester since it started 4 years ago, and I don't think she will be bested by a newbie."

"Who wins it?" Catherine asked. She heard scoffing again from the debating duo sitting with them at the table, as if the question was dumb.

"You're looking at her kid," said Elisabeth, with a mischievous grin.

Catherine was beat red with embarrassment. She should have known Elisabeth would be the top teacher in the school. "So, I don't suppose you would want to divulge any secrets as to how you managed to get the students more involved?" Catherine pleaded.

"Honestly? No. Not that I think you are much competition, but I like to win too, and giving away secrets is not how you win" she replied as she finished off her cucumber sandwich in one large bite.

"I see. Well, I might be competition. I had one student reach silver level today," Catherine countered, hoping to get a response out of Elisabeth.

"Who?" Elisabeth queried, suddenly no longer gloating.

"Lucy Gamble," Catherine proclaimed proudly, then added, "The whole class gave her a standing ovation when they heard. I was surprised."

"I see. Why were you surprised? That is quite an achievement."

"I was surprised because when I went to school, the kids who did well were picked on, not applauded," Catherine replied.

"Did you think that maybe one of the reasons everyone is encouraging to Lucy is because her father is a foreman at the mine? He could fire half their dads and they would be on the street or reassigned to another city. You didn't know that, did you? The ties to the mine control a lot of things around here, Catherine."

"I guess there are a lot of things I don't know. Josh Armstrong was out of class today. I just realized Larry Armstrong must be his father, right?" Catherine asked.

"Yes, why do you ask?"

"My boyfriend said Larry died yesterday at the mine in a collapsed corridor. They are closing the mine until Monday for his funeral on Sunday. You didn't see it on the news last night?" Catherine inquired.

"Yes, I did. But, I didn't realize the man that died had a son in high school. That is very sad. Do you plan on going to the funeral? Did you need someone to go with you?" asked Elisabeth.

"I hadn't thought of that. I will be watching my boyfriend's dog Rufus this weekend and I don't want to leave him at the house alone with my dog Sass," Catherine responded.

"I forgot you had a boyfriend. How is that handsome young Anthony? If only I were 30 years younger, you would have some competition there too," Elisabeth proclaimed with a smile and a wink.

"He is fine, handsome as ever. He was part of the crew that pulled Larry from the rubble. He isn't even going to the funeral. I guess his hunting trip that he's been planning with his buddies is more important."

"Hunting trip?" inquired Jordan as he sat down next to Catherine. The dynamic duo of arguing teachers had just gotten up and left, leaving room. Jordan seemed less forlorn and gloomy than usual as he pushed aside the dirty napkin left on the table to make room for his cup of Udon noodles. She had never seen him purposely sit next to anyone before, this was new.

"Catherine was just telling me about her boyfriend Anthony, and how is he going on a hunting trip this weekend and leaving her with his dog Rufus," said Elisabeth. "Your head is looking better Jordan, though that isn't saying much."

"Thank you for your kind words, as usual, Elisabeth," Jordan rejoined, casually ignoring the insult. "It takes a year to get a license to hunt anything other than fish around here, and then there are limited windows for hunting specific game. Elk, for instance, is only in October for two weeks. That is probably what he will be hunting this weekend."

"If I wanted a boring lecture, Jordan, I would take your class," Elisabeth said as she got up to leave. "Tell Lucy congratulations on the silver merit achievement for me, Catherine. You'll need four more in your class if you plan to come anywhere near close to me in winning the homeroom party merit reward," she declared as she patted Catherine on the back and left with her typical grin.

"Four more silver level students? How in the world does she do it?" Catherine pondered aloud, incredulous.

"She is lying, as usual, she likes to pull your leg if you haven't noticed," said Jordan.

"Really? Why do I always fall for it then?" replied Catherine.

"Because you are young and naïve," stated Jordan, casually.

"Thanks," Catherine answered as she was starting to understand why Jordan sat alone most days. "Thanks for the explanation about the hunting as well. I was starting to think Anthony was a bit callous for not going to his co-worker's funeral."

"So, your boyfriend works at the mine in the tunnels then?" asked Jordan.

"Yeah, he loves rocks. I mean, really loves rocks! I didn't realize how much until I saw him caressing a tunnel wall last night," she replied.

"You went to the mine last night?" exclaimed Jordan, looking shocked and somewhat angry. "Do you realize how dangerous that was? The tunnels are very unstable. The blasting they are doing is not safe. Did that not register in your pretty little head when you heard a man died there yesterday?"

Catherine felt reproached, and a bit indignant. It truly did not occur to her the mines could be unstable when no one was there and there was no mining going on.

"We were the only ones there. It seemed all right to me," she declared.

"What were you doing there?" Jordan questioned.

"I wanted to see something," Catherine responded.

"What?" Jordan asked. "Please, tell me what could have possibly persuaded you to enter a dangerous mine in the middle of the night."

Catherine wasn't sure how to answer the question. *Should she tell him about her dreams and that strange mechanically enhanced man and his inane warnings to stop the mining? How he had said they had found another lab and she wanted to see if there was a lab in the mine just so she could prove whether or not the man in her dreams was real?* She didn't know what sounded more insane: dreaming of cyborgs or thinking a man from her dreams might be real. As she opened her mouth to try and explain, the bell rang for class.

"Another time then," Jordan stated as he quickly devoured his bowl of noodles, then jumped up to leave. "You look awful today, by the way. You should try getting some sleep instead of running around in mining tunnels trying to get yourself killed. What do they call it? Beauty sleep? It would help with the dark circles under your eyes," and with those words of wisdom he was gone.

Catherine got up to go to her next class. It would be medieval literature, and she was looking forward to putting in a movie about Geoffrey Chaucer's *Canterbury Tales* and taking a nap.

On her way to class the phone band on her left arm vibrated. It was a text from Anthony, asking what time she would be home so he could drop off the dog. She started to type her simple reply "5ish" when she tripped over a student who had been bent over in the hallway tying his shoelaces. She managed to tuck and roll but the fall launched her digiTeacher Controller down the hallway, right at the feet of principal Sanjay Repalle, who was standing just outside her classroom door.

"Walking and texting is forbidden in the hallways for a reason, Miss Newton, even for faculty," he announced. He was a tall, dark ash-skinned Indian man with big brown eyes and no hair. He had a regal appearance that reminded her of a senator, and right now he looked very intimidating as he loomed over her rumpled figure lying on the hallway floor.

The poor student she had tripped over was kind enough to help her up as she apologized for not paying attention. He ran away quickly afterwards, not wanting anything to do with the situation that seemed to be unfolding with the faculty.

Principal Repalle picked up Catherine's digiTeacher Controller and inspected it, saying, "These controllers are very expensive, my dear. Please try to be more careful. Thankfully, this one appears to remain undamaged at present."

"I'm sorry, sir. I will try to be more careful," she said as she looked down at her vibrating phone band and cleared the screen quickly; Anthony had just sent a funny picture of Rufus's tongue licking the screen, with his eyes so wide you could see the whites at the top and bottom. *Did he put peanut butter on the screen?*

"Please see me after class, Miss Newton. I would like to discuss how you are doing here so far. Good day," he declared as he walked off into the crowd of students parting like the Red Sea all around him as if he were Moses. The way he said "Good Day" always seemed like some sort of commandment; she almost wanted to click her heels together and give him a salute. Or bow to him like he was a king. He sure ran this place like he was king.

Even as a teacher it never felt good to be called into the principal's office. Especially a principal that just caught you texting and walking over students. She was not having a good day. Thankfully, the fall was on her right side and her phone band was okay. She let Anthony know she was going to be home closer to 6 now that she had to meet with the principal. He texted back with "lol badass." He was definitely a bad influence. That picture of Rufus was hilarious though. She looked at it again three more times throughout the day.

After the nap in medieval literature, she got a second wind and was able to make it the rest of the day without further incident. She did spend the entire afternoon dreading meeting with the principal though. *How bad could it be, really?* she thought. Besides assaulting her fellow teacher, Jordan, with a door the other day, and the texting and walking today, she was a model teacher. Well, unless you counted all the times she came in late through the back door. *He didn't know about that? Right? Oh man, she was a terrible teacher!*

The closer the time came to the final class ending, the more anxious she was getting. By the time the closing bell rang, she was so anxious she jumped in her seat at the sound. She heard muffled laughter from the class as she dropped her digiTeacher Controller on her desk and let out a pitiful, squeaky noise. It was time to head to the principal's office, to meet her fate. *Would she be re-assigned?*

Mr. Repalle's receptionist was busy typing up what she could only imagine was demerit letters to parents when Catherine walked into the administrative lobby. The receptionist, Mary Kingsley, was a short, chubby woman in her mid-fifties who looked like Shirley Temple, with a wide grin and a head full of curls. "Ah, we've been expecting you, Miss Newton," she said with a warm smile. "Go right on in, dear. He doesn't bite."

"Thank you, Mrs. Kingsley. What a lovely dress you are wearing," Catherine replied, trying to stall going into the office. "Are those flower blossoms on the hem?"

"Thank you, dear," she said as she sat up to show the tiny sunflowers along the edges of the skirt. "I always wear yellow on Fridays. It's the cheeriest color for the best day of the week," she added, then whispered, "Its okay, go on in." Mrs. Kingsley had seen right through her stalling efforts. She was probably used to everyone being scared of the principal.

Catherine straightened her back, brushed off her skirt and walked right up to the principal at his desk and said, "Good afternoon, Mr. Repalle" a little too loudly, as he looked up somewhat startled.

"My lovely, Miss Newton. Thank you for coming. Please, have a seat," he said as he put down his digital notebook, likely the principal's version of the digiTeacher Controller that she had been given on her first day of school. She wondered what he could do with his controller. Probably everything from sound an alarm at the school to rate the faculty on their performance. He sat back in his chair and said, "I realized today in the hallway that I haven't spoken to you since you arrived in August at the beginning of the school year. I know this is your first assignment and you have no family, so it must be lonely for you here in Desert Grande. I hope you are adjusting well to the desert and to the life of a school teacher?"

"Yes, sir. All of the students are great," she lied. *What was she supposed to say? The students were either annoying slackers or overachieving workaholics.* "I even have a silver level merit achiever in my homeroom. As far as adjusting to life in the desert, I am almost used to all the quakes now. I hardly notice them, except the big ones of course, like the one we had the other day."

"Ah, I forget the mine does make quite the impression on those who are not from here. It was unfortunate about your student Jonny Ricker falling and hitting his head in class during the last quake. The janitor said there had been a trail of blood from your homeroom to the nurse's office. That is why it is important for the students to remain seated during class, Miss Newton."

"Yes, sir. It won't happen again, sir, I promise," said Catherine quickly. She had forgotten about the sitting rule.

"Please, you do not have to call me sir, Miss Newton. I just want what is best for my faculty and staff, and all rules are there for a reason. We must maintain our integrity. We are the pillar of the community after all, the central rock on which this small mining town stands. I am a bit worried about you though. You look like you haven't slept in days. Is the workload too much?" he asked with genuine concern in his voice.

"No sir, I mean, Mr. Repalle. I just had trouble getting to sleep last night."

"Are you having nightmares?" he asked, suddenly leaning forward and very curious.

She was taken a little back by the question. "Actually, I have been having some weird dreams since I got here. You would think I was crazy if I told you," she said with a little uncomfortable laugh. *What sane person dreams of cyborgs?*

"This is a safe space, Miss Newton. You can tell me anything," he said earnestly.

Catherine seriously doubted that she could tell him anything, and was starting to wonder if that controller of his could send faculty to the mental hospital as well.

"Well, I keep having dreams where this man tells me to 'stop the mining'," Catherine replied, leaving out the part about the man being mechanically enhanced.

"Why does he want you to stop the mining?" he asked, looking at her intently.

"He won't tell me why the mining needs to stop. He will say just that it is getting more dangerous. Last time he said that the mining needs to stop or it will wake him, or worse, his brother."

"Wake him and his brother, you say? Hmmm ..." He sat back in his chair in contemplation. "So, it sounds to me that maybe your subconscious is not happy with all the quakes and this is interrupting your sleep. I can understand the quakes can be disturbing if you aren't used to them. Rest assured, Miss Newton, there is nothing to worry about. I've been here for over 15 years, ever since the mining company first got here. My brother Alluri owns Greggo Sands and our family was assigned here when he came to open the mine. The quakes have intensified in the last few years. I am not sure what they are up to in order to warrant such a big blast as they had Wednesday. I can see how that could be disturbing. Jonny wasn't the only one knocked down, and I have had complaints from other faculty members as well. I am sorry you are losing sleep. My brother has great respect for human life and works diligently to ensure the mining is done in a safe and professional manner. Unfortunately, quakes and tunnel failures are unavoidable. At least you can rest assured that there will be no quakes this weekend; the mine is closed for Josh Armstrong's father, Larry. He died in a collapsed corridor yesterday. Are you aware? It was a tragedy."

"Yes, I am aware. It is very sad. I heard he had three children. I didn't see Josh in class today, and I expect he will be out for a while. I think the funeral is this Sunday," Catherine said.

"Yes, I plan to be there. Will you be attending, Miss Newton?" he asked.

"Regrettably, I have other obligations so I won't be able to attend," she replied but immediately felt callous and followed up with, "How safe is the mine? I mean, this kind of thing doesn't happen very often, does it?"

"This tragedy is a rare occurrence indeed. But, I would not say the mine is a safe place no matter what my brother tries to assert," he paused for a minute, looking contemplative. "For instance, it is dangerous enough that one should not be wondering around the mine in the middle of the night. I hope you keep that in mind, Miss Newton," he said, pointedly and sternly, leaning forward for emphasis. Once he could see the shock register in her eyes that she realized he knew she had been in the mine last night, he stopped staring so hard and leaned back once again. "I am glad we were able to talk today, Miss Newton. Please, enjoy your weekend and I hope you get some rest. Feel free to come by my office anytime .... during the day. Good day."

As Catherine walked out of the room, a chill went down her spine. *How did he know she was at the mine in the middle of the night? Did Jordan tell him?* She walked in thinking he was going to re-assign her, only to get chastised for not getting enough sleep because she was wondering around the mine in the middle of the night. *Did everyone know everything about everyone in this small town?* It was a small world if the principal was the brother of the owner of the mine. She had mistakenly assumed the owner had to be someone named Greggo given the name. *Maybe Greggo Sands was a place? Another mine?*

There were two things she did know when she got into her car to head home. One, she was going to sleep unquestionably well tonight. Two, that thank God it was Friday! *Woo, hoo weekend!*

CHAPTER 4

Take a Hike

The weekend was going by too quickly. The days were getting colder so her hikes with her dog were getting shorter. Today, however, it felt extra-long because she had two dogs. Sass and Rufus where quite the pair. Sass was beautiful, elegant and a lady as she pranced along the trail right next to Catherine. Rufus was a half-black, half-white mix of fat fluffy shepherd. He was as distracted as a dog could get. He pulled ahead, weaving left and right along the trail, sniffing everything and everyone in sight. Catherine was getting bigger calves from digging in to hold Rufus back. Sass seemed amused.

Whenever a stranger would come up, Rufus was all over them, super friendly. He would jump up and lick them from head to toe, probably looking for crumbs of food. Sass would growl at anyone who came near her, super unfriendly. People had no idea how to react to the mix of the two dog's responses; neither was good. Rufus was large enough to knock over a full-grown man in his attempt to find food and Catherine constantly had to warn people not to try to pet Sass or she would bite. So, Catherine tended to look for less populated trails to avoid running into people when she hiked with both dogs.

Desert Grande had plenty of trails all throughout the valley and mountainside to choose from, thankfully. Today, Catherine decided to hike in a forested area near the east red rock mountains that reminded her of Montana where she grew up. The red dirt and rock was still foreign, but the evergreen trees and shrubs were as similar to the northwest as it got here in the desert. She was able to find a small dirt trail that followed a creek leading off from the main trail that it seemed everyone wanted to take today. After a few minutes away from the main path she felt she could finally breathe easy and enjoy the fall day. There were pink flowers on some of the bushes that were losing their petals. Their shades of pastel mixed with the grey and red rocks in the creek as they fell and drifted by.

She found a large log that cut across the creek like a tiny bridge and had mushrooms growing all along the sides. She sat on the log, inspecting the little mushrooms and let the dogs sip from the creek. She took off her shoes and socks and then let her tired feet cool in the stream. She couldn't help but feel at peace listening to the water trickle along the rocks and the rustle of little critters in the woods, splashing her toes to make ripples in the water.

Every now and then a raven would squawk, eliciting a small barking rampage from Rufus. Sass jumped up on the log and laid her head on Catherine's lap; she seemed to share in her contentment. Rufus jumped on the log and sniffed at the little mushrooms though didn't seem to find them appealing enough to eat. *Thank God!* she thought as she tried to imagine wrestling with Rufus over questionable mushrooms.

Catherine felt like she could sit on the log forever, but it was getting late. As she was putting her shoes and socks back on she could hear footsteps approaching. Sass was up and looking straight behind her, growling. Rufus almost jerked her backwards into the creek as he lunged towards the other side of the trail, in the opposite direction from where they had come. Someone was coming from deep in the woods.

As Catherine attempted to rein Rufus in, she saw the origin of the footsteps, a tall man in a jacket with the hood covering his face. He walked fast, with what looked like purpose. He seemed familiar.

"Jordan?" she blurted out.

"Catherine? How did you recognize me?" Jordan said as he pulled back the hood of his jacket. He walked closer to where she was sitting with the two dogs on the log.

"It was your walk. It is very distinctive. You're always looking like you are headed in a beeline straight for something important," she answered.

"I see. What are you doing out in the middle of the woods at dusk?" he asked as he tried, unsuccessfully, to not be knocked over and licked from head to toe by Rufus. He barely missed falling into the creek.

"As you can see, it is hard to keep Rufus off of people and the main path was a bit crowded today. I took a detour because I just needed some peace and quiet, and my arm needed a rest from wrestling Rufus off of people," she said as she pulled Rufus off of Jordan. "What about you? You look like you are up to no good with that hood up, all alone in the woods."

"I *am* up to no good," he replied with a smile. "I was just at the lake. It is about 2 miles north of here."

"What were you doing at the lake? Trying to catch a virus so you could get out of class?" she inquired as she pulled out some treats from her backpack to give to the dogs. "Did you see any mosquitos?"

"It is too cold for mosquitos. The whole virus thing is a lie anyway, and I am going to prove it. I know Greggo Sands is up to something; they have people all around the lake right now," he stated.

"What do you mean they have people all around the lake?" she said, puzzled.

"I mean, I saw people in white suits and masks, carrying what looked like test equipment, walking up and down the lake, looking for something. The suits had the Greggo Sands symbol on the sleeves. You do realize the lake has a direct run-off from the mines? I think they spilled something into the water and are trying to clean it up," he proclaimed.

"Why make up a story about viruses then? Why not just come out and say 'Hey, we spilled something, stay away from the lake while we clean it up'?" Catherine pointed out.

"The whole town relies on the mines, without the jobs that the company brings there would be no town. If the mines were implicated in the deaths of anyone who went to the lake they would have to close the mine for investigation and that could cost the whole town," he answered.

"But no one has died, right? I mean, none of the viruses are deadly from what I hear. They just cause strange reactions, like black scars on your skin or red welts or something, right?" Catherine said. Jordan was looking confused, and sullen as he sat on the log next to her. "I have only been here six months, so I might be missing something," she added, somewhat to console him.

"You are right. But, there is no mistaking what I saw. Plus, how does mining for viruses make any more sense than covering up toxic waste? You can't mine a virus, Catherine. The company is obviously cleaning something up at the lake," he insisted. "I am going to figure this out if it is the last thing I do."

"You know, there is something I want to figure out myself. How did Principal Repalle know I went to the mines the other day? Did you tell him, Jordan?" she asked, crossing her arms in disapproval.

Jordan countered with, "What do you mean he knew you went to the mines? Why in the world would anyone tell the brother of the owner of the mine that you were parading about looking in the tunnels while no one was there?"

"That's the thing, I didn't tell him. He showed up outside of my classroom right after I talked to you at lunch on Friday and asked me to meet him in his office at the end of the day. I thought he was going to reprimand me for hitting you with that door and that maybe he found out about all the times I have been showing up late. I was convinced I would be re-assigned but instead he gave me this speech about caring how I am doing, etc. ... and then ended it with a warning to not wander around the mine in the middle of the night!"

"Well, I didn't tell him," he replied. He paused for a minute, looking at Catherine without expression, then continued with, "You, perhaps, should not have told me either. What were you doing, anyway?"

"I wanted to see something. See, I had had this dream ..." She stopped herself. Was she actually going to tell him about her strange dreams? She didn't want him to think she was crazy. "It is getting late, we had better head back. I didn't bring a flashlight," she said as she got up from the log and crossed over the creek to the dirt trail.

"I see, a dream led you to stroll through dangerous tunnels all alone," he said as he followed behind her on the trail.

"I wasn't alone. I was with my boyfriend, Anthony."

"Oh yes, the famously handsome miner who loves to hunt," he said.

"Famously handsome?" she laughed.

"Isn't that what Elisabeth says?"

"Well, he is probably the most handsome man I have ever seen, but looks aren't everything you know."

"What is more important than looks?"

"Well, for one, having things in common is pretty important. Communication is a big one too. And great chemistry, of course," she said. She was starting to feel a little uncomfortable talking about this with Jordan. She hardly knew him, and what she knew about him so far is that he was paranoid and sullen, not the best traits in a person.

Rufus must have seen a squirrel, because he decided to try and rip Catherine's arm off to get to a nearby tree. Catherine liked her arm, so she let go of the rein in time to save it but not in time to stop from falling flat on her face in a pile of muddy leaves. Jordan was right beside her in a flash, helping her sit up and then heading over to go get Rufus from the tree. She sat on the trail, picking the leaves out of her hair, and spitting the mud from her mouth. Jordan was grappling with Rufus, trying to get him away from the tree that the squirrel had run up. Sass came over and started to lick Catherine's face. Jordan managed to calm Rufus down and lead him back over to where Catherine was sitting, still a bit dazed.

"You've got a small cut on your cheek. I've got some Neosporin and Band-Aids," Jordan declared as he removed his backpack to pull out a first aid kit, a small cloth and some water. He drenched the cloth in water and started to wipe her face clean. "I guess we are both clumsy when we are distracted," he said with a smile.

"Ha! Yeah, I can hardly see the welt on your head anymore," she replied as she brushed his hair off his forehead to check out the bruising from his encounter with the nurse's office door windowpane. There were flakes of gold in his brown eyes that she never noticed before, and his lips seemed so soft. She could feel her heart starting to beat faster and her body began to feel warm all over. As he applied the Neosporin his fingers lightly grazed her cheek and she felt flutters in her stomach. *Wow, talk about chemistry!* She blushed as the thought entered her head and turned away from Jordan to see Sass looking at her sideways.

"Umm, ah, so, Anthony, that's my boyfriend, left his phone band at the mine and we went to go get it because he couldn't live without it over the weekend. That's why I was at the mine in the middle of the night, rescuing my boyfriend's phone," she declared.

"I see," he said as he applied the band-aid and offered a hand to help Catherine to her feet.

"Yes, I came along for the adventure," she said as she put her hand in his hand. He pulled her up and she stumbled forward into his chest. Her heart was beating so fast she could hear it thudding in her ears. She was in his arms, looking up into his golden-brown eyes that were drawing her in like deep, unexplored caves. He was looking down at her, expressionless, dead still. Her heart skipped a beat as he leaned forward to remove another leaf from her hair.

"So, you are an adventurer?" he asked. "What did this adventure into a mine have to do with a dream?"

Catherine pulled away. What could she say? How to begin? "I have a lot of dreams, vivid dreams. I always have, ever since I was a little girl," she answered while fidgeting.

"And you dreamt about going into the mines at night?" he inquired.

"No. Remember Wednesday, when that huge blast went off?" she said as she started to walk along the trail. She still wasn't sure if she should be saying what she was saying, but now that she was saying it she might as well continue.

"Yeah, the day you hit me with the door, how could I forget?" he said as he followed behind her along the trail.

"Well, that night I had a dream. There was a man, I've seen him in a few dreams actually, and he always tells me to 'Stop the mining'. Like I can stop the mining, right? Anyway, that night he said they found one of his labs. The next day when Anthony was telling me about his day, he mentioned they had come across something that looked like a lab. His supervisor told him it was an old Navajo tunnel though. I know it sounds crazy but I just wanted to see it for myself. It seemed like such a weird coincidence, you know?"

"From what I recall, the Navajo did not have tunnels in this area; they weren't a tunneling people. I can do a little research on the area though, just to make sure," Jordan responded. After a brief silence, he said, "What did your boyfriend think of the dream?"

"I didn't tell him, I just said I was curious about the lab," she replied.

"I see," he stated as he walked on the trail behind Catherine. "Did the man say anything else in the dream?"

"Yeah, he said that the mining was dangerous and that it might wake him, or worse, his brother," she said. "I know, I sound crazy."

"Well, it is just a dream," he replied. He walked for a few seconds, then added: "It does seem odd that he is telling you that he is asleep in a dream."

"What do you mean? He was awake and taking to me in my dream," she responded.

"No, he said not to wake him, which meant he was asleep and so was his brother," he pointed out.

"Great, now I am super wacky, dreaming about sleep-walking cyborgs!" she exclaimed.

"Wait, what? You never mentioned he was a cyborg," he said while laughing. "So, you are dreaming of a dreaming cyborg? Is his brother a cyborg too?"

"Yeah, I have very vivid and weird dreams. Now you think I am insane for sure," she said, cringing.

"No, it was just a dream. I wouldn't worry about it, really," he laughed, then added: "I do wonder why you didn't tell your boyfriend about it though. How serious is the relationship anyway?"

"Pretty serious, I think. He's Catholic and wants a big family right away. I swear, last time I visited his sister she tried to measure me for a wedding gown!" she proclaimed as she stopped on the trail and turned to see how Jordan was doing handling Rufus. He had both hands on the reins and was still being dragged through the mud.

"You don't sound too happy about that. Do you not want to get married?" he inquired as he looked up from Rufus long enough to almost be dragged down.

"I don't know. It is all so fast. We have only been dating for four months and we haven't even ..." she was about to say 'had sex' when she cut herself off. That was more than he needed to know. *Wow, was she just going to tell him everything that popped into her head today?*

"Haven't even what?" he asked, looking perplexed.

Catherine was trying to think of something fast. "We haven't even gone camping yet," she stated. That was all she could think of, she wasn't a very good liar. *Camping?*

"Yes, a good camping trip can certainly tell you a lot about a person," he said with a laugh.

"You sure do laugh a lot more when you aren't at school," she declared as she continued walking down the trail.

"Well, I have to keep appearances or those students wouldn't be afraid of me anymore. A stern look of authority, with severe gravity keeps them in line," he stated with the firmest face and voice possible. It was disturbing. He obviously had years of practice.

They were at the parking lot off the main trail already. *How did they get there so fast?* Catherine wondered.

"My car is that way," she said, pointing left.

"My car is that way," he said, and pointed in the opposite direction. "I guess this is goodbye. Let me know if you want someone to go 'camping' with, my schedule is pretty open," he professed as he took her hand, gave it a gentle kiss and then placed the reins to Rufus in her palm.

He was walking away before she could open her mouth to try and respond. It was probably a good thing too because she had no idea what to say. He had guessed what 'camping' meant, and when his soft, warm lips had touched her hand she knew the chemistry was unmistakable because the fluttering in her stomach and the flushing of her skin went off in coordination. She began to wonder about how Italian he was. His last name was Muntz, so he had to be somewhat German. Most of the time he had that expressionless, yet superior German attitude when he was at school. But that smile, and those eyes. They conveyed so much passion it was almost overwhelming. Her roommate in college had dated an Italian guy; he was passionate indeed!

Catherine had to shake herself to some sense. Nothing was ever going to happen between her and Jordan. Anthony was her man, and even though they had never had sex, she was sure there would be plenty of chemistry when they did, based on all the heated make-out sessions that they had shared so far. The last thing she needed right now is another guy confusing her feelings for Anthony; they were already confused enough as it was.

She got the dogs in the car and sat back while the autopilot took her home. She spent the car ride home looking in the mirror as she removed debris from her hair and cleaned the mud off her neck and ears where Sass and Jordan had missed.

When she got to the house she could see Anthony's car in the driveway. He wasn't due back until tomorrow. Rufus saw the car too and started jumping and going berserk to get out. As soon as she opened her car door, he ran right to the other car and jumped at the door. Anthony must have been sleeping in the car because he sprang up and opened the door.

"Hey, Babe! I thought you were going to be out all weekend?" Catherine questioned as she walked up to the car. "Is everything all right?"

"Yes," he replied as he gave her a firm kiss and hug. "We managed to get three Elk in one day! That was all we were licensed to get this season, so we were a bit too successful. Man, I managed to shoot a 7-point buck with one arrow! Rodge was pissed because his buck was only a 5-pointer. Steven got a 4-pointer. Three bucks in one day and those guys are wining about not getting to put that 7-pointer in their living room, like we could share. Ha!"

"Should I be expecting an elk stew anytime soon?" she asked.

"No, we usually just keep the racks and heads for trophies and sell the meat. Rodge already brought the bulls down to the butcher this afternoon. Elk stew does sound good though. I haven't had anything since lunch. I came straight here after I went home to shower. I was hoping to surprise you. Oh wait," he said as he reached into the car. He pulled out a bouquet of wildflowers. "I found a whole field of flowers when we were out hunting, I figured you might like them."

"They are beautiful, Anthony. Thank you!" she exclaimed as she gave him another kiss. "Let's go inside and I can see what you might like from the combinator." With that they headed inside. She removed her coat and gloves and placed them on the hanger in the entryway. She filled two bowls each of food and water for the dogs and then looked up her phone band to check the combinator options for the humans. She lifted the band from her arm and pressed the button to straighten it for holding out in front of them so Anthony could look at the options too.

"Let's see, we could have tuna casserole or chicken lasagna. That seems to be about it for two people. There is enough Salisbury steak for one though. I usually do my shopping on Sundays, so we are a bit short on options. If you want, I could order Salisbury steak for you and when that is done I could have tuna casserole," she offered.

"Okay, that sounds like a good plan. Salisbury steak it is," he proclaimed as he gave her a kiss on the forehead. She placed the order in the app on her phone band.

"What happened to your face?" he asked as he touched the band-aid on her cheek.

"Oh, Rufus tried to catch a squirrel. He and the squirrel were fast, I was slow. I ended up face down in the mud," she replied. "Speaking of mud, I wouldn't mind taking a shower. Can you watch the dogs? Sometimes they fight over food when Rufus finishes before Sass and he is still hungry."

"Sure, Babe, no problem," he answered as he learned back and turned on the south wall to ESPN.

As Catherine washed off the mud and twigs from her hair, she kept going over the conversation she had with Jordan in her head. *Why did she just blurt out everything in front of him, with no filter? Maybe because it felt like she could tell him anything and he wouldn't judge her?* She had told him so much already. *Why couldn't she talk to Anthony like that? Maybe she should just try harder to open up to Anthony? Maybe she could start with telling him about her dreams and see what he would say? That's it. It was decided!* She would tell him about her dreams tonight.

Catherine got dressed in a light blue silk shorts and tank-top nighty and went downstairs. Anthony had already started munching on his Salisbury steak and potatoes. Rufus was sitting at his feet drooling and begging for pieces from his plate. Sass was curled up in her bed in the corner.

"Yes! Go, Go, Go!!" Anthony yelled as he jumped up from his seat, fork flinging potatoes that Rufus was more than happy to clean up. Catherine looked over to see a man running with a football get taken down by three other men.

"Did he make a touchdown?" she asked, trying to sound like she cared. She really wasn't a football fan, but every guy she had ever me was a fan.

"Almost. Sourier caught an interception and ran for 40 yards, now the Buffaloes have the ball," he exclaimed, not looking away from the screen the entire time he talked. He sat back down, still so completely engrossed that he wasn't even looking at the food he was scooping into his mouth. It looked like they would be watching the game tonight.

Catherine walked over to the combinator in the kitchen. Anthony had left the door open so her tuna casserole hadn't started yet. She shut the door and then went back to the entryway to pick up the dog bowls to put in the dishwasher. She set the Rhomba to clean up the mess around the doorway where the dog bowls had been. They must have fought a little over the food because it was everywhere. She then picked up her hiking shoes next to the door. She looked for Anthony's shoes and realized he never took them off. They were on his feet, which were on the coffee table. She went over to him and took off his shoes, trying to avoid breathing due to the smell of his feet. *Didn't he say he just took a shower?* she thought. She set the shoes by the entryway in the shoe cleaner hatch and then took the wildflowers he had brought her into the kitchen to find a vase. She placed the flowers in the vase on the coffee table next to his feet. She was hoping the proximity would help hide the smell. She then sat down and cuddled on the couch next to Anthony. *Maybe they could make out during commercials?*

"Do you want me to stay the night?" he asked, looking down on her curled up next to him. "I can control myself if you can. I have never slept with a woman before. I think it would be great to cuddle like this all night long, don't you?"

"I would love that," she said. It was an exciting thought, though she wasn't sure if she could control herself. She had never just "slept" with a man before either. It would give her more time to try and talk to him. Right now, he was so engrossed in the game it was impossible to say more than a sentence or two.

When the game finished she took him by the hand and led him upstairs to the bedroom. Her alarm was a digital projection on the ceiling that tracked time and weather conditions as images floating by as sunshine, clouds, rain, a starry sky, etc. She could set it to real time weather, or select another option or sky pattern. She even had Hubble telescope images to choose from, which were her favorite. They lay there for a few minutes looking up at a starry sky representing the current conditions, with little meteors that passed once a minute. He laid her head on his chest and then he put his arms around her, pulling her close to his side.

Ok, if you're going to talk, talk now! she thought. "Do you have any strange dreams, Anthony?" she inquired, thinking the question was a good transition to talking about her dreams.

"No, I never dream, or I never remember them anyway" he declared. "I mean I have dreams like goals and things I want for my life. Like a family, kids, you know. I've told you this stuff before. Definitely nothing 'strange.' I want to be a good father, teach my kids about mining, geology, hunting. Even if I have daughters, I want them to hunt too. Be good with a bow and arrow like their dad, you know? Man, a 7-point buck! That was a nice one, I am looking forward to mounting that in my living room!"

Catherine could imagine Anthony being a great dad. She could picture their kids running around, adorable and adventurous, hunting in the woods. As she was distracted, thinking about kids, she heard a rumbling growling. The growling turned into a spurt of snorts, followed by what could have passed for a chainsaw. It was shocking; it was coming from Anthony! He was snoring, and it was loud! This was something he should have warned her about because she didn't have any earplugs. He also had a tight grip on her with his arm around her, holding her oh so close to the gaping source of the cacophony. She couldn't pry herself loose; she was stuck! She lay there, miserably awake, wondering what in the world she had done in her life to make her deserve to be tortured by a wailing gargoyle throughout the night.

CHAPTER 5

Just a Day at the Job

Anthony was a humble man who wanted a modest life. He knew he was not the smartest man and he never intended or even thought to go to college. He got a job directly out of high school working in the mine to support his family. His favorite part about the job was blowing things up, that's why he signed up to be a blast helper from the start. What he lacked in book smarts, he made up for in street smarts and leadership skills. He was able to work his way to crew lead in just a few years and he was on track to be the next foreman. If he was going to do a job, he was going to do it well.

He always strove to do what was right by his family and for God. He began each day with a prayer, thanking God for his blessings. Today, he made sure to thank God for Catherine and allowing a night with her without falling for temptation. Holding her in his arms, he felt complete. He had fallen asleep so quickly when he spent the night at her place this past Saturday. It was probably the best sleep of his life.

He felt they were very compatible. She had the book smarts to his street smarts. She reminded him of a teacher he had had a crush on when he was 12. He loved how great she was with kids too because he planned to have at least six.

His whole family was pushing him to marry Catherine, convinced she would convert to Catholicism as soon as they were engaged. He didn't need much convincing; he had fallen for Catherine from the start. Ariana, his youngest sister, helped him pick out a ring this past Sunday. Gretchen, the second youngest sister, had aspirations to be their wedding planner and had already tried to measure Catherine for a wedding dress when she wasn't paying attention. His parents were thrilled and couldn't wait for grandchildren.

This next Thursday, on their weekly date night, Anthony was planning to propose to Catherine. He had to come up with a good spot, and he was still trying to work out the words to say. He was excited, and ready for the next step in his life.

Everything was coming together for him and he could hardly sit still with anticipation.

Monday morning work went by in a flash as his team dug further down Tunnel One where the corridor collapsed last Thursday on Larry's crew. They were putting in extra supports today to ensure no further collapse, and Foreman Gamble came by to inspect the work himself. When Anthony went back to the washing station to clean up for lunch, Foreman Gamble pulled him aside and asked if he would meet him in his office when he was done eating.

Anthony had no clue what the meeting was for, and he didn't stress about it either: he would find out soon enough. *Maybe he was looking to fill Larry's position already?* That would be a promotion with training. He put it out of his mind for the time being. He was starving and looking forward to reminding Rodge and Steven about the buck shoot this weekend during lunch. They were already in the cafeteria showing pictures to a couple of the other guys from their crew when Anthony came in.

"Hey Rodge, you tell them I brought down that 7-pointer with only one arrow?" Anthony asked as he sat down next to Steven, who was chowing down on some beef stew. Steven and Rodge were both a couple of years younger than Anthony, and had joined his crew two years ago. They had all hit it off instantly and had been inseparable ever since.

"Yeah, you know I let you have that one. I pointed him out to you and the next thing I know, you were up and shooting. You spooked the whole herd and if we hadn't happened across that second gang then both Steven and I would have been pissed and you know it," Rodge declared. Rodger Lombardi was a short, dark Italian with a hooked nose. He had a little bit of a gut and an attitude big enough to make up for his small stature.

"You pointed him out? Ha!" Anthony laughed. "Yeah, right! I was locked on him before you said anything and you know it. It was your arm movement that spooked him, that's why I had to take the shot right then. Isn't that right, Steven?"

"Huh? What?" Steven said, looking perplexed and annoyed. "You know I wasn't looking, we've been over this already," Steven urged, between mouthfuls of stew. "We caught 3 bucks in one day, that's amazing! Who can say that? Who cares who saw the first buck, let it go! We all went home with good trophies for the season."

Steven Chan was very tall and thin, despite his veracious appetite. He was half-Chinese and half-Irish, with green slanted eyes and a few little freckles on his cheeks. He usually had the most sense of the trio despite being the youngest.

"It matters because I get to take home a sweet rack to mount on my wall, right above my fireplace," Anthony gloated. "You are taking good care of my trophy, aren't you, Rodge?"

"What kind of guy do you think I am, man? I brought all three by the taxidermist this morning. He said they should be ready in a few weeks," replied Rodge. "Speaking of trophies, how's that hot little teacher of yours? She like those flowers you, so delicately, picked for her?"

"At least I have a girlfriend. Maybe you should think about taking a shower every now and then, Rodge. The circling flies might decide to leave you alone long enough for a girl to see you," Anthony responded, jokingly.

Anthony finished off his stew, wiping the bowl with the last of his cornbread and gulping it down in one bite. "I've gotta run. Boss man says he wants to meet with me."

"What's old Gamble want with you?" Rodge asked.

"You thinking he wants to promote you? Maybe give you Larry's job?" Steven asked.

"I don't know, but he sure didn't want to meet with you two losers so I guess it is a promotion," Anthony said as he smacked Steven on the back. "I'm headed out to the shed. Don't do anything stupid while I'm gone."

The shed is what they called the three-story, cement office where all the bosses, finance and HR spent most of their day. All their desks were set along the perimeter of each floor, facing inward with glass separating the offices from the center. There were several working elevators in the center, each marked by a circle on the ground. When someone on an elevator was about to enter the floor, the ground would light up and buzz. If there was an object or person on top of the circle, the floor wouldn't open. Else, it would open and whatever was above or below would be moved using a clear tube into the circular area. Then the tube would leave and it would just be the person standing there. The tubes utilized a pressurized vacuum system that was highly efficient and very fast, even with large objects. In the very center of the room was a giant pillar. The pillar had various news stations projecting on all four sides. Above and below the stations were live feeds from cameras planted within the mines. The floor was 15- feet tall, and every three feet, on each of the four sides, there was a live display. The displays and stations would change and rotate periodically.

The first time Anthony had been to the shed was also the last time he had been there: when he was initially hired into the company over four years ago. He had forgotten how fast everyone walked, moved and talked in the shed. The constant flashing of the projections in the center and the movement of the tubes whistling by was a whirlwind, and he couldn't image anyone being able to get anything done with that distraction.

Gamble walked out of the office three cubicles up to the left and waved Anthony over. Anthony walked forward, slowly, keeping close to the glass and as far away from the elevator tubes as possible. The constant movement in the center gave him a little vertigo. Even from where he was standing he could feel the air move as people went through the tubes. He didn't want to get any closer for fear of being sucked down a tube.

"Anthony, I am sure you know why I asked you to come to my office today," Gamble stated, simply, as he crossed his hands on his lap and sat back in his seat. He was a stout but firm man, with steel blue eyes and freckles almost covering his face. His thinning auburn hair was missing from the front half of his head, which shone with beads of sweat.

"I'm sorry sir, but I have no idea," Anthony replied, honestly. He gingerly took a seat in the chair across from Gamble at the large office table. The table was fully topped with pictures of his family, a large black briefcase, a collection of rocks from the mine as well as three computer monitors.

"Did you think we wouldn't find out? We have cameras everywhere. Even when we are shut down, they continue to run. I should fire you, right here, right now," Frank Gamble threatened as he turned his right most monitor around to show two shadowy figures looking around a room with a flashlight. The image was dark and hard to discern, but when the man holding the flashlight looked up and pointed it at the ceiling, his face was clear as day on the camera for a brief second. It was Anthony, looking for those ventilation shafts in the middle of the room that he had thought might be a lab.

"What in the world made you want to do what looks like some kind of spy investigation, in my mine? I got heat from Mr. Repalle himself this morning. That whole area is closed off due to radiation. You realize that you and your little teacher girlfriend are lucky to be alive?" Foreman Gamble asked angrily. "What were you thinking, young man?"

"I was just trying to impress my girlfriend, honestly sir. I had only come in to get my phone band from my locker and she wanted to explore. I didn't realize there was a radiation leak, sir. If I had I wouldn't have gone down that corridor. She had never been in a mine before. She was curious and I ...." Anthony continued to explain but Frank was no longer looking in his direction, something on the other side of the glass wall had caught his attention. Anthony turned around to see what had caught his eye.

On the other side of the wall, an old gray-haired man with a large tool belt around his waist full of tools had appeared in one of the tubes. He had started to walk quickly towards the glass of Foreman Gamble's office and then he abruptly fell. There was blood coming from his eyes and ears and he was convulsing on the floor, coughing up blood. Several people had come out of their offices to see what was going on but Gamble bolted out and yelled at everyone to stay back. He pressed a few buttons on a small device at his waist and then told Anthony to go get the briefcase off of his desk. Once Anthony brought him the briefcase, he punched a few numbers into the control panel on the top and it opened. There was what appeared to be a hazmat suit inside the case on one side and on the other side were four injectors filled with differing colored fluids. In addition, there was also a small device inside that Foreman Gamble reached for first after putting on a pair of gloves and a mask. He then ran the device over the forehead of the old man. It kept beeping and turning red, but Gamble tried it over and over.

"This is not happening," Gamble whispered, closing his eyes. The old man had stopped convulsing and his empty eyes were staring straight up at the ceiling.

"What did you say?" Anthony asked as he moved in closer, leaning down towards the old man to see if he had a pulse.

"Everyone stay back!" Gamble yelled, pushing Anthony back and almost knocking him down.

Three of the circles lit up at once, several people had to take a step back towards their offices to make way for the elevator tubes. Men in hazmat suits appeared with briefcases similar to the one that Foreman Gamble had opened next to the man on the floor.

Foreman Gamble shook his head and said, "This one is new, check where he came from. We need to contain this, NOW!" He motioned towards Anthony and said, "Take this one too, he needs to be debriefed and quarantined."

Before Anthony knew what was happening, two of the men had him by the arms and were taking him down one of the tubes. All he could see was light whizzing by, he felt like he was going a million miles an hour and then he felt weightless as the tube decelerated to a smooth stop. It all happened in a matter of seconds. He was brought to a large room that looked like a prison center with nothing but 10-foot steel doors all around. He was placed in the room behind one of the huge doors and the men were gone before he could even speak.

Anthony turned around in a circle, taking in the room. It looked like a doctor's office inside. There was a locked cabinet with medical appliances, with a built-in sink that had a soap dispenser. There was a doctor's table and a small rotating chair. Anthony sat on the doctor's table and waited.

After what felt like an eternity, another man in a hazmat suit entered the room saying, "Hi, I'm Dr. Steinman. I believe you may have been exposed to something dangerous and I will need to examine you."

Dr. Steinman motioned towards the table and said, "Please have a seat." He then walked over to the locked cabinet and removed what looked like a long syringe. "This may sting a little," he said as he placed the needle in the back of Anthony's neck. There was a petite box on the bottom shelf of the cabinet in which the doctor placed a few drops from the needle. It beeped three times and a red light appeared on the top. The doctor quickly turned around and smiled. "It appears you are all clear. I will be right back."

With that, the doctor was out the door with the little black box in hand. About 15 minutes later, the door opened again but this time it was Foreman Frank Gamble that entered the small room. "I bet this is very confusing for you, Anthony, am I right?" he asked as he sat in the chair next to the cabinet.

"Yes sir. Will that old man be okay?" Anthony inquired.

"No. It seems that he has died of a stroke. It is never easy to see a fellow coworker die, even when they are 76-years-old and still trying to work like they are in their 20s," Foreman Gamble replied, mournfully.

"But, why the hazmat suits and why am I here if he was just having a stroke?" Anthony questioned, bewildered. None of this added up right.

"Listen, Anthony, I need to level with you. You do have a family, Anthony? Two sisters, a mother and an Aunt here, from what I remember, right? You wouldn't want anything to happen to your family, am I clear, Anthony?" Foreman Gamble asked, pointedly. "Here at the mine, we are all one big family. We're very protective of our own family too. We must all work to protect our family. You've been part of my crew for over four years now and today when you helped me with the briefcase and the old man it was another example of the quick thinking and hard work that has earned you crew lead status. Leadership, you know, is all about setting the example. Sometimes you do not have all the answers, but you have to do what is right for your family. Without the mines, this city would not exist. Our family, would dissolve. Again, I ask, you wouldn't want anything to happen to your family, would you, Anthony?"

"No, sir. My family is the most important thing to me, sir."

"Good. I am glad to hear that. Before your little investigation adventure with your girlfriend, I was considering you for training into Larry's position as lead blast engineer. Now, I am not sure if I can trust you. I need you to prove to me that I can trust you," Foreman Gamble insisted.

"I am willing to do whatever is necessary, sir," Anthony said, reflexively. He was still in shock.

"Good. For now, know that everything we have done today is to protect you, because you are family. I don't ask questions of leadership, and they have not explained anything to me and I am okay with that. I need you to be okay with that. Are we clear?" Foreman Gamble questioned.

"Yes sir," Anthony responded, knowing there was no other way to answer the question.

"Also, no more nighttime adventures in the corridors; it is not safe. Are we clear on that as well?"

"Of course, sir. It will never happen again," Anthony pleaded.

"Thank you. I will be keeping an eye on you, Anthony. Please do not make me regret my trust in you," Foreman Gamble insisted.

Gamble pressed a button on his waistband and it opened the steel door. He then led Anthony through the hallway and into one of the elevator tubes. The deceleration at the top made Anthony feel like his blood was being pulled into his feet and almost made him black out. When he could see clearly, he saw that he was face-to-face with the pillar of flashing news stations and video feeds at the center of the offices where he had been earlier. Everything seemed back to normal, people in their offices going about their day as if nothing happened.

"Now, get back to work," Gamble announced as he headed into his office and shut the glass door behind him.

Anthony was dumbstruck and walking in a daze as he headed back down to the mine. There was a long passageway along the cliff face that led from the shed to the mine. He stopped, and while holding onto the guardrail, he threw up his lunch over the side of the cliff. Down below he could see the clear blue lake that had been carved out by a glacier millions of years ago. The whole area seemed blissful and serene as a gentle breeze blew past and left sparkling ripples along the lake and set the trees in motion. Anthony wiped his mouth and continued forward towards the mine.

Family. The most important thing to Anthony was family and he was pretty sure Foreman Gamble had just threatened his family. He would do anything to protect his sisters, mother and aunt and that included keeping his mouth shut about everything that happened today. He didn't like to lie, it was against his religion, but not saying something was not the same as a lie. So, he planned to just forget about it and never bring it up. *That was the right thing to do, right?*

He stopped again on the bridge to say a prayer and ask God what to do. He stood there looking out at the mine and back to the shed. He stared at the lake below, and couldn't help but notice how peaceful the whole area was this time of day. He noticed a helicopter coming into the helipad, and Alluri Repalle, the mine owner himself, walked out to greet a group of men and women waiting for him near the shed entrance. Whatever was going on, it looked like they had everything under control and he had never heard of anything going on before now. This was all way above his pay grade.

That man was very old and really could have died of a stroke for all he knew; he had never seen anyone die of a stroke before. After what Anthony had done, getting caught snooping around the mine in the middle of the night, he felt lucky to still have a job. After what he saw today, he felt lucky to be alive. And, if he kept his mouth shut, he might just get that promotion after all.

By the time he got back to his shift, everyone was cleaning up to go home. He walked to the washing station and began to clean his hands. He noticed a small bunch of dark red dots that were coming off in the water in streaks. It must have been blood splattered from the old man when he was coughing and writhing on the floor. Anthony decided to use a little extra soap this time, just to be sure he got his hands clean.

"So, what did the Foreman want with you all afternoon?" Steven asked as he started to wash his hands next to Anthony.

"Yeah, you were gone all day. Man, you look pale, are you okay?" Rodge inquired with concern as he came up to the other side of Anthony at the washing station.

"Let's just say you might be looking at the next lead blast engineer," Anthony responded with as big of a smile as he could muster. That wasn't lying, Foreman Gamble did hint at him getting Larry's job.

"No way, man! That is awesome. Did you start training today? Is that why you were gone so long?" Steven asked.

"No, I haven't started training yet. We had a long discussion about leadership," Anthony responded. "And, we talked about how he didn't know anyone except me that could deal with you two lazy bozos that can't drill a blast hole to save your life."

"Is that so? Well, I'll have you know I drilled three blast holes without your supervision today, and they are perfect," replied Rodge.

"Perfectly uneven. Hector had to go through and ream the holes you drilled just to get the explosive pouches in," declared Steven.

"Oh, and yours were better?" Rodge retorted.

"Hey, I never said I was perfect! You're the one saying your crappy blast holes are perfect," Steven exclaimed as he shook his wet hands dry in Rodge's direction, splatting him in the face with hot water droplets. Rodge responded with flicking water at Steven from the running water, getting it on Anthony as well in the process.

"Children, please! See, this is what I was talking about, a couple of bozos," Anthony said as he took a towel off the rack and proceeded to twist it, then flick the end of it at the back of Rodge's rear end. Rodge jumped and almost landed in the washing station, then splashed water at Anthony's face in defense. Steven went for another towel off of the rack and Anthony battled him back.

They were interrupted when second shift started billowing into the washing room to get ready. Anthony dried off his arms and face with the towel he had been using to fight off Rodge and Steven. He noticed a little red come off from the back of his neck where the needle had gone into his skin. A chill went down his spine as he was suddenly reminded of the day's events. He threw the towel into the bin with the others and got his belongings out of his locker.

"Just another day at the mine, just another day at the mine" Anthony said aloud to himself as he got into his car to head home. He planned to forget everything he could about today.

CHAPTER 6

Boss Man

Alluri Repalle sat in his helicopter, looking over at the view below. The wilderness of America was magnificent: he could see a herd of horses playing in a river and red boulders all around shaped like ancient guardians of the wild. Sitting across from him, and deliberately not looking out the window, was his head of research and development in Russia, Sasha Mikhailov. Her knuckles were white from how hard she was clutching the briefcase on her lap. He asked how she was doing and she produced only a strained smile on her pale face. Apparently, she wasn't a fan of heights.

"Don't worry, you're perfectly safe," he said with as much authority as he could to try and ease her anxiety. He was used to having authority and responsibility from a young age. He was the third child, and second eldest son of 10 children in a highly prestigious Brahmin Hindu family. His father and mother had both filled various roles in politics back in India. He rarely saw his parents while he was growing up, and became very close to his siblings, helping to teach and raise them. He strove hard to be successful to show a good example, and to be seen as honorable in his parent's eyes. He came to America when he was 16 and he earned dual degrees in mechanical and metallurgical engineering from the Colorado School of Mines. He followed those with an MBA from Harvard before becoming employed at the mining company Greggo Sands. After several quick promotions, he became the CEO and bought the majority share in the company so that he could run it exactly the way he saw fit.

Then the war came. The Great War of Dust they called it. Even though it lasted just a few short years, the aftermath of the radioactive dust across the planet left most areas uninhabitable. Five of his siblings and his father died in the war, two more died slowly just a few years after from the dust. Sickness and death was all around him for years, so he poured his devotion and energy into his work, expanding the mining company and investing in new research and technology.

When his eldest brother and mother took an assignment here over 15 years ago, he had no idea the mines in the area would end up being the crown jewel of his company. In fact, he didn't even know if they would produce anything of value. It was his brother Sanjay who persuaded him to invest more in the old mines, to support the build-up of the new community. Luckily, he found high levels of bauxite, which was a key ingredient for the energy harvesting ceramic roads his company had been developing over the last decade. But, what was discovered recently was much more valuable, and more dangerous.

Alluri stepped off the helicopter at the landing pad above the main governing building for the Desert Grande branch of Greggo Sands. He and Sasha were met by several members of his staff and then escorted down to the offices below. Sasha discretely headed straight down to the research floors below while Alluri made the rounds through the offices, greeting as much of the staff as he could. He found that the best way to keep track of what was going on in his company was to engage with employees at every level. Sometimes the lower level engineers and supervisors would let slip details that the upper managers tried to keep hidden from him because they did not want to let him know they didn't have control over absolutely everything.

"How is the expansion coming in Corridor One Mr. Gamble?" he said as he approached the office of the head foreman for the site, Frank Gamble, who was apprehensively waiting for him outside the door.

"Couldn't be better, we are making great progress now that we are back to work today. We're spending extra time reinforcing as we go to ensure no future collapse," replied Frank Gamble, shaking Alluri's hand with vigor. There was a sternness to this foreman than he always appreciated; it helped him keep a tight crew.

"Good," declared Repalle. Then he brought Frank a little closer and said soft enough for only him to hear, "And the little incident with the curious couple?"

"Nothing, just a young man trying to impress his girlfriend," whispered Frank sincerely, looking confident, though still shaking Alluri's hand.

"We've all been there, my friend, haven't we?" said Alluri as he patted Frank on the back, which seemed to cue Frank to finally release his hand. Women were more trouble than mines. His wife still expected rubies and diamonds whenever they got into an argument. That reminded him, he would have to get her a gold bangle just for taking this last-minute trip, with no notice, or he could expect grief when he got back that night.

He looked around for more employees to visit, giving Sasha more time below. There weren't many more offices on this floor, and it was getting close to the end of first shift. The head of HR was pregnant, and he wanted to make sure he congratulated her on the blessing of her second child before making his way down to the Research Department. He found her office across the tubes, and was able to pop in just as she was packing up to leave. Afterwards, he typed a code into his belt and the tube took him to where the real research was taking place, 10 stories down.

Sasha Mikhailov was there waiting for him in a glass enclosed inspection room. She and Dr. Steinman were in quarantine, in full gear, examining the body of the old man who had died earlier this afternoon. Alluri stood outside the lab looking through the glass and listening into the intercom for the full report.

"It is both miraculous and frightening, sir," said Sasha, with her strong Russian accent.

"Yes, it is unlike anything we have seen before," explained Dr. Steinman. "All other enhancements have been viral. So, when he tested negative, it was assumed he may have died of natural causes. That was until we were able to examine his brain. There was a residue covering most of the synaptic tissue. Upon examination it was found to be a neurotoxin excreted by an unknown, gram-positive bacterium."

Dr. Steinman walked over to a microscope, and turned around a computer monitor to show moving bacteria suspended in liquid as he said, "We have found traces of the bacteria in his blood. However, we found none on his clothes or body, nor in Tunnel Three where he had been working last week before we closed it down for radiation. It looks as if the bacteria survives for long periods of time, dormant, but it is not resistant to our high heat cleaning methods. So, most traces are probably destroyed. It was likely kept in the form of a fine powder in one of the glass containers that were shattered during the blast last Wednesday."

Sasha interrupted with, "It seems Mr. Grayson here was heading up the initial clean-up crew and came across some broken glass that he failed to mention." She lifted his right hand, which appeared to have a large cut. "He must have cleaned up all the evidence, fearing reprisal."

"A bacterial neurotoxin? Fascinating!" said Alluri. "Can we synthesize any for further testing from his blood? What does the excreted neurotoxin do exactly? How did it kill him?"

"From what we can tell, it enhances neural activity. His brain and nervous system must have been firing at exceptional rates right before he died, given the amount of damage we found. We are already synthesizing the neurotoxin and growing a culture of the bacteria for further testing," replied Dr. Steinman.

"This would be the first enhancement we have found to increase brain activity," Sasha quickly added.

"This is also the first to prove deadly. How does increased brain activity cause death?" Alluri inquired.

"I believe it was a combination of his advanced age and the amount of initial exposure. The aged immune system was unable to clear the excess toxins as they built up," replied Dr. Steinman.

Sasha added, "Yes, the brain and nervous system basically overheated from excessively, externally stimulated activity."

"How confident are you in your assessment? You said the bacteria was found in his blood. Is there any possibility of contamination to other employees?" asked Alluri.

"It is hard to say. We will need to conduct a thorough investigation of the clean-up crew, Mr. Grayson's family, and those that came in contact with him during his death," replied Sasha.

"The clean-up crew have already been examined, no cuts found and no bacteria in their blood. Mr. Grayson had no family, and his two cats have been eliminated and disposed appropriately, just in case. There were only two individuals that came into contact with him during his death and we are monitoring their activity until we find a suitable treatment," added Dr. Steinman.

"Monitoring? We need them in quarantine. Until we know if this spreads by any means other than direct blood contact, or if it poses a threat to anyone but the elderly, or those immune compromised. We can't take any chances," Alluri declared, shocked that the doctor had released anyone out of the confines of the lab who had been contaminated, even if it was a bacteria and not a virus.

Dr. Steinman looked dejected and responded with, "Yes sir, we will move them to quarantine immediately."

"Does the bacteria respond to standard antibiotics?" asked Alluri.

"Yes. We will need to do further testing to see how long the toxin takes to fully clear. For all we know, a normal, healthy individual maybe able to eradicate both the bacteria and toxin without antibiotics. We'll have to bring in test subjects... I estimate we will have more answers within two weeks if we start immediately," Sasha explained. Dr. Steinman nodded in agreement.

"Good. You will have all the resources you need to begin testing straightaway," responded Alluri. He liked the idea of a product that could require re-exposure, that meant increased profitability. He could see this as the next "smart pill," finally something he could sell outside of the black market.

"How has the clean-up of the Quinta virus leak been going?" Alluri asked.

"Fairly well. We still don't know how they are leaking into the lake. Every passage and run off has been checked repeatedly. I believe there must be more corridors within the old compound that we have not found," said Dr. Steinman.

"Or, more plausibly, your men are not being careful with the shipments," responded Sasha. She and Dr. Steinman just stared at each other. This was an argument Alluri had heard a dozen times, unfortunately.

"So far, we have been lucky. Every virus has not been deadly, but who knows what we will find as we continue to dig? We all need to strive to be more careful." Alluri responded as he began to think of ways to ensure no further damage could be done. *Maybe a new company safety initiative? Employees needed to feel comfortable coming forward with reports of minor injuries, like cuts, but how would he motivate them? Safety Stars program?*

"Sir, we have new data from Test Subject 17," said Dr. Steinman, interrupting Alluri's train of thought. "He is in Room 5, would you like to see? It is quite fascinating."

"Yes, of course," replied Alluri. "Lead the way."

Dr. Steinman and Sasha both left the lab and went through the cleaning room to disrobe. Alluri was steered further down into the research facility and to a large steel door. Dr. Steinman entered a code into his belt and the door opened. Inside a large room, on a small cot, sat a man wearing only light blue cotton pants. His face, chest and arms were covered in black streaks and his eyes were bloodshot, but he was smiling as he said, "Nice to see you as usual, Dr. Steinman. I see you brought company?"

"Yes, Gerry, this is Mr. Repalle and Miss Mikhailov. They have come to see what you can do," replied Dr. Steinman. "Can you please demonstrate?"

"As you wish," Gerry responded as he bowed his head slightly and walked over to a weight bench. He picked up a large barbell, with several weights, with one hand. He then flipped it into the air and caught it with the other hand. Next, he took one of the weights from the end of the barbell and broke it in half with his head, grinning like a Cheshire cat the entire time.

"Remarkable!" exclaimed Alluri. From what he could tell, the weights on that barbell added up to about 300 lbs. He walked over to pick up one of the pieces of the weight Gerry had smashed with his face, a metal coated cement. He tried to smash the piece against a large bar and the reverberations he felt back into his arm from the impact caused him to drop the piece to the ground with a loud clang. “The latest Quinta virus looks promising. Do we know how it works?”

“The virus takes over the cells in the muscle fiber, causing it to produce a concentrated carbon fiber similar to graphene in structure. The resulting muscle tissue is 100 times stronger than normal, and 10 times denser,” explained Dr. Steinman. “It also can help the body withstand large electrical currents, though I am not sure Gerry would want to demonstrate that right now, would you?”

Gerry didn’t not look enthusiastic. He just stood there rubbing his right arm where the skin looked red over the black streaks.

“Sasha, have you found anything dangerous about this new virus? How is the antivirus coming along?” asked Alluri.

“The muscle transformation, once initiated, is irreversible. They become a permanent carbon coating, like a tattoo on the muscle tissue. However, the anti-viral we have created, if administered early or before exposure, can limit and even prevent initiation of carbonization by the virus. In addition, the virus must be injected directly into muscle tissue in order to spread, so there is no worry about indirect contamination,” replied Sasha.

“So, it is synergistic with the last 4 viruses we have found? Does Gerry here have the other four as well?” inquired Alluri, looking over to Gerry, who was now smiling again because he wasn’t going to have to demonstrate the shock proofing effects.

“Yes, Gerry is the first to have all five,” Dr. Steinman said quickly, smiling and patting Gerry on the back. “If the muscle enhancement was not backed by the tendon and bone reinforcement, that little flip would have ripped his arm right off. The other two enhancements that cause increased liver enzyme and red blood cell production we believe were designed to aid in the large amount of cellular changeover needed for virus propagation. So, yes, they are extremely synergistic. Whomever developed these had a clear focus.”

“Yes, a focus that we will be able to take advantage of. The Russians and the Chinese are both finding the first four in great demand. Now, with the Quinta virus, soldiers like Gerry here will be the new elite force of the world," declared Alluri. Gerry looked quite pleased with himself, and very healthy. Except for the bloodshot eyes and the fact that just below the skin there were black streaks running all along his muscles. "Are there any ... negative side effects?"

"None that we have found," said Dr. Steinman. "All 20 test subjects have had improved health, strength, and even speed. It appears the firing speed of the new carbon tissue is also 200 times quicker than normal fast-twitch muscle fiber."

"It just seems too good to be true," said Sasha. "No negative side effects? I would find it hard to believe if all my testing did not confirm little chance of ill effects. It all seems positive. Even virology has come back with little chance of contamination; subcutaneous injection is the only means of dispersion in all five."

"I agree, Sasha. It does seem too good to be true. Especially with our latest findings, improved physical ability combined with mental stimulation," responded Alluri.

"Mental stimulation?" asked Gerry eagerly.

Alluri instantly regretted mentioning the latest findings from the bacteria. Gerry was obviously hooked on his enhancements, and wanted more.

"Yes, I did not realize it!" Dr. Steinmen said, enthusiastically. "Faster muscles only equals faster reaction time if the synaptic tissue is firing faster. We should start trials immediately with the bacteria and the viruses combined. This would take the entire system to the next level, with extraordinary possibilities!" exclaimed Dr. Steinman with emphatic nods from Gerry.

Sasha gave Alluri a look he had seen a thousand times, one that let him know how much of an idiot she thought Dr. Steinman was in wanting to move forward so quickly to human trials. He had been this reckless with each new virus, and seemed to be getting worse at moving forward without much testing.

"Let Sasha finish her tests with the mice, Dr. Steinman. Just because we have been lucky so far, does not mean that our luck will continue. Be patient, we will know more in two weeks," responded Alluri. Dr. Steinman looked like he was about to say something, then he cleared his throat and nodded. Sasha looked pleased.

"Now, I need to get back before my wife makes me sleep in the garage for the next week. Is there anything else I need to see?" said Alluri. "Sasha, I assume you will be staying here for the next few weeks. Do you need anything?"

"Wait, she is staying here?" asked Dr. Steinman in shock.

"Yes. Miss Mikhailov and I both believe the status quo here would benefit from having our head of research in its midst for a little while. She may also be able to solve the problem of the leaks we have been having into the lake," announced Alluri, with authority. He wanted to make sure Dr. Steinman knew he was being watched, and to be on his toes. The leaks into the lake were unacceptable, and there had been whole shipments of product disappearing lately. Something was going on, and he was sure Sasha's presence here would either root out the issue or resolve it.

Seven years ago Dr. Steinman was a regular general practitioner assigned to the mine. Now his responsibilities far outstripped his credentials. He had done a fine job in adapting, but Alluri was beginning to question his motives.

The three moved out of Gerry's room, through the steel door and into the main research floor. They walked a few feet towards where the tubes where but Dr. Steinman suddenly stopped and turned around.

"I didn't want to say this in front of Gerry, but we have had some negative side effects," said Dr. Steinman.

Both Alluri and Sasha were alarmed; this was the first they had heard of anything remotely negative about the remarkable enhancements they were finding and synthesizing for years. They both looked at each other and crossed their arms over their chests at the same time. When they realized they had both done the same thing, they both uncrossed their arms at the same time as well. Finally, Alluri cleared his throat and said, "Continue" to Dr. Steinman.

"The viruses are synergistic with each other, but they take a lot out of the body, even with the increased red blood cells and liver enzymes. Gerry is not our only test subject to take all 5 viruses, he is the only one who has survived."

"What do you mean? I thought all of the viruses caused enhancement effects," said Sasha. "All of my research has indicated positive results."

Alluri could see she was going almost as pale as she had in the helicopter as she started to mutter something he didn't understand in Russian. He felt a bit nauseated himself, *how many deaths?* When these viruses were discovered, he did everything in his power to ensure the safety of everyone working for him and in the town. He would have kept them buried or destroyed them had they had any negative effect. This news from Dr. Steinman was quite a shock, and hard to believe given the extensive testing they had performed over the last seven years.

"Yes, individually they have enhancement effects. But, when combined, especially with the last one, the Quinta virus, they take too much out on the nervous system. Some of the test subjects have already died," Dr. Steinman continued, but Sasha interrupted with, "Why are we just now hearing about this doctor? How many have died already?"

"Two over the weekend, numbers 18 and 20, and 19 died just this morning. Please, I am not sure how much longer Gerry has to live. I believe the new bacteria is key to his survival; he may not have two weeks for your tests to complete," explained Dr. Steinman, looking directly at Sasha. She was staring him down with overt suspicion. She began to open her mouth to say something he was sure to be an insult directed at Dr. Steinman in Russian when Alluri interrupted with, "Go ahead, doctor, if it will save Gerry's life. Only Gerry though, no other human test subjects, understand?"

"Yes sir, of course. Thank you," replied Dr. Steinman. "Excuse me, I need to go make preparations for Sasha's stay here and ensure the rooms are ready for the necessary experiments. I assume you are done with me for now?"

"Yes, of course. Thank you, Dr. Steinman, I appreciate your efforts and progress," responded Alluri. He waited a minute for the doctor to enter the tubes and be out of earshot before he turned to Sasha and said, "Is there anything you need? I want to ensure your efforts here are not in vain."

"I assure you, I will be quick and thorough. As soon as I find anything, I will let you know," she responded. "I find it highly suspicious that we are just now hearing about any deaths. He did not mention a thing to me when I came down; he only focused on the old man. I find his reticence disturbing. I will route out everything he is keeping from us. Be assured, he will speak freely soon."

Sasha Mikhailov was the most competent researcher Alluri had ever met, he was sure she would do exactly what she said. She looked off in the direction the doctor had gone with a scowl, fists clinched.

"I feel like I have been down here all day. I am starting to feel claustrophobic!" Alluri declared, attempting to ease the tension.

"You own a mine and you get claustrophobia? Odd," responded Sasha looking at Alluri quizically.

"I am a mine owner, not a mine worker," replied Alluri, laughing as he made his way to the tubes. Sasha pressed a few numbers into her belt and gave him a little nod. He would have nodded back but he was already flying towards the offices above.

His was met with empty, dark silence. First shift had ended, and the only workers left were in the mine, not the offices. The center column still displayed activity in the mine, but the images were dark and there was no sound. The news stations were turned off, the lights in the offices were off and the windows showed the sun had already set. *Where did the time go?*

When he reached the heliport outside, he saw his pilot waiting. He was sitting on a bench playing a game on his expanded phone band. From what he could see through the glass, it looked like some kind of puzzle game with little stuffed animals that looked like kittens navigating a labyrinth. When he noticed Alluri standing there, the pilot replaced the band on his right arm and stood up stretching, then said, "Your wife is not going to be happy, Mr. Repalle, and I am pretty sure Zales is closed by now."

Alluri cringed, looking down at his phone band; it was already 8:15 pm. He had been married for over 25 years, and the one thing he knew for certain is that tonight he would be sleeping in the garage.

CHAPTER 7

History Lesson

Jordan always had a fascination with anything historic. Particularly wars in the great empires of ancient Rome and China. He spent the majority of his youth in libraries, nose-deep in book after book on the rise and fall of ancient civilizations. He had probably been so interested because when he was a youth he was living through the fall of one of the greatest civilizations, The United States of America. Even before the first bomb struck LA, he knew it was impending. The sudden large military spending, the loss of the gold standard, Russia's loss of key holds in the Middle East, and especially the rapid rise of India and China in technology and industry were all tell-tale signs. By the time the first bomb dropped, he had already convinced his parents to take an extended summer vacation in Wyoming.

Living through the disaster and reading about it later in history books were two different things. In real life, there was sudden panic followed by years of complete isolation from what civilization that remained. The reality was illness everywhere due to radiation dust covering all of the North American continent. Those who did not die in the initial blast either died in the following weeks or were left caring for those who were dying even more slowly, such as Jordan's parents. They died two years after the dust reached Wyoming. There was no help, but there were also no invaders to fight because the whole world had fallen apart. It was just death, loss and loneliness. It would be years before communities came together again with the help of the International Alliance to re-establish what remained of the people of the United States and Canada.

According to history, when President Trump retaliated against North Korea for the first bomb that made it into USA by basically obliterating all of North Korea, everyone else who had a nuclear bomb decided to use theirs at once. Russian decided to launch an attack on all major US cities simultaneously, as well as major targets in Europe. Anti-ballistic missiles were able to stop most of the bombs, but the few that got through were enough to cause total worldwide chaos. China took advantage of the disaster, with their own interests being control of all of Asia. However, they were stopped in their pursuit by India and Russia. India with the help of USA military overseas and British allies that remained in Europe had taken out Pakistan. Their coalition had conquered through most of the Middle East into Saudi Arabia by the time they stopped. After three and half years of bloody warfare, India and their allies were caught by Russia, who controlled the vast majority of Europe to the North, and China, who controlled almost all of Asia on the east.

The continental USA was left in nuclear dust, isolated and alone, no longer even seen as a threat with China, India and Russia emerging as the global leaders. International laws were set in place to completely remove all nuclear technology and put limits to military spending by any one country. The large increase in military spending that Trump had pushed for in the USA was seen as a direct threat to Russia, and was their excuse for the attack.

What was left of the United States and Canada pulled itself together on Christian values, hard work and community which they believed was the pillar of what had made the nation great.

The war was also blamed on the greed and selfishness of capitalism, and due to the help of China in re-establishing the economy and law, current communities were heavily influenced by communist order.

That was history. But, the reality was that nothing seemed all that different now than what Jordan could remember from his youth before the bombs and dust. He still spent the vast majority of his time in libraries and researching on the Internet. People still went to work, the grocery store, and home every night. Technology was still advancing at a rapid pace, selling to the highest bidder, capitalism or no capitalism. Everyone and their brother was taking advantage of the vast land and mineral resource of the Americas that had previously been protected, similar to right before the war. Plus, the superpowers of India, China and Russia were in a cold war standoff that could blow up any second. To Jordan, it felt just like living in the USA before the war.

His interest in the rise and fall of civilizations was still strong, even after living through a fall. Today he was researching the Indian tribes that lived here before Europeans settled the area. He had started looking up Navajo details to prove to Catherine they weren't a tunneling people and had come across some interesting information about viruses as well that might help him answer what was going on at the mine.

He was particularly interested in signs of viruses that wiped everyone out. He did not expect to come across an article from the 1860s about an illness that wiped out the entire settlement that was known as Mesa Heights. The illness was blamed on a nearby Native American population, which was quickly dispatched by state militia.

He had never heard of Mesa Heights. Supposedly, it was a mostly Dutch population that had migrated west for gold mining. He did a little more research and found that this entire desert region was once called Mesa Heights. Despite its past, it had become a thriving mining community again until the 1950 when it was wiped out by another strange illness. After this last incident, the entire town was abandoned.

The name of the town, Desert Grande, wasn't introduced until 15 years ago with the arrival of Greggo Sands. Until then, there was practically no population.

Jordan never knew any of this, mostly because his past searching was on the history of Desert Grande. Now he had a treasure trove of information, and it was both thrilling and frightening, by searching for hits on Mesa Heights. What was the mysterious illness that kept wiping out the population in the area? Were there any survivors who could tell the tale from the 1950's? Most of the people here were assigned within the last 10 years, himself include, when Greggo Sands decided to make it a model town for their new ceramic roads.

Jordan performed a search of Census data from the 1950s, finding no population. Though no one remained from the 1950s, anyone who lived there pre-war might know more about the area and its history. He then searched 1960s, then 1970s with nothing. However, he found a few families that moved here in the 1980s. It was probably considered a retirement community by then because almost everyone was over 60 and very few families had children.

He finally found one with children who might be alive today. The Jahren family consisted of four people, two were kids. According to the 1980 Census, both Martin and Beth Jahren's occupation was listed as research scientist. They had two young sons: Clifford and Daniel, age four and seven, respectively. Census data indicated that this family remained in the area at least until the 2010 Census. He wrote down the address listed on file and the names listed for the two boys.

Jordan then performed a search for any news articles on Daniel Jahren, finding a news article that stated both him and his brother had opened up a research department and were hiring in 2007 in southern Colorado. Another article written in 2010, as a homegrown pride feature, had a picture of the two brothers. The men were dressed as doctors, accepting an award for advancements in prosthetics at an international medical convention. The last article in 2017, unfortunately, was an obituary. It listed both Daniel and Clifford as being assumed deceased following an explosion at their research facility. The explosion had killed everyone inside. No more new articles followed and the newspaper went out of print less than a year later. The research facility must have been the primary business in the town of Mesa Heights, because everyone left town and there was no one left according to the 2020 Census, the last census taken before the war began.

The research into the two Jahren brothers had reached a dead end, literally. Jordan was disappointed. He had hoped to use the address on file and track one of the brothers down to discuss the history of Mesa Heights. He wanted to know about the mysterious illness that wiped out the population in the 1860s and 1950s. Now he had even more questions and no answers.

Jordan sat back from the computer at the library and began to rub his temples. He stared at the picture of the two brothers for a while; they looked so proud and happy it made him sick. Suddenly, he realized he saw something odd about the younger brother, Clifford. There was a small amount of what looked like black streaks coming down the side of Clifford Jahren's hand as he held up the prosthetic arm for the picture. The streaking pattern looked exactly like the description of the latest virus discovered at Lake Holt, the Quinta virus.

That made Jordan think of something Catherine had said in the woods. *Didn't she say that she had dreamed of a "cyborg" who had said something about a brother, and a lab?* These were brothers, who worked on prosthetics and ran a lab in the local area. This seemed like too much of a coincidence. Jordan printed out the news article with the picture of the two brothers to show Catherine.

What exactly did Catherine say? He had been behind her while she was talking, ignoring most of what she was saying, taking in the ample view. She had a gentle sway to her hips as she walked that he found mesmerizing. She had said something about a cyborg man being asleep in her dream. That had been a bit strange. Dreaming of a dreaming person.

He would have to ask her more at school. It would give him a reason to talk to her, which he found pleasant. Not that he expected anything to come from it; he was twice her age and had been alone most of his adult life. He had no idea how to incorporate someone into his life right now, and hated change. But, he enjoyed making her smile, and her nattering wasn't all that unpleasant compared to most. He especially liked the way she looked with her hair down, in a mess, with a few leaves stuck in it ... with her breathing heavy ... his mind began to wander, then he remembered he was in a public library and pulled his thoughts out of the gutter and packed up to go home. His research on the viruses could wait until tomorrow.

Monday couldn't come soon enough. The article Jordan was keeping in his left pocket felt like it was made of burning coal. All he wanted to do was hand it to Catherine and see what her reaction would be –impressed he hoped. His students were extra irritating today. Year after year they were getting dumber and this year's class was, by far, the dumbest. Not one could name the first president of the United States, much less the last. If the information wasn't right in front of them, or the event wasn't happening right now, they didn't care.

"One merit for whoever can answer the next question," Jordan announced, hoping that would get their attention. A few students seemed to perk up at the offer. This merit system had its flaws, and he never had too much success getting involvement. *How did Elisabeth do it?*

"Name one of the Indian tribes that once lived here in Colorado." Jordan's offer was met with blank stares all around. "Just one, take a guess, anyone?" Jordan continued. *Not a single student could name a single tribe, not a single one!?!* Jordan was pacing up and down the aisle between students and trying not to lose his temper.

"I got one, Mr. Muntz," chimed in a tall, lanky, dust-blond-haired stoner in the back of the class named Edward Paulson.

"Go ahead, Mr. Paulson," Jordan replied, hoping for an answer that wouldn't make him want to throw his digiTeacher Controller against the wall.

"The Shoeshiners," Edwards said, meekly.

"Shoeshiners? You mean Shoshone?" Jordan responded.

"Yeah, man, the Shoeshiners, they all got wiped out by Big Foot," Edward said, barely containing his laughter.

"Thank you, Mr. Paulson, but there were no 'Shoeshiners' in Colorado," Jordan declared, irritated enough for the large vein in his forehead to start to pulse. He rubbed his temples with his left hand while his right hand shook slightly from the restraint of holding onto his controller.

"Of course not anymore, they got wiped out by ..." Edward began.

Jordan interrupted with, "There was never any 'Big Foot' either, Mr. Paulson. There was, however, a Native American tribe called the Shoshone, of whom Sacagawea belonged. Does anyone remember her significance in American history?"

"She helped Lewis and Clark scout the West," answered Angela Freeman, a bone-thin, bleach-blond sophomore with big blue eyes and fake dark eyebrows.

"Thank you, Miss Freeman, that is correct. You just earned yourself a merit," Jordan replied. "Sacagawea worked as a translator, and proved invaluable at ensuring the Lewis and Clark exposition's safe passage through territory that was predominately controlled by the Shoshone at the time."

The bell rang and everyone began to quickly leave and Jordan announced, "Tomorrow, we will discuss more about the Native Americans of this area. Please do your research in order to be prepared for questions in class."

Angela presented her digiStudent to get her merit and quickly left the classroom. Edward came up right behind her and asked if he could get a merit too, for his participation.

"Mr. Paulson, you are lucky that you are not at Principal Repalle's office right now, you understand?" Edward looked confused, but Jordan just gave him a blank stare until he gave up and walked away.

Jordan sat down at his desk and felt a bit troubled. He pulled out the paper in his pocket that he planned to show Catherine. Did she care about history? What was he doing, trying to impress her with knowledge? He thought about throwing the paper away, about skipping lunch.

His next class was senior level world history. He knew these students well. Most had classes with him for the last 3.5 years, so they knew him well too. Not one student was smiling once they walked into the room and saw his demeanor. No one liked pop quiz day, and when he was in a bad mood, it was always pop quiz day. As he put a current map of the world on the front wall, he heard groaning all throughout the classroom. He smiled; their misery made him feel just a little better.

"Pop quiz. Please use the map shown to mark the controlled territories of the major superpowers of the world. Then, mark each of the major countries described in class last week that no longer exist since WWIII," Jordan Muntz declared as he sat back in his chair to take in the wonderful, terrified looks on the students' faces.

The bell rang and the class did not move, they were all still staring at the wall in horror and busy typing into their digiStudents. Muntz turned off the front wall and stated,

"Please submit your final answers now, or none of your work will be counted." He thought he heard a few cuss words from the back of the class; that almost brought a smile to his face.

There were a few stragglers, so he decided to count down aloud "5, 4, 3, 2 ..." and by then all had submitted their answers. "Thank you, I look forward to grading these this afternoon."

"It looks like your whole class is going to a funeral, Jordan. What did you do to them?" Elisabeth asked, standing right outside the doorway.

"Pop quiz," replied one of the students morosely, as he brushed by her on his way out of the door.

"Yes, I just thought I would check to see if the class remembered anything I said last week," Jordan responded. "From what I can see, they did not."

"A quiz on a Monday? You are particularly evil, Jordan, especially considering most of these students did have to go to a funeral this weekend," said Elisabeth as she headed out to the faculty lounge, shaking her head and patting one of the forlorn kids reassuringly on the back.

Jordan followed, a few steps behind. He watched as she engaged some of the students with little waves of her hand, and smiles, even a "hello, blah blah blah." *How was she always so cheery? Why did the students like her so much?* He was exhausted just being witness to it all. Maybe Catherine was right, maybe Elisabeth was on drugs. That thought made him smile. *Sign me up for the happy drugs!* he thought as he pictured himself walking through the halls, high fiving the students, skipping even.

Jordan was in line behind Elisabeth at the combinator in the faculty lounge. She turned around to see the little smirk on his lips and then acted like she was going to pass out as she exclaimed, "Oh my god, Muntz is smiling, everyone!"

"I don't believe it," Jordan heard behind him, then turned to see that it was Catherine, smiling herself, dimples and all, looking up at him with those doe-brown eyes. She had her hair down today in little waves around her face that made her look even more sweet and innocent than usual.

"He must have had a good weekend marking student papers with F's I presume," stated Elisabeth. "Your schadenfreude finally giving you a high, Jordan?"

"No, just wondering what kind of drugs you're on, Elisabeth," he responded nonchalantly, no longer smiling and face back to the controlled expression he worked so hard on perfecting all these years.

"Oh, the best kind of drugs. Sunshine, clean air and exercise. I spent the weekend backpacking in the San Juan National Forest with a group of friends and my vitamin D levels are peaking. You should try getting outdoors sometime," Elisabeth said. "You might stop looking like Skeletor's cousin 'Bob the snob.'"

"I don't think the wilderness works that way with him, Elisabeth," Catherine replied. "He looked just as grouchy as ever when I came across him hiking Saturday."

"Now that is a story, you two went hiking together? What did handsome Anthony have to say about that?" Elisabeth asked as she pulled her Tikka Masala out of the combinator. She stayed at the line, bringing the bowl up to smell her food, savoring it almost as much as she was savoring the looks on both Catherine's and Jordan's faces as she eyed them both up, down and sideways. "Wow, you both look like you were caught doing something naughty."

Jordan looked over to see Catherine blushing. It was then that he recalled the conversation about "camping," and the kiss he placed on her hand as he left her in the parking lot of the trailhead. He felt protective of her, and wanted to defend her.

"We ran into each other. She was out walking her boyfriend's dog. Don't you have anything better to do than to start rumors and gossip Elisabeth?"

"I thought you said you were going to the funeral this weekend, Elisabeth," said Catherine. "Did you skip the funeral to go camping?"

"I did go to the funeral. I support my students in their time of need, unlike you two. It was Sunday afternoon; I got back Sunday morning. It was very sad to see the Armstrong children dealing with the loss of their father. They read a poem together and barely made it through. It seems the whole family is going to be relocated to Oklahoma, so that is good news," responded Elisabeth. "I have family in Oklahoma, a cousin, I wouldn't mind being re-assigned there myself."

Jordan retrieved his Tikka Masala from the combinator and couldn't decide what to do. He wanted to sit with Catherine so he could show her the paper, but if he sat down now she might not follow him to his table. He decided to take a little extra time getting utensils and napkins, then casually stood next to Elisabeth.

"How many children did Larry Armstrong have, Elisabeth?" he asked.

"Three. They were 17-, 10- and 4-years-old. Josh was the only one we all knew, the other two were too young. His wife is a homemaker, so she is getting re-located to be near family to help raise the children. She didn't seem that sad. I speculate that Larry might have been abusive," Elisabeth replied.

"There you are spreading rumors again, Elisabeth. What proof do you have?" Jordan questioned. She always seemed to be in everyone's business.

Elisabeth responded quickly with, "Experience, wisdom and age, my young friend. When my husband died, I was a mess. I could barely hold it together. She was almost cheerful. The only time that I saw her cry was when her children read that poem, though I don't think a single person in the room didn't cry."

"What makes you think he was abusive, Elisabeth? That seems like a far-fetched claim," Catherine inquired as she got her lunch and headed towards the nearest empty table. Elisabeth and Jordan both followed, taking the vacant seats on either side of Catherine.

"Just a hunch," she said, noticing that Jordan had followed them to the table. "Speaking of hunches, what exactly went on during this 'accidental' hike together this weekend? How did you get that cut on your cheek, Catherine? Are you being abused? Jordan, did you abuse her?" Elisabeth remarked slyly. She then began digging into her curried chicken and rice, scooping it up with pieces of naan bread. She would suck the masala off of the bread before eating the bread, which Jordan found repulsive and irksome.

"Nothing, really. Anthony's dog, Rufus, nearly ripped my arm off chasing a squirrel up a tree. He threw me right into a large pile of sticks and mud, that's how I got the cut on my cheek," Catherine responded. "No one is abusing me. Please don't spread those rumors, Elisabeth!"

"So, Jordan threw you into a pile of sticks and mud and he is not abusing you?" asked Elisabeth between bites.

"No, the dog, Rufus, threw her," replied Jordan. "That dog is a beast, he could have killed her."

"He is a lot to handle, but I love that furry monster," Catherine stated, beaming. Before Elisabeth could say anything snarky, Catherine added, "I love the dog, not Jordan, and no one is abusing me, okay?" She started picking at her food; she had gotten the palak paneer, a creamed spinach, and looked like she was regretting it.

"Where was Anthony?" asked Elisabeth. "Oh wait, he had that hunting trip, didn't he? Convenient. When the cats away, the mouse will play."

"What are you implying?" demanded Catherine.

"She's just messing with you again, Catherine. She knows damn well nothing would ever happen between the two of us; she just likes to rile you up," said Jordan, still somewhat jilted by the "I don't love Jordan" remark Catherine just made.

"You are particularly entertaining, my young friend," replied Elisabeth, laughing. "Oh, to be young and innocent again!"

Jordan was picking at his meal as well. Not because he didn't like the food, tikka masala was one of his favorite dishes, but because he was trying to work up to pulling out the folded paper in his pocket to show Catherine. He finally just reached into his pocket and slid it over in front of her.

Jordan looked intently to see Catherine's reaction. She delicately unfolded the paper, then gasped aloud clenching her chest. She began mouthing the words in the article aloud as she read.

"Passing notes, are we?" inquired Elisabeth as she leaned over to see. "Next, you will be playing footsie under the table."

"It's none of your business, Elisabeth," Jordan responded, pushing her hand back as she tried to reach for the paper. He then took a big bite of his naan and sat back in contentment. He was enjoying gloating over Elisabeth's scowl and Catherine's attention on the object he brought. Catherine obviously was fascinated.

"Where did you find this, Jordan?" Catherine demanded and then she whispered, "How is this possible?"

"I was doing a bit of research in the library, searching old news articles in microfiche, and I came across this one. I thought you might be interested based on what you told me the other day. I plan to do more research tomorrow; you are welcome to join me," he responded, but quickly regretted the invitation. Catherine had looked up quickly, blushed, and looked down even more quickly. She was looking a little too intently at the paper now, as if trying to not to look at him.

"Sounds like a date to me," said Elisabeth, smirking.

She sure knows how to make an awkward situation worse! Jordan thought.

"I can't. I have to prepare midterms, and then I have to grade them. It will be a busy week for me, I'm sorry," Catherine replied, hesitantly. She seemed to be picking her words carefully, so not to hurt his feelings. "I'm already behind grading the last-minute assignment I gave my Medieval Literature class Friday afternoon."

"I understand," Jordan replied, quickly finishing his meal. As he was getting ready to leave, Catherine grabbed his hand and looked up at him and said simply, "Thank you."

"I'll let you know tomorrow what I find during my research tonight," he replied. He was feeling mixed emotions, mostly thrilled. Her hands were so soft and delicate. He looked over to see Elisabeth shaking her head at him, again. He gave her as blank a stare as he could and hurried away.

CHAPTER 8

Dream a Little Dream of Me

Catherine spent her evening grading the two-page essays she had assigned her class on the video of *Canterbury Tales.* Unfortunately, some of the kids had decided to follow her example and take a long nap during the video. She had just marked up the fourth student who thought the tales were about something silly like chocolate rabbits that lived in medieval times in a town called Canterbury England, where they now make all kinds of chocolates. *There is no way they could have gotten that from watching the video!* She put her digiTeacher Controller down long enough to rub her temples and take a few deep breaths. It was partially her fault, she did sleep through the whole class and set a bad example. *Maybe if she let them all slide on this assignment no one would rat her out to the principal? Why did she give them this assignment in the first place?* That's right, she had thought telling them they would have an essay on the video would make them pay attention and not look back and notice her sleeping. She was obviously wrong.

Sass picked up her head from Catherine's lap and then jumped up to plant a few licks on her cheek. "Thank you for the kisses, sweet lady," Catherine said as she scratched behind Sass's fluffy ears. She looked over at her phone band to check the time. The rest of the grading would have to wait for tomorrow; it was already past 10 p.m. "It's time for bed, isn't it?" Sass gave a little, 'woof' in confirmation.

Catherine made her way to the bedroom with Sass at her feet. She was too tired to even shower tonight; she would just have to wake up a little earlier to take one in the morning. She threw on a nightgown and plunged right into her sheets. She set the alarm to display the milky-way galaxy spinning above her. It was always so soothing to watch and it was guaranteed to put her to sleep right away. Staring up at the ceiling, her mind started to move through the events of the day, processing what was important for retention and everything else to forget-me-land.

Her mind stopped at lunch, with the smug look on Jordan's face as he handed her a folded piece of paper. The visual impression of what was inside that piece of paper would be forever burned on the back of her eyeballs. Two brothers, heralded by the local press and accepting an award for advances in prosthetics research. The face of the eldest brother stood out like it was painted in gold fairy dust in her mind's eye. Her body even remembered her reaction to seeing the article, and was replaying it for her as she thought about it again. For a second, her heart had stopped and she had forgotten to breath. She was staring at the man who had been in her dreams. A person she had never met in her entire life and thought was a figment of her imagination. *It was beyond coincidence, wasn't it? What did it all mean?* She had done such a good job of putting him out of her head all day, but now it was all she could think about.

She felt a shaky chill all throughout her body that ran deep into her bones and she pulled her sheets and comforter closer. *What did this all mean?* That thought kept repeating, over and over. *Maybe the mysterious cyborg man from the news article would be in her dreams tonight and she could ask him more questions? Maybe he would actually answer this time, now that she knew who he was and she confronted him with his identity?* She almost laughed at the idea of confronting a figment of her imagination. *Why not?*

She needed to relax her mind to fall asleep, which meant she needed to stop thinking about the news article and clear her head. She let her mind keep processing the rest of the day as usual and took deep breaths to relax. The rest of the day moved by in a flash and faded. The images ended with her imagination producing giant chocolate rabbits getting their heads cut off by her digiTeacher stylus and the chocolate heads landing on the desks of students in her classroom that hadn't been paying attention.

As her thoughts and reactive images faded, she began to fly straight into the stars from the projection above her bed. In her dreams the Milky Way was made of milk. As her hand glided over to grab a twinkling blue star the milk dispersed all around her. The white milk became fluffy clouds encompassing her. The clouds then dissipated into a finer and finer mist. As the mist cleared, the surrounding scene became a red cliff overlooking the city of Desert Grande. It was a cliff she had hiked by several times since she had been assigned to the city, but she had never gone up to the top. She had wanted to go to the top, and had looked up and wondered what it was like many times but there was no trail to the top that she could find.

Her bare toes were on the smooth surface of petrified sand dunes that made up the top of the cliff. It was noon on a sunny summer day and the rock sparkled like a million little stars. There were little pools of clear water in the recesses of the cliff face, with dragonflies skipping across the water. The dragonflies glowed in all colors of the rainbow. The air smelled like the jasper trees and sage bushes of the surrounding woods. She opened her arms to feel the warm summer breeze blow through her silk nightgown, sending her robe flying back behind her like a cape. She felt like the wind moved around her body and hugged her like the greeting of a long lost friend.

"You look like a goddess," she heard behind her, in an all too familiar voice. She turned around to see the golden eyes of the mechanical man she expected. The normal flickering of his eyes where replaced by bright reflections from the sun. It was unsettling and almost looked like they were flashlights. The bright noon sun was suddenly a sunset, with muffled rosy tones. The flashing eyes were no longer blindingly bright, but subdued like the sunset.

"You have such control. Such vivid dreams. I find it irresistible to watch you," he said with a smile that did not reach his eyes as he walked over to within a foot of Catherine. There was a metal click and the sound of moving gears with every movement of his body as he moved closer.

Catherine could see the familiar, but completely foreign, symbols move across his eyes clearly from this distance and was trying to make them out. The symbols looked like something from an Aztec ruins, possibly the Nahuatl language, but with numbers mixed in and possibly Latin.

"Do you know why I am here?" he asked, breaking her stare.

"Yes, you want me to 'close the mine.' Hey, if I have such control over my dreams, then why would I dream of you telling me to do something so ludicrous?" retorted Catherine.

The mechanical man began to laugh hysterically. "Ludicrous?" he laughed more, the sound becoming more and more maniacal. "You have NO IDEA of the dangers that will be unleashed if they continue!"

"Then tell me all about it, Dr. Daniel Jahren," Catherine replied haughtily. The news article that Jordan had given her earlier was unmistakable; this man was the older brother of the two doctors, the one named Daniel Jahren. Of course, in the article he had hair instead of a half-bald head and half-metal plate with small objects sticking out the side that looked like they could be antenna.

He looked at Catherine with as blank an expression as she had ever seen, except there was something very cold about his eyes that sent shivers down her spine. She pulled her robe around her instinctively, even though it was a sunny, warm day. She had no idea what he was thinking.

"You are remarkable," he finally said, but with still no expression on his face. It was almost as if he was purposefully trying not to betray his feelings.

"So, you are Daniel? How are you in my dreams? What is so dangerous about the mines? How can I stop the mining? Why should I be the one to stop the mining? What is truly going on here?" Catherine demanded, pouring out the questions like canon fire. The barrage took Daniel back a step or two, literally. He walked back with every question. Then, he looked like he might walk away or disappear in his normal flash. But, after a terribly indecisive minute that made Catherine hold her breath, he finally decided to stay.

"Your dreams call to me, you wouldn't understand how I ...." he began but seemed to be troubled. "I just want to sleep. I need to sleep, Catherine. The digging is going to wake me up."

"And that is dangerous? How?" she asked.

"You know my name, which means you should know something about the viruses that have been part of the history of this area, correct?" Daniel inquired looking at Catherine, who was looking very confused at the moment. "Ah, I can see that you don't know about the viruses. History is a funny thing ... easily erased, easily changed, easily buried. You need to ask about the viruses, then you will understand. There's more ..." he looked at her, seeming to weigh his words and continued, "but that should be enough for anyone to stop digging in that godforsaken tomb of a mine."

"Viruses? Like the ones at the lake caused by the mosquitoes?" asked Catherine, perplexed. Those were the only viruses she knew about, and none of them were deadly or dangerous as far as she knew. "Jordan did say that he thought the mine had something to do with the viruses at the lake."

"Jordan? Who is Jordan?" Daniel seemed very curious, stepping forward again towards Catherine.

"He is just a co-worker, a History teacher actually: Jordan Muntz. He was the one who found the article about you and your brother working on prosthetics research and development that had your name," Catherine replied. *Why did he care who Jordan was?*

Daniel walked to within a few inches of Catherine, looking down on her ominously. He then closed his eyes. He began to flicker in and out of Catherine's dream. He disappeared fully for a minute, but without his typical flash of light that tended to wake Catherine up.

"This Jordan has very jumbled dreams, but he clearly has a thing for you," Daniel said as he re-appeared.

Catherine was blushing. She knew Jordan liked her. If the kiss on the hand after the hike wasn't enough, when he asked her over today to do "research" with him it sounded a lot like a date request. "What is wrong with someone liking me?" she asked, abashed.

"I see," he stated, looking down on her intently. He then disappeared again for another couple of minutes and when he came back he was frowning and said, "I would watch out for this guy. He is not what he seems and his intentions towards you are ... troubling." He looked like he highly disapproved of Jordan.

"Why should you care about his intentions towards me?"

"You are ...." Daniel paused, then continued with, "special to me."

"So, I am supposed to not have a relationship with a man because a guy in my dreams who says that he 'needs to sleep' thinks I am special to him?" Catherine replied, completely confused. She didn't know if she was flattered or angry.

"No, he is not what you think. His dreams are ..." he looked as if he was trying to think of what to say then continued with "disturbing. They indicate an unstable mind."

"Well, he seems to be the only one who knows anything about what is going on around here. And you don't seem to want to tell me anything. Who should I trust?" answered Catherine.

"I am sorry, you are right. I don't think you understand how special you are, how special all of this ..." he stopped himself. He then walked over to the edge of the cliff, near one of the little ponds and opened his arms, looking around at the rose-colored sunset scene, on a cliff overlooking the city. A purple glowing dragonfly landed on his finger, and he laughed as he continued, "Not everyone can dream like this, Catherine."

"Is that why you visit me?" responded Catherine. "To play with my dragonflies and watch the sunset?"

"Yes, and no," Daniel replied, slowly. "I do enjoy your dreams, and miss them when I can't find you. Why did you not sleep the other night? There were two nights where you were gone this week."

Catherine was swiftly disturbed at the thought of this man watching her *every night* and wasn't sure if she wanted to say anything. She was having trouble wrapping her head around how any of this could even be real; she was in a dream right now talking to a cyborg, after all. She finally answered, "My boyfriend, Anthony, he kept me up snoring all night one night."

"Boyfriend? I would never have thought you had a boyfriend. Why is he never in your dreams? Is this a new relationship? Most people dream of their significant other on a regular basis," Daniel inquired, quite shocked, stepping even closer with each question, and seemingly looming by the end. He was looming over her a lot tonight. He had never been this close before and this was the third time he had come so close in one night.

Catherine didn't want to answer; she didn't know how to answer. He had a point. Her dreams were filled with the things that made her happy, and Anthony was never in them. That probably wasn't a good sign for their relationship.

"What is his name?" Daniel said in a tone that made it sound like an order.

Catherine knew he was likely going to do that flicker and eavesdrop thing he had just done when she mentioned Jordan, but she was curious what he would find: "His name is Anthony Grant."

Of course, she was right. Immediately, Daniel flicked in and out, then he was gone. Catherine waited, he was gone for a while before he appeared again. She had been sitting cross-legged on the edge of the cliff, playing with her dragonflies. She was getting them to create a glowing rainbow around her when he materialized beside her and made them scatter in every direction.

"Anthony is sick. You must stay away from him," Daniel said, this time it was definitely an order.

"Sick? Like what kind of sick?" Catherine demanded as she stood up to face Daniel. She was very confused. Last time she saw Anthony he was as healthy as an ox. *Did he mean he had a mental illness? Like was he dreaming of sheep or something?*

"He was exposed to one of the tests we were running at the lab. We could never control this specific strain we had developed very well; it was unpredictable. So, we ended the experiment fairly early after a few test subjects died. Most tolerated the side effects of the neurotoxin well, but some had what we called a 'runaway reaction.' We were able to save a few of the runaways if we caught it in time. Once they started to convulse and emit blood from their ears and eyes, the only thing that could stop the overheating in their cerebral cortex was ice administered directly to the carotid arteries followed by intravenous penicillin," Daniel explained. He looked at Catherine and in a grave tone stated, "Don't kiss him, the contaminant is spread via bodily liquids, like saliva. Especially don't ..."

Catherine knew where he was going and interrupted with, "Don't kiss him, right? That's convenient. Don't kiss my boyfriend. For how long? Shouldn't I just get him some penicillin?"

He looked at her for a minute, seemingly weighing his options. "Sure, get him some penicillin," he said, "If you can get it to him in time."

Catherine didn't know what to think, but something made her believe she should be very worried about Anthony right now.

"He brought you into the mine? What did you find?"

How did he know that? Catherine thought, he must have seen something in Anthony's dream, or hers, though she didn't remember dreaming about going into the mine. "Nothing much, just some rectangular holes and broken glass. I wanted to see if you were real, if the lab you mentioned was real. I still find it hard to believe in your ... existence," Catherine responded as she struggled internally to figure out just what she believed.

Daniel walked forward and looked Catherine directly in the eye and said, "I am real. And you are in real danger if you don't get that mining stopped now."

Chills ran down her spine. His eyes were mystifying this close and his presence emitted a pulse in the air that could be felt and heard in low vibrating tones. In fact, looking this close to him she could see ripples warping her dream coming off his body. She answered him with, "Why? Just because you will wake up? What is so dangerous about that?"

"I told you, look into the viruses. You wouldn't understand the rest, and I would have to show you ... it's just too dangerous," replied Daniel. He looked down on her, his face was inches from her face now. He was almost a foot taller but was leaning down and then he reached his hand towards her hair. From this vantage point she could gauge his expression a little better and the look in his eyes verged on pain. "Just, close the mine, okay? Goodnight," he said as he closed his eyes.

"Wait, how?" Catherine asked, in vain. Daniel had already disappeared in a blazing light. *How did he do that? Actually, how did he appear in her dreams at all? This was all just so bizarre!*

The fact that he watched her every night was creepy. But his existence proved the ability to appear in and look at other people's dreams. The thought of anyone being able to look into another person's dream was exciting. *How did he do that? He said she had extreme control in her dreams, maybe she could too?* Anthony might die and she wanted to see him and warn him. She closed her eyes and concentrated on Anthony.

Images of Anthony flashed in front of her and then settled on him lying in a hammock, holding up a turkey leg like a microphone, singing in between bites of turkey. It was never-ending turkey, because after each bite the turkey leg would reform. He sounded like Frank Sinatra, singing 'The Way You Look Tonight.' The whole screen was a bit blurry and besides the hammock, turkey leg and singing Anthony in Hawaiian hula-dancing-girl boxer shorts ... there was nothing. Just white fogginess everywhere else. Everything and everyone, including the hammock were just suspended in nothingness.

"Anthony?" Catherine almost whispered. She couldn't believe it! *Was she imagining this or was she in his dream?* It didn't seem like her typical dream; it was all so unclear, unsubstantial.

"Catherine?" Anthony said in shock. He went to get up out of his hammock and instead flipped upside down, turkey leg flying into the air. The spinning hammock suddenly stopped and he was standing where the hammock used to be. His clothes had changed as well; he was now wearing what he wore on their date last week. He leaned down to kiss her and the whole world changed; they were now lying down in her bed. The bed was only half formed and the entirety of her room was dusky mist.

"Wait, I have to tell you something," Catherine said, shocked that he was so forward in her dream: he was trying to undress her! "You're sick, you need penicillin." He continued to kiss her, she wasn't sure he understood. "Anthony, Babe, listen, you're sick."

He wasn't listening. She couldn't change the scene to make him move away or listen. She normally could change anything in her dreams and the inability to change made her feel panicked and almost claustrophobic in the all-encompassing darkness in the room. *Maybe she was actually in his dream and that is why nothing was changing?* She closed her eyes and imagined the cliff from earlier. She was back, but Anthony was gone.

She closed her eyes again and thought of Anthony. She opened her eyes again and was standing in her bedroom at the edge of a not-fully-formed bed, watching him make out with what appeared to be her. Except the other her was dressed in somewhat the same nightgown but not quite. The version of her making out with Anthony looked different too: her hair was up like she wears it to school and her hands were all over him pulling off his clothes, which she hadn't been doing. Then, the other her began to undress herself. Catherine had to look away, because it all felt positively weird and uncomfortable to watch. Catherine closed her eyes and when she opened them again she was back on the cliff overlooking the city below.

Could she have really just visited Anthony's dream? He was normally not that sexual. Maybe it was just her projection of him? She could text him in the morning to see if he had any weird dreams. If he didn't remember his dream or if she didn't truly visit his dream then she would have to tell him about the penicillin he needed in person. If she told him about the penicillin she would have to tell him how she knew he needed the penicillin. That would be a fun conversation that she didn't even know how to begin.

She sat on the cliff, looking out at a purple sunset fading into city lights for miles all around. She usually just let her dreams take her wherever, enjoying the view. But, now she was wondering about all the lights across the valley. *Did they mean something? Were there people down below?*

She decided that she would focus on one of the lights below. It became stronger and came into focus. A street light in front of a house flickered into a small boy sleeping in blue pajamas on a red racecar bed. Next thing she knew, she was standing on a toy race track with toy cars flying all around her, bouncing off the track. Above her was the little boy. He was now a giant holding the flying cars that she had seen bouncing above and beside her on the track. He looked down at her and put down one of the cars so that he could reach for her. As his giant fingers came close to gripping her she closed her eyes and concentrated on the cliff she had been standing on earlier. When she re-opened her eyes, she was back on the cliffside.

Her heart was beating fast. She waited on the cliff for her heart to calm down and her breathing to get back to normal, staring down at the lights. *Where they all people? Who were they?* The lights flickered, some going out completely, some coming on for the first time. As she looked down at the lights, she felt connected. There was a hum in the air that vibrated in her bones and pulsed with the lights. As she focused on the pulse, she felt like all the lights at once were drawing her in and the pulse was getting stronger within her. She pushed away the pulse and all the lights went out at once. The valley below was dark. Slowly, the lights came back on, one by one. *What had she done? Did she just wake up everyone in the whole town?*

Was this all just her imagination? Daniel, the cyborg, had turned out to not be just her imagination. The picture Jordan showed her today proved he was real. *But what did that mean?* All along she had felt that his appearances were different, deep down. That is why she wanted to go into a dark, dangerous mine in the middle of the night when Anthony presented an opportunity. The fact that she found what looked like a lab, after Daniel had mentioned it in her dream, almost made her believe in and of itself. She just didn't want to believe yet. But she had to believe once she saw the evidence literally staring her back in the face from the news article.

The more she thought about Daniel spying on her, the more it gave her chills. Those golden flashes of strange symbols in his eyes was haunting. They made her feel so exposed, almost naked. She suddenly looked all around her on the cliff to see if he was watching her again. She was alone, and thankfully clothed in her silk nightgown and robe.

The cliff began to feel softer and softer beneath her. As she sunk into its embrace there was a sunrise forming over the valley below, glowing in soft yellow and orange as the sky above her was turning blue. There was an alarm ringing in the distance, getting closer and closer and it was drawing her away. She wondered how much of this she would even remember when she awoke.

CHAPTER 9

A Little Pep in Your Step

Catherine opened her eyes and sat straight up. She reached for her phone band and immediately texted Anthony, asking him to meet her for lunch. She was surprised to see another text message from a strange number. All the message said was, "We need to talk." She texted back, "Who is this?" and stared at the screen in bewilderment. She waited a couple of minutes. No response. She needed to get in the shower now, or she would be late, again. She put down the band and got ready for work.

In the car ride over, she kept looking for a reply from either Anthony or the strange number. It was driving her crazy and she was so distracted looking down at her arm that her driving was crazy. She eventually had to put her vehicle on autopilot going down her favorite hill because she hugged a couple of the turns a little too tightly, knocking a few rocks down the steep hillside into the trees below. She never noticed how far of a drop it was from that hillside until she almost went over with the rocks.

She managed to make it in one piece to homeroom, right as the bell rang. Everyone was already seated and she pulled out her digiTeacher Controller to take rollcall. Only Jonny and Lucy were missing. Jonny hadn't been back since last week because he was out with the flu. Lucy never missed class, and she was never late. *Maybe she went to the bathroom or was running an errand for another teacher?*

"Has anyone seen Lucy Gamble today?" Catherine asked, with no response from the class. They all looked like they just woke up and hadn't slept very well. Some even had crust in their eyes from the sandman still, and a few were sleeping! One Chinese student, Peter Liang, appeared to be not only sleeping, but drooling down the side of his shirt. She made a little knock on her desk and cleared her throat to try to wake the sleepers. They barely moved. Only Peter woke up, just to wipe his face on his sleeve and then put his head down on his desk to go back to sleep. Another student in the back, Tracy Brooker, had a small mirror out and was picking at zits, hoping that it would be hidden by her long hair hanging down on both sides of her face.

"I see that everyone is ready and excited for the day. Let's check the events. Ah, we have a pep rally today," she said and was met with groans and rolling of eyes from nearly everyone awake. "Are any of you participating in the show?" She had completely forgotten about the pep rally herself. Usually they put on a good show here at Desert Grande High School. The dance team, band, glee club and drama club all taking turns or working together to bring out school spirit.

"Not if we can help it," mumbled Jack Fairchild, while looking into his digiStudent Notebook. He was a quiet student who normally didn't speak in class, and was fairly withdrawn. He was always doing his homework on his Notebook during class and it looked like he never paid attention. Somehow, despite the lack of attention in class, he always managed to get good grades. He looked up from his Notebook, surprised he had said anything aloud himself.

Everyone looked so down and out, even more so than a typical Wednesday. "It looks like you could all use a pep rally. The comradery, the coming together to support each other, creates bonds and improves morale. I know the academic decathlon team that is going to nationals will appreciate the cheers and support. Plus, you get to leave fourth period early," Catherine said with as must gusto as she could muster this early in the morning. They got to leave fourth period early, but that meant her lunch break was extra short today and she was hoping to meet with Anthony as soon as possible to warn him about ... *What, a cyborg telling her in a dream he was sick and needed penicillin??* The thought was so ridiculous, but she still sensed Anthony might be in danger and wouldn't be able to live with herself if something happened to him.

She felt her armband pulse and looked down to find Anthony had texted back, "Sure, 11:30, park near mine. You bringing lunch?" Her heart jumped. She would have to skip the pep rally, and probably be late for her next class, and now she needed to pick up lunch too! She punched in the route into her navigation and searched to try to figure-out where she would get food on the way from the school to the mine. There weren't many restaurants that way. She started looking up meal options that were available and then she got another text. The strange number that had texted her earlier finally responded, "Jordan Muntz. I'm outside your door."

How did he get my number? Catherine thought. "Class, I'll be right back," she said as she turned the north wall to News Channel 4 and slipped out the door. No one even looked up, half were snoring.

"We need to talk," Jordan almost commanded as he grabbed Catherine by the arm and moved her away from her homeroom door and into a side hallway. His grip was very tight, and he looked like he hadn't brushed his hair or shaved today. "What did you get me into?" he demanded.

"What do you mean?" Catherine responded, completely shocked by his appearance and question. She pulled her arm from his grip and said, "How could I have gotten you into something? You look terrible. Did you even shower this morning?"

"The older brother from the article I gave you yesterday, he was in my dream last night. Except, like you said he had changed, he looked, walked, moved like he was a machine. Or, at least partially a machine. At first, he just stared at me with those golden eyes of his and then disappeared. Then he comes back just to put his arm through my chest, rip out my heart and begin to laugh maniacally as he squeezed my heart to a bloody pulp in front of my face. I get the distinct impression he doesn't like me," Jordan declared, emphatically.

Catherine had to stop herself from laughing, or even smiling though she thought the entire thing was funny. *Macho Jordan, upset over a dream?* "It was just a dream, Jordan, pull yourself together," she finally managed to get out.

Jordan was not amused. And quite frankly, it was hilarious to see such a tough guy upset over something so silly as a dream. He opened his mouth to say something then looked at Catherine putting her hand over her mouth to hide her smile and then he stopped. Sulking, with his normal grumpy demeanor, he said, "I would think that you of all people would understand."

"It isn't real; it is just a dream," Catherine tried to reassure him, but it just seemed to turn his mood darker. Okay, Jordan was not handling this very well. Maybe he wasn't used to having nightmares.

"Not real? That was the most real dream I have ever had! I did some more research yesterday. This guy Daniel Jahren and his family buried their research, and their research facility to hide something. He and his brother are supposed to be dead. Dead! How is he in our dreams? And how did he find me? Did you tell him about me?" Jordan asked.

Daniel was dead? That didn't make any sense. "I might have mentioned you in my dream last night. I think I spoke highly of you though. I said you were the only one who knew the truth that I could trust," Catherine answered, trying to recall the details of her dream. She couldn't remember everything; it was a dream, after all.

"I know the truth? Great! I don't know the truth. But I bet I know more than you, else you would be scared like me right now. I need to show you my research. You obviously have no idea what is going on, or refuse to believe what is right in front of your face. This is real, Catherine, it isn't just a dream. Is nothing real to you? You need to see what I have found. Can you come by my place after school today?" Jordan requested.

"I have so much grading ..." Catherine was trying to form excuses to not be alone with Jordan. She didn't know what would happen between them after the hiking trip when he mentioned he would go "camping" with her anytime. She was loyal to Anthony and she was sure he wouldn't want her alone at Jordan's place either. But, really she was curious about the research he had done and wanted to make him feel better; he was obviously very upset. She finally said, "I guess I can probably make it if I hold off grading a few essays. Text me your address later."

Jordan looked slightly less gloomy as he quickly headed back towards his classroom. She caught herself rubbing her arm where Jordan had gripped her; he had been so upset he probably left a bruise. *By a dream?* She had been dealing with

Cyborg Daniel showing up in her dreams for months and it didn't bother her too much. *Maybe knowing that he was real hadn't fully sunk in? Was she in some sort of denial state? What did Jordan know that she didn't?*

"Taking a break, Miss Newton?" said Principal Repalle. His voice made Catherine jump away from the wall she had been leaning on and spin around to see him standing not three feet away.

"I'm sorry, sir, I just ... was heading to the bathroom," Catherine lied as best she could.

"You look like you have been sleeping better. Have you been having any more bad dreams?" he inquired.

Catherine was taken back for a second. She had forgotten that she had mentioned her dreams to Mr. Repalle. *What had she said?* "Yes, I still seem to be disturbed by the rumbling from the mines. That man keeps visiting my dreams and telling me to 'close the mine.' Ridiculous, right?"

"Well, we don't want that, do we? I mean, if the mine closed, what would happen to this town? We would have to close down the school. You don't want to be re-assigned, do you, Miss Newton?" Mr. Repalle said. He let the message sink in, then he walked away with his signature phrase, "Good day."

Catherine decided to head towards the bathroom, just to add a little substance to her lie and maybe splash some cold water on her face. She walked into the bathroom and heard some weak sobbing in the far stall. There were small sneakered feet, pigeon-toed and pointing down, that abruptly picked up off the floor. Whomever it was, they didn't want to be seen.

"Hello. I know you're in there. Are you okay?" Catherine queried, tentatively.

The sneakered feet dropped back down and the door slowly swung open. It was Lucy peering back through teary green eyes and wiping off wet cheeks. "Miss Newton? I am sorry I was not in homeroom," she said as she started to cry again.

"It is okay, Lucy. It is just homeroom. I am sure with your merit level you can miss a few homerooms with no consequence," Catherine responded as she took some paper towels to dab on Lucy's cheeks. "What's going on?"

"I'm just not feeling well. My head is pounding and my mind is racing. I finished all my homework for the entire week yesterday afternoon. I haven't been able to sleep either," replied Lucy.

"Well, have you been by the nurse's office?" asked Catherine, concerned.

"Yes, Nurse Betty Green said I was fine. She offered me two aspirin but I haven't taken them yet ... I just don't like taking pills," Lucy answered.

"Well, aspirin has been known to help with headaches, Lucy. You said your head was pounding, right? Two aspirin is pretty safe. How about we take that aspirin and get back to class? If you are still not feeling well we can go back to the nurse's office and insist on a more thorough check-up, okay?" Catherine offered.

"Okay, Miss Newton. If you think it will help," Lucy said as she pulled the aspirin out of her pocket and went over to the sink to get some water to drink the pills down.

"Good. I will walk you back to class and I will mark you as here this morning in homeroom. Does that make you feel better?" Catherine asked as she held Lucy's hair back to drink the water from the sink. Lucy nodded emphatically, water spilling down her lips. She seemed a bit flushed, and Catherine could feel the heat radiating from her forehead. Her eyes could be seen much better in the bright light above the sink. They looked different, her pupils were very tiny and it made her already large eyes look even larger.

As they walked out of the bathroom, the bell for class was ringing and students started pouring out of the nearby rooms. Lucy was off in what was likely the direction of her next class before Catherine could even take a step forward into the passing throng. *I guess she didn't need that homeroom mark on her Notebook,* Catherine thought as she headed to her classroom.

As she was walking towards her class she got a buzz on her phone band on her arm. She tried to ignore it so that she didn't trip over another student. She hurried to her classroom. When she arrived, she first had to turn off the news channel. Next, she had to put up the questions for the reading assignment today. Finally safely at her desk, she looked down to see that the buzz had been a message from Anthony saying he got called into a meeting and couldn't make lunch. He asked if they could meet after work.

"Sure" she replied, "same place?"

And he texted back immediately, "Yes, 5ish."

Great. It was going to be nerve-wracking waiting that long to talk to him, but she would have to power through. *Wait. She had to meet Jordan after work too!* Maybe Jordan could wait a bit later tonight, tomorrow even? She didn't like the idea of going over to his place after dark. She'd have to ask him at lunch, though she didn't think he was going to be very pleased based on his actions earlier.

Oh no, the pep rally! She realized the pep rally today would go through their normal lunch hour, and then she would likely not have time to catch Jordan before the end of the day. She would just have to make it over to him somehow, or text him, which just seemed too strange right now. And find lunch. Which reminded her, she had been so busy worrying about text messages this morning she had skipped breakfast too. She'd probably pass out if she didn't eat all day, so that was her Number One priority as soon as she could find a break.

Her normal empty fourth period was now a mad dash to the faculty lounge combinator to grab a meal and find Jordan before she had to be at the pep rally. Unfortunately, she wasn't the only faculty who had forgotten her lunch and the line was longer than she expected. Jordan was nowhere to be found. The line was barely moving. There was always the salad bar; that would be quick. Not hot, and not the scrumptious smelling pizza that was the special of the day, but it would work to keep her from passing out later. Catherine left the line and headed to the salad bar. She was able to sit and eat for a few minutes before the announcement came on the intercom for everyone to head over to the pep rally. She heard grumbles from the faculty who had stood in line the whole time and would now miss lunch.

As Catherine left the teacher's lounge she was almost run over by the band making their way to the gymnasium. The marching band also decided to start playing the school fight song right as they passed by and she had to duck to miss being hit by a crashing cymbal and then a bass drum hammer flying in the air towards her head.

Was she just accident-prone or where these kids trying to kill her? She couldn't decide. She kept a comfortable distance behind the band, just in case. Plus, the narrow hall made the sound of the band reverberate so loud it made the lockers shake. The clamor was enough to make anyone want to stay back. She continued to follow the band into the gymnasium, which was a mistake. She didn't realize that right behind her the dance team had formed and she was sandwiched in-between like Act Two in a three-act show. As they entered the gym, all she could think to do was smile and wave like a celebrity. Then she quickly walked over to the bench area where the other teachers had gathered. She was sure that she was blushing red the entire time, and that gave it away that she wasn't supposed to be there, plus she could see Elisabeth almost doubled over laughing.

She watched as the dance team came out into formation, kicking in unison until the drum rolls from the band that had formed into a block behind them stopped. The band began to play one of the Top 40 songs on the radio, something by someone named Jazzy Duke. The song was about club crawling or beer hoping or something. The hip gyrations from the young girls seemed highly inappropriate and the tuba players behind them swayed back and forth heavily, with hip thrusts at key emphasizing phrases in the song. When the show was over, Principal Repalle came down to the center of the open gym with a microphone to announce the decathlon team. A small group of students in black blazers with gold insignia arose and began filing down from the center of the stands, high fiving everyone on their way.

Lucy Gamble was one of the students in uniform who were gathering next to Principal Repalle at the center of the gym. She was the only one Catherine recognized besides a very tall student, Edward Paulson, from her fifth period, who usually had a very relaxed disposition. Apparently, this was the best decathlon team in the state four years running and everyone was excited to kick off this year in the same direction. A teacher she didn't know very well, Linda Trego, was obviously their advisor, given her presence below and the absolute look of pride and exuberance she had on her well made-up face. She looked like she belonged in the '90s, and was attempting a pure Madonna knockoff from head to toe.

As Mrs. "Madonna" Trego began to introduce each student, Catherine could see Lucy looking more and more pale. By the time it was Lucy's turn to take the microphone and say a few words, her hands were visibly shaking. She reached out to take the mic and immediately dropped to the floor and began convulsing. Catherine ran straight to her and could see blood coming out of the young girl's eyes, ears and nose. Lucy's forehead was burning hot. Catherine couldn't help but think of her dream last night. *Could Lucy be exposed to the same infection as Anthony, the one that Daniel had described?* There was no time to guess. She pointed to Edward Paulson and told him to get ice and then asked Nurse Betty for as much penicillin as she could find, especially shots. Catherine told everyone to stand back and out of the way as she turned Lucy on her side so she wouldn't choke on her tongue from the convulsions.

Edward came back quickly and they placed the ice all around Lucy's neck and under her head. Nurse Betty was running in heels as fast as her little feet could click away, carrying several large syringes, yelling "I'm coming! I'm coming!" down the hallway. She seemed to be taking forever so Catherine got up and met her in the hallway, grabbing the syringes from Betty and running them back the rest of the way to Lucy. When she got to Lucy, she suddenly realized she had no idea what to do with the needles.

"Gluteus Maximus!" yelled Nurse Betty still running to get to the center of the gym.

"Stick her in the butt!" a student yelled and was met by giggles that were quickly subdued by the stern look of Principal Repalle.

Oh right, the largest muscle group was the glutes, in the posterior. Catherine injected Lucy as fast as she could with as many of the syringes, making her right hip look like a pin cushion.

"One of those was Tylenol to help bring down the fever. What made you think she needed penicillin?" asked the nurse as she dabbed the blood from Lucy's face.

Lucy had stopped convulsing and was staring straight ahead, pupils as tiny as pin pricks. If it wasn't for the high speed at which Lucy was breathing, she would look like a rock because she was so stiff.

"I ... I ... um ... don't know," replied Catherine as she brushed back Lucy's hair and tried to think of what to say next. She looked up, everyone was staring at her. "I've seen this before," she finally said, then added, "I think it would be wise to give everyone who was in close contact with Lucy today penicillin as well, just to be safe."

Principal Repalle immediately gathered the decathlon team and their horrified advisor. "Has anyone else been in contact with this young lady?" No one in the gymnasium said a word; you could have heard a pin drop. He followed up with, "Teachers, please ensure all students are back in their class as soon as possible, as orderly as possible. Demerits should be given for any stragglers. Everyone, please head to your fourth period. Good day."

"How much penicillin do you have left, Mrs. Green?" asked the principal.

"That was everything I had. I will have to call in some from the hospital. They are pretty quick and they are on their way already. In the meantime, I think it is best to keep this small group quarantined. Let's bleach all our clothes to be safe. We'll all have to change into gym clothes for the day until they are done. That includes shoes and socks," replied Nurse Betty Green.

"You don't expect us to bleach the BLACK decathlon jackets do you? The gold embroidery is going to fray in those industrial machines. It will ruin our team!" yelled Linda Trego. "My lace jacket will never make it! It will be destroyed! And my gloves!"

"Now, now, Mrs. Trego, it is only clothes. It is what is in the team's heads and not what they wear that the judges are interested in for the decathlon," Mr. Repalle said as soothingly as possible to a frantic Linda who looked like she was about to have a nervous breakdown.

Lucy began to grumble and sit up, ice chips falling all around her. She looked down and saw the needles sticking out of her leg and began to scream.

"Lie down, dear, you've been through a lot," the nurse cautioned as she pulled the needles out of her leg. Seeing the needles must have been the last straw for Lucy, because she then fainted into the pile of ice chips.

Even though she had just fainted, Catherine was relieved to see Lucy doing better. She looked calm, her breathing was easy and the bleeding had long stopped. It looked like the penicillin and ice was the right call. And that made Catherine worry about Anthony. He could be convulsing on a floor right now somewhere and she couldn't even get to him until after work. She would have to swipe an extra shot of penicillin to bring to Anthony when the syringes showed up from the hospital. She just hoped she could get it to him in time.

CHAPTER 10

Sunset on the Valley

At the last bell, Catherine tried to find Jordan to let him know she couldn't meet him tonight but he was long gone and she didn't want to linger in the halls too long. She felt more than uncomfortable running around the school in nothing more than gym shorts, a school T-shirt, and tennis shoes. She filled out the shorts a little too well and her long bare legs were not something students were used to seeing. She had to yell at a few small groups of pubescent boys for ogling. She passed by Mrs. Trego, who was still crying over ruined clothing, and said her condolences. She couldn't help but notice Linda was wearing an extra-large school gym shirt that she had rolled the sleeves up and ripped on the side to make a bow tie. *This lady was obsessed with '90s fashion!*

Catherine decided she would just have to text Jordan, sending him "Can't meet tonight, rain check?" before heading out to the park near the mine to meet up with Anthony. It was freezing outside and the laundry was still not done. She rummaged through her car and found a long sweater in the trunk that would have to do and put the extra penicillin shot in the pocket. It had not been easy to get, and she had to lie and say they had miscounted earlier when giving everyone shots. She wasn't sure, but Principal Repalle had given her a look and she thought that he might have suspected something. She didn't care; she needed to get the shot to her boyfriend or he could die.

Catherine texted Anthony to let him know she was on her way, and it worried her that she hadn't heard from him since the earlier text when he changed the plans to later today. While she was staring at her phone band, a text came back from Jordan, "Tonight, no rain checks."

Urgh! So, she would have to deal with eccentric Jordan tonight. It had been too long of a day already. *He was freaking out about dreaming of a cyborg? Really?* She had been dreaming of Daniel Jahren and his golden eyes and jerking mechanical movements for months now. It wasn't a big deal. It was just a dream. Of course, he never threatened to kill her in her dreams. *But, it is just a dream and you can't kill someone in a dream, you can't even hurt them! Jordan had his heart ripped out and he was fine, didn't he realize that?* He probably just needed someone to listen to him. He seemed like such a lonely guy.

"Okay, late date w Anthony," texted Catherine, telling the truth but also trying to remind him she had a boyfriend. She waited a few minutes for a reply, nothing came back from Jordan.

She looked out into the desert around her. There were large dark clouds on the horizon to the east. A storm was brewing and would probably come in tonight. Most of the sky was clear and the distant sun was beginning to turn the fringes to a dusty red. She felt chills as she looked out into the expanse. Something felt different about the day that she couldn't quite wrap her mind around.

The car pulled itself up to the park near the mine and she put it in manual to find a parking spot near some picnic benches. That reminded her, *she had forgotten to grab anything to eat on the way!* She sat in her car shivering, looking at dinner options she could pick up near the area when Anthony would eventually arrive and want food.

Three tiny knocks on her window made her sit straight up and almost jab herself with the shot of penicillin in her pocket that she had been absent-mindedly fondling. Anthony was outside her window smiling with a big handsome grin. She jumped out of the car and gave him a big hug. She had to move her face quickly out of the way when he reached to kiss her lips.

"Here, you have to take this!" Catherine proclaimed as she straightaway handed Anthony the syringe, pushing him back.

"What is it?" Anthony asked, looking down at the needle in confusion.

"It is a shot of penicillin. There is something going around and I think you might have caught something," she said.

"How would I have caught something?" Anthony looked worried.

Right then her armband vibrated and a text message from Jordan with his address and "Tonight!" popped up on her screen.

"Is there something I should know?" Anthony asked.

"I had a dream you were sick. Then this little girl at school today got sick the same way as you had in my dream. They used penicillin on her and she got better and I just thought it couldn't hurt to give you some too so I got this from the nurse," Catherine said as she cleared her text messages from her screen. She had spent all day coming up with that lie so she didn't have to tell him about dreaming of cyborgs.

"Well, that is odd. You see, the reason why I couldn't come to lunch today was that I was brought in to get a shot of penicillin from the on-call doctor at work. He said he noticed something in my last physical and they wanted to make sure I was in great shape, and they said that they want to take good care of me at the mine ... Are you sure there isn't something you need to tell me?" he asked, looking down at Catherine's arm band. He had apparently noticed the text from Jordan.

"No. I mean one of my co-workers wants me to come over tonight and discuss some history about the mines and viruses ... he is a bit paranoid, full of conspiracy theories. I promised him I would hear him out," replied Catherine.

"Him? And you don't think it is inappropriate for you to meet a male co-worker at his house at night, alone?" inquired Anthony, crossing both arms in front of his massive chest.

"It is, I am sorry. I will cancel, look, right now ..." Catherine said as she texted back Jordan to let him know she couldn't make it. Anthony was frowning, but he looked satisfied with the text, for now.

"You look cold. What are you wearing?" he asked, checking out her gym clothes.

"Oh, that little girl that I mentioned who almost died today during the pep rally, Lucy Gamble, had an infectious bacterium. Everyone around her when she went into convulsions and was bleeding had to have their clothes bleached and had to change into school gym clothes," Catherine replied. "I was one of the few who were right next to her when she got sick, so I lost my clothes to the laundry machine."

"Lucy Gamble? That wouldn't be Forman Gamble's daughter?" Anthony asked.

"Yes, I believe she is his daughter, why?" Catherine replied. Anthony looked pale.

"Monday, a man died in convulsions on the floor and Forman Gamble was there ..." started Anthony.

"And so were you?" interrupted Catherine, eyes wide, everything was coming together. That must have been how Anthony had gotten exposed to the bacterium.

"Yes. Lets walk for a minute, it will warm you up," Anthony said as he pulled Catherine's sweater around her, slid the syringe in her pocket and put his hand on the small of her back to lead her down the trail towards a large canyon overpass bridge.

Anthony stopped when they got to the center of the bridge and he said, "Catherine, there is something going on at the mine. We aren't just finding rocks down there ..."

"Viruses? Like the lake viruses? Is that what you are finding? Jordan said that there were people from the mine in white suits at the lake on Saturday," Catherine interjected. *Was Jordan right about the viruses? Was Daniel?*

"Jordan said, huh? I don't know. All I know is that I was brought somewhere that I didn't know existed on Monday after the incident with the old man that died. It had to be ten stories below the shed, a lab. They threatened my family, Catherine. They knew about you too, that we had come to the mine together to get my phone band and had explored the tunnels. If Lucy almost died, that means they are not as in control as they want us to believe. Whatever is going on, I don't think we are safe ... I need to keep my family safe," Anthony said, looking flustered.

Catherine was in shock. *A hidden facility at the mine where they hid viruses?* Now this was more than just a coincidence. *Was everything from her dreams going to end up being real?*

"What are you going to do, Anthony?" Catherine asked. He had never looked so shaken. He stood there looking out into the red sunset, black clouds coming out of the east. There was a distant rumble, and a flash that lit up the canyon.

"Do you think they will re-assign us to the same place?" Anthony at last asked, looking down at Catherine. His dark look had changed to one of love and hope, and he continued with, "They will re-assign us together if we are married."

"What are you implying? Why would they re-assign us?" Catherine barely got out as she watched Anthony get to one knee and pull out a ring. It had a beautiful, heart-shaped ruby that was cupped in golden hands. *He was proposing, now?!?*

"What do you mean re-assign us?" Catherine asked again. She was trying not to look at the ring, as if that would make the whole situation disappear if she didn't acknowledge the ring.

"Will you marry me, Catherine? I couldn't stand to lose you," Anthony asked.

"Lose me? I ... I can't. We have only been dating a few months, Anthony. This is just too fast." Catherine was surprised at herself, she had said it: it was too fast. But what was he planning to do that would lead to them re-assigning them?

"I know it is soon, but you are the best it is ever going to get for me and I know it. From the day I met you, I knew you were the one," Anthony said, still looking up holding the ring, in hope that she would say yes.

"I just can't, Anthony. Please, it is too soon," Catherine explained.

"I understand," he said in the end, getting up from the ground.

"I'm so sorry," she pleaded. Her chest was starting to hurt. It felt like they were breaking up and she wanted to cry.

"Then I hope we get re-assigned to the same place, or that you can wait for me," he said brushing the tears from her cheek with his big fingers.

"What are you planning to do, Anthony? Please don't say you are going to do something to the mine ... are you?" she inquired, hoping she was wrong.

"They threatened my family, they threatened you. That old man didn't die of a stroke. What they are doing, playing around with viruses and bacteria in secret, it just isn't right and it needs to stop. I can stop them. I should have sooner. I feel like a coward," he replied. "You know they offered me a promotion? And that is all I was thinking about ... Is Lucy Gamble okay?"

"Yes, we got her ice and penicillin immediately and she recovered fairly quickly," Catherine said.

"I am glad no one died. They must have known she was sick and let her go to school. How could they have let her into the school to infect others like that? They need to be stopped," he insisted, working himself up.

"I don't think they knew she was sick," Catherine started, then struggled to think of how to explain that she was the one who knew what to do with Lucy.

"What do you mean? They knew Forman Gamble and I were exposed. They gave us both penicillin today and asked us if we had any contact with anyone since the incident. So, they knew he went home to his family," he said.

"Well, they might not have known it would spread so fast or affect her the way it did ... see I was the one that treated her. Like I said, I had a dream last night, and you were in it. That is why I wanted to meet you for lunch, to tell you what happened ..."

"Do you dream about me often?" he asked, blushing, probably thinking about the naughty things he had done in his dream the night before.

"Umm, well, I have been having these warning dreams, about the mine. See, this man keeps telling me that it is dangerous and needs to be closed. Last night he told me you were infected and needed to be treated with penicillin. He told me all about the bacterium and how it works and when Lucy showed the exact signs he was talking about I knew what to do to save her life," Catherine explained, thankful to finally get it all out.

"I see. Do you think it is Jesus you are dreaming about?" Anthony asked, sincerely.

Catherine tried not to laugh. She knew he was serious. The idea that a golden-eyed cyborg was Jesus Christ in any way was too funny. "No, if anything, this man seems dangerous himself." Anthony just stood there, looking out into the canyon below and back towards the mine.

"Anthony, what are you planning to do? Should we go to the police, tell them what you saw?" she questioned.

"The police would never believe me. I am not sure I believe me," he said. "Besides, no one in this town wants the mine to shut down."

Catherine was shivering and trying to rub her arms to generate a bit of friction. The sun was set and the temperature had dropped a few more degrees.

"You need to get home, get into some warm clothes and get some rest. It sounds like you had a rough day," he told her as he hugged her close and rubbed her arms to generate frictional heat.

"I will be fine. I am worried about you. I don't want you to do anything dangerous," she insisted.

"I will only do what is right, and what needs to be done to protect my family," he said as he held her and led her down the path back to the car. She kept trying to think of what to say to stop him. But, from everything she knew about him, once he put his mind to something there was no changing it.

As he put her into her car, and set her destination, he whispered one last thing that sent chills to her bones: "I hope to see you again one day, my love." Then he pressed the autopilot and shut the door.

Catherine couldn't believe it. What was happening? One minute she was thinking she was going to save his life with this shot of penicillin, the next it seemed he was going to put that life in danger to shut down the mine. And she could do nothing to stop him! Well, nothing short of warning the cops, or Mr. Repalle could call his brother and ... what? Shoot Anthony?

She sat there, stunned, in her car while it drove her to the coordinates Anthony had set, which was her house. A vibration woke her from her stupor. Her armband was buzzing again, and it was Jordan, insisting that she meet him now. After a minute of contemplation, she decided to put in Jordan's address instead of her own into the navigation system. *Maybe Jordan could help her figure out what to do about Anthony?* She let him know she was on her way.

The car ran down a long, windy, upward road and into denser and denser trees on a hillside just east of the mine. The path became rough, and the road had turned to gravel a mile back before the car finally pulled up to a log cabin. The cabin had only one dim porch light on and a second light coming from the living room window. Everything else was pitch black all around, and there wasn't another house or street light for at least five miles. The place was secluded and dark, somewhat like Jordan himself.

Jordan opened the door and came out onto the porch with a small lantern to greet Catherine as she climbed the stairs.

"You actually came," he said, letting her into his house.

"Yes, I was with Anthony. He didn't want me to come here. He didn't think it was appropriate and I agreed with him so that is why I texted you I couldn't come earlier," she replied as she walked through the door into the warm living room with a log fire going in the fireplace. Besides the fireplace, the room was stark and bare, with only a recliner, small table and a TV. The back wall behind the recliner was made of a stack of books. Definitely the home of a reclusive, bookworm bachelor.

"What made you change your mind?" he asked as he handed her a drink that smelled and tasted like mulled wine.

"I think Anthony is going to do something dangerous tonight. I think he might blow up the mine!" she replied.

"What? Why?" Jordan exclaimed.

"He thinks that they are working on viruses in a deep underground lab and that it is dangerous. He said they threatened his family," she replied as she sat down cross-legged on the floor next to the fire to get warm, sipping on the wine.

"Well, that is what I wanted to talk to you about," Jordan said as he sat across from her in his recliner. "They *are* working on viruses at the mine. But not ones Greggo Sands made themselves, ones they are finding from an old facility that was buried in late 2017. And, before that, the viruses they were working on wiped out this whole area twice before. These are very dangerous viruses that have been linked to this town since before there was a town. I was doing some research on it all, and I finally put it together. Those brothers, the ones that are 'sleeping' as you say, in your dream. Well, they were part of experiments that dug up things here many years ago. And they buried themselves to try and stop the things they found," Jordan replied in grave tones.

"And you had to have me over tonight to tell me that?" Catherine asked.

"Well, I couldn't just tell you at school during lunch for Elisabeth to hear and spread all over town that I am a whack-job. Plus, I only came in today to talk to you. After the dream I had last night, I know they can't contain what they are doing at the mine. I plan on boarding up and riding this out right here, a safe distance from contamination. I have enough provisions for two to last a few years. It is manageable."

"So that is your solution, hole up and hide from it all?" Catherine replied. She was starting to feel a bit tipsy and noticed her speech was slurring.

"Yes, it worked for me last time during the dust. This will be no different," he explained.

"Whas in this drink, manitisss stoong ..." was the last thing Catherine remembered saying. And, as her vision went from blurry to black her last image was of Jordan quickly catching her before her head hit the fireplace.

When she finally opened her eyes again, she found her wrists tied together and attached to a bed headboard by a knot. She was lying in a bed covered in a large flannel blanket. She was still in her gym clothes underneath the blanket, thankfully fully clothed. The room was dark but when she rolled over she could see Jordan, asleep next to her. She kicked him sharply with her left leg; he must have forgotten to tie her up completely.

"What are you thinking, you crazy paranoid idiot!" she screamed, trying to get a few more good shots in with her feet as he wrestled her down.

"This is for your own safety, Catherine! They have no idea what they are doing with those viruses. I am trying to help you!" he yelled as he held down her legs.

"This is crazy, Jordan. You can't just kidnap someone!" she screamed.

"I don't want to be alone," he said. "Last time, I had to watch my parents die and then I was alone for years before they found me. I don't want to be alone again. I can't be alone again."

"I'm sorry, Jordan, but this just isn't the way to make friends, okay? You could have just asked me to stay here, you know," she declared.

"I don't want just a friend. I know you feel it too. Deep down. I think you'd want to stay here with me. You just have to give it time, and we don't have time. So, I had to do something," he insisted.

"Jeeze. What is it with men!" Catherine professed. "Jordan, please let me go. I need to stop Anthony, and I was hoping you would help me; I'm afraid he will blow up the mine."

"No, he has chosen his fate and I hope he gets buried with the mine like the Jahrens did," Jordan replied.

"Jordan, please let me go," Catherine asked softly. "I promise we can talk. Just untie me."

"No. We can talk tomorrow. And if you kick me again I will tie up your feet too. Goodnight," he said as he turned over and tried to sleep.

"They will wonder were I am tomorrow at work. They can track my car, my phone, my texts with your address ... they will find me here. You will have to let me go, eventually," Catherine added.

"Not if everyone is dead, they won't notice," Jordan remarked, still turned away and trying to sleep.

"Why would everyone be dead? No one has died, except the old man yesterday anyway ... Look, the bacteria that killed him and made Lucy sick isn't that deadly and is treatable with penicillin. You are overreacting," Catherine replied.

"That bacteria was nothing, and it is only one of the many things they have buried in those labs the mine is trying to get into. I saw what these viruses can do. Daniel showed me after he ripped out my heart. There is no stopping that mining company from digging, which means they are going to open up Pandora's box any day now and it will be a long time before anyone goes looking for you. Especially now, with Anthony off to blow up the mine. I am not overreacting."

He stopped talking for a minute and took a few deep breaths then continued with, "Look, if your boyfriend manages to blow up the mine and stop it all, I will let you go as soon as we know none of the viruses escaped. Deal?" Jordan asked.

"No, no deal. I want to be let go now! I don't want Anthony to blow up the mine and I don't want to lay around here for days waiting for everyone in the town to die!" Catherine exclaimed.

"Too bad. Goodnight." Jordan responded, nonchalantly.

What in the world was with this guy? Was he really fully convinced that any day now viral Armageddon was going to be unleashed? She lay there staring at the impressive knot on the bedframe and the tie job around her wrist. He must have been a Boy Scout. Her father had taught her a thing or two about knots though, and she was prepared with teeth to rip the tie to shreds if she had to when he finally fell asleep.

She lay there waiting to hear him snore, which he never did. However, his breathing became regular and he seemed pretty still. She began to slowly pull at the rope until it began to slide free, one knot down. He had been pretty thorough. She began on the second knot and felt movement to her left, suddenly she saw a hand over the knot.

"Impressive. I was trying to keep you comfortable, but it looks like you want to be difficult," Jordan said as he pulled her hands above her head and re-tied the knot. "Goodnight," is all he said as he turned over once again to go to sleep.

Great! She was really stuck now! Jordan had fallen asleep already, confident in his knot. Catherine lay there wondering how the heck she was going to get free in time to stop Anthony, and if there was anyway of stopping him at all.

CHAPTER 11

Blowing up the Mine

Anthony knew one thing, how to blow something up. That is all he had been doing the last four years at the mine. He also knew how to get explosives and exactly where he wanted to put them. What he didn't know was how he was going to do all of that and not get caught before he executed his plan. There were cameras everywhere and guards at all times. He knew he had to wait until the guard was lowest, right after 2 a.m. when there was a shift change. He also wanted no casualties. He couldn't live with himself if he knew he had murdered someone. Most importantly, for the plan to work, he needed access to the labs. As far as he knew, there was only one person that could get him into everywhere he needed to go tonight.

"Dr. Steinman, thank you for agreeing to see me," Anthony said as he reached out to shake the doctor's hand. They were outside the main entrance to the shed, where Dr. Steinman had just opened the door to let Anthony into the building.

"Anytime, that is what I am here for. I am sorry you are still not feeling well. You said your head hurt? Are you running a temperature?" the doctor asked.

"Yes. I think I might have a fever, and my head is pounding," Anthony answered as he slid inside the door. The doctor was busy locking the door behind him and Anthony could easily get to the belt Dr. Steinman wore around his waist that controlled the elevators and all of the entry points. Of course, Anthony had no idea what the access codes where, so it was no use getting to the belt without "convincing" the doctor to help him. He had to wait until the right time, where there were no cameras watching.

A tall, thin woman with short, slicked-back, strawberry-blonde hair and a stoic face walked up to greet them as they entered the lab below. She didn't say a word as she walked beside Dr. Steinman as they all headed towards one of the steel-doored rooms. Suddenly, she jabbed the doctor in the neck with a syringe and held onto his back, releasing the liquid into his vein. He spun around and punched upwards into her arm that was holding the syringe while using his other hand to push her whole body away by her throat. She flew back against the wall, bashing her head, and was instantly knocked out. The doctor pulled the syringe from his neck and his eyes got really wide for a second as he looked at the half-emptied contents, then he fell to the ground himself. Anthony caught the doctor about halfway to the ground and gently placed him on his back. He checked for a pulse at the neck and put his head down, with his ear to the doctor's mouth, listening for breathing. Nothing: no pulse, no breath. *She had killed him! But why?* He emptied out the syringe onto the doctor's jacket; it was just a clear liquid that smelled a bit acidic.

Anthony walked over to where the lady had landed and checked her pulse and breathing. She was still alive, just knocked out. He sat her up against the wall, bracing her neck. He did not know what to do. She might attack him if he woke her up, but he couldn't just leave her. He decided to shake her a little bit, and she responded with reaching out and clutching both of his arms and screaming. Which, of course, made him jump backwards and scream himself.

"I'm sorry. I didn't mean to scare you, I am actually here to help you, Anthony," the lady claimed with her hands still up, open palms out to show she was unarmed with any more syringes. She had a thick Russian accent.

"He's dead. You killed him," was all Anthony could think to say.

"Yes, he was going to kill you. He has killed several people. I saved your life. I was actually sent here to investigate what has been going on and I came across some very disturbing evidence this afternoon. Here, look at his arms," she said as she lifted up his lab coat to reveal dark streaks running up his muscles. She opened up his shirt and revealed the same dark streaking. "Quinta virus. He has been conducting illegal experiments on himself and others, then destroying the evidence. I found the bodies earlier. I knew he would figure out why I was here soon and I would end up in one of those barrels too."

"Barrels? What barrels? Who are you? How do you know who I am?" Anthony asked in a barrage.

"Sasha Mikhailov, head of Research and Development for Greggo Sands," she said as she reached out to grab his hand. "I was sent here by Alluri Repalle himself, yesterday. And you are Anthony Grant, a simple miner who was in the wrong place at the wrong time yesterday when a member of your crew, a Mr. Theodore Grayson, died suddenly exposing you to a dangerous bacterial infection for which you were treated with penicillin earlier today," the woman said as she rubbed the back of her head and neck absently.

"So, you came out yesterday just to investigate the old man's death? I am not buying that you didn't know about the experiments going on down here," Anthony said. Her story just didn't add up.

"No, I came out here yesterday to find out why traces of viruses have been continuously found in the nearby lake. Mr. Grayson's death was accidental, and also the first and only non-mining related death that anyone in the company knew about. Until now. Let me show you something," she stated as she stood up and began to walk over to the doctor's body. She removed his belt and brought it with her as she walked down the hall. Anthony followed reluctantly.

Sasha directed him into the tubes, where she entered in a number into the doctor's belt and the tube sucked them upwards. They landed on a sparsely cemented room that opened out into a cave that was dimly lit with led lamps. The entire cave was full of stalagmites and stalactites. There were beacon-like ribbons running along the walls, with little bits of quartz jutting out in between. The sound and smell of a distant waterfall filled the air. Sasha guided him down into the darkness of the expansive cave until they came across a river inside. There were three barrels located along the cave wall near the river's edge.

"Look inside," was all she said as she pointed her flashlight at the barrels.

Anthony opened the lid and found the jumbled-up remains of a dark-haired, muscular, young man with black streaks along his skin. His bloodshot eyes were open on his disembodied head and he was staring straight back up. There was blood coming from his eyes, ears and mouth, similar to what he had seen on the old man when he had died yesterday.

"This man couldn't have been dead for very long," Anthony said as he closed the lid and opened the next barrel. Another dismembered young man, this one with no black streaks on his skin, lay inside. "Or this one," he added. He didn't know much about dead bodies, but from hunting he knew that they would start to rot pretty soon if left outside like this and these didn't smell at all.

"Yes, all three of these men were killed in the last 24-hours alone. Who knows how many were killed before now. He's been throwing the barrels into this river, which heads out into the lake after going down a waterfall. I suspect the lake is so deep that the barrels get pretty wedged-in when they fall down the waterfall, about 50 feet from here. Likely, the viruses have been escaping due to leakage from cracks or ...."

"Viruses leaking?" Anthony interrupted.

"Yes, viruses. During mining here about seven years ago, we came across a lab that had been buried. We found viruses that could be used to enhance physical attributes and health. Nothing deadly, nothing dangerous. However, it was outside the scope of the mine crew here and kept with another division. My division. The labs here were created because we needed quarantine areas in case we came across any other viruses that might not be so friendly. We also needed someone to handle the quarantine process, so we put Dr. Steinman in charge. We have found three labs and five viruses so far during mining activity in the area. However, Dr. Steinman has taken it upon himself to conduct more research than was authorized and I do not know how far it all goes. I do know that you would likely be in one of those barrels if I hadn't stopped him tonight," Sasha proclaimed.

"I am sorry, but it is hard to say thank you for saving my life when I feel like hiding viruses in the first place puts you on the wrong side of all of this as well," Anthony replied.

"I am not a murderer, I am a scientist!" Sasha exclaimed.

"Yet, you experiment with viruses that you know nothing about. Viruses that were developed by someone else that you know nothing about. You play god, and it is wrong," Anthony declared.

Sasha just looked at him as if he had just said the sky was made of Skittles.

"We need to stop the mining. These labs, these viruses, were buried for a reason and we have no right to dig them up," Anthony stated as matter-of-factly as he could, looking her dead in the eye to ensure she knew how serious he was as he took the belt that had belonged to the doctor out of her hands.

"What do you plan to do, Anthony?" she said, with her head turned sidewise and her eyes narrow. She looked like a bird inspecting a worm.

"I am going to blow up the mine," he replied, simply, as he walked over to the tubes. "You can help if you want."

"There are twelve stories of labs here, with over $1 billion in synthesized viral product ..." she began as she followed behind Anthony.

"So, you're killing people for money?" Anthony asked. He wasn't slowing down and was not deterred by her spouting figures of money.

"Are you willing to kill innocent people too?" she finally said when she saw he was un-phased.

"What do you mean? What people?" he demanded.

"I don't know how many people are here in quarantine. I don't know how far the deception goes and how many people were brought into the labs. Dr. Steinman had his own agenda; he had at least seventeen other test subjects that I knew about. Like I said, there are twelve stories of labs and quarantine rooms, and possibly people in those labs or rooms."

"Then we will have to go to each of the twelve stories and every single room and clear them all out. Maybe helping me clear this mess out will help you clear your conscience in working with deadly viruses and bacteria that you just found laying around and used to make money," he said as he looked down into her steel-grey eyes. Her scarlet cheeks and pouty lips indicated his message had gotten across.

"Alright, I will help you disable the mine. But, I do not want to blow the whole thing up. I hope that isn't what you expect to do, is it? Blow the whole thing up? Who knows what kind of backlash on the mountain that would have. We know we haven't uncovered everything that was buried here, and who knows what consequences that would have if those labs were to be disturbed. This has to be a controlled demolition," she demanded.

Anthony nodded his head in agreement. Of course he planned a controlled explosion. He knew exactly what to do to close off each of the passages and disable the lifts in the shed. He looked down at the belt in his hands and suddenly realized that his original plan would never have worked without the help of Sasha. He had no idea how to work this belt, what numbers to press to open rooms, elevators, or anything. He had known that, and had planned to force the doctor to enter the required keys. But, he hadn't realized until now he would have had to twist the doctor's arm pretty hard to get him through a twelve-story facility to search for people.

"It is going to be a long night. Let's start from the bottom," Sasha said as she punched the code into her belt that sent both of them rocketing downward into the tubes.

~ ~ ~

Catherine must have fallen asleep waiting for Jordan to go to asleep again so she could work the binding on her hands. She was no longer at Jordan's, but was somehow standing in front of a red door with yellow reflective tape around the edges. She realized she was looking at the door she had entered when she and Anthony had snuck into the mine to get his phone band. She reached for the handle right as the door opened and Daniel walked out.

"What are you doing here, Catherine?" he asked. "Back for more exploring?"

"Exploring? No. I don't know how I got here or why. Actually, I didn't even mean to fall asleep. Last I remember, I was trying to work out the knot in the rope Jordan had tied me up with," she answered, honestly.

"Jordan! I told you he was trouble. I told you to stay away! You never listen, do you? Why does he have you tied up?" Daniel yelled as he punched the mountainside to his right and the rocks fell into a thousand pieces of shining dust at the impact. The whole cliffside was rumbling.

"It was an emergency. See, I came over to his house tonight to try and get him to help me stop Anthony from blowing up the mine," she explained. "Anthony has it in his head that is the only way to stop people from being killed around here and he is so hard headed, I didn't think I would be able to convince him to stop."

"Anthony wants to blow up the mine? Tonight? What do you mean blow up the mine?" Daniel demanded.

"I mean, I told him about you and my dreams finally and he thinks that it is not right and that the viruses need to remain buried. He is so stubborn! He thought you were Jesus ..." Catherine tried to think of how to explain Anthony to Daniel, and it seemed impossible.

"Oh, I am far from Jesus. I told you to stop the mining, not blow up the mine! Blowing up the mine is the last thing that needs to happen! It could destabilize the entire region! The mountainside has already suffered enough damage from when we buried our facilities," Daniel replied.

"So, you did purposefully bury yourself alive? Who would do that?" Catherine asked, stunned to find that everything that Jordan had told her was true. "Are you dead? Are you a ghost?"

"Ha! No, I am not a ghost!" he laughed, then paused for a minute, looking down into the valley. "I did it to stop the very thing your boyfriend may release tonight, something far more dangerous than you can imagine ..." he trailed off in thought, eyes flashing in strange symbols. "What are his plan?" Daniel finally asked.

"I don't know. Honestly, I am guessing that he is going to blow up the mine. I know his specialty is explosives, and I know he said he had to protect his family. Then he said something that made me think he thought he might never see me again and it scared me. He seemed sure to do something tonight, and I didn't know if I should stop him or how ... that is why I went to Jordan," Catherine explained. "I needed advice and he seems to be the only one who knows anything around here."

"That's right, you are currently tied up in the clutches of a mad man that you think you can trust. This Jordan. Why exactly has he tied you up?" Daniel was looking at her intently and he took another step forward and asked, "Has he done anything to you? Has he hurt you?"

"No, he drugged me with some wine and then tied me to his bed. He said he doesn't want to be alone when all the viruses get out and kill everyone. He hasn't hurt me; he just seems lonely," she replied. "I feel sorry for him, really."

"Most lonely men don't drug and kidnap people, Catherine. He is insane and you are in more danger than you know. So innocent. You should have listened to me ... Now, I am going to have to rescue you," he insisted.

Catherine laughed, "Rescue me? You are a dream, a figment of my imagination, you can't be real."

"I am real, Catherine, haven't you figured that out yet? Are you still in denial, after everything that has happened?"

"Okay, so say you are real. You said it yourself, you are asleep somewhere, buried I assume."

"I am real, Catherine." Daniel said gravely. "How exactly do you plan to escape Jordan's bedroom ... unscathed? He has dark plans for you, and you have no idea how much danger you are in. Is nothing real to you?"

"I will figure something out. And I will stop Anthony. I can manage. I don't need your help," Catherine declared. Somehow, the thought of Daniel awake and in the real world was more frightening than the idea of being stuck as a prisoner of Jordan's.

"Strong. Independent. I like it. Foolish. But I like it," Daniel laughed. "Your innocence is a gift, and a curse."

"I need to go, I need to get those ropes undone and get to Anthony before he blows up the whole mountainside," she replied.

"I will see you soon," Daniel said, with a smile and a sense of finality that was unnerving.

Catherine tried to ignore the knot in her stomach that was forming as she looked into his eyes. She closed her eyes and tried to concentrate on waking up. When she opened them again, she was in a dark room, hands tied up behind her head to a cast iron bedframe. It was still nighttime and Jordan was asleep next to her on the bed.

She began to wiggled her wrists to clear room in the ropes. She had pretty flexible wrists and was able to twist her right one backwards to catch hold of one of the three knots with her ring finger. It felt like hours, but she was finally able to get her left hand free. Once her left hand was free, she pulled the knot out of the bedpost holding her right hand and gently slipped off the edge of the bed.

She lay on the floor for a second, listening to Jordan's steady breathing. When she was sure he was still sound asleep, she slowly crawled along the floor on hands and knees towards where she hoped was the living room in the pitch-black house. The floors, along with everything else in the cabin, were all wood. The wood floor below creaked with the weight of her body and it sounded like gun blasts to her hears in contrast to the dead of the night. Her heart was beating so hard, the thuds in her ears sounded like canons to go along with the creaky gun blasts. She could barely see and used her hands to feel her way in the dark as best she could, trying not to knock anything over or run into something.

The lights came on and, in less than a second, she was being lifted into the air. She kicked as hard as she could, throwing her arms and head back at the same time. The movement knocked Jordan back and down to the floor. She managed to get behind his back, then yanked his left arm backwards while putting her knee on his spine. She used the rope that he had tied her up with to wrap around his arms and tie in a knot behind him. She was raised on a ranch in Montana; she used to rope calves for fun, and tying Jordan up proved even easier.

"Stay down, Jordan. I am going. I need to stop Anthony," she said as she got up to leave. He tried to stand up and she kicked him in the shin, knocking him down.

Jordan was writhing in pain on the floor but managed to get out, "You can't stop it. The viruses are coming and you will die if you don't stay with me!"

"Jordan, you are crazy. Goodbye," she replied as she escaped, seizing her phone band and purse off the counter and heading out the front door. She jumped into her car and turned it on in manual mode so she could immediately back out. She knew that rope wouldn't hold Jordan for long and wanted to get as far away as she could, as fast as she could. She turned around as she accelerated backward all the way along the gravel driveway. She then spun the car around as the road turned out to lead back down the hillside, throwing up rocks and mud everywhere.

The road was dark and desolate; there were no lights except from her car and she was driving like a mad woman. The twists and turns in the gravel caused the car to slide several times. It didn't help that there were potholes full of water all along the path down. The storm she had seen earlier at the park near the mine must have come through in the night while she was asleep because not only were the potholes full of water but there were several tree branches on road.

Just as she was thinking about slowing down, there was a loud explosion. She instinctively turned left to look in the direction of the sound and the resulting swerve of the steering wheel caused the car to nearly go off the side of the road. She slammed the brakes and the tires slid 20 feet in the loose, muddy gravel. *The explosion, was it the mine?* she thought as she got out of her car to see if she could tell where the blast had come from. She looked in the direction she had heard the blast. All she could see was darkness all around and all she could hear was the sound of bullfrogs and crickets in the bushes next to the car. Something slithered on the ground at her feet and she jumped back in the car with a little yelp. *She hated snakes!* She took a few deep breaths while clutching the steer wheel.

Just as she started the car again and headed down the hill, another explosion rocked the hillside. This time, it knocked down a few boulders that began rolling towards her car. She hit the accelerator and dodged the rocks. She was busy navigating boulders, tree branches and potholes when another explosion slashed through the air and pounded the glass of her car with a loud bang.

This explosion was the strongest and it caused her car to bounce slightly down the gravel road. The road kept shaking after the blast, and the rumbling was getting louder. She looked in the rearview mirror and she could barely make it out, but it looked like everything she had passed earlier was coming down behind her. The rain from the midnight storm, and the explosions she had heard, must have triggered a landslide in the soggy hillside.

The last thing she remembered, she was hitting the accelerator to the floor and trying not to look at the mountain of trees, boulders and mud coming down behind her in the dim light of the rising sun.

CHAPTER 12

The Aftermath

Anthony couldn't believe it; he had done it! It helped that there ended up not being a single living person in the entire twelve floors of labs below the shed at the mine. After the first four floors, Sasha and he had split up the search: even floors for him and odd floors for her to inspect. She was waiting for him on the main floor of the shed when he was done with his search. They had found the explosives next, and planted them at the base of the elevators on the main floor of the shed first, to trap all entrances to the labs below.

The guards and miners working the night shift in the mine had to be cleared before the explosives could be set in the entrance. Sasha was instrumental in coming up with a way to get everyone out safely. She had hatched a plan to call a biohazard drill and get all of the minors out to the main yard where she could safely "quarantine" them while Anthony was able to go in and set the bombs needed down the corridors. She injected each of them with a serum Benadryl mixture that would put them all to sleep quickly, so they couldn't go back into the mine before Anthony was finished.

Anthony set a 5-minute, timed detonation at the mine entrance and then headed back over to the shed to trigger the bombs there by a remote from a safe distance in the parking lot.

Everything had worked out perfectly, as planned. Anthony was sitting in his car, looking out at the rubble in satisfaction, waiting for Sasha to come back from the yard where she had left the sleeping guards and minors. Just as he saw her figure in the low light of the emerging dawn, unexpectantly, another explosion rocked the entire cliffside. The explosion was so strong it sent Sasha flying and even caused Anthony's car to bounce a few feet in the air as he clutched the steering wheel to avoid being thrown through the window. When the rumbling finally stopped, the entire parking lot was riddled with large cracks and the whole mine looked like a giant rock pile. The bridge over the lake that had gone between the mine and shed no longer existed and half the cliff face had fallen into the lake.

Anthony got out of the car to take in all of the damage. As he looked over towards the lake, he noticed a forming whirlpool. All the water in the lake was being sucked into something big that must have opened up with that last blast.

"What did you do!?!" Sasha yelled as she ran up to his car and tried to punch him in the face. He wrestled her back, holding onto her fists.

"I didn't do it! I swear. I set two blasts, not three. I have no idea where that last explosion came from. I swear!" he exclaimed.

"You've destroyed everything!" she yelled.

Anthony had no idea what happened. There was no way that last explosion came from the mine or the shed. It had to have been far deeper, and much further into the mountainside in order to trigger the entire cliff face falling down. The ground began to rumble again, but this time it was coming from a distant hillside. *The shock must have destabilized the entire region! Who knows how much damage would accumulate by the time the destruction hit the full light of day!* he thought.

"I trusted you, and you ...." Sasha began but Anthony quickly interrupted.

"Trusted me? Did you really go and check the floors or did you set that bomb? I know I didn't set the bomb. There was no need, I just wanted to shut down the mine, not destabilize an entire region putting hundreds of people's lives in danger! You are the one playing around with dangerous viruses, not caring about people's lives. You are the one who doesn't care about people's lives." Anthony said, accusingly.

"I saved your life. I helped you with your hair-brained, half-witted plan. I have everything to lose here. My career, my reputation ..." Sasha said as she leaned against Anthony's car, running both of her hands through her hair, clutching her head as if it hurt to even think about what had happened.

The distant rumbling on the hillside stopped and the sun was starting to peak over the horizon. Both Anthony and

Sasha were leaning against Anthony's car, trying to take it all in.

"It's over," Anthony finally responded. "We did it, and it is over. So what if our detonations set off something else. It was probably something in the old buried labs that would have probably gone off eventually anyway, and killed everyone working in the mine if we hadn't set if off when we did."

Anthony looked over at Sasha, who looked quite upset still. She was rocking back and forth with her arms crossed over her chest.

"No more viruses. Everything has collapsed and is buried. No one was hurt, I don't think anyone lives on that hillside over there ...I hope," he said as he looked over the landscape and paused for a minute. Had they killed anyone accidently? Whatever the consequence, it would have been more severe had they let things go the way they were with Dr. Steinman in charge and with more mining every day into God knows what was in those labs.

"The murderous, treacherous Dr. Steinman is dead thanks to you and he can no longer kill any more innocent people. You should be happy, Sasha. You can now ask God for forgiveness," Anthony declared as he leaned back against the car next to Sasha, pointing out at the rubble all around, trying to calm her down.

"That is easy for you to say; you can just go back to your life. I have all of those men in the yard as witnesses. When they wake up, I need to be long gone. No one even knows you were here except me and the now-deceased Dr. Steinman," Sasha explained.

"My life will change. The mine is closed. This town will close and everyone will be re-assigned. Everything I have worked for my entire adult life is gone and I will have to start all over. Worst of all, I'll probably even lose my girlfriend. We had just started dating, but I knew she was the one ... but she wouldn't say yes to marrying me when I asked her tonight. She said it was too soon ... So, we will likely get assigned different towns and you know how that goes," Anthony said. Now he was the one running his hand through his hair and looking distraught.

"Well, that's her loss, a handsome man like you could have any girl he wants," Sasha said as she looked up at Anthony with a smile. "Speaking of leaving this town ... I need to get out, quick! At least before those men in the yard wake up and realize what happened. Can I get a ride?" she asked, looking as composed as she could while brushing the dust off of her clothes.

"Sure," he replied as he got in the car. "You know, you did the right thing," he said as she sat next to him in the car. She looked over at him with that sidewise look she favored for a while, then eventually nodded her head in agreement. As they drove out of the parking lot, bouncing back and forth on the cracks all throughout the cement, he looked over to her and said, "Thank you."

She smiled back over to him and said, "Finally!"

~ ~ ~

There was Daniel, in the middle of the hallway, at the high school. He had both hands up and was yelling: "What have you done! Why can't you ever listen!" Right next to him was a man in a wheelchair, looking out at Catherine ominously. He looked like he could be Daniel's brother, but his face and body were so warped with tubes, plates and prosthetics that it was hard to see much of what was human anymore. What was human was covered in black streaks and looked fully integrated into the wheelchair-like contraption in which he was sitting.

Gravity had lost its hold and the whole world felt upside down. *Was this a dream? Really, it had to be!* Catherine thought as she tried to blink away the lights flashing in the hallway full of books and people floating weightless and stunned. Her fellow teacher Elizabeth looked at her in horror and confusion. *As if this was her fault!* Just because the shadowy man at the end of the hallway was speaking to Catherine didn't mean she knew anything about anything.

The only thing Catherine knew was that this wasn't a dream. She couldn't change a thing, she couldn't make anything stop and she had never seen Daniel's brother like this and he had never been in her dreams before. *This had to be real!*

"Why can't this be a dream?" she said aloud. Then it was over. The lights were back to normal. The cyborgs at the end of the hallway were gone, and everything (and everyone) that remained fell to the floor with a thud and a few grunts. Her whole body hurt with the fall and she lay groaning on the floor.

Elisabeth, who was normally peppy and nice, was giving Catherine a mean scowl. She was deadlocked, looking at her for an explanation. The gaze that could kill from Elisabeth was interrupted by Jordan, who clutched Catherine by the arm and dragged her to her feet. In an instant they were heading to the principal's office, as if she was in trouble.

"Jordan, did you see what I saw?" she asked.

A quick nod was all the reply she could get. Elisabeth was up and on her feet, marching right behind them, scowl gone and replaced with bewilderment.

"Do you think he will listen?" Elisabeth asked.

Catherine responded with, "I don't know why; he never listened to me before ..."

Jordon interrupted with, "Yes, but that was before the whole world was turned upside down in front of half the school. How can he not believe you, how can anyone?"

As they reached principal Repalle's office, Jordan let go of his grip and pointed her to go into the room. Catherine entered and opened her mouth to speak but nothing came out.

"You have to stop the mining," Jordan said from behind her. It sounded like a echo of Daniel's warning and jolted Catherine to speak.

"Yes, there is something buried there that needs to stay buried or we are all in trouble. It has to stop now," Catherine explained.

"What do you mean?" Principal Repalle asked.

"I mean, I just saw two cyborgs in the hall yelling about mining waking them up and that we were all going to die!" screamed Elisabeth.

Prinicpal Repalle was on his feet, "Two cyborgs?"

"Yes, and they want us to stop the mining. They have been telling me for months, and I know I told you already and you blew me off but I know your brother runs the mine and you can stop the mining any time," said Catherine.

"You're right. I can stop the mining but that would mean the end of this town and re-assignment for everyone, including my family and we happen to like it here," Repalle responded.

"You won't like it when there are viruses from the mine that kill everyone and everything you know and love ..." Jordan began but was quickly interrupted by the principal.

"Viruses? What do viruses have to do with the mine?" he asked.

"The mining has uncovered buried labs from before the dust where they were experimenting on viruses. The two cyborgs were brothers whose family owned and ran the labs," Catherine explained.

"I see, and they appeared in your dreams to warn you?" Repalle asked.

"Yes, they are in some kind of coma or something I don't know. Daniel would never explain anything. But, they appeared here somehow, in the hallway, today, just now, and threatened to kill us all. We have to stop the mining, we have to shut down the mine," Catherine pleaded.

Repalle looked at the three teachers and after a minute picked up his phone band and opened out the screen for all three to see. He dialed his brother and said only five words: "Shut down the mine, now."

There was silence on the other end, apart from the static of the line, and then finally a response: "Okay. As you wish, brother. It is done. Good day, Sanjay."

"Good day, Alluri," Repalle said as he turned off the screen. "The mine is closed."

"The mine is closed," Jordan said with visible relief as he walked out of the room.

"The mine is closed," Elisabeth said, patting Catherine on the arm as she walked away.

"The mine is closed," Catherine repeated to herself, hearing a faint echo and feeling the room wobble all around her and the lights go dark.

~ ~ ~

Catherine opened her eyes to see a white light above her. She couldn't move her body, and could barely open her eyelids. She tried to speak, but all that came out was a weak, rattling groan. She heard voices to the left and tried to turn her eyes to see.

"They have closed the mine, for good," she heard a soft female voice say.

"I know. What do you think will happen? Do you think you will get Oklahoma? I have family in Wichita. I will probably get assigned there; it is number one on my list," another slightly older female voice replied back.

Catherine felt a gentle hand on her arm as it was lifted to place a blood pressure cuff around her bicep. She felt a small device being placed on her finger, and a thermometer was stuck in her mouth, under her tongue.

"I sure hope I get Oklahoma!" said the first voice.

"I think she is awake, Kate," said the second voice, coming around to Catherine's left side.

"Hi, Catherine, how are you feeling?" the voice that belonged to Kate asked.

"I ... where am I?" Catherine managed to get out as the face of a beautiful young, dark-haired nurse appeared in front of the light.

"Dear, you were in an accident. You were stuck in the rubble of a landslide for two days before the crew was able to pull you out," said the voice to her left. "I'm Mindy, and this is Kate, and we are the nurses who have been taking care of you. You're in the hospital, dear."

"Mindy! You are scaring her. Look at her heart rate, it just jumped to 145!" Kate exclaimed as she opened up the blood pressure cuff and removed it as well as the device from Catherine's finger and then said, "All of your vitals are looking good. You'll be able to go home in no time."

"What do you remember last, dear?" Mindy asked. She had a sweet face, with pretty, bright blue eyes and fluffy brunette hair.

"I remember ... driving ... an explosion ... did someone ... blow up ... the mine?" Catherine inquired, barely able to get out any of the words, her throat was so hoarse.

"Blow up the mine?" Kate laughed, "What in the world would make you think someone blew up the mine? There was an earthquake that caused a hole to open up under the mine and collapse most of it into the lake. Everyone is saying how lucky it was no one was hurt."

"Except you of course. You see, the earthquake caused the landslide that crushed your car and pinned you ...." Mindy began.

"Mindy! What did I say!" Kate whispered very loudly. "How about I get you a saline drip? You sound a bit hoarse and are probably just a little dehydrated," she continued as she walked over to hang a bag from a nearby hook and then place a connector into the IV in Catherine's left arm. The flush of the IV tasted nasty but the cooling fluid was making her throat feel better already.

"Is ... the mine ... closed?" Catherine asked.

"Yes, it looks like there is so much damage that is just isn't worth it to the company to dig through the rubble," Mindy answered.

"And, they are worried about more earthquakes I think. They just decided this morning. They had been talking about continuing digging all week. The owner of the mine, Alluri Repalle, unexpectedly came on the news and announced it. It was a shock to everyone. We can turn on the news and find out more if you want. Channel 4?" Kate asked as she used a small controller connected to the bed to turn on the far wall to the local news channel.

"Get your assignment sheets ready and updated everyone. We just got word on how they will be handling the re-assignment now that the mine will be permanently closed. They have announced that they will be moving us all out in phases, beginning in two days. My top three are Oklahoma, Grand Rapids, and Lincoln City. How about you, Don?" said a blonde woman with big hair and an even bigger smile sitting at a grand news desk. The man to her left was dark-haired with a few grey streaks and had sad doe-brown eyes. He didn't look nearly as happy as she did, with visibly slumped shoulders.

"Well, Grace. I haven't updated my list in 8 years because when I met my wife I knew I wanted to stay here in this beautiful valley forever. My three kids and I are not looking forward to starting over anytime or anywhere," replied Don.

"Oh, this is so depressing, Kate. I thought you were the one wanting to cheer her up. She's been asleep for a week and this is the first thing we show her?" Mindy interjected as she turned off the TV and went over to the windowsill. "Look, your boyfriend has been bringing you fresh flowers. He should be here soon; he visits every day."

"Boyfriend?" Catherine managed to get out. So, Anthony had made it out of the mine alive!

"Yes, quite the handsome fellow, I say," Kate beamed, and Mindy nodded in agreement.

"You're a lucky lady to have a ..." Mindy started, but Kate interrupted whispering "Not if they don't get assigned the same place."

"Don't worry, he'll be here soon. Just press the nurse button on the controller if you need us for anything," Mindy continued and then she and Kate left the room.

Catherine stared up at the ceiling light, trying to wrap her mind around everything. She couldn't move anything and could barely move her head. She had no idea what damage had been done to her body in the accident, and was afraid to ask. *Had she really been asleep for a week?*

The hallway at school with Daniel and his brother appearing in front of everyone, her and the other two teachers asking the principal to stop the mining ... *It had all been a dream? Truly? Maybe it felt so real and she couldn't control it because she had basically been in a coma? It had felt so real! Was that Daniel's brother, or did she imagine him?* She could never have imagined something so horrible.

"I am so sorry, Babe," she heard Anthony say as he sat down on the chair next to the hospital bed. He leaned over and kissed her softly.

"What ... happened?" she asked.

He was silent for a while, which was not typical for him at all. He must not want to tell her. He got up and closed the door and then came back to sit down.

"I blew up the mine ... I didn't know it would cause a landslide. I didn't know it would ... hurt you," he finally said.

"Why ... why ... Anthony?" Catherine replied.

"They were experimenting with viruses that they had no God-given right to mess with. They threatened my family, and they threatened you. I had to put a stop to the evil. You are the one who told me the mine needed to close," Anthony declared.

"Close ... not blow up ..." Catherine said, weakly. Anthony was obviously very upset.

"How did you even get on that hillside? You were the only one hurt, out of everyone. Of all the people and all the places to be ... I feel like God is punishing me," Anthony replied, mournfully.

"Jordan ... helped ... stop you," Catherine insisted.

"Jordan? That male teacher who wanted you to come over in the middle of the night? Where you at his house?" Anthony asked.

"Yes," Catherine said and then tried to say more but Anthony interrupted before she could get her voice to work right.

"Now it is starting to make sense ... you spent the night at his place, didn't you?" Anthony began, angrily.

"No ... not like that ... I," Catherine tried to get out.

"I see it now. God didn't punish me. He is punishing you for your adultery. I did what was right to protect those I love and those I thought loved me back," Anthony said, righteously.

"Please, no ..."

"Catherine, sin is sin. It was six in the morning when that landslide got to your car. You had to be coming back from his place ... you had to have been at his place all night!" Anthony began, furiously, and then stood up. "I am not God, and I would never punish you like this," he looked down and caught his breath for a moment, then continued, "but what you did was wrong and only God will forgive you." Then he was gone.

Catherine was so angry. Anthony was stubborn to a fault and never did listen to her, but not even letting her explain? She closed her eyes and groaned. The room began to shake and the lights began to flicker. She opened her eyes and everything stopped. *Was that an aftershock from the earthquake?*

She took a few deep breaths to calm down. She was probably going to break up with Anthony anyway. They would have likely been re-assigned different cities. And, he had blown up the mine like an idiot! So, it was his fault she was in this hospital bed right now because it was that explosion that caused the landslide. If anyone should be asking for forgiveness, it should be him!

She heard steps coming into her room. The sound of machine gears turning and a mechanical clang as it touched the floor. It sounded like ...

"Miss Newton, we meet at last, in the flesh," said an all-too-familiar voice.

"Daniel?" Catherine asked as she saw his smiling face above hers in the light. Except, his eyes were a warm hazel green. They weren't their usual glowing gold with flashing symbols that crossed his vision. He had a bit of a stubble brown beard too, instead of the neat goatee, and a full head of wavy brown hair instead of the half plate and half shaved head in her dreams. He was wearing a doctor's robe, but underneath his body was still covered from neck to toe in black, including his hands.

"That would be Dr. Jahren, Miss Newton, and you wouldn't be in this mess if you had just listened to me from the beginning," he answered.

"The mine, it's closed," she replied.

"Yes, you did finally close the mine like I asked. Congratulations on that, by the way. I knew you could do it. I couldn't believe they were still going to dig after the collapse. They must have been making pretty good money off of the research they had stolen and didn't want to abandon their treasure trove. Sanjay ended up persuading his younger brother Alluri after your incessant dream haunting over the last week," he elaborated for her. "It seems Sanjay's influence on his brother was the key, as was your ability to influence Sanjay."

"You're ... welcome," Catherine stated. It was all finally sinking in. Her dreams were real. The influence she had in dreams was real, and what she experienced in the dreams was real. It was all real, and it was all also a dream.

"If you had stayed put at Jordan's, I would have come to save you. I wish you would have listened. But, you wouldn't be the exceptional woman I know if you just did what everyone else told you, now would you?" he said, pulling her chart from the wall.

"Now what?" she said, knowing the answer might not be what she wanted to hear but knowing that whatever was going to happen, her entire world would not be the same.

"Like I said before, you are special to me, and now ... I have special plans for you," he replied as a spark of gold began to flicker in his eyes.

= = =

CYBORG
DREAMS
THE BURIED PAST
H.A.
BURNS

To Julie Cooperrider for her unfailing kindness and generosity without which I would never have been able to write.

Prologue:

Cliff usually let his dreams take him wherever they wanted. Today he dreamt he had rockets for legs that were jetting him up into a lavender sunset. Blue fire roared from his metal appendages. Pulsed beams shot from his hands and created circular clouds radiating for miles, getting bigger and bigger as they dissipated.

He laughed as a giant eagle landed on his left shoulder, hanging on for the fiery rocket ride. He spun in circles to see if the bird would get dizzy and fall off. It clutched on effortlessly, peering calmly down with piercing, beady eyes.

Cliff stopped spinning, the bird flew out in front of him; it was leading him forward. He followed it until it landed on a juniper brush jutting out from a red rocky mountain cliff.

He recognized the cliff when he looked down to see a teenage girl hanging on the edge and screaming. He turned and fired a pulsed blast back at the bird for taking him there to see her, but the eagle had already disappeared.

The whole scene changed as his anger welled up. The rocks around his feet started to levitate and the cliff broke apart as he screamed. The horizon in every direction was soon filled with floating rocks and broken mountainside. There was rumbling and tumbling until it exploded into rusty dust.

What was left after it cleared was Cliff standing in a dark office of a hospital, the details coming more into focus. He stood behind his brother, Daniel, who was sleeping at his desk at work at the UCLA neurology department. Daniel faded in and out of focus. Cliff noticed an odd object on his brother's desk – it was a small microchip.

He held the microchip up for inspection and a woman's face appeared behind it. She smiled and held out her hand to take his. As their hands touched, he rocketed forward into bright, shimmering light. The light broke into a world of glimmering, spiral skyscrapers surrounded by ships in the air. Tiers of the skyscrapers were layered with trees. It was amazing, it was beautiful ... it was the future.

When Cliff awoke from the dream, he couldn't help but feel sudden claustrophobia at the dark grey walls surrounding him. Panic struck as he blinked into the dim florescent bulbs of a laboratory, burrowed deep within a cave. In comparison to his dream, the reality in which he awoke was a nightmare.

Chapter 1

Home Sweet Home

Beth Jahren's feet sank into soft mud, hitting the hidden riverbed before she even knew there was a river bed to hit. The mud began sucking her into a trench within the cave she had been exploring with her husband, Martin. In the sketchy light given off by her kerosene lantern, the rock and muck below were one and now her boots and muck were one as well. She fell back onto her butt with her feet flying into the air, boots no longer attached. The ends of her socks dangled off her toes.

"Well, there goes another pair of boots, honey," she said, slinging mud behind her in the direction her husband had last been seen inspecting the cavern walls.

"Huh? What did you lose this time? Hummm ... You should see these petroglyphs. I speculate we are in close proximity to what we are seeking," he said, not even peeling his eyes away to gaze in her direction.

The cave was pitch black except for the shifty light brought in by the reconnoitering couple. Beth could barely see her husband behind her. He stood near the back wall of the small alcove deep within the Colorado mountains. He flicked his wavy brown hair out of his glasses as he inspected the walls in unwavering intrigue – lamp at his nose and hair often dangerously close to being lit on fire. He was a tall, stout, and proudly German biochemist who was on a mission. He had a one-track mind: to find the remains of the individuals who lived in these caverns years ago and to harness the remnants of a lethal virus that wiped them all out. At least, that's what he hoped.

"I think I found that river we've been hearing. It's mostly mud right now though," Beth explained while trying to salvage her shoes and becoming more and more entrenched. "I think a little further up we might reach water."

Her long, dirty-blonde hair was tied in two loose braids hanging down the back of her green polyester jumpsuit that was now mostly red-brown as it was covered in iron infused sludge. She squinted her bright, ocean-blue eyes out into the distance as far as she could see with the limited light from the flickering lamp. The alcove they were in had stalagmites, snowy quartz cubes, and wet, dripping walls. Every flash of light revealed minerals gleaming different shades of reds, creams and browns.

"Good, good, hummm ... Yes. I see, here! There, yes, hummm..." Martin mumbled, completely engrossed in thought and humming enough for it to be a song.

"You know, honey, you aren't making any sense," Beth replied, looking back towards her husband who had his nose about an inch from the cavern face. His sharp mind was obviously scattered by the variety of etched and painted objects and symbols on the wall.

"A river you say? Hummmm ... I think this petroglyph is telling us to follow a river to 'The Death of a Thousand Deaths.' How interesting. Hummm ... What does that even mean? Hummm ... A thousand deaths of a death ... Quatsch!" He still had a thick Bavarian accent although he had lived in the USA for the last 15 years. The accent didn't help in him making sense to Beth right now. She was staring in his direction in complete bewilderment, mouthing in horror the term 'death of a thousand deaths.'

He finally broke away from the wall and gazed in the direction where his wife was struggling in the mud. "Honey, I think you are making the situation worse."

"How can I make a thousand deaths worse? That isn't a nice thing to say, Martin!"

"No. The situation in which you are completely covered in mud and have no boots. The suction is pulling all your belongings under. Tugging like that isn't helping you. Might I suggest you use your walking stick to poke a hole near the shoes and allow air to move. Then you will be easily able to scoop them out. I would also suggest you attempt this from a hard surface so that you are not pushing yourself in further. I am sure you can find a rock to sit on to attain the proper leverage. Where is your walking stick?"

"Remember, I lost it back at the entrance when I got it wedged and it broke in half." She began looking for a rock and tried to ignore the condescending tone from her husband – he was only trying to be helpful, probably.

They met at John Hopkins University in Maryland while taking organic chemistry together their second year and they'd been inseparable ever since. He kept her grounded and focused. She taught him how to get out of the books and experiment with real life and not just life in the laboratory. In fact, if it were up to him, they'd probably live in a laboratory.

"Oh, that's right. Well, here, use my walking stick," he said as he carefully maneuvered to where she was encumbered. He made an obvious show of how to determine proper footing with his stick the entire way over to Beth, to drive in the message. She purposefully ignored him so that she didn't strangle him or shove his head into the mud when he eventually arrived by her side.

"So, what is this "death of a thousand deaths" you mentioned?" She was finally pulling herself out of the muck and onto a large rock that he'd pointed out for her. The rock had been right next to her the whole time. But, he wasn't smiling smugly or anything when he pointed it out; no way he would do that! She didn't look at him – just in case – or she might just smack him with his own walking stick.

He sat on another rock next to hers and helped her get her boots free, although he spent more time cleaning his glasses from the sludge tossed up in the struggle.

"I believe it is in reference to what we are searching for..." he began.

"Death of a thousand deaths?" she interrupted.

"Yes, yes that's, well, my interpretation anyway ... Probably the virus that wiped out the ... I suspect Navajo tribe? Yes, it is doubtless the Navajo carved out these tunnels."

"We're making progress then!"

"Yes, yes ... Maybe." he continued, still working on getting her shoes out of the mud, now wrestling the right one with his wife. "Truly, it could be anything from a burial site for the dead to the location of a bat cave of blood sucking creatures ... I know how much you love bats."

She stopped wrestling at the mention of bats. Bat guano was good for a wide variety of applications and she was thinking about a venture one of her colleagues had discussed for a new mascara line. He seized the break in her struggle as an opportunity to poke and pull according to his plan, wrenching free her right boot at last. He tried – unsuccessfully – not to smile too smugly, evoking the ire of his wife.

"The markings on the cave were inscribed at separate times, and most likely by several civilizations. Who knows where this all started ... why and what they did ... the symbols are unclear and the message is mixed. As far as I can tell, and mind you I am no expert, some of the messages are just about large game to the east, one is about following a lake to a river..."

"We found the river bed!" she said, scooping up a handful of the sludge that was bringing her back to childhood memories of mud-pies and fire-flies out in east Pennsylvania. "So, that means we're close, right?"

"I am an expert in viruses, not petroglyphs, honey. It is tough to say. The large stone work symbol over there..." he pointed and held his lantern towards an odd granite stone that stood out amidst the limestone and quartz. Beth couldn't see any symbols from this distance but she nodded anyway to get him to continue.

"It indicates a great amount of deaths that lead to deaths. I postulate if we follow the river we will find out more," he was trying to sound matter-of-fact but she could hear the anticipation in his voice that meant he was onto something big.

"That's sick!" she exclaimed as she wrenched her last boot free, inadvertently flinging muck into both of their faces. "Sorry, honey. I promise to try not to be such a spaz."

"Yes. Well, it certainly baffles me how you have managed to survive this long without me. Let's stay near the cave wall, away from the mud. You can use the stick to check the ground from here on out, agreed?"

"Agreed. This mud isn't so bad. It is probably full of microorganisms and minerals that aid in detoxification and cellular regrowth. We could bottle it up and I bet I could sell it to snooty women for facials back east. That's if lab testing shows it's viable, which I'm sure it'll be. Want to collect some and test it out?" She put a little bit on the tip of his nose and on hers.

"That's my wife – always making the best out of any situation. Gets entrenched in the mud so resolves to give herself a facial while postulating a marketing plan," he said, chuckling to himself and unpacking a few glass jars from his backpack to collect mud samples.

Beth got her boots back on, the mud jars full and back in the backpack, and her footing worked out. Then they were able to continue their long quest in the dark. They stuck close to the cavern wall, following the sound of the running water up ahead until they got to another alcove, this one the largest they had encountered yet. The opening in the ceiling height alone had to be hundred feet from the sound of their boots and breath echoing around them and emptying out into the fathomless distance.

What was more exciting was that up ahead they could see light reflecting off of a massive, bright mound. It was stark in comparison to the void of darkness inside the cave that seemed to swallow all light and sound at its infinite edges. As they approached they could see the giant, dingy, yellow mound was composed of layers of matted straw wrapping smaller bundles. Each layer was a few feet thick, stacked neatly in an ascending pyramid reaching at least ten feet high.

Martin brought his lamp up to the end of one of the wrapped bundles within the layers. He pulled back the straw cloth to reveal the remains of a black, shriveled foot.

"Get out your gloves, honey!" Beth exclaimed. He was so forgetful when it came to safety sometimes. "Who knows what could be in those remains!"

"You do realize these remains have been here a very long time. The likelihood of a live virus or bacteria that is dangerous is absolutely minuscule."

"I just have a bad feeling, okay? I know it is probably just 'superstitions bred into me from societies' ignorant obsession with the plague,'" she said this while holding her fingers up in quotations. She was quoting him and they both knew it. She continued, "but you never know what we could find down here. Any risk is too much in my opinion. It wouldn't hurt to wear gloves and take a few extra precautions. For me, honey, okay?"

He said nothing as he pulled out a pair of gloves, a glass vial, some small bags, and a razor. He was excited to have finally found exactly what he was hoping to find – dead bodies. It had been weeks of cave diving in southern Colorado with no evidence of plague before they found this cave, where they had spent the last few days exploring without finding anything until now. One breach of protocol for a brief second and his wife went on a nagging spree. He shoved the gloves on grumpily.

Dead bodies made Beth squeamish, and she was particularly nauseated today. So, she eyeballed the petroglyphs on the wall near the mound to keep from hurling her lunch. She had no idea what any of them said – she just liked to trace her finger along the indentions in the rock. When she proposed the idea of searching for ancient viruses to harness for his oncolytic research, she was simply trying to get her husband's mind off of his mother's recent passing. She never expected they would find anything.

"At least it isn't a bat cave full of ravenous blood suckers ready to pounce that they were writing about," she said while squinting at a symbol of several x's surrounded by swirling lines radiating out into straight lines. "Though, bat guano would also make some good products for snooty ladies too, you know, that we could sell. I know someone who'd be interested..."

"Would you like to help me?" he asked, yanking at a body to remove it from the mound. It was solidly wedged and not moving much as he pulled.

"Urgh! You know I don't have the stomach for dead body stuff," she said, putting down her bags and replacing the thick hide gloves she'd been wearing with the disposable latex ones they'd brought just in case they found something. The whole time she was changing gloves, her husband was impatiently glaring at her. So, she delicately placed them on her hands one finger at a time – just to annoy him further. She then slid her arm deep into the straw-clothed pile to get a good hold on the body.

"Ready?" he asked, the annoyance echoing in his voice if not shouting out of his wide eyes gleaming in the flickering light.

"Ready," she said and then tugged at the body to pull it from the mound right as a large, hairy spider ran straight up her forearm with its eight fuzzy, freaky legs. She screamed, let go with a backwards jerk, and then launched the spider as far away as she possibly could.

"Ah! I told you I had a bad feeling! There IS something alive in here!" she screamed.

"It was simply a tarantula, they aren't dangerous," Martin replied, holding back mirth at her irrational antics.

"Do you think there are more? I'm not touching that thing if I end up covered in spiders!"

"Too late," Martin said as he plucked another spider off of her shoulder.

"Aaaaahhhh!" she screamed, jumping up and dancing around in a circle scanning for more spiders on her body.

Martin had fallen backwards with Beth when the body came out of the mound in a quick rush and he was now rolling on the ground laughing. He obviously found it highly amusing that she was dancing and spinning. His laughing increased when she started hopping around like a little kid throwing a fit.

"I can feel them, they are everywhere!! Martin, they are everywhere, get them off!" She stomped her feet and her two braids flopped wildly. She couldn't have cared less what he thought. She hated spiders with a passion that involved blood-boiling, skin-crawling dread at their touch.

"I think you scared them all. Please, you're making my ribs hurt," he said, trying not to gaze at his normally beautiful and refined, PhD in microbiology, wife. Right now, she appeared absolutely ridiculous covered in muck and throwing a tantrum over tarantulas.

When she finally calmed down, she took his walking stick and started poking at him in the ribs, "I'll make your ribs hurt!"

He easily avoided the jabs, yanked her down onto him on the ground with the stick and gave her a big kiss, saying,

"Come on, we need to get back to work before more spiders come to get you." Her gregarious smile after the kiss turned to a frown and an expression of determination quickly.

"Let's get booking!" she said.

"From the appearance of this piled heap of bodies, I think we have found what we have come for ... this skin is treated with ... tar, I suspect, from the smell" he said as they examined the body and collected various tissue and bone samples in the low light. "Not much assiduousness was taken to swathe these in this straw-like sheeting. This is a positive sign of a virulent outbreak, the most advantageous kind I need for synthesizing an amalgamate."

"Let's hope so. I know you'll be the one to find a cure, Martin, I just know it. You're the most brilliant man I've ever met." She put the small collection of samples her husband was cutting away into containers and then carefully into her backpack. She was still trying not to look in the direction of the dead body. Man, the sight was sickening!

"There, I think that is enough. Unless, of course, you want to try another body?" he asked.

"No thanks! I think we should put this one back exactly how we found it for now too, out of respect for the dead."

"Respect? They are dead; they don't care about respect," he said as he begrudgingly helped his wife shove the body back into its place in the stack. She knew how he felt, but she was stubborn. Even though she knew her logic was irrational, it was hard to break superstition. Especially when she had an eerie feeling in the dark.

"What do you say we find out where the river ends? It sounds like it could be a waterfall. I could use a shower. I still feel like spiders are all over me, crawling ... Uuuugh! And, I think the mud is leaching my skin bare."

"Bare skin you say? Skinny dipping in a waterfall sounds like a great way to end this successful venture. Brilliant idea," he replied with a wide, mischievous grin.

The waterfall turned out to be inside the cave, only about fifty more feet from where the straw mound of bodies was found. The two climbed down to the bottom to find a secure place to put their belongings before jumping into the water.

They were happy to find a small opening to the cave as well. It was the first break to the outside world they had seen in hours of spelunking through tunnels, alcoves, and crevices. The cave opening was just a few feet from the waterfall. It had a small ledge and a grand view of the rocky mountain valley below. It was already dark out, but the moon was full and bright on a clear, brisk, starry night.

"You don't get views like this in Maryland!" she exclaimed, taking in a deep breath of the clean air wafting in on a summer breeze. Then she began pulling off all her clothes and belongings – troublesome boots first.

"Not covered in mud anyway," he replied while staring at his disrobing wife. Then he gave her a wink. He could not care less about the view of the rocky valley and was more interested in her curves.

"Come on, let's jump in," she said, giving him a gentle kiss while removing and then setting aside his glasses. He was already kicking off his shoes and had detached his backpack.

The sizable pool beneath the waterfall was cool, but not too cold with the desert valley summer heat emanating from outside. So, the shivering was minimal as they warily slid into the unknown depths.

The water had been purified from years of filtering through the rocks of the mountainside. The moon was low and large, and the stars were numerous enough to accumulate into a blanket of sparkles over the water. Jutting outcrops of quartz also picked up the light, making the room glow in light pinkish jagged streaks along the cavern walls.

"Isn't this the most beautiful thing you've ever seen, Martin?" she said, pulling her hair out of the braids to clean out the sludge and marveling at the twinkles and glittering glistening on the walls and water.

"Yes," he said as he cleaned some muck off her cheek, and continued with, "though you did appropriate my spectacles. So, I am half-blind at present."

"I have a great feeling about this place. What if we bought some land out here and stayed?" she asked, filled with excitement at the idea that just came into her head. She bit her lip, "that's bananas, isn't it?"

"Well, the inheritance from my mother could subsidize rudimentary land; but, we would need to endeavor to create something habitable. And, by some means, build a facility for my continued research," he replied.

"You're considering it?!?" she exclaimed, completely surprised he would regard the idea as serious. Then, her mind began racing at the possibilities. "You don't think it's too far out?"

"My mother was all I had. I spent my life seeking a cure to save her and now she is ... she is..." he swallowed hard. It was still difficult for him to accept his mother's death. He had worked so hard, for so many years to save her. In the end, he had a solution but was unable to administer the serum due to concerns by the hospital staff. Concerns that generated paperwork and wasted precious time. Time she didn't have. Institutional bureaucracy prevented from saving his own mother's life. He fought the anger and swallowed hard again. "There is nothing left for me back east, except you Beth," he explained. "You are my everything now."

"You know you couldn't save your mother. The cancer spread too fast and came on too quickly this time. Your research is going to save millions more, though. I just know it," she said, coming over to Martin, to hold him. She pushed back his wavy hair from his face, staring deeply into his eyes and kissed him. "You are everything to me too," she said and laid her head on his chest.

"What about your family? Won't you miss them if we move all the way out here to Colorado?" he asked, squeezing her warm body close in the chilly water.

"What? My narcissistic mother and manic-depressive sister who thinks that because I married an atheist German I am somehow Eva Braun?" she replied. "I still love them, but man – they drive me bonkers! I could use a little distance, I think."

"Your mother is a narcissist?" he asked, perplexed. She'd always been so nice to him just to make her xenophobic jabs behind his back less believable – so she never mentioned them. Her mother was the most manipulative person she'd ever met, she could use a break from it all, really.

"Oh, she's the definition!"

"Your sister thinks I'm Hitler?"

"Hey, we're married now: the bones are falling out of the closet," she laughed. She'd been avoiding telling him these things because she didn't want him to dislike her family. But, knowing the truth now might help convince him to stay here in Colorado.

"Well, you know how much I like skeletons," he said right as a shooting star flashed across the night sky, lighting the whole valley.

Beth closed her eyes and made a wish on the shooting star, then said, "These caves are perfect for laboratories. The temperature and humidity are naturally controlled. These Navajo tunnels and alcoves have been around for God knows how long so they must be reasonably stable. We can make a research facility in no time and then you'll have free reigns on your work." Her eyes were shining in the starlight, and she was getting more excited with every word. "Free reigns, imagine what you could accomplish!"

She looked up to see her husband deep in thought with a quizzical brow, then added, "I can sell the mud to pay for the upgrades to the tunnels and to make a nice house down in the valley."

"You're rather confident regarding that mud," he gave her a curious expression and held her at arm's length, probably wondering what had gotten into his wife.

"Well, I will have to run a few tests on it, but yeah. I think the stuff could sell. I have a good feeling about it. There is a ton of it back there, untouched. I'm sure the land has other resources too. Not to mention this," she held up a handful of water and let it slip through her fingers as she continued with, "natural spring water we are desecrating. We could sell that too."

"We're not desecrating it yet," he said as he brought her closer for a kiss.

"We'll have to get rid of the spiders," she said, pushing him back.

"Yes, of course," he was trying to bring her closer again but she was swimming away.

"And the dead bodies. I mean, we can't keep those around." She continued moving further away.

"Of course, no dead bodies." He was chasing her in the pool.

"Maybe we should find those bats," she said playfully as she jumped out of the water, "bat guano is good money too."

"I'm not so sure there are any bats, honey," he said as he climbed out and began carefully searching for his glasses so he could have a better chance at catching his wife, who continued to elude him in a blur.

"Too bad. We could use the extra income right now, with a growing family," she smiled, looking down at her stomach and rubbing it with her two hands.

"You're...?!?" he said, putting his hand on her belly, overcome with emotion.

"Yes," she nodded. "I think this is a much better place to raise a family too, don't you think? Away from east coast politics and my insane family."

"I don't know what to say ... I am overwhelmed!" he had both hands in his hair now, on top of his head and he was grinning from ear to ear. "We've been trying for years. I didn't think it would happen!"

"Maybe it is all the fresh air we've been getting lately, running around in caves."

"Right, fresh air in caves ... Ha! I don't know what to say!"

"Just say 'Yes.' To this place, and a new life."

"Yes!" he laughed, picking up his wife and spinning her around in the moonlight.

Then she covered him in kisses and said, "Welcome home then, honey. I have a great feeling about this place!"

Chapter 2

Let's Take a Walk

Tsintah Hunt had seen quite a few strange people in her life, but this family was the most peculiar. Nothing like the people of her native tribe. Their large Craftsman house was full of experimental test set-ups. Microscopes, vials, and all sorts of machines were strewed all over. Weirdest of all was that half the kitchen was taken up with a system of pulleys and levers directing the flow of coffee through the house. It was set according to a giant German cuckoo clock in the entryway that ran many of the other tests as well.

Part of Tsintah's job was to make sure the two young sons of doctor Beth and Martin Jahren didn't get any of the coffee passing through the kitchen and the hallways. For some reason, the Jahrens found that particularly important: no coffee for the kids.

Primarily, she was paid to feed the children regularly and make sure they didn't get into too much trouble that would distract the doctors from their unremitting investigation into god only knew what. For her part, Tsintah felt getting the kids outside of the chaos in this mad scientist lair was her biggest daily challenge. That made taking the boys on a walk her most important endeavor of each day.

The eldest son, Daniel, was a bit easier to wrangle than his younger brother Cliff. At ten, Daniel knew he needed to let off some steam. He welcomed daily walks in the wilderness. So, he was easy to coax outdoors most days. The only exception was when one of his tests was not working out well – then there was no breaking him away. Cliff, seven, almost always had several experiments going at once. So, it was harder to get him to drop them all at their various stages.

Tsintah began her search for the boys in the large house by calling their names. She had no idea where the kids' parents were either; there were so many passages, nooks, crannies and hidden doorways in the house. The doctors were constantly disappearing. When they were around, they would suddenly pop out of nowhere with a cup of coffee in hand.

A loud bang reverberated in the house. It sounded like it came from one of the front rooms. Tsintah headed in that direction.

"Daniel, it is time to take a break," she said when she found him in his favorite location, the den converted into a library. He had his face buried in a rather large book with several others open around him on a grand mahogany desk. There wasn't an inch of wall space in the room that didn't have a book, and more books arrived weekly. The doctors felt the education of their children meant extensive reading on anything and everything, and that is exactly what the books in the room represented. A novel by Jane Austin sat on an encyclopedia of invertebrate, an atlas on a tome of poetry by Poe.

"Miss Tinny, is it already that time of day? Okay. I'm almost at a good place. Need help with Cliff I bet, huh?" Daniel replied while still moving his finger along the page, continuing to read as he talked. He wrote a note in his journal and then picked up another book. He compared it to the first one, wrote another note and then finally put his pen down before standing up to stretch. He was a dark haired, lean and amiable boy that took heavily after his father.

"Yes, I can't find him and that noise sounded like trouble," she said staring down at Daniel's notes in his journal. It appeared as if he was reading another native American language, one unfamiliar to Tsintah. "What was that you were writing?"

"Oh, I found some information on Aztec languages that I'm exploring. It's fascinating. The symbols are each a whole sentence. I'm trying my own method of translation ... using the dots here, see..." he said, flipping between pages of different books to show off what he was learning and then pointing to the dots above some strange symbols.

"Were you looking for me?" said a meek voice from behind where the two bents over the books.

"Cliff, sweetie! Yes, it's time for our daily walk. Are you ready to go? What's that on your face?" Tsintah asked, walking over to the pint-sized, chubby-cheeked Cliff standing in the doorway. Black smudge shrouded his face and blonde hair, and his eyebrows were scorched.

"Were you dismantling fireworks again to see if you can get your trains to go faster?" Daniel asked.

Cliff nodded, he was still in a daze. "There was a spark on the track ... I must not have cleaned up well..."

"Awe, poor thing. You're lucky to still have your eyebrows!" Tsintah said, brushing back his eyebrows with a small comb after wiping his face clean with a cloth. She always wore a blue-jean, bejeweled fanny around her waist that was packed full of useful things – like combs and washcloths. If she could fit more stuff in it, she would. "Come on, let's get some fresh air."

"Yeah, the fresh air should clear the smoke out of your lungs, little brother," Daniel said as he tussled Cliff's hair. "I'm ready. Where are we heading today, Miss Tinny?"

"Can we go by the lake?" Cliff asked, "I had a dream about the lake last night."

"Oh, Cliff, it wasn't a nightmare again, was it?" Tsintah inquired as she hurried the boys out of the house before they became sidetracked.

Distractions were everywhere. There was another dose of coffee moving down the conveyer belt that they had to duck under when leaving the den. On the kitchen table there was a mock-up of the entire rocky mountain range. It had simulations of volcanic eruptions on a timer, and it was going off.

Even more distracting was the cat. It was riding around on the train set, holding on for dear life. Cliff must have managed to get the train moving at close to 40 mph! Somehow the cat had become attached by the claws to one of the railcars.

"No, not exactly a nightmare..." Cliff said, detaching the cat from the train and putting her down on the floor. Her black and white hackles were up and her bright green eyes were as wide as could be, whites showing and everything. She stayed there, petrified for a few moments before realizing she wasn't riding the train anymore and then she fled under the china cabinet.

"We should take out the trash before we leave," Daniel announced, pressing a button next to the cuckoo clock that started a conveyer moving. Levers and handles activated in the kitchen, one of which got stuck on the lid of the trash can and couldn't quite lift it up.

"I can fix this," he declared, running over and moving a lever at the sink that kept clicking, "It's not getting enough torque, the bag must be over full."

Oh no, something to fix! It was the worst kind of distraction for these boys! Tsintah thought.

"Let's just do it the old-fashioned way today," she said, pulling the bag out of the trashcan and hurrying out the door. She pushed Cliff ahead of her. She knew if she let them get diverted with fixing the garbage disposal system then she might never get them out of the house today.

The trash system usually went out the front window and right to the barrels outside. So, she had to lift a conveyer belt and move a pulley system aside just to attempt to open the lid of the barrel.

"'Work smarter, not harder,' Mom always says," remarked Cliff under his breath to Daniel, who had just come outside from the kitchen where he had been fixing the lever system. Cliff was smiling as Tsintah struggled to get the trash put away. She tried to ignore his comment and smug little grin.

She was not very tall, and the trash barrel was larger than her. Clamoring and stumbling, she felt she might fall into the rancid waste bin of steaming goo trying to push back the heavy conveyer system above. Thankfully, Daniel took the bag and placed it into the barrel while she held up the contraption they called a lid. Daniel even gave Cliff a stern scowl, then shook his head at him for not helping her.

"All of this technology, it is making you boys lazy," she said, pinching one of Cliff's chubby cheeks. "Hard work gets your blood moving and keeps you healthy. I know a good path out to the lake from here. Let's head out."

Tsintah put a hand on each boy's back and led them out of the yard towards the sparsely wooded desert beyond. Finally, she had them out of the house! Success! she thought, breathing in the clean air while taking satisfaction in her triumph.

They took a red dirt path made from wild horses that were common in the region. The summer heat had turned the path into a fine dust but the horse prints were still visible.

"So, what was this dream you had Cliff?" Daniel asked, breaking the silence on the trail, "and stop shuffling your feet."

Cliff had been peering off into the distance, eyes unfocused, mouth slightly ajar and feet barely picking up enough to move forward but just enough to kick rocks annoyingly in every direction. "Well, I can't remember much ... I remember the lake, and a girl with a big smile ..."

"A girl?" asked Daniel. He had snuck a Rubik cube in his pocket and was working on how many moves it took to solve it without looking. He dropped the cube when he heard the word 'girl' come out of his brother's mouth, and lost count of his moves.

"Yes, she was very friendly but then she stole something of mine. I can't remember what," Cliff said and immediately went back into contemplation, followed by shuffling feet and rock kicking. "It was my GI Joe set I think," he said at last.

"Stop shuffling your feet! Did you even tie your shoes today? You're dragging your laces through the dirt!" exclaimed Daniel.

"Here, let me help you," Tsintah said bending down to fix Cliff's shoes. The laces were undone from all the shuffling and covered in dirt. "You should be more careful, you could trip over these things."

"I think I will get Mom to buy me some of those Velcro shoes I saw on TV and then I won't have to tie these bogus things again," said Cliff.

"Velcro?" Daniel asked, bending down to help with the right shoe. The laces had tangled and collected debris, including some thorns. Tsintah didn't even have to warn him, he was already carefully pulling out the thorns before tying the laces.

"Yes, it is a new material they are using to replace shoelaces. No more tying would be great!" Cliff declared.

"I'll have to check that out. You still shouldn't shuffle your feet, Cliff. It is annoying." Daniel said.

"I feel tired," Cliff moaned, "How much further to the lake, Miss Tinny?"

"Another mile or so. We just started, are you okay? Would you like a Fruit Roll-up? It will give you a little more energy," she offered, and pulled out a snack for Cliff from her handy bejeweled fanny-pack.

The treat seemed to satisfy him for a little while. He was a little bit chubby, especially in the lower half and calves, and was always hungry. He needed to walk much more than his lean older brother. Both boys took after their German father heavily and would likely be just as broad and tall one day. But, the younger brother had his mother's dark blue eyes and dirty blonde hair. Daniel had his father's wavy brown hair but he had the strangest hazel eyes; they changed from every shade of brown, including almost golden in the sun, all the way to a deep hunter green. Tsintah couldn't help but stare at them sometimes, they were so mesmerizing in their uniqueness. Everyone in her tribe had dark brown, straight hair with equally dark eyes and nowhere near as pale of skin. Skin that is turning red, oh no! she realized

"Oh, I forgot! I need to put sunscreen on you boys," she swiftly announced, dishing out the liquid from her trusty bag. She began slathering Cliff's face first. Their mother would throw a fit if she brought them back red and they had already been out for 15 minutes in the desert.

Daniel put the Rubik cube back into his pocket to get his sunscreen slathering. He wasn't much shorter than her even though she was a grown woman, whereas he had just turned ten this past August.

"Are you getting smaller?" he asked her with a smile and a patronizing pat on her head.

"Very funny..." she began.

"Hey, see what I found!" Cliff held up a lizard's tail an inch in front of her eyes. He then ran off giggling. The shock of the sudden lizard tail appearance caused her to squirt sunscreen into Daniel's face.

"I'm so sorry, Daniel!"

He flung-off the excess sunscreen into the dirt while squeezing his eyes shut and groaning at the stinging liquid. She took a tissue for him out of her pack and asked: "What happened to the rest of the lizard?"

"He likes to collect the tails. Sometimes he feeds them to the cat," Daniel explained. Tsintah must have appeared as horrified as she felt at the suggestion of feeding cats lizard tails because Daniel continued with, "The lizard's tails grow back. It is alright, the lizards are fine. Good source of protein for the cat too."

That somehow didn't ease the gut-reactive revulsion to the idea of ripping off reptile appendages for fun. She was still staring warily over at Cliff, brow furrowed.

Daniel had cleared the excess sunscreen out of his eyes. He peered over at the concerned nanny wondering how to console her. "You know, fish would be better for the cat. We have never been fishing. Is there fishing allowed at the lake?"

"Yes, though we can't fish today because I didn't bring any equipment. I can bring a couple of poles and show you two next time we're there though." Tsintah said, motioning Cliff to come back from the lizard chase he was on over by a pile of rocks.

They continued walking, enjoying the early autumn breeze carrying the scent of sage and threadleaf. Daniel and Tsintah followed a few feet behind Cliff, who was zig zagging on a sugar high up ahead along the path. He was still managing to shuffle his feet along the dirt though, kicking up a dusty red haze in front of them.

"We have to have a pole to catch fish? Don't your people catch them with your hands?" Daniel asked, sincerely.

"Pardon?"

"I'm sorry, I just assumed..."

"That I am a backwards, backwoods ... barbarian catching fish with my hands?" she interrupted, fervently.

"I'm sorry, Miss Tinny. I've never been fishing. I've only read about it."

"Yes. Well, you have a lot to learn, including about fishing." she tried not to be angry. These boys had very little social exposure because their parents homeschooled them. The doctors felt the local school was inadequate.

Maybe she could bring them to the reservation sometime to get acquainted with others? Oh, not a good idea! she realized almost as soon as she had the thought. Her family and most of the tribe wasn't very happy with the Jahrens after they bought the old mine and most of the surrounding hillside.

The 'improvements' to land over the last decade without any consult just made the situation even worse. The Jahrens thought that buying the land meant they could do whatever they wanted with it. Some of the tribe members were furious, and likely would cast blame on the kids. Poor kids, they were doomed to be ostracized simply because of their parents' mistakes, she thought.

"I'm grateful to have you to teach me, Miss Tinny." Daniel was such a sweet boy. She gave him a hug and they continued walking in silence, enjoying the crisp air and warm sun rays.

Upon arriving at the lake, they were surprised to find they were not the only ones. A few families had come to take refuge by the water – it was a caravan of campers. The threesome passed along the waterfront and said 'hi' to the picnicking families sprawled-out on blankets in the grass, apparently enjoying lunch.

The Mesa Heights area was utterly secluded, being not on any main Transamerica path or near a national monument. Consequently, visitors were scarce. The population of the town was barely over 100, with most of the residents getting close to 100 themselves – here to retire. That also meant even local residents were rare at the lake. The Navajo reservation to the southwest was the largest town for miles. So, for the boys, it was typically Native Americans they would see in the area, not Caucasians in campers.

"We should, perhaps, go ... they keep staring at you Miss Tinny," remarked Cliff, noticing that some people must not have ever seen a full-blooded native by the ogling she was being given.

As they headed back into the woods, an upside-down head popped out right in front of them, stopping all three in their tracks.

"Hello!" said the fluffy, curly, blonde-haired head. The head happened to be attached to a young girl dangling from a branch by the knees. She wore a blue jean jumper and white t-shirt with a little purple pony on it. She had on rainbow socks inside white Velcro tennis shoes that Cliff walked around to inspect. She did a little flip to get out of the tree she was hanging from and stood smiling. With one hand on her hip, her glancing eyes taking in all three with excitement, she held out her other hand for anyone to shake.

"Hi," said Daniel first, taking up the outreached hand.

"I'm Amy, Amy Shipley. Nice to meet you!" she said, shaking his hand vigorously.

"I'm Daniel, Daniel Jahren and this is my brother, Cliff. This is our nanny, Miss Tinny."

"You have a nanny? Do you live here? We're all just passing through but the Johnsons over there are having problems with their transmission. So, we might be staying a while. What's there to do around here anyway? Caves? Canyons? Ancient cities? I think I saw a cave up there that I'm gonna to try to explore tomorrow..." Amy just kept talking and talking and Daniel had no idea what to do but stand there and nod.

Cliff took Tsintah's hand and pulled her away, leaving Daniel to fend for himself. "It's the girl from my dream," he whispered when they were at a respectable distance. She took a step back in shock. Cliff never made things up and having someone appear out of a dream was not normal.

"Are you sure?" she whispered back.

"Yes. Dimples, smile, big blue eyes ... Is she going to steal my GI Joe set Miss Tinny? I won't let her!" he declared and crossed his arms over his chest in defiance.

"No, that isn't how dreams usually work. They're never literal. It's all symbolic. And most of the time, they don't come true ... I..." she didn't know what to say. Was Cliff a dream-walker? This wasn't the first time he seemed to have a predictive dream, but it was the first time someone showed up out of his dreams.

"What do you mean? I thought dreams were supposed to come true. On TV they are constantly say things like 'dream,' 'keep on dreaming,' or 'I have a dream!' What do you mean they don't come true?" He was stomping his feet, trampling the grass and throwing a mini-temper tantrum.

She held his arm and faced him towards her, then said, "What I mean is that most dreams are simply your spirit speaking to your mind in symbols to help you connect more deeply with your inner desires. Does that make sense?" That stopped his stomping enough to make him think. He scratched his head and squinted his eyes up at her. She wasn't sure what part of what she had said confused him.

"No, what spirit?" Cliff said after a bit of contemplation.

"Your spirit, your soul." She was shocked at the question. "You've heard of that, right?"

Cliff shook his head, eager for an explanation.

"It's the thing inside that makes you ... well You." Tsintah tried to put the right words together but the shock was tying her tongue. These kids had no religious education except for books, and Cliff preferred only books that helped him with his inventions and experiments. Unlike his brother Daniel, who explored all aspects of life.

What did their parents even believe? Were they Christian like most of the other white people she had met? Tsintah realized she had never asked.

They rarely watched TV and usually only to turn on the nightly news. Cliff did have the TV on sometimes when working on his train set, he liked to watch cartoons. She understood then that Cliff had probably never heard of a spirit or a soul his entire life, and he was 7!

"I don't like her," Cliff declared, still cross in attitude and in arms and staring at the little girl fifteen feet away.

Daniel and Amy were getting along great. He was showing her his Rubik cube and she was showing him her Chihuahua that had been tied to the tree she'd been climbing. They were sitting under the shade of an old cedar, smiling and giggling.

"It looks like your brother may have a new friend," Tsintah said, "You should be happy for him. You two never get to meet people."

"He better not let her near my G.I Joe set!" Cliff yelled, loud enough for the two under the tree to hear. They completely ignored him.

"Oh, stop it, Cliff! I told you that dreams aren't literal," she explained. "She isn't going to steal anything. Little girls are sugar and spice and everything nice, don't you know that?"

"You said that dreams don't come true; but, there she is, explain that!"

Tsintah thought for a minute, not sure what to say. It was rare when someone had predictive dreams like Cliff. She would need to consult her sister, who knew far more about dream-walkers than she did. But, for now she should let him know what she remembered about dreaming. She just thought of something she heard about once. "Sometimes, when important people come into your life you can have a dream that foreshadows them. It's never happened to me but it has to other people I know. The spirit world doesn't operate in the same time and space that we do."

"So, you are saying that I have a 'spirit' and that it is from another dimension?"

Wow, that was a good take on it, especially for a seven-year-old, she thought.

"Yes," she affirmed. "This young woman must be important. And, she's not going to steal anything from you; that's not how it works."

"How does it work?"

"Well, what did you feel when you thought of your GI Joe set?"

"What did I feel? What kind of bogus question is that?"

"Searching your feelings, they will reveal the truth your spirit is trying to tell you." That much she knew for certain. Everything in a dream has more to do with how you feel about the images and happenings than anything else.

"Search my feelings?" Cliff asked, kicking rocks. "Like using 'The Force' from Star Wars?"

The kid knew about Star Wars but not about spirits and souls! TV was not the best way to raise children, that Tsintah knew for certain.

Cliff picked up a rock to throw it at the girl. "I feel like I don't like her!"

Tsintah managed to stop his arm in time for the rock to land just a foot from Daniel and Amy's feet. "I think it's time to head back," Tsintah announced loud enough for everyone to hear. This conversation was getting too deep and she wasn't sure their parents wanted her talking about such things. "We'll talk about this more later, okay?" she whispered to Cliff.

~ ~ ~

"Nice to meet you!" Amy said to the three, waving goodbye. Daniel waved at Amy as he was walking backwards, being dragged by the arm by his nanny. He then turned around and started skipping along the path home, excited to have made a new friend.

"So, I found out about the caravan of people here. They might be here for a while. I may, possibly, be able to help with the transmission problem the Johnsons are having. I will see if we have a book on that at home," Daniel said, smiling from ear to ear and stretching his crisscrossed hands out in front of him like he always did when he proposed a new project to work on.

"I don't like her Daniel. I don't think you should go back and see her again," Cliff said. He was still sulking while ambling along the path kicking rocks and shuffling his feet.

"Stop shuffling your feet! Your shoe laces are going to come undone again," Daniel said, purposefully ignoring his brother's request to not see the girl again.

Cliff stopped shuffling his feet but then started marching fast towards home. That compelled Daniel to want to keep up, so he started marching beside him. Then they started going faster and faster until they were running.

Miss Tinny didn't even try to keep up with them, she knew how competitive they could get. Daniel tried not to embarrass his little brother too much, so ran just fast enough to be slightly ahead of him. Cliff was tiring out but determined to get past Daniel. Cliff was becoming redder and redder, and more out of breath ... until finally he tripped on his own feet – or his laces had become unstrung again. All Daniel saw was him doing a diving face plant from the corner of his eye.

"Are you okay?" Daniel attempted to help his brother up. Cliff merely pushed him away. He searched for Miss Tinny, with her bag of Band-Aids and ointments, but she had been lost long ago at the start of their run. She was far behind on the trail now.

"No. I think something is wrong. My legs feel ... weak," Cliff said as he tried to get up and was having trouble standing. His legs were buckling from under him whenever he tried to put weight on them.

"Let me help you," Daniel pleaded.

"No! This is your fault, you made me run. You like that girl!" Cliff yelled.

"My fault! I didn't make you run, and so what if I like a girl!" Daniel yelled back.

"I had a dream that she is going to steal my GI Joe set! Miss Tinny says it means something about my spirit but I just don't like that girl, okay?"

"Come on now, that girl doesn't matter. She will be gone in just a few days. I am here, and I am your brother. Let me help you," Daniel asked.

"I don't know what is wrong with me. I feel so weak and I can't stand it!" Cliff said in frustration. He picked up a handful of rocks and threw them at a tree.

They sat there for a few breaths, Daniel felt like maybe Cliff just needed to calm down.

"Don't worry, Mom and Dad will know what to do," Daniel said, reassuringly placing his hand on Cliff's shoulder. "Let's just get home."

Cliff sat sulking for a minute before he nodded, indicating with a pouty lip and chin up that he would accept help at last, but wasn't happy about it. Daniel lifted him up, putting his arm around his shoulders.

"Do you think they will let me have some of their coffee? I mean, it always seems to give them energy," asked Cliff.

"That stuff smells gross. You really want to try it?" Daniel asked, looking back along the trail for signs of their nanny. "Hey, if we get there before Miss Tinny, we can swipe you some without asking, okay?"

"Deal!" said Cliff, grinning at the idea of getting past his nanny to get to the coffee she was sworn to protect.

Chapter 3

Food for Thought, and the Cat

Unfortunately for Cliff's and Daniel's aspirations of sneaking some coffee, their father was standing in the kitchen and staring at the cuckoo clock when they stumbled through the front door.

"What happened?" Martin immediately took hold of Cliff from an exhausted and out of breath Daniel.

"We were running and he fell," Daniel answered. "He said he was weak. We haven't had lunch. Maybe he is just hungry?"

"Hungry? Where is Miss Tinny?" Martin lifted Cliff onto the kitchen counter in one smooth motion.

"She is coming..." Cliff started to say but just then the nanny walked through the door, answering the question in the flesh.

"Tsintah, what happened?" Martin demanded, his attention still on Cliff, who was looking forlornly at the coffee.

"Hi, Dr. Jahren," Tsintah said calmly standing just inside the doorway. "Cliff's been dragging his feet all day, and he'd been more tired than usual."

"I see," Martin said, feeling his youngest son's forehead and then looking at his palms. No fever, no sweaty palms. He did have a slight sunburn and was a bit flushed, nothing alarming.

"He got upset because Daniel was talking to a little girl we met at the lake today. He tried to race his older brother home. I let them go ahead. From the markings in the dirt on the path that they left, it looked like they might have gotten into a fight."

"We didn't get into a fight! I noticed he'd been shuffling his feet all day too but he ran fine before he face-planted into the dirt. I helped him home ... I hope there's nothing wrong with his legs. Maybe he's just hungry?" Daniel jumped up to sit on the counter next to his brother and nudged him. "I'm hungry too."

"You better get your mom, Daniel. She is in the third study, you know the code. Schnell!!" said Martin.

Daniel jumped down and headed out right away. He knew that when his father started using German, things were going to get intense.

"Tsintah, we will no longer need your services today. Thank you for the detailed explanation of events and we will see you tomorrow." He was already pushing her out the door, he didn't need any of the locals butting into family affairs. If there was something seriously wrong with his son, it was none of their business.

"Thank you, sir, let me know if there is anything I can do," she tried to say as she was being walked out backwards.

"Father, we haven't even had lunch yet!" Cliff whined.

"Oh, stop whining! You aren't hungry. How does this feel?" he said, poking and prodding at Cliff's legs. He lifted Cliff's arms up and made him hold them out as he tested the strength of each arm, pushing down slightly.

"Fine. I feel fine, just weak. Ow!" Cliff yelled when he dinged him below the knee cap with a ladle. Cliff's reflexes were not good – it took too long for his leg to kick up and it barely moved. "And I AM hungry. I'm always hungry!"

"What happened?" Beth said, gliding into the kitchen and giving her youngest son a little kiss on the forehead.

"He fell..." Daniel started to say.

"He is suffering from muscular atrophy..." Martin started at the same time.

"I'm just hungry..." Cliff began, simultaneous to the other two.

Beth peered around the room at the three guys talking at once, then held up her hand to shush them all. Cliff's stomach growled in the brief silence loud enough for everyone to hear.

"See!" said Cliff, grabbing his belly with both hands.

"Martin, make the poor boy a sandwich!" she said, and gave Cliff a big hug.

Twenty minutes later (and a few turkey, bacon, lettuce and tomato sandwiches between the foursome) and they were all feeling better.

"So, who's up for a trip to Denver?" Beth asked when they were all done, carrying plates into the kitchen. To Martin's surprise, she decided to help him with the dishes.

"When?" Daniel asked, gazing up from the journal he was writing in on what should have been a dining room table. He had the journal propped between the Olympic Peninsula and the Cascade Mountains in the Rocky Mountain display that took up most of the room.

"Denver! Can we go see the new Star Wars movie?" Cliff asked, starting a drum roll with his hands in excitement on the kitchen counter where he was still seated.

"Yes, Cliff. And, we'll visit our friend Dr. Jorgensen while we're there," Beth suggested.

"The rheumatologist we encountered at that conference in Orlando four years ago? I would hardly call him a friend," Martin replied, handing her a freshly washed dish to put away. "Though he is the single individual we are acquainted with who would have a more thorough comprehension of the predicament than us."

"We could run preliminary tests ourselves ... But yes, David Jorgensen is a specialist and I want my son to have the best care available." Beth was looking through the cabinets trying to figure out which one the plates were typically stored. Daniel took the plate from his mom and put it in the cabinet behind the three-foot coffee-making contraption.

"How about I start some tests now, and you give David a call to arrange a time?" Martin could not argue with her sound logic but needed to check a few things himself first before relying on another's expertise.

"Sounds like a good plan, honey," Beth said. She dried her hands with the dishtowel and went straight for her rolodex next to the phone to search for the doctor's number.

"Cliff, we're going to the basement," Martin said, picking him up and flinging him over the back of his shoulders. Cliff hung on like a gorilla baby, crossing his legs around his father's waist.

"The basement? Can I come Father? You never let us in the basement," Daniel pleaded.

"No, Daniel. It is prudent not to conglomerate in that space. I am confident you have an abundance of studying to do: some CLEPs, or GED, ACT perhaps SAT's pre-exams? You must have adequate preparation for college entrance." Martin said, sternly for severity's sake. "Unless you need me to assign new work..."

"No thanks, Father. I've got plenty to keep me busy," Daniel quickly interjected, heading grudgingly towards the den.

"I've never been in the basement. What's in there?" Cliff asked almost right into Martin's ear. Cliff had laid his head on his shoulders and his mouth was less than an inch away. He tried to ignore the moist, turkey-sandwich smelling breath on his neck as he walked.

"You will see," Martin replied. He pushed open a side wall in the back of the house that opened into a tunnel lit with candelabras-like lanterns strung together with large green cables going straight into the mountainside about 100 feet from the house.

The basement was no basement. It took a few minutes of walking in a dimly lit, damp tunnel and then going through a substantial metal door to reach "the basement." The door needed a combo to open because it was made from an old bank safe. Once open, they arrived in Martin's personal work space – a laboratory built into the side of the mountain.

He sat Cliff down on one of the lab chairs, saying "Don't move, I need to prepare some solutions." He headed over to a large yellow cabinet full of chemicals.

It was an expansive and heavily cluttered room. Not particularly well lit either. There were desk lights on each table, but they were mostly off to save power. Everything was wired to cords bundled up together and leading out to the back of the room where there was a large generator. Between books on the floor, and vials, beakers and test equipment on every shelf, there was hardly any space to move around. But, most days it was just Martin so there was no need for more room.

"What kind of microscope is that? I have never seen one like that before," Cliff asked, staring straight ahead at a massive microscope connected to several metal boxes and a vacuum chamber. The magnification portion of the scope was completely surrounded by a rectangular glass enclosure.

"Oh that, it is an experimental electron microscope. Don't move and don't touch anything," Martin said, coming back over to place a container of rubbing alcohol on the desk. He swiped Cliff's hand away from the microscope and then spun him around in the chair.

"Wow, Dad. How many computers do you need? Is that a Commodore 64?" Cliff inquired, he was now spinning himself around on the chair and checking out the 'basement' in 360.

"I need as many as it takes," Martin yelled over to his son from where he was mixing chemicals under a fume hood that was very loudly clearing the air.

"What are those?" Cliff pointed over to a set of enormous refrigerators full of blue vials, and beakers of red liquid sitting next to a four-level shelf full of small jars with the tiny organs of various creatures.

"Those are refrigerators," Martin replied over the noise of the fume hood and then walked back to where Cliff was sitting. He pulled some needles out of a drawer and placed them on the counter. He started rummaging through a few more drawers until he found some cotton balls.

"Duhh, what's IN the refrigerators?" asked Cliff, slightly annoyed.

"My work," Martin replied, "This may hurt a bit," he wiped down Cliff's right arm with alcohol-soaked cotton balls and then drew some blood.

Cliff gave a slight wince when the needle went into his arm. "So, what are you working on?"

"Oncolytic virotherapy," Martin replied, curtly. "You know that, or have you forgotten?"

"Oh yeah. I thought it would be, you know, cooler or something."

"Not glamorous enough for you, son? Trust me, it astounds under the microscope."

"Really, can I see?"

"No."

'C'mon!"

"No." Martin said as he removed the needle. He then put the three vials of blood he had taken into a spinning centrifuge. He put a small cotton ball onto Cliff's arm and said, "Hold this down for a few minutes."

"C'mon Dad!"

"No."

Cliff opened his mouth again, but Martin put up his finger and squinted his eyes, which only made Cliff emulate him and giggle. So, Martin smacked Cliff's finger back and then spun him around on the chair again.

"Have you had weakness in your legs before today Cliff? How long have your calves been that swollen?" Martin asked.

"I don't know, Dad." Cliff stopped the spinning to let him examine his legs a bit more.

"Try to think."

"Hummmm ... I had trouble climbing a hill a couple of weeks ago. Been extra hungry lately. So, a couple of weeks, maybe? Nothing as bad as today though. Do you know what is wrong, Dad?"

"Precisely, no ... we shall find out more from the tests running. In Denver, our friend will perform more thorough examinations that should lead to a conclusive answer."

"Am I gonna die?" Cliff was making a sad face, pushing out his lower lip and opening his eyes wide in mock shock and dismay.

Martin tried not to make eye contact with his son, the situation was severe and he knew Cliff wasn't prepared to know the details. It was wise to wait until all the results were in, no need to say anything that will make anyone worry. "We will all die, one day. But you, my son, are going to live a very long life," he assured Cliff, pulling playfully on his son's protruding lower lip.

"You aren't giving him SAL-142 are you Martin?!!?" Beth exclaimed. She had just come into the room and all she heard was the last thing he had said.

"No, but that isn't a bad idea!" he declared, jumping up out of his chair and towards one of the refrigerators that held his latest salix alba concoction.

Beth stopped him, taking him by the arm and pulling him aside to whisper, "That is highly experimental, don't you think? Especially with your family history of cancer? It could be dangerous."

"Yes, of course. We should hold off to find out what Dr. Jorgensen says first, honey. Of course. Oh, what about BNR-73? I suggest we initiate immunization with that one if we proceed with SAL-142." Martin whispered back, getting more excited. Beth motioned him to shush, he was apparently whispering too loudly. He adjusted his glasses in irritation.

"No, Martin. I think this is a dangerous road to even think about starting down. It is one thing if we experiment on ourselves, it is another if we start inoculating our children. They don't even understand the risks." The irritation in Beth's voice added an unmitigated volume that made her prior shushing seem quite hypocritical.

"What risks?" Cliff asked, startling the two by unexpectedly standing right between them. Standing. He hadn't stood since falling down earlier. Beth and Martin were flabbergasted at both the standing and where he was standing. "You're experimenting on yourselves? How?"

"So, you are feeling better already? Walking okay now?" Martin inquired, no longer feigning to whisper, holding onto Cliff's arm in case he needed support. He glanced over at Beth, who was still speechless.

"What risks? What experiments? Do you have something to make me better?" Cliff was quite invigorated. "Will I get super powers like spider-man? Can you make me grow a tail like a lizard?"

"We do have a lizard amalga..." Martin began to say before getting a nudge from his wife.

Beth shook her head, gave Martin a look of consternation and said: "No, son. We are going to Denver to a specialist. We have an appointment on Friday, so we need to go upstairs and start packing right away."

"That quickly! I assume you managed to contact David directly?" Martin didn't expect for the doctor to create an opening in his schedule so rapidly, he was touted as one of the finest in the country and he expected it might take weeks for him to find time to see his son.

"Yes, and I already discussed some of the symptoms. He has a good idea of what it is ... we'll find out more soon," her voice was breaking and she was blinking away tears. That was a very bad sign.

"We can fix anything, together," Martin took her hand and brought her in for a hug. He gave her a kiss on the cheek and she relaxed into his arms until he yelled "Don't touch that!" right into her ear, unintentionally. He meant it for Cliff who was about to lift up the glass rectangular enclosure next to the microscope.

"Ouch!" Beth exclaimed, "I think I am going to go deaf!" She rubbed a finger on the inside of her ear to dull the pain.

"Sorry, Father. Sorry, Mom. Is that a wasp under there? Its huge!"

"Yes, it is a tarantula hawk wasp. We are utilizing them to expunge the tunnels of all the tarantulas. Their venom is proving advantageous in some of my experiments and your mother is analyzing their gland structure under the microscope," Martin answered. "You must not touch anything here. The wasp carcass needs to remain in vacuum for the electron diffraction to function and you destroyed the seal."

"Honey, maybe I should take him back upstairs?" Beth said. "I think seven-year-old's and a lab full of deadly viruses is not a wise combination."

"What deadly viruses?" Cliff was about to open one of the refrigerators before his mother ran over and stopped him.

"Yes, I have enough serum for the tests I need to execute. I'll be above ground in a few hours with the anticipated results," Martin said. He had already begun working on re-sealing the rectangular enclosure. He turned on a loud vacuum pump; the sound of which, combined with the centrifuge and fume exhaust running, made the room too unbearably noisy to pursue further conversation.

~ ~ ~

"Mom, why do you want to kill the tarantulas?" Cliff asked, holding Beth's hand as she led him up to the main house through the mountain tunnel.

"Because they are hairy, evil, 8 legged things from nightmares that make your skin crawl and stare at you with strange, creepy eyes of dreadfulness!"

"So, you have nightmares about spiders?"

"Yes, they're the most horrible creatures, pure evil."

"I like Spider-Man, and spiders. I wouldn't mind being bitten by a radioactive spider and becoming a super hero. I don't have nightmares about spiders. I have nightmares about little girls stealing my GI Joes – now that is pure evil!" Cliff insisted, nodding as he talked.

"Little girls stealing you GI Joes?" Beth laughed; she couldn't help it. Spiders were far worse than little girls, but maybe not to little boys.

"Yes, and I met one today, she was horrible."

"You met a little girl? Where?" This was the first she had heard of it. They had focused on telling her about Cliff's fall and subsequent muscle weakness and not any of the events leading up to it.

"At the lake. Daniel talked to her. She told him that her caravan was stuck there for a few days. So, she could come steal my toys any day. You won't let her mom, will you?" Cliff begged, stopping her walking by yanking on her arm.

"Of course not! No little girl is going to steal your toys, I promise. Why would you think that?"

"She did in my nightmare," Cliff said, sulking and refusing to move further through the tunnel.

"It's only a dream. They mean nothing. It is merely your brain firing off images processed throughout the day. You probably saw something on TV with a little girl. Then, you played with your toys. When you went to sleep, your brain simply put it all together. Dreams have no meaning, they are purely jumbled non-sense."

"Miss Tinny says it is my 'spirit' trying to tell me something and I should look into my feelings," Cliff said, peeking up curiously at her. He clearly wanted to see how she would react, and it was important that she set some facts straight about the matter.

"Miss Tinny has very different beliefs than we do, and that's okay. Lots of people have different beliefs because of their culture or religion. From a scientific standpoint, dreams have not been proven to have any significance. They are just random thoughts being stimulated by events firing off in your brilliant imagination. Do you understand?"

She waited for him to acknowledge what she said, and he nodded. He still looked troubled.

"Little girls are nothing to be scared of, and they seldomly steal. I'll make sure no little girl even comes into this house if you like." Beth did not know how else to re-assure her son and she was going to have a word or two with Tsintah.

"Okay, Mom, thank you," Cliff said, sighing a breath of relief at last. She tried not to laugh, he was that bothered by a little girl?

"I do have one more question for you, honey," she began, taking his hand between both of hers, kneeing down so she was at his level to look him directly in the eyes, "What did you do to the cat?"

"I didn't do it, the cat jumped on the train," Cliff insisted. "I swear, it wasn't my fault!"

"Well, Dr. Whiskers hasn't gotten out from under the china hutch all day. Can you coax her out? Maybe give her a treat?"

"Oooh, I can give her this!" he exclaimed, digging a lizard's tail he must have collected on the trail earlier from his back pocket and suspending it in front of her face.

"Oh my! Sure. I'm sure she would love that," she said, trying to smile through the natural grimace response to seeing a dead piece of animal flesh wiggling so close to her nose. "You know, you seem to have a lot more energy, and you are walking fine now ... did your dad give you something down there? Did you get into anything? Be honest. I promise, you won't be in trouble."

Cliff appeared guilty: if the blushing and eye aversion didn't give it away, the fidgeting feet and hands sure did. Finally, he said, "I took a sip of dad's coffee on the desk while you two were talking. I'm sorry! It tasted nasty!!! I don't know why you like it so much. I won't drink it again, ever, I promise! Really, I promise!"

"Honey, thank you for being honest. You know coffee is off limits. We have a strict rule about that for a reason." Beth said. Well, that explained the sudden jolt of energy! But the sudden walking? What in the world in that tarry concoction of Martin's could have done that? she thought. She slid open the wall at the back of the house and led Cliff through. "Whatever made you want to break the rule today?"

"I was feeling so tired and you always look like coffee gives you energy. Dad sat it down right next to me, you two weren't looking ... I just thought it might help. Are you going to punish me?"

"Not today, though I may have a word or two for your father. We will find a better medicine for you when we go to Denver. No more, okay?"

"Yes, mom. Can I go feed the cat now?"

"Of course, honey," she said as she kissed him on the forehead and patted him on the back. "I'm just glad you're feeling better."

Cliff ran off gleefully towards the kitchen, dangling lizard tail in tow, saying "Here, kitty kitty ... I have a treat for you!"

Beth went into the master bedroom to start packing for the trip. They would need to leave first thing in the morning and she had a full family worth of bags and things to get ready.

"Mom, can I stay? Please? I want to see if I can help fix the transmission problems the campers at the lake are having," Daniel walked into the room and wasted no time making a request to his busy mother who was loading up suitcases.

"No honey, we all have to go," she replied off hand while trying to count the number of shirts she had pulled from the closet. "One, two, three ... Yes, that should be enough. How can you help with a transmission problem? You haven't studied auto mechanics yet, have you?"

"I know. I can't find anything on cars, trucks or RV's in the house. Maybe we should order some?" Daniel was so kind hearted, always wanting to help others and fix problems. A trait Beth wanted to encourage.

"We might be able to find something in Denver for you to study. There are a few great bookstores we can go to."

Daniel stood in the room, watching his mother pack. She had thought the bookstore idea would have him elated, but he appeared contemplative. He started to help her pack by folding some of the stacks of clothes she had shoved into a suitcase. Beth loved planning, but hated organizing. Daniel was so detail oriented, like his father. It was nice to have the help.

"I still want to stay ... I promised Amy I would come back to see her tomorrow..." he said at last after moping for a few minutes.

"Amy? Is that the little girl you and Cliff met today?" she said while going into the bathroom to get toiletries.

"Yes, she was very nice. I told her about the eastern cliffs and she wants to climb them. She says she has climbed the Grand Canyon and every great canyon west of the Mississippi."

"I see. She sounds like a very impressive young lady." She could tell that Daniel really liked this girl, he had never spoken like this about anyone before.

"Yes, she is." He said, pointedly gazing down at the clothes he was folding extra carefully. "She might leave before we get back." He looked up with those sad eyes a mother never wants to see and can hardly resist.

"I can't just leave you here by yourself!" she exclaimed – it was getting harder to say no.

"I won't be alone. Miss Tinny can check on me. I promise, I'll be good." The hope in his voice was heartbreaking.

"I don't know. We would need to see if she is even available..." She hadn't finished her sentence before she was interrupted with Daniel yelling "I'll call her now!" and running off. She had planned to call Tsintah to watch the house while they were away anyway, but she wasn't expecting to ask her to watch her eldest son too.

Two minutes later she heard him hollering from the kitchen, "Mom! She says she can stay here! She wants to talk to you! MOM!" The words got increasing louder as he was running from the kitchen to the bedroom to tell her the good news.

"No running through the halls! You might trip!" Beth put down the shirt she was folding, wondering how she had been convinced to leave Daniel at home alone. She followed him through the hallway, being towed by the arm the entire time, then picked up the phone sitting on the kitchen counter.

"Hi, Tsintah. Daniel let you know we're heading out of town?" she wound the twisted phone cord connected to the wall absent-mindedly around her index finger and paced back and forth. Daniel followed her around, trying to listen-in on the conversation.

"Yes. I have no problem staying there and watching the cat and Daniel. I can tell he is very excited. I'm sorry you are having to go to Denver though. I hope it is nothing too serious," Her voice replied over the phone, the speaker making her sound older and distorted, with a bit of a crackle.

"Thank you. I hope so too. We're leaving first thing in the morning. We'll likely be back Saturday evening. I'll give you double pay for all three days for the inconvenience. I appreciate your help."

"Oh, it's not a problem at all! I'm happy to spend time with Daniel, he's such a bright and sweet boy."

"Thank you again, Tsintah. I'll see you in the morning, 6 am. Thank you."

"Yay!!" Daniel yelled and hugged her when she hung up the phone.

Beth tried to untwist the cord that she had nervously twisted even more than before. Somehow during the brief conversation, she'd managed to get it wrapped around her leg, arm and even in her long blonde hair.

"Now you need to be careful with this girl, Amy. If you go climbing you need to bring your own gear and do the standard check from the checklist in the gear bag. Most importantly, you're not allowed to go anywhere without Tsintah, are we clear?" She used as mommy stern of a voice as she could manage.

Daniel was nodding in-between hugging.

"Miss Tinny can climb a cliff like a mountain goat, she loves them!" Daniel exclaimed.

"She loves mountain goats?"

"No, cliffs ... climbing. Maybe she loves goats too, I don't know. Oh, don't forget the book on transmissions when you go to Denver; I want to help my new friend if they haven't gotten it fixed by the time you get back."

There were few people in the area and it was good for her kids to make friends at any opportunity. Not having companions their own age was probably very hard on them and she felt like a horrible parent because of it. She had hoped more people would move to the town with kids, but in the last 10 years it was still mostly retirees.

"You aren't coming with us?" Cliff asked. He had Dr. Whiskers in his arms, and she had the lizard tail sticking out of her mouth. Beth held back a reactionary gag at the sight.

"Mom said I can stay and go climbing with Amy. Miss Tinny is coming to watch me."

"You're going to miss Return of the Jedi, are you sure you want to stay?" Cliff said, he seemed a bit in disbelief.

"You can tell me all about it and I can wait and see it when it comes out on VHS like we have seen all the rest." Daniel replied, unfazed.

"You aren't going to let that girl come over to our house while we're gone, are you?"

"Don't worry Cliff, I won't let her anywhere near your GI Joes," Daniel said, petting the cat, who was chewing on the lizard tail and appearing quite content, purring in Cliff's arms, eyes almost sparkling green.

Beth stared at her two boys and wondered how one could think so poorly of girls, and the other was so excited to meet one. With how much exposure to other people her kids were getting living here, she was surprised they even knew what a little girl looked like. I certainly must find a way to get more people to move to this town! she thought as she went to finish packing for the trip.

Chapter 4

Little Girls and Games

Amy Shipley spent her life on the road going across the United States of America from one national park to the next and everywhere in between. It was all she knew, besides her family. Her father was retired Army, a full-bird Colonel. Her mother was 20 years younger and loved adventure. Her younger brother, Doug, was three and barely talking, still in diapers and a snotty pain-in-the-butt that kept her mom busy all day cleaning up mess after mess. Her family had three Chihuahuas, but her favorite was Mimi. The other two generally just liked her mother. Mimi was Amy's best friend and went with her everywhere.

Amy loved meeting new people, especially boys. Unfortunately, where they were stuck now no one seemed to pass through. She'd been bored to death the last few days waiting for anyone to show up.

Her parents had relegated her to the lake area yesterday because her dad decided he wanted to fish and play cribbage with the Dukes instead of go hiking like she wanted. She'd gotten her rock skipping game down to an art before she started climbing trees to look for a better view of the valley.

Then she saw him: Daniel Jahren. He was the most interesting boy she'd ever come across. He'd showed her how to solve a Rubik's cube in ten moves, and she'd never even seen one solved before. Plus, he knew the entire area and said he could show her how to get to the top of the mountain near the lake.

She was so excited to see him again that she got up early and was out walking the tree line. She paced back and forth in the wet grass with only the sound of birds and the lapping of the water at the lake to distract her from her thoughts. Her fluffy purple socks were soaked with morning dew. Urgh, I've been up and about for an hour now. Where is he?? she thought.

The Ryans were hosting breakfast. The aroma of pancakes and sausage wafting through the air made her mouth water. But she didn't want to miss seeing Daniel come through the tree line first because she was afraid the Johnson twins would get to him and steal him away from her. Last night they had asked her like a million questions about him, his brother and his nanny. None of them had ever seen a Native American as a nanny before and she had looked so beautiful and mysterious.

Daniel's chubby little brother Cliff didn't seem to like Amy, he even threw a rock at her dog! She hoped he wouldn't be coming back today. He was probably a total brat, just like her own pants-craping younger sibling.

Mimi was getting dizzy following Amy around, pacing at the forest edge, and started to bark and whine. Her smooth and fluffy brown hair was standing up straight and her cream-colored paws were turning dark reddish-brown from the dirt. Amy picked her up and kept pacing, brushing off the grime from Mimi's tiny feet and cradling her to keep her warm.

"Did you chase him away being such a ditz, Amy?" Sarah Johnson asked. Her twin, Rebecca, mirrored the look of snide condescension she was directing at Amy. They dressed alike, talked alike and sometimes even walked alike, probably just to annoy and confuse everyone. The only way she could tell them apart was that Sarah had a one-inch, dark brown birthmark on her neck in the shape of a melting crescent moon and Rebecca was slightly taller and leaner. The dark auburn hair, large hazel eyes and perfectly porcelain skin accentuated their pink lips and rosy cheeks. They reminded her of well-crafted dolls. Their only flaw was a pig-like nose, and a snooty attitude to match.

"No, you're the airhead that chases everyone away, Sarah. Daniel said he'd be back today. He swore," Amy grimaced, staring into the tree line. Great, she was going to miss breakfast and the Johnson twins were ready to pounce on Daniel the minute he walked out! "Either of you want to get me a sausage?" Her request was met with disdain. "For Mimi?" Her stomach was rumbling, and Mimi gave a little bark of concern.

"Go get breakfast yourself! You're obviously hungry and poor Mimi deserves better," Rebecca said, petting Mimi who was licking what was likely the syrup from pancakes off of her fingers.

"Did you make Daniel pinky swear he would be back?" Sarah asked.

"No, I..."

"Lame!" Rebecca cut her off and snickered.

"I ... I'm going to go get something to eat," Amy said, the empty pit of her stomach growling louder and feeling heavier with each insult from the Johnson girls.

She dashed away towards the Ryans' old 1967 Volkswagen RV to get breakfast before they packed away the last morsels of delectable goodness. They made the best pancakes and today they had put wild berries in them, and even put the berries in their homemade syrup. They were every bit as delicious as they had smelled! she thought as she tore into a large pile of pancakes drenched in syrup and topped with fresh berries and cream. The thin sausages that came with the pancakes weren't the best, a bit freezer burnt. Mimi didn't mind finishing them off though.

Amy still kept her eyes glancing towards the tree line, but she had a gut-sinking feeling it would be unavoidable that the Johnson girls were going to snag Daniel today. She would have to fight them for his attention.

Before she was done eating, Amy's worst fears came true. Daniel stepped through the tree line, with his neat native nanny, and the Johnson girls swiftly surrounded him.

What were they saying? Dang it!

She shoved the remaining berries and pancakes into her mouth as fast as she could, getting blueberry juice all over her face and sending little bits to the ground that the dog happily seized with her tongue.

"Thank you, Miss Jude!" Amy said with a full mouth to old Jude Ryan, who was hunched over and hosing down a large pile of dishes. Amy went to hand her the empty plate but she was in such a rush that she didn't quite make Jude's gnarly, feeble hand for the transfer. The plate dropped into the mud puddle on the ground created from the dish washing overspray. "Dang it!" she muttered. She decided to pick the plate up and put it and both her hands into the hose water to clean off the debris. But she ended up splashing poor Mimi. "Dang it!" she said again, a little louder. Now she had to dry off the dog and her hands.

"You might want to clean your face, dear." Miss Jude Ryan said, "You've got berry juice all over."

"Dang it! Dang it!" She kept muttering to herself the whole time she was cleaning off the mess she had made in her rush. Every second she was wasting was agonizing because she was not getting over to where Daniel and his nanny were talking, and she wanted to hear everything!

"Thank you, Miss Jude!" she yelled, running off with Mimi all wrapped up in a towel.

"Dead Man's Pass is too steep for children. I'd advise taking the fork at Siphon Draw to the left and head to a smaller embankment for today. We can try something different tomorrow if all goes well," Amy heard the native nanny say as she approached with Mimi.

"Amy, are you really going rock climbing? Isn't that dangerous? What did your Mom say when you asked her?" Sarah said with what sounded too close to a patronizing tone disguised as concern. She was standing far too close to Daniel for Amy's comfort too.

"I think you should stay here, we can play games. We know all sorts. Have you ever played 'Red light, Green light' or 'Bones'?" Rebecca asked, standing so close that she was practically sandwiching poor Daniel between her and her sister.

"I think we should play 'Red Rover' and go get Jack Williams to help. It'll be fun!" Sarah was jumping up and down slightly as she spoke, and she kept touching Daniel's arm, which Amy found very annoying.

"Hi Amy," Daniel finally said. Amy was beaming and gave Daniel a big, tight hug that made his eyes look like they were going to pop out of his head. He was wearing khaki pants and a grey cotton shirt with a small pocket in the front. He looked cute, clean and perfectly well dressed. A little too clean and perfect for the outdoors, really. He brought a large duffle bag and a backpack, and best of all, his nanny! She was smiling at Amy with those mystifying dark eyes and had her knee-length-long, black hair back in one compact braid. All she brought was that bejeweled fanny pack, the same one she had been wearing yesterday.

"Hi Daniel," Amy replied. "Mimi says hi too." She held the pooch up to Daniel for kisses but Mimi just barked – yapping and snapping wildly. She hurriedly pulled the dog back. "Sorry, she doesn't know you very well yet."

"That's okay," Daniel said. "I brought all my gear for climbing Dead Man's Pass like we talked about yesterday. Miss Tinny doesn't think it is a good idea though. So, we might have to start with something a bit easier today until we can prove to her we are both exceptional climbers. You don't mind, do you?"

"I didn't know we needed gear, why do we need gear?" Amy wondered. She hadn't realized that the cliff at the edge of the mountain was that steep. She might have over exaggerated yesterday about her climbing skills. Technically, she had never been climbing. How hard could it be though? She could figure it out.

Daniel opened his mouth to talk but was quickly interrupted by Rebecca, "You didn't tell your mom about climbing then! I'm going to tell her! I bet she won't let you go!"

"Rebecca, come on!" Amy exclaimed, she knew that her hopes of running off on an exploration of the mountains with a new friend were now dashed completely. Technically, she wasn't even allowed to leave the lake area today. If her mom knew anything about her going off climbing she would be in big trouble. She'd have to settle for hanging out with the twins for sure now, and with sharing her new friend. "Daniel, maybe there is something we can do here instead, for today. Have you ever played 'Red Rover'?"

Daniel looked just as disappointed as Amy felt, and he was frowning at Rebecca and Sarah who were peering over (quite self-satisfied) at Amy. "What is 'Red Rover'? Is it a board game? A puzzle?"

"No dummy, it's a playground game. You've seriously never heard of it?" Sarah laughed derisively.

"I've never played a playground game," Daniel admitted and was meet with snickering from the twins.

"We're going to have to teach you everything, aren't we?" Sarah said.

"Don't be mean to Daniel, Sarah," Amy scolded. Sarah's acidic attitude had driven off more than a few new people and everyone knew it. Amy didn't want her ruining this for her, so she snuck a hand behind Sarah's back and gave her hair a nice yank to ensure she got the message. Then she smiled and pretended like nothing happened.

"I'll go get Jack," Rebecca shouted, already running towards the Williams' large, white and tan Winnebago.

"Who's Jack?" asked Daniel.

"He's the Williams' son. He's about your age, 11?" Amy replied. She didn't like Jack, he once pushed her down into an ant pile. Later, when she was crying to her Mom while she was washing the ants out of her hair, her mother told her that little boys sometimes do mean things to girls they like. It never made sense to her that a boy could be mean to a girl that he liked. So, she generally avoided him if she could, she didn't want more ant bites! "Do we have to invite him?"

"We'll need more people if we're going to play, silly." Sarah remarked. "Do you want to join us Miss Tinny?" Sarah's tone was slightly politer, but she was still being obnoxious in Amy's opinion.

"I can, but I'd prefer if we played a less violent game than 'Red Rover,' something like 'Red light, Green light' might be good," Tsintah recommended. "Or 'Blind Man's Bluff'?"

"Oh, yeah, 'Blind Man's Bluff' would be fun! Who wants to be 'it' first?" Sarah exclaimed. "I know, we can play 'Rock, Paper, Scissors' to see who goes first. Whoever loses is 'it.' Ready?" she held her right hand in a fist over her left palm, leaning forward towards Amy.

Amy put Mimi down in the grass and faced off against Sarah. "1, 2, 3 ... go!"

"Rock beats scissors! You're 'it'!" Sarah shouted.

"Gosh dang it!" Amy declared, stomping her foot and causing Mimi to bark and run around in a circle.

"Rock beats scissors?" Daniel inquired, apparently confused. He must not know any games! Amy thought, but she was nice enough to keep that to herself, unlike Sarah.

"Haven't you ever played 'Rock, Paper, Scissors' before? Do you live under a rock? Geeze!" Sarah said, exasperated by Daniel's ignorance. Amy slipped her hand behind Sarah's back again and pulled her hair. This time Sarah put her hand behind Amy's back and pulled her hair too, making Amy grit her teeth and stomp on Sarah's foot. Then she smiled even bigger than before. Daniel seemed not to notice any of it, thankfully.

"I live in a house," Daniel replied, still just as confused and appearing a bit hurt with his shoulders slouched and chin down, kicking at the ground and not looking up at the two little girls. Tsintah put her hand on his back, comforting, while glaring disapprovingly at Sarah.

"I will explain that one later, Daniel. For now, we need to learn the rules of 'Blind Man's Bluff.' It's pretty easy..." Tsintah began but was interrupted by Amy.

"Ooh, let me tell him!" She begged, and with an approving nod from the nanny, she continued, "I will be blindfolded, as I am 'it', for now, and you and everyone else will have to stay here in this grassy area ... Umm ... we need something to mark it off ..." She took hold of his duffle bag and placed it 10 feet away. "Okay, between here and that tree," she was pointing at the large cottonwood tree, "and from the tree line there to that park bench is the game zone. You can stand anywhere in this area. They're going to blindfold me, spin me around until I'm dizzy and then everyone has to pick a spot to stand while I count to 10 slowly. I'll have to find everyone, and when I do I have to identify that person without taking off my blindfold. If I guess right, then that person is 'it' and we start again. Got it?"

He nodded and smiled a cute little grin at Amy that made butterflies dance in her belly. Mimi started barking and running around her feet.

"I need to go tie Mimi to the tree so she doesn't run off, I'll be right back," she said, heading over to the giant cottonwood that made up the north end of their established play area.

"If you guess wrong?" he yelled as she left. "How will you know those two apart? I can't even tell them apart with my eyes open," he was pointing at Sarah and Rebecca, who had come back with Jack. The girls were giggling and Jack was sizing Daniel up.

"So, you're Dan?" Jack asked with his chest flared and nose up in the air. "I'm Jack Williams, the only sane one around here." He held out his hand for a shake.

"My name is Daniel, not Dan. The insane don't know they are insane, you know," he said with a half grin and then added, "or maybe you don't know." He gave him a very strong handshake that left Jack knowing he wasn't to be messed with and made the twins giggle some more.

"Ha, very funny," Jack pulled his hand back and rubbed it. He wasn't used to being challenged and obviously wasn't sure what to make of it. Jack was slightly taller, but leaner than Daniel so they were probably evenly matched for strength. Neither boy looked ready to find out just yet.

"Daniel does bring up a good point, one of you will have to wear or do something different somehow so that we can tell you apart," Amy insisted, coming back and standing right next to Daniel who was facing off the twins and Jack. "It really isn't fair to the rest of us."

"Life's not fair," Rebecca said, sticking her tongue out. "Get over it, you'll just have to figure it out."

Geeze, she was just as irritating as her sister! Would Amy have to step on her foot too in order to get her to act nicer to their guest?

"How about I just sit this one out." Sarah offered. "Miss Tinny, do you want to meet my mother? She would love to meet you! She's been trying to make turquoise jewelry like the necklace you're wearing. You don't make jewelry, do you? Did you make that?" Sarah took the nanny by the arm and led her towards the end of the RV park to their blue and white GMC Motorhome before anyone had a chance to stop her, including Tsintah.

"Okay, that's settled then. Let's play!" Rebecca announced, pulling out a flowered scarf to use as a blindfold and grinning wildly.

After an hour, they switched from 'Blind-Man's-Bluff' to 'Bones' and then went to hand games, like 'Patty Cake.' Amy even got to teach Daniel the rules of 'Rock, Paper, Scissors.' By the time Tsintah and Sarah returned a few hours later they were all sitting in a circle clapping their hands together singing 'Rockin' Robin' with Mimi snoozing in the middle. "Tweet! Tweet! Tweet!" they shouted in unison when Sarah and Tsintah arrived.

"Miss Tinny! I have never had so much fun in my life!" Daniel jumped up to take Tsintah by the hand. "You have to play with us!"

"It's time for lunch. Did you want to eat what we packed, or do you want to visit with the Johnsons, they offered bologna sandwiches and grape juice," Tsintah used a neutral but polite tone in her voice. She then frowned with a slight shake of her head to Daniel when the Johnson girls weren't looking.

Amy couldn't help but chuckle. That sounded awful! "We're having fish tacos today. My dad's been fishing all morning and I'm sure they'll be delicious and fresh. My mom makes the best lemonade too ... oh, please come!"

"We've got the 49ers game on, if you want to come eat lunch at our Winnebago," Jack offered. His father had a 6-inch black and white tv with three channels. It was the envy of the whole caravan, even though it took them an hour to set-up the giant antenna it was hooked up to every time they stopped.

Everyone was staring at Daniel, begging their case and waiting for a decision on lunch. He was turning red, scratching his head and darting his eyes between them all. Finally, Amy just took him by the hand and directed him over towards her parent's aluminum Airstream, leaving the other three kids behind in dejection. You snooze you lose! she thought.

He smiled over at her and let out a long sigh of relief. It was nice holding his hand. He had learned all of the games today so rapidly and never had to be told the rules again, nor did he break any ... unlike Rebecca and Jack. She'd caught them both peeking out of their blindfolds during 'Blind-Man's-Bluff.' He was so smart! And so charming glancing over at her through his wavy brown hair that he kept tossing out of his face.

"Thank you, Amy," he said. "I've had so much fun today. I didn't want to hurt anyone's feelings, everyone's been so nice to me."

"Nice? Jack is a cruel nitwit and Rebecca is a stuck-up twerp!" Amy blurted out, realizing she sounded kind-of snooty herself as she said it. Her mom always said, "If you can't say anything nice, don't say anything at all" and she had just bad-mouthed her own friends the first chance she got. Not nice! She blushed and held her head down in shame. "Sorry, I guess that they aren't so bad. They're my friends and I shouldn't have said that."

"Do you have a lot of friends?"

"Sorta. I mean, I guess I do. I meet new people all the time and in all places; from national parks to Walmart parking lots. Some stay with the caravan for a week simply because they have the same destinations in mind. Others stay for years for the company." As they walked through the park, Amy explained to Daniel more about the different families and how the caravan of RV's that her family traveled with had formed organically over the years.

There were currently six families traveling together. A week ago, it had been nine but three didn't want to stay and wait for the Johnsons' RV to get fixed when they found out it would likely be another week before all the parts would arrive for the transmission repair.

"If you stay for the bonfire tonight, you'll get to see the best in everyone. Especially with you here, they'll want to show off their talents."

The Arabies played guitar, harmonica and sang. The Johnsons father played guitar too, and had a small drum set that they let anyone bang away on. The Dukes were good storytellers: they were a couple in their forties that made money publishing articles and books for a living. They liked to test their stories out on the group, some were a bit too dark for Amy's tastes and gave her nightmares. The Ryans were in their late 60s, retired, and mostly told stories about their grandkids from letters they received along the way at the established Post Office boxes. Amy and her Mom liked to recite poetry and dance.

"Sarah and Rebecca have their flaws but every now and then they will sew-up little jackets for Mimi and the other dogs and we put on a dog fashion show."

"A dog fashion show? How fascinating ... It's nice to have friends," he was looking down at her hand holding his as they walked. "I almost forgot! I brought you this." He pulled out a stone that was in his front pocket. It was shinny and black, shaped like a triangle, with chopped, razor-sharp edges.

"What is it?" She asked, taking the stone and rubbing the smooth top, trying not to cut her fingers on the sharp parts.

"It is an obsidian arrowhead. I shined it up for you yesterday myself. It's an ancient Native American tool and it came from this mountainside. See the red?" he took it back and moved it so that the sunlight caught the different colored elements set in the dark stone. "It has flecks of iron in it like all the rocks around here. That's what makes them red, the iron oxide." He placed it gently in her palm and closed her hand over it, then put his hand over hers. "I thought it would be great for you to remember me by," he peeked up into her eyes for a brief second but then quickly looked down at his hand.

Amy was overwhelmed, this was the neatest thing she had ever seen! Tears welled up in her eyes. She decided she wanted to give him something too but couldn't think of anything she had that was anywhere near as cool. An idea popped into her head and before she even knew what she was doing, she had given him a full-on kiss. Right on the lips!

They both looked at each other in amazement. Amy had never kissed a boy before. She kissed her dolls, her mom, even Mimi ... but never a boy! From the look he was giving her, he had never kissed a girl either.

"What was that?" Daniel finally asked after a long wide-eyes pause. The fingers of his left hand drifted to his lips.

Amy smiled, took his hand, and said, "Something to remember me by."

Chapter 5

Cliff on a Cliff

It had been six and a half years since Amy Shipley graced Mesa Heights with her presence. Daniel had been going to school at Mesa College in Grande Junction for most of those years. He was home for the summer and at his old desk in the den. The heavily worn-in chair and warm sunlight coming in from the window were almost as comforting as Dr. Whiskers laying curled up on his lap. He petted her absent-mindedly while going through a box of letters from Amy.

Amy's parents had decided to settle in New Mexico so that they could send her younger brother, Doug, to school. Doug had turned out to be too much for their parents to handle home-schooling and he needed special education. At least with her family settled down he could get regular letters from her. Lately she had been sending him poems. The latest had his whole family chuckling for the first time in a long time. It was titled "Fat Cat Fall-ee:"

I wants a treat but you're takin' a bath
I wants it now, or I'm gonna' be mad
I'm on a ledge, I'm having a cow
I wants a treat, I wants it now!
Meow, Meow, Meow, Now!

Dang it, I slipped, now I'm all drenched
An icky feeling, and I'm entrenched
I have to get out, so I pounce
I hurl my huge belly, bounce
Pounce, Pounce, Pounce, Bounce!

Down I go again, Oh, this isn't right!
I'm stuck in the tub, try as I might
Sliding under, claws can't grasp
A desperate, wet, hairy mass
Splash, Splash, Splash, Fat-Ass!

What willful negligence, what disrespect
I'm in dreadful hot water, up to my neck
Laughing, mean human, mocking me
You won't be laughing, if I pee
Hehe, hehe, hehe, flee!!!

It was about Amy's kitty Pumpkin's misadventure with the bathtub, and how he was now too fat to get himself out of the tub but tried and tried non-the-less. She said he weighed 25 lbs. and still ate everything he could find but no longer begged her for treats when she was taking a bath after the 'incident' that inspired the poem.

"You're not re-reading that poem again, are you Dude?" Cliff remarked, bounding side to side into the room on crutches that he had rigged with springs and a shoulder strap that went around his back for support. Cliff's condition had deteriorated. He had been diagnosed with a severe form of muscular dystrophy and his parents had given up on Dr. David Jorgensen's help long ago. They were relied solely on their own methods now.

"No," Daniel protested, folding-up the most recent letter from Amy and slipping it away casually, trying not to notice Cliff's tone or the fact that he was on crutches today.

If Cliff was on his crutches, it meant he wasn't having a good day, because most days he could get around without them. The apparatus made it to where Cliff could be hands-free some of the time while walking. But that wasn't the only reason he wore it, he was also starting to lose muscle strength in his arms and he didn't want to admit it.

"Are you in love? Is she your girlfriend? Daniel and Amy sitting in a tree, k-i-s-s-i-n-g!" Cliff sang. He smacked the desk leg with his crutch at every letter of 'kissing' for emphasis. The cat jumped up and out of the room, not wanting to be any part of the conflict.

Cliff had gotten a bit chubbier from all the steroid treatments he had been given, and his hormones were out-of-whack so his cheeks were splotchy, filled with acne and stubbled with hair despite him being only 13. Daniel had grown almost a foot and a half in height, but Cliff was barely

4 inches taller than he had been at seven years old. Clearly, he acted as immature as he looked.

"No, she is just a friend. At least I have a friend," he said and immediately regretted it when he saw Cliff's face turn dark.

Both boys were so much younger than any of their classmates, so it had been hard to make any friends. Cliff had been at Mesa College for the last year and he had it worse than Daniel. Not only did no one want to be his friend, but there was a group of jocks that went out of their way to make his life miserable, and once pushed him down a flight of stairs. The girls were worse, though well meaning. About once a week one would ask him if he was lost and needed to find his mommy.

"I don't need friends; most people are idiots anyway. Just a waste of time, just like those letters. You could be doing so much more with your time than wasting it on writing letters about fat cats in bathtubs to some dumb girl you hardly even know."

"I've known Amy for over six years now. She's my best friend." Not only was Amy Daniel's only real friend, but she called him her best friend too, signing every letter with BFF (Best Friends Forever), which made him feel extra special.

"Yeah, in letters. Would you even recognize her if you saw her?"

"I would. She'll be here today, so you'll see." More exciting than the letters, and humorous poems, was that Amy was coming back to Colorado. Her parents missed being on the road and she had managed to convince them to take a detour through his town on their way from Zion National Park in Utah to Garden of the Gods in Colorado Springs. Daniel couldn't wait!

"Today? Wait, what? You've got to be joking?"

"Yes. Today. No, I'm not joking. I'm meeting her out at the lake this afternoon." Daniel took the grey metal box he kept Amy's letters in and put it on the top shelf of the cherry-wood bookshelf that was next to the desk. The den now had several bookshelves all along the walls to help organize the many books. There were less books in the room as well, because the boys now utilized the campus library for their studies. Daniel kept the box up there because he knew it would be hard for Cliff to reach. He'd also put a combination lock on the box after opening it once and finding scribbled snide remarks on a few of the letters.

After a minute of silence, Cliff unexpectedly asked, "Can I come?"

"No. We're going to hike up to climb Dead Man's Pass and you're in no condition today to make the trip." He also didn't want him there, but he didn't want to hurt his little brother's feelings.

"You know I can always drink some of that foul coffee Mom and Father put God-knows-what in ... let me come!" Cliff pleaded. Their parents refused to tell them what was in the drink, and still didn't want them to have it saying 'it isn't good for growing boys' and left it at that. But, Cliff was right – there was definitely something in that mixture that made him have movement back in his legs, temporarily. The two of them had managed to sneak a few cups and experiment. The biggest problem (besides the taste) is if Cliff didn't keep drinking it he would end up a crazed and half-dead mess within 24 hours afterwards. He'd also be in crutches for a week, which is a steep price to pay for one day of movement.

"I thought you didn't like Amy, and you're willing to drink that concoction to see her, what gives?" Daniel was not liking the idea of sharing his time with Amy with Cliff.

"So, you get to have a friend and I don't? Are you ashamed of me? Do you not want me seen by your friend?"

"Of course I'm not ashamed of you!"

"Or is it that you are going to go make-out with her and don't want me around?"

"If it means that much to you, you can come. Don't worry, we aren't going to make-out. We're just friends," Daniel said to placate his little brother, knowing that Cliff was behaving strangely but still wanting to make him happy. "You'd better go gulp down a pot of that stuff now though, I was just about to leave out the door to head down to the lake. And, more importantly, you better not let Mom, Father or Miss Tinny catch you!"

Cliff bounded out of the room leaving Daniel to wonder how he was going to manage getting all three of them through Dead Man's Pass. He would need to load up more gear. He started packing the extra equipment and realized he would also need some more food. So, he headed into the kitchen in time to see Miss Tinny getting duped by Cliff.

He was snagging the coffee behind her back while he distracted her by knocking down a pile of boxes near the door with one of his crutches. "Dr. Whiskers strikes again," he said, laughing and then taking sips in between words continuing with, "That cat sure is clumsy!" He knocked a glass down from the sink. "She's probably going senile. What is she, almost 14 now?"

"The cat isn't senile, what are you up to Cliff? Daniel, you look like you are up to something too, what's going on?" Miss Tinny was good at sensing when something was not quite right. She had her arms crossed and was glaring up at the two boys. She hadn't grown an inch, so both boys towered above her. She stood her ground though and her presence and demeanor was plenty intimidating enough to make up for the height.

"We're going to meet Amy at the lake this afternoon," Cliff answered for both of them.

"That's right, we're just in here getting food for a picnic that we're planning with her," Daniel had to be careful of what he said and knew if he mentioned the pass they intended to hike then Miss Tinny would not approve.

"Well that is exciting! Amy, of all people, coming into town! Cliff, do you mean to hike and picnic as well? Today doesn't look like one of your good days," she said with concern in her voice and eyes on his crutches.

"I'm fine, I was just testing out some new springs I installed, see," he unstrapped the contraption and set it to the side to prove his point. He lifted his hands up, but then leaned back against the counter to hide the fact that he was still a bit unsteady. It took a minute or two before the coffee kicked-in and it hadn't quite kicked-in yet.

"Should I come with you? I just put a casserole in the oven, but I can pull it out and start it later," Tsintah suggested.

"No, that's okay. I can watch Cliff, he'll be fine. I'm sure Dad is looking forward to that casserole," Daniel didn't want her to come up with any excuse to come along or start to think too much on it so he decided they should undoubtedly leave as soon as possible.

"Okay. Tell Amy I said 'Hi.' She was such a sweet young lady. It's so nice that she has kept in contact with you all these years. Are you sure you don't want me to come along?"

"No, we made plans already for today. Maybe tomorrow before she leaves." If she came along he would never get to show Amy the best view of the valley. He had even hidden the climbing gear in his backpack instead of the normal duffle bag so that Miss Tinny didn't suspect anything. "I'll get my bag. Cliff, don't forget to grab the peanut butter and jelly sandwiches!"

They managed to get out of the door without the nanny or parents intervening. Miss Tinny was very protective, even though she really wasn't their nanny anymore. She was more of a housekeeper and cook, lately. Their parents didn't have time for much of anything except research and had just kept her full time so that no one starved and the house didn't fall apart. She was like a second mom to the boys, or a first mom as their mom was kind of like a second dad.

Their mother was quite the entrepreneur in addition to her research. She had always made plenty of money from capitalizing on the patented drugs their father had developed, and the natural resources from the land they owned. But, a few years ago, she had started a manufacturing facility and research center in town to work on a larger variety of drugs in hopes of curing Cliff. The center only hired around 50 people, bringing them in from all corners of the world. But, it had boosted the economy up enough to have a McDonald's and a Walgreens, employing even more people. The local population was now up to almost six hundred people. Managing the business and having to participate in town hall meetings in a growing city meant that they never saw their mother.

Daniel and Cliff spent a lot of time with each other, especially now that they went to school together too. However, they hardly ever went out or did anything fun anymore. In fact, they hadn't gone to the lake since Cliff started getting sick.

It was pleasant walking out in the invigorating, June air. The familiar sage smelled wonderful and the trail was nice and dry because it hadn't rained in over a month. There were lizards basking on rocks and ravens cawing in the branches. They even heard a rattlesnake rattling in a bush. Daniel made a sport of counting the number of jack rabbits that were startled and went bounding into the woods – ten so far.

Cliff was keeping quiet, which was superb, and managing to keep up with Daniel's fast pace. The only thing that would make this day better would be seeing Amy. Would he recognize her? She had sent him pictures, but it had been years.

When he got to the lake, he knew her right away. She still had the same fluffy, curly blonde hair and bunny-like gait, and big dimples framing a big smile. When she saw him, she came running and had her arms wrapped around his back in a flash that left his head spinning. He felt like he was in a dream, he couldn't believe Amy was standing right there!

"Hi Amy, remember me?" Cliff asked, holding out his hand. He figured she must not have heard him because she was just staring at Daniel, smiling. Daniel and Amy were just standing there, staring, smiling like fools. "Umm, Amy? Hello! Hello!"

"Oh, I'm so sorry! Hey, Cliff!" Amy gave Cliff a hug, and continued with, "Of course I remember you! Duh! What's happenin'?"

Daniel felt like the world stopped and there was only Amy. She must have felt the same. She had grown into a beautiful young woman; her baby-fat cheeks were gone and she had curves under her skimpy tank top and cut-off jeans that he was trying not to notice too conspicuously. "Are you ready to climb up the mountain? Do you need to change into something that...?" He was trying to think of something to say that didn't make him sound like a pervert.

"What, you don't like my outfit?" she said, spinning around. "I cut these myself and added these jewels, she was pointing to her butt cheeks and the heart rhinestones on each of the back pockets.

"Sparkle butt, classy," Cliff laughed derisively and was met with a frown from Amy that made Daniel want to hit Cliff, hard. He didn't know why, but all he wanted was to see her smile.

"Where's your nanny?" she asked, staring at Cliff. That was probably one of the worst things she could have said. He was sensitive about how short he was, and she was practically calling him a little kid.

"Miss Tinny is busy, she said 'hi' though," Daniel reached out and took Cliff by the arm, half to re-assure him and half to hold him back.

"We're too old for a nanny, don't you think?" Cliff glared down at Daniel's hand on his arm and shrugged him off. "Daniel didn't want her to come because she wouldn't want us to climb the mountain. I think it's a dumb idea too."

"Oh, she's such a sweetheart," said Amy. "Maybe she can visit us tomorrow morning before we leave?"

"I'll ask, I'm sure she wouldn't mind. Come on, let's go. The sooner we get to the top, the sooner we can enjoy the view. There is nothing like it in the whole valley," Daniel could barely holding back the urge to start running towards the trail. He'd been talking up the view to Amy for years and they were so close to going now!

"Can I bring Mimi? She loves escapades," Amy begged, then started singing 'On an Escapade' by Janet Jackson. "Ooh, I need to get my Discman! I'll be right back."

A few minutes later, after having to deal with Cliff shaking his head and saying "Really?" every time Daniel made eye contact with him, Amy was back with Mimi and a dark grey, square CD player that she had clipped to her right pocket.

"Like, you so have to listen to this," she said to Daniel, putting her headphones on him as they walked the trail. It was 'On an Escapade' playing. "I think, like, it should be our theme song for the afternoon. What do you think? It's so rad."

"Theme song?" Cliff questioned, "We have a theme song?" The two just walked ahead and ignored him. He was being grumpy, and Daniel was still wondering why he had even wanted to come along. He followed along behind them, muttering and shuffling his feet all the way to the cliff face.

"Okay, we're at the point where we need to gear up," Daniel said as he dropped his backpack and started pulling out rigging, blocks and pulleys.

"Wow, you're like totally serious. Okay, I trust you," Amy smiled, watching amused as Daniel set her up. He tried not to blush while pulling the rigging over her scantily clad body.

"We might have to put Mimi and your Discman in my backpack. They'll be okay, we'll be at the top in no time. Hopefully she doesn't eat all the food in there."

"Oh, you brought food! Like, you are so prepared!" Amy giggled.

Cliff giggled, mocking Amy. Daniel shot him a scowl that shut him up.

"Cliff, did you need me to strap you up too, or do you remember how to do it yourself?"

"Of course I can do it myself! I'm not an idiot," Cliff glanced at Amy and snickered.

Daniel didn't like how Cliff looked at Amy when he said idiot. He had to fight a strong urge to hit him again.

They managed to make it up the mountain without too bad of an incident. Cliff slipped once, but Daniel succeeded in stopping him well before he went too far – thanks to the harness. It took a lot longer than he expected, over an hour. Amy was in pretty good shape, she had strong climbing legs and made the ascent look easy. It was Cliff that was slowing them down and having the most trouble. But, he made it up despite his difficulty.

"Oh my god, like this view is so like, super rad!" Amy exclaimed when she reached the top. "Mimi has to see this! Poor thing must be so scared." She opened Daniel's bag and pulled out the pintsized dog that had been yapping half the time they were climbing.

"Wait until you see the view from the cliff over there," Daniel said, pointing to the far side. He was busy helping his out-of-breath younger brother out of his gear.

The cliff had a grand view of the valley below. The cliff face was petrified sand, with little pools of water in areas where the sand had swirled and juniper brushes spread out sporadically. Amy sat down cross-legged, only a foot from the edge. Daniel put his backpack down and sat beside her.

"I'm ready to eat something. Daniel, can you hand me one of those peanut butter and jelly sandwiches?" Cliff asked, he was planted in front of Amy and blocking her view. "And a cranberry juice?"

While Daniel was busy opening the backpack, Cliff tried to sit. He almost landed on top of both her and Daniel.

"Oh, that sounds good. And while you're in there, get my CD player, we could use some Janet Jackson up here," Amy requested and moved over a few inches to let Cliff sit in between them so he wasn't right on top of them.

Daniel pulled out the CD player first, handing it across Cliff and over to Amy. He then started digging around for the sandwiches. They ended up being squashed fairly thoroughly with little paw prints. They were still edible though.

Amy laid back to eat her sandwich, and Daniel moved his backpack behind Cliff and laid back as well so he could be next to her and so Cliff couldn't get in between them again. They enjoyed staring up at the clouds passing by while eating the afternoon meal.

"Delicious!" she said and went to put the plastic bags they had used away in his backpack. "What's this?" she asked, pulling out a piece of paper.

"Oh, a poem I wrote for you in a letter I was going to send, want to read it?" Daniel had been excited to send her the next letter and brought the poem thinking it would make a perfect spot up on the mountain to see her reaction. "I had a dream about you and it inspired me."

"You dream about me?" she said, coyly, smiling and unfolding the paper. She had to set Mimi down to read it.

"Let me see that!" Cliff demanded, snatching the letter from Amy. "Daniel never said he had a dream about you. I'm the one who has dreams about you."

"What, you have dreams about Amy?" Daniel asked, perturbed at both the idea and him snatching the letter before Amy could read it. Then he remembered the first time they met and Cliff's ludicrous GI Joe dream and said, "Oh yeah, never mind."

"Never mind what?" she asked.

"Right before we first met you, Cliff dreamt about you and then thought you were a thief." Daniel said.

"No, I didn't!" Cliff was keeping the letter out of reach of both Amy and Daniel, who were trying to snag it back.

"How could you have a dream about me before you met me?"

"Exactly, I think he was just jealous because I had made a friend." Daniel explained.

"Miss Tinny said it was because you were important, but I don't think you are that important," Cliff remarked.

Amy looked at both boys and raised an eyebrow. "I'm flattered, but can you give me that back, I wasn't done reading it..." but as she reached for the letter the wind blew it out of Cliff's hands.

Mimi barked and went running for the paper, stumbling right over the edge of the cliff.

"No! Oh, No!" Amy was panic stricken.

There was a steep drop about 4 feet and the dog had landed on a tiny ledge with a thud and a sharp squeal that was heart wrenching. The three teenagers looked down to find the poor dog was still alive, miraculously.

"We have to get her!" Amy declared, climbing down before anyone could stop her.

"Wait, it's too dangerous!" Daniel was too late to get to her. She was already on the flimsy ledge and she had no gear on and no ropes attached. She'd just picked up the dog when the ledge fell out from beneath her feet. He reached for her hand and caught her in the nick of time.

"Help!" she screamed, clutching onto Mimi with one hand and desperately holding onto Daniel with the other. She would need both hands if she were to lift herself up. Daniel was barely holding onto her and unable to pull her up by one arm. "Help, please help!"

"I've got her," Cliff announced. "Get the dog." He took hold of Amy's arm so that Daniel could let go and maneuver for the pooch.

Daniel reached down and snagged her collar to jerk her up, freeing her from her frantic owner. She had been whining from the pain of her injuries. But, when she got into his arms, she started growling and biting and he almost lost his grip. He fell backwards trying to calm the crazed and wounded Chihuahua.

The terror in the little dog's eyes was nothing in comparison to what was about to happen; because the next thing he heard was a scream that would haunt him for the rest of his life.

Chapter 6

Blood is Thicker Than A lot of Things

Daniel sat straight up in his chair, he had fallen asleep studying again. He was dreaming of her: screaming, falling, reaching out to clutch a hand that wasn't there to take. The pain was as real as the day it happened.

His heart ached. He needed to see her again.

She was at the UCLA department of neurosurgery, the same place he got his PhD. The same place in which he now worked but in a different wing of their hospital. She had been in a coma for over ten years, and no one expected her to wake, her brain activity was less than 30%.

He could never give up, he had devoted his career to neuroscience and had left for LA as soon as he had gotten his residency at the best hospital he could find. He procured her a spot at the brain injury research center so he could be as close to her as possible.

They had surgically removed the injured and dead tissue a long time ago from the initial trauma, but she still wasn't waking. He was currently studying different electro-stimulus, or neuromodulation, approaches but didn't want to risk anymore damage and most of the work being done was high risk.

He heard a knock on his door, "Dr. Jahren? You're needed in the west wing. Charlie Abram may be speaking." The voice and knock came from one of his post-doctorate students who had been working the night shift.

"Thank you, I'll be right there," he was still in a half-awake daze as he pulled his white coat on over his scrubs. He was about to leave when the office phone rang. The caller ID said it was his parents in Colorado.

"Hello?" Daniel answered softly, voice still not fully awake.

"Hi, honey, it's your mom. We need you to come home. Your brother has gotten worse, we need your help," the voice on the other end of the line was strained. It sounded like she'd been crying.

"What happened?" Daniel couldn't help the tone of anger and annoyance creeping into his voice. He knew what probably happened, what he feared Cliff had finally done.

"I will tell you more when you get here. How soon can you make it?" The desperation in her voice was barely masked.

"I'll be on the first flight I can book."

"Okay, honey, see you soon," she hung up before he could ask her anything else. He almost didn't want to ask anyway. What had Cliff done now?

Daniel knew it had to be serious if his mother was calling, she never called. He talked to Tsintah, his old nanny, more than he talked to her. He rarely talked to his father or his brother either, they were consumed with treating Cliff's muscular dystrophy, despite his rapid decrease in functionality and their constant failures. They resented that Daniel didn't help and never understood why he devoted his life's work to helping people he didn't even know over his own family.

But, he loved Amy. He had fallen in love with her at 10 years old and didn't realize it until he thought he lost her forever after the accident. He would find a way to wake her up; at least, that is what he had been telling himself for over a decade. So many years. It was getting harder and harder to admit he might never bring her back.

In the meantime, he enjoyed helping the patients that he could, and training the next generation of doctors on the most advanced neurological developments on the planet.

Each patient was unique, and as he helped them he felt he was one step closer to seeing Amy open her eyes and smile. For instance, the patient who was waiting for him, Charlie, had a traumatic brain injury that was inoperable and resulted from a chronic subdural hematoma that had gone unnoticed for weeks. Daniel was trying direct current pulses to activate some of the dead brain tissue. Specifically, he was hooking up electrodes to the left temporal lobe and shocking Charlie regularly in order to help him regain his speech and left side of the body functionality.

Before he could call the travel agency and book his emergency ticket, he had to follow up with Charlie and ... he needed to see Amy. More importantly, he had to coordinate treatment for the both of them, and several other patients, while he was gone. He pulled out his BlackBerry, scrolled through his contacts. He would be calling in favors all night. It was a lot of trouble. If Cliff isn't dying, I'm going to kill him! he thought, and then immediately felt pangs of guilt and shame. What if he was dying? He forcibly put the thought out of his mind but added urgency to his efforts in making arrangements.

~ ~ ~

The taxi pulled up to the stone and cedar, single-story house he had called home for so many years. The cool air of the night, chirping of crickets, and howls of a distant coyote pack were all there was to greet him when he stepped out of the cab and onto the moonlit gravel entryway. The sights, smell of iron laden dust, and sounds brought back memories of a time of innocence he had suppressed for so long. How many years had it been? Eight?

Coughing down the rush of emotion entering his throat, he thanked and paid the cab driver. He forced himself to take a step towards his old home. An ever-increasing sense of foreboding crept into the pit of his stomach with every step towards the dark doorway shrouded with shadows in the dead of the night. By the time he reached his hand out to knock on the door, his heart had already begun to skip beats. It didn't help that the door opened silently before his hand even touched it, without anyone on the other side. The anxiety and confusion were only somewhat alleviated when he noticed a video camera above the door. His heart was still thudding in his chest, but he managed to smile and wave at the camera before pulling his luggage into the darkness within.

Less than a second after he closed the door behind him, the lights in the hallways came on. The kitchen and living room that had been full of gadgets and gizmos he and his brother tinkered with as children were now bare and cleared of any sign of the unique minds that dwelled in the house's hidden lower regions. A soft light came on automatically as he entered the kitchen and he noticed a note on the counter.

"You know the code, porcelain," Daniel read aloud and flipped the paper around looking for more information. Porcelain?

He looked around the room, taking in all the changes and yawning from the jetlag. Where were his parents? he wondered. It was just like his family to greet him with riddles instead of hugs.

He was about to head towards the den when his BlackBerry buzzed with a page that read 'LAB7.' Oh, so they were in lab 7. Was porcelain the lab door code somehow? Usually the code was alphanumeric. It was then that he noticed there were dishes in the sink. There were never dishes in the sink. It was one of his father's pet peeves. One of the dishes was a porcelain tea cup. His parents didn't drink tea, they drank only their 'special' coffee. On the bottom of the cup there were tiny letters 'R33L28R4.' Now that was about right for a door code. Why the added security?

He pulled on the third book (Hansel and Gretel) in the hallway bookshelf next to the old cuckoo clock that his father had brought from his hometown in Bavaria. The clock and bookshelf were some of the few things that remained in the now almost barren house. Although it was barren, it was neatly decorated in minimalist cream tones that made it look like the cover of a magazine. An elevator door opened up where the bookshelf had been and he pressed the B3 button to descend into the mountain. There used to only be a staircase and tunnel behind the bookshelf, they had installed another nice upgrade.

Laboratory 7 was their most secure lab, located furthest into the mountain than any other lab, at least it was when he was here last. Who knows what they had installed since. It took him ten minutes of walking through the tunnel to get to the steel door. Again, his head was filled with foreboding accentuated with a heartbeat that was pounding hard in his chest as he turned the dial of the combination lock on the door. Right twice to 33, left to 28 and then right again, stopping on 4.

His mother's dark grey-blue eyes were bloodshot and filled with tears as she flung her arms around his neck as soon as he entered the room. "I'm so glad you are here, honey. You're our only hope," she said softly in his ear between choking on tears.

He had never seen his mother cry. She was the most stubborn, outrageously positive person he had ever met in his entire life. She made the best of every situation and fought every obstacle in her life with a smile and a laugh. It was staggering.

He held her tighter as the tears threatened to burst from his eyes, he couldn't stand to see her this way. When he pulled himself together he gripped her shoulders with both hands, pushing her far enough away to look her dead in the eyes and say, "What can I do? What has he done?"

"The reaction has spread, it has gotten to his thighs, it's killing him!" she screeched, causing a round of screeching in the room. Monkeys screeching, and loud. It was only then that Daniel took a look at his surroundings.

There were cages of monkeys, rats and mice lined against the wall to the right, and to his left was a chemical mixing room and clean room. Straight ahead, behind his mother, was a figure lying on a bed and surrounded by plastic sheeting separating him from the rest of the room. His father sat in full bio-hazard gear beside him, his head down and shoulders slumped.

"I'll suit up," he said, not taking his eyes off his father and brother. "What are we dealing with, virus or bacteria?"

"It is a new virus, Tribus, that Cliff formulated himself. He'd been working with carbon nanotubes and managed to create a virus that turns cells into mini carbon factories; initiating and spreading monolayers through surrounding tissues," she was saying all of this while walking over to one of the monkey cages that had a large polycarbonate wall. It was quarantined from the rest of the primates. "It proved very effective for Artie here, we had to put him in a special cage after he ripped open the last two. His muscle density has tripled and his strength has more than quadrupled since he had injections of Tribus in each major muscle group."

"What is that black streaking along his legs?" Daniel asked, noticing vein-like black marks along Artie's muscles visible even through the fur.

"Some of the carbon escapes and goes into the veins and surrounding skin, embedding itself like a tattoo," she replied. "It's a purely aesthetic side effect, and nothing compared to the gains in muscle strength. Cliff was so excited, he..."

"What happened?" Daniel demanded.

She swallowed hard. "He injected himself yesterday, in both calves. I told him not to, but he didn't listen. I wanted him to test directly on human tissue samples first, but he couldn't wait. Just like his father, never planning for when things go wrong. Did you know they wouldn't even quarantine any of this at first, I had to insist!"

"I can believe it. Do we know if the virus is contagious? How does it spread?"

"For now, the virus must be inserted into the tissue directly, but you know how viruses can evolve. These two think they are masters of everything. If he had just listened to me..."

"Mother, what can I do?" Daniel interrupted, trying to pull her back to the situation at hand.

"The damage is ... irreversible. I'm afraid if we don't remove the injured areas soon, he will die," she couldn't even look in the direction of her son as she spoke. "We have everything you need. He's on 30 mg of morphine already and 100 mcg of Propofol. We have methohexital ready too ... Please, I can't lose him!"

"You want me to remove his legs?" Even though everyone in the room was technically a doctor, he was the only one who had ever performed surgery on a living being.

She nodded.

"I brought a few things myself. Deep down I knew something like this would happen, eventually. He has always been reckless," Daniel said scornfully while pulling out his gear and donning latex gloves. His glanced over to see his strong, easy going and proud mother sobbing so hard that she was hiccupping.

"I will help him. It will be over and done before you know it. Maybe this will teach him to listen to reason, and his mother, for a change," he said while holding her close for a hug, rubbing his hand up and down on her back to try and comfort her. "Hold your breath and then have drink, it will clear up those hiccups. At least, that is what my mother always told me," his effort at cheering her up was rewarded with a faint smile, interrupted only by more hiccups and tears.

"Get a drink," he said sternly and moved quickly towards his brother's bedside, sliding on a mask as he marched forward. He needed steady hands – that took a clear mind right now. And focus. Focus on the task at hand. He took a deep breath then walked through the opening in the plastic tarp hanging from the ceiling.

His father promptly stepped aside and pulled the blanket back to show Daniel the extent of the damage. Both legs were black as charcoal, with bulging dark veins and skin that was like petrified wood from his calves up to almost mid-thigh. Cliff was conscious, but he was glaring at the ceiling with a blank stare and set jaw. Daniel knew Cliff didn't want to hear 'I told you so' but expected exactly that from his older brother.

"We'll have to cut from here to start," Daniel pointed to the middle of Cliff's thigh, an inch above the damaged area. "We'll place the tourniquet here. You know what all these are," he showed the clamps and tools he had brought, Martin nodded. "Where is the blood?"

"I have four pints of o- available, will that be enough?" Martin asked.

"It'll have to be," Daniel replied, it might not be enough. Anything could go wrong.

"Put me out, now. I don't want to hear this, I don't want to know. Please," Cliff begged. His father immediately went to the drip and turned up the Propofol and started prepping the barbiturate. He had Cliff out in less than 2 minutes while Daniel laid out and organized the equipment.

After placing the tourniquet on the right leg, they began cutting the skin where they would peel it back for post operation wrapping of the femur stub. They clamped the peeled flesh just below the tourniquet. Martin lifted the leg and found that on the back side the dark streaks had begun to move closer to the area they were cutting and the muscle beneath was beginning to blacken.

"Will it be sufficient to cut here?" Martin asked.

"We're cutting up here, we just need the skin in that area."

"Was zur Hölle?!?" he heard his father exclaim, realizing how high his son had planned to cut. They were cutting almost to the tourniquet, which was just below the groin. Cliff would lose both entire legs.

Daniel began digging his fingers into and pulling the muscles back to clamp down the major arteries. "Hand me another clamp," he said, reaching a bloody hand up while concentrating on stabilizing a delicate vein.

When he was done clamping, he pointed to the groin area and said, "I will need you to ensure that stays out of the way of sharp objects as we proceed. If a clamp slips, or a tendon pops, muscles could spasm and he could jerk around. I am pretty sure you want grandchildren and he will never forgive either of us if we screw up. Also, keep a close eye on his vitals and the drip. Let me know if anything changes and if we start running low on meds. Are you ready?"

Martin nodded, somberly.

He could hear his mother cry out from across the room as he turned on the electric blade. All the animals in the cages cried out with her. Daniel put it all out of his mind, he had to focus.

Over an hour later, they were done. All four pints of blood were needed, but both legs were successfully removed. It hadn't been easy, he'd even had to chase a disappearing tendon in the left leg. But, Cliff was now stabilized and on a saline drip, his morphine at 60 mg.

His mother had gotten coffee, and she'd stopped crying and hiccupping. She was at a lab counter across from his father who sat quietly sipping coffee too. He was jotting down the day's events in a scientific journal with one hand while holding her hand with the other.

Daniel stood looking at the monkeys in their cages; they never had monkeys when he was a kid. "I bet you wish you were swinging from a tree, Lulu, don't you?" he said to the female, dark eyed, black and white capuchin in the cage in front of him labeled 'Lulu.' She showed her teeth by pulling her lips back and biting the cage bar, then she held onto the bars with all fours and bounced up and down. "Yeah, me too. I always did love trees."

"Thank you, son," Martin said, one hand resting on Daniel's shoulder. He had come to stand next to him in front of the monkeys. "You did amazing work."

"Thank you, I ..." Daniel started to say but found himself choking on his words. He wanted to scream, "it should never have come to this!" but there was no point. His father had always encouraged Cliff to push barriers and take risks. It was his fault and he knew it.

"You like the monkeys? They are proving to be particularly useful. We should have had them years ago."

"Sure, is that why there is added security? Did you steal these from a zoo?"

"Steal? You know we would never steal anything."

"Just do illegal experiments involving deadly viruses and bacteria. Now on, what I suspect, are illegally acquired primates."

"Not everything that is illegal should be. The rules set in place are for profits by the pharmaceutical industry. The bureaucracy in this country is rooted in greed, at the cost of human lives."

"Oh? Is that what you told Cliff? Before you allowed him to inject a highly experimental drug into his own body?"

"Allowed him? He didn't even ask me what I thought ... I ... your mother ..." Martin peered over at Beth for help, but she looked away.

Daniel didn't even want to look at his father, who was holding his head down staring at his feet. Lulu started jumping up and down, and wailing.

"The added security isn't for the primates and it isn't to hide illegal work. It is due to the threats we've been getting from the local tribes. Didn't Tsintah tell you?" Martin said as he reached his hand in to comfort Lulu.

"No, what threats?" Daniel couldn't believe Miss Tinny wouldn't tell him something like that.

"Your mother has been stalwart at the city council for development of her business, and we have been expanding in the tunnels. We needed more lab space. Some of the natives are unappreciative of what we are doing with the land. We had to fire Tsintah, we caught her trying to get into the labs."

"No wonder she never mentioned it. Why didn't you tell me?"

"The phone lines may be tapped. We are contemplating installing a fiber optic system throughout and encrypting all communication. We are not sure who we can trust right now."

"If they only knew what else you were doing here..."

"We are being safe..."

"Oh, you are?!? Do you call that safe?" Daniel turned his back to the monkeys and was pointing at his brother.

"It is crucial work ... we are so close to a cure for so many things ... We have not had an incident in all these years, and your brother was so hopeful."

"I know father, I know."

"How long will you stay," Martin asked and Daniel knew what he was going to ask next. He wanted him there, to help with his research; his all-consuming search for a cure for cancer and a cure for MD.

"No longer than I need to in order to make sure he recovers well. Hopefully just a few days. I have patients that need me in LA and I have..."

"She is never going to wake up Daniel, give-up!"

"Would I ask you to give-up on your research? Have you found a cure for cancer? For MD? Simply because I haven't found a way to wake her from a coma yet, doesn't mean she won't wake up."

"My research has already helped millions of people's lives and will save billions of lives once I find a cure. Cancer kills 22% of the population and just about everyone on my side of the family. She is just one girl."

"I help many people, one at a time. It is my life."

"Schwachsinn! What kind of life is that? You have no friends, no girlfriend. You don't have a pet ... I suspect that you do not even have a plant!"

Daniel knew he was right. He had inherited his dad's obsessive nature, and his drive to want to solve the impossible. Unlike his father, he didn't have a woman in his life that did what his mother did – pull him out of the lab and into the world. He loved a girl who was in a coma. He really did have no life.

"I know a marvelous young woman I met at a conference, she would be perfect for you, honey," his mother said as she came around to his other side. He was now cornered by both parents, with monkeys at his back. That heart pounding feeling of dread he felt earlier was returning. She continued with, "I was thinking about hiring her to run my new department, researching and perfecting bat guano for a new cosmetic line. We've finally found a bat cave and I want to make use of it."

"You finally found a bat cave, huh? You're in a bat cave, you're both batty!" Daniel exclaimed. "Look" he pointed to his sleeping brother. "Will you never learn?"

"He made that choice himself, and he paid the price." Martin declared.

"Will he stop?!?" Daniel shouted. "Will he ever stop?!?"

"Yes," a faint cry came from the bed. All three standing turned at once, in unison, to face the now awake Cliff. "Daniel ...if you had been here ... I know you ... I know you would have stopped me ... I need you."

Daniel didn't know what to say, there were tears forming in his eyes and he felt pressure in his throat rising up to choke him as his breath was caught in his chest. He knew it was true, deep down, he knew he was the only one his brother ever listened to ... and if he had been here ... maybe his brother would still have his legs.

"Okay ..." Daniel could hear his mother gasp at the simple but poignant word. He glanced over at his father, who was smiling proudly. "I will need to go ... to make arrangements..." he couldn't let himself think about what this meant for Amy. He was sandwiched again by both parents, only this time with hugs.

With the two of them this close he couldn't help but notice that they appeared as if they hadn't aged a day since the last time he saw them. It had been 8 years. Some signs of aging should be present. Not to mention, he couldn't quite tell how old they were. From the lack of wrinkles around their eyes to the tightness of their skin, they could both pass for early 30's. But, they were technically in their late fifties. Daniel had been in LA long enough to spot plastic surgery, so he knew there could only be one explanation.

"I have one condition," he said and his parents looked at each other, concern flashing between their eyes. "We can't have any secrets between us, understood?"

"Of course, son." Martin insisted, and Beth nodded in agreement.

"We would never keep a secret from you," she said.

"No secrets? Okay, then you have to tell me what is in that coffee."

Chapter 7
Microchips and Membranes in Men's Brains

Susan Aldean spent the last three years doing nothing but writing letters to universities and institutions across the world. She was sick of writing and even more sick of waiting on responses. On a whim, she decided she was going to walk right into an office today, to talk to one of the local doctors who had not given her an answer. Maybe she could convince him if she was face-to-face. It was worth a try.

Dr. Jared Daniels was a professor in neurology at UCLA and specialized in Parkinson's disease and other disorders of the brain that her invention would be perfect to treat. She'd sent him an envelope containing a disc that had all the data on the successful tests her team had conducted on mice. It included photo copies of the accolades her ICMod had gotten in Scientific America, and a proposal letter explaining she needed human test subjects that he could provide.

Bravery was the name of the game today. She was willing to brave the two-hour stop-and-go traffic through LA, using it as an opportunity to practice her elevator pitch, over and over. She was willing to brave the Santa Ana's almost blowing her briefcase out of her hand as she struggled against the wind to close her car door in the parking lot of the medical center. She was willing to brave anything to have a chance to convince someone her research was worthwhile.

"I'm looking for Dr. Daniel Jared," she said to the woman in scrubs behind the counter at the neurology department.

"You mean Dr. Daniel Jarhen?" the middle-aged, dark-red haired woman replied with a quizzical brow while continuing her activities of marking-off papers and sorting folders.

Susan was taken aback, that didn't sound right. Had she said the wrong name? She was a bit dyslexic and English was not her first language. She was far more comfortable in her native French.

Before Susan could answer her back, the woman behind the counter pointed to the man walking in from the elevators down the hall and said, "You're in luck, there he is right now. Really good timing, he's been out for over a week with a family emergency." She held her hand over her mouth then continued, "Oh, I shouldn't have told you that!" She leaned over the counter and whispered, "Don't tell him I said anything."

"Hi Nancy, how are you doing this morning?" The male doctor who had just come in from the elevators asked. Susan's first thought was that he appeared as if he could be a movie star. He was tall and had a broad, muscular build. Plus, he had full lips, a chiseled jaw and dreamy hazel eyes. He also looked young enough that she would have thought he was an intern.

"Fine. Just fine, Dr. Jahren," replied the women in scrubs. "This lovely young lady is here to see you."

"Hi, I'm Dr. Susan Aldean from the ICModTech Research Group here in LA I've been writing to you for the last six months and I would like to discuss with you my research proposal," she said while shaking his hand firmly, to show confidence. Finally, it was time to use that elevator pitch she'd practiced, "I have an innovative, implantable microchip that can..."

"I've never heard of ICModTech, are you sure you sent your proposal to the right address? I typically send rejection or acceptance letters within ninety days of receiving them."

"I..." Susan began. Had her dyslexia struck again? She went to open her briefcase to check her copy of the letter. But, as she opened the right latch, the left latch flung open and all of her papers came flying out. She bent down to chase the pages, but her head struck against the young doctor's hard enough for her to see only stars. He must have bent down to pick up the papers at the same time. By the time she could see anything else, she saw that all of her papers were back in her briefcase and it was closed and on her lap. Did she black out?

"How are you feeling?" the young doctor asked as he handed her a cup of cold water. "You may have a concussion. Can you stand up?"

"I'm alright. I need to talk to you about my research..." she replied as she held onto her briefcase with both hands while Nancy and the doctor hoisted her up by each arm. She stood steady and said, "Thank you" as they released her to stand on her own. "I'd like to show you my proposal."

"You are persistent! I believe I can take a few minutes to hear you out. Come to my office," the doctor said with a smile. He was far too cute to be a doctor!

Susan sat down and couldn't help but notice the nameplate on the desk in front of her and then read it aloud, "Dr. Daniel Jahren." She knew that was definitely not right when she heard herself say it. She was pretty sure she needed a Jared Daniel. She might just die with embarrassment.

"You can call me Daniel. Please, let me see your research," he asked with an outreached hand.

Susan decided to hand him her papers even though she knew there would be the inevitable: "No, this is not at all something I'm interested in. Good day, maim." Her head was pounding, and she kept sipping the water as he shifted through her papers. She started to notice that she would take a sip every time he turned a page and then had to stop herself and tried to look around the room for a distraction.

The office was bare except for an impressive array of awards, diplomas and certificates on the wall. There were a few rocks, and oddly, a dream catcher, on his desk next to his computer and office phone. No family pictures. No girlfriend pictures. She checked his hand instinctively, no ring either. How can a guy this handsome and successful be single? What is wrong with him? He was probably married to his work, like her.

Nancy came in quietly and handed her an ice pack for her head. Susan thanked her and went back to staring at the office furniture and trying not to stare at the cute doctor.

"So, you have developed a promising implant to stimulate the dopaminergic neurons of the substantia nigra," he looked up and Susan nodded. "I am particularly interested in this part about 'improvement in motor response and overall brain activity' that you mention," he looked up again and Susan nodded again and he continued: "I have a patient, Charlie, that has been doing well with an electro-stimulation implant, but he continues to have significant motor loss in his left side. Could this device be altered to provide feedback to an electro-stimulation unit already installed?"

"Yes, of course. They have very similar modalities..."

"How soon can you have your equipment here and ready to go?" he interrupted briskly.

"Today! I can come back in an hour ...wait, maybe three depending on traffic." Susan couldn't believe her ears. She was going to be able to work on a real-live-human-test-subject for the very first time! She had waited so long! She jumped up and immediately had to sit right back down. Her head was pounding!

"Dr. Aldean, you have a concussion."

"You can call me Susan."

"Susan, you need to rest for today. If you are feeling better, come back tomorrow. I'll still be here. Take some Tylenol and rest, agreed?" he said gently. He shuffled her papers neatly back into the briefcase and securely set the latches.

"Thank you, I'll be back first thing tomorrow," she picked up her briefcase from his desk, getting up much slower this time. She was having trouble looking into his eyes and was feeling that same nervous feeling she always got when a cute guy was around. Great, I have a silly crush! She thought as she headed out the door, trying not to run.

~ ~ ~

Susan had spent the last two days in a lab at UCLA near Dr. Jahren's office. She was matching her implant with a rudimentary electro-stimulation device. Most of her time was spent writing the code needed to provide a feedback loop between the two and a mock-up to represent neurotransmitters. Apparently, Dr. hottie-Mc-Jahren (that's what she was calling him in her head anyway) wanted her to provide stimulus simultaneously at multiple locations and increase the implant output based on measured EEG activity in the left hemisphere of a brain trauma patient. It was a novel approach, and ambitious. Exactly the kind of work she thrived on. It wasn't the ideal patient trail she had planned for the

ICMod technology, but it tested the limits enough to provide significant data for forthcoming applications. And, if all went well, it was patentable.

"Is the system configuration complete, Susan?" Daniel asked, handing her plain, black coffee from the break room in a Styrofoam cup. He was drinking coffee from his usual container; a dark grey thermos that had his name on it and "Do NOT Drink" in big, red, bold letters. He was serious about no one touching his coffee, though she doubted anyone would touch it considering how awful it smelled.

"Yes, I just ran my last test simulation. Thank you for the drink," she said, carefully sipped the piping hot beverage. He was leaning over her shoulder to look at her Compaq Presario screen, he could apparently read C from the way he was scanning the code. This was the closest he had ever been and she couldn't help but notice he smelled like shaving cream and burnt coffee beans.

"I think it would be best if you were near during the surgery." He was looking at her for a response to something ... did he just say he wanted her near?

"During surgery? Are you sure you want me in the room? I've showed you all you have to do is press the spacebar ... it's fairly straightforward." Her specialty was the microchip and software, and her doctorate was in electrical engineering, not medicine. So, she typically wasn't in the room when one of her teammates installed the implant onto a mouse. Also, it didn't help that her hands weren't that steady when dealing with such delicate matters. Plus, she was a bit accident prone in general. "Are you really sure?"

Daniel laughed, he was starting to get used to her and was well versed in the plethora of little accidents that she was prone to already. The amount of accidents was directly proportional to the level of her nervousness, and in this case, the handsomeness of the doctor she was working with.

"Okay, I'm ready then. Prep the patient!" she almost shouted as she picked up her laptop, knocking her Styrofoam cup down and off of the counter. Daniel must have anticipated the sudden movement and had the cup in hand before it spilled a drop. He was pretty good at averting her disasters.

"I should keep you around all the time," she said without thinking, then blushed at the thought of him around all-the-time. Oh God, did he think she was hitting on him? She probably sounded psychotic wanting him around all the time, like Misery or something. Oh God, did he think she was going to be like Kathy Bates' character? "I didn't mean it like that I..."

"That's okay, I know what you meant," he interrupted, chuckling to himself.

He definitely thought she was flirting. That was a good thing, right? She was terrible at flirting, at least on purpose.

They first headed into the patient's, Charlie Abram's, room and began questioning him to make sure he understood the procedure and risks. He had limited speaking ability but was still able to verbally agree and sign a disclosure notice for the experimental procedure.

Susan set up her laptop and equipment in the operating room and waited for Daniel's team to prep the Charlie and initiating the gory stuff. There would be three other doctors and support staff involved, and they needed to go over the operation together before starting. She would basically be there to witness and ensure the feedback loops were operating before the implant went into his brain and then run a brief calibration program. Charlie would be under conscious sedation, with localized anesthesia, so they could get his feedback.

While the other doctors were in the hallway talking procedure, she looked around the room for anything she could trip over or knock off of something. She made sure any and all objects were far away from where she would be standing.

Once everything began, the whole process went by quickly and smoothly. The interface functioned well with the electro-stimulus device previously installed. The implant seated in the desirable spot of the cerebral cortex without damaging the surrounding tissue. All thanks to the remarkably steady hands of Dr. Jahren. It couldn't have gone better.

After Charlie was moved to recovery, Susan found herself standing outside the operation room door, in a daze. They did it! They actually did it!

"I'm impressed," Daniel said as he was washing up. "That went nicer than I thought."

"You're impressed with me? You're the one that just cut into a human being and..."

"Can you take a compliment?" he asked, and held her gaze with his gold-flecked hazel eyes that she found so mesmerizing...

"Humm ...?" she finally asked, not realizing she had spaced out, staring into his eyes.

He laughed. At least he found her quarks funny. Some people thought she was annoying when she was constantly knocking things over and spacing out. She even found herself annoying.

"Are you hungry?" he asked. "What are you doing for dinner?"

"I'm ... ummm ..." What was she doing for dinner? She hadn't even thought about what she would do after the surgery, except maybe lurk around Daniel's lab until she could run her full program on the patient.

Wait, was he asking her on a date?

"Do you like BJ's?" he inquired.

"Do I like WHAT?" she was scandalized at what he was suggesting.

"There's a BJ's Brewhouse right around the corner, it's one of my favorite restaurants. We should celebrate your achievement today. I'll even buy you a Pizookie." He had a confused look that spoke volumes about his innocence.

Susan was blushing red as a beat, but managed to get out, "What's a Pizookie?"

"It's a hot and gooey cookie topped with ice cream, delicious!" Daniel replied. "Let's go."

They managed to get to the restaurant alive and in one piece, but only barely. Walking a few blocks should not be a life-threatening fiasco. But, with how distracted she was today, mishaps were bound to happen.

The first accident was on the stairway leading down from the hospital. Susan turned around to talk while walking backwards, failing to realize there were stairs behind her until she almost went flying down them. Then, at the curb to cross the street, she tripped and almost fell right into traffic. Talking while walking was definitely not her best skill. She was merely trying to explain her fascination with Parkinson's disease and helping people like her uncle and Michael J. Fox. Both times Daniel saved her before she fell to what might have been her death.

"So, do you make a habit of saving the lives of falling women?" Susan asked as they were seated at their table in the restaurant. For some reason, that question had the opposite effect on Daniel she was hoping for – it produced a dark frown instead of a bright smile. He sat there, quietly, deep in thought.

"What did I say?" she asked, obviously she had hit a nerve. "I'm so sorry, are you okay?" Maybe he was finally sick of her bad jokes.

"I didn't ... I couldn't save her..." he said and glanced back in the direction of the hospital.

"Who couldn't you save?" She turned her head back towards the hospital and didn't see anyone. "One of your patients?"

"Amy ... she was my childhood friend ... we were climbing ... and she fell ... and ..." he was speaking very slowly, controlling his words and taking deep breaths in-between as if it just happened.

Susan quickly realized the severity of her mistaken words. "Oh my god! I'm so sorry! I had no idea! I didn't know your friend died like that. I'm so sorry!"

"No, no, it's okay. She didn't die, she's in a coma. Here." He was staring in the direction of the hospital. "But, I couldn't save her ... I can't wake her up." He gazed at Susan with tears welling up in his eyes.

"Good Evening! My Name is Linda, and I will be your waitress. Can I start you off with something to drink?" said a bright and cheery, middle-aged woman with bleach-blonde hair pulled back in a bun and smile wrinkles three rows deep on either side of her mouth.

The cheerfulness of the waitress was in such stark contrast to the mood of both Daniel and Susan that they both took a breath at the same time. Then they focused all their attention on Linda.

"I'll have a beer," Susan said, "a Hefeweizen if you have it." She peered over at Daniel again and then asked the waitress, "Do you have something bigger than a pint?"

Linda shook her head.

Daniel cleared his throat, forced himself to smile and said, "May I have a water, no ice, with a lemon slice on the side? Please? Thank you, Linda."

"I'll be right back," the waitress said, scurrying off in the busy restaurant.

Normally, Susan would pick-on a guy that goes to a brewhouse and doesn't order a beer but she didn't feel like this was a good time. She was left not knowing what to say so she fiddled with her napkin nervously.

"I'm going to miss this place," he said, scanning the crowded restaurant with a half-smile.

"What do you mean?"

"I'm leaving in two weeks to go back home to Colorado. I've already put in my notice with the medical center. My brother is not well, and my parents need my help."

"Two weeks?!?" she exclaimed, dumbfounded. This was the first time he mentioned anything about leaving. "What about Charlie? We've only begun, what will..."

"The staff all know, and he will be in good hands."

Susan sat quietly stunned, completely speechless. They just met and he was going to leave her so soon. Leave her ... It all made sense, his research, his friend in a coma ... and he was finally giving up ... that's why it shook him so bad when he talked about her. He was going to leave his friend Amy too.

"What about your childhood friend Amy, in the coma? Are you leaving her here?" She wanted to add a "too" on the end of that question, but she bit her tongue.

"Yes. She has been in a coma for over 10 years, with limited brain activity. I can no longer waist my life hoping she will wake-up."

"But, the implant ... when I was doing my patent research I stumbled across another recent implant patent used for deep brain stimulation. It was specifically designed to wake people from comas ... they were stimulating the vagus nerve directly with various pulsed frequencies ... Is that something you've tried?"

"The vagus nerve, that is odd. I've looked into pulsed frequencies. But, no, we haven't tried them. It is all very new, very risky. I don't want to hurt her. I'm not going to try something on her that hasn't been well tested on others."

"But, you are willing to hurt Charlie? To take a risk on Charlie? The ICModTech implant can be easily adjusted to emit similar frequencies to the patent I saw ... if the tests go well with him, would you be willing to help Amy?"

"What do you mean, you can easily adjust the frequencies? I have only tried DC on my patients ... isn't your implant DC based?"

"No. My paper clearly states that it produces a time-varying electric field through electromagnetic induction."

"Ah..." Daniel said, he looked a bit embarrassed and Susan got the impression he wasn't as familiar with electrons and neutrons as he was with electrodes and neurons. "I think I was confused when I read 'increase the levels of dopamine in the brain through direct neuron stimulation' and assumed that meant direct current like the devices we are having so much success with presently."

"I did hit you in the head right before you read my research proposal."

"Yes, you did," he chuckled. "Or I hit you? I think it was a mutual bashing. Though, I think you got the brunt of it because you were out cold for a few minutes and ended up with a concussion."

"Ouch, was I? Wow, all I remember was seeing stars. Come to think of it, you didn't even get a bruise, you must be very hard headed!"

The waitress came back with the drinks, and asked, "Are you ready to order?"

Neither of them had even looked at the menu. A burger with a beer at a brewhouse was probably a safe bet, "I'll have a cheeseburger and fries," Susan said.

"May I have a steak, medium rare, and a side salad. Please," Daniel replied with a less forced smile this time and handed the waitress both menus. "Thank you, ma'am."

"Coming right up," Linda's big smile was accentuated with a golden-brown lipstick that she must have been trying to match with the brown scrunchie in her hair.

"So polite, that is a rare trait in a man these days," Susan pointed out.

"It must be my country upbringing," said Daniel. "I grew up in a small town. By the way, where are you from? I couldn't help but notice an accent. I would say French but it almost sounds Spanish."

"I'm from Toulouse, in the south of France. So, you were very close."

"Oui? J'ai toujours voulu aller en France!"

"Tu parle français? C'est encore plus rare que d'avoir des manières pour un Américain."

"Yes, well ... I speak several languages, but most Americans feel it is rude to not speak English all the time, especially in public." He scanned the room pointedly – they had already gotten a few glares as they spoke.

"Well, maybe you should go to France. I could show you some fantastic restaurants in Toulouse where they love it if you speak French." Susan couldn't believe she had said that. Oh, I just met you, cute doctor, let me take you on a trip to Europe!

"I'm sure you could. I don't think I'll have much time for site seeing anytime soon though. I need to go home and help my family in Colorado."

There it was again, that mention of leaving that left a pit in Susan's stomach and made her mouth dry. She took another sip of her beer, a gulp really. Where did half of it go? Maybe it was the beer getting to her brain already, be she realized she couldn't let him leave.

"What about Amy? What about trying the ICModTech implant on her? Are you going to leave her here and let the other doctors work on her? Or, do you not want to work with me anymore?" Okay, that last part was definitely the beer talking, she needed to slow down!

"You're incredible truly. Somewhat accident prone, but incredible. Honestly, I mostly decided to work with you because I thought that at least if Charlie doesn't get his motor skills back, he will still be much happier. He has been fairly moody and depressed, and increasing his dopamine levels before I leave made me feel like I was giving him a nice going-away present."

"So, you are going to leave me here to wake up Amy, without you?" There was a look in Daniel's eyes, like a fire had been lit. It let Susan know she was right to guess Amy was the bait she needed to keep Daniel from heading home.

"Do you actually think it will work? We have to make sure that Charlie is okay, and responds well ... but, do you actually think it will work?"

"I would bet on it," Susan replied. Now all she had to do was figure out how to get her ICMod to wake someone up from a coma, and she had less than two weeks to do it or the dreamboat of a man sitting across from her was going to be gone for good.

Chapter 8

Oh Brother, Where Art Thou

Cliff dreamt he was flying up into a lavender sunset, with rockets for legs. Blue fire issued from his metal appendages, and he shot pulsed beams from his hands that created circular clouds radiating for miles, getting bigger and bigger as they dissipated.

He laughed as a giant eagle landed on his left shoulder, hanging on for the ride. He spun in circles to see if the bird would get dizzy and fall off. But it hung on easily, looking down at him calmly. When he stopped spinning, the bird flew out in front of him, leading him forward.

Cliff followed the giant, white faced, bald eagle with rainbow glimmering wings until it landed on a juniper brush jutting out from a red rocky mountain cliff. He immediately recognized the cliff when he looked down from it to see a young girl hanging on and screaming. He fired a pulsed blast at the eagle for taking him to this place but the bird had already disappeared.

The whole scene began to change as his anger welled up. The rocks around his feet started to levitate and the cliff broke apart as he screamed. The horizon in every direction was filled with floating rocks and broken mountainside until it all exploded into red dust.

What was left after the dust cleared was Cliff standing over his brother, who was sleeping at his desk at work at the UCLA neurology department. There was an object on his desk, a small microchip that Cliff held up to inspect. As he examined it further, a woman's face appeared smiling. She held his hand and led him forward to a world of bright shimmering light ... there were ships in the air flying around metal skyscrapers layered with trees ...

Cliff awoke in pain. His legs were still healing and he was trying to ween himself off of morphine. He looked down at the stubs where his legs used to be. He felt complete apathy. Maybe he should feel something, but he just didn't. He had hated his legs for so many years. They failed him and continued to fail him more each day until they were useless objects relegating him to a wheelchair. Now they were gone.

He lifted himself up onto the wheelchair next to his bed and rolled over to the lab to go straight to work. He began the day by tweaking a prototype leg that his mother ordered from a scientist she'd met at some conference. It was nothing like what he wanted. What it could be. What he imagined.

He heard his father come into the room but didn't turn around. Martin had been tip-toeing around him for over a week now and the super vigilance was annoying.

"I'm sorry to be the bearer of bad news. I received a call from Daniel, he isn't coming as soon as he planned. It turns out he has come across a new implant that may help wake Amy up and he wants to attempt it before he returns home," Martin sat next to Cliff, who was still not facing his father.

Cliff threw the small screwdriver in his hand across the room and exclaimed, "Why can't he just give up on that white trash, good-for-nothing tramp?"

"I am unsure son, I believe he loves her..." Martin reached out and gathered the other tools on the table, slid them into a drawer and was eyeing Cliff warily. "How is the morphine withdrawal? It is reasonable to add more if your symptoms start to get too much for you, you needn't be ashamed..."

"I can handle it!" Cliff yelled. He rubbed his temples and leaned over his workbench, head in his hands. This wasn't his first outburst since the incident, and it wasn't like him to lose his temper so easily. At least, not since he was a child. He felt like a child and hated being treated like one. But, if he wanted to be treated better, he needed to start acting like an adult. Maybe his father was right, maybe it was just the morphine withdrawal?

"I'm sorry dad." He turned to face his father, who's concern was evident. He looked away, he hated seeing pity. "Perhaps I do need to add a bit more morphine for a few days." The truth was the pain didn't bother him, it made him feel alive. But the withdrawal symptoms were turning out to be less manageable than he thought. Moodiness, irritation and outbursts of rage.

"The average person would crumble under the weight of the struggles you've endured and you've managed to thrive your whole life. One accident does not define a person," Martin put his hand on Cliff's shoulder. "I'm proud to call you my son. When you have completed these prosthetics, they will be the most state-of-the-art legs anyone could have..."

"Yes, anyone. Much stronger," he said as he thought than rotting flesh legs, and continued with, "capable of so much more. I'm fitting a power unit here," Cliff pointed to an area close to the top where they would attach to his pelvis, then continued, "and I'm planning to install an electro-gel membrane kneecap. I haven't decided on the hydraulic system quite yet."

"Brilliant work! Is there anything I can do to help?" Martin sounded genuinely pleased with the progress Cliff had made in such little time, and while getting over major surgery. It might be because he thought that the cocktail of enzymes, anthocyanins, and phenols he had injected was working well. He had immune supporting cocktails down to an art; after all, they were his bread and butter.

"Yes, fix Tribus. If I'm going to be strong enough to wear these things," he held up the prosthetic leg, "I'm going to need that formulation to work."

"I am unsure if that is the most..."

"I know it will work. I need it. Dad, please?" he turned to look his father dead in the eye, still holding onto the leg and trying not to lose his temper again.

"Okay, son, but we need to initiate testing on human tissue, and thoroughly vet the stability. It may take a while to..."

"Of course," Cliff interrupted, turning back to his work and pulling out a screwdriver from the drawer his father had slid all the tools into. He didn't want to hear it was going to take a while. Focusing on his work would help distract him from the set-backs.

"Well, we both have work to do it seems. I will get started." He patted Cliff on the back and then said: "I'm proud of you, son. I hope you know that, no matter what happens ... I love you."

Cliff hardly ever heard his father say he loved him. He looked up to see pride mixed with pain in his father's eyes, and a tinge of pity that was like a razor blade slowly going across a glass beaker in his mind. But, he managed to smile and say, "Thanks dad, I love you too."

Cliff had so many ideas of what he could do with cybernetic legs, but he needed his brother's knowledge of neuroscience. He didn't just want a prosthetic, he wanted legs that responded to his mind like they were his own. He knew that with his brother's help they could make exactly what he needed. There were universities all over the world already working on it, and if they could do it, so could he!

Dammit, why couldn't Daniel get over Amy! Daniel knew Cliff needed him, yet he was still wasting his time with her. What could he possibly be working on that could wake her up from a coma that she had been in for over a decade?

Wait, the dream he had last night ... it was already fading, but ... there was something ... he had had a dream of her ... and a microchip ... He learned a long time ago to pay attention to his dreams. Especially when he had a dream as vivid as the one he had last night. It always meant something important was right around the corner.

What if Daniel did wake her up? What would she say to him? Cliff quickly went online to buy a plane ticket, he needed to be there and make sure she didn't wake up!

~ ~ ~

This wasn't the first time Cliff was in public in a wheelchair, nor the first time he was in LA. But, it was the first time he was in a wheelchair in LA with no legs, and the looks of sympathy coupled with averted glances were driving him insane with rage. He bit his lip and continued on, ignoring as much as he could. By the time he and the cab driver (who was carrying all of Cliff's luggage) made it into his brother's office, he was humming a Buddhist mantra to stay calm.

"Cliff! What are you doing here? Is everything okay?" Daniel asked, getting up from behind his desk and rushing over to check on his legs as he wheeled himself into the room.

Cliff had to shoo him off, waving his hand away and then saying, "I'm fine. I'm fine. I heard you were staying here to wake that ... Amy. And, I just couldn't wait. I wanted you to see what I was working on and I knew you could help me."

Cliff motioned to the tall man in black, standing behind him holding several large suitcases and said, "Randall, you can leave those here, thank you."

"You never were very patient, little brother. What have you brought for me?" Daniel asked, curiosity piqued at the luggage being set down in the room and no longer focusing on Cliff's legs.

"Open that suitcase and see for yourself."

When Daniel unzipped and lifted the top, his eyes went wide and he pulled-out a large object. "Wow, and it's so light! What did you use?"

"I bought a prototype from a German manufacturer and re-designed it in carbon fiber. I used electro-gel for the kneecap and titanium for the hydraulic tubing. I altered the feet with my spring-loaded design I already had for my crutches."

"What is this area for? Is that a power supply? What does it power?"

"I was hoping you would tell me, for now it only powers some of the hydraulics ... but what I want is for those legs to feel like my own. I want them to work like my legs..."

"Cliff, I'm not sure that is possible..."

"It is possible! I've seen it. Look at those papers, there are studies. And all over the world..."

"But Cliff, I have never done anything like this before..."

"You can do anything you put your mind to Daniel. If you choose to use your mind for something useful like this."

Daniel was holding up the leg in one hand and the papers in the other, looking at the two. Cliff could see his mind racing, getting excited – he would solve this problem. Daniel could never back down from solving a problem.

"Wow, what is that?" said a soft, female voice with a slight foreign accent from behind Cliff's head. As she walked in front of him to reach out and take the leg from Daniel, Cliff had to catch his breath. He recognized her, from his dream ... and she was even more lovely in person. Soft brown hair, cut to her chin and doe brown eyes. She was the one with the microchip.

"Dr. Susan Aldean, meet my brother Cliff," Daniel said. Just as he said that it looked like she was noticing someone else was in the room. She turned backwards to look at Cliff, at the same time as bending to sit down on the corner of the desk, and also reaching out to shake Cliff's hand. It must have been a bit too much to do at once because she missed the desk and then spun around to try and catch herself. She realized she still had the leg in her hand and tossed it upwards so she could hold onto the corner of the desk.

This theatrical folly appeared as if it was normal to Daniel. He not only caught the leg mid-air, but also caught Susan within an inch of her face smacking right into the corner of the desk.

"Thanks, Daniel. Again. I'm sorry." She was smiling up at him and he was grinning down at her and he had his arm wrapped around her waist.

Cliff had to clear his throat to break the tension and let them know he was still in the room.

"Sorry, Cliff was it? Wow, good looks run in the family. It's a pleasure to meet you," she said, not even noticing the wheelchair or his legs.

Cliff was flattered. He wasn't used to compliments. He'd only had a few his whole life and only when he would go down to the tavern for a drink to get away and try to be normal for a day ... and mostly from drunken tavern whores that he wasn't at all interested in hearing compliment him.

"Cliff was just here to get my help with this prosthetic he designed," Daniel said.

"You designed this? It's amazing. Genius is another trait that runs in the family it seems." She smiled at Cliff and he felt butterflies in his stomach. She had that petite librarian look that he always found sexy, and those little pointy glasses she had on just added to the effect. "What is the power supply for?"

"It is for the neural-interface network that Daniel is going to design for me," Cliff was staring Daniel in the eye and not breaking eye contact. He knew he needed to press him to keep him on track.

"I see. I could get this battery much smaller. And you'll need electrodes that interface directly with the nerve endings..."

"Susan, you don't want to help do you? Cliff will drag you off to Colorado if you keep talking like that and I need you here to alter the ICMod," Daniel said, half playfully, half seriously.

"ICMod, is that a microchip?" Cliff asked. This Susan was turning out to live up to his dreams.

"Something like that. It is an implantable integrated circuit I designed to create pulsed signals deep in the brain, stimulating neurotransmitters. Particularly the ones responsible for dopamine production. I'm making alterations to attach it to the vagus nerve so that we can attempt to bring Daniel's friend Amy out of her coma," Susan replied while running her hands along the prosthetic leg and poking at the gel in the knee. "This is brilliant, by the way."

"Daniel, if you don't marry her, I will!" Cliff heard himself exclaim before he even knew he had the thought. That statement made everyone in the room blush and look around nervously. "Sorry, I'm still on a lot of pain medications from my recent surgery. I don't usually propose to women I just met, usually." He gave Susan a wink, and she glanced over at Daniel, who was scowling at Cliff.

"Oh no, it's fine. I need to go get back to work. Daniel, I should be ready to run the full program on Charlie by 2:30 this afternoon, if I leave now anyway. It was nice meeting you Cliff!" she attempted to walk out of the room while saying all of that but only managed to trip over a suitcase and then catch herself on Cliff's wheelchair.

He held her hand so she could steady herself as she got up, and he couldn't help but notice how soft, delicate and warm to the touch her skin was. He also couldn't help but notice she wore heels. "You know, it would be easier to walk if you wore flats."

"You would think so, but no..." she whispered loudly, shaking her head. "Besides, I love heels, and I just wouldn't feel very French anymore without them."

"French? Parlez-vous français?" he asked.

"Bien sûr!" she replied.

"Yes, of course you would speak the language of love."

Both Cliff and Daniel watched as Susan exited the room. "Now that's the kind of girl Mom would want you to take home, Daniel," Cliff said when the door closed.

"What does that mean? As opposed to who?" Daniel stated indignantly.

"You know who," Cliff said with disdain. "Look what you've done. You've made me come all the why out here to beg you to help me. Do you know what kind of debacle I had to put up with at the airport? I couldn't bring any of the vials father made with me, TSA took them all. I sure hope he didn't put anything ... you know ... risky in them."

"Are you kidding me?" Daniel shouted, "Cliff, you're joking, right?"

"You wouldn't come to Colorado, so I had to come here."

They both sat in silence, staring each other down. Daniel broke the gaze first, his eyes sliding down towards Cliff's legs for a mini-second and then away quickly.

"I want to help you right now, Cliff. I do. But, I made a promise to myself, and to her, that I would do everything I could. If the tests go well with Charlie today, we'll start on Amy soon after. Since you're here, and if it takes Susan a while to configure the ICMod, while she does that I can help you with your prosthetics. Deal?"

"Deal," replied Cliff. "So, what is the 'deal' with you and Susan. Is she single? Are you two, umm, together?"

"No, no, no. We just met a few days ago. Why?" Daniel replied too rapidly, he could be so naïve when it came to women. So, she was available. Cliff felt relieved. She probably had no idea how obsessed his brother was with that girl Amy, but she soon would.

"Can I watch her run the program on, Charlie was it?" Cliff asked. "This ICMod microchip sounds interesting. I have more questions I would like to ask her."

"I bet you do." Daniel said, peering sideways at Cliff, eyes squinting.

~ ~ ~

"It feels like ... warmth emanating from the inside of my skull, and I feel ... good? It's hard to describe. But hey, I'm describing it! Wow! Don't I sound good!" Charlie Abram said not long after they began the program. He had wires coming out of the back of his shaved head, electrodes on both sides of his skull and down his neck and he had on an EEG head cap.

"Yeah Dad, but you look like a cyborg," his three-year-old son said, sitting on his mother's lap next to the patient's bed.

"Yeppy, Cyborg Chucky they are going to call me, mwarrrr!" Charlie exclaimed as he tickled his son's belly, leaving the kid squirming and giggling in his mother's arms.

"You do sound like yourself again, and look, you are using your left arm!" his wife said, overjoyed.

"We're going to step down the power now. We need to see what maintenance level we are going to have to keep to continue to see benefits," Susan adjusted the stimulation and continued stepping down the power levels and checking Charlie's response until he showed visible signs of deterioration in speech or movement.

"600 milliwatts, I can work with that," Susan said. "I'll have my contacts in Idaho generate a compatible power unit. If we're lucky, it will be here in less than a week. When we are done hooking that up we can remove most of the wiring and" she looked down at the three-year-old and smiled "he'll not look so much like a cyborg anymore." Charlie's son giggled when she said 'cyborg' as he apparently loved the word.

"You have friends in Idaho that can make an implantable, micro-sized power supply in under a week? That's impressive," said Cliff.

"It's a microchip manufacturer that has a research and development division working on novel product lines. I help them with fresh markets, they hook me up with some of their latest tech. And, because they already have all the manufacturing and production set up for solid-state devices, most of the hard part is already in place for fabricating the necessary components. This makes it easy for ICModTech to acquire one-offs for our wide-ranging uses. For instance, right now they are generating an integrated circuit for cell phones that can capture photographs to the same resolution as a 35 mm film camera."

"Who would want to use their phone to take pictures? I'm more interested in the power supply. You mentioned earlier that you could get me a better power supply for the prosthetic. Is it from the same manufacturer? Are you thinking lithium-ion?"

"Yes, we'll have to evaluate your needs to configure your..."

"Stop right there, we are working on configuring the ICMod for deep brain stimulation at the vagus nerve next, not for prosthetics. I told you both, we can work on that later," Daniel interrupted, visibly perturbed at Cliff.

"Daniel's right, one thing at a time..." Susan began but Cliff didn't want to hear her agree with his brother, so he interrupted.

"Don't you have to make sure there are no negative side effects with Cyborg Chucky here first before you open up Amy?" Both Susan and Daniel looked at Cliff questioningly, they weren't biting on his bait. Charlie's implant was the epitome of success, after all. "Fine. But, Daniel, you promised to get started helping me with the prosthetic while Susan works on configuring the ICMod."

"Okay. Let's get started then. First, we need to know what we're dealing with." Daniel took hold of the back of Cliff's wheelchair to wheel him out of the room.

"Here," Cliff reached over before Daniel could stop him and removed the EEG head cap from Charlie. The he put it on his own head. "Go ahead and run some tests..."

"Sorry, Charlie," Daniel apologized. "My brother here is very curious about what we are doing with your implant, it is state-of-the-art." He then sat back down at the computer and removed the leads to the electrodes on Charlie's head. "Cliff, Susan's software only works if it is talking to her ICMod, and this particular set-up is special. The EEG you put on your head, though it may make you look like a cyborg," Daniel smiled down at the giggling little 3-year-old who loved the word 'cyborg' and then went back to the computer and continued, "it can only tell us so much, it has a feedback loop to ..."

Daniel was deep in concentration, he had stopped talking in mid-sentence.

"Daniel? Are you okay?" Cliff asked.

"Your frontal lobe ... I've never seen anything like this ... what are you thinking about?" Daniel asked, in awe.

"Nothing, I was just imagining being a cyborg..."

"Well, you are either using far more of your brain than a typical human being or you have far more neural connections in your cerebral cortex. I want to get an MRI done ASAP. I've never seen anything like this before, it's amazing!"

"What are you seeing?" Susan asked. "You do work with mostly coma patients Daniel, so your basis of comparison is low." She said as she was putting away her equipment and walking over to Daniel's computer. "Wow, you weren't kidding!"

"Susan, don't let this distract you. I will see you in the lab later, go..."

"Geeze, has he always been this bossy?" Susan asked Cliff.

"You noticed too?" Cliff laughed. "And stubborn to a fault once he sets his mind on something he wants."

"I'm not the only stubborn one here," Daniel chimed in.

"That kind of neural activity would be perfect for..." Susan began but Daniel interrupted with, "Susan, don't you need to reconfigure the ICMod for Amy?" He turned away from the computer, crossing his arms on his chest and tapping his foot.

She was obviously intrigued. Cliff wanted to know what she wanted to use him for, but Daniel was not happy with her attention on Cliff. That only made him smile even bigger at his older brother.

"You're right, Daniel. I'll get started right away," she said and patted Cliff on the shoulder. "It'll have to wait until later then. Charlie, thank you for being such an ideal patient. I'll be back in a few days with the upgrades."

Cliff watched Susan leave the room then noticed Daniel was glaring at him. That made Cliff wonder if the EEG could read his mind and not just his brain activity.

Chapter 9

Amy On An Escapade

It was here! Susan held the highly anticipated yellow envelope in her shaky (caffeine-induced) hands. I'd been three weeks of 12-hour days, 7 days a week and multiple test configurations. And an ungodly amount of coffee. But now she was finally able to try-out her adapted ICMod on a coma patient.

All she'd had to go on was the diagram for a recent USPO patent, and her knowledge of how the nervous system interacted with micro-electrodes. She was trying something different, not just simple pulses of DC energy, but waves of complex signals at varying frequencies and power levels. She wanted to have the option of both simple DC and complex waves just in case one worked better than the other.

It took everything she knew to make it work. She'd needed to get the specifications to her friends in Idaho at least a week in advance of when they planned to put in the implant. Since then there'd been nothing to do but tweak the software and anxiously wait for the updated ICMod to arrive. And it was finally here!

"Ready?" Daniel suddenly said from behind her, startling her and making her drop the package in her hands. Thankfully he had good reflexes and was able to snag it before it hit the ground.

"Yes, when do you want to install the implant? Knowing you it will be this afternoon." Susan was talking rapidly due to caffeine jitters. It also made her voice have a bit of a squeaky vibrato. Plus, lack of sleep always made her a bit talkative. "It's this afternoon isn't it? Now, I bet it's now? I bet you want to install it now. I'm ready, let's go! You're ready, right?"

"Yes, we can go immediately. I've had two interns and another doctor on call for the last few days waiting on your package. When they can get here, we can begin. I've already paged them."

"You're very, umm, how do I put it? In control?" Susan said. He was so commanding, competent, efficient ... he wasted no time and he seemed a step ahead of everyone else. Everyone except his brother of course. She still hadn't quite figured Cliff out.

"Is that a bad thing?" Daniel asked, intrigued and sipping on his coffee.

"No, quite the opposite." Indeed, his ability to command any situation practically drove her crazy with desire and she wanted to tear that white coat off of him and ... Wow, pull it together Susan! She thought as she pulled the rubber hair band she kept on her wrist and let it go. "It's probably a good trait for a brain surgeon to have – being in control, having everything figured out."

"Ha! Yeah, you don't say?" he laughed. He looked sideways at the rubber band on her wrist, he still hadn't asked why she started wearing it over a week ago. "Where is Cliff? I thought I would find him with you, it seems I have no control when it comes to him."

"No one does, he's all over the place. We should call him wheels, though I'm not sure he'd like that," she said and then saw Daniel shaking his head vigorously. "Well, he was here earlier, asking a million questions about the software updates ... I don't know where he went."

"I'm sorry, I've been trying to keep him away but..."

"No need to be sorry, I like his company. He's very sweet."

"Oh?"

"Yes. The other day he brought me flowers, lilies. Oh, and he also got me chocolates – my favorite Belgian ones. And he's always getting me lunch and asking how I'm doing, how my work is coming along. He's attentive..."

"He's just trying to distract you."

"Oh? Is that it? Just distracting me?" She didn't know what was going on between the brothers, but it seemed they were fighting over her these last few weeks and she liked every second of it.

Daniel opened his mouth to say something but a vibration at his waist caught his attention. He pulled off the little, black, square pager clipped to his belt and said, "It appears as if the other doctors are ready, it's time."

The two headed over to the patient quarters and ran into Cliff about to go into Amy's room. "So, you got the news?" Daniel asked as they approached, holding up the package in his hand.

"Yes, of course. I thought you were already in here, actually. I was looking for you," Cliff said, positioning himself between them and the door to Amy's room.

"Well, whatever you have in mind for me is going to have to wait. We were about to move her into the operating room," Daniel declared impatiently.

"Already? Are you sure you don't want to run a few more tests?" Cliff asked, then looked to Susan for support. "You're ready?"

"Yes, we're ready. Hopefully we'll all be celebrating tonight when it's over. Don't worry, we're only installing the device today and turning it on to make sure it works. We don't want to stress the patient too much in one day," she answered, dropping her mouse into his lap when she leaned over to console him by patting him on the shoulder. Then she went to grab it back but thought better of it – reaching for his crotch was not exactly lady-like.

Cliff breathed a sigh of relief, while Daniel had the opposite reaction – clenching his fists and putting on a strained smile. She looked from brother to brother, a bit confused. Daniel reached down into Cliff's lap to retrieve her mouse then handed it to her along with the package.

"Let's go," he said, walking around to behind Cliff's wheelchair and moving it out from in front of Amy's door. "Cliff, shouldn't you be wearing your mods? Why are you still in this thing?"

"The god forsaken legs are too bulky and unresponsive. I hate them. I want something that feels like my own legs, in my mind and in my body."

"What you are asking for simply doesn't exist..."

"Yet!" Cliff interjected. "Daniel, I know if we work together we can make them!"

"Yes, yes, of course ... but for now at least try to wear the ones we have created so far to get used to them, okay? Have some of my coffee here if you need a smidge of, you know ...

nerve." Daniel said, giving his brother a wink and handing him his grey thermos.

"Nerve, right..."

Was that an inside joke? she thought.

"Next time I see you, you'd better be in the prosthetic mods," Daniel then pushed his little brother down the hall in the opposite direction saying: "Now go, we have work to do!"

~ ~ ~

There was a whistling sound, like a train in the distance coming closer and closer. Except, it never came. Amy tried to open her eyes, to look around and see if the sound was coming from behind her and found that her entire body was paralyzed. Fear gripped her. Her whole body was now vibrating to the sound of the distant roaring whistle in her ears. She felt her breathing, her heart beating hard in her chest and the numbness of pure immobility. Behind her eyes she imagined the train or whirlwind that was making the sound coming for her, but it never came. Her mind was trying to make sense of the vibrations in her body, she felt out-of-sync. Then the frightening roar surrounded her and she wanted to scream. After a few seconds she realized she was still alive. It had consumed her and she still felt her body vibrate but it was in sync with the roar in her mind and ringing in her ears.

Why couldn't she move? She wanted desperately to move something. She focused on her eyes, but nothing. What kind of monster was holding her eyes closed? It was as if each inch of her body was made of lead, sealed in cement. She wanted to weep in frustration, to cry out.

She started to hear voices echoing around her, getting clearer through the whistling roar and ringing rush that filled the dark void in her mind. A male voice, almost familiar, was speaking. She focused on his voice. He was saying something about increased brain waves ... Another voice, a woman, chimed in excitedly asking to ... continue testing?

Amy felt a sharp jolt in her head that left her wanting to scream but she couldn't. She couldn't even weep. What had they done? Was there something in her brain??? She felt her skull vibrating, the vibrations getting stronger and stronger and then her body began to convulse uncontrollably.

She felt herself bite her own tongue and could taste the blood, acrid and filling her mouth. She wanted to shout for them to stop but couldn't even control her tongue to stop it from getting bit again and again. The blood and her tongue were choking her.

Hands came from nowhere, touching her body, holding her down. They were foreign and felt plastic. Gloves? They shoved something into her mouth. Her eyes flung open on their own and started to move side to side. She could hardly see anything. A light above, blurry. It was stark and glaring, and it hurt as her pupils tried to adjust. She tried to blink and couldn't.

The jolting vibrations in her head abruptly ended, and her body convulsed a few more times and then stopped as well. She was still paralyzed. Her eyes were left open, but she could still hardly see and she had no control.

The familiar male voice was talking again. Was he talking to her? She could barely make out what he said from the ringing echoes in her ears and head. But, she concentrated all she could on his voice. Then she heard him say clearly "I think she is locked-in. We need to stop!" and afterwards there was nothing as her consciousness faded in a pleading whisper.

~ ~ ~

"I'm so sorry, Daniel..." Susan began but Daniel raised his hand to stop her from continuing. He was merely sitting there next to the hospital bed, staring at Amy, holding her hand.

"It's ... it's okay," he said at last as he stood up slowly, laying Amy's hand softly on the bed. "We are making progress, it will all be worth it when she's back with us at last."

"I can make some modifications ... I read something about music being particularly effective and..."

"Yes, I've tried music therapy on some of the less severe cases. Occasionally it seems to be effective, but it was never very reliable."

"It isn't exactly music therapy I was going to suggest."

"What do you have in mind?"

"Well, I was wondering what would happen if we played music transposed to lower frequencies that resonate within the brain cavity?"

"Go on."

"Maybe couple that with similar frequency combinations coming from inside via the ICMod, say in the Theta or Beta brainwave range? On very low power, of course."

"Yes, I was going to suggest lowering the power as well." The scowl he was shooting her was probably in reference to the jolt that had caused Amy to go into convulsions. She had no idea how an extra 0 ended up in a few lines of her code that ran the process of stepping down the voltage. Instead of going down, it had gone up to an unsafe level, one that could have caused permanent damage with the amount of current it was drawing. She'd had to frantically take manual control over the program to bring the voltage back to a safe level.

"By introducing sound with lower resonate waves in a familiar pattern we might stimulate a varied response across the brain. How does that sound?" Susan asked, then laughed at herself. "How does that sound, ha ..." Daniel did not look amused. "See, I'm talking about sound and said 'how does that sound' ..."

"Yes, I know. It's just not funny." Daniel was still upset, clearly. He usually found her banter somewhat amusing, or at least pretended to. "When can you start the modifications?"

"No need, I built-in the capability already. I simply need to select a musical arrangement and do the transposition. I anticipate it would be ideal if the song was something familiar to her, that she knew from her childhood. Do you know a suitable song? As her childhood friend?"

"I'll need to think about that. She should rest for today. It must have been frightening for her to be locked-in like that."

"I can only imagine ... I'm not even sure what 'locked-in' is, exactly." To her it looked like they had awoken Amy. She had moved and opened her eyes. Just when she thought it was successful, Daniel had gotten frantic and made her stop the program completely.

"It is a state of consciousness between a coma and full awareness. Like purgatory in the body. Where you are aware of your body and your environment but completely incapacitated. Some patients can control the movement of their eyes, but it seemed she couldn't even do that. Her brain was showing close to normal activity, a conscious level. So, she was aware … for the first time in over a decade. And yet, unable to move or talk. That must have been terrifying. I would hate to put her through that again, or worse, leave her in that state."

"Tomorrow then?" Susan asked, but instantly felt callous at the suggestion when Daniel's shoulders visibly slumped and he looked back over at Amy … longingly? "How close were you two, exactly? Sorry if I'm being too personal. I get the feeling you are very connected."

"She was…" he began to speak but looked like he didn't know the words or didn't want to admit something. "She was my first true love. We met as children and became especially close. I didn't have too many friends growing up and she was my best friend. She is special to me."

Wow, was he in love with Amy? Susan thought. It was starting to make sense why he was so protective and sensitive when it came to her.

"Did you wake her up?" Cliff said loudly breaking the silence between them as he entered the room. He was wearing his prosthetics and the clanging sound they made on the floor was a sharp interruption to the tense conversation Susan and Daniel were having.

"Those look fantastic! And look, are you taller than me?" Daniel said as he stood adjacent to his brother and put his hand above his head to measure the height difference with his fingers. "Wow, I'd say a full inch taller. How is the movement? Walk around!"

"Yes, sir," Cliff replied, sarcastically, and smiled over at Susan.

Susan gave him a shrewd nod – she knew how commanding Daniel could be.

Cliff regulated the forward motion of each leg with a small red button he had embedded into his fingerless, leather gloves. There was a rhythmic pulse to the movement from the hydraulics, and it was somewhat jerky. So much so that Cliff was visibly straining to keep from wobbling. He moved about the room quickly though, taking large strides. "I can work out the hydraulics to smooth out the motion, but the delay is bothersome between the switch and the leg."

"I told you, I will work on the neural interface when Amy is awake," Daniel said, looking perturbed again and sitting back down at his chair next to Amy's bed.

"We're close. She opened her eyes and moved today. We have a plan for tomorrow." Susan explained.

"She moved?"

"Convulsed, really." Susan was still ashamed that her program almost killed Amy. "There was a small glitch in the program. It won't happen again, I promise."

"She looks fine though, Susan. I'm sure you can easily fix whatever went wrong with the voltage."

"Did she say something went wrong with the voltage?" Daniel looked up at his brother and his jaw was set, fists clinched.

"I think he could gather that from the fact that she convulsed, Daniel," Susan wasn't sure why he was so suspicious of Cliff. Did he really suspect intentional foul play?

"What is the plan for tomorrow? More electro-shock therapy? Isn't that what you are, in essence, doing?" Cliff asked, with the typical disdain he always showed when it came to Amy.

"We're going to use music synergistically. But we need a song that will work. Something familiar to her, and I can't think of anything," Daniel replied, forlorn.

"What about that Janet Jackson song 'Escapade' that she loved so much?" Cliff offered. Daniel tensed up and become visibly angry at the suggestion, staring at Cliff with daggers in his eyes. "What? That might shock her back into life."

"What's the matter? Why is that song..." Susan began but was quickly interrupted by Daniel.

"Cliff knows exactly why," he said.

"If it is a strong memory, that could be enormously helpful Daniel. We should try it." Susan explained. The more of a connection someone had with a song, the more brain activity would be stimulated when listening to it. Everyone knew that who knew anything about music therapy.

"Okay ... if you think it would work, we can try it tomorrow," Daniel said tentatively.

"Why tomorrow?" Cliff asked.

"She needs a break, we have put her through an unforgiveable ordeal today," Daniel replied.

"So, you can push me around and make me do whatever. You have me running around in quasi-formed prosthetics and drinking 'coffee' just to move them but your precious Amy gets a break just because she had a few extra jolts?"

"She was locked-in..." Susan began and was interrupted by Cliff. These guys really liked to interrupt her!

"I don't care. All you're doing is playing music. Waiting is just wasting an entire day of my life where we could be moving forward. Have some balls!" Cliff ranted.

"Wow, you're a selfish ass, aren't you?" Daniel retorted, standing and walking up to be face to face with Cliff.

"Play the music! Wake her up! Get it over and done with, now!" Cliff demanded. "I'm sick of waiting around and wasting my time here."

"Cliff, remember I still need to find and configure the song," Susan said. The guys were about an inch from each other's face and had their fists ready. She had no idea how to calm them down.

"I have it on my iPod, we can download the mp3 right now." Cliff pulled out the small white device from his pocket and held it up. Neither Susan or Daniel responded, they were both speechless. So, Cliff took the opportunity to head over to the computer and begin downloading.

Daniel was still tense, and the latest bit of information made him look even more angry with his brother. But, he sat back down on his chair next to the bed. He kept staring at Amy with a longingness that Susan was starting to find irksome. "Do it," he finally said.

Why would he be mad that his brother had 'Escapade' by Janet Jackson on his iPod? It must be another inside thing between brothers that she didn't get, like the coffee.

"I'll start the transposition," she took control of the computer from Cliff after he finished the download. She thought she saw him quickly close another screen, though it might have been iTunes.

Cliff stepped away and back towards Daniel. "The sooner this is over and done, the better, for everyone."

"We'll play the song from the speaker at the same time as I generate the respective internal waves," Susan said. "The combination, along with a micro-shock to the neural network near the vagus nerve, should have some effect. So, prepare yourself."

Both Susan and Cliff were looking at Daniel for a command, or a movement, or anything to say he was ready. He was as still as granite. This was unlike him to not take charge. But it seemed that when it came to Amy he was a different man. Unsure, unsteady.

"Oh, come on!" Cliff said and then reached across Susan to hit start.

The music began to play. There was no response. Susan was too afraid to touch the voltage regulation after last time, so she simply let the program continue. Cliff was staring at her with a blank expression and Daniel's eyes were locked on Amy.

About a minute into the song, Susan decided to increase the microcurrent intensity manually, being extra careful about how many 0's were involved at each step up.

Amy's hand began to twitch and Daniel leaned over her, taking hold of her hand. At about 3 minutes into the song, when Janet yelled 'Let's Go!' Amy sat straight up, screamed and reached her hand out into the air so fast that it hit Daniel right in the face and knocked him off of his chair.

Daniel was on the floor and Amy was sitting up, looking around the room. When she saw Cliff's legs, she gasped in a raspy voice. "Oh my god! What happened? Who are you? Where am I? What happened to my voice?" Her speech was barely more than a horse whisper, but discernable nonetheless.

"You were in a terrible accident Amy. What is the last thing you remember?" Daniel asked, sitting back in his chair and holding onto his bloody nose. "Cliff, can you get me a tissue?"

Cliff brought him the whole box and remained standing between Amy and Daniel. Daniel shoved one tissue up each of his nostrils and then held his head back.

"Cliff? Like little Cliff? You ... your legs ... and you're so much older ... Daniel? Is that you, Daniel?" Amy asked, in shock while squinting her eyes and blinking repeatedly. She then held her head and laid back down onto the bed with a soft moan. Her voice was getting louder but still sounded extremely horse.

"Yes, you've been in a coma for over a decade," Daniel explained.

"A decade? Where are my parents? Mimi? Oh my god, Mimi?" Amy was crying in between words.

"Your parents died in a car crash not long after your accident. Your dog Mimi, I don't know ... she was old even then, so I don't expect..." Daniel stopped talking. Amy was already enormously upset about finding out she was in a coma (who wouldn't be?) and telling her about her parents and Mimi dying was probably not the first thing she should be hearing right now.

"My parents are dead?!?" Amy wailed in between guttural, choking sobs. It sounded odd with the bright music of 'Escapade' still playing in the room. Susan didn't want to shut the music off just yet, because she didn't know what would happen if she did.

Everyone in the room was silent, except for Amy. No one knew what to say.

"What? What happened to me?" Amy asked, after weeping for a short time and then feeling the top of her shaved head.

"You fell off of a cliff chasing that stupid dog and hit your head." Cliff insisted. Daniel hit him in the leg and then regretted it instantly as the clang against his knuckle sounded like it would leave a solid bruise. Cliff just looked down and smiled as Daniel tried to flick the pain away while biting his lip.

"I did?" Amy asked, closing her eyes and wiping her tears. "I fell off of a cliff?" she opened her eyes and squinted at Daniel, "I can't remember, why can't I remember?"

"It will all come back to you in time, don't worry," Daniel said soothingly while rubbing his bruised knuckle and scowling at his brother.

"Well, she did hit her head pretty hard. I'm sure not all of her memories will come back. Some won't be correct either, I'm sure," Cliff said. "Who knows what kind of jumbled mess her mind is in, or what crazy things she might think."

"Actually, we should see what happens without the ICMod stimulus," Susan said. "Daniel, Cliff? Ready?" Both guys nodded together so she hit the off switch on the computer.

There was dead silence in the room, no one was even breathing. Amy lay there with a blank expression on her pretty face, tears rolling down her pink cheeks and pouty lips. Susan never realized how much she looked like Goldilocks until now.

"I felt a buzzing in my head, and it stopped. What was that?" Amy asked, forehead scrunched. Everyone let out a sigh of relief, breathing again.

"It's a microchip we inserted to stimulate brain activity," said Susan. "It is what brought you out of your coma."

"Who are you?" Amy asked, peering at Susan quizzically. "Do I know you too?"

"No. My name is Dr. Susan Aldean, and I'm the one that designed the microchip," she answered, proudly. "Daniel is the one who installed it though."

"Wow, you must be super smart," Amy said, swallowing hard. "Thank you for waking me up. Thank you both."

"Yes, she is remarkable." Cliff kissed Susan on the cheek, unexpectantly. She blushed and looked over to Daniel for a reaction but he was just staring at Amy, in awe. Were those tears in his eyes?

"Well, it looks like my work here is done. Daniel?" She didn't know what she was hoping for, but at this moment her heart was breaking because Daniel wouldn't even look at her.

"Come on Susan, let's leave them alone. I have an idea for what we can do with the ICMod next," Cliff said as he put his hand on the small of Susan's back and led her out of the room. As she walked out of the door, she turned her head to see that Amy and Daniel were now holding hands and looking at each other, longingly. It was all so sickeningly sweet.

Chapter 10

Wedding Bells and Cells

The weather was always pleasant in California, and Susan needed a break from the lab. So, a jog in the sunshine was perfect medicine for the dark mood she'd been in. As she was coming back home from her run, she decided to stop and check the mail. Her endorphin levels were high as she thumbed through the contents of her mailbox, humming to the music in her headphone. That is until her fingers stopped on a fancy envelope. She opened it to find an invitation to the wedding of Dr. Daniel Jahren and Amy Shipley. She almost threw the letter in the trash instantly. Then she thought about stomping on it – burning it maybe? The runner's high she had was now gone and all she felt was rage and frustration.

She walked into her house and laid down flat on the couch, tossing the mail on the coffee table and staring blankly at the ceiling. Six years and she still felt the same. Would she ever get closure? The more she thought about it, the more she thought she should probably go to the wedding. Maybe she would be able to finally move on? Cliff had been begging her to come to Colorado for years to help him with his family business. But it was his family, particularly his brother Daniel, that she didn't want to have any business with!

After they had awoken Amy, it was as if Susan no longer existed in Daniel's eyes. What a prick! She thought.

She was perfectly satisfied with her life in LA She had been enjoying great success with her ICMods being implanted to help Parkinson's patients and had even gotten FDA approval. Now, ICModTech was using her devices everywhere and for various application. The company was at the leading edge in the research of patients with severe and un-responsive ADHD, anxiety, depression and even epilepsy.

Cliff even had her design a modified ICMod for amplifying his brain signals to control his prothesis. It was working out well, at least that is what he kept saying. She steered clear of him, mostly because he reminded her of his brother. Daniel the prick! Urgh!

Why couldn't she just feel the way she did about Daniel, for Cliff? He was brilliant and handsome too. His brain was fascinating – she had never seen anything like it. It made her want to do more research on dreamers, which is what she had been studying for the past few years. The only thing that stood out about Cliff was that he had strong, frequent, lucid dreams in comparison to most people. He was more intelligent too, but this was beyond that. The anterior of his prefrontal cortex was dense, and when he slept his brain lit up like the fourth of July.

After conducting an open call for lucid dreamers, she found that her intuition was correct. Many shared the same metacognition abilities and brain density. None so remarkable as Cliff's, but all similar. She was thinking about looking into Native American dream-walkers next, because Daniel mentioned once that his Native American nanny said Cliff was a dream-walker.

With a new microchip, she might be able to project what these strong dreamers where seeing onto a computer. Basically, because they had such conscious and vivid dreams, their brain waves were more stable and focused. The strong signals would help her to hone in exactly what algorithms she needed to project thought. It would be the next step in human evolution, projected thought!

Susan heard the song 'Dreamweaver' play from the kitchen, that could only mean one thing. Cliff was calling her cell phone, again. Likely to ask her to come work for his company, again. She grudgingly got up and picked up the flip phone from the counter and put it on speaker. "The answer is 'NO,' Cliff," she said before he could say anything.

"Hi, Susan. It's Daniel." With those words Susan's heart skipped a beat and her mind went blank. "Are you there? Hello?" She went to sit down on the stool next to her kitchen counter, almost falling off but then catching herself.

Susan had to clear her throat, it felt like it had a knot. "Hi. Yes, I'm here."

"Good. I am sorry we haven't kept in touch. I've tried calling, but you always seem to be busy."

"Yes, I am very busy."

"I'm sorry, Susan. I never meant to hurt you."

Tears started to well-up in Susan's eyes. He waited six years to call and tell her this? "I'm fine. Why are you calling?"

"Well, I knew you would answer from Cliff's phone and I had to talk to you. It would really mean a lot to Amy and me if you came to the wedding. She adores you and she thinks you are 'The Angel that saved me with microchips' she says." He said this with such joy in his voice that Susan almost threw the phone. "Did you get the invitation?"

"Yes, it came in the mail today."

"Good, will you at least think about coming?" he waited for a response but Susan was biting her lip, trying to hold back a torrent of words she wanted to say. "Cliff misses you, he would love it if you came. He might try to kidnap you and make you work in his lab, ha ha."

Susan was shocked, did he really just say that? Cliff probably would try to keep her there!

"I'm just kidding. I wouldn't let him kidnap you, Susan. I promise. Honestly, he does miss you. We all do. Will you at least consider coming to Colorado for the wedding?"

"I'll think about it," she said at last.

"Good, I'm glad. Amy almost wanted to make you a bridesmaid, can you believe it?"

Susan scoffed. She could believe it. Amy was so adorably innocent that it was hard not to love her, even if she was the only thing standing between Susan and the man of her dreams.

Daniel continued with, "but I talked her out of it."

"Thanks!" she exclaimed, the last thing she wanted to be was a bridesmaid.

"It would mean so much to her if you came. I'll let you go now. I know you're busy."

"I'm..." Susan began, but was at a loss for words. "I'm glad you called," she realized she was as she said the words. "Goodbye," she said and it felt like letting go.

"Goodbye."

Susan sat there, stunned. She felt like a weight had been lifted off of her shoulders. Did she finally let go of her feelings for Daniel? Could she move on?

Dreamweaver started playing again and she picked up her phone, this time with less confidence as to who was on the other end and said, "Hello?"

"It's me, Cliff! So, you're coming to Colorado?!!?"

"Wow. Patience is not one of your virtues is it, Cliff?"

"You know it. I've been dying to show you around our new facilities. We've been hiring like mad lately, getting the prosthetics into manufacturing. We could most definitely use a brilliant engineer like yourself on our staff and I would ensure a weekly bonus of Belgian chocolates was on your desk."

"Daniel said you were going to kidnap me."

"Oh? Daniel said I was going to kidnap you, did he?"

It sounded like Daniel got hit with something. She heard an "Owe" and something or someone falling to the floor with a thud. "Hello!" she finally said to get Cliff back on track with the conversation.

"Oh. Sorry, Susan. Daniel accidently knocked over a vase just now. I'm so happy you will be coming up! There is so much I want to show you. How have the studies on the dreamers been going? Found anyone as good as me yet?"

"No, you're still the odd ball out. But I have found a few interesting ... similar ones ... but..." She wanted to say that she hadn't decided to come up yet when Cliff interrupted, as usual.

"Good! I've been talking to a guy in Japan named Pat Morichi, who specializes in harnessing the power of blood flow for nano devices. We might be able to start powering your ICMods with something far more sustainable than lithium-ion batteries. What do you say?"

"That all sounds very interesting, but I have a life here in LA and..." And what? she thought. She had a Siamese cat named Franklin and an aloe Vera plant that she sometimes called Bo-Bo ... both would be fine in Colorado. If she was finally over Daniel ... It did sound like compelling work and she could do her dream-walker studies anywhere. Heck, she would probably find some in the large Native American population near their facility. But, was she over Daniel?

"Just promise me you'll give me a few days when you come up for the wedding and I promise you I won't have to kidnap you to make you want to stay, okay?"

"Okay ..."

"Fantastic, see you soon!" he said, gleefully.

Urgh, did she just agree to go to the wedding?!? Wow, Cliff sure was manipulative! She always seemed to say 'yes' when she meant 'no' with him. That's why she liked to start the conversation with a 'NO' to get it out before he could stop her. At least she had six months to decide how she felt about Daniel before the wedding and prepare herself.

Did Cliff say nano blood motors? Or machines? Was it chemical or physical? That sounded intriguing and would help with some of the heating and power problems she'd been having with the smaller mods. Maybe she should email him now, just for a little more information.

~ ~ ~

Daniel couldn't be happier. He was sitting in the hotel lobby bar, sipping on a glass of sparkling water and greeting family and friends as they stopped by to check into the hotel for his wedding. He had everything he had ever dreamed of. A beautiful bride to be. A nice house on a hill. He'd even convinced his family to stop doing dangerous and illegal work – except for the coffee, they couldn't give that up. They had a legitimate research and development company now, focused on prosthetics development. It was much better than the mud wrap and mask company that his parents had used as a front for their illicit research for years.

Tomorrow he would be married and starting a whole new chapter of his life with Amy. When she had first awoken, her mind was that of a 15-year-old girl and she was all alone in the world. He had no idea how to take care of her himself. So, he had sent her to a boarding house for women. A place where she could learn and adapt to the world. Their feelings for each other only grew stronger over the distance. They would email each other every day like they had written to each other as children.

She still didn't know about his family's ... umm, unique? ... ways of viewing research, but she never needed to because they had all promised to do the right thing when Daniel came back to help with the prosthetics neural networking. As far as she was concerned, they were all ethically saints and Cliff had lost his legs in a car accident.

"So, do you want the best man speech tonight at the rehearsal or tomorrow at the wedding?" Cliff said, walking up to Daniel and putting his hand on his shoulder with a tight grip.

"Ouch! That's quite the grip you have there," Daniel replied. "Are you nervous?"

"Sorry," he responded, loosening his hold. "Not really, there isn't much to say: 'Glad you're awake Amy. Now go have fun making babies with my brother?'"

"Funny."

"Seriously, what do you want me to say?"

"I don't know. I still have to work on my vows."

"What? Aren't you mister 'poetry?' I would have thought your vows were written months ago!"

"It's just that these words are more important than any other. It is a promise for the rest of my life, and I keep my promises."

"That you do, and she is lucky to have you!" Cliff said, patting Daniel on the back so hard it made him cough.

"Cliff, are you trying to crack my back?!?

"Sorry, umm ... I need to go started writing my speech. See you later tonight!" Cliff hurried away, pulling down his sleeves as if to hide something on his arm. He was behaving oddly and that was never a good sign, knowing his brother.

"Is this seat taken?" a soft, female voice asked next to him.

"Susan!" he exclaimed, turning to see his old friend. He thought about giving her a hug but it felt awkward so he just put out his hand for a handshake. That felt even more awkward so he pulled it back at the last minute. She went to take the hand while she was about to sit on the bar stool and when he pulled it back she fell forward, almost landing in his lap.

"Sorry!" They both said at the same time. You could cut the tension with a knife.

She had been in town for a week. But it practically seemed as if she had been avoiding him because she hadn't said a word past "Hi" when passing through the halls of their new facilities with Cliff.

"Your research laboratory is amazingly state of the art. You must have good investors," Susan began and hailed the bartender with, "I'll have a scotch on the rocks, make it a double. Thank you!"

"Yes, the funding is ... not important. How have you been doing? Has Cliff convinced you to stay?"

"He is trying, he can be very convincing."

"Tell me about it!"

There was awkward silence again. The bartender returned with the drink and Susan downed it in one gulp and said, "Another!"

"Wow, are you okay?"

"Fine. I'm fine. I just spent the day with Amy. Looking at all the flowers and wedding décor. She even had me and a few other ladies from the boarding house she went to making these little fans that have the wedding program on them. Adorable. Really, quite adorable."

The bartender was back with another drink and this time Daniel put his hand over the top of the glass before Susan could gulp it down. "You don't look fine, Susan." She looked like she was about to cry, actually.

"Did I ever even have a chance, Daniel? I know I was just too successful. If I had waited, maybe no woken Amy up..."

"What do you mean? You saved her life! I had given up on her and was going to leave ... who knows what UCLA would have decided to do."

Susan slid the glass from under Daniel's hand and started to sip the scotch, not taking her eyes off of him. She appeared as if she was wondering something about him. He was completely muddled and felt anything he said was wrong. He had apologized for leading her on. He hadn't meant to. He had started to have legitimate feelings for her before Amy was awake but once she was back Amy was all he could think about. It wasn't his fault. It wasn't her fault. It just was. He had spent over a decade, losing hope every day, working to get Amy back. How could he explain that to Susan?

"You're a remarkable and beautiful woman," he said at last. "I'm sure there have been plenty of men who have tried to make you theirs, right?"

Susan scoffed, sipping her scotch. "There is this one guy. He's a dream-walker, like your brother. He volunteered for one of my research projects. He is part Native American, part Irish. He's a charmer. He'd asked me out a few times before I finally said yes about a month ago. His brain is unlike any other and surpasses even Cliff's."

"Don't tell Cliff! You know how competitive he can be and how proud he is of that special brain of his. Why is it that you two never got together? He has been pinning for you for years!"

"I don't know ... I guess I don't trust who I am around him?" she stopped to think for a minute, taking draws from the scotch. "I get caught up in his schemes and ideas so quickly. I don't want to be another one of his li'l groupies. Have ya seen the lates set? Those three scientis tha never leave hisside at the facilaty? Is ... issa ... is like they worshap him or somethan, is kinda creepy!"

"No, I never noticed. Are you sure you're okay? Are you coming to the rehearsal dinner? I need to start heading over to the restaurant now."

"No. Is think I'ves had enough weddi..." she hiccupped and continued with, "excuse me, 'stuff' for the day. I'lls see ya tomorrow," she said as she shot back the last of the scotch and stumbled back towards the lobby elevators.

"Do you need help getting to your room?" Daniel yelled after her, concerned because she was obviously drunk and upset.

"No, no, no ... iz fine! Go! Go to yur Amy!" she exclaimed as she got into the elevator and left.

The hotel was fairly safe, but he asked a bellman to go check on her just in case before he headed out the door.

There was a garden patio set aside for the wedding party at Dominic's steak house and it looked like he might be the last to arrive. The summer air was warm in the Colorado desert even this late in the evening and today was particularly hot. There were misters and lights hung along the beams overhead that cast a foggy shadow over the area. Three large banquet tables were shaped in a U for the party, and every seat was full. His bride-to-be was sitting right in the center. She was in a delicate, pink, ruffled, mermaid shaped dress with a low back and no sleeves. He long curly blonde hair was set in a twist to the side and her bare, tanned shoulders shone in the candlelight from the table. She was handing out gifts to her bridesmaids when he came behind her and kissed her gently on the cheek, whispering in her ear, "You look exquisite, my dear."

"Oh, you finally decided to arrive?" she replied back, jabbing him with one finger in the chest. "Where have you been? Someone said they saw you in the hotel lobby bar with another woman, getting drunk!"

"Me? Getting drunk? I've never had a drop of alcohol in my life!" he laughed.

"Oh, that's right," she said, abashed. "Well, you're still late. Sit down so we can get started." She motioned to the wedding planner they had hired, and that must have been a que for the activities to start. Daniel had no idea what was going to happen. He had left the planning to Amy. She had very specific ideas and he did not want to get in the way of making her happy by throwing in any of his ideas in the mix, even if everything did turn out pink – which it did.

"Tonight, we celebrate the union of our two most beloved friends, Amy and Daniel," the neatly dressed, pant-suited planner said. She then clapped her hands to generate applause from the crowd. "We would like to start off the night showing a video prepared by the family to highlight their very special relationship." She pressed a button and a white screen came down. She turned on a projector and it showed pictures of the two of them as children.

Watching the display, Amy went from laughing out loud to giggling and back, and Daniel found it hard to not look at her dimpled smile the whole time. "Your mother found some hilarious pictures of the two of you boys as children. And Miss

Tinny, I had forgotten about her! Where is she?" she whispered to Daniel.

"She had a falling out with the family a few years back..." he didn't want to tell Amy that Tsintah had found out what really happened to Cliff. Then, after getting fired for snaking into a lab, had refused to go anywhere near them. When she found out where they had gotten some of the viral compounds used to derive Tribus they almost had a full Native American uprising on their hands. He had to think of something to say to Amy, quick. "Cultural differences. About how we were using the land near the mine."

"That is sad, I liked her very much. Maybe I can work out an environmental plan that the native tribes will like? It could be my thing. I could be, like, an ambassador or something."

Daniel kissed her on her forehead, he treasured her optimism. "That sounds lovely, dear."

The pictures continued, until a delightful shot of Amy's old Chihuahua 'Mimi' showed up. Amy gasped, holding her hand over her mouth. Daniel put his arm around her, he could feel her shaking.

"Are you alright?"

"I..." she was fixed at Cliff, eyes wide. Cliff was scowling back at her, fists clenched. He never did like her, but he could at least have some empathy for his soon to be sister-in-law's weak mental condition. They should have never included her dog in the slideshow!

"Turn it off!" Daniel yelled. The planner quickly hit the stop button.

"I..." was all Amy could get out. She started scanning around the room in a daze as if she was lost. "I'm sorry. I think I need to go lay down. Excuse me," she said as she got up to leave.

Amy's maid of honor, Amanda (a pleasant, black lady she had met at the boarding school) got up and said, "I'll make sure she gets safely to her room." She was used to Amy's sudden spells. Even after all these years Amy's mind never fully healed.

Amy reached over and squeezed Daniel's hand, "I'll be alright, I just need to rest." Then she shot a glance over to Cliff and shuddered visibly. Daniel looked at Cliff in confusion, had he done something to Amy?

Cliff noticed Daniel was staring at him and quickly pulled away from the table. He tossed his napkin in his seat and then stormed off.

The wedding planner didn't know what to do. The bride, maid of honor and best man had just left the table. She was just standing there completely flabbergasted.

Thankfully Daniel's mom stood up and gave a toast to try and ease the tension. "My handsome son was able to awaken sleeping beauty; but, alas, she still needs her beauty sleep!" she said as she clanged the side of her champagne glass with a spoon. "To young love, and real-life fairy-tale endings!"

Daniel's father followed with another speech about how proud he was of his son and how he hoped to have many grandchildren. The night continued with him having to engage with relatives he had never heard of before and colleagues of his mother's he had never met. The entire time he was worried about Amy. He was also disturbed that his brother had not returned so he could ask him why Amy seemed frightened of him so suddenly. He was able to excuse himself eventually and hurried straight to Amy's room.

Amanda was sitting next to Amy, brushing back her hair with her hand and singing a lullaby when Daniel walked in.

"How is she?" he asked.

Amanda got up and picked up her purse, readying to head out. "She's fine. Simply a little frazzled, you know."

"Yes, I feel better now. Amanda has such a sweet voice. I love hearing her sing." Amy smiled, eyes still closed as she lay in bed.

There was a knock on the door. Daniel opened it to find the bellman with a package. "Another wedding present arrived," he said, handing Daniel a white box with a dark red ribbon. The note just read, "Congratulations!" and nothing else. The bellman was gone before Daniel could ask who it was from.

Amanda took the package and declared, "Oh, how lovely! Amy, do you want to open this one now? I know how much you love presents, it might cheer you up."

"Are you sure that is a good idea? We don't know who it is from." Daniel insisted.

"I'm sure they merely forgot to put their name on it," Amanda scoffed. Amy was already opening the present. Inside was a beautifully decorated ceramic tea pot. "Oh, isn't that a nice gift!"

"Yes, I love tea!" Amy said as she was trying to open the lid but couldn't.

The mental spells left her a bit weak sometimes. Daniel took the teapot and placed it on the counter, saying, "We'll make tea later, dear. Get some rest!"

"I'll be going now. See you tomorrow, Amy! Goodnight!" Amanda exclaimed, sauntering out the door.

Daniel sat down next to Amy and she started to open her mouth to say something when his phone began to ring. It was Cliff. He had a few choice words he wanted to share with him, so he flipped open the phone and walked out into the hallway.

"What did you do to Amy?" he demanded.

"Nothing, what did she say I did?" Cliff replied.

"She didn't say anything. It was just that look you were giving her ... and she was trembling..."

"She has brain damage Daniel, and you know I have never liked her."

"Why did you storm off?"

"I was just mad that I had spent so much time trying to figure out the best man speech and she had to go and ruin it with her little episode."

"What? You're that mad about a speech?"

"Yes, and I'm mad she wouldn't even let you have a bachelor party too. What kind of best man am I anyway that I can't even throw my brother a bachelor party?"

"You know I don't drink Cliff..."

"Well, I do! And you could at least meet me in the lobby bar for a drink, pretend we can have a bachelor party."

"I don't know, Amy is out of it..."

"Oh, let sleeping beauty sleep!"

"Okay, I'll go. Just one drink." Daniel acquiesced.

"Okay, are you heading there now?"

"Yeah, I am already in the hallway."

"Good, see you soon!" Cliff said, hanging up.

Daniel hung up the phone and started to walk towards the lobby but remembered he hadn't said goodbye or given Amy a kiss before leaving. He went back towards the room and right as he reached for the door he heard a loud explosion followed by ringing in his ears. The next thing he knew he was pinned between the door and a hallway shelf. The mirror behind him had shattered into pieces showing thousands of reflections of fire and smoke cascading around him. The pain in his legs was intense and the door holding his body down was on fire. The last thing he saw before losing consciousness was the arm he had used to reach for the door. It was three feet down the hallway, still holding the handle.

Chapter 11

Mindful Mind Full of Mods

There were voices talking in hushed tones. Two women and one man, arguing. The chatter awakened Daniel's mind. The grogginess in his head transitioned to awareness of a heavy body laid down on a hard bed. He opened his eyes to look towards the sounds and could barely make-out three blurry figures coming in and out of focus above him.

"He should have the right to decide what he wants. Just because you are his father, doesn't mean you have the right to make decisions for him," Daniel's mother's voice could be heard clearly from across the room now.

"She's right, let him decide," Susan's voice was subdued, but distinguishable and coming from one of the three figures above him.

"I'm overruled, apparently. It is a moot point, he is awake now regardless: observe," Martin's voice announced from the blurry figure on the right.

"What ... happ ... happened?" Daniel asked. He saw all three figures looking down at him, heads almost touching in a triangle blocking-out the glaring florescent light above and turning them to shadows.

"There was an explosion, son. It appears there was a remote detonation device inside a ceramic container in the hotel room. You're lucky to be alive," Martin said, in somber tones.

"Yes. We're all glad you're alive, honey," Beth said, coming up to his right side while his father was talking, and taking hold of his hand. He realized he couldn't feel his left hand. He winced as an image of his arm in the hallway suddenly flickered in his mind.

"Amy? Is Amy ...??" Daniel already knew the answer before anyone could say a word. Tears began rolling down his cheeks and his chest began to ache.

"I'm so sorry, honey. It was swift, and painless. She was such a lovely girl. She deserved so much more in this life." Beth was unable to hold back tears herself as she spoke.

"Bellman ... he ... he brought us ... a ... a ceramic tea pot ... he might know ..." Daniel was having trouble getting out the words. His throat kept clenching and it felt like his vocal chords where collapsing.

"Yes. Amanda already told the authorities. The bellman said he didn't remember coming to the room when he was held for more questioning by the police," Martin explained. "They did a lie detector test and also found a heavy dose of flunitrazepam in his system. Consequently, they presently have no leads."

"We were all hoping he would remember something for the longest time, but..." Susan said.

"Cliff ...where is Cliff?" Daniel demanded.

"I'm right here, brother," he heard his younger brother's voice coming from the shadow next to his father. "I've been here the whole time. I'm so sorry for what happened to you ... I'm ... so glad you're alive!"

"Did you ... did you..." Daniel couldn't quite bring himself to ask the question that was burning in his brain. Cliff never liked Amy and his actions had been suspicious. But, could he accuse him of such a horrible thing? Of murder?

"Cliff came up with some great ideas for modification for you Daniel. He's quite the wizard when it comes to prosthetics. I can have a master ICMod made for you in no time. It'll have the new nanogenerators we've recently developed. It'll make it to where the mod can be completely hidden, no wires coming out. I will have to go to Japan with Cliff to work it out, but from the papers he sent me..."

"That's right. Susan and I are working together again and we'll have you better than new ... you'll be invincible!" Cliff interjected.

"I promise I'll do everything to make you feel whole again, Daniel." Susan's words were like ice in his chest, highlighting his loss ... not of his body, but in his heart. Amy was gone, he would never feel whole again. Tears rolled down his cheeks without restraint.

"We should let him rest," Beth said.

"Right, we all have work to do," Martin said and the four shadows were gone, replaced by the blurry, bright light of a hospital ceiling.

Daniel closed his eyes and wept until the void of sleep eased him into an oblivion he never wished to wake from.

~ ~ ~

Months passed into years, and years faded away the pain. Everything took longer than anticipated. Technology and the heart never reacted as expected. While Cliff and Susan worked the nanogenerators in Japan, Beth and Martin worked with Daniel to accept his new life. To accept the pain and loss in his heart and in his body. The love they showed him, and to each other, was inspiring. By the time Susan and Cliff came back from Japan, Daniel was ready to try again. To live again.

The new prosthetics they had him try finally trying on today weren't that bad. In fact, they felt like extensions of his own body, only his body felt bulky, heavy. "I see what you mean, Cliff, about the weight," Daniel explained. "I never understood before; but, you're right – it's cumbersome."

"How about the Mod?" Cliff asked. He had started to call the ICModTech microchips Susan created 'Mods.' They'd just gotten back from Japan two days ago with the latest version and installed it within the hour of arrival. Cliff's small team of scientists had spent the last 48 hours calibrating the controls with Susan's direction.

"I feel ... better, and of course it provides seamless control of the prosthetics," Daniel answered, proudly. He didn't know how to explain it, but he felt happier these last few days then he had ever felt in his life. Did Susan add an extra dopamine stimulus package to his Mod? Knowing her, she would, for him, he thought. "I feel too good, really."

"Yeah, the neurotransmitter stimulation can have that effect. You'll get used to it," Cliff smiled.

And then you'll want more!

That was a strange thought, where did it come from? Daniel thought, looking at Cliff, who was grinning like a Cheshire cat. "Did you say something?" Daniel felt Cliff's attention focus inward and away from him.

Is he reading my mind? Daniel heard in is head, only it 'sounded' like Cliff's voice in a strange way.

Are you reading my mind? Daniel asked in his head.

"No," Cliff said aloud. Then realized what had just happened and looked appalled, eyes wide and mouth agape.

"Has this happened to you before, Cliff? With any of the other Mods?" Daniel asked, concerned they had gone too far this time, or that his brother had been keeping the side-effect secret.

"No, I swear!" Cliff exclaimed.

He answered that maybe too quickly? Daniel thought, staring down his brother.

"Why are you swearing?" Susan asked, entering the room with her laptop, glasses having slid down her nose. She was dragging wires behind her that she would no doubt trip over any second and ... Daniel caught her as she tripped. He also snagged the computer she had flung from the air too. "I see the neural network interface is firing well. That arm speed was just as fast as your normal reaction."

"Oh, so you tripped to test the Mod?" Daniel laughed. He had missed her quirkiness, she always kept him on his toes.

"Right, I'm that good," she winked, sarcasm seething.

"Cliff and I were just noticing ... Umm, how can I put this? An unexpected connection? Cliff?" Daniel hoped he might have a better idea of what to ask.

"Our minds ... they appear ... linked..." Cliff was talking too slowly, he was obviously struggling with how to describe it ... or didn't want to.

"We can read each other's mind, Susan. Is that an intentional design element?" Daniel wanted to get directly to the point.

"Holy Mother of God!! No!!!" Susan exclaimed while falling back into the chair behind her and grabbing her forehead. She was in complete shock and disbelief. "What is it like? Do you hear a voice or is it just a perception of thought? An image? Oh My God, this is incredible!"

"I heard him ask me a question as if it was aloud," Cliff relinquished.

"I heard him thinking to himself," Daniel expanded.

"You did?" Cliff asked and Daniel nodded.

"Yes. If I think about it, I can feel a measure of what you are feeling..." Daniel started to concentrate on the impression he had in his head that he was starting to identify as coming from Cliff.

No, no! Please give me my privacy! he heard Cliff scream in his head. The echoes in his skull were deafening. But, what was even stranger, is that it shook him physically as well and the lights began to flicker in the room.

"What was that!?!" Susan asked, looking from brother to brother and up at the flickering lights.

"I ... I don't know..." Daniel said, sitting down next to Susan and rubbing his forehead. It felt like Cliff had punched him with a sonic boom in the center of his brain. Not nice, little brother, he said in his head to Cliff. "What have you done, Susan?" he asked aloud.

"Nothing! I well ... I added a few modifications Cliff and I discussed that might be beneficial for you..."

"Beneficial?" Daniel interjected. What kind of crazy augmentations had Cliff convinced her to put into his brain?

"Yes, but this is unexpected and..." she stopped mid-sentence, eyebrows scrunched while she sat there thinking for a minute. "I'm guessing here ... but, I think because you are so genetically similar, your brain waves may sync better. I saw a study on it once, I think it was on the Discovery Channel? It was on genetically similar people. Identical twins. For instance, they tend to almost be able to read each other's minds ... some say that they do read each other's minds. The Mods enhance your brainwaves to control the prosthetics, and they must be amplifying more than just the ones for motor control."

"I'm not so sure I like this," Daniel finally said, after letting all of that sink-in.

"I'm not so sure I like this, either," Cliff declared, staring at his brother and sending out what felt like a threat to not go into his head or he might be sorry. Cliff then strode out of the room, fists clenched.

"So, you think it is only because we are brothers that this is happening? Are you positive?" Daniel asked.

"No ... I ... umm," she was staring in the direction Cliff had gone. "Maybe ... You can try it on me, let's see," Susan faced Daniel, gazing intently at him and obviously thinking hard about something. Daniel could sense nothing, except his own heart beating faster while peering into her eyes. He felt drawn to her, an attraction that he hadn't felt in a long time. Was it the Mod?

He shook his head.

She moved her chair closer to his and then continued, "Okay, I'm thinking of a number between 1 and 10." Daniel did not hear a single thought, or feeling, or anything coming from Susan other than the warmth of her body and the scent of her orange blossom perfume. It was intoxicating and he suddenly wanted to kiss her but stopped himself.

"Maybe it is the duel Mod interaction? It is probably only because you BOTH have an amplification Mod for your prosthesis. That, combined with the fact that you are genetically similar, could explain the odd interference the two of you are experiencing. Most of the Mod's I've built are for stimulation, not amplification. So that would explain why we haven't seen this kind of thing before," Susan explained, appearing worried. She got up and was checking the hallway Cliff had stormed down.

"Perhaps. We can try-out your theory on another prosthetic patient who has a Mod right now. Do you want to see if Bill can read my mind? It's worth a try. I want to see how far this goes." Daniel had a pretty good idea of what Cliff might have done with the Mod technology, and none of this was likely an accident. He always wanted more – more amplification, more control. Though it was hard to believe that even Cliff was chasing mind reading technology.

Susan nodded and followed him reluctantly down the hallway towards the main facility.

Bill was a veteran who had lost his legs in Afghanistan and volunteered as one of their initial trials a few years ago. He now worked at the facility as one of the operators on the manufacturing line. As they approached, Daniel said in his mind Turn around.

Bill turned around from the shipping bins and greeted them with a big smile, "The miracle-working geniuses! What do I owe the pleasure of your company?"

Say 'Monkey wrench' Daniel said in his head, projecting his thoughts towards Bill.

"Monkey wrench ... sorry, I think I am developing Tourette's! Ha, ha," Bill laughed and looked embarrassed, staring at Daniel quizzically. Daniel could feel Bill's embarrassment, could sense his troubled thoughts.

"I just wanted to check on you and see how you're doing, you look well!" Susan said, then gazed over toward Daniel, unsure of what to say next. She, of course, had no idea what was going on. Daniel wasn't about to tell Bill that he could not only read his thoughts but control them. He did have to give Susan an indication that he was trying-out her theory.

"I'm thinking of a number between 1 and 10, got any idea?" This time Daniel wasn't projecting his thoughts, he was just thinking.

"Three?" Bill guessed. "That was an odd question, was I right? What's up?"

Susan opened her mouth to say something but Daniel put up his hand to silence her. He'd been thinking of the number seven. Now he thought I need to get back to work and projected it at Bill.

"I need to get back to work," Bill said while walking backwards away from them. "It was nice seeing the two of you again. Thank you for the legs, I'm forever grateful!" He turned around and hurried away down the assembly line towards the optical inspection booth that he normally operated.

Daniel waited until they were out of earshot in a nearby hallway, away from any doors or cameras for him to let Susan know what had just happened.

"That can't be right, are you sure?" Susan whispered, loudly.

"I'm sure. I could practically control his mind and he couldn't even read mine. I heard his every thought when I focused on him. I could even feel what he was feeling!" Daniel exclaimed in hushed tones.

“Shushh...” she said, looking around and then up at the camera at the end of hallway. “We need to talk somewhere else, somewhere private.”

“Why?” Daniel asked, suspiciously now wondering exactly what special modifications she used in his Mod. He wouldn’t put it past Cliff to slip something into the programming, but he also felt that the good mood he was in (despite all of this and everything before) had something to do with her.

She tiptoed close to him, raising her chin to his ear and the euphoria that ensued could not be natural. Did he feel this way about her before? “The lake. Noon. Tomorrow. Come alone. It is important. Tell no one and guard your thoughts,” she said as softly and as close to his ear as she could before rushing off.

Daniel watched Susan walking away and tried to sort-out his feelings. Was she always this beautiful? His heart was pounding and his skin was flushed, he felt excited but not worried or anxious. This didn’t sit right in his mind, but he couldn’t quite place why.

What were you two talking about? Cliff demanded in Daniel’s mind. His heart jumped at the sudden invasion but he kept calm.

We were talking about the new Mod, we may need to make an adjustment, Daniel said back in his mind, looking down the hallway to where his brother was standing, only 20 feet away.

I want to show you something, come with me, Cliff said in his head. Daniel felt compelled to follow him, compelled! It made him wonder how much control Cliff hand over his mind after the interaction with Bill.

What interaction with Bill? he heard Cliff ask inside his mind.

I just wanted to see if Susan’s ‘genetically similar’ theory was correct, which it seems to be Daniel lied as he projected an image of Bill being completely confused and thought about him guessing the wrong number. He then tried to guard his thoughts as much as he could by focusing on the objects and things around him. On walking. On the feel of his new legs and arm.

I see, Cliff replied casually in his mind.

Daniel almost felt amusement coming from his brother before there was nothing. Cliff was either good at muting his thoughts or he had none. Daniel tried not to think about protecting thoughts or Bill or Susan or anything and just focused on his new legs as he came closer to Cliff.

They were walking side by side now, toward the elevators in the back that led to another, deeper facility. The rhythmic pulse of their legs was in sync and the metal on metal clank of both of their appendages was ominous entering the dead silent elevator.

Cliff was guarding his thoughts so well that Daniel was having trouble following them and every time he tried he felt a push backwards, almost physically. He glanced over to see a small smile creep onto the side of Cliff's lips that sent chills down his spine as the elevator plummeted to the depths below.

"I want you to meet our onsite propulsion engineer, Ran McNaulty." Cliff was talking aloud now as he strolled out of the elevator.

"Why would we have the need for a propulsion engineer, Cliff?" Daniel asked aloud as well, following in stride.

"One of the benefits of the new Mods is that they generate their own energy. But, you'll notice we kept the larger power systems on the prosthetics," Cliff stated nonchalantly, walking down the hallway before he reached a steel door. He punched in a code and opened the door wide, with a hand out to usher Daniel in first.

"Dr. Jahren, and Dr. Daniel Jahren, I presume? It is a pleasure to finally met you!" An older gentleman, about 60, with peppered grey hair and a stubbly, matching beard said with hand out to shake Daniel's. He was wearing the blue cotton overalls with company logo that was the standard issue uniform for engineers in their facility.

Daniel shook his hand and was looking around the giant room that gave the impression of being an airplane hangar dug into the mountain. Even smelling of jet fuel. It was filled with what appeared to be small rocket engines and other devices that could be grenade launchers for all he knew. What is this!! he yelled at Cliff in his head.

Cliff shook his head and rubbed his temple but before he could say anything Ran started to talk.

"Now that you have gotten used to your prosthetics, I'm sure your brother has told you about the enhancements we have been developing for the military," Ran announced.

"A secret military funded project, Cliff?" Daniel said, aloud.

"Yes, need to know only. I wanted to show you how much more you will be capable of, and you deserve to know what your hard work has led to."

"What has my work led to?" Daniel asked, concerned and annoyed. All he ever wanted to do was help people, not blow them up. Everything in this room looked like a weapon.

"Attachable robotic propulsion systems and sonic blasters mostly, but the latest enhancement device is my favorite." Cliff beamed as he walked over to an arm that lay on the table. "Go ahead, switch it out."

Daniel immediately removed his left arm and placed the one on the table over his interface. He turned it left to lock it in and then could feel it sync into his mind. He opened and closed the fist, noticing a hole in the middle of the hand than was wound-up like a solenoid inside. It wasn't until after he put the arm on that he even realized he was going to do it and Cliff was smiling like he was up to something. He tried to put those thoughts out of his head.

"You'll want to be in a narrow passage, or hallway when using this one ... here, we have a test range built." Ran led them over to a room on the right wall. It was filled with tennis balls and bowling ball sized objects of different weights and materials. "Hold your arm out and concentrate on the center of your hand," Ran directed.

Daniel held his hand out and there was a buzzing in his arm, followed by a sonic wave that pulsed in the room at a low frequency that he could hear and feel. The objects scattered about the room started to levitate, tennis balls first. As he focused harder, the larger objects began to levitate higher. It was amazing! He could feel the pride and exuberance flowing from his brother and couldn't help but mirror the feeling.

I almost want to cut my own arm off, just to be able to have this one, he heard Cliff say in his mind. He understood, the power was overwhelming.

"What else do we have?" Daniel asked, unable to control his excitement and unsure if the source was him or his brother. He would be keeping this arm though, no matter what.

"These legs use liquid hydrogen fuel and can fly for about 30 minutes on full burn; but, we have modified them with a sonic interrupter that helps maintain altitude and can generate a glide for up to 2 additional hours," Ran explained showing off a pair of 'legs' that looked more like rocket thrusters.

Daniel felt Cliff's heart beat faster and his pride double as Cliff stroked the metal legs. Titanium additive manufacturing he heard his brother say in his head.

"This is what I like to call a 'sonic sickener.' It can generate tones that cause severe headaches and induce vomiting." Ran pointed to the first hand on a table with three different metal hands. "This one is fundamentally a Taser, and this one shoots off bullets from the pointer finger like a gun. They are all exchangeable with the one you have now. Look and see."

Why wasn't I told about any of this before, Cliff? Why am I just now finding out? Daniel asked in his mind, turning to face Cliff.

You were so preoccupied with Amy and wanting a 'normal life,' he said in his head with dripping disdain and ... hurt?

Did he feel hurt that he wanted to be normal? Daniel thought, completely confused.

"I didn't think you would understand," Cliff said aloud. His emotions were wild. One minute he was staring at the hardware around the room with pride and excitement and the next he felt hurt and guilt. The rollercoaster of emotion was overwhelming and Daniel was starting to have trouble breathing.

"Am I missing something?" Ran asked the two of them. He'd been gazing from brother to brother, who'd been staring at each other, not saying a word (from his perspective) for the past few minutes.

Cliff smiled, then turned to face Daniel.

Suddenly all Daniel could think of is how much work went into making these dreams come true and how state-of-the-art each and every device was. "This is legitimate, government work, right?" he asked, aloud.

"Of course!" Ran and Cliff both exclaimed at once.

"Well, then, lets test these babies out!" Daniel said, excitedly removing the levitation hand and replacing it with the sonic sickener. "Who wants to go first?"

"Whoa, very funny!" Cliff laughed, holding up his arms as if he was being accosted by a cop, but in his head he was calling his brother a few curse words.

Ran held his arms up too, not wanting to volunteer either.

Daniel laughed, until he noticed something on Cliff's arm. Black streaks going down the muscles in his forearm. Cliff quickly pulled down his sleeve.

"Cliff!!" Daniel yelled, the lights in the room began to flash and all three men looked around. He took Cliff by the arm and ripped back his shirt, revealing the extent. "Tribus? Really?"

It isn't Tribus, father fixed it. He's calling it Quinta, he added two more ingredients to stabilize the reaction. Cliff was looking at Ran and back to Daniel, speaking to Daniel's mind. Ran doesn't know about this. This is not sanctioned. I know. I'm sorry but the prosthetics were too heavy and my body was still ailing. The MD was too much and Quinta is the only thing that could stop it.

"Am I missing something? What is Tribus? What is wrong with your arm Cliff?" Ran asked.

"Just a bad tribal tattoo," Cliff lied as he tried to fix his slashed sleeve to cover the black streaks.

"I'm guessing Mom and Dad know all about this, am I right?" Daniel asked, aloud.

"Of course," Cliff answered, aloud.

"Yes, your parents helped set-up the contract years ago. It was your mother who hired me," Ran proclaimed. "We actually went to school together. She hasn't aged a day since I met her. That mud business must be working-out well for her."

More like coffee! Daniel thought, hearing the echo of Cliff in his head. They both chuckled.

"You have quite the remarkable family," Ran said. "Most of the ideas for this technology came from Cliff, I just put it together."

"Yes, we have quite the family!" Daniel said. It was hard to be mad at his brother when the brilliant work around him was so extraordinary. Maybe it was the new Mod, but he felt more connected to Cliff than ever before. And, now he was sure Susan had added an extra dopamine enhancement to his Mod because he knew he should be angry or upset or even disgruntled with his family's usual breaking of every known law and ethic. But, he just felt exhilarated.

Cliff was smiling, and Daniel couldn't help but match it with an equally big grin.

Chapter 12

Arrested Development

Susan sat cross-legged on a wooden park bench, gazing out at the lake and nibbling absentmindedly on a bag on Funyuns when Daniel arrived right on time, right at noon. He placed his hand on her back as he sat down next to her and said, "Hi Susan." He had a smile so devastatingly handsome that it made her heart melt but also made her painfully aware of her own onion breath. She packed away the snacks into her backpack, uncrossed her legs and looked around to make sure they were alone.

"I think the coast is clear," he whispered to her, with barely muffled amusement as he feigned to look around as well.

"Did you talk to your brother after I left? Did he tell you to do anything?" Susan asked, unabated and serious.

Daniel was not the same. He was acting different and it was slightly unsettling. He was so happy, unnervingly happy. She hadn't seen him happy in years, not since Amy's death. The new Mod she'd placed had an extra stimulus package to help drive him out of his depression and an extra bit of amplification based on Cliff's feedback. But, it was having a far different effect than she'd anticipated. Were his emotions being amplified by hers?

"Yes, and yes. Why?" Daniel asked, still smiling like a buffoon and leaning closer to Susan. She could smell his breath. See the gold flakes in his hazel eyes. Feel the heat of his body next to hers. She was starting to forget why she was here – he had that effect on her. Unfortunately, she wasn't wearing her rubber band on her wrist to snap herself back out of it anymore.

He asked, "Are you okay, Susan? You look ... dazed?" as he hugged her next to him and rubbed his hand up and down her back to comfort her. That didn't help. The closeness and heat of his body took over her mind.

"I'm fine ... how are you?" was all she could think to say as she stared into his eyes, leaning towards him, pulled in by his magnetism.

"I've never felt better, truly! What did you put in my head, Susan?" he asked as he straightened her glasses. "Do you want me to fix these? The left side is crooked." He didn't wait for an answer as he removed the glasses and bent the frame back. "There, that looks more even," he said, placing them on her face while softly brushing her hair back behind her ears on either side.

"What did you put in my head..." she repeated out loud, not quite catching on, staring at his full lips. "I'm not..." she began but was interrupted by those full lips on hers. It was a full minute before she could catch her breath, much less try to finish her sentence. He had kissed her! How did that happen?

"I'm sorry, was that okay?" Daniel asked, still inches from her face and holding her close with his right arm around her waist. The endorphins released in his warm breath were making her giddy and her glasses a bit steamy. She had to take them off again and wipe away the condensation.

Susan wanted to stay in this moment forever. She had dreamt about it. Wished for it. Wondered how those lips would feel on hers for so long. Years! She'd wanted him to kiss her for years! It did not disappoint. He was an incredible kisser, as gentle and as adept with his tongue as he probably was with his fingers during surgery. Before she knew it, her finger was touching his lips, gliding over the contours ... But, this was not okay! Not in the least okay! What was happening??? She should have better control over herself!

"I can't!" she said at last. "I'm seeing someone, and this isn't right – it isn't fair to him."

"Who?" Daniel asked, unfazed and going in for another kiss. She couldn't help but dissolve into his arms and relinquish control to his thorough hold on her. He moved her, body and soul, and she didn't even feel like she was in reality anymore.

A few minutes later, or an hour? Time had stopped. Susan pulled herself together and pushed Daniel away enough to catch her breath. They sat there, foreheads touching. His hand on the back on her neck holding her fervently. Her hands on each of his shoulders, keeping him at a safe distance.

"This isn't right, Daniel."

"This feels very right to me, Susan," he implored, looking her straight in the eyes, which, at the distance they were from hers, melded together to make him look like a cyclops. That funny thought helped pull her back to reality.

She took his hand from her neck and held it in between hers. Such a large, strong yet delicate hand. She looked down at his left hand and finally noticed he was wearing a new prosthetic she had never seen before. "What is that?"

"Cliff showed me this yesterday, after you left. It is a secret prototype for the military. You'd love what it does. But, if I told you, I'd have to kill you," he said, teasingly. "I'm kidding! It affects gravity. I'd show you, but it has to be used in a confined space for the waves to build up enough to lift anything."

"Cliff making secret weapons for the military, great! I thought things couldn't get any worse! Daniel, there is something I have to tell you." She tried to get every word out before she lost her train of thought again to his full lips. "Cliff is controlling people and has been for years! I'm not sure he knows it, but he will probably figure it out soon after what happened yesterday."

"Cliff has always been manipulative, Susan," he replied. "What makes you think he is 'controlling' people? We tested out the Mod, it only affects others with a Mod, right? Is he..." he stopped and looked a bit annoyed, then continued with, "do you think he is controlling me?"

"Yes, Daniel. I do. I'm sorry."

"How? Why? Right now?"

"No, not right now. Of course not right now! Unless ... is he here? He's not here, right?" she said as she looked around to make sure Cliff wasn't hiding in the park or waiting in Daniel's car.

She was pretty sure that if Cliff was close, he wouldn't be too happy about them making out and would have stepped-in a long time ago. He'd been asking her out for years and it took everything she had to tell him 'No' because of how persuasive he had become. But it was exactly his manipulative tendencies that made her not want to go out with him in the first place. He had been even more persistent and aggressive ever since she came to Colorado, and she was afraid to even bring up the guy she was dating.

"How can I know if he is trying to control me? How can I stop him? I felt like I had a fairly good handle on him yesterday," Daniel stated.

"I don't know. You probably won't be able to tell. Plus, he might not even know he is doing it. The Mod is amplifying more than what was intended, that has become very clear today."

"What do you mean?"

"I mean, have you ever felt this way about me before, Daniel?"

He pulled back and thought for a minute. "I've liked you since the day I met you, Susan. If it weren't for Amy, I think we would have been together a long time ago. I think you know that too."

Susan was shocked. Hearing him say aloud what she had thought for so long seemed surreal. Could it be he was just finally over Amy and ready to love again?

"Why do you think it is amplifying my feelings?"

"Because you have never kissed me before..." she was not able to finish her sentence before he kissed her again.

"It feels right to me," he said, smiling and caressing her cheek.

"As much as I want it to be real, I don't know..." she began but was having trouble putting a finger on what was wrong. "I don't trust it, it feels ... sudden. And, I know Cliff has more control than you know."

"I am in control." He was getting angry. "You know I am always in control."

"I don't think so, Daniel. I ran some tests while we were in Japan that I found disturbing, like source code in the microchip that shouldn't exist. After what happened yesterday, I realized it was that his brain figured out how to integrate and use the Mod for telepathy."

"Yesterday, you told him that the telepathy was only due to our genetic similarity."

"I had to think of something to say. I don't trust what Cliff will do once he knows his capabilities."

"I have the same capabilities too, right?"

"Not exactly. Your Mod is a different, an advanced version. It has more capacity and enhancements, so you will likely not be as susceptible to his control as say, Bill. But, we both know Cliff's prefrontal cortex is ... special. He could override yours, you might not be able to stop him," Susan explained. "Once he truly realizes the extent of his abilities, there may be no stopping him from doing whatever he puts his mind to."

Daniel did not look very happy anymore. The lightheartedness, and lovi-dovi-ness of the new Daniel had been replaced with a grim look of determination that she had seen often before when they had worked together years ago. In a way it was comforting to see him back to himself. But, her heart still sank and her lips were aching for his. It wasn't meant to be, though, and she knew it. She took a deep breath, let it go slowly and tried to focus on the dilemma at hand.

"I've been working on designs to enhance the output of similar patients, for imaging purposes. I think I told you, I've been working with dream-walkers?"

"Yes, I remember. You were a bit drunk, so I wasn't sure how much of what you were saying should be taken to heart."

"I wasn't that drunk!" Honestly, she didn't remember drinking that much, but couldn't remember much else of that night. That bartender had given her a strong scotch on the rocks. She only remembered ordering two drinks. She'd never been drunk on only two drinks.

"You stumbled away and fell into the elevator, Susan. I had to send the bellman to go check on you."

"Is that why the bellman went to my room?" She had wondered about that, and continued with, "huh ... okay, anyway, dream-walkers seem to have the same brain patterns as your brother. Remember, I told you I found one that was stronger, better than Cliff?"

"Yes, where are you going with this? That is the guy you are seeing, isn't it?"

"Yes, it is, but that isn't the point. The point is that I think that if I work with him, I can develop a microchip that can stop Cliff from controlling you. Or, at the very least, allow you to overpower him. I need to understand more how it all works with Darren..."

"Darren, that's his name? So, you want to leave and go back to Darren?" Daniel asked, holding her hand tightly, then pulling her close for another kiss. "Does Darren make you feel like this?"

"I ... I can't ... But, we both need to leave! Get as far away from Cliff as we can. He's probably already figured it all out by now and it is dangerous for..."

He kissed her again, holding her close before saying: "How about we just run away together instead, Susan? Get as far away from here as we can together. Leave Cliff to his own devices."

"Run-away together?" The thought had never crossed her mind. Of course, she never expected Daniel would ever reciprocate her feelings for him – not after what happened with Amy.

"Yes, just me and you. Maybe, Seattle? Though, I might rust with all the rain." He laughed and held up his left hand. "Or, you could finally show me your hometown of Toulouse."

"But, my work. Your family..." as much as the idea of running away appealed to her, she had never been one to run away from a problem. Or leave the world with a legacy she never intended to create. Did Daniel not understand the implications of Cliff having telepathy?

He tried to kiss her again, but she had to stop him. And as much as it hurt her to do it, she had to bring up the hard truth he was unwilling to face. "Who knows what Cliff will end up doing ... are you sure you trust him? The incidents surrounding Amy's death, the way he always despised her ... I ..." Susan felt the tension in Daniel immediately, his posture went ridged and his jaw was locked. "I ... I'm not saying that he..." Susan couldn't continue. She wasn't the only one who speculated that Cliff might have had something to do with Amy's death, but no one would say it aloud. No one dared. The whole town didn't. Cops and all.

"He couldn't have ... he is my brother, he couldn't have..." he was staring out at the lake, void of emotion on his face and eyes looking like they were seeing miles away.

"You can't..." Susan didn't know how to finish that sentence. Daniel, with his current Mod, might be the only one with a chance at controlling Cliff. And Cliff just couldn't be left to do whatever he wanted ... not after what happened with Amy.

If only Daniel could learn to manipulate the Mod the way Cliff did and focus his mind. If she could get him an improved chip, that would be even better. But, for now she had to help him as best she could. "Do you ever dream, Daniel?"

"Not in a long time, not that I remember. When I did, it was only bits of nightmares. Why?" he asked. He had moved away from her already, and the aching distance felt like a deep cold chasm.

"There are some that believe that in a dream state we can access the 'collective consciousness' of humanity. It is where all human minds can connect, have you heard about this?" Susan asked while looking around for an ant pile ... there had to be an ant pile around the lake somewhere ... ah ha! She got up and walked over to kick the ant pile, causing complete chaos for the ants.

Daniel had been following Susan around, confused at her sporadic behavior, "So you think this access to the collective conscious by dream-walkers is somehow tied to the ability to use the microchip for telepathy?"

Wow, he didn't miss anything! He put that together quick! she thought as she nodded.

Susan pulled a Funyun out of her bag and placed it down next to an ant that was all alone on the sidewalk and placed another Funyun a few centimeters away but not next to any ant. "Watch. Look how this little ant can't pick up the snack ... and look, here come several family members to help out."

"They probably smelled the onion."

She was suddenly self-conscious of her breath, but she cleared her throat and continued, "No, see how none of them went to the other Funyun, even though it was just as close to the group as the one here. The only difference was there was a single ant here – he called for help. This experiment has been done before, several times in labs. The ants, they can sense when other ants need help. They have a communal mind. They use it all the time and that is how they are able to accomplish so much together."

"So, this is your collective conscious experiment? Dream-walkers are ants-like humans?"

"Yes, I think people who are dream-walkers are more in tune with the collective conscious, and make much better telepaths if ... say, their abilities were enhanced. The Mod pushes and amplifies brainwaves. Yours uses the energy of the blood to produce the power needed, and it is limitless. You haven't had it for very long, so there is no telling what you will be capable of."

"I never wanted this, Susan. And Cliff is the last person on Earth who should have this capability." He was watching the ants intently and then looked to her and said, "You truly believe I can stop him?"

Susan couldn't meet his look, she glanced away. 'No' was the answer she had in her head but instead she said, "Cliff's Mod is still regulated by the outer power controller, but he wants a new one installed. He asked for it the other day and I said I would get him one made once I went back to LA. Honestly, I never intended to give him any upgrades. I could install a less advanced version instead ... but we would have to keep it a secret from him until then ... and that might be possible."

"Do you think it is just the latest versions and dream-walkers that it would do this for? Or could this affect everyone with a Mod? Did you design this on purpose, Susan?"

"No, of course not! You know my intentions. I always wanted to help those suffering from debilitating illness and disease. Not mind control!" she was offended he even suggested she had purposefully unlocked human telepathy.

"I'm sorry, you just seem to know a lot about it for someone who says they didn't do it on purpose," Daniel inquired. "I know the EEG was originally designed by a doctor wanting to explore telepathy. Did you know that? His experiments failed, and I never expected that anything would come of your Mods besides the shortsighted, personal goals I had."

"My goal was Parkinson's, you know that ... everything else has been an accident," she replied while thinking of all the sideways twists and turns in her research that had led to this moment.

"You are prone to accidents," he chuckled.

"I'm worried about you Daniel. Now that you have this new Mod installed, your brain is more open, it's like a doorway. Cliff is far more advanced than you, he's not only a dream-walker, but he has had years with his Mod. If you want to resist his persuasion, I think you'll need to work on your dreaming skills. Learn to become a lucid dreamer. It's your only chance."

"How would I do that?"

"For one, try and remember your dreams every morning when you wake up. Have a diary, and write down what you remember and..." Susan stopped what she was saying, standing up at the sound of police sirens coming into the park.

"They are coming to arrest you for kicking over that ant pile," Daniel joked. "And littering with those Funyuns. Better hide the bag and clean the dirt from your shoe."

"Very funny." Susan couldn't help but feel concerned, and Daniel stopped smiling when four police cars stopped right in front of them, lights on and forming a barrier to any exit.

A Sheriff, middle-aged, lean and grizzly got out of the foremost vehicle. He had his hand over his holster, the other hand with cuffs already out, and gruffly stated, "Are you Dr. Susan Aldean?"

"Why, is there something the matter?" She stood still, looking at the group of men in uniform forming around her. Their faces were graven and intent as if they expected her to flee at any second.

One of the officers opened the backseat door of his car and Cliff appeared as if summoned. "Yes, that is Dr. Aldean," he remarked. "It is best that you not resist, Susan."

"I'm afraid I'm placing you under arrest. You have the right to remain silent, anything you say or do ..." The sheriff continued but Susan didn't hear a word he was saying, she was in complete shock as her arms were being forced behind her back and the hard, cold handcuffs were being placed on her wrists.

"Sheriff Osbourne, there must be some mistake," Daniel began. "Look, you've known me my whole life. I tell you this woman is innocent of whatever it is you think she has done!"

"She is being charged with the murder of your fiancé Daniel. We have found compelling evidence that she is the one who planted the bomb."

"WHAT?" both Daniel and Susan said at the same time.

"That is absurd! Why would I want to kill Amy? Daniel, you don't believe this, do you?" Susan pleaded, gazing up at Daniel for defense while he was merely standing there gaping.

"How? What evidence?" Daniel finally asked, holding the Sheriff by the shoulder with his mechanical arm. The Sheriff's eyes went wide, seeing the formidable prosthesis for the first time.

"I, umm..." Sheriff Osbourne took a deep breath and continued, "I received a call yesterday, from the bellman at the hotel. He said he finally remembered who he had seen last and where he had seen the suspect 'present' before – in her room. He still couldn't remember much else, including how he got home or even delivering the present. It is clear he was drugged, that was established. We did a check of her credit card transactions and found the purchase of a ceramic tea kettle the day before, one that matched the description the bridesmaid, Amanda, gave."

Daniel's grip on the officer got tighter and the Sheriff was now wincing and bent forward, holding onto the metal hand with both of his own. "Please, Daniel!" he yelled.

"It's true, Daniel. It's all true," Cliff said, coming over to stand next to his brother, placing a hand on his shoulder.

Daniel released the officer, who dropped to the ground. He then glared at Susan with the coldest expression she had ever seen in her life, with eyes like black holes. "You wanted me to think it was my own brother? You almost had me convinced! Amy trusted you, she loved you! I loved you!"

Susan's heart felt like it was going to pound out of her chest. Her head was spinning and her lungs felt like iron.

What was happening? Think Susan, think! "The bellman did come to my room. You sent him, you said so yourself ... I did get a teapot for Amy, but ... I was so drunk, I don't remember anything after the bellman came knocking, asking how I was ... I could never have ... I would never have ... you must know that ... Daniel?"

"Take her away, I can't even look at her," Daniel said, walking away with Cliff by his side. Neither man even turned to look back at her as they got into Daniel's car and drove away.

Sheriff Osbourne had his hand on her head and was pushing her into the back of his patrol car before Susan could open her mouth to plead her innocence. How could he believe that she could kill Amy? How could anyone believe that she could kill anyone?

They all had to know it was Cliff ... he must have figured out that she knew and ... she never should have asked to meet Daniel alone yesterday! Cliff must have overheard, he must have gotten the bellman to call the Sheriff!

She should have run yesterday. Her instincts had told her to run. When she saw what happened between Daniel and Cliff, and what Daniel could do to Bill ... she should have run! But, she had wanted to help Daniel, to warn him ...

How in the world was she going to get out of this mess? She was staring out the window of the back seat of the cop car, out into the red rock desert that was beginning to look like hell to her. She should never have come to Colorado!

Cliff had complete control over everyone, and no one could see through it. Or chose not to. Did he set her up from the beginning? Did he take her present and drug the bellman? He had to have! Which meant there was more to this than just overhearing a conversation yesterday.

What motive could he possibly have in trying to implicate her in all of this? Jealousy? She could see that he might be annoyed or frustrated that she would chose Daniel over him ... but not to this extent.

Think! What happened in the last 24hrs??

He had always wanted her close, wanted her to come to Colorado and work for him. She had just told him yesterday that now that Daniel was fully recovered she would return to LA ... Was this an attempt to keep her here? A sick, sadistic attempt to force her into some kind of agreement to work for him? That bastard!! Whatever he wanted, and whatever it took, she would never, EVER, EVER give it to him!

Chapter 13
Dreams and Things

Daniel stood on a cliff, overlooking the grand desert valley below. He came back here often in his dreams. He was pulled to it, as if his soul was not through with it. His subconscious wanted him here. He hated coming here, this is where Amy had fallen so many years ago. He sat down on the red rock, cross-legged, waiting for what this dream would bring him next.

"You know the truth, dear Daniel. Admit it and you will be free," the familiar voice of his old nanny, Miss Tinny, could be heard from behind him. He turned around, but she was not there ... only rock fading to more rock.

He turned back around to face the edge and saw Susan, one hand outreached. She was holding on for her life from the precipice, like Amy had been so many years ago. She begged him to help her. He refused to move, to get close to the edge, and then she fell screaming.

Daniel awoke bolt upright in his bed. He picked-up a notebook from the nightstand and jotted down everything he could remember ... his mind already reaching for details that were slipping away. Was it Susan or Amy falling? Was it his mother or Miss Tinny's voice he had heard? How did he get to the cliff?

He was getting better at remembering, but it was still difficult for him. It didn't come naturally like it did for his brother but he knew it was important for him to get better at it if he was to have any chance to find the truth and face it. To ease his troubled mind.

Susan's arraignment seemed like yesterday. She had the motive, the means, no alibi, and all the evidence pointed to her. He still couldn't believe she did it though, not fully. That she was the one who murdered Amy. His recurrent dreams kept reminding him that deep down he thought she was innocent. He knew that is what his dreams meant. But, he also knew that if she didn't set the bomb then ... he didn't want to think about it. There was only one other person that it could be.

And, if it was Cliff, how could he have ...? How? How could he get himself to admit he thought his little brother was capable of murder?

His mind kept bringing him back to the day in the park Susan was arrested, and all the words she'd said. How he felt when he was with her. How close he had been to running away with her ...

If Susan was right, and innocent, working on his dream skills was the only thing he could do for now to prepare to face Cliff. And eventually challenge him mentally to force-out the truth.

In the meantime, he had been struggling to not let anyone know that he still suspected Cliff. Because if Cliff found out Daniel suspected him, who knows what he would do. If he was capable of doing the things that he may have already done then more murder was not out of the realm of possibility. He shuddered at the thought and pushed it out of his head.

Daniel worked with Cliff every day on prosthetics for new patients. Often veterans who could not afford care. They also worked on weapons for the military, and for personal use. Side by side, and with his parent's support. The family had never been closer. And when they were working together it was so easy to forget the past; to shove the horrors aside and focus on the help they were able to give so many.

Today they were testing out an acid solution his mother designed for one of the projectiles used in the launch packet Cliff had developed. An ideal family gathering for accusing your brother of murder. Right. Best to keep those thoughts out of his head.

When would it be the right time? When Susan was in prison for another year? Ten more years? If Susan was innocent, how could he do this to her? Every day she was in prison would be on his hands forever, and the guilt and conflict were eating him up inside.

Daniel had just reached the research facility when he guarded his mind. Then he set to thinking about the work at hand. His father greeted him at the entry to the military bunker where they would be doing their testing today. He had two thermoses of coffee in his hands and handed one to Daniel.

His parents still didn't know about the telepathic link between the two brothers, or the Mod's opening the mind to manipulation by those with more advanced Mods or more advanced cognitive abilities. Cliff never mentioned it and Daniel figured with Susan in jail and unable to fix the problem that it was better to not bring it up either.

"Thanks, Father. How are you today?" Daniel asked while drinking from the welcomed thermos of steaming energy.

"I have been having troubling headaches, to be frank. I may step out for a bit today," Martin admitted, uncharacteristically, then continued walking forward as if he has just said, "I'm fine."

That admission stopped Daniel in his tracks. He had never known his father to be ill. The coffee was invented by him for that sole purpose! To keep the cancer at bay that plagued his brain and it had worked for decades to prevent any kind of illness, including even aging. His father never had headaches. Was this his way of him telling him the cancer was back?

"What?" was all Daniel could get out.

Martin ignored the question and kept walking. He was such a proud and stubborn man. Admitting the cancer relapsed was admitting failure. The last thing he ever wanted to do was admit failure.

Daniel's mother was waiting for them in the back of the hangar-like complex within the mountain that they had reinforced for weapons testing. She was wearing a jet pack with an attached flame thrower nozzle converted for acid spray. The goo-ified remains of rubber dummies were oozing in front of her. Their stench was noxious and that was with loud fans blowing out into sizable ventilation shafts at the furthest wall to the south of the great open room.

"You're too late, boys!" she yelled over the noise of the fans. "These guys are deep-fried slimers now!"

"I see, honey. You couldn't wait?" Martin asked his wife, leaning over to give her a kiss on her cheek right below the chemical goggles she was wearing. Her hair was pulled back in a blonde braid that hung down to the middle of her baggy, blue coveralls and she had on giant black chemical gloves that came to her elbows as well as large, black boots that came to her knees.

"I tried to stop her, but she simply felt like those dummies deserved to get it this morning," Cliff said, coming from one of the locked research rooms and carrying another chemical bag and nozzle. He was dressed similarly to his mom, but with goggles on top on his head. "I was working on getting this one to create a mist. I added a nebulizer; but, we would have to contain it in another room. We need a smaller area if we are to test out a mist."

"You'll need a full suit and mask as well, for a mist. Not just these cotton threads," Beth suggested. "I probably should have worn a mask, this stuff sure stinks and those blowers are barely pulling the fumes out! Likely I inhaled a good dose of carcinogens I'll regret later."

"Is it because Father is sick that you are being more reckless than normal, Mom?" Daniel asked.

"You told him?" Beth said, throwing off her gear and gloves. She reached over to Martin to check his pupils with a small flashlight that was sitting on the counter next to him. Even she knew it must be bad if he was admitting any symptoms.

"It has advanced unpredictably fast, honey," he said. "I don't think we can hide it anymore."

"Told him what? Father is sick? What's going on? What are you hiding?" Cliff demanded.

"Dad has a glioblastoma that he has been self-treating for years, Cliff. Didn't they tell you?" Daniel said, shocked that his parents were able to keep something like that from Cliff all these years. Daniel had figured part of it out when his parents gave him the formula for the coffee, and the rest by confronting his father. He'd asked him if he could examine him, possibly operate if needed and Martin had refused help. He had his own methods of treatment and felt like brain surgery was a last resort.

"No! But your research, oncolytic virology ... isn't there a cure in there somewhere, in all those viruses you dug up?"

"No, there isn't son. There are treatments, enhancements, remedies..." Martin seemed to lose his train of thought, and sat down, somewhat wobbly. After a deep breath he continued with, "there is one virus that we haven't tried..." he gazed at Beth and she shook her head. Then he said, "your mother would never let me test it on myself. And, it has to be altered to my DNA first ... it is a particularly virulent strain, prone to shifts."

"If the virus evolved after mixing with his DNA, it could become highly unstable and even kill him. And, it is extremely contagious ... we decided this a long time ago, that we would stop working that strain." Beth looked forlorn and wasn't unable to take her eyes off of her husband. "But, I never expected that we wouldn't find anything else after decades of research ... and that the coffee would stop working."

"How bad is it, father?" Daniel asked, realizing the gravity of the situation, locking eyes with his brother Cliff, who's jaw was firmly clasped in the shared rage and helpless frustration they felt so strongly in the moment together. He could feel his brothers surprise and ... betrayal? He felt betrayed they had never told him. You have to know that father is too proud to admit failure, Cliff.

"I'm just happy to spend any moment I have with my family," Martin said, in a humbled resignation that sent despair into Daniel's heart like a knife and he felt the anger well up inside Cliff to a dangerous level.

"That is unacceptable, Mother, that we can't try this virus of his. Simply unacceptable! If there is any hope, we have to try." Cliff was focused hard on his mother, and Daniel could feel the determination in waves pulsing through his anger and frustration. "You know we can keep him in quarantine until he stabilizes; and, if the strain evolves we can deal with it when it comes. This is an acceptable risk, we have to try!"

Surprisingly, Beth was nodding her head as he spoke. She appeared to be in a daze.

"Yes, you're right Cliff ... we have the facilities now to contain this ... and the alternative is just as unbearable to me as the risk," Beth explained, both hands holding her husband's head gently. "We have to try."

"Are you sure, honey?" Martin was gazing into his wife's eyes, which were filling with tears as she nodded.

Daniel couldn't believe what he was hearing. He was no expert in viruses, but for his father to be this hesitant about using one, at the risk of his own life, meant that this strain was very dangerous indeed. He would have to ensure everything went smoothly. "How long will it take to prepare the sample with the altered DNA? Will you be able to perform the alteration in your condition, father? Can I help?"

"Yes, I will need to move everything to the quarantine labs. I think, 48 hours? I'll know more then," Martin explained.

"I'll bring in a team. I have three scientists in mind that can help..." Cliff began.

"Not those three that keep following you around, Cliff? Ferris, Dawson and Lobbs?" Beth was flustered and more annoyance entered her voice with each name she dropped.

"Yes, they are the best we have and I know I can trust them. I'll have them help you set up, Father, and prepare the chambers in case you need to stay for a while," Cliff insisted. "It will be good to have help."

"Right, and which of them knows about the dangers of not following the proper protocols around viruses?" Martin asked. "How to determine if there has been an antigenic shift?"

"Lobbs is a microbiologist, and I am sure Dawson and Ferris took some biology, they are doctors, after all," said Cliff. "It matters more who we can trust now than anything."

"I'll show them where to go then. Daniel, can you clean up this mess?" Beth said as she led Cliff and Martin out of the room and left Daniel standing there in disbelief.

He stood in silence for a while. Then cleaned up the rubbery ooze, placing the remains in large hazmat barrels.

As he was leaving the room he glanced over at the rocket legs Cliff had been developing ... which gave him an idea. His family would be distracted over the next 48 hours ... What if he broke Susan out of jail? He could be out and back before they even noticed anything was missing. This might be his only opportunity!

He didn't know for sure if she planted that bomb, but his heart sank at the thought of her in prison for life knowing that her love for him is what put her there. Maybe if he finally helped her, his recurrent nightmares would go away and the turmoil inside of him would subside.

Daniel took the rocket legs, a laser blaster, and one of the black Kevlar suits and then headed out the ventilation shaft.

~ ~ ~

Susan was settling into her top bunkbed with a self-help book called "Let. It. Go." She had heard of other martyrs going to jail and becoming wise by reading a ton of books, and she thought that maybe improving her mind was her best bet to keep her sanity.

Her bottom bunk mate, Lana Perez, was a Hispanic woman who had robbed a bank with her ex-husband, thinking they would be the next Bonnie and Clyde; but, they hadn't even made it past the first heist before being surrounded and tasered.

Lana was nice. She'd been here a year already and had taken on the hobby of doing hair for the other ladies in her corridor. She'd offered to give her some blonde highlights and Susan didn't dare refuse. She wanted to fit in because it looked like she would be here for a while. The highlights turned out more pink than blonde, but her hair was the least of her worries.

The night was drawing on, and she was beginning to fall asleep when she noticed an odd smell, like burning electric wires. Then she felt the heat coming from the wall next to the window. She looked over to see there was a bright orange, square outline forming on the wall and it was getting brighter. There was a low hum, getting louder.

"Christ! Lana, get back!" she whispered loudly as she jumped down and pulled her dozing roommate out of her slumber on the bottom bunk. She got as far back against the far wall as possible, pulling the half-asleep Lana close.

The square outline was now completely formed, and then the wall burst forward, revealing a metal hand extended. On the other side of the wall, floating in mid-air, was Daniel of all people! He was dressed all in black, with a jet stream coming out of his legs. She was more surprised at who was there than that there was a cyborg outside her jail cell – she'd thought it would be Cliff who would eventually come for her. She was convinced Daniel hated her.

"We have to go now, we don't have much time," he said as he lifted her into the air and out into the desert nightscape with the surprised Lana waving 'bye' from the open 3rd floor cell wall. They were moving at incredible speed, and she had her face buried in his chest because the wind was blasting her eyes. He had on a protective helmet and goggles, and he held her tight enough to almost crack a rib but she didn't mind. He had come to save her!

They stopped in a wooded area near the highway and he landed down gently, debris flying in all directions.

"Here is some money and a dress," he said, handing her a wadded-up cloth over a purse. "Down the road about a mile, you'll find a greyhound bus station. I suggest you take a bus and disappear."

Susan was not sure what she had expected him to say, but 'take this and disappear' was not it. It hurt that he was so cold.

"Why are you helping me, Daniel? Do you still think I killed Amy?" She asked as she pulled over the dress while pulling off the tan and black coveralls underneath. She kicked the coveralls into the bushes.

"I don't know, but..."

"Right, Cliff has you believing whatever he wants..."

"I don't know what I believe, Susan!"

"Did he tell you he came to me, in jail? Several times, actually. Offered to get me out if I would work for him. Saying he forgives me for killing Amy, but that you never will. As if I didn't know that he did it, that he set the whole thing up!"

"He visited you in jail? What did he want you to do for him?"

"He's out of his mind, Daniel! Can't you see that? He has figured out that the Mod's could be altered to control people, to control everyone, not just people with Mods. He wants a master Mod to control everyone! He wants me to develop it for him and I refused."

"I don't know if I can believe that, Susan."

Susan was looking at Daniel in the low light of the crescent moon: half machine, half a broken human being who had lost so much at the hands of someone who should love him the most – his own brother.

"I'm so sorry, Daniel," was all she could say. He was so broken, in so many ways.

He reached his human arm out to her and pulled her close for a kiss, a kiss filled with tears from the both of them.

"I'm sorry too, Susan. I have to go, before they find out I left. And you have to get out of this state."

"Thank you, Daniel. For everything."

He blasted off, leaving her coughing on desert dust. She looked down at the cash in the small purse, it had to be over $400,000! That should buy a bus ticket or two! She wondered if her cellmate had jumped out of the hole in the wall. Maybe Lana thought she was still dreaming. Seeing a cyborg appear and jet out had to be fairly un-expected after waking up from a nap. Hopefully she knew better than to tell anyone who had broken her out of jail.

Daniel was always so prepared. Dress, purse, money ... he must care about her. If only he could admit that his brother was pure evil, sent from hell to inflict harm on all humanity! Okay, maybe that was too much. Cliff was an evil bastard though, for putting her in this predicament!

Now she was a fugitive and had no idea where to go. All she knew was that she wanted to get as far away from Colorado, and the Jahren family, as she possibly could get and never come back!

~ ~ ~

Daniel finished replacing and cleaning all of the gear he had used just in time for Ran to come into the bunker.

"Trying out the goggles?" Ran asked, pointing to his head.

"What? Yes, the visibility is great. IR was a nice touch for night vision," Daniel replied, removing the goggles he had forgotten to take off and trying to play it off. He realized the dirt on the goggles was likely all over his face as well.

"Yes, the night vision can come in handy. Where is your family? I thought you were testing the new acid wash technology today?"

"Something came up with my father, he's sick," Daniel explained, heading towards the door to avoid any more questions he had no idea how to answer without further implicating himself. "I should go check on him now, in fact."

"That explains why your mother has been acting strange lately..." Ran began, obviously wanting to continue talking despite the fact that Daniel was walking away. Daniel made it to the door before hearing. "Please, stop, there is something I need to tell you!"

Daniel halted and turned around to see Ran biting his lip and wringing his hands, completely unsure of what he was about to say next but desperate to say something.

"Your mother and I ... umm, no, let me start over ... Cliff, he ... he can be quite persuasive, you know, and ... we know Daniel, we know what happened. I'm sorry," Ran was stammering.

"What are you getting at, Ran? What is it that you know?" Daniel asked, more confused than ever.

"There is another bunker. Your mother had me work on it and keep it a secret. She never trusted Cliff, and I can see why. Please don't tell Cliff! He can't know. Here, take this key. The door is in the far wing of the third level basement. There is a cut-out in the side of the rock that if you go past, you'll miss it," Ran explained. "You'll understand when you see it."

"I don't understand." Why would my mother build another bunker and keep it secret from Cliff? What did she know? Daniel thought.

"Cliff has an insatiable appetite for power, Daniel. None of this will ever be enough for him ... can't you see that?" Ran looked scared, and as if he might be regretting telling him any of this.

"I think I know my own brother, Ran." Daniel took the key from Ran's shaking hand and hurried off in a metallic-clanking fury down the hallway to find this other bunker.

The third level basement was not fully finished, there was more chopped rock tunnel than hallway as Daniel walked around looking for an enclave in the mountain that could hold a door. He walked by it three times before he noticed the opening. He pulled out the key and unlocked the door.

This was not a military weapons bunker! There were computers, beds, and barrels of the family brand coffee. It had supplies enough for a small city ... and incubation pods? Was his mother planning for World War III?

He strode over to one of several 7ft long tubes that he was guessing was an incubation pod. It had a touchscreen display with temperature controls and tubes coming out for liquids going into the ground. No liquid nitrogen as far as he could tell and the temperature only went down to -20 degrees centigrade. He pulled-up one of the floor panels next to the pod and there was an intricate system of tubing underneath. He opened one of the tubes and recognized the black liquid by the smell. This pod was definitely designed to sustain someone indefinitely.

This was not what he expected to find tonight. Ran and his mother must know something he didn't. This explained nothing! He was now more confused than ever.

He locked the room and put away the key, heading up towards the main facility to find his family. How many secrets were they keeping between them? Communication was not their best family trait, it never was. But this, this was on a whole new level. Plus, he had to keep this from Cliff as well? Another tangled web to navigate.

Chapter 14
A Reckoning

Beth sat anxiously waiting next to her husband's bedside. She was dressed in full bio-hazard gear and it was excruciating not being able to touch him. But, they were taking no chances until the virus ran its course, which was carrying on longer than expected.

She had never seen her husband like this, and it felt like it was killing her to look at him. Martin appeared to have aged a decade in the past week and lost a significant amount of weight. His face was wan, with dark circles under his eyes and his breathing was shallow and labored. They had been together so long, and part of her thought they would both live forever. She never wanted to think about life without him, she just couldn't.

She held his hand as best she could through her thick gloves and closed her eyes, focusing on breathing deeply. "Follow my breath, honey," she whispered. He followed her breathing, taking in deep breaths. "Breathe from your stomach," she explained, while putting her hand on his abdomen, "here." His breathing got stronger and longer, and he smiled up at her lovingly. The thin-skinned cheeks and frail lips drawn was enough to make her heart break at the same time as give her hope.

"How is he today, mom?" Cliff asked, coming in to sit next to her in full gear as well.

"Better, I feel like he is getting better. How are you?" Beth couldn't help but notice the dark circles under her youngest son's eyes that were evident even through the plastic mask.

"I don't know why this is taking so long to work ... it's maddening!" Cliff had both hands balled into fists on his lap and was staring down at his own mechanical legs.

"You of all people should know, some things can't be rushed. It's barely been more than a week."

"Yes, of all people," Daniel said, coming in the back door with a rhythmic pulse and the sound of metal on the floor. He began donning his suit to enter into the cordoned-off bed chamber. When he got to his father, he began the usual routine of checking vitals and listening to heart and lungs.

"He's improving. And I have more good news. The last scan came back with no evidence of the tumor, so the virus has wiped his brain clean," Daniel was staring down at his father and trying to smile while delivering the good news, but it was obvious it hurt to see him in this condition. "Father, is there anything you would like us to get you?'"

"Coffee!" Martin exclaimed, with a half-smile and a twinkle in his eyes. In a shallow, wheezing voice he said, "Also, approximately 2mg of SAL-157 twenty minutes proceeding a booster of BR-76 and 25 mg of Benadryl." He took a few shallow breaths, coughed and continued, "And, my brain is not wiped clean, son. Hand me a Sudoku, honey. I'll prove it!"

"Honey, a Sudoku won't prove anything!" She should never have brought those into his bedchamber. He was obsessed. Plus, he was solving all the good ones before she could get to them. "We all know you are still smart as a whip."

"He's improving? Then why does he look so..." Cliff started but didn't want to finish the sentence after he caught her concerned glance.

"The virus has taken a toll on his body, it doesn't just attack the cancer. Biomarkers are all getting better though ... at least than they were a few days ago ... he's stronger than he looks," Daniel was once again trying to make everyone feel better, but she wasn't sure he wasn't lying about the biomarkers based on Martin's appearance.

"We should give him Quinta. He will get stronger, much quicker," Cliff suggested.

"No!" everyone said at once.

"Why not? Daniel, you took it. I took it. Look how much stronger we both are with minimal side effects. He would get better so much quicker if..."

"Daniel, you took the Quinta virus?" This was the first Beth had heard of it, she thought her first born son was wiser than that. She thought Cliff must be lying. Her mind was frozen in a panicked rage waiting for Daniel to answer her question.

"The prosthetics, they are heavy and Quinta makes them feel like nothing," Daniel explained. "I guess I felt like I had nothing to lose, mom, after what happened..."

"Nothing to lose? How about me? Or your father? Or your brother? I can see Cliff doing some hair-brained thing like injecting himself with that monster of a concoction, but you Daniel?" Beth was standing, hands on hips and fully irate before she could stop herself.

Losing her temper was the last thing Martin needed to witness, so she began taking deep breaths to calm down. "It was bad enough when I found out your father and Cliff were working on that behind my back, but when I found out Cliff had injected himself ... and now you!" The deep breathing wasn't helping, and her temper was mounting. She felt like a deep breathing purple monster about to explode. "I can't deal with this right now," she said while exiting out of the bedchamber. She tried to let out a little of the anger she felt by throwing pieces of bio-suit into the donning booth with voracity.

Maybe it was the thought of losing her husband, and seeing him in such a horrible condition, but her ability to deal with Daniel's negligence was just too much right now. He was supposed to be the responsible one in the family! The only other one she could trust. She felt like everything was spinning out from under her control, and she needed to be in control.

Planning. Planning made her feel in control. If all things fail, go to plan B! She always had a plan B, or C, or D. And if that failed, E.

When life throws you a reckless maniac for a son, you have a responsible son who can keep him in line. Now, what did she have? A husband barely alive, and two senseless sons. Calm down! she said to herself. There must be more going on here.

This was not like Daniel, and she needed to figure out why he would do something so reckless. The Quinta virus was barely stable and had unknown side effects. However, one known side effect that was not to be taken lightly was added aggression and instability, which Cliff had been displaying since day one.

Daniel knew better! But, he had changed so much since Amy's death, and there was something he was hiding from her, she could feel it. She needed to figure out what, now. But first, she needed to calm down so she could think straight. Breath! Count to 10 ... 1 ... 2 ... 3 ...

~ ~ ~

I would never have guessed you would break the woman out of jail who killed Amy, Cliff said to Daniel in his mind as they sat next to their father, who was now sitting up and sipping on a thermos of piping hot coffee.

Is that why you told Mom about the Quinta virus? Daniel asked, in his mind to Cliff. To expose my reckless nature? What are you trying to do, Cliff?

Why did you do it? Do you love Susan? Cliff demanded, pushing the question hard against Daniel's skull, enough to make him wince. You know I wanted her for myself.

Yes. Yes, I do, Daniel said, fighting back his brother's presence in his head, and at the same time realizing that he did love Susan. Wow, I love Susan, despite everything she's done? he thought.

Cliff was gone, he removed himself and it felt like a band-aid being ripped out of the inside of his skull. It was enough to make Daniel lose his balance and almost fall forward.

Susan is a special person, I wish things could have been different, Cliff said in his head, he genuinely felt strong affection in the statement. Daniel could feel it coming through into his own mind and mixing with his own thoughts so much that it was hard to distinguish individual feelings.

She's long gone now, Cliff. We'll never see her again, Daniel let him know, showing an image of her walking down the road towards the bus stop in his head.

I see, Cliff said, smiling and getting up to leave. Daniel felt a sudden panic, had he given away too much? Cliff would not be able to find her from only that simple image, could he?

"Where are you going?" Daniel asked, aloud.

"I'm going to find something I lost, brother. It should be a good distraction from all of this," Cliff explained, aloud, while swiftly taking off his suit in the donning booth and heading out the door.

"Good idea, Cliff. It will keep you out of trouble, I am sure," Martin said. "Daniel, can you hand me that Sudoku your mom left?"

Daniel tossed the Sudoku to his father and tried to follow Cliff out. He yelled, "Wait!" but Cliff was long gone, he moved quickly with the prosthetics and the Quinta virus giving him speed.

"Where is your brother hurrying off to, Daniel?" his mother asked, standing in the hallway, leaning back against the stone wall with her arms crossed.

"He is going to look for something he lost, that's what he said anyway ... are you okay, mom?" He knew she was mad at him, if her squinting eyes and pursed lips didn't say it themselves.

She seized him by the arm as he tried to head down the hallway in the direction Cliff had left. "Why do I get the feeling there is more that you aren't telling me? What other secrets are you holding, son?"

"My secrets?" he whispered loudly, looking down the hall in both directions. "My secrets? Come with me!" Now seemed like a good time to clear things up, with Cliff distracted.

He brought his mother down into the third basement, through the enclave and into the hidden disaster bunker. She followed, silent and sullen. "What is this, mother?"

"How did you find out about this? I told Ran not to show you unless..." Beth looked stunned. "You found out? You know Cliff killed Amy?"

"What?" Daniel was more shaken than he could stomach, and he suddenly wanted to throw up. He didn't know if it was hearing those words out loud or knowing that his mother knew that made him more sick. Ran knew. Others knew. The world was turning black. Was he about to pass out?

"Wait, you didn't know?" Beth looked thoroughly baffled.

"Of course I didn't know! Who else knows? Why didn't you tell the police?" Sickness was gripping him and he was trying not to hurl. He let his anger wash over him and held onto that to steady his stomach.

"I couldn't tell the police ... I'd just found out the day before he had injected himself again with the Quinta virus and I didn't want them to find out about that too."

"How did you find out?"

"He'd wanted to be strong for when Susan came to town. He was acting aggressive and irrational and I confronted him..."

"Not about him injecting the virus, about him killing my fiancé!"

"I'm sorry, it was obvious. His behavior ... his hatred for her ... and I knew where he got the drugs he used on the bellman ... Plus, Ran noticed some of the explosives were missing from the bunker. It just all added up."

"So, you have Ran keeping our dark family secrets too. How much does he know? I know he doesn't have a clue about the viruses. Now, I think he has another secret..."

"What new secret?"

"I had just gotten back from..." he held his stomach and felt dizzy, sitting down on one of the chairs next to the computer station. God, Susan had been innocent this whole time! "breaking Susan out of jail. When Ran gave me this key." He held up the square gold key for his mom.

"So, it was you who broke her out! I thought it was Cliff. I've been trying to figure out where he stashed her away. I assumed he was going to hold her prisoner until she gave him what he wanted, whatever that might be."

"What? Who all knows about Susan? Am I the only one who couldn't see she was innocent? How could you let him..." Daniel had no words, the amount of betrayal he felt was overwhelming, topped with the guilt for letting Susan go to jail.

"He is my son, Daniel ... he has always been troublesome. But I never expected for him to do what he did. I blame the Quinta virus for his erratic behavior, he took it right before the incident ... and it's a monster concoction ... He felt so badly afterwards and worked so hard to get you better ... he loves you."

"He felt badly?!? Erratic behavior? Amy was innocent! She deserved better."

Daniel looked at his mother, as if seeing her for the first time. Her eyes were filled with tears and her hands were clenched. She stood up straight and said, "There is nothing we can do for Amy. I am sorry, Daniel."

They stood there in silence, at a stalemate. Years had passed. Years of deception and now that the truth was out he almost wished he never knew. Daniel's insides were churning and settling until he said, "And this, what is all of this? What are you afraid will happen? The apocalypse?"

"Yes, after what happened. Yes! I didn't know where your brother would stop, or if he would stop. I don't know what he wants, but I have a bad feeling. When I have a bad feeling, I make plans, I prepare."

"Well, that you did!" he extended his hands out into the room of supplies, incubation pods, computers, beds and devices he hadn't even have a chance to fully inspect yet. It was enough to last his family decades, that much he did know.

"I planned to tell you about it. When the time came ... but it never seemed like the right time."

"Yeah, I know the feeling..." The rush of anger was gone, and the guilt. Now he felt empty and alone. Alone with his own dark secrets. Was he ready to tell his mother?

"Daniel, what is going on between you and Cliff? It is like he has control over you. It was always the other way around. And he got you to take Quinta? I can't believe it! What has changed? What happened to you?"

His mother noticed he was being controlled? Was he being controlled? Did Cliff have a hold on him? Daniel thought. Susan said he might not know if he did have control. Was Susan right about everything?

"It is the amplification type Mod. We can hear each other's thoughts, read each other's minds. Except he is much better at it than I am. Susan said it had something to do with him being a dream-walker, about the way his brain is wired and that it was better able to use and control the microchip in ways she never expected," Daniel explained. "I've been trying to learn, to fight back, but I don't know if I can tell my own mind anymore."

"I see, now that makes sense why Cliff would want Susan," Beth leaned back against the computer desk, one finger on her pursed lips, peering off into the distance. No doubt she was making more plans.

"So, Susan was right all along," Daniel said aloud. "And innocent."

"Yes. And you broke her out of jail thinking she was guilty? Why?"

"I ... love her," Daniel replied simply. "I couldn't let her go to jail for loving me, but I couldn't forgive her for what she did, what I thought she did ... and now Cliff is going to try to find her."

"What do you mean?" That made her sit back up in her seat.

"Susan is the thing that Cliff lost that he went to go find," Daniel explained. "She told me he visited her in jail. He wanted her to build him a master Mod, one he could use to control everyone. Not just people who have a Mod installed. She refused. So, he left her in prison until she changed her mind. She can be quite stubborn and she's better at resisting Cliff than most. Even without enhancement he is highly persuasive."

"I see. Well, don't worry. I am sure she is long gone," Beth said, reassuringly putting her hand on his shoulder.

"And if you're wrong, mom?"

"Let me deal with your brother. With the Mod, you are no match for him. I'm sorry but you have changed and not for the better. You stay here and take care of your father, get him healed!"

"And what will you do with Susan when you find her? Will you let Cliff do to her what you let him do to Amy?"

"What I let ...!!!" His mom was furious, but so was Daniel, eyes ablaze and locked on her in accusation. "I had no idea he would harm her, I had no idea what he was capable of..."

"But, now you know! Don't let him hurt her, mom, please!" Daniel begged. "Cliff has to be stopped. I've been in denial for so long ... but, I think you have been too."

"I don't know if I could..."

"Me either..."

They were both looking around the room, and both sets of eyes fell on the incubation pod at the same time. They didn't have to read each other's minds to know what the other was thinking, and it was a good plan.

"Like I said, you take care of your father, and I'll take care of Cliff," Beth said solemnly.

~ ~ ~

It had been over a week since both his mom and brother disappeared and Daniel's father was not improving. In fact, over the last few days he'd actually gotten worse. He was going in and out of consciousness, losing more and more of his mind every day. The last Sudoku puzzle he completed was the day they'd left.

Daniel's three helpers, the scientist Cliff had assigned to work on the virus, had no clue what to do. They had been picked for their ability to keep the family's dirty secrets after all, and not for their expertise.

Dr. Steven Lobbs wanted to reformulate and try again. He was in his early thirties, self-assured, tall, dark and lean. He was younger than Daniel but thought that because he appeared much older that he was somehow in charge. The power struggle was annoying, but not something he wasn't used to. Daniel had stopped aging around 22, when he first started drinking the family coffee. So, people often thought he was much younger than he was. It was one of the only negative side effects of drinking the brew – so long as you kept drinking it an ignoring the taste anyway.

Dr. Brooke Dawson was a very attractive, tall brunette and a thoroughly respectable scientist who specialized in organic polymers. She had developed several new implants and had 14 patents, making her the top scientist in the company. She had a good head on her shoulders but was somewhat pessimistic. Her theory was that the virus had evolved and it was too late, they should let it run its course and start funeral arrangements. Daniel couldn't let himself come to that same conclusion, and he found himself frowning at her more often than not.

Dr. Jack Ferris was blue-eyed, red-haired, short and pudgy. A self-proclaimed genius, he'd come straight out of grad school in biomedical engineering at Cornell to work for Cliff six years ago. He was young and eager to test any and all new technology, at any risk. He was almost as aggressive as Cliff and wanted to inject the Quinta virus (of all things) into his father. That was an unacceptable solution. Cliff must have left him with that notion because he had been persistent about it from the beginning.

Thankfully both Lobbs and Dawson agreed with Daniel that the Quinta amalgamate was not something that should be mixed with another, possibly shifting, virus. Tribus had been extremely unstable and it had taken Martin years to fix it. It was likely anything could tip that delicate balance.

Between the four of them, they were at an impasse. None of them could agree on what to do next. Martin's consciousness had faded so much that he had no input to break a tie or offer a new suggestion. Daniel was learning towards Lobbs' idea of reformulation but wasn't sure how much he had learned from his father before his mental state had deteriorated. Lobbs was, after all, just a microbiologist. Likely they would try a new formulation today if Martin regressed further overnight.

Daniel entered the quarantine room and was beginning to don his gear when he noticed the bed was empty. He quickly ran over to the other side of the bedchamber, "Father?"

He heard a whimpering (interchangeably with fits of growling) sound coming from behind the curtain in the corner. He slowly pulled back the curtain to see his father curled up in the fetal position, rocking back and forth on the floor. He was wearing only blue cotton nurse pants, and there were black streaks all over his body.

Ferris! Damn you Ferris! Daniel couldn't believe he had gone behind his back and injected the Quinta virus. Martin's teeth were bared and his eyes were squeezed shut. There was froth coming out of his mouth as if he had rabies. He was jerking in spasms, snarling. His muscles were so wound up and he had lost so much weight over the last few weeks that his body was nothing but veins, muscles, bones and sinew hardened together.

"Father? It's okay. It's me, Daniel," he said while getting on his knees and approaching slowly on all fours. The whimpering was being replaced more and more by growling and he stopped moving forward because it was starting to sound more like a cornered wolverine than a human being. He got up and stepped back, hitting the emergency button on the side of the bed.

Where were those three buffoons? Where was Ferris? How could he inject him and then leave him like this?

The sudden movement of reaching for the emergency button caused Martin to open his eyes, staring directly at his son. It was the scariest thing Daniel had ever seen: eyes full of dark red blood – they were so bloodshot. There was something very frantic in the way he was sneering now, and animalistic. "Father?"

"What's going on? What is the emergency?" Lobbs said, entering the room, with Ferris and Dawson not far behind.

"Stay back!" Daniel yelled, turning to look at the doorway. His father growled and snarled at the abrupt sound which made Daniel jump back. His metal foot slipped sideways on the partially torn curtain on the floor, twisting and turning his leg. He fell down, hitting his head on the hospital bed, going dizzy, seeing stars.

When he opened his eyes, he was face to face with the froth mouthed, black streaked and bloody-eyed creature on the floor. The last thing Daniel saw were claws slashing towards his face. He experienced shearing pain in his skull as the beast gorged out his eyeballs in a clawing fury. Screaming, he kicked Martin back with his metal legs and heard him slam against the far wall.

His head was throbbing and all he heard was what sounded like wrestling and screaming as the three doctors attempted to reign-in Martin who was fighting like a rabid animal fueled by the power of the Quinta virus.

Daniel felt his left eye dangling from his face and reached forward, blind, feeling for his right eye with his human hand. He eventually came across a bloody mass on the floor, squished. He swiftly passed out from the pain and shock.

Chapter 15

Fully Integrated Cyborg Functionality Test Commence

Daniel saw bright flashes and twinged with the intensity. The flashes coalesced into a computer interface. There were screen selections in English. He opened his swollen and ripped eyelids to see light pour through, flooding out the interface.

"What is this?" he asked.

The voice of Dr. Brooke Dawson answered in her typical dead-pan monotone, "It is an organic light-emitting diode interface built into a willow glass, wrap-around backplane in a fully integrated visual stimulation virtual reality simulator I developed for blind patients."

"Oh, that's all?" Daniel answered, sarcastically.

"We'll need to calibrate it, as soon as you are ready, of course." Brooke replied. "It essentially uses the remote power and brainwave amplification technology you developed with Dr. Susan Aldean to aid in the ease of operation. Or, more simply put, we will be able to use your thoughts to calibrate the new eyes I have installed."

"Thank you for putting it simply for me, Dr. Dawson."

"You're welcome. Are you ready to start?"

"Should I close my eyes? I can barely see the interface with the light pouring through."

"I think it would be best if you kept them open. Any calibration would be better in the state in which you use the implants. Let's begin."

"Okay."

"Think 'Up' while saying the word out loud," Brooke said as she touched the up arrow on her computer, which was connected to both eyeballs via electrical leads.

"Up," Daniel responded.

"Good, now think 'Down' and say that as well," she continued, hitting the down arrow key. "Now 'Left', and 'Right.' Good!"

He acquiesced with all commands, though not particularly liking being told what to do. He hoped this would be over soon.

"Okay, think and say, 'Main Control' and now, 'Select'," she commanded.

"Now let's test out the interface. Think 'Main Control' and use the up, down, right, and left arrows to move through the commands. Think 'Select' to make a selection. You can always go back to the main control by thinking it as well."

There were ten different visual patterns to select from, and over a thousand languages. The vision system went from 20/20 to macro, micro, fish eye, and about 20 other versions of enhancement. "You developed this for blind patients, Brooke? Really?" he finally said aloud.

"I wanted to be thorough," she explained. "If you are going to do something, you might as well do it to the best of your ability. Don't you agree, Dr. Jahren?"

"Yes, thank you. This is exceptional work," he said as he sat up and looked at her. Her bright blue eyes were no longer blue, they appeared closer to violet, almost red. Though neither color described it, colors in general were muted. "Why aren't your eyes blue anymore?"

"The OLED has trouble with producing blues, unfortunately," she explained. "There is a German team working on it, but the technology just isn't quite there yet."

He couldn't help but notice a cut on her face, with black streaks coming out, and her arm was bandaged and in a sling. More black streaks were on her arm as well. Was she always that skinny?

"I am sorry about your arm, and your face. How is my father?"

She seemed a bit sweaty, and her eyes were bloodshot. Not a good sign, she was starting to look like Martin had right before he'd been found on the floor. "He's ... rabid. He's in quarantine. We had to put in a plexiglass confinement. We're all in quarantine, in fact. I don't think it is safe for us to leave. I put on a full bio-suit to go get those implants for you, and even then Dr. Lobbs was cautioning against it."

"Why? Do you think that ... that the virus has spread?"

"There is no doubt in my mind, Dr. Jahren. You are the only one who has not displayed any symptoms in the last few days. Dr. Lobbs and Dr. Ferris are in a worse condition than I am, and I am deteriorating rapidly."

"What do you mean, deteriorating rapidly?"

"The combined effect of all the immunotherapies ... maybe even the coffee ... it is unclear. We are not sure if it was the Quinta virus injection, but R.V. 321J-2017 has shifted and now produces something uncharacteristically violent, mind numbing and highly contagious. I sustained only a scratch on my cheek and arm nine days ago and already my mental capacity and health are greatly minimized."

"Nine days? It's been nine days?"

"Yes, Dr. Jahren. Dr. Ferris was not so lucky. He was bitten and went into convulsions within hours. Dr. Lobbs was able to confine your father but sustained several injuries. We worked together on coming up with a temporary solution for whatever this nightmare is that we are dealing with. But, Lobbs has not regained consciousness since yesterday. I will likely follow suit. As, although I was the least infected, I've still been symptomatic since the onset of this ordeal. It's inevitable, we are all doomed."

"I sustained more injuries than you but I feel fine. Why am I not sick?" Daniel asked.

"That is a very good question." Brooke was looking increasingly ill as she spoke. "I should probably go lay down and think about that," she said as she got up to go to one of the hospital beds in the fully crammed room, closing the plexiglass door behind her.

There were five plexiglass holding chambers within the room around five beds. The furthest one down had Daniel's father, snarling and growling at the doorway. Ferris was in the one next to his, curled-up on the floor and whimpering. Lobbs appeared as if he was sleeping soundly on his bed, but he also looked like he had lost weight and was covered in Quinta virus streaks. He must have gotten scratched in several places. They all looked terrible, sickly and thin.

Daniel didn't know what to think. He felt fine besides a bit of a headache from what must be eye strain. There was only slight pain from the sewed-up cuts on his eyelids. Understandable, given he had his eyeballs ripped out only nine days ago. Had he really been out for nine whole days? He looked at his bedside IV and noticed barbiturates. Dawson must have had him on anesthesia for the operation and had just kept him out for the pain until the implants were fully installed.

He had been entirely exposed when his father attacked him. Was it because he already had the Quinta virus that he was unaffected? Not likely, his father's health had deteriorated rapidly before the Quinta virus was administered. For all he knew, all that did was make him stronger, not less sick.

He stood there, looking at his father who was in a mindless rage, not even capable of knowing to reach for the door handle ... bloodied claws sliding down the plexiglass ... mindless, vacant, bloody eyes ... Mindless! Was it the Mod that made Daniel resistant? Was the Mod protecting his brain from the deterioration of the virus? Stimulating brain activity? There was only one way to find out.

"Wake up Dawson, I need your help. I think I might have found a solution," he said knocking on her plexiglass door. She looked like she was not doing well, but she was going to have to pull herself together, they had brain surgery to perform.

Ferris volunteered his father for the Quinta virus, so Ferris was going to get the Mod first. He was not exactly a willing patient. They had to shoot him with a tranquilizer and wait for him to stop writhing on the floor. Brooke was strong, having the Quinta virus running through her veins, and was more help than he could have hoped for, even being sick. She had been helpful in getting all the equipment while he went to get a handful of the latest Mods Susan had left. Both of them were forced to go out in full biogear, and thankfully it was after hours at the facility so they hadn't run into anyone.

Daniel had worked with Ran to develop what he called a 'surgeon-helper' robotic hand for a military contract that proved useful. This was the first live surgery for which Daniel had the opportunity to use it. It was more stable and precise than even his own hand, and that was saying something.

"Merely a simple upload, and then wait? Correct? I have never performed one of these before," Brooke admitted after the operation was complete.

"I've performed several. Yes, just hit that button once we are ready to go. I'll dose back the anesthesia and we will be able to tell if he can regain consciousness."

"Okay, ready."

They waited for what felt like an eternity for Ferris to open his eyes, which were still fairly bloodshot. "What happened? What is going on? Why am I strapped down?"

Brooke was wheezing, but she said, "Oh, thank god!" as excitedly as she could. "Can I pass out now?" She was one tough cookie, obviously giving it everything she had to hold it together until the end. Her adrenaline push must have worn off at the sight of success, because she was slumped over and barely holding onto her seat. Daniel helped her to her bed.

"One down, four more to go," he said, scanning around the room.

~ ~ ~

Beth had been searching for Cliff for weeks with no success. Always one step behind him. How hard could it be to find a man with metal legs? He hid them well, it seemed. Even Susan was better at hiding than Beth expected. She must have known Cliff would come looking for her and knew to stay out of reach. Smart girl!

She was beginning to feel more and more unsettled and had a strong urge to return home. She had a bad feeling about her husband, even though Daniel had said he was improving and the cancer was gone before she left. She got the feeling he might be lying to spare her feelings and keep her on track in the search. She hated giving up, but she couldn't shake the feeling that she needed to return back to Colorado, now.

Plus, Cliff was not answering his phone anymore. The constant questioning him where he was had likely given away her intent to follow him, and he was no longer engaging. She had tracked Cliff's last phone call to Seattle. She spent her days going from one coffee shop to the next, mostly near bus stops and crowded areas.

Today she was waiting in a small coffee shop on first avenue watching people pass by outside, hoping to see her son. Instead, she saw Susan. Recognizable despite the chopped pink hair and the fact that she had her face hidden behind some flowers she was holding up conspicuously. Was that a bouquet of wildflowers from the farmers market?

Beth ran out the door and yelled, "Susan, stop!"

Susan looked back, saw her face and bolted in the opposite direction, surprisingly fast in heels. It didn't last long though, as Susan tripped on a storm grate and went flying forward, almost into an intersection. Flowers scattered in every direction.

"I'm not going to hurt you dear, I'm here to help," Beth explained, helping Susan up off of the ground. "Let's get somewhere out of sight."

"How did you find me?" Susan demanded once they were in a parking garage stairwell. The bum urine smell made it clear what this stairwell was typically used for.

"I was trying to find Cliff..."

"Cliff! Is he with you? Is he here!?"

"He's out trying to find you..."

"I have to go!" Susan tried to run up the stairs but Beth caught her and brought her back down.

"I know, Susan. We all know..."

"Oh, we do? So, you know that your son is a murderer? Does Daniel know? Where is Daniel?" Susan's voice was breaking as she spoke Daniel's name.

Was she going to cry? Did she expect Daniel to meet her in Seattle? Why? Beth thought.

"My husband is ill, Daniel is taking care of him. He is no match for Cliff anyway, not after the Mod you put in his head," Beth accused. "Cliff practically has Daniel at his beck and call."

"I didn't know that it would do that, honestly. I was only trying to help people. How could I have known? I might be able to design something that can fix it, that can make Daniel more resilient. But I need my lab ... and another dream-walker," Susan explained. "And, I don't know how long it will take."

"I see. I may have a better plan. You'll need to come with me, do you trust me?" Beth asked.

"No! I don't. What would you do if Cliff showed up, right now? You let him murder Amy. Who would stop him from murdering me?"

"Like I said, I have a plan. I won't let him harm you, Susan, I promise."
"Does Daniel know about this plan of yours?"

"Yes, he helped me come up with it ... he loves you."

She could see Susan's eyes welling up with tears, even though she was trying to put on a tough face. "Alight, what is this plan of yours?"

~ ~ ~

Cliff had been scouring Seattle for weeks. In pursuit of the elusive Susan. This was the strangest city he had ever been in, and the greenest. It was a stark contrast to the harsh, desert landscape of his childhood.

The people were different too. Not a single person looked twice at his odd shaped legs under the dress pants he had thrown on over them in order to be more inconspicuous. Most everyone had their heads down under hoods – shuffling about in the drizzling, cold rain. Oddly, no one carried an umbrella. After the first week he tossed his umbrella too and bought a rainproof hooded jacket like the locals. The apathy of the people matched the dreary chill that reached through and into his bones.

Today he was settled in front of three large glass spheres filled with offices and greenery. It was a mix of technology and nature that reminded him of the dream he had where he first saw Susan and her microchip. Like the sparkling, green, futuristic city. A place he thought she might be drawn to.

As he stood there, he realized he'd made most of that dream come true. He'd awoken to the nightmare of his life and – through perseverance, vision and dedication – achieved everything he set out to accomplish. Rocket legs. Sonic blasters. Power in his veins that defeated his disease. He had the strength and ability to go wherever he wanted, whenever he wanted. In fact, he attained a level of ability far beyond human. Superhuman, in fact.

But, he wanted more. There was so much more the whole human race could achieve!

What was that world he saw in the end of his dream? Not one of divided, idiotic politics and old money families controlling the masses into destitution. For what? For the sole purpose of greed. His dream was so much more. It was one with flying vehicles, buildings like this one in front of him. With larger, spiral buildings up above and greenery all around.

The world needed to be led to it's destiny, and the idiots in charge were not at all capable ... at least not in his lifetime.

Susan was the key to bringing that world to life, and he knew it. His dreams always came true, one way or another. He was going to make it happen, and she was going to help him, like it or not. With her by his side he could do anything. They had come so far together already. The Mods. Nanogenerators. If only she hadn't fallen for Daniel. Why did he have to go and mess everything up? If only she had wanted to stay in Colorado. If only she could see his vision. See what they could be together.

She was proving to be better at hiding than he thought and he was not good at being patient in seeking her out. It was driving him mad. His fists were clenched at his side, rain dripping down his knuckles which were blue with the cold. Where could she be hiding? He hailed a cab and asked to go to Pike's Place Market. Maybe she was buying flowers, she always loved flowers.

~ ~ ~

"Ferris, what made you think that injecting me with the Quinta virus was going to help the situation?" Martin was lucid, sipping on coffee and almost back to his normal self besides the obvious toll the virus had taken on his body.

"Cliff demanded that I do it if things were not going well. I was following his last command," Ferris admitted. "He said it would make you stronger, and it did."

"Yes, well ... I believe it had no effect on the mental depreciation, and only made the predicament worse for your when you tried to rein me in," said Martin.

"Thankfully the Mods are working. I can see that you are feeling much better. Your mental clarity is astounding, actually," Daniel could sense his father's mind working, and it was like a well-oiled machine. Focused and methodical.

"What do you mean, my mental clarity is astounding, son?" Martin was quick to catch his slip. Daniel was able to read everyone's mind in the room now that they had a Mod, and he was finding it difficult to tell what was said aloud and what was not. "I feel ... connected, to you, son. To all of you."

There were nods around the room. Can anyone hear my thoughts? Daniel asked in his head, projecting outward. More nods around the room. "Okay, try to speak to each other."

He felt a faint impression from his father, and the other doctors in the room were gazing in Martin's direction as well. There was nothing from the other three. The Mods they all had were of the older variety, not the more enhanced one Susan had created specifically for Daniel. They were closer to the one in Bill's head, just enough enhancement to run the prosthesis. Just enough to enhance brain activity against the virus. Martin must have a strong mind indeed if he was able to project thoughts with the older version.

"Well, it looks like I need to find a more suitable solution for this virus. I don't like having my mind in the hands of another person – even if it is my son's," Martin was quick to catch on to the situation. The other three scientists in the room took another few seconds for what he said to sink-in and then stared at Daniel in awe mixed with fear.

"Yes, I agree. Unfortunately, we'll need to be in quarantine until then. I'm not sure how fast this will spread if it gets out," Daniel added. "So far, we know that subcutaneous inject of bodily fluid is the fastest method of transfer. In addition, given Dawson and Lobbs only received cuts, and somehow ended up with the Quinta virus as well, there is more going on than I know. In the past, Quinta was only transferable straight into muscle tissue."

"You are quite correct. This combination of pathogens appears decidedly contagious and may even be airborne," Lobbs added. "I would say that it is deadly as well, given the only cure is brain surgery and how fast and thoroughly the illness took hold."

"I agree. The risk is too high to leave." Dawson eyes were the least blood-shot of the bunch and her pallor was improving. However, Daniel could hear her say in her head, We might as well work on our tombstones. He wasn't sure how much of that attitude he would be able to stand.

"You mean, we have to stay here until we find a cure? In this room? How long will it take?" Ferris demanded, unable to hold back his mounting panic.

"Calm down, I am sure with the five of us working on it, we'll have a solution in no time," Lobbs added. "Correct, Dr. Jahren?"

"On the contrary, only one of us has the expertise to establish even the protocols for such an endeavor. The rest of us are dead weight," Dawson concluded in such an indifferent tone as to make everyone in the room sink into depression.

"We have everything we need to synthesize a cure. I cannot guarantee a timeframe, but I will endeavor to deliver as efficiently as possible," Martin offered, but no one in the room felt any better about the situation.

"What happened here?" Beth said, entering through the chamber door.

"Stop, honey!" Martin exclaimed. "You will need to be in full gear to enter the room ... we have had an incident."

"What's going on? Why the plexiglass enclosures? Daniel! Your eyes! What happened to your eyes!" she said, walking toward her son.

"Stay back Mom, please!" Daniel yelled and Beth kept her distance.

"You're infected to? You like fine, except for your eyes. They look like mirrors, with flashing symbols, are those implants?"

"They look like mirrors? All I see is a computer interface. I haven't had time to work-out the intricacies."

"Yes, Dr. Jahren. There is a setting to project an image of more natural eyes. It is under the 'Eye' command, in 'Projections.' I uploaded a picture similar to your original hazel. Can you see it?" Dr. Dawson explained.

Daniel was able to find the picture and select the impression using his thoughts, it was seamless technology. "Is that better Mom?"

"Yes. Though, I think there is a bit more gold in the green than normal. What happened? Why did you need implants? Why can't I come closer?"

"Honey, the virus evolved to not only attack the cancer in the brain, but to shut off neural activity as well. In effect, it caused all but the most rudimentary of brain functions to be eliminated. Through deductive reasoning Daniel was able to find a solution and install Mods in all of us to re-stimulate cognitive function. However, we do not know how contagious we all are In addition, anyone who comes into contact with us may rapidly infect others before even showing symptoms."

"Do you mean a complete loss of higher order thinking?" she asked and was answered with nods. "Well, it was designed to attack glioma cells. It looks like you all have Quinta virus as well ... how did that happen?"

"Ferris," Daniel said calmly to his mom but in his head he was furious. He glared over at Dr. Ferris. Ferris held his head as if he had a headache, rubbing his temple and frowning sorely at Daniel. "He said Cliff commanded him to do it."

"Cliff? Is Cliff back?"

"No, and I'm guessing you didn't find him if you are asking that question." Daniel answered. For goodness sake, was there to be no good news today?

"He specifically ordered that if Martin took a turn for the worse I was to personally administer the Quinta virus," Ferris explained.

"Cliff ordered you to do that and you just followed him blindly?" Beth's voice let everyone know she was more than annoyed. "And you Daniel, you didn't want to tell me that things were going badly?"

"What could you have done? Everything happened so quickly ... and we just finished installing the Mods..."

"Do you ... um ... did you tell them ... the other effects of the Mod, Daniel?" Beth was trying to ask about the mind control without giving it away. Everyone in the room knew what she was saying though. They all nodded at once. "I see."

"I will find a cure, and we will remove these microchips, honey," Martin assured.

"Until then, Mom, you might want to make sure everyone stays clear of here, especially a certain someone..." Daniel knew his mother would catch on about Cliff. If Cliff knew he could control everyone in this room with a single thought, who knows what he would do with that kind of power.

"Right, well ... I will leave you to it then. Good luck!" She was backing out of the room, eyes wide with a strained smile on her face. She was never a very good liar.

Chapter 16
Buried Alive

Beth ran through the corridor, franticly trying to come up with a new plan. This news did not fit well with her current plans at all. She had just set a lure for Cliff to come back and if he came back now and found out what happened it could have devastating consequences that she didn't even want to think about. She needed Daniel's help getting Cliff into the incubation chamber, except he was now stuck in quarantine. Who could she possibly get to help her? Who could she trust? Ran!

Ran was in the military development bunker, as usual. He was toying with the acid wash tech when she burst through the door, huffing and puffing, "Shit just hit the fan, Ran!"

"Well, it was bound to happen. Which shit, which fan?"

"An out of control virus ... a homicidal madman, pick one?" she said between breaths.

"Same old news in your family Beth, what's new?" he laughed, likely thinking she was joking.

"Thanks," she said, stopping to catch her breath. "I found Susan, she's at the main facility upstairs as we speak. Cliff could be back at any moment. We need to get him into the incubation chamber before he finds out what happened to his father and the rest of the team."

"What happened to his father? Is Martin okay? What team?"

"I ... umm ... wow," she realized she hadn't told Ran about the secret oncolytic research utilizing deadly viruses. "Martin has grade IV glioblastoma..."

"My god, I had no idea. I knew he was suck but ... I am so sorry. Is that why you been gone? Everyone just disappeared ..."

"Yes, and no. Daniel and a team administered a developmental virus that was able to clear out the tumor cells."

"That is good news then?"

"No, the virus shifted into something dangerous, deadly even. Then the whole team got infected, they're all in quarantine."

"I see," Ran's typical light hearted, humorous dispositions was beginning to turn as he realized the gravity of what she was saying. "And the homicidal madman? I am assuming you mean your son, Cliff? And why are we putting Cliff into incubation, Beth? What has he done now?"

Beth looked at Ran as if he were an idiot for a minute before she remembered that he didn't know about the Mod mind control problem. "I found out why he framed Susan. It wasn't what we thought, it wasn't to keep her from Daniel. Cliff wants her to build something for him, that he can use to control people's minds."

"Well, that is a problem. So, why did you bring Susan back here? Isn't that like bringing the sheep into the lion's den?"

"I had to get Cliff back here, where we can properly handle him."

"Putting him into an incubation chamber is the proper way to handle your son, Beth?"

"At least until I can figure out what to do with him, yes! I can't have him running around killing people and he has already figured out how to use his current Mod to control others. Who knows what he will do next?"

"He is controlling people already? How?"

"Yes. Susan tried to explain it to me..."

"Susan tried to explain what to you, Mom?" Cliff said, walking in behind her. "Where is Susan, by the way? I know you found her."

"I..." Beth's eyes were wide and looking at Ran for help. He was looking at her in confusion. She picked up the closest thing she could find, which happened to be the acid wash tech, and pointed it at her son.

"Whoa! Whoa! Mom, what has gotten into you? What did Susan, a convicted murderer by the way, tell you?"

Beth glanced down at the device in her hands, could she bring herself to pull the trigger? Ran was right behind her, but she knew he was no match for her son. Not only did Cliff have several weapons built into his legs, but he was about as strong as King Kong with the amount of Quinta virus in his body.

"She said ... that you were blackmailing her, to force her to work for you. Is that true?"

"All I did was offer her a way out of prison, if she would come work for me. Is that so bad? Mom, put the weapon down. We both know you could never use that on me."

"I let her come and get some of her things from the lab, she's in the main facility," Beth said as she slowly lowered the acid wash down onto the table. She was following Ran's movement from the corner of her eye, he was circling to the left of Cliff. Ran had an idea, and she knew it. So, she made sure to lock eyes with her son, and keep him for looking in Ran's direction.

A sonic blast left Cliff choking on vomit, Ran must have found a sonic sickener and activated it. That wouldn't stop Cliff for too long though. She picked up a wrench, thinking she might be able to knock Cliff out when he flung her back with a simple twist of his wrist. She could feel her ribs crack when she hit the corner of the metal table behind her, and her head was spinning from the pain.

Ran had reached the acid wash pack, but Cliff had him three feet in the air by the collar bone before he had even flung his mother aside like a rag doll. Beth was unable to see anything more from below the desk where she landed. But, she heard screaming from both men and the sound of breaking bones. The next sound she heard was the door slamming shut.

Her breathing was strained. She could feel a rib piecing her lung and it was getting harder to breath. She tried not to think about the extent of the internal damage, and especially tried not to move too quickly as she crawled over to where she had last seen Ran.

Ran's blank eyes were staring out from his twisted body, which was dissolving slowly into the acid on the floor. She quickly looked away, squeezing her eyes shut and trying to remove the image now seared into her brain. Ran had been a friend for over 30 years. How could her son have done that to him?

There was a trail of blood and green ooze leading out to the doorway, Cliff was injured. He would probably be heading straight for Susan though. She opened up her pocket to pull out her cell phone, no bars. Great! Well, of course not, she was in the bunker. What was she thinking? It was getting harder to concentrate on anything through the stabbing pain in her side. She needed to get help, she could feel her lungs filling with blood.

There was no stopping Cliff now. She hoped that Susan would turn out to be smarter than all of them and just run as far away as she could from this place.

~ ~ ~

Cliff needed to get to a medical room straight away. He removed his soiled shirt and wiped as much of the acid off as he could, but his chest and right arm were burning so badly it was hard to think. He didn't even want to look at his arm, he knew it wouldn't be salvaged.

Things had happened so quickly, he didn't mean for any of it to happen. Ran was dead. He could see his blank eyes staring at him through his skull. It was self-defense. Ran had tried to kill him. And his own mother? Had she tried to kill him too?

He found a wash station and rinsed ... the pain was excruciating. The water swirling into the drain was blood red, and he knew he had to stop the bleeding before he passed out. He took off his belt and wrapped it around his right shoulder.

In desperation, he reached out in his mind for his brother, Daniel. "I need your help, brother," he projected, sending images of his arm. He had never tried to reach him over such a large distance and didn't know if it was possible but he knew he had little time.

Cliff? Cliff is that you? Where are you? he heard Daniel respond in his head. He was only able to send jumbled images back to him. He tried to focus on his location. His mind was fading as he fell to his knees in the haz-mat shower. Help me, please!

When Cliff opened his eyes next, he was staring at lights on the ceiling. He was laying in a hospital bed. The pain was gone. He could feel his brother's presence in the room. And his fathers. Odd. "Father?"

"Yes, son. I'm so glad you made it. You lost a lot of blood," Martin replied from somewhere to the left of him. He tried to move to look over to his father but found that he was strapped down to the bed. His mind was a bit fuzzy as well, did they have him drugged?

Yes, Cliff. You are drugged, he heard Daniel say in his head. What did you do to Mom, where is she? I saw you hurt her. Where is she? The thoughts were like bullets in his head, pounding and ricocheting off his skull. Too intense, too focused.

I don't know. She attacked me. Ran attacked me, he replied in his head, trying to form the thoughts. She's in the bunker, the military bunker.

"Father, we'll need to gear up again. It looks like mom is injured as well and in the military bunker," Daniel said to Martin aloud.

"You have a military bunker?" Ferris said.

"I'm not surprised," said Dawson.

Cliff realized he could feel everyone in the room the same way he felt his brother. And, that meant one thing. He reached out to Ferris and told him to knock-out Daniel. He heard a smack, them a crumpled thud. He told Dawson to unstrap him. His brother obviously overestimated how much consciousness it took to exercise control over the earlier Mods. He could practically control these three without a Mod.

"Why is it that you all have Mods?" Cliff asked, sitting up and looking around the quarantine room while pulling out the IV in his left arm. His right arm was gone and he was bandaged from the neck down to his waist on his right side. "Put him in one of those rooms," he told Lobbs, who immediately drug Daniel into a quarantine plexiglass holding area. "What is the purpose of these enclosures?"

"The virus evolved, son. The effect was lack of brain function except primal necessity. Daniel was able to install Mods that invigorated our minds. Adeptly finding a solution before we all wasted away. Unfortunately, we are stuck in quarantine until we can come up with a permanent answer that does not involve invasive surgery."

"I see. I believe we need to go find out what happened to mother, let's go." Cliff said, and everyone in the room stood up at once, as if on command. Cliff smiled, it was nice when no one argued with him.

They reached the military bunker and Beth could not be found. There wasn't much left of Ran, just a pile of ooze on the floor. His mother must have gone to find Susan and warn her. They would no doubt be in the main facility upstairs.

"We should get in bio-hazard gear, son. We don't want an epidemic on our hands," Martin cautioned, putting his hand on Cliff's good shoulder. Cliff shrugged it off and walked around the room picking up pieces of gear.

"We don't, father?" He came across the interchangeable arm, he'd always wanted to try these out for himself. He had to use a Kevlar vest to strap it into place for now. Thankfully the pain medication was still working as he pushed the interface into his shoulder socket, hoping not to disturb the stitched-up wound before he could apply adhesive gel to seal it. Success, he felt his new arm come online. He opened and closed the sonic blaster hand, working each of the fingers one by one to get used to the control.

"That's right, son. If this virus gets to the facility above, it could get out. We don't have a cure. Who knows how many people could die."

"But, we do have a cure. We are the only ones who have a cure, the solution, in fact."

"The Mods are not a solution, son. I can develop a real cure, I just need time."

"Imagine, if you will, a world where no one argues with you. Wouldn't that be nice?" Cliff was imagining it himself, and it had so many possibilities.

"What are you suggesting?" Martin asked, gazing up as sirens began to go off.

"That's the beauty of it all, Father. I no longer have to suggest anything." Cliff ordered all four of the people to line up behind him and follow him through the door ... and that is exactly what they did. He didn't even have to say a word.

~ ~ ~

Had it been days? Maybe hours? Beth finally made it up to where she had left Susan. Susan turned out to not be as smart as she had hoped because she was sitting there at her laptop, fiddling around with her darn ICModTech when Beth stumbled in and said, "You're lucky it's me and not Cliff, now run!"

"What happened to you?" the girl said back to her, still not running ... coming over to help her sit down.

"A little accident. Listen, things are worse than you can imagine. Wow, I don't even know how to explain this..."

"I've been watching the monitor. I saw Daniel bring Cliff into a quarantine room with his father and those three scientists that were always following Cliff around. Then everyone left Daniel and went into that room you came out of where there are no monitors. What's in that room? What's going on?"

"You've got to be kidding me?" Beth glanced over at the monitor in the quarantine room and saw Daniel laid-out on the hospital bed. She pressed a button and it sent a loud buzzing noise into his room and an intercom blared, "Daniel, wake up!"

"Mom? Are you okay?" Daniel said, rubbing his head and sitting straight up.

"Yes, I'm fine. What happened?" she lied but there was no time to talk about her injuries right now.

"The worst thing imaginable, that's what."

Beth knew what that meant and got up to reach for the emergency switch for the building, smacking it hard. She needed to evacuate everyone before Cliff made it up, virus in tow. Water was now coming down from sprinklers and the alarms were wailing.

"Susan, you need to leave. Never come back here, do you hear me?"

"What about Daniel, is he okay?"

"I'm sorry but Daniel has been infected with a deadly virus. Cliff is about to bring that virus into this facility. There is only one way to stop him, and you had better not be anywhere near when I hit that button, dear. Now, Go!"

"I can't leave him!"

"Susan," Daniel said from the quarantine room. "I need you to listen to my mom. Cliff is on his way, and if he gets to you ... please, you have to leave."

"No, I am not leaving! What can I do to help? There must be something I can do."

"Leave, go to your dream-walker, Darren. Forget about this place. Forget about me, it's too late for me."

Beth was finding Susan's inability to understand the gravity of the situation infuriating, she was not listening to reason. She would have to come up with something to distract the girl, quick. "There might be someone who can stop Cliff, another dream-walker who lives very close. Miss Tinny, the kid's old Native American nanny. She taught Cliff everything he knows. She's at this address." Beth scribbled the reservation address on a torn-off piece of paper and handed it to Susan. "It's not far from here. Go now and find her! Hurry!"

"That's right! Maybe she can overpower Cliff, or convince him to stop, she is the only one! Go!" Daniel said, aiding in the ruse to convince Susan to leave.

Susan looked like she wasn't sure. Buy it girl, buy it!! Every breath and every second she wasted was irksome, but Beth tried to keep her cool. "Please, you're our only hope." That seemed to make Susan put some pep in her step. She shoved her computer and equipment into her bag and took the slip of paper with the address.

"I love you, Daniel," she said, "I'll be back for you soon, I promise!" She blew a kiss to the monitor and left out of the room.

When Susan was safely out of earshot, Beth said, "Can you get out of there? I've got a plan!"

"Yes, Cliff didn't realize these chambers were only made to keep mindless people at bay," Daniel explained while opening up the plexiglass enclose to demonstrate.

"What would happen if I set off an EMP?" Beth asked.

"That would likely kill everyone with a Mod down here. If not instantly, then eventually because the virus would take over."

"So, it would destroy the Mods?" She asked, looking at the monitor outside the military bunker. Cliff had just opened the door and was leaving.

"Likely ... I guess it would depend on the shock of the blast ... where are we going to find an EMP? Don't tell me, I think I can guess..."

"I'm going to go try and stop them from coming upstairs, you hurry as fast as you can! They have just left the bunker."

Not very many people were in the building today, but she had to make sure everyone was out. She could feel her right lung filling with fluid, and she wasn't sure how much time she had left. The only thing that mattered now was stopping Cliff. She didn't want to die knowing she let lose an epidemic on the world. That would not be her legacy.

She spent all her energy and concentration on checking all the monitors and yelling over the intercom at the stragglers who thought it was just a drill. She saw Susan running out of the building and was glad that she had made it out. "Good girl," she said, and then she left to go downstairs. There was only one solution to dealing with Cliff now ... and it involved a big red button and not a nanny.

~ ~ ~

"Stop right there, Cliff!" Daniel demanded. "I don't want to have to use this!" Daniel meant every word. He really didn't want to use the round, glowing object in his hand. He didn't know if it would be completely ineffective or fry everyone's brains in the room, including his own. In fact, he really didn't even know exactly what it did, only that it was in the drawer labeled "EMP" in his mother's apocalypse room.

Put it down, he heard Cliff command in his head. Daniel resisted with everything he had, his body wanted to follow the command and he kept having to tell it to persist.

He looked to his father and felt a strong connection. Father, can you resist him? he said in his mind. Hold him back. I've got a syringe, if I can just inject him! He felt his father struggling to break free.

Daniel raised his hand and used the anti-gravity mechanism built into his prothesis to throw everyone off balance, hoping that would help his father distract Cliff long enough for him to free his mind. It worked! They were all in the air in the hallway. Cliff was caught completely off guard.

Martin had Cliff pinned to the side of the wall and Daniel almost reached him when Cliff kicked his father in the chest. Lobbs and Ferris took hold and started to pummel Martin mid-air. Dawson bounded towards Daniel in a rage, knocking the syringe out of his hand.

There was only one thing he could do now – set off the EMP. He pushed himself backward from the wall and threw the grenade-like device down the hallway, towards his brother. Cliff caught it in his hand and tried to toss it back before it exploded. But, Martin latched onto Cliff's hand, pulling him close in a tight embrace with the device wedged between.

A deafening explosion rung in all their heads and there was a flash of light before everything went dark. They all fell to the ground at once in a hard thud of flesh and metal on the floor.

Daniel, miraculously, retained consciousness despite the worst headache imaginable. Dawson had been flung on top of him in the blast, and he pushed her unconscious body aside. His vision was taken out by the EMP, and he could see nothing as he crawled down the hallway using his one flesh arm towards where he had last seen his brother. He felt through the bodies on the floor and he found the syringe. He then located his brother's mechanical arm, reached up to his neck and stuck in the needle delivering anesthesia that would make him unconscious for hours. That is if he ever regained consciousness from the blast.

"Good job, son," he heard his mother say over the intercom down the hallway, the blast radius must have been small. "You might want to try that remote power trigger I know you were smart enough to pick up."

"You do plan for everything, don't you, Mom?" he said as he opened up a small metal box and removed the battery-like object with a tiny blue button on top and held it down with his thumb. His vision came back online, the interface at reset. He still had an excruciating headache.

"Obviously, I taught you well how to prepare," she laughed but then started to cough and wheeze. "Check on your father, he isn't moving."

Daniel could now move all of his appendages, which meant that his Mod, thankfully, wasn't fried. He had been the least close to the blast though, and had Dawson covering him, so he wasn't sure about the rest of the people in the hallway.

He moved Martin's body off of his brother and found a large hole in his chest where the EMP must have exploded in Cliff's hand. He was dead. His father was dead. Likely instantly during the explosion.

Daniel stared up at the camera in the hallway and knew he didn't have to say anything to his mother. She saw. He didn't know if he could speak those words anyway.

"I should never have let it get this far..." he heard her say into the intercom, voice breaking. "Now ... now everything has fallen apart. Your father ... He was the only one who could find a cure, Daniel. I'm sorry, but..."

"I know, Mom ... we can try, though..."

"I have to do this..."

"Do what? What are you going to do? Are you coming down here?"

"I can't ... it's too late for me anyway. You know what to do, where to go..."

"What do you mean it is too late? Mom? Please, don't leave me!"

"I don't have much longer. And someone has to hit the button, it is the only way."

Daniel's eyes could no longer fill with tears, but his heart was heavy and he had only one thing left to say, "I love you."

"I love you too son," was the last thing he heard his mother say, right before the entire world around him shook.

~ ~ ~

Cliff's face was oddly peaceful behind the glass of the incubation pod. Daniel couldn't help but stare at him and wonder how he could have done this to his family. His parents were dead. They had always seemed invincible to him. Now they were buried in rubble. The whole facility above was rubble. There was no way to reach the outside world without a substantial amount of explosives that could significantly destabilized the mountainside and possibly bury him alive. It was better that he didn't try anyway, he was infected and had no clue how to find a cure.

What was there for him up there anyway? Susan? It was better she thought he was dead. For her sake. For the world's sake.

He thought about ending it all, blasting everything to bits. But ... Dawson, Lobbs, Ferris ... they were all innocent, and deserved a chance. He walked down the line of pods, checking settings and vitals. They had each survived the blast. He had to go on, for them.

He would find a cure, one day, somehow. Until then, he needed to rest. He slid into one of the pods, closed his eyes and welcomed the deep slumber that ensued.

= = =

CYBORG DREAMS

THE AWAKENING (VOLUME 3)

H.A.
BURNS

ABSOLUTELY AMAZING eBOOKS

ABSOLUTELY AMAZING eBOOKS

Published by Whiz Bang LLC, 926 Truman Avenue, Key West, Florida 33040, USA.

Cyborg Dreams: The Awakening (Volume 3) copyright © 2018 by H.A. Burns. Electronic compilation/ paperback edition copyright © 2018 by Whiz Bang LLC.

All rights reserved. No part of this book may be reproduced, scanned, or transmitted in any form or by any means, electronic or mechanical, including photocopying, recording, or any information storage and retrieval system, without permission in writing from the publisher. Please do not participate in or encourage piracy of copyrighted materials in violation of the author's rights. Purchase only authorized ebook editions.

This is a work of fiction. Names, characters, places, and incidents either are the product of the author's imagination or are used fictitiously, and any resemblance to actual persons, living or dead, businesses, companies, events, or locales is entirely coincidental. While the author has made every effort to provide accurate information at the time of publication, neither the publisher nor the author assumes any responsibility for errors, or for changes that occur after publication. Further, the publisher does not have any control over and does not assume any responsibility for author or third-party websites or their contents. How the ebook displays on a given reader is beyond the publisher's control.

For information contact:
Publisher@AbsolutelyAmazingEbooks.com

To xxx.

CYBORG DREAMS

THE AWAKENING (VOLUME 3)

Chapter 1

Dreams Do Come True

Catherine Newton dreamt she picked dandelions from the cracks of a derelict parking lot. California lilac bushes grew in fields surrounding the rough and fractured pavement. Her bare feet carefully tiptoed as she gathered a yellow bouquet. The lilac at the edge of her vision rippled in a breeze that brought the salty scent of the sea instead of the sweet perfume of flowers. She peered out in wonderment at the waves within the bushes. They peaked and dipped like an ocean.

Then he appeared in the ripping field. His bright eyes reflected the baby-blue sky. He was covered in tubes and electronics and sitting in a heavily modified wheelchair.

Is he staring at me or seeing something beyond? she wondered and turned around to see what was behind her. He was across the field there too. She turned again and again; but, no matter where she looked, he was there. It felt wrong, he didn't belong in her dream.

Wake up! she thought.

Catherine sat bolt upright in a hospital bed, shuddering. *Why did he have to stare like that?* Every night he appeared in her dreams he got more persistent.

She removed the palm-sized, flat disc remote-controller from its magnetized location on the side of the bed. She propped herself up using the disc. It controlled everything in her hospital room – from calling a nurse to turning on the far wall to project the latest news.

She sipped on the small cup of juice one of the many nurses had given her while she'd slept. It was difficult to keep track of all the nurse's names because so many came in and out of the room throughout the night and day. However, they all knew she loved the cranberry cocktail as much as she loved sleep. The congenial nurses would try not to wake her when checking on her IV, filling back up a small pitcher of ice water, or bringing snack packs with little juice cups she continuously sipped.

She let the dream fade away and focused on drinking her juice. Being waited on hand and foot made her feel somewhat spoiled. However, the offering to help her shower was a bit awkward. At least they didn't ask her if she needed help to the toilet. She didn't even want to think about what had gone on while she'd been in a coma for a week.

The hospital staff couldn't have been treating her any nicer. Still, she couldn't wait to leave and get back to her normal life –whatever that was now.

"Ready to go home, Miss Newton?" The familiar voice of her doctor sounded from the entryway to her room, along with the familiar metallic clang of his footsteps as he entered.

Dr. Daniel Jahren would almost seem normal if you didn't look too closely or listen too hard. If the sound of his footsteps, or the distinct swooshing of hydraulics maneuvering his legs didn't give it away, then vigilant inspection of his eyes would. The quick flashing symbols glowing just at the edges of his irises were tell-tale signs he wasn't completely human.

"I thought you had special plans for me Dr. Jahren?" Catherine answered back. Just a few days ago, she would have thought she was dreaming if he'd walked into her room. Now he was sitting next to her bed on a small stool, scanning a digital clipboard, scrolling through notes on her electronic medical chart.

"I do," he replied and continued his evaluation of her vital statistics without skipping a beat. He appeared right at home making selections in her chart while talking, not even pausing for a second as he read, confirming medications and speaking at the same time. "I need to show you something first. I think we both learned the hard way that seeing is believing for you." There was a glint in his eyes as he spoke that went beyond amusement.

"Right. Well, it's not every day that a cyborg from your dreams appears in real life. Who would believe that without seeing it themselves? No normal person would take what a cyborg tells them in a dream seriously. Heck, I thought I was going batty when you kept popping up in my dreams. Most people never dream about cyborgs, you know. Much less two cyborgs that –"

"What do you mean *two*?" He suddenly stopped what he was doing and watched her intently.

"What do you mean 'what do you mean'?!? Your brother! The one in the wheelchair with all those tubes coming out. His name is Cliff, right? He's even more unnerving than you are, he just stares at me." She shuddered again, remembering the dream she had awoken from merely a few minutes ago.

Now Dr. Jahren was staring at her too. His expression was spookily similar to his brother Cliff's in her dream. Thinking about them looking at her made her instantly aware of her appearance. *When was her last shower? Yesterday morning?* She ran a bandaged hand through her long, dull-brown hair and pulled it to the side. He was still staring. He was like a stone statue, and completely unreadable. So, she cleared her throat and that successfully brought him out of his stunned silence.

"Are you sure?" he asked, still in a stunned, contemplative pose and becoming increasingly pale.

"Am I sure? How many cyborgs do you think are out there? I've never heard of or even seen one in real life except for you ... why do you think it was so hard for me to believe you existed?"

He sat there thinking for a few more moments, then asked, "He doesn't speak?"

"No, just stares. Why do you ask? Is that important?"

"I see."

"You see what?"

Silence.

"How long has he been in your dreams, Miss Newton?" he asked after a few moments.

"Please, you can call me Catherine. I don't know ... umm ... the last two or three nights maybe?"

"I need to go check on something," he said, standing up in a swift move that sent the stool flying.

"You're leaving? Do I still get to go home today?" She couldn't help but reach out to him and pull on his white jacket to try and stop him from leaving her there. She was worried about her dog, her house, her life ... she'd been begging to go home every day since she awoke.

"Yes! Yes, of course. Go home, rest up. I will come for you."

"Wow, that doesn't sound creepy at all." She let go of his jacket and raised an eyebrow.

He gathered the fallen stool and sat back down next to her bed and then held her hand, saying, "I'm sorry, Catherine. You are more important to me than you know right now. It will all make sense soon, I promise." There was a hint of a smile passing his lips. It was a brief moment of tenderness that ended when his hand began to shake and a profound sadness pulled down the sides of his full lips and wrinkled his forehead.

The emotions he had ran so deep that it almost brought Catherine to tears. She wanted to console him but didn't know how or why. She barely knew him but knew they had a connection she didn't understand.

He turned away and stood up. "I'm sorry to leave you. I'm sure you'll be fine going home now ... as long as you stay away from *Jordan*, of course. You've learned your lesson to listen to me now?"

"I ..." she began, then felt herself flush in shame. Going over to Jordan's cabin is what landed her in this hospital bed. "I don't plan on going anywhere near Jordan. I had no idea – "

"I don't want to hear any excuses," he interrupted. "I warned you. I don't trust Anthony either, he's reckless. But, at least we don't have to worry about him anymore."

"Yes. That stubborn idiot wouldn't even let me explain why –"

"Why you had to go to the house of a psychopath that is obsessed with you in the middle of the night?" he asked rhetorically as he marked something on her chart which he set into a docking station on the wall. The station and her bed lit up green, as did her wristband.

The green lights would have made her ecstatic if the moment hadn't been ruined by what he'd just said. She countered with, "I didn't know –"

"I warned you!"

"I thought you were a figment of my imagination! C'mon!" At the time he told her, she was dreaming. He was a dream. He had only ever been in her dreams. She still didn't even know how he had climbed out of her dreams and into her hospital room. His sudden appearance was another thing he was waiting to show her and refused to explain.

"Well, I am real. We've established that, correct?"

Catherine hurled the dark disk-shaped remote at his head. He caught it mid-air. It would have been more assuring if it had hit him, and more satisfying. "Yes," she said, sulking.

"I'll come for you soon. Go home and relax." He tossed the remote onto the bed and walked out the door.

She tried not to be so sullen. She simply didn't understand men and hated that they all wanted to tell her what to do, expecting her to follow their instructions like a loyal dog. How could she have known that Jordan would try to kidnap her? At the time he seemed like the only sane person she knew in this small desert mining town.

"Miss Newton, would you like me to order you a ride home?" chimed a bright voice that disrupted her brooding. The request came from the smiling mouth of a head peeking sideways in her doorway. The head belonged to a short, bald, Pilipino nurse who had a habit of just sticking his head in, as if that was less intrusive.

"Yes, please. Thank you, Robbie," she answered back, finishing off her cranberry juice.

"Okie dokie," he said, head disappearing before she could ask him to close her door.

Catherine got out of her bed and was amazed at how steady she was walking already as she crossed the room to close the door. She hurriedly put on the outfit one of the nurses had generously left for her. Not exactly her tastes: silvery leggings, stiletto grey boots and one of those modular lighted sweatshirts that depicted a different image depending on your mood. She got the feeling the clothing items were from a lost and found bin. She slipped the miss-matched ensemble on under her robes because people tended to knock and not give very much notice before barging into her room.

How is it possible that I'm moving so quickly? she pondered.

Barely a week ago she was squashed in her car under half of a hillside. The nurses kept remarking on how they'd never seen anything like it: broken ribs, broken wrist and a skull fracture – and the bones were already healed. It was miraculous. Every day since she awoke from her week-long coma she'd felt better and better. She unwrapped her wrist and moved it around. No soreness, nothing. She didn't even have a cut or a bruise.

There was a rapid knock followed swiftly by the door swinging open and nurse Robbie announcing, "Your car is ready out front. Let's see your wristband." With a deft motion from a handheld scanner, the band opened and fell into his open palm. He put it in his pocket and asked, "Do you need any help out? Want to bring any of those vases of flowers with you?"

"No, they're all from my ex-boyfriend, Anthony," she said as she closed the door behind her and walked with Robbie down the hall. Her sweatshirt began changing to a dark red as she stomped away, heels clicking on the floor.

Anthony had diligently brought in new flowers every day for the entire time she was in a coma. How could his feelings have turned so quickly when she awoke and hardly got out a few words? *Because he was a 24-year-old hot-head!* Merely the thought of his misunderstanding and assumptions made her furious.

"None of my business, I'm sure." Robbie must have noticed her dark look, or red sweatshirt ... or that she was barreling down the hallway trying to drive holes into the tile with her stiletto boots.

She halted her stomping and took a deep breath. "It's okay, Robbie. Really." She wanted to quickly change the subject so she asked, "Was there anything that Dr. Jahren left in his notes for me for follow up?" She trailed Robbie through the labyrinth of gurneys and nurses busily tending patents but stopping to wish her farewell. They headed to the end of the hall where there were four elevators, one already open.

"Doctor who?" He pushed the elevator button and it descended to the main level. He then peered up at her as if he was wondering if she was okay.

"Dr. Daniel Jahren ... the cyborg?" When she said it, she realized the doctor was always alone in the room with her. He was always by himself. *Oh god, had I been hallucinating this whole time?* she thought. Her heart started to beat faster and she had to catch herself on the cold, steel elevator wall.

Robbie looked absolutely confused and reached out to help her stand straight. "A cyborg doctor? I think that head injury of yours has made you see things. Should I get you a wheelchair? Are you sure you're alright? You don't have to leave if you feel uneasy." His brow was creased and he glanced nervously over at the elevator buttons, which made her concerned he would stop its descent and take her back up to her room for a brain evaluation.

Catherine swallowed hard and shook her head. Nothing made sense. "Dr. Daniel Jahren: tall, broad shoulders, wavy brown hair, rusty beard ... likes to dress in all black under his white medical jacket."

He flashed a relieved smile and nodded his head. "You mean your doctor, Dr. John Smith." The elevator landed and he led her gently out into the lobby. "He's a recent transfer. He isn't a ... what did you say, a cyborg? Though, thinking about it I could see how you would say that – he's a bit cold, robotic. I don't blame him, getting transferred here immediately before they decide to shut down the mine and the whole town finds out they're getting transferred out."

"Dr. John Smith?" Catherine couldn't help but laugh at the obvious fake name. "Robbie, you don't think there is anything strange about him? What about his eyes? No golden glow?"

"No, he has normal hazel eyes from what I remember. Miss Newton, you did suffer a traumatic head injury. Hallucinations are common, though I didn't see any signs of them written in the doctor's notes. Are you sure you are okay to go home?" He held her up by the arm and kept a close eye on her progress towards the sliding glass doors.

"Yes, of course! Only a head rush from the elevator, I'm sure." She wasn't sure. In fact, nothing felt sure anymore. She simply wanted to get home.

They walked through the hospital doors together and he pointed towards a sleek, red hover vehicle on the right of a crosswalk. "Your ride." He guided her over to the open passenger side door, it rose automatically when they approached.

"Thank you, Robbie."

"It was our pleasure, Miss Newton." He gave her a hug and helped her into the passenger seat, belting her in. "Best of luck to you." With his large, infectiously amiable smile, Robbie waved bye and then walked away.

She sat comfortably on the lustrous synthetic-leather seat. Not many people could afford the new hover tech. She was amazed that the hospital would offer this lavish vehicle as a home transport. She touch-typed into the navigation module the address for her house and the car started the trip. She laid her head back and closed her eyes as the autopilot carried her home.

Home sweet home. Maybe when she got there, things would feel normal again. Maybe. She sure hoped so.

After a minute or two spent relishing the thrill of being out of the hospital, she opened her eyes. She watched the red rock and white roads of the small mining town in southern Colorado pass her by in a blur as the vehicle smoothly zoomed to its destination.

Catherine's mind began to race like the car. She was sick of feeling crazy, of feeling unsure of herself. She knew what she saw. What she heard. Going over it all in her mind she knew, deep down, that the healing wasn't ordinary and neither was 'Dr. John Smith.'

When the hover vehicle approached her house, she noticed another car in the driveway and she knew exactly who it belonged to: Anthony. *What was he doing here? Wasn't he furious with her?* Two days ago he had stormed off, accusing her of cheating on him with Jordan. As if she would ever cheat on him!

She held the magnetic key over the door lock and heard barking on the other side that made her heart skip a beat. She couldn't even open the door fully before being tackled by two dogs. A fluffy white poodle and an even fluffier sheep dog mutt – big enough to knock her backwards. She was covered in doggie kisses that threatened to smother her to death.

"Sass! Rufus! Oh, I missed you two! Yes, yes, I love you too. Please, let me breathe!" she said, wrestling with her poodle Sass and Anthony's dog Rufus. She sat on the front porch with the dogs as the door swung gradually to reveal her burly, way-too-handsome-for-his-own-good, ex-boyfriend sitting on the couch in her living room. He had his head down and hands clasped together. *Was he praying? Yes, his lips were moving and his eyes were closed.* The anger she'd felt earlier had mostly dissipated at the sight of her dog, safe and sound in his care. Now she didn't know what to think. *Had he come to his senses? Or was he praying for her 'adulterous' soul?*

"Anthony, thank you for watching Sass for me. I was so worried about her." She took off her stiletto boots at the door and wasn't sure what to do next because Anthony wasn't talking, but he also wasn't leaving. She stalled by filling up a bowl of dog food for each of the pooches.

Finally, she closed the door, braced herself and then walked over to sit next to him on the couch. He turned his face away from her, but she said, "Will you please let me explain what happened?"

No response, he refused to even look at her. Tears were welling up in her eyes with frustration. The cold shoulder, the rejection, the loss of the months-long relationship ... it was all hitting her.

Her voice broke as she said, "I went over to Jordan's house to see if he could help me stop you. I knew you wouldn't listen to me. I didn't know what else to do. You wanted to blow up the mine!"

He still wouldn't look at her. His eyes were closed. His knuckles were white – he was holding his hands tightly together with dark rosary beads dangling between his fingers.

"I wasn't having an affair, Anthony. I can't believe you would think I would do that!" She caught a brief glance from him before he looked away again. "When you wouldn't listen about not blowing up the mine, I contemplated alerting the cops but Jordan called me again and ... and I thought he might help. His intentions were never good, you were right about that ..." She heard Anthony mumble something but didn't quite catch it. "But ... but I didn't think he would do what he did. He tied me to his bed and –"

"He did what?" Anthony turned to face her and she could see his eyes were either red with lack of sleep or that he'd been crying.

"He drugged me. He wanted to kidnap me from the beginning. I had no idea. He was afraid more deadly viruses would get out of the mine any day and thought that keeping me there was the best way to protect me."

"He tied you to his bed?" Anthony was looking at her intently, a smoldering inferno lay in the depths of his stare. "He didn't ... ?"

"No, he didn't do anything to me. He thought I would be more comfortable on the bed, it wasn't sexual at all. He thought he was protecting me somehow. It was ridiculous. It took me all night to work the ropes to escape because I had to wait for him to fall asleep. I ran out as fast as I could, got in my car and was driving down the hillside when I heard the explosions you set off. The next thing I knew, I was waking up in a hospital bed. They told me I was buried under debris for two days, and in a coma in the hospital for a week – so my voice wasn't exactly working when I woke up. You barely let me get out a sentence before you assumed I cheated on you!" Her righteous anger started to rise up again, remembering waking up to his questions and subsequent condemnation.

Anthony unclasped his hands and reached out to wipe her tears. "You really are innocent, aren't you?" He was on the verge of crying himself. The rage in his eyes replaced with remorse and compassion.

"I can't believe you would think I would do that, I just didn't know what to do –"

"I'm so sorry, Babe," he said, pulling her close in an embrace that only made the water rush from her eyes as she sobbed. "I assumed ... I ... you deserved so much better than that. I truly am sorry."

They sat there for a few minutes until her weeping subsided. She wasn't even sure what had made her cry like that. Was it the ability to finally tell him the truth and have him listen? Or detailing the trauma she'd endured? Was it the embrace that she longed for? Feeling the comfort of home in his strong arms after such a horrible few weeks? Right now, she didn't want to think about it, she solely wanted to be held and cared for.

After a while he opened from their embrace, wiped more tears from her cheek, then gave her a gentle kiss on the lips. She was distinctly aware of the fact that she hadn't brushed her teeth or fixed her hair. She pulled away in shame and said, "I'm sorry, I need to shower."

"That's okay, Babe, I don't mind." He tried to run his hands through her greasy hair like he wanted to make-out but she caught his hand midair and pushed him back.

"Don't go, there's more we need to discuss," she said and hurried up to the bathroom upstairs.

"Okay, Babe. I'll be right here." He leaned back, grinning and laying his heavy-booted feet on the coffee table.

As the hot water poured over her and the smell of lavender shampoo filled the air her mood instantly got better. It was the little things of home that she'd missed so much. She tried to enjoy every moment.

Less than a half hour of bliss later, she came back downstairs in her super comfy, pink sweats, and sat next to Anthony to cuddle. Unfortunately, the first thing he said was, "How can they let a man like that be a high school teacher? He needs to be taught a lesson or two." He held up both of his fists when he said the word 'two.'

Catherine pulled away, recognizing that tone of voice. "No, Anthony. Don't do anything foolish! He's probably stuck up in his cabin all by himself due to the landslide over the road. Being isolated is punishment enough for him."

"No, they cleared the road days ago," he said, getting up and putting his shoes on by the door. "You're too innocent to understand, and too nice of a person."

Catherine went over to him and placed a hand on his arm, "Please, Anthony. Please don't go." All she could think about was trying to stop him from doing something foolish, again.

"I don't know what kind of man I would be if I let some other man kidnap my girlfriend and I did nothing about it." He shook his head the whole time he spoke. "Not the kind of man I'd respect. Not the kind of man you deserve for your husband."

"Anthony, please –" she began but was interrupted with him pulling her up flush to his body and kissing her passionately. The kiss made her sink into his embrace and forget about everything for a brief second. Then he was out the door before she could think straight again.

Why would she believe that Anthony would listen to her anyway? He never did. The man was about as impulsive and hot headed as they came. She'd told him there are deadly viruses at the mine and the first thing he did was try to blow up the mine. So, of course, when she tells him her co-worker kidnapped her, the first thing he does is run off to beat the man up.

She glanced over to see Rufus and Sass both peering at her sideways. She snagged the white tennis shoes from the wooden shoe cubby, slid them on and dashed out the door. She didn't think Anthony would kill Jordan, but there was no telling what Jordan would do to Anthony.

Thankfully the jetted red car from the hospital was still out front. She lifted the hover vehicle driver-side door up, and got in. She went to type in the address for Jordan's place and she realized she didn't remember what it was. She missed her armband, it had all her information. Too bad it was crushed. She searched the map for the approximate location of Jordan's cabin in the woods and set the target point as the destination. Hopefully that was close enough.

When the car glided down the familiar winding hillside, a route she'd taken every day to work for the last four months, she thought about how much she'd miss this place. With the mine closed, everyone would be transferred soon, including her. *Where would they send her? Another small town, of course.* She couldn't even imagine starting over and being an English teacher again. It felt like a lifetime ago–so much had happened in the last few weeks. Anthony blowing up the mine, Jordan kidnapping her, the landslide landing her in a hospital bed with a cyborg doctor from her dreams in attendance. It was a lot.

The phone in the car began to ring, the number was unidentified. Likely the hospital wondering where their hover vehicle was being taken off to. She pressed the answer button on the main console to try and explain before they sent the car, and her with it, back to the hospital.

"Hi, Catherine. I know you are not going where I think you are going," Dr. Jahren's voice clearly stated from the other end.

"Where do you think I'm going, 'Dr. John Smith'?" she rejoindered. "How did you find me anyway?" She felt like the he might jump out of the back seat like a rabbit out of a hat.

"Oh, magically of course," he laughed. "You're in my car."

"Oh." That made sense, it was state of the art and not like anything she'd ever seen. It could be from a dream as much as he was. "Why is it that no one knows your real name or that you're a cyborg? How's that even possible? Am I seeing things? Am I going crazy?"

"It is easy to persuade people to believe what they want to believe. You are not crazy. However, you are not at your house. Where are you going?"

"Are you spying on me?" she asked, trying to delay the inevitable.

"No, I am trying to protect you."

"Why does everyone seem to think I need protection?" She couldn't quite decide if she felt angry at him or ashamed of herself for actually needing protection.

"Catherine, where are you going?"

Catherine swallowed hard. "I'm going to Jordan's house."

"I'm starting to think you like to do exactly what I tell you *not* to. Do you enjoy putting yourself in harm's way or simply being rebellious?"

"Anthony is going there, he found out the truth. Well, he finally let me tell him the truth anyway ... and who knows what Jordan will do to him when he gets there. That big buffoon has no idea how dangerous Jordan is."

"So, what I am hearing is that you are going to rendezvous with the two people I asked you to avoid. The *only* two people."

"Urgh! What I'm hearing is that you don't understand that I care about Anthony. I have to help him."

"I see."

"Good." A sullen defiance that she wasn't used to feeling was starting to emerge again. Why did he make her feel so, so ... urgh!!

There was a brief moment of silence, and the tension was pulpable. She could hear him take a deep breath and sigh before he said, "He's not right for you. You know that, Catherine."

She couldn't answer. What right did he have to tell her how she felt? But, it was true, she knew it. She knew Anthony wasn't right for her but it didn't matter. She cared about him. Jordan might kill him, and it would all be her fault.

More silence, more tension. But, her jaw was set and she was determined to go to Jordan's house where the car was speedily taking her as she sat there staring out the window. That's if Dr. Jahren didn't remote in and override her directions, which he could do at any second.

He broke the silence with, "I'm on my way."

"What? What do you mean you're on your way?"

"I'll be there before you get there. Goodbye." He hung up.

Oh, man! This isn't good! She tried to take the car out of autopilot and into manual mode to drive faster but got an "unauthorized" message in flashing red letters. *Great!*

A hot head, a psychopath and a cyborg converging ... all with the intent of 'protecting' her but truly only flaunting their own egos. *What could go wrong?*

Chapter 2

Fight or Flight

Pounding, banging, disrupting. Whoever was out front, they weren't welcome. Jordan pulled out his 1000-volt Winchester Cripto-Bolt 2032 from the closet by the front door and yelled, "Go away or I'll shoot!" He took position next to the door jam and peeked through the adjacent window pane.

There was a thunderous crash and a booted foot appeared where the door used to be. The next thing Jordan knew, he was wresting with an over six-foot tall beast of a man intent of knocking his lights out.

"Who the hell do you think you are?!?" he tried to say while dodging the man's fist coming at his face. "Get out of my house!!"

"I'm the man who's going to teach you a lesson on how to treat a lady," said the intruder while he tried, unsuccessfully, reaching for the Cripto-Bolt.

Jordan bashed the guy with the butt of the weapon on the chin, knocking him back against the entryway wall. A boot came up and hit Jordan in the face as the guy flew backwards. All he saw were stars, but he managed to hold onto the Winchester, shooting blindly towards where he last saw the guy fall back. He was rewarded with the sound of writhing on the floor.

When he could see straight, he stood up and pointed the barrel right at the head of the intruder. "Get out! Next shot will be on full power." He switched the setting as he spoke.

The jerk on the floor kicked up the weapon and slid his boot behind Jordan's calves in a swift and unexpected motion. Jordan fell backwards with burning calves. His head landed on the edge of his recliner which caused the world to spin around him. He struggled to keep hold of his weapon with the heavily muscled man using brute force to get the upper hand. If he'd had his old M-16, the guy would be dead by now. Unfortunately, those weren't legal anymore.

Jordan managed to get the intruder's head in a vice grip, with the weapon across his throat and a knee to his back when he heard a low voice from the doorway say, "I suggest you both cease and desist."

Jordan thought the voice sounded familiar and it brought his attention away long enough for the thrashing combatant to lurch forward, tossing Jordan off his back. Then the guy hit him in the jaw with a wild right hook.

The next thing Jordan knew he was waking up sitting on his recliner. The sour smell of vomit filled the air. Blinking, he scanned the room for the source of the stench and found it next to the burly, dark-haired man that had busted open his front door. The guy now lay crumpled in a ball, holding his stomach and groaning. *What happened?*

"You have a concussion, sit back," said an eerily familiar voice coming from behind him. He caught a black-gloved hand from the corner of his eye, then felt the iron grip on his left shoulder pushing him back into his seat.

"Who are you?" Jordan asked the stranger. He had a bad feeling about this guy and was trying to place where he had heard his voice.

"I'll explain everything when Catherine gets here, *Jordan*." The voice above his head was deep and menacing, with a tinge of contempt as he said Jordan's name.

"Catherine? Catherine Newton?" Jordan asked. Ever since Catherine left he'd worried the cops would be knocking on his door any day. But, from the interaction so far, he knew neither one of these guys was from Central.

"Yes."

The man on the floor was still groaning and holding his stomach.

"What happened to him?"

"I employed a mild deterrent, he will recover."

"A mild deterrent?" grumbled the jerk. He opened his eyes, and they went wide as he stared up at something behind Jordan's head.

Jordan instantly wanted to look up too, to see the guy behind him. But, he held back, defiantly not letting the stranger know he cared.

"What did you do to him?!" Catherine's voice was high and clear from the busted-open entryway of Jordan's cabin. She rushed to the fallen man, avoiding the mess on the floor with a graceful side-step.

"You know him?" Jordan asked and was met with a quick scowl before she was consumed with helping the intruder to his feet.

"He'll be fine," said the ominous voice behind Jordan's head.

"He better clean-up that mess and get me a new door. What right do any of you have, barging into my house?"

"I'm sorry, Jordan. Anthony is –"

"Don't apologize to this maniac, Catherine!" said the man currently leaning on Catherine for support and dripping chucks of vomit from his football jersey. The falling pieces of ... breakfast scramble? ... made Jordan wince almost as much as seeing large boots obliviously driving the gunk into his carpet.

Anthony? Was this the infamous 'handsome Anthony'? *He doesn't look that handsome*, Jordan thought. It makes sense though, with Anthony's comment about how to treat a lady. Catherine probably told Anthony about Jordan's failed attempt to detain her for her safety.

"As far as I'm concerned, you're both maniacs," said the voice from behind Jordan's head. The iron grip on his shoulder let loose and the man walked around to help Catherine with her still wobbly-legged, barbarian of a boyfriend.

As the gloved man came into view, a chill went down Jordan's spine. It couldn't be ...

It was like watching a nightmare come to life in front of his eyes. Standing in his living room was one of the Jahren brothers who had owned a local prosthetics company. A company that recently Jordan found out was also involved in illegal viral research –decades ago, before the war. Not many would recognize Daniel Jahren, because the man was supposed to be dead. But, he'd ripped Jordan's heart out in a lifelike, intense dream that left him with nightmares for days. That was hard to forget. Daniel appeared far less like a cyborg in person than he did in Jordan's dream, but he still recognized the face and mechanical movement as he walked.

Jordan was speechless. He wanted to run but was stunned and immobile, mouth agape.

"I'm not here to hurt you," Daniel Jahren said, helping Anthony over to the only piece of furniture in the room, a burlap recliner that was about the size of a small couch. They sat Anthony on the opposite end of where Jordan was already seated, and way too close for comfort.

"Right, who are you? Why do your eyes glow?" Anthony replied. "And what was that ... that pulse? ... that you used on me? Is it radiation? Am I going to die?"

Daniel laughed a deep rumble that barely touched his eyes. "No, you won't die from the sonic sickener." He lifted a black glove from his left hand to reveal a metal prosthetic with an intricate design in the center, similar to a speaker. "It uses sonic waves only."

Jordan didn't like the way Daniel was now standing so close to Catherine, almost on top of her and in between her and Anthony. It was as if he was trying to protect her. Protect her from what? Her own boyfriend?

"I think we all deserve an explanation," Jordan declared.

"I don't think anyone needs to explain a thing to a lunatic who likes to abduct innocent women," Anthony retorted, seething face less than a foot away and practically foaming at the mouth.

"Whether or not you deserve or need an explanation, I will give you one," Daniel moved over to the wood-burning fireplace across from the recliner and sat down on the empty hearth. "Because I need your help."

"Help? Who are you? What are you?" Anthony motioned for Catherine to sit down next to him on the recliner as he moved over towards Jordan to make room for her. Now he was way too close and Jordan had to squeeze his fist to keep from punching the man.

Jordan found it intriguing that Catherine looked down at the new open spot, stared warily at Daniel and then walked away. Surprisingly, she chose to sit two feet away from Jordan's left, near the window, on a pile of books.

"Aren't you supposed to be dead?" Jordan asked, breaking the awkward silence between the three men all staring at Catherine.

"Yes." Daniel said matter-of-factly.

"'Yes,' you are dead, or 'yes' you're supposed to be dead?" Jordan tried to get clarification. Seeing this machine-like man made him wonder how much human remained. His question was met with a glare only.

"He's obviously not some kind of zombie, Jordan. He's real, flesh and blood ... mostly. You can see that with your own eyes, so stop antagonizing him." Catherine scowled and crossed her arms. The daggers in her eyes clearly indicated she hadn't forgiven Jordan for drugging and tying her up. He'd only done it so she couldn't leave and get killed, and she had no idea how much he'd worried about her since she left.

"Catherine, do you know this ... man?" Anthony asked. He'd moved back to his original position at the far end of the shared recliner. However, the putrid smell remained and Jordan was starting to understand why Catherine wanted to be next to the open window. Eggs smell a thousand times worse coming out than going in.

"Yes. No. I mean ... it's hard to explain ..." she began but trailed off. Apparently, she hadn't told Anthony about her dreams about cyborgs like she'd told Jordan ... fascinating.

"Catherine, let me try." Daniel said. "My name is Dr. Daniel Jahren. I know it is hard to understand, but I have been asleep deep within the mine for the better part of two decades. It was the three of you who, in fact, woke me up."

"That's not possible. You look like you're the same age as me, maybe younger." Anthony alleged.

Jordan found it hilarious that a man shows up with metal legs that look like rockets, says he's been asleep in a mine for decades and reveals a prosthetic hand that can reduce him to a helpless mound on the floor and all Anthony could think about is how young the guy looked.

"Good observation, Anthony," Daniel said and Jordan couldn't help but chuckle. "Like the viruses I'm sure you have become aware of, my family also perfected other drugs. One in particular that produced the effect you noticed."

"It was your family that created the viruses? What gave you the right to play God?" Anthony demanded. "What you created was unnatural. People are dead because of you."

"Didn't you bury yourself alive to protect your dark secrets?" Jordan had put the destroyed research and development lab and viruses together a few weeks ago while searching through the town's history. Who knew what the Jahren family was keeping deep in the mountain? Whatever it was, it was too dangerous for even them to allow to escape. The greedy mine owner was too blind to see that. Jordan had known what they were digging up was not going to end well for anyone and had remained safely in his cabin ever since he'd found out. He'd tried to keep Catherine safe too, but, she'd run out on him.

"You are correct," Daniel glared at Jordan with such hatred that it gave him goose bumps. Did his eyes just flash gold? How human was this guy?

"You said we woke you up, what do you mean?" Catherine asked. "Why were you asleep?"

"I've spent years in and out of hibernation. At first, I stayed awake relentlessly searching for a cure ..."

"A cure? For what? What else did you cook up in your labs?" Anthony queried.

"I understand your fear. Frankly, I'm just as concerned. I found out today that the very thing I have been trying to keep the world safe from has escaped."

"I sealed all the entrances to the mine, to keep your unholy experiments locked away." Anthony started to explain but then his eyes narrowed and he leaned forward. "That last blast ... was that from you?" Daniel nodded and Anthony continued, "Well, that uncontrolled blast left half the mountainside, including the mine, in rubble. How could anything escape?"

"There are secret passageways and tunnels that even I do not know about in that mountain. Besides, it was not just anything that escaped ... it was someone –my brother."

"Your brother has a virus?" Catherine chimed in right as Jordan opened his mouth to say the same thing. He gave her a quick smile, but she ignored him, leaving an empty pit in his stomach.

"Yes, and no. He carries something that has the potential to destroy the human race, or enslave it."

"What do you mean, 'enslave it'?" Anthony asked.

"Yes, this moron has a point. How can a virus enslave the human race?" Jordan countered.

"That is my brother's Cliff's goal: complete control. He developed something that ..." He gazed at Catherine, and then down at the ground. He sighed, leaned forward and cleared his throat. "There is a deadly virus, virulent, fast spreading. Humanity could be wiped out in a manner of months. I had to bury Cliff in the mine to stop him after he murdered both of my parents and tried to release the virus. When I awoke almost two weeks ago I thought he was safely still in hibernation, but it seems he escaped while I was tending to Catherine in the hospital."

"So, humanity is doomed." Jordan declared and everyone's glares were aimed at him. "Isn't that what you're saying? Correct me if I'm wrong; but, if he has escaped, then so has this deadly virus."

"No, we are not doomed, Jordan. There is still a chance I can stop him. But, I need your help." Daniel took a moment to make eye contact with each person in the room. When his eyes landed on Jordan, a feeling of urgency filled him. A feeling that felt foreign, and made him uneasy.

"How can we help?" Anthony asked when Daniel's eyes reached him. Anthony was on the edge of his seat, leaning towards Daniel as if magnetized.

"Why didn't you dispose of your brother? Put a stop to the threat years ago?" Jordan didn't understand this man. "Why put a threat like that in hibernation just to be dug up to destroy the world one day?"

"I am not a murderer, *Jordan*." The tinge of contempt when Daniel said 'Jordan' was not lost on him and he wondered why Daniel would have a problem with his name. "Nor am I a psychopath that can just 'dispose' of my own brother. Besides, I thought I could find a cure, given enough time I –"

"Decades weren't enough?" Jordan snorted in derision.

"Jordan, please." Catherine chided.

"There is someone who can help. She was developing something that could stop him," Daniel stated, looking at Catherine with his right eyebrow raised. Jordan thought he saw a glint of gold and a symbol appear in the iris of Daniel's eye.

"Great, let's go find her." Anthony said, and then stood up as if to head right out on a mission.

"Last I heard from her, she was working in her lab in LA."

Jordan began laughing, he couldn't help himself. Anthony swung a fist at him and Jordan leaned back, caught the fist and twisted Anthony's arm, causing him to fall to his knees.

"Enough! Stop it Jordan!" Catherine exclaimed and Jordan let go, eyeing Anthony warily in case he tried something stupid again.

"Why are you laughing, Jordan?" Daniel asked, somberly.

Jordan took pleasure in seeing Anthony sit back on the recliner rubbing his arm at the elbow.

"While you were busy sleeping and *not* working on a cure to the virus, the whole world went to war ... starting with a nuclear blast to the heart of LA," Jordan said, not caring how much condescension was oozing out of every word.

"I am aware of that," Daniel's eyes flashed gold again and, with the look he was giving Jordan, his words about not being a murderer were coming into question.

"Then you are aware that the likelihood your friend, and whatever she was working on, is long gone."

"I'm sorry, Dr. Jahren. Jordan is right, there were few survivors," Catherine said, sincerely trying to console him, as if he were a friend.

"Please Catherine, call me Daniel."

Jordan couldn't help but shake his head and snort, "Not to mention the entire area was blockaded off by a 70-foot concrete wall that runs the entire length of what was previously California, Oregon, Washington and even Canada."

"No one asked for a history lesson, or can you not help yourself?" Anthony snidely remarked.

Jordan's mind was filled with about a million ways he wanted to break every bone in Anthony's body.

Daniel simply stated, "I am aware of that as well; however, I have reason to believe the research she was working on is still secure."

"How can we help you? There is no way in or out of California as far as I know. Are you planning to take your hovercraft?" Catherine inquired.

Jordan added, "A hovercraft is not going to work, they are programmed for only 5-10 feet above the ground. The regulation is to reduce the need for a pilot's license, and limit people from trespassing. You'd need an actual aircraft, and government access, to get through the guard wall."

"And that, Jordan, is why I need your help." Daniel wasn't smiling, he obviously wasn't pleased to be asking for Jordan's help.

What did this machine-thing know? What made him think he could help? Jordan wondered.

"I know someone with an aircraft, and maybe someone with access too." Anthony's statement had everyone's eyes on him. "She may be willing to help, to stop the virus."

"Who is this 'she' you're talking about?" Catherine asked, her previously pale cheeks flushed red with a tinge of jealousy.

"A woman I met while setting the explosives in the mine. She risked herself to help me and, for that, she is now on the run. See, even though the news story is that an earthquake caused the destruction at the mine, she was seen on camera getting the night shift out and drugging them before it happened. She had nowhere to go so I let her stay with my sisters. She knows Alluri Repalle, who owns a helicopter we can use ... possibly."

"I seriously doubt Alluri would let her use his helicopter if he thinks she had anything to do with the destruction of his mine," Jordan said, pointing out the obvious.

"Then we 'borrow' it, and Jordan can fly it for us and get us into LA," Daniel added. "Anthony, do you have any idea how to get Alluri and his helicopter here, tonight?"

"I'm not sure, but my friend, Sasha, she would know," Anthony replied. "I'll have to go back to my sister's place to talk to her."

"What makes you think I can get us into LA in Alluri's helicopter?" Jordan asked. There is no way this guy, this thing, knew anything about Jordan's past. Or did he?

"Because you were an Army pilot, and secret operative for the U.S. government before you 'settled down' to your teaching life here ... would you like me to elaborate?"

How the hell did he know that? Jordan's heart pounded and he tasted metal. The last thing he wanted was to help this guy, but he knew it was always better to stay in the eye of the storm than in its wake.

"If we need the helicopter by tonight I should leave now. Catherine, are you coming with me?" Anthony asked as he sat up, walked over and reached a hand out to her to help her up from the pile of books.

"I need her with me, to assist in gathering all the equipment we will need for the trip." Daniel clipped the words, head tilted toward Anthony and he didn't blink the entire time he spoke. "We will meet you later tonight. Be ready by seven p.m. at the heliport in front of the lake, near the mine."

Anthony left as if on command. Odd. You'd think he'd put up more of a fight than that over letting his girlfriend stay in the care of a cyborg, or even just a strange man he'd met today. Very odd indeed.

Catherine sat back down, somewhat dazed and confused as she watched her boyfriend abandon her there.

"Jordan, I'm going to need your help as well, to gather the supplies we'll need –"

Catherine interrupted Daniel with, "Why do you really need me? What were you going to show me earlier?"

"He was probably just going to take you back to his evil lair and keep you there for experimentation."

"That's not funny, Jordan," Catherine said.

"I find that ironic, coming from you," Daniel said, eyes flashing again.

"Why do your eyes keep flashing? Are you even human?" Jordan countered, standing up and staring down the cyborg. He was instantly sorry he asked because Daniel's eyes lit up bright white like two flashlights, almost blinding him.

"I'm more human than you are, sociopath." Daniel was now up and towering over Jordan.

"Stop it you two! Jordan, why do you always have to piss everyone off?" Catherine placed herself in between the two men, putting her hand on Jordan's chest. "Sit down and let Daniel explain things, please."

Jordan was sitting down before he even thought about it. Did she push him? His head was spinning and his vision was still a bit spotty from the brightness of Daniel's eyes. Thankfully, the cyborg's eyes were back to normal again.

Catherine started to sway like she was going to faint before Daniel caught her and set her down on the reclining loveseat.

"Are you okay?" Jordan asked. She was paler than normal, and perspiring.

"She is fine, no thanks to you. Simply a head rush from getting up too quickly. Do you have any vegetable juice or fruit juice?"

"Preferably without anything 'special' in it, like last time," Catherine added with a sideways glance and matching scowl.

"I have grapefruit juice, will that work?" Jordan replied.

"Yes." Daniel ungloved his right hand and put his fingers on Catherine's wrist, checking her pulse. That hand appeared human, unlike his left.

"I hate grapefruit juice –" she began but was cut off by Daniel adding, "It will make you feel much better until I can get you more BRX-27."

"More what? What have you given me?" Jordan heard her ask, her voice slightly cracking, while he selected grapefruit juice on the combinator screen in the kitchen. He impatiently waited for it to fill up a cup and have it ready in the output window. He could feel the part-man, part machine in his living room staring holes into the back of his head as he reached for the glass.

"The administered immunotherapy is the reason you are even able to move right now," Daniel tried to whisper. "You need a tapered dosage every 6 hours for the next few days or you will suffer severe withdrawal symptoms."

"Why are you giving her cancer treatment?" Jordan asked as he handed Catherine the glass of juice.

"It is not for cancer, it's to treat the trauma she received after escaping from you and ending up being crushed in a landslide at the bottom of the hill," Daniel said with contempt, suggesting it was all Jordan's fault.

"If you are implying that I caused her injury, you are mistaken. I have only ever wanted to protect her." Jordan locked eyes with Daniel, eying Catherine in his peripheral to gauge her reaction. He was still ashamed of what he had to do and hurt that she didn't see things his way. "I know for a fact that landslide was caused by an explosion at the mine, and from what Anthony said a few minutes ago, an explosion that *you* caused."

"What are you insinuating?"

"I'm not. I'm saying it outright: you are the reason she was injured, not me."

Catherine had been shaking her head as they argued. "Neither one of you protected me that night, and both of you put me in harm's way. You can blame each other all you want, but eventually you will have to take some responsibility for your own thoughtless actions."

Jordan tried to defend himself, opening his mouth at the same time as Daniel but Catherine stood up, turned to face them and said, "In the last few weeks I've been stalked, drugged, kidnapped and almost killed. What I want to know is, is why?" Her eyes were on both Jordan and the machine-thing, Daniel.

Jordan didn't understand her angst towards him. If anything, the cyborg from her dreams showing up and telling everyone his family created a deadly virus that was now loose upon the world and threatening all of humanity was complete validation for Jordan's actions. That was exactly the reason he'd given her the night he'd 'kidnapped' her.

Daniel stood up and put a hand on Catherine's shoulder, his expression was one of concern and frustration as he approached. "I am sorry you have gone through so much, I truly am."

Catherine put her hand on his metal hand, and lifted it, grimacing. Jordan was up and in between them so quickly that it made Daniel step back.

"Sorry, I ... I did not mean to hurt you." Daniel's shoulders slumped and then he proceeded to put gloves back on both hands. "It has been a long time since I interacted with people ... I ... I should never have left." He turned and glared at Jordan, as if he was the reason the cyborg was here now. "Unfortunately for everyone, I did. Decades of isolation ... and now I need to go back in there, to retrieve the gear necessary to enter LA and ... only you can truly help me, Catherine. Now is not the time for explanations." Again, another annoyingly accusatory glance in Jordan's direction. "Now, we need to go back into the mine."

Chapter 3

Sisters to the Rescue

Anthony's car pulled into the driveway of his sisters' place and he realized he didn't know how he got there. Last he remembered, he was sitting in the living room at that kidnapper Jordan's cabin. Odd.

His was still scratching his head when he placed the magnetized key over the lock of the wrought iron entrance box. Gretchen flung the intricately designed, double paned wooden doors wide open before Anthony could put his hand on the handle.

"Ant! What are you doing here? Why didn't you call ahead?" she asked, standing with a hand on each bulbus hip and still wearing her dental assistant smock from work.

At first Anthony thought she was getting ready for work but then noticed the state of her make-up and the wrinkles in the blue cotton and realized she'd slept in her clothes and had probably just woken up.

"Wow, you smell awful!" She held her nose and fanned away from him while stepping backwards so he could come inside. "What's that on your shirt?"

"I'm sorry, I ..." he began but his trail of thought ended when he saw Sasha sitting down on the couch in the living room. "I need to talk to her about something."

Sasha wore his sister Gretchen's Buffaloes jersey, and that's it. Gretchen was about 10 sizes bigger than Sasha's perfect hour-glass frame, so the shirt fit down to her knees like baggy pajamas. Sasha had her cropped strawberry blonde hair down without any of whatever she normally used to slick it back, and no make-up either. It was the first time he'd ever seen her so relaxed and natural. The look suited her. She grinned at him with that little half-smile she favored.

"Uh-hummm," Gretchen cleared her throat and glared at him.

"I'm sorry, I ... what was I saying?" Anthony hadn't noticed he'd already moved into the living room and sat next to Sasha on the deep cushions of his sisters' super comfy, burgundy couch.

"You weren't saying anything, Ant. Are you okay? You look like a mess; did you get into a fight?" His sister still stood near the doorway, squinting at him with her arms crossed. "Your face and neck are bruised."

Anthony nodded. "Yeah. And I'm starving too. Lost my breakfast." He sniffed himself, then lifted his shirt off and threw it at Gretchen.

"Ewe, gross! Thanks a lot, butthead. I guess I'd better toss it in the wash before it stinks up the *entire* house." She left to go into the laundry room behind the kitchen.

Anthony yelled, "Thanks, Grety!" after her.

She yelled back towards the living room, "Did you eat something bad? Did Catherine's combinator make a bad egg scramble?" Gretchen walked back into the room and leaned against the hallway wall between the living room and kitchen. "Mom made lasagna and brought half over last night. I think she went to your place and dropped off the other half, she didn't realize you were still watching Catherine's dog."

With her thick Russian accent making words a bit choppy, Sasha asked, "I didn't realize your mom made it. She doesn't have a combinator?"

Gretchen glanced over Anthony's head to Sasha to explain, "Mom still refuses to use the combinator, says it makes everything taste like chemicals and cheese doesn't melt right. Plus, the lasagna's based an old family recipe with a not-so-secret ingredient," she held her hand next to her mouth and whispered, "Kalamata olives." She rolled her eyes and continued, "She actually thinks that if she puts the recipe in the machine it'll steal it and the lasagna will end up at Maggiano's or something. So silly." She rolled her eyes again and threw up her hands. "Anyway, Ant, I'll go get you some. Be right back."

"What did you need to talk to me about, Anthony?" Her accent was so strong he had to replay the words again in his head as he stared at her pink, sensual lips. She was still grinning, but now leaning back, relaxed. She had the large football jersey pulled down over her knees, which were up almost to her bountiful chest. Her bare feet were on the couch next to him, mere inches away, and even they somehow seemed sensual, with delicate painted toes. She was an attractive woman, but now that Anthony was back together with Catherine, he felt guilty even noticing ... or thinking about how those lips felt when they'd made out yesterday. "Anthony? What is it?"

He glanced back in the direction his sister had gone and whispered to Sasha, "I met a cyborg today, he said he came out of the mine."

She sat upright, pulling her knees out of the jersey and planting her feet on the floor so she could lean close to Anthony. The light-hearted countenance she had earlier was replaced by steel blue eyes that could freeze your soul. "A cyborg?"

"Yes, at least I think that was what he was." Anthony was still whispering. "He had rocket thrusters for legs and his hand had a ... well, I don't know what it was, sonic something-or-the-other ... but he used it to cause me to up-chuck. The rest of him was human, I think."

"What did he look like?" Sasha's hand grasped onto his right bicep, and she squeezed hard as she demanded information. "Eyes? Hair? Height? Any distinguishing features?"

She made him feel like he was being interrogated in a prison camp, and he started to perspire. Anthony straightening his spine, cleared his throat and then lifted his right arm up onto the back of the couch, smoothly breaking Sasha's grip. The other arm he placed on the arm of the couch. He was hoping to appear more relaxed as he took a deep breath and answered her barrage of questions. "I don't know ... he was about my height, a little slimmer. Had brown hair and hazel eyes, a goatee that was rough around the edges, you know, five o'clock shadow ... why?"

"Did he say what his name was?" she asked and when he didn't answer right away, she asked again with more urgency, "Anthony, who was he?"

"I don't know ... umm ..." After a few more seconds of scratching his head he recalled, "Daniel? Daniel Jared or something, I don't remember exactly."

"о мой Бог!" she exclaimed, swearing in Russian.

"What? What is it?" Anthony didn't have to speak Russian to know that wide-eyed expression meant she recognized the name.

"That isn't possible ... he's supposed to have died in 2017."

"Yes, that's what Jordan said ... that Daniel was supposed to be dead."

"Who is this, Jordan?"

Gretchen and an incredibly delicious smelling lasagna entered the room, causing Anthony to lose his train of thought. He had three bites in his mouth before his sister answered Sasha with, "I know who Jordan is, he's the guy that Catherine cheated on my big brother with. No wonder you got into a fight! Did you beat him up?"

"No, well yeah. I knocked his lights out, as a matter of fact," he replied with a mouth full of cheesy goodness and as big of a grin as he could muster while chewing. Man, the sausage's spice was incredible! Ooh, and the olives complimented the gouda cheese so well. He'd had his mother's lasagna a hundred times, and it was always magnificent.

"So, what happened? Did Jordan show up at Catherine's place? Was she there too? Is she out of the hospital? I'd like to give her a piece of my mind! I might put her back in the hospital!" Gretchen waived around a piece of garlic bread as she spoke. She was the female version of her brother: she had Anthony's curly black hair, his Irish temper and was built like a brick wall. No doubt she'd put Catherine in the hospital if she had the chance.

"It turns out, Jordan kidnapped her." Anthony was still a bit ashamed that he'd accused his girlfriend of cheating and left her alone in the hospital. He held his head down in shame, but continued to eat the tasty meal his mother made.

"No! No way! Man, this is like a soap opera!" Gretchen said. "I've got to tell Ariana!" She ran off to the back of the house yelling, "Ariana! Ariana, you won't believe it! Get in here!"

In less than a minute she came back in, pushing in front of her a sleepy younger sister. Ariana was still crusty eyed from her mid-morning nap. She must have fallen asleep reviewing the latest case from Arnie Gustad's law firm. Just hearing her talk about the cases was enough to put Anthony to sleep.

"Whaaaaat?" she asked through a yawn. "What's the emergency, Grety?"

"Tell her, Ant!" Gretchen thrust Ariana towards Anthony as she spoke. Ariana almost fell on top of him before shoving back at her big sister and grumbling something under her breath that made Grety gasp and move to the other side of the room.

"Catherine came home from the hospital this morning and finally told me what happened. That maniac, Jordan, lured her to his place and then, of all things, tied her to his bed. He'd planned to keep her there indefinitely but she escaped. Who knows what other perverted plans he had for her."

"He did what?" Ariana's mouth was agape. She stood there in her pink camisole nightgown like a zombie – her bleach blonde and straightened hair half stuck to her face from drool and the rest of her hair in every other direction.

"Did Jordan follow Catherine to her place this morning?" Gretchen asked, sitting down on the chair near the fireplace, on the right side of the couch. She had her legs across the chair arm, and squeezed a fluffy white throw pillow against her stomach like she did when she watched one of her favorite rom-coms.

"No, I went to his cabin to teach him a lesson ... a lesson that ended with a nice right hook to the face!" Anthony said in between swallows, cleaning the last smidgen of sauce from the plate using the garlic bread Gretchen had flung about earlier.

"She claims he kidnapped her? I thought you mentioned she had conspired to meet him alone and you caught her cheating." Sasha pointed out.

That was partially true ... he hadn't 'caught' her cheating. Catherine did plan on meeting Jordan ... but, Catherine also said she didn't know Jordan's intentions and thought he would help her.

"How can you trust her?" Sasha seemed nearly as upset now as when she'd heard about the cyborg. Her arms were crossed, so were her legs. Her lower lip was slightly pouty as she pushed herself back into the right nook of the couch.

"I only saw that he was contacting her on her armband, asking her to come over ... and then when she said she was coming back from his place at 6 in the morning I assumed –" His words were disrupted abruptly by a throw-pillow smacking him upside the head.

"You dufus! How could you have treated her like that! I wanted her to be my new sister!" Ariana yelled at him in between pillow smacks. "Tell me you apologized?!?" That was more of a threat than anything.

"Where is she now? Where is Jordan and the cyborg?" Sasha asked. She was back to her serious voice and steel eyes that made her seam like a robot herself. It wasn't very attractive.

"A cyborg? What?!?" Ariana exclaimed, ceasing her pillow beating of Anthony. Gretchen joined her on the, "What?!?" part.

Anthony regretted letting Sasha kiss him yesterday morning. He'd been in a fit of anguish over Catherine's adultery, spilling his heart out when she'd seized his face and planted her lips on his. Those cold eyes wanted an answer now, so he said, "They are at Jordan's cabin."

"Where is Jordan's cabin?" Sasha asked.

Neither Sasha or Anthony were paying attention to Gretchen and Ariana's questions and they were getting visibly annoyed, huffing and puffing even.

Anthony's focus was on answering Sasha, and trying to figure out how to tell her about needing a helicopter without giving away too much information to his sisters, "It doesn't matter, they are probably gone by now, back into the mine."

"But the mine is closed, the earthquakes destroyed it." Ariana pointed out. "Why would anyone want to go in there?"

Sasha gave Anthony a knowing look. Neither had told his sisters why Sasha was really here. He'd made up an excuse about a co-worker who'd lost her house during the landslide.

"The cyborg said the explosion ... umm, I mean earthquake, woke him up and released ... and released him somehow. I need Sasha's help to ... to help him get back into the mine." Anthony hated lying, especially to his family. But, the less they knew the better if Central ever came asking questions. He didn't want them imprisoned for knowingly aiding and abetting a criminal.

"You're not going back in there! It isn't safe!" Gretchen declared.

"That's right, the News said it was too unstable to mine anymore." Ariana added.

"The cyborg wants to go back into the mine?" Sasha asked, brow crinkled. She wasn't quite getting what Anthony was trying to say.

"What do you mean 'cyborg'? None of this makes any sense, Ant." Gretchen loomed over his head with her throw pillow ready to knock some sense into him and Ariana still had her pillow ready above his head as well.

"Anthony, I think we should tell them the truth." Sasha's words were daggers, how could she betray his trust like that? Now he wouldn't hear the end of it until his sisters knew everything.

Of course, both of his sisters at once started yelling. In between pillow smacks he heard only fragments of, "Truth? What truth? Have you been lying to us!?! How could you? Tell me!" before he yanked both pillows away and flung them behind the couch.

"I didn't want to get them involved, Sasha!" Anthony cared more for his sisters than his own life. What he'd gotten involved in at the mine with Sasha was both illegal and dangerous. "That was the deal, remember?"

"If what you said is true, we will need all the help we can get. Keeping secrets from your family will not keep them safe from what is to come ..." Sasha's eyebrow was raised to an ungodly level.

"From what? What do you know Sasha?" Anthony demanded. "I haven't told you about what the cyborg said yet ... how do you know what is to come?"

"I know that Dr. Daniel Jahren and his family tinkered around with some of the most virulent viruses and much more. There was a cybernetics division that produced something that we have been searching for, for years, and have been unable to find or replicate. Your government did everything in its power to hide this research, or the Jahren family did everything in their power to keep it from them as well."

"So, what you're saying is that they, this family of doctor Jahren's, created cyborgs?" Ariana asked.

"Far more than that. All of their technology has so much potential ..." Sasha didn't finish her sentence; her eyes were far off and you could practically see her mind racing at the possibilities.

"Daniel claimed that the third explosion was from him, and that we woke him up." Anthony explained further.

"What do you mean you woke him up? What explosions? Who's Daniel?" Gretchen spoke in a whisper that vaguely sounded like hissing, as if she were mad and enthralled. She'd moved the dirty dishes over and plopped down right across from Anthony on the coffee table in the center of the living room.

"Daniel is the cyborg. The earthquake ... it wasn't an earthquake at all ... ." He didn't want to explain anything, he didn't want them to know the danger they were all in. He wanted them to remain innocent.

"Oh my god, Ant. What did you do?" Ariana's mouth was open again, the morning breath reminded him of dirty mop water spewing into his face. She'd taken up a seat on the arm chair next to him and was breathing right down on him.

Anthony didn't want to speak, he looked to Sasha and she nodded for him to continue but he didn't know where to start.

"Your brother is a hero. He saved the entire town, maybe the entire world. He found out that the company we both work for, Greggo Sands, was recklessly using viruses and bacteria from the old Jahren laboratories buried in the mine. He convinced me to help him set explosives to close all the entrances. I was seen on camera before the explosions, he wasn't. That is the true reason why I am here." Clearly and succinctly, Sasha revealed everything.

"Anthony, is that true?" Ariana had one hand on his arm, the other covering her mouth. She must have seen the grimace he'd made last time she opened her mouth and realized she hadn't brushed her teeth yet.

Gretchen shook her head, her eyes were welling up and she turned away. "Why didn't you tell us?"

"I had no idea how this would end. I only wanted to keep you safe ... from the viruses and from the consequences of my actions."

Gretchen patted him on the knee. Ariana bent down and gave him a hug, saying, "You're such a sweet older brother."

"What doesn't make sense to me is that the cyborg needs help getting back into the mine," Sasha pointed out.

"He doesn't ... I made that up ... I didn't want to tell them ..." he stared back at his weepy eyed little sisters, "but the real issue is that something has escaped the mine. The cyborg, Daniel, said if we don't help him stop it then all of humanity is in danger."

His sisters both gasped. Ariana signed the cross by using her right hand to touch her forehead, then the middle of her breast, then the left shoulder, and finally the right shoulder. As she did this, she said, "In the name of the Father and of the Son and of the Holy Spirit, Amen."

"I need to light a candle!" Gretchen declared and left the room in a hurry.

"Did he say what it was that escaped?" Sasha demanded, brilliant eyes focused so hard on Anthony that they were moving quickly from his left to his right eye. It was disturbing.

"He said ... he said ... his brother escaped with a," Anthony peered up at the ceiling, then closed his eyes, "wait, his brother had a virus? Or was a virus? I don't remember. But he said his brother had to be stopped and we had to ... had to ... had to go to LA? Yeah, LA." Anthony couldn't understand why the information was so fuzzy in his head. He remembered feeling like he needed to get out of there and find Sasha immediately and now he was wondering why.

"Oh my God, what did I miss? What's in LA?" Gretchen came back into the room holding a large glass of wine and sat down hard on the chair next to the sofa.

"What happened to the candle?" Ariana crossed her arms and stared holes into her sister's head. Either disapproving or wondering why she'd only brought one glass.

"So, we need to go to LA? Is that what you need my help with, Anthony?" Sasha sat back and her eyes were still moving but you could tell it was from what she was thinking in her head, not from trying to read his face. She was coming up with a plan already, he just knew it!

"Yes! Yes! We need a helicopter, and I said I knew someone who could help ... umm, you." Anthony was wringing his hands, trying to work out the details. This person, this machine had asked for his help and he was so ready to give it, but why?

"Catherine!" he exclaimed and stood right up. *How could he have left her there with them!?!? What was going on?*

Everyone else stood up too, all yammering versions of "what?" and "Catherine?" that he had to shush them all vigorously while waving his hands.

"They have Catherine ... that psycho Jordan and the cyborg ..."

"I'm sure she's fine. Did they give a time and place where they wanted the helicopter, Anthony?" Sasha asked, standing up next to Anthony and laying a comforting hand on his bicep.

Ariana bit her nails and Gretchen took rather large gulps of red wine.

"Yes, I remember that clearly. Heliport by the lake, by the mine, at seven pm." Was he starting to think more clearly? That information seemed burned into his brain.

"Okay, there is only one person we know that has a helicopter ... and you think he will listen to me?" Sasha had her half smirk on again.

"Who?" Ariana took her fingers out of her mouth long enough to ask, then started chewing immediately after.

"Alluri Rapalle, the owner of Greggo Sands." Sasha replied.

"You know the owner of the mine?" Gretchen asked while trying to get her sister to stop biting her nails and but also protecting her glass of wine from her younger sister at the same time. "Get your own, Ariana!"

"Wait, who are you, really? Is your name even Sasha?" Ariana sat down on her hands to keep from the nervous biting habit.

Sasha put her chin up and her quirky smile was gone as she said in her thick accent, "Yes, my name is Sasha Mikhailov, and, up until recently, I was the VP of research and development for all of Greggo Sands' Russian division."

Anthony could hear his silly sisters oohing and ahhing and he rolled his eyes at them until he saw a grimace from Sasha that made him want to snag one of the pillows to protect himself from a punch to the face.

"I think I might have a plan." Sasha's words caused a cascade of events. It started with Anthony sitting down on the couch confidently, Ariana falling backward from the sudden movement and Gretchen tumbling over her sister, with her wine glass in tow.

He glanced around the couch arm to see both sisters tangled and covered in wine. Anthony hoped that whatever plan Sasha had didn't include those two clumsy dufuses.

"Can I help!?" Ariana asked, and so did Gretchen, as they untangled on the floor.

Of course, they would ask to help! Anthony thought as he practically smacked himself in the forehead with his right palm. He shook his head vigorously and stated as clearly as possible, "No, absolutely not!"

"I may need Ariana to –" Sasha started to say but Anthony didn't care what she thought, he interrupted with a hard, "No!"

"But!" Ariana tried to say.

"No!" He would not risk his baby sisters. It was already bad enough that they knew as much as they did. There had to be a way to get the helicopter without them and he would do it himself if he had to. Maybe call Alluri and ask to meet him then … his thoughts were disrupted by Ariana slapping him in the face. It was so weak it didn't even sting, but it shocked him.

"You don't get to tell me what to do!" Ariana stood two inches from his nose and pointed a finger straight at him. "If Sasha says she needs my help, I'm helping! Why do you think you can save humanity and leave us here to worry? Huh? Why?"

"That's right, Anthony Connor Grant." Gretchen reared up next to Ariana and they were now side by side with matching arms crossed and had on their meanest faces.

"Seems you are overruled, Anthony. Besides, all I need is for Ariana to make a phone call. You and I can handle the rest." Sasha explained.

"What about me?" Gretchen whined.

"If all goes to plan, we'll be heading into LA tonight. We are going to need someone to watch Rufus." Sasha pointed out.

"Oh great, I get dog duty? That dog takes the biggest dumps!"

"Oh, and Catherine's dog too, Sass," Anthony added and was immediately punched in the arm. "Why so violent? How did I get such abusive sisters?"

Ariana made a biting face at him and winked. He was sure if he pressed the matter he would feel her teeth.

"She's only going to make a phone call?" Anthony asked and was answered with a simple nod from Sasha. He took a deep breath and let it out. "Okay." It was only a phone call … how bad could that be?

Chapter 4

Bunker Basics

"Are you serious? I'm not going in there! No one said anything about swimming!" Catherine was not keen on the idea of going into an unstable mine, but this? No way! When Daniel pointed at the entrance he intended to take them through and said it was at an opening under the lake she decided her best reaction was to sit on her butt, cross her arms and flat-out refuse. "I'm not a robot! What if I can't hold my breath as long as you can?"

"It is simply eight feet down and maybe thirty feet of swimming to reach the opening. Catherine, you can easily hold your breath. I will aid you, it will take only a few seconds." Daniel towered over her and held his hand out to encourage her to get off her butt and back on track. His metal legs were inches from her face. The legs had tubes and gears all over and were more reminiscent of a motorcycle engine than a human appendage. She glared at the legs, refusing to meet Daniel's eyes or move from her spot in the dirt.

"Are you going to carry me through as well? You may think thirty feet takes only seconds, but- to us normal humans- holding our breath and swimming that long is no simple task." Jordan added.

Catherine still didn't understand why Jordan was here in the first place. Actually, she didn't understand why she was either. What could she possibly do to help?

"Why do I need to go in? Can't I just stay here?" She stared at the water and shook her head to let them know she wasn't happy about diving into the frigid depth on a cloudy fall day, much less into the underbelly of an unstable mountain.

"When I was a 'normal human' child I could swim the length of an Olympic sized pool while holding my breath. This is not even a fifth of that distance." Daniel had the most callous look and tone whenever he answered Jordan. There was no mistaking that he despised him to the core. Jordan handled it poorly, almost egging him on. No doubt he would be completely annihilated in a fight, so Catherine figured Jordan simply couldn't have a good attitude to save his life, literally.

"You said it would take seconds? Do you mean 5 seconds or 105 seconds? Ballpark?" She asked, hoping for the five seconds.

"I will get you through as swiftly as possible, ten seconds maximum. Deal?" Daniel still held out his black-gloved left hand, beckoning her from her sulking spot in the dirt. She no sooner put her hand in his than was yanked up and into his arms.

"Deal." She said quickly while moving backwards away from the robotic grip and then brushing the dirt off her clothes. She stopped as soon as she realized how idiotic she appeared, cleaning herself off right before going into a lake. "Are you coming, Jordan?"

"How can I refuse," he answered, watching Daniel with the blank, cold expression he'd perfected for his high school history class students.

Despite his off-putting countenance, she knew the only reason why Jordan would be following them. He certainly hated Daniel, so it wasn't to help him. Jordan's feelings for her made her go from flattered to frustrated in a hot second.

"Shall we go?" Daniel's black-gloved hand was outstretched towards her again.

Catherine turned from glaring at Jordan to peering up at Daniel, who had a glint of a smile in his golden eyes. She nodded and extended an arm, then was snatched up and flying into the air in a roaring flash.

"Take a deep breath." Daniel demanded and when all the air she could fit was in her lungs, they plunged into the frigid water.

She closed her eyes and pushed her face against Daniel's chest as she counted to ten in her head. *One, two, three ...* The pressure on her ears and nose was intense. *Four, five, six ...* He held her with such a tight grip that her lungs hurt and her ribs felt like they might crack. *Seven, eight ...* The pressure was gone and she hovered above a pile of rubble in the dark. The only light was coming from the cyborg in front of her, eyes gleaming bright as he stared down at her. He held her gently now in his arms.

"Are you okay, Catherine?" he asked. His eyes were back to a more normal, slightly-glowing hazel. He pushed back the hair from her face and then helped her stand steady as she tried to find her own footing among the slippery rocks. "How do you feel?"

For goodness sakes, how did she feel? She wondered that herself. He had a way of disarming her, of peering into her soul, that she couldn't help marvel at. He was holding her, was looking at her, like she was a long-lost lover. In her dreams he was so visceral, so surreal. In real life he was still intimidating, but the flesh and bone man had much more trouble hiding his emotions. And his emotions were strong – overwhelming at times. So strong she swore she could feel what he was feeling. Loneliness. Loss. And he needed her, that she knew for certain. Needed her desperately. He was waiting for her to answer, but all she could think to say was, "I don't know."

He leaned down towards her, and she thought he might kiss her and her heartbeat quickened. But, he turned away and said, "I need to help Jordan." He sank into the water, abandoning her to shiver in the pitch-black cave.

Catherine's mind was confuddled. Daniel was a handsome doctor and had a confidence about him that she found rousing ... but two days ago he was a dream. A dream! Now she blindly followed him into a death-trap mine. She worried about her own sanity.

"Echo!" she yelled, hoping to hear enough to figure-out how big the cavern was around her. There was a delayed and faint echo back, so she guessed the area in which she was standing had to be immense. That was good, she hated confined spaces, especially ones that had the essence of bat guano stinging her nostrils. It was about room temperature, but still cold due to the wet clothes clinging to her body. She rubbed her arms to keep warm. She dared not move for fear of falling off her precarious perch and diving right into the river that was probably less than a foot away.

A light come up in the water, and it burst in waves with the two men flying up and onto the rocks next to her. Daniel's eyes had changed into two exceedingly intense, white beams. He dropped Jordan off nowhere close to as tenderly as he had set her down a minute or two ago.

Jordan laid on the ground gulping air and coughing, before roaring, "That was far more than 30 feet you jackass!"

"Quiet! This area is unstable and yelling may cause a collapse," Daniel said in hushed tones.

"Bullshit," Jordan countered, but he wasn't nearly as loud. Catherine put out a hand to help him up but he refused it and got to his feet on his own.

As soon as Jordan was up, Daniel stared further into the cave and said, "Stay ahead of me and continue where the path is illuminated. The faster we move, the quicker your bodies will warm up."

Catherine began to walk carefully over the multi-colored, large rocks. The footing was treacherous and often Jordan reached out to catch her when she stumbled. She stubbornly refused his help like he had refused hers earlier. She heard nothing behind her except a swishing-air sound, signifying that Daniel was levitating above, versus navigating through, the rubble.

After nearly an hour the debris cleared and became a smoothed-out stone pathway. The walls even narrowed into an arched, grey-walled hallway. The rushing air behind them stopped and metallic clanging began.

"Stop." Daniel stated from behind after they had walked fifty feet down the path. "Turn left."

To the left was an enormous, bunker-like doorway hidden in the tunnel in such as way that they would have missed it had he not pointed them directly at it.

Daniel lifted a control box, pulled out a large metal key and inserted it. There was a loud clicking noise, followed by the sound of gears moving and then the doors began to glide open, spilling light into the hallway.

Catherine wasn't prepared for what lay behind the entrance. A military bunker? A research laboratory? Both, but on a whole other level. Vehicles, computers, chemical tanks, robotics, large barrels of coffee and so much more. It was an entire aircraft sized hanger full of supplies. Enormous, and well stocked. A visual display station for communications sat to the right, with old-fashioned computer screens that had to be a full inch thick.

"What are those?" Jordan asked, pointing to oblong, coffin sized containers set in a row towards the center of the room. Five of them were ajar, clear lids opened straight up on a vertical hinge. Near each container was the same type of devices she had seen in her hospital room, used for measuring vital signs and administering drip intravenous drugs.

"Hibernation pods." Daniel said and strolled over to a 40 foot high, 100 foot long shelf of labeled brown boxes.

"Why are five of them open? I thought you said it was just you and your brother," Jordan said as he wandered around the empty vessels. Catherine noticed a crevice in the ground and pointed it out. Jordan slid his finger along the edge and lifted it up. Beneath the stone slab was tubing that ran from the pod to deep within the ground. There was black liquid that had spilt from cracks in some of the pipes. "This is no research laboratory. What is this place?"

"My home for the last twenty years," Daniel answered, not looking up from a sizeable bag that he was filling with items from the boxes. "I need each of you to carry your own supplies." He threw two tan rucksacks over the counter he was standing over. "We will need to pack for at least a week. I have a Geiger-counter and contamination suits in this bag as well as a reverse osmosis filtration unit that we can use to collect water. There is a shelf of MRE's over there. Select what you would like to eat and fill your packs." Daniel indicated a middle shelf full of boxes with labels like beef stroganoff and spinach tortellini.

Catherine opened the box labeled chicken and rice, and found numerous brown and black bags inside. "What are these?"

"Each bag has food as per the label," Daniel explained. "They also have utensils, napkins, dessert and sometimes gum as well as a heating element and a drink inside. It is a full meal, about 2000 calories. Not the best tasting food, but it will sustain you."

"These are military grade MRE's. My favorite was always the beef stroganoff." Jordan said while loading a few of his favorite into his back pack. "What about weapons? Won't we need those?"

"No. I do not expect many people will have survived the blast and subsequent radiation contamination and depravation from the supply chain of modern society. Unless you have information that I am not privy to, *Jordan*." Daniel stopped what he was doing long enough to glare at Jordan, then a confused expression crossed his face and he went to a different shelf to rifle through a crate.

"And if there is someone who survived, you plan to handle them yourself?" Jordan yelled after Daniel's back. He shook his head, and went back to shoving food his own bag. "That's plenty, Catherine." He told her, "You don't need to cram the whole bag full."

They chucked the filled bags on their back and went to find Daniel. When they got to him, Jordan asked, "It will be dark when we get there, do you have flashlights? Or do we have to rely on you for light as well?"

"Right, good idea. This way." Daniel led them a hundred more feet into the bunker where even more shelves full of boxes made up aisles and aisles of supplies. The flickering lights above dangled from a fractured stone ceiling and fragments of rock and dust fell on the shelves.

Daniel opened a box full of long sticks with a clear face on the end. "You will need batteries as well." He handed Catherine and Jordan each a stick and then charged ahead, expecting them to follow behind him without question.

"Those are flashlights," Jordan was bemused by Catherine's bewildered look when Daniel handed her the stick and stomped off without explaining what it was. "I know you're used to the flat appliques but these are what they mostly used twenty years ago."

Catherine labored to keep up with the tall, long-legged men competing with each other over who could take a bigger stride. She still felt a bit faint from the medication withdrawal, and began to perspire and breath heavier.

They marched past an aisle of work benches covered in various human body parts made of metals, plastics and composites. Daniel paused to select a prosthetic arm. He removed his glove and then rolled up the long, black sleeve of his thin turtleneck shirt made of a rubbery synthetic material. His entire left arm was made of cybornetics. A clockwise twist and snap was all it took for it to detach. Catherine caught a glimpse of a socket-like opening in his shoulder under his sleeve before he raised the prosthetic from the bench into place. His eyes flashed when the arm clicked into place and Daniel began to move his fingers, testing out the new attachment. When he was satisfied, he rolled down his sleeve and put the black glove back on. He began walking forward again, leaving the old arm on the bench like a spare part.

"What does that one do?" Jordan asked, joining Catherine in stalking behind a fast-moving Daniel navigating through the aisles. He'd been checking out all the prosthetics on the table, and had even tried getting one to work without success.

Daniel didn't answer. He halted in front of a metal case and then unsealed the cover, cool air billowed out. He reached in and handed Catherine and Jordan each several one inch long cylindrical objects. "These are batteries for your flashlights. Open the top and put three inside, tipped end pointing outward."

She followed his direction but the light did not come on. "It doesn't work."

"You have to turn it on," Jordan replied, sliding a lever on the side of the flashlight that made it shine brilliantly.

"Oh, thanks." Catherine started to have a vague memory of using similar items back when she was a child in Montana. It was a long time ago. Many of the objects in the room were unfamiliar. The world of lighting in particular was vastly different. Lights were flat and built into a wall, not dangling from wires hanging from the ceiling or coming out of a stick. "How do you know so much about all of this outdated technology?"

"I was a teenager before the war ... how old do you think I am?" Jordan pulled out the batteries from her flashlight and said, "You will want to keep these separated until you need them or the batteries will run out quicker."

"I didn't think you were that old, maybe 45? 47?" Catherine answered while shoving as many batteries as she could into the front pouch of her backpack. Memories of being stuck in the pitch-black cave by herself only a short while ago made her want to have light at all times.

"He is 39, but I think he appears a decade older too," Daniel added, smirking.

"You may look as if you are 22, but according to census records, you're closer to 70. So, I wouldn't be grinning if I were you, old man. If you are human, that is."

Catherine gasped, she had never thought about how old Daniel must be, but 70? Wow. Ancient.

Daniel cleared his throat and said, "That reminds me, there are a few more items I need to procure. Meet me at the entrance." He left, speedily moving further into the bunker past large tanks that had colorful diamond symbols with numbers inside the four quadrants of the diamond. Some tanks had a yellow square with black skull and crossbones.

If Greggo Sands had found this place, it would have been a lot harder to try and pass it off as another Navajo tunnel.

The lights began to flicker and vibrations in the ground shook the room enough to heave up dust. She and Jordan passed each other a look. They didn't have to say a thing as they both started moving hurriedly towards the exit.

"How is it that he has cybornetics that are so advanced but gives us these ... flashlights?" she said, waving about the bulky light stick while striving to meet Jordan's stride.

"That is how technology works. Developments only happen with funding and a lot of bureaucracy. From what I read, the Jahren's had top of the line prosthetics, and that was only what they wanted people to know. Like the viruses, so much of what they did they kept secret ... and developed technology no one has ever seen. Plus, I have a feeling that whatever is powering these cybornetics isn't something the government wanted the public to know about."

"What do you mean?" she asked loudly and while sucking air. She struggled to follow closely behind Jordan's long-legs as he spoke and she was falling further and further behind. The rucksack had to weigh at least 40 pounds. She wondered how she would carry it for a day, much less a week in LA.

"What I mean is that this technology wasn't just buried in the mine. It was left buried by the U.S. Government as well." He stopped and turned to her as he spoke this time. She almost ran into him, she'd been staring down at her feet, willing them to move faster. "Do you need me to carry some of that? Let me take a few of those batteries."

"You and your conspiracy theories, Jordan." She said, unloading her pack into his. That dropped a good five pounds.

"Ha! I was right though, you have to admit that," he claimed smugly and helped her get her backpack back on.

"No, you thought the mine was dumping waste into the lake. You didn't believe there were viruses until I mentioned how strange it was that they would make-up five different viruses as a smokescreen. Then, when you found out there actually were viruses you over-reacted and tried to hole-up in that cabin of yours, expecting the 'end-of-days'."

"I was right! Admit it! What are we doing here but trying to stop a virus that is going to destroy humanity. If that isn't end of days, what is?"

Catherine shook her head, and stomped away. He was obviously still trying to convince her that it had been in her best interest to be tied up in his cabin, to protect her from the viruses. When she got to the closed exit she threw down her backpack and sat on a chair near the computers to the right of the bunker doors and stewed. After a few minutes she had to admit that Jordan did have a point ... they were trying to prevent the total annihilation of the human race ... weren't they? "Exactly how are we supposed to stop anything, Jordan? What are we even doing here? What are *you* doing?"

Jordan stammered, started to talk a few times but didn't get out a decipherable word. He finally put his bag down and sat next to her. "All my life I have felt an impending doom."

"That explains a lot," she quipped.

He scoffed and continued, "I've been alone for so long. I watched my parents die slowly from the dust. You don't know what that's like. Your parents probably coddled you to college.

When you lose everyone you love, it changes you. I pushed everyone away. I ... I liked it that way." He turned away from her so she couldn't see his face, but she could hear the suffering in his voice.

"You're wrong, I do understand. My mom died when I was two, and my dad ran off and died when I was ten. But, I don't go around kidnapping people."

"Catherine, you are always surprising me." A rare smile crossed his usual grumpy face for a brief second. "How did you get out of those ropes?"

"I was raised by my uncle; his name was Houdini," she joked.

"Come on," He snickered. He had a full smile now, and it reminded her how attractive he could be when he wasn't purposefully being a jerk.

"Being raised on a ranch in Montana has it's perks, I guess ... you get to know ropes fairly well. Those were some pretty good knots you made, took me hours to work them out."

"I underestimated you ..." He opened his mouth to say more but then glanced up. She followed his eyes towards Daniel coming towards them. He had on a completely different outfit that covered his rocket-legs completely, down to booted feet. He carried two bulky bags that he set on the counter between them. "More MRE's, spare clothes, blankets and a tent. Jordan, you will have to carry one of these temporarily. When we rendezvous with Anthony and his friend we will give them each one."

Jordan lifted the bag and winced, giving Daniel a sideways grimace. "Fine."

"Change into these." Daniel pitched them each an entire outfit similar to his new clothes, including a nice warm jacket with a hood and some masculine looking boots. "Put the cotton socks on first, then put the wool ones on over them."

"Military uniforms, nice touch. A bit out of date, but they'll work," Jordan stepped behind one of the shelves, taking his clothes with him. Catherine went behind another, thankful of the privacy the stacked boxes provided.

"What are you doing?" Catherine asked when she came back to the communication hub. Daniel had moved to a bench and pressed buttons on a large rectangular box that began to light up, along with the old computer monitors all along the counter.

"We need to check on your boyfriend's progress," he explained while typing and turning on applications. "I put a tracker on his ... shirt ..."

The screen showed what could only be described as the inside of a washing machine. Suds and all.

"Genius," Jordan added, zipping up his jacket and coming to stand behind Daniel, next to Catherine. She was used to seeing Jordan in baggy clothes, and the jacket Daniel had given him fit snug. She'd assumed the baggy clothes he usually wore were meant to hide his middle-aged pot belly. But he had a flat stomach, and nice wide shoulders too. He looked ... sharp.

"I also put a tracker in his car," Daniel opened another camera view and it showed past a car window. The vehicle was sitting in front of a charming green colonial house with white trim. The garage door was open.

"That's Gretchen and Ariana's place, his little sisters," Catherine said. "He did say that 'Sasha' was staying with them."

Daniel moved through a few more camera views on the computer screen. They displayed various rooms and places. Then he opened one showing the heliport near the mine. A sleek, silver helicopter with the Greggo Sands logo (white crescent moon over a red mountain) on the side of the tail was parked in the center. Its twin engines were not moving, so it was at rest.

"Let's go," Jordan announced.

"Not so fast. Observe." Daniel pointed to the pilot and two guards standing near a bench with a clear glass overhang on the far right of the helicopter. He switched views back to the one inside Anthony's car. The passenger side door opened and an attractive blonde woman sat inside. Anthony walked around the front and sat in the driver seat, then inputted directions into the navigation system. He was such a gentleman, always holding the door open and letting a lady in first. Though, when he did it for another woman it made Catherine feel a twinge of jealousy.

"He will know she is lying, Sasha. I will never forgive myself if she is hurt because of this," Anthony spoke to the woman as the car backed out of the driveway and into the street.

Sasha leaned towards him and put her hand on his thigh, saying with a strong eastern European accent, "She understands the risks. We all do. It is her choice."

Catherine leaned forward, practically breathing down Daniel's neck as he flipped through other screens on another monitor and typed something or the other. Why wasn't Anthony moving Sasha's hand off his thigh? Who did she think she was, holding onto him like that? Sasha was still holding his thigh! Anthony peered down at the woman's hand and reached his hand towards–

"They are heading over to the heliport, as should we," Daniel said, abruptly switching off the computers and turning around to find Catherine's scowling face two inches from the screen that just went black before she could find out what Anthony was going to do about Sasha's hand. Daniel grinned like a scoundrel as he said, "There is one last item before we leave. You may enjoy this one."

Chapter 5

Copter Convergence

Fire and brimstone, that was an apocalypse. Not this – not withering death. Would Alluri Rapalle's name go down in history as the one who exposed the world? He contemplated his fate, sitting in a café, alone on a stool near the window. He waited, anxiously fiddling with a ceramic mug filled with an untouched dark brew.

As he thought about it, he realized all the signs were there all along. Each new discovery adding to the last, but each more powerful. The final virus, labeled Quinta, should have been enough on its own. None of the best scientist money could buy understood the mechanism for how it could turn muscle cells into graphene-making factories.

Sasha had always been discrete in her plans, and was now definite in her threats. She'd left her coded threat in a message on his private line, one only a handful of people knew. He knew the code, knew what it meant. The message played over and over in his head, "The seventh sign, you broke the seal. Neumon's Desert Grande, 7pm." Efficient. Brief. Horrifying.

"Would you like another cup of coffee, Mr. Repalle?" asked the mild-mannered waiter wearing the all-white Neumon's uniform. The uniform made the boy a walking billboard that advertised the daily specials on the front and drink prices down each sleeve in an ever-changing graphic display.

"No, thank you. I'm fine," he replied with a strained smile and a brief glance up to see the waiter gaping down at him in awe, apparently searching for something more to say.

"So.. so.. sorry you had to close your mine, Sir," the lanky young man stammered. "Will ... ummm ... will the principal be transferred to your hometown now? He's a great principal, sir! The best! Ummm ... I ... I hope I get transferred to his new school ... is there a Neumon's there, sir?"

Alluri's older brother, Sanjay, was the reason he was closing the mine – but no one knew that. "Unfortunately, I don't have control over where principal Sanjay Rapalle is transferred. But, I can tell you there is a Neumon's in every town I have ever been." Another strained smile, with an added awkward silence for a few heartbeats before the boy finally left him in peace.

Peace and quiet, the whole reason why Sanjay convinced Alluri to open the mine here in the first place. Sanjay wanted a small town to live a 'normal' life. He practically put this town together brick-by-brick himself. Yet a week ago he'd begged Alluri to end it all.

A dream, he said. He'd found out what they'd dug up, and forced a confession. Alluri still didn't know how Sanjay knew about the viruses. The excuse that the knowledge came to him in a dream was ridiculous. Someone must have told him, was it Sasha?

He heard a broom fall, and a cup shatter. "Sorry! Sorry, sir," the boy yelled back from behind the customer counter.

Was the kid working by himself? Maybe the other staff members were already transferred? No, only a few dozen families left since his announcement that meant the end of this town. The boy being alone was probably because Alluri was the only customer in the café this evening. Likely it simply wasn't a popular time to get a cup of coffee and Neumon's only needed one employee to cover the shift.

Alluri went back to his thoughts, ruminating while staring out the window into the empty parking lot. Tumbleweeds blew across the white pavement made of his company's latest energy-harvesting ceramic, Briatech.

Shutting the mine down was no issue at all. He had several others that could produce the same minerals, including bauxite used for the ceramic mixture. The Briatech roads were already being used in other towns, so the city had served its purpose for Greggo Sands as a model town for the energy-harvesting technology. Even the treasure trove of research uncovered in the tunnels that tripled the company's profits was already being mass produced overseas for the big three powers that be-India, Russia and China.

It wasn't shutting down the mine that bothered Alluri, it was having to confess to his older brother.

It was a full confession too, detailing that he had been involved in illicit activities. That he'd found something that should have stayed buried and sold it to the highest bidder. The disappointment in his brother's eyes unsealed a well of shame in his soul.

Emptiness, and regret. That was what Alluri felt.

Why had he done it? Profits were high ... but besides the Briatech, not much innovation was going on at Greggo Sands. Exploring the laboratories in the mine was pure fascination, curiosity really. And, he thought he had it all under control.

At seven pm his arm started to vibrate. He rolled up his shirt sleeve to see a call from the same unknown number that delivered Sasha's cryptic message. So, she wasn't meeting him here after all? He tapped the prosthetic behind his ear and answered, "Alluri speaking."

"I need to borrow your helicopter, Mr. Rapalle," said a soft female voice endeavoring to sound monotone, and with a fake British accent that made him want to laugh.

"Who is this?" Alluri knew it wasn't Sasha. Sasha had too thick of an accent to pull off a fake voice like the young lady on the other side of the line. Plus, Sasha wasn't so stupid that she would think something like faking a voice would even work.

"If you want to redeem yourself, you will do as I ask," she threatened.

"Why should I listen to you? Who are you?" Redeem himself? Had his brother Sanjay put one of his students up to this?

"We don't have time, Mr. Rapalle. It is not underselling it to say that the fate of humanity is at stake, and only you have the power to help."

A canned, ridiculous response. "I'm hanging up now," he stated.

His finger was mere centimeters from the button by his ear when she exclaimed, "Wait! Sasha said to tell you 'The seal was buried alive the entire time' – those were her exact words."

"Where is Sasha? Why did she set those detonations and kill Dr. Steinman?"

"What? She killed someone?" The fake British accent was gone, and he could tell the caller had a touch of an old New Yorker's Brooklyn accent.

"Yes. She is very dangerous. Tell me where you are and where she is and I will help you."

"I ... I ... she ... I ..." the young woman cleared her throat and began her fake accent again, "There is only one way to redeem yourself. Leave the helicopter on the helipad at sunset, unattended. That is all." The young woman dropped the connection and Alluri's armband went back to default mode.

When the call ended, Alluri reflexively took a swig from the coffee mug in front of him. Bitter, cold and the beans had an awful burnt residue. He spit the acidic black liquid back into the cup and yanked two napkins out of the holder to wipe his mouth in disgust. The typically bitter brew was far worse when cold and he wasn't even sure why he'd ordered it. He hated Neumon's coffee.

"I'm sorry Mr. Rapalle! I'll get you another one!" The lanky waiter took the mug and ran off to the espresso machines.

"Don't worry about it!" He called after the kid, but wasn't sure he was heard or the barista purposefully ignored him.

Alluri thought about the phone call, and tried not to think about the awful taste in his mouth as he scowled after the boy. The seal was buried alive meant only one thing: the Jahrens were still alive. How was that possible? Had Sasha uncovered their hideout? Had they taken her captive and were the Jahrens manipulating her now? The knowledge brought more questions than answers.

The Jahrens were the true owners of most of the town, including the entire mountainside. When the bauxite mining revealed tunnels leading to laboratories years ago, Alluri hired an investigator to uncover everything about the town's history. The seal was broken meant that whatever the Jahrens had feared would escape had escaped. Whatever it was, they'd feared it so much they buried themselves and all their research in a massive explosion 23 years ago ... sealing it, and themselves, away from the world.

He tapped his fingers on the counter, gazing out at the scarlet horizon. The sun would set soon. "The seventh sign, you broke the seal." Repeated over and over in his head.

~ ~ ~

"I told you, if he decides to help then the guards will be gone right after sunset. If not, all we have to do is deal with them and we have the helicopter. Simple." Sasha was becoming annoyed by the constant questions from everyone. She knew her plan was brilliant. She'd already lured Alluri into town, along with his helicopter. What more could they ask?

"I asked for the helicopter to be ready by seven pm, not sunset," said the supposed 'cyborg' towering over her. He was as intimidating in stature as he was in his scrutiny. Ever since he'd popped up out of the water in a small, circular submersible 20 minutes ago he hadn't taken his eyes off of her. It was like he was scanning her. Which he could be, she had no idea what he was capable of. He was absolutely intriguing, and terrifying. Nothing like what she expected. He was tall, dark and unexpectedly handsome. But most shocking was that he was about 50 years younger than he should be. This couldn't be Dr. Daniel Jahren – impossible. Was this an android built by the Jahren family to protect their secrets? She wanted to poke him, he looked so human ... exactly like the pictures she'd seen of Daniel from records Greggo Sands dug up of the area. She wanted to take him into her laboratory and cut him open to see what was inside.

Daniel turned his concentration from Sasha to across the lake where the helicopter sat on the Greggo Sands helipad. It was barely visible from their vantage point by the lake-side park marina.

"Look, they're leaving!" Anthony shouted back from his hiding place ahead in the sage bushes at the top of the hill. He motioned them to come up from where they were standing by the boat dock below.

"So, the man does have a soul." Sasha whispered to herself. She was never sure if being honest with Alluri would be fruitful. He was a businessman after all, even though he started out as a scientist like her. He must have gotten her message and decided to he needed to redeem himself.

She followed Daniel and the girl he hovered next to constantly, Catherine, to Anthony's bushy hideaway on the hill. The three of them laid down next to Anthony when they reached the top. Anthony let her peer through his rifle sight to see the empty helipad.

They'd come equipped with Anthony's hunting gear. As the sun went down, Anthony prepared to take aim using his tranquilizer rounds. Jordan, the supposed high school teacher, was on the ground next to him with Anthony's other rifle. He, begrudgingly, let Daniel peer through his rifle sight. Jordan had directed Anthony to the right area for a sniper shot, and handled the weapons like it was second nature. Teacher indeed. His every action, look and word was too well calculated.

"Let's get to the chopper," Sasha announced. "Before Alluri changes his mind."

"My thoughts exactly," said the 'cyborg' calling himself 'Daniel' who smiled for some reason. "But, first we need to load-up."

Daniel proceeded to rocket into the air and in a flash he was down the hill and levitating over a round submarine by the marina. The whole group quickly followed down the hill to gather at the floating orb. The three of them (Daniel, Jordan and Catherine) had arrived in the orb earlier, at seven pm on the dot. After Daniel unloaded several bags to the dock, he pressed a button on the top of the sphere. The thing sealed itself and then sank back into the water with barely a ripple to show it had ever existed.

More technology Sasha had never seen. It was her job to know technology, so having the spherical submarine disappear without being able to inspect it was irksome.

Daniel landed in a gusty rush by the pile of supplies he'd unloaded and handed each person an ample, heavy rucksack to carry. The petite girl, Catherine, labored with hers. Such a pale, weak thing. Anthony doted over her though, offering to carry her bag as well. The child at least had the pride to refuse. Why she was here, it was unclear. She was sick and obviously slowed the entire party down as they made their way to the helicopter on the other side of the lake.

"Jordan, are you familiar with this model?" Anthony asked when they reached the helipad. He motioned for Sasha to help him remove the mooring cable attached to the retractable landing gear and tail blade.

"Yes, but I will need to rig it to start because no one thought to leave us the ignition pad," Jordan answered, heading towards the front of the craft after digging around in the cockpit.

"Stop, I have an easier solution," Daniel said, entering the cockpit and fishing out a black disc and an old-fashioned hand-held computer from his rucksack. He held the disc over the main navigation system in the center. The screen of the laptop began running through combination sequences. All Sasha saw were numbers and screens flashing open and closed so quickly it was hard to follow. Some kind of security decryption routine. After about 30 seconds the whole cockpit console lit-up. The engines outside the windows moved to take-off position, there was a buzzing and then the blades extended outward.

"Everyone, get in," Daniel commanded, shutting off and putting away his equipment.

"You'll want to fasten your seatbelts," Sasha added. She'd been in this contraption half a dozen times, and *always* wore a seatbelt. There were rumors that over 100 people died testing the initial models of this aircraft in China before it was deemed flightworthy. This was one of the most dangerous commercial helicopters ever built, but one of the fastest, reaching 270 knots. The technology was awe-inspiring, but the danger and her fear of heights combined meant she would be clutching her bag and staring straight in front of her until they landed.

Daniel took the co-pilot seat on the left and threw his bag on the floor in the back where Sasha was already belted in. Jordan was apparently a seasoned pilot as well as a sniper – adeptly flipping switches all over the cockpit and checking gauges. Anthony helped Catherine get her backpack off so the poor girl could jump in after she'd tried propelling herself up a few times with no success. Catherine then decided to plant herself in the seat behind Daniel, facing straight toward Sasha. Anthony sat next to Catherine, back to back with Jordan in the right pilot seat of the cockpit. The aircraft could seat seven tightly. But, with all their luggage shoved in the back, it was a snug fit with only the five of them inside.

"Are you alright, Babe?" Anthony spoke to Catherine, whose eyes were opening and closing, fluttering like she was about to pass out. He held her face in his hands.

"She needs to drink this," Daniel opened a vial into a plastic container of clear liquid. The purple fluid from the vial turned the water red. He handed the bottle to Anthony.

Where did the vial come from? How acidic was that water if it became red, or was the clear liquid even water to begin with?

"Babe ..." Anthony patted her face. "Babe, wake-up! Please, drink this."

Catherine opened her big doe-brown eyes long enough to see the bottle moving toward her lips and she drank it – gulping and choking, spilling it down her jacket. Her, Daniel and Jordan all had matching outfits: tan camouflage head to toe and apparently made of water-resistant material because the liquid beaded up and rolled down – leaving no signs of wetness.

"What's wrong with her?" Sasha asked. She knew next to nothing about this young woman, except she was Anthony's 'girlfriend' and some kind of high school teacher ... was it English? She could pass for a high school student.

"She was in an accident two weeks ago. Her healing has been accelerated, but at a cost. We will all need to keep an eye on her. Without her, none of this matters." Daniels words were puzzling. As he spoke, Sasha felt his intentions. Sasha's heart beat harder, her head felt like it was going to explode. It was frightening.

"Why?" Jordan asked, breaking the poignant tension in Sasha's head and chest. "Why is Catherine so important to you?"

At first, Sasha was confused by Jordan's words. Of course Catherine was important! She was vital! That was all Sasha thought and felt. Then, after a few seconds she realized those thoughts made no sense. Jordan had a point, why was this girl important? What's more ... why did she feel so strongly all the sudden? There was more going on here ... wait, were Daniel's eyes *glowing*?

"Glaring at me with those eyes is only going to make my night vision worse," Jordan answered with amusement in his voice. This guy had balls, he was pissing a cyborg off and thought it was funny! Great, the pilot was suicidal.

"Guys, we need to leave, now!" Anthony pointed toward the end of the helipad where three men were running towards the helicopter. "Go now! Go!" he yelled.

"Take off!" Daniel demanded.

Jordan pulled back a joystick in the center of the cockpit and the aircraft careened forward and up. Bags went flying about as he swiftly shifted the helicopter up and around at a 45-degree angle turn. Beams of light exposed the freshly broken-up boulders forming the mountainside where the entrance of the mine used to be.

Sasha felt squished down into her seat as they rapidly gained altitude to make it over the high peak. Jordan flipped a switch and she could hear the landing gear retract. From what she could see, it was going to be a close call getting high enough so that they didn't ram into the mountain at high speed.

She closed her eyes and didn't realize she'd held her breath until the helicopter leveled out and sped forward at a smooth, even velocity. She breathed a sigh of relief and opened her eyes to see the last rays of a blood-red sunset illuminating their right. The sparkling lights of the town of Desert Grande shown faintly below, serene as the sparking sky above.

The town passed by in a matter of seconds and the aircraft headed directly into the darkness beyond.

"Fly us into LA, safely, Jordan. That is all you need to worry about." Daniel had his left hand clasped onto the handle above his door, the other on the back of Jordan's seat. The tension in his body and voice indicating he wasn't a fan of Jordan's piloting skills. Daniel wore dark black gloves, but beneath his left glove the hand was odd, with a circular shape in the center and knotted knuckles. He moved his hand down before she could inspect it further, then turned to face the back seat and said, "Anthony, secure those back packs before they knock someone out."

Sasha helped Anthony buckle two bags into the empty seats next to her. They found a cargo rope on the sidewall that they extended and crisscrossed over the other three on the floor between them. Anthony gave her one of his charming grins, and a simple 'thank you' that made her heart skip a beat before he went back to coddling his girlfriend.

Static-filled chattering came from the front console, apparently the local flight control frequency. She caught few words, but heard one phrase that made her concerned they might be followed: 'what is your destination, over.' Jordan turned off the channel and unscrewed something from the top of the cockpit, then hurled it out his door in a loud rush. He slammed the door shut and said to Daniel, "That reminds me, exactly where in LA are we going? Do you have a map?"

"If we head 30 degrees southwest at 300 miles an hour, we should arrive in approximately 2.5 hrs," Daniel replied, words almost undecipherable from the noise of their flight–roaring engines competing with wind howling and swirling around them.

"And the wall? How do you plan to get past the defenses?" Jordan's harsh tone carried well above the noise.

"That, Jordan, is the only reason why you are here," Daniel answered. The two men were now in a staring contest.

"What defenses?" Sasha had no idea there were active defenses. The wall was built decades ago, during the war – which was long over. Plus, this was not a military aircraft. If there were any air to ground missiles, they wouldn't stand a chance.

"And if old codes don't work?" Jordan asked, eyes glancing back at Catherine, concern visible despite his stone façade.

"What codes?" Anthony took time away from helping Catherine sip her red elixir, and attempted to pay attention to the men arguing in the front.

"It tastes like cranberry cocktail ..." Catherine was so mousy and adorable when she spoke. Even Sasha had trouble not smiling at her little hands holding the bottle and sipping so cutely. Delicate features, a sweet smile. Oh, but Sasha wanted to hate her! Anthony couldn't be more in love with the girl, and that alone was reason to despise her.

Jordan's words seethed with sarcasm and disdain as he said, "The walls along the west coast were set-up during the war as autonomous, meaning they will shoot down anything not having the code needed for a particular entry point. This forces us to come in from 100 miles south, as the closest code I know is for the San Diego entrance. What makes this even more ... how should I put this? Fun? Is that if I switch on the navigation, Central will likely scramble a jet to take us out well before we get there. So, we will be flying blind, hoping to make the correct entry point. Oh, and let's hope they didn't change the codes in the last seven years."

Was Catherine sobbing? Anthony wiped the tears and kissed her gently on the forehead and both cheeks, saying: "Babe, it's going to be okay. He's just a jerk, remember? We'll be okay, I promise. God is with us." He hugged her as best he could, being belted securely into a seat over four inches away from hers. The he began to pray: "Yea, though I walk through the valley of the shadow of death, I will fear no evil: for thou art with me –"

"Here, give her this," Daniel produced two white pills from a translucent, flexible bag in his jacket pocket. Vials? Pills? How many drugs did Daniel have? She knew they had only scratched the surface of what the Jahrens hid, and he brought some of it with him, apparently.

Sasha thought briefly about rummaging through Daniel's bag, to see what all he brought but a quick glance from Daniel's glowing eyes made her realize that was a terrible idea.

Catherine took the pills, no questions asked. Swallowed them down with the last of the red liquid then smiled briefly before passing completely out. Anthony instantly freaked out, of course.

"She is fine, those were sleeping pills. She needs rest," Daniel stated.

"Do you have anymore of those?" Sasha asked in all seriousness. She hated flying almost as much as she hated seeing Anthony holding Catherine and tenderly caressing her sleeping head on his shoulder. Two to three hours of this and she would probably jump out well before they reached the wall.

Chapter 6

Rough Landing

Beep. Beep. Beep. Beep.

"Turn the helicopter around, now!" Anthony yelled, waking Catherine from her slumber and causing her left ear to throb–his loud mouth was less than an inch from where her head lay on his shoulder.

She spun around as best she could in her seat to see they were speedily approaching a sizeable, well-fortified cement wall with cannon barrels on top – aimed right at them. The X shaped lights ahead on the wall flashed red in sync with the 'Beep' noise, which was high-pitched and deafening even this far out as it blared every second.

"No! I know what I'm doing. Sit back and shut up!" Jordan said, hastily pressing a button in the front of the cockpit. Catherine realized he was producing a Morse code signal through the speaker system.

"Brace yourselves, this might get bumpy." Daniel warned.

Catherine had no idea how to brace herself any more than she already was, being fastened in with a x shaped belt over her chest and another belt on her hips. She turned her head around and pressed it back against the seat and gripped tightly onto the seatbelt crisscrossed over her chest. She stared straight in front of her and noticed Sasha completely passed out. Lucky, she would die peacefully in her sleep while the rest of them had to experience the impending doom.

Beep. Beep. Beep. Beep. Beep.

Catherine squeezed her eyes shut – they had to be right over the wall by now! She waited for the inevitable missile fire.

Beep. Beep. Then it stopped.

"Oh my God, did we make it!?!" she yelled, rotating around in her seat towards the cockpit to see only blackness ahead through the front window.

"Yes, we have passed over the wall," Daniel answered, turning in his seat to offer her an assuring smile. His face was practically flush with hers and his humid breath smelt like coffee and ... tree bark? He appeared relieved and, to everyone's surprise, said, "Thank you, Jordan."

"Anytime. I always love a good adrenaline rush." Jordan's sarcasm wasn't enough to take the smiles off anyone's faces. Well, anyone awake. Sasha had her head back and mouth wide open, drool dripping down her cheek.

The view from the cockpit window was shrouded in night as far as the eye could see. She knew the entire west coast was decimated, but what little she could make out from the helicopter beams was other-worldly. They passed over what used to be the city of San Diego, and it was clear more than just nuclear weapons had taken their toll. Most of it was overrun by seawater. Either the water level had risen, or the subduction plate had sucked the coast down into the ocean.

"That's new," Jordan said, peering out at the ocean waves lapping against a domed building covered in seaweed and driftwood.

"What's new?" Anthony asked, gaping in awe. No doubt at the enormity or multitude of structures poking through the ocean like Catherine. Likely he'd never seen any city so large in his lifetime. Catherine sure couldn't remember anything so expansive, she was too young when it all got blown to bits.

"The ocean used to be ten miles west of here," Jordan shook his head. "Are you sure you want to continue? I doubt LA will have faired any better, and we probably won't have fuel to ... Wait, what?!?" He tapped a gauge with his knuckle. "We're close to empty already!"

He reached for the joystick and Daniel put his hand over it, saying, "I brought extra fuel."

"Ha! How much fuel do you think this takes!?! You can't get far on a five-gallon container of Biozene, and you don't have enough room in that bag of yours for anything bigger."

"Head north and when we get to an adequate landing area, I will show you." Daniel's confident words made everyone relax after Jordan's panic episode. Surely Daniel had the technology, he was well prepared.

"That's if the entire city isn't under water." Jordan snorted, ruining the feeling of ease Daniel had created.

After Daniel and Jordan's bickering ceased, Anthony leaned over and gave Catherine a delicate, brief kiss. No sooner than he said "I told you we would make it, Babe" the fuel light came on, illuminating the dark cabin in a tangerine glow and removing his grin.

"Just keep flying." Daniel's voice was less reassuring this time, even he had been startled by the sudden fuel light.

Everyone quietly, anxiously sat staring out the windows. Catherine was afraid to blink. She watched through the front window for signs of a dry place they could land. For a while there were no more buildings and she only caught glimpses of hilltops being crested by waves.

"Over there, what's that?" Catherine spotted a white object and pointed ahead to the northwest. The closer they came, the more white objects came into view. After a few moments flying towards where she'd point, it was clear that the ocean ended in a suburb of sun-bleached, flattened, wood houses adorned with palm trees. It went on forever. "My God, there are so many!"

"There! Land there," Daniel steered them to a parking lot of a ruined, gigantic shopping center. The sparse number of vehicles left on the lot were in poor condition, as was the pavement. There were chasms, cracks and whole areas lifted and slanted sideways. Earthquakes must have riddled the area.

Jordan managed to find a decently flat and unobstructed place to land among the heavily creviced and cluttered parking lot. Hoovering over it, he pressed a few buttons and switched on something that caused the bottom of the aircraft to make noise.

"Don't worry, Babe. It's only the landing gear." Anthony must have seen the confused panic on Catherine's face. He patted her leg and then held her hand. It reminded her of when Sasha had put her hand on his leg and she scowled at Sasha, who was still drooling in her sleep.

After setting the helicopter down smoothly, Jordan turned off the engines and shut off all of the lights, exterior and interior, saying, "No reason to draw attention to ourselves, just in case."

The sound of breathing, Sasha's soft snoring, and the eerie glow of the cyborg's eyes were all there was. It was a start contrast to the previous howling wind and churning rotor blades. The cabin of the aircraft felt far more confining and intimate than it had only moments ago.

Jordan unstrapped himself and turned to glare at Daniel, then Anthony and then down at Anthony's hand holding Catherine's. Daniel just glared at Anthony.

Anthony ignored the both of them and squeezed Catherine's hand tighter. He leaned towards her for a kiss but was interrupted by Daniel putting his hand on his shoulder and saying, "Anthony, unstrap the bags and start unloading. This should take less than an hour. Jordan, you're welcome to help too."

Catherine opened her mouth to offer aid but thought better of it as she watched the guys get to work. The last thing she wanted was to become a liability tonight, getting in their way, or worse–passing out while she held an important wrench or something. Best to stay put. Maybe she could fall asleep again. Sasha sure was snoring away without a care in the world.

The cabin was cozy-warm and the thick jacket she wore was snug as a blanket. Catherine closed her eyes, easily drifting asleep despite the sound of men bashing away outside the front of the aircraft.

She awoke in what felt like a second later to Sasha shaking her. Sasha had her hand over Catherine's mouth. She put one finger over her own lips in the universal shushing sign.

"I heard something outside," Sasha whispered. "Do you know what happened? Where are the guys?"

"Outside. Refueling." Catherine carefully unbuckled her two seatbelts and made her way into the empty cockpit left side seat for a better view of where she'd heard the men banging away in the front before she'd fallen asleep. Sasha came up and sat in the pilot seat to the right. They heard nothing coming from outside, and could only see cracked pavement ahead in the moonlight. Where *were* the guys?

Catherine turned to quietly ask Sasha in her ear, "What did you hear?"

The right door opened and in a heartbeat Sasha was snatched out by an indecipherable figure. Catherine's heart tried to beat out of her chest and she held her own hands over her mouth so she didn't scream. She gaped into the blackness beyond the open door, petrified.

Something out there moved like a shadow in the night. Then the world went black.

"This one fainted," a foreign female voice said and Catherine felt a hard object poke her in the ribs. She opened her eyes and the first thing she thought was, "Am I dreaming again?"

She wanted to pinch herself but found her hands were tied and so were her feet, and a soft cotton cloth covered her mouth. The rough-rope bounds between her hands and feet were attached with a rope segment that was designed to prevent her from reaching up to her face to remove the cotton gag.

The scene in front of her could not be real. A figure, no more than 3 feet in stature but with the head of a fully-grown man sat on the back of a Komodo dragon. The giant, scaly lizard dribbled saliva next to Catherine's boots as its forked, white-blue tongue flicked in and out of its mouth. Its beady black eyes blinked in contemplation of no doubt eating her for dinner and it had sharp black claws that scratched the cement floor as it lumbered about with the dwarf on its back. The man held the rains of the beast using, not two, but three arms! The extra arm came right out of the center of his chest. He wore a golden robe over silken pants with black, Chinese dragons embroidered down the sides. He had on slippers and small brimmed hat to match. His hair was silver and he had a jagged burn scar that ran from above his upper lip down his cheek towards his chin.

"We used the tranquilizer on the other four," the female voice coming from Catherine's right said.

Catherine took her eyes off the unbelievable golden dwarf on a lizard long enough to notice the women surrounding him. Every one of them wore black and red Asian fighting uniforms with a three-inch golden dragon logo on the arm. Their eyes were the only thing exposed except for the woman to

Catherine's right, who had her mask off. They wore knife belts all down their legs, full of sharp objects coated in black except for the tips. Each woman also had a utility belt and a variety of weapons. Some had swords, some had weapons Catherine had never seen. Chinese assassins, or Ninja.

This must be a dream! Catherine thought, closing her eyes and repeating *WAKE UP!* over and over again in her head. Dwarfs on dragons with a band of female assassin warriors was about as outrageous as cyborgs. But the cyborgs turned out to be real. She opened her eyes and they were still there.

"I think she might faint again," said another Asian woman behind her and to the left. The comment caused scattered laughter throughout the room. Catherine turned and noticed the woman who'd spoken had more red and some gold in her uniform, and no mask. She had the same Chinese dragons on her pants that the man on the lizard had, and she wore two swords on her hip. Blades hid beneath intricately designed wrist guards on both of her arms.

"Wake up the rest. I want to talk to the one with booster legs. Right now, he has a leg up on his competition," said the golden dwarf overlord.

Laying around her, and currently being rudely zapped awake by electric sticks, were her friends–all similarly tied and bound. Except for Daniel, he had sharp mesh-metal net around him and four hooded warriors ready to slice him with swords as soon as he opened his eyes.

She watched all of them go through the same shock and awe at the scene unfolding in front of them ... all except for Jordan, who was actually devilishly grinning.

"That ugly smirk is familiar. Jasmine, remove the scraf." The Chinese woman with the extra gold in her uniform followed the dwarf's command and removed the gag from Jordan who instantly began speaking in a foreign language. The only word she could decipher was 'Tripod.' The rest sounded Chinese.

The dwarf replied in the same language and must have given orders to have Jordan unbound because the woman, Jasmine, cut his ropes away.

Daniel began to try to speak through his gag and shook his head.

Jordan spoke more in Chinese, nodding towards Daniel, who glared at him with glowing eyes.

"I believe not everyone in your party agrees with you, Luca. Let's see what your mechanical friend has to say." The dwarf spun the index finger of his left hand once clockwise and then pointed towards Daniel. The female fighter on Daniel's right slid the scarf off of his mouth and then swiftly went back to directing her sword at his throat.

"We have no time for this! If we don't stop Cliff now than everyone here will be dead or under his control in a matter of months! Lord Tripod, we need your help to fin –"

The dwarf made a swift motion with his center hand, fingers flat and squeezed to the thumb and there were suddenly four sword tips on Daniel's neck close enough to give him a shave. "You dare come into my territory and ask me a favor? You should have listened to your friend. That will cost you."

Another hand motion, this time from Lord Tripod's center arm – all fingers pointing up. The party of robed warriors followed him out of the jail cell, swinging the barred gate shut behind them with a reverberating metal clank. Cast iron bars, six inches apart and with sharp points coming out like thorns made up the whole twenty foot opening of the large cell. The rest of the room was pure cement, floor to ceiling, with no windows. On the far-right corner of the cell was a sink and a yellow and black streaked toilet that filled the room with a nostril-burning sourness that would be hard to forget, if they ever made it out alive. Across from their cage was another cage filled with bandaged and weary-eyed men wearing nothing but black pants with red embroidery made from the same silken material the female assassin warriors wore.

"And I thought I had a talent for pissing people off," Jordan snidely remarked, helping Catherine with the ropes on her legs. She'd worked her hands lose on her own and removed the ropes and her gag as soon as the door slammed shut. "If you play along, we can be out of here in a matter of days, minus a few supplies."

"That simple?" This time Daniel was the one with a sarcastic tone. "And if I can't deliver on your promise?"

Catherine and Jordan began untying Daniel's ropes. She had no idea how they would remove Daniel's netting until Jordan produced a small knife he'd hidden in his boot. The sharp knife easily, and surprisingly, cut through the metal mesh. She decided to leave Jordan with Daniel, as there wasn't much she could do. She crawled over to help Anthony, who was yanking unproductively on his bounds.

"What did you say to him?" Catherine asked Jordan, who ignored her and glared at Daniel. "How do you know this 'Lord Tripod', Jordan?" She removed Anthony's gag, and peered in wonderment at his hands ... he'd somehow gotten even more entangled in the ropes. "Or should I say, Luca?" Catherine asked as she carefully untied a grateful Anthony.

Jordan didn't answer, he continued cutting the wire mesh and glaring threateningly at Daniel.

"Luca Puglisi here, that is his real name, is a spy. Or was, until he was forcibly 'retired' for illicit activities," explained Daniel. "He told Lord Tripod I can –"

"What I did was save everyone here from being breakfast for Tripod's brood of pet Komodo dragons –"

"Everyone? Except –" Daniel began but was interrupted by Jordan.

"What, you don't think you can fight all of the sudden? Wasn't it you who smugly said we didn't even need weapons because no one could have survived out here this long? I guess you don't know everything." Jordan finished cutting the mesh and slid the knife back in his boot. Then stood up and began to pace along the bars, staring into the cell across from theirs that held the bloodied and bruised men.

Anthony tried to help Catherine untangle Sasha, who'd managed to get her own hands free already and didn't need much aid. He yanked on the rope and Sasha winced before he gave up and then asked, "Tripod wants Daniel to fight one of those giant lizards?"

"No, you idiot. The dragons eat the losers of his gladiator matches, or anyone he doesn't like. He'd kill you himself if you hurt one of his pets. He loves them as much as his wife,

Jasmine." Jordan explained and then sat down in the back-left corner of the cell. "Plus, one bite and you'd bleed to death, that is if you lived to get away from them."

"So, you aren't a history teacher after all." Sasha had on a quirky half grin, like she'd figured-out a puzzle. She stood up and stretched. When she leaned forward to reach her ankles Anthony stared at her ample cleavage popping out of her tight white shirt. Like everyone else, she'd taken off her jacket in the hot, confined cell and now her full-hourglass figure was clearly defined. Even her butt in the air in the skin-tight cargo pants was drawing attention from Jordan.

Catherine cleared her throat and scowled at the two men, elbowing Anthony, who blushed scarlet and looked away quickly.

"No, I am at high school teacher. Unfortunately," Jordan replied, leaning his head back against the concrete wall behind him.

"How is it that you know this 'Tripod'?" Anthony took a seat against the back wall a few feet from Jordan, who had wisely planted himself in the corner furthest distance away from the toilet. Anthony motioned for Catherine to take the spot to his left on the floor. The spot across from Anthony, and along the far right wall near Jordan had quickly been taken up by Sasha. She now sat smugly with her legs forward and put one thick booted ankle over the other. The Russian sex-doll rubbed her wrists where the rope had been. Anthony's legs were laid forward as well, a few inches from Sasha's boots. When he saw Catherine glance down at the close proximity he pulled his legs up to his chest with his muscular arms around them. Catherine decided to plant herself straight across from Jordan and in between Sasha and Anthony so she could keep an eye on both of them.

"Go ahead, tell them. Or do you want me to, Luca?" Daniel stood behind Catherine. He towered above the three people who were now circled around Jordan on the solid concrete floor. Concrete that could suck every bit of warmth out of any body part touching it. It felt good in comparison to the sweltering air around them.

"I prefer Jordan, Luca brings back too many memories that I would rather forget." Jordan's whole demeanor was different somehow, relaxed. Like he'd given up a façade and could be himself.

"I bet," Daniel said, eyes flickering in symbols as he inspected his mechanical legs and arm for damage. The Asian warriors had chopped off the bottom of Daniel's pants to expose the mechanical parts and sliced off his sleeve too.

Everyone else went back to staring at Jordan, waiting for an explanation.

"Alright!" Jordan breathed out in frustration, ran his hands through his hair -holding and massaging his head for a minute before he put his hands down and said, "At 16 I was recruited by my uncle, who was a Sicilian Don smuggling drugs in and out of Puerto Rico." His voice was different, his words rose and fell with a slight Italian accent. Had he been faking all along? "He got caught and I, 17 at the time, was given a choice ..." His attention was drawn away for a second as Daniel began to pace by the bars along the opening, tapping on each bar as if checking their integrity. Producing a repetitive pinging sound as the metal from his prosthetic middle knuckle met the iron.

"Continue, please," Sasha requested, pushing her arms back behind her and managing to raise her chest even higher.

Catherine watched Anthony like a hawk, and he was having trouble not ogling Sasha. There was definitely something going on between him and his 'friend.' Catherine rolled her eyes and focused on Jordan's story.

"My choice was that I could spend time in a jail cell, like this one, or join the military. I chose the latter of the two evils. I tested high enough on the ASVAB that –"

"What's the ASVAB?" Anthony interrupted to ask.

"The military entrance exam –when we had a military. It is the test everyone took to find out what jobs they qualified for. It had several parts, gauging aptitude for various special duties. My scores drew the attention of Army Intelligence. But, not even a year after I entered the service, all hell broke loose with Kim Jong-un firing that nuclear missile at LA. They formed the wall immediately, fearing an invasion and –"

"Yeah, we know, we don't need a history lesson," Anthony said, yawning.

"Fine. To make a long story short ... given my 'background' one of my first assignments was to 'deliver packages' in and out of the wall. Tripod was one of my contacts. I'm surprised he's still alive. He's far better funded now too."

"What were your packages?" Sasha asked offhandedly, her eyes were now on the pacing cyborg and her head was cocked to the side.

"Mostly locked briefcases – sometimes people, sometimes information." Jordan studied Sasha, as if her question meant more than the obvious.

"You put people in briefcases?" asked Anthony. "Is that what Tripod did? Chop people up and put them in briefcases?"

"No. He had ties to China, obviously. What was left of the government at the time found those ties useful. He is unstable though, and not to be trusted."

"So, how did you end up as a History teacher in Colorado?" Catherine had to know. His life sounded far more interesting than hers, and she still wondered how she'd ended up an English teacher.

"The government was falling apart and the major powers were making moves, using everyone as pawns to –"

Daniel laughed and said, "Oh, that is your excuse? Brilliant."

"You read a few notes in a military file and you think you know the situation? Us humans have to make hard choices sometimes. You'd know that if you still had a beating heart. Let's just say I fell in with the wrong movement and was forced to retire. The identity and location were ideal –"

"Tell that to the real Jordan Muntz." Daniel's pacing had stopped and he leaned back against the right wall with his arms across his chest staring straight at Jordan.

Catherine saw Jordan in a whole new light. It made sense, he never fit in with the simple Colorado lifestyle or as a teacher. He was a terrible teacher. That was the one thing she'd felt like they had in common, but now she didn't know if she knew Jordan at all. No wonder he always kept to himself.

What did he have in common with anyone? What could he even say about his own life? His past?

"If you're such buddies with this guy 'Tripod', why did he leave you in the cell with us?" Anthony asked, feigning to be unimpressed.

"I never said he was my buddy. The man is insane. He has certain rules ... and requires a price to –"

"What price?" Catherine interrupted, her voice almost a squeak. All of their belongings were commandeered, so what more could they offer? She cleared her throat and said in a more audible tone, "What price?"

"He loves entertainment, and you must entertain him by fighting." Jordan spoke directly to Daniel when he said 'you'. "If you do, you will be rewarded and can make one request. If you don't ..." Jordan trailed off, insinuating a foul demise.

"Lizard food." Anthony chimed in.

"Exactly." A dark look crossed Jordan's face as he realized he'd just agreed with Anthony, so he added, "Maybe you're not as dumb as you look."

"You made a deal for Daniel to fight in a gladiator tournament or something, in order to entertain him?" Catherine asked. "If Daniel wins then we can all leave in a few days?"

"It is not that simple ..." Daniel's gaze was locked with Jordan's and he didn't finish his sentence.

"Why? What do you mean?" Sasha broke-in, looking back and forth between Daniel and Jordan, her right eyebrow raised to an ungodly level. Catherine tried to mimic her, but couldn't quite get her eyebrow that high.

Daniel's next words were nearly as menacing as the glare he was giving Jordan as he said, "Because someone is going to die first."

Chapter 7

Are You Not Entertained?

The dome shaped arena brimmed with clamorous spectators crammed into wooden bleachers that stacked up at least 15 rows to the overly raftered ceiling. Catherine was surprised to see that people wore normal, modern clothes. For some reason she expected more traditional Chinese robes like those worn by Tripod and his bodyguards. The people in the stands instead wore synthetic micro blends with digital integration for their electronics. The fashionable, sleek cut, body-hugging styles resembled those hanging in her own closet at home. It dawned on her that the company she'd ordered her outfits from, Invargo, was a Chinese company.

How could so many have survived the war, dust and isolation? How could Central not know about all of these people? Catherine thought from her vantage point, standing in a barred dugout, eye level with the coarse dirt on the arena floor.

She felt faint, and barely able to stand. A side effect, Daniel claimed, from not having received her medicine in almost 24 hours. She leaned on Anthony and Daniel so she could see what was happening on the battlefield. They had been watching battle after battle for hours, and now it was time for the final event.

Jordan stood in the middle of the dirt floored fighting area, fifty feet away. He'd strolled to the center with that familiar long stride like he owned the place. He was dressed from the waist down in the gladiator standard black and red pants, but wore nothing else. From where Catherine nervously watched, she could see he had only a light patch of black hair running up his stomach to his pectoral muscles. Chest muscles that were bigger and more defined than she'd expected, along with the impressive ones on his arms and shoulders. He typically wore baggy clothes, maybe to hide his physic so that he would be underestimated? There was a cross on his left pectoral over where his heart would be, it had a rose in the center wrapping its vines around the four quadrants.

Catherine knew from watching the other fights that Jordan had been allowed one shield and one weapon. However, he'd chosen only a sharp, thin sword that he held in a loose, relaxed grip at his side as five burly gladiators approached, attempting to surround him. He stood tall and unmoving, but his eyes followed the men. She couldn't tell if his confidence was bravery or suicidal and she feared he might die in a matter of seconds.

Jordan made a deep lung with his right leg while leaning backwards. He skewered a man that had tried the same on his right. The blade went clean through the ribs, into the heart and out the man's back.

Catherine gasped in shock, the movement was so sudden. Jordan lunged like a coiled viper.

Jordan stepped to the side of the skewed man to retrieve his sword using the leverage of kneeing him in the stomach. The knee served a dual purpose, as it knocked the man down. He fell like a sack of potatoes, sending up dust. He oozed blood as he writhed in his final death throws.

Jordan didn't blink as he faced the four remaining opponents. Now he had two swords.

Catherine guessed he preferred two weapons to a shield, that's why he hadn't brought one. Such confidence. Such arrogance.

Two of the remaining gladiators attacked him from the right and left at once. Jordan used his swords to scissor cut the right man's weapon brandishing hand off while wheel barrel kicking the one of the left in the face.

Catherine gripped the concrete in front of her, barely able to keep up with Jordan's lightning fast movements. How had he dodged the axe from the guy on his left? All she saw were Jordan's feet in the air and then the man fell to the ground.

"What the hell was that?" Anthony professed, in awe.

When Jordan landed back on the ground he ducked because a third attacker nearly sliced his head off. He used the body of the one-armed man as a shield when the fighter with the axe barreled down on him. He spun right and glided one sword into the back of each of the axe welder's lungs.

Catherine couldn't believe how simple and easy Jordan made it look to kill people. It was hard to believe this was the same guy she'd accidently bashed in the head with a nurse's door merely a few weeks ago.

Before Jordan could remove the swords from the man's body, he had to drop under a swooping sword from a warrior coming from his left. The broadsword lopped off the axe welder's head in a bloody rush. Jordan spun behind the gladiator, getting on his knees on the ground. He jumped up, back to back with the fighter. He reached around behind his head to grab the guy by the neck and then crouched down. In one swift motion, he tossed the guy over his shoulder while snapping his neck.

The adept precision and simplicity of Jordan's movement was admirable. Catherine felt strangely, and embarrassingly aroused. She couldn't take her eyes of the fight.

The final man leaped forward with a kick that landed Jordan on his butt in the dirt. The fighter plunged a spiked spear downward as Jordan threw dirt upward and rolled to the right. Jordan's lean figure obviously had the dual advantage of not only making him viper-quick but also a harder target to stab.

While attempting to wipe the dirt out of his eyes, the last man standing fell backwards to the ground. Jordan had rolled around and kicked the guys legs right from under him.

"Man, he's quick!" Anthony exclaimed.

"Look at his scars, this isn't his first battle." Sasha added.

Jordan used the side of one of the abandoned shields to crush the fallen man's windpipe and crack his ribs. The fighter lay there choking as Jordan got up and confidently walked with his long-legged stride to retrieve his sword from the dead axe welders back.

"That was ... amazing," Catherine admitted. Daniel peered down at her with his typical unreadable expression, but she got the impression he knew how Jordan's skills had made her feel and it made her blush in embarrassment. She swiftly went back to looking at what was going on in the arena and tried to ignore Daniel's gaze.

The uproarious chant of the crowd 'Kill!, Kill!, Kill!' was more unnerving than the amount of blood spilt when Jordan held the man by the hair and slit his throat.

The crowd cheered the name, 'Luca! Luca! Luca!' Jordan somberly dropped his sword and took deep, calming breaths as he stood still to wait for Tripod and his armed guard to approach. His demeanor indicated he didn't relish the murder or applause.

"Ah, what a battle! Though, you could have made it last a bit longer, that was less than 30 seconds. Five fighters, bravo! You haven't lost your touch, Loco Luca." Tripod sat smirking on his extra-large lizard.

"I request the girl be freed with me, and her medicine returned to us. You can do what you want with the rest."

His words were outrageous. Do what he wants with the rest? Was his intention all along to get rid of everyone? Catherine was just as confused as when she'd found out he would be fighting today and not Daniel. When they'd come to take Jordan, she'd been absolutely flabbergasted, along with Anthony and Sasha. Daniel had said nothing, knowing exactly what was going to happen, of course.

"This is part of the plan," Daniel whispered to Catherine, the first explanation she'd gotten from him all day. "It will be alight, just go with it."

"Which one? The Russian bombshell or the mousy little one?" Tripod asked.

Jordan pointed to Catherine.

"You know the rules, one request for one battle." Jasmine protested, standing to the right of Tripod with her left hand readied to unsheathe her sword. "Freeing yourself and the girl is two –"

"I make the rules!" Tripod interjected. "Besides, she is hardly alive, look at her. Humm ..." He sat there thinking for a few seconds. "Let's make a deal. You can stay at my palace with your little trophy and her medicine tonight. But. And this is a big butt, like yours sweet cheeks," he proceeded to pinch Jasmine's butt. She slapped him so hard in the face that he almost fell off his ride. He mouthed 'worth it' with a wink and smile to Jordan, then continued his bargain: "The big butt is that your machine-friend has to defeat my *prize* fighter tomorrow or all three of you die."

Jordan glanced back in Daniel's direction and then nodded, "Agreed."

Two male warrior guards wearing all black, with no red in the pattern like the women, made their way into the dugout. They had giant gold dragons on their backs. Daniel motioned for Anthony to let go off Catherine and the guards yanked her from the trench and up onto the arena floor. The crowd cheered again, and some made lewd comments when she got flung into Jordan's blood-speckled arms.

He held her close, aiding her to walk as they were led down into an underground tunnel by three members of Lord Tripod's personal bodyguard. After about 50 feet, they arrived at a weapons room and then were brought into an adjacent supply room full of bags. Jordan directed them to search the jackets for a small black bag of purple vials, which they soon found and handed over to him.

When they got to a flight of stairs Jordan gave Catherine the medicine and then picked her up into his arms, carrying her like a child. She held him around the neck, saying nothing as she laid her head on his sturdy shoulder. She could see the five o'clock shadow on his face. He was always clean shaven at school, but a little facial hair suited him better. He looked more rugged. A rugged, chiseled warrior.

She was confused about how he made her feel. There was a raw, primitive, attraction ... pure chemistry as strong as it was when he'd kissed her hand in the woods and offered to take her 'camping.' This close to him it was hard to think of anything else. The way he fought all five of those men with such confidence and skill was frighteningly exhilarating, and she was definitely ashamed of herself for the thoughts that were going through her head.

"Are you okay?" he asked. "You're breathing harder, is there something wrong?"

She was mortified that he'd noticed. "I'm okay." She tried to think of something else and control her breathing. He was dangerous. Daniel warned her – Jordan was not mentally stable and she shouldn't trust him. For goodness sakes, he'd kidnapped her! Plus, they hadn't officially gotten back together, but she was pretty sure Anthony thought he was her boyfriend. She sure hadn't dissuaded him. And there was Daniel. An enigma, but he moved her in a way she'd never felt before.

"Your room," a lady dressed in formal, ancient Chinese attire opened an arched double door and pointed inside. Catherine hadn't even noticed when they were no longer going up stairs. "Be ready in an hour for the banquet."

Jordan put Catherine down inside, said something in Mandarin and made a small bow. The lady bowed back and closed the doors. There was a distinct locking noise. So, they weren't free to leave.

The room had a shaggy red carpet and was full of multi-colored, vibrant floor cushions. An an extra-large, ten-foot-round cushion in the middle had a few animal skin throws, pillows and blankets on it, including one throw that was made of lion skin with the head still attached. Along the wall was a rack of robes with matching pants and slippers beneath, organized by size and in every color imaginable. The embellishing designs were elaborate, some had peacocks, some tigers. The only thing they had in common was the silken material and the dragon logo on the sleeve. There was a large, keyhole shaped, red doorway that opened into a bathroom with a luxurious marble jacuzzi-tub. The tub was absolutely fabulous and big enough to fit four people.

"I feel bad that we get to come here while the rest of our friends have to stay in a jail cell." Catherine ambled over to plop down onto the main circular cushion.

"I don't," Jordan snorted. He came out of the bathroom with a cup of water, emptied a vial into it and passed the red liquid to Catherine. He sat down right next to her and watched her drink a few sips. The icy chill in her bones faded and the room began to feel warm, likely from the raw heat coming off of Jordan's toned body. She tried not to look at him, facing ahead toward the bathroom as she slowly drank, increasingly aware of her own lips touching the glass.

"I'm going to take a shower, you're welcome to join me." He winked as he said it, but didn't wait for her answer before heading straight into the bathroom.

Her jaw dropped as he took off his pants and stood beneath the steaming water falling from a large, circular showerhead in the corner of the bathroom. There was no shower door or curtain. She could see every hot inch of him, and he had quite a few inches that he was lathering up with soap.

She closed her mouth and turned around to face the other way. How long had it been since she'd been with a man? Not since college, and Jordan made the guy seem like a little kid in comparison ... They were only thoughts, but she still felt guilty. She got up and started to hunt through the slippers, searching for ones that might fit so she could distract herself from thinking about the naked Spartan warrior in the bathroom.

"Do you want me to start a bath for you?" Jordan asked, coming into the room wearing only a towel and drying his thick black hair with a second one.

"Please," she replied and gulped down the last of her medicine while watching his back as he strolled away, spotting several scars – and a couple of bullet wounds.

She found a pink outfit that matched a pair of shoes that fit comfortably and laid them out on the bathroom counter. "Do people not wear underwear here?"

He slid open one of the bathroom counter drawers to reveal varying lingerie, and was smiling like a Cheshire cat.

She lifted one of the bras up and it was completely see-through, she would barely consider it lace. The underwear wasn't much better. "I see."

Jordan chuckled, "Your bath's ready. Don't worry, I'll look the other way." He opened another drawer and took out some regular men's underwear, then sauntered back into the bedroom, hunting for a robe in his size.

Catherine kept one eye on Jordan as she swiftly disrobed and eased into the hot suds. *God it feels so good!* Was all she could think for a few blissful seconds. It smelled like jasmine and every muscle in her body slowly relaxed. She closed her eyes and tried to take it all in. Her mind wasn't cooperating, the last 24 hours flashed in front of her lids: high-jacking a helicopter, almost being shot down, being abducted by a lizard lord and having to watch dozens of men brutally hack each other in an arena. So much for relaxation.

"Here's some shampoo, and the soap and rag are on your left." Jordan placed a normal-looking, slender, cylindrical bottle of shampoo next to her head, causing her to open her eyes. He parked his butt on the toilet next to the tub and toyed with a towel in his hands. He'd put on maroon pants but nothing else and was peering down at her with smoldering dark-brown eyes. "Need any help?"

"No. And you can leave that towel there and go back into the bedroom, thank you very much." She tried hard to scowl at him while lathering her hair in shampoo.

"I like it here," he replied, not moving.

She felt like she was flirting with the devil. She dunked her head under the bubble shrouded water to remove the soap and when she came back up he was still there. Her scowl was apparently having no effect. Probably because her gaze kept flashing to his bare, muscular arms and chest. She could see the tattoo much more clearly, and noticed it had a banner beneath the rose on the cross. The banner had a name written inside – Maria.

"Who's Maria?" she asked, thankful the soap bubbles hid her butt and foot scrubbing activities beneath the water.

He glanced down and traced the name with his finger, tenderly. "She was my first love. A feisty Mexican fighter." He chuckled at first, but then his eyes looked out as if seeing something far beyond the room. "We met in the trenches, on the wrong side of the wall." He got up, placed the towel on the toilet seat and went to lay down on the circular bed. He clasped his hands behind his head and closed his eyes.

Catherine climbed out of the tub while holding the towel up, just in case Jordan peeked. She wrapped the towel around her figure and tried to find the least revealing underwear she could, which turned out to be a skin-tight black one-piece that she had to lace up in the front and that made her boobs look like they were about to fall out. She put on the pink robe and matching pants and slippers then joined Jordan on the bed-cushion-thing. “What happened to Maria?”

He turned to gaze at her with eyes reddening with tears, or maybe exhaustion. “We were coming out of a club one night, and a rival gang opened fire.” He swallowed hard, turned away and closed his eyes tight. After a few deep breathes he continued, “She died on a sidewalk … drowning in the blood filling her lungs as she lay in my arms, *begging* me to help her … and … I couldn’t help her.”

The shock of what he’d scarcely been able to tell Catherine hit in waves. At first tears welled up and her throat clenched, then the questions came. *How did watching the women he love die affect him? He was in a gang? Was Maria the reason he was kicked out of the Army? Did he avenge her?* She wanted to ask, but she bit her lip instead. He was studying her, probably waiting for a response, so she said, “I’m sorry … I … I can’t imagine how that must have felt.”

“I need to shave,” was all he said as he got up and went into the bathroom, leaving her there wondering why he had told her what he did. It was so intimate, so deep. The man had many layers and was not only baring his body, but his soul to her this evening. Was he purposefully trying to draw her closer to him? If he was, it was working.

There was a knock on the door, followed by a 15-minute warning from one of the ladies of the house.

Catherine dried her hair and hardly had enough time to put on the make-up she’d found in one of the bathroom drawers before another lady came in to escort them out.

They were led into a grand banquet hall with a long rectangular table in the center. Only about 20-30 other people were in the lavishly-decorated room, mingling. Formally dressed servants passing out frosted beer mugs and wine glasses among the guests. There were scarred men, evidently successful gladiators, with beautiful women by their sides. There were even scarred women with strapping young men clinging to their heels.

The lady that brought Jordan and Catherine from their room announced, “Today’s Champion!” and the crowd burst out in ‘hurrahs’ and ‘hurrays.’

Jordan guided Catherine through the room by putting his hand on the small of her back, and shook hands with the other successful gladiators congratulating him. Two trumpet blasts came from the back doors and Tripod and Jasmine entered, followed by several of their personal bodyguard. He took a seat at the end of the table and then made a hand motion to allow others to be seated. Jordan and Catherine were directed to the center seats, across from a large bowl of fruit.

"To congratulate Loco Luca returning from his early retirement, we have a special treat." Tripod made a motion with his right hand and three fully concealed assassin came in with a bound man in green denim coveralls. He had a black cloth over his face, and a bird logo on the side of his sleeve. "In your honor, champion."

The three led the man up to a staging area next to an axe stuck in a piece of driftwood. An assassin removed the black cloth from the man's face and forced him to kneel. The captive had a salt and pepper beard and a balding head to match. He scanned the room and locked eyes with Jordan right away.

Jordan tensed, but showed no other outward sign on his stoic face that he either recognized the guy or thought anything of what was about to happen.

Another hand motion from Tripod, this time using his middle arm, and a man dressed like one of the arena guards but wearing a hood approached the stage. He pulled the axe out of the wood block, then moved the wood into position in front of the captive. The executioner placed his boot on the man's back, forcing his head onto the block and then lifted the axe into the air.

"Any last words, forsaken scum?" Lord Tripod asked.

"Rot in Hell!" was all the man said, then spit towards the table.

Tripod pointed his fingers downwards, and the axe fell, chopping off the head and causing it to roll onto the banquet hall floor.

Catherine gasped when she saw the man's eyes blink and his lips turn down in a frown. *This was a present for Jordan?*

Many of the guests clapped, including Jordan who said something in Chinese to Tripod and bowed his head.

Catherine was the only one who was completely appalled and tried not to look in the direction of the man's head on the floor. "Did you know him?"

"Now is not the time," Jordan softly replied. "We should eat."

Catherine glanced around the room and noticed everyone had begun to fill their plates and mouths. She couldn't remember her last meal, but she had absolutely no appetite.

Jordan handed her a roll and butter, then whispered, "It is considered very rude not to eat." He might as well have said "you will be next on the chopping block if you don't eat now" by the way he said it.

She swiftly stuffed the bread in her mouth and tried to put on the best smile she could muster with the nausea threatening to flush out her medicine. Jordan tried to comfort her by rubbing up and down on her mid-back.

"So, which one of these men has the distinct honor of being your prize fighter, Lord Tripod?" Jordan asked, and began collecting olives and cheese for his plate and sizing up the other fighters in the room.

"None," Tripod answered simply, proceeding to devour a giant turkey leg. Or, maybe the turkey leg only seemed giant because Tripod was so small he had to be propped up in a booster seat.

"Really? When do we get to meet him?" Jordan had that blank look Catherine was starting to recognize meant he was calculating his next move carefully.

"What makes you think it is a him?" Jasmine had a smug grin.

Did that mean it was a woman? Catherine thought.

"Tomorrow, at the arena," Tripod answered, winking at Jasmine.

Catherine noticed movement out of the corner of her eye ... Komodo dragons ripping apart something in green. She didn't have to look to know it was the remains of the beheaded man.

The ornately attired servants bringing food to the table kept watching Catherine and glaring at her empty plate.

"Eat," Jordan insisted, and then whispered softly in her ear. "You'll need your strength for later." She gave him a harsh look, and he laughed and said, "later as-in tomorrow" before lobbing a small sausage stuffed in a biscuit into his mouth and setting another one on her plate.

Catherine gulped down the glass of red wine in front of her and her lips tingled from the alcohol. She watched as Jordan jam-packed her plate with food. She tried to nibbled on some cheese and wondered what she would regret the most if this turned out to be her last meal.

Jordan leaned over, his masculine odor almost as intoxicating as the wine, and filled her glass back up with Merlot. She passed him a smile, "Thanks."

The look he gave her, with those eyes like deep, mysterious caverns, made her start to wonder something else instead. She was now wondering what she would regret the most about later that night in bed.

Chapter 8

Dance Until the World Falls Down

The grand banquet room was empty –devoid of people and decoration. A towering 10-foot-tall stone fireplace with a lavishly sculpted mantle was now where the decapitation staging area had been. Catherine sat at the center of the table in the chair she had earlier, wearing the same pink silk robes. There was nothing on the table–it was bare wood and a darker color than she remembered. The only sound was the roaring of the fireplace, crackling as it burned giant logs.

She had the distinct feeling she was being watched. It reminded her of the dreams she had of Daniel, "Daniel, are you there?" It made sense that he would want to talk to her tonight. She caught movement in her peripheral vision. "Daniel?"

There was no one there. Only a dress. It hung by the double doors Tripod had come through with his entourage at dinner. A puffy sleeve ballgown adorned with pearls, lace and sparkling diamonds. The bottom had to be five feet wide. It had extra material and bows in the back like something out of a fairy tale.

The room grew dimmer and music began to play –a wistful waltz on a grand piano somewhere in the darkness beyond the light of the fire. The sound growing stronger and stronger as the room grew darker.

Silver pitchers of water, glistening glasses, and silver trays of food appeared all over the table. Jewelry and mirrored boxes too. All baroque antiques. The only light in the room now came from the wavering radiance of the fireplace, creating playful reflections and shadows with the shiny silver and prismatic glass. Catherine opened a square jewelry box in front of her and drew out a long necklace mode of full-carat diamonds. The diamonds glittered mesmerizingly from the flames.

A deep shadow moved in the room, something blocked-out the light. She put down the necklace and peered over to the hearth to find the fancy dress hovering a foot from the flickering blaze. The brightness of light behind the dress made its cloth appear black in contrast.

Intrigued, Catherine glided up from her seat at the table and strolled towards the dress in a trance-like state.

She was startled when the dress suddenly began to move to the music, swaying left and right – possessed by an invisible, graceful dancer. It traveled across the room, swaying and spinning, before pausing to bow in a friendly curtsy in front of her. A tendril of the lace that dangled from the left sleeve reached out towards her –it beckoned her to dance.

She held out her right hand and before she knew it, she was whirling along the floor, dancing with the dress. The music was delightful, a fun waltz and she enjoyed dancing. She felt like she was flying, moving up and down, round and round with the three-quarter beat rhythm. The room blurred as she spun, getting lighter and brighter. Through the blur she noticed figures appearing. Other dancing couples, wearing masks. The had room transformed-now bright, loud and full of people. The fireplace and table were gone. Everything and everyone had an iridescent glow.

She tarried from her spinning dance to take a closer look at the decadent costumes worn by the other dancing couples and then realized the dress she'd been dancing with was now on her body.

The feeling that someone was watching her increased. So many people filled the room now, all wearing masks. She searched for who made her feel uneasy. The costumed couples drank, danced and laughed. Some gawked at her like she didn't belong while holding up masks of grotesque beasts of fantasy, mocking her and laughing.

She caught a glimpse of herself in the reflection of a silver pitcher on a serving tray and held up the pitcher to inspect her appearance. Her hair was done-up puffy with pearls and other jewelry. It matched the creamy white lace and adornments of her dress. It was grand and beautiful. She was as gaudy as anyone there, only she didn't have a beastly guise.

One of the masked men lowered his disguise long enough for her to see his eyes. She knew him, but she couldn't quite place how or where she'd seen those piercing blue eyes. He danced away with a partner and several other couples sashayed between them. She tried to spot him again but everyone kept moving. He had distinctive feathers in his shirt and hair, and his mask was like an eagle but it was all white and tan. His outfit matched her own in colors and textures of creams and lace.

She gave up and turned to leave the dance floor, and he stood before her. His mask was completely gone now. He pulled her close and began to dance with her, lifting her onto her toes. She said one word, "Cliff?"

"You know who I am?" he answered with a beaming smile. "You look very lovely tonight. So much like someone I used to know. I could dance with you forever." He had his brother's thick eyebrows, high cheeks, full lips and defined jaw. If he dyed his hair brown, grew out facial hair and put in golden contact lenses he would look *exactly* like his brother.

Was he trying to look more like Daniel for her? she wondered. She was used to seeing Cliff in a wheelchair with tubes and electronics coming out. A forlorn cripple who never spoke.

He stared intently down at her, and danced with skill and a smooth grace.

Catherine didn't know what to say. All she knew about him is that Daniel said Cliff wanted to kill everyone with a virus, or control the world somehow. After a few moments of being dumbfounded, she asked, "How did you find me?"

"This is my dream, you found me," he replied, evidently perplexed. "How is it that you keep appearing in my dreams? I don't even know who you are ... but I feel drawn to you."

The room revolved faster and she was getting dizzy. If this wasn't her dream, then how did it look so real? Whenever she had visited another person's dream it was always so obvious–malformed and losing details along the edges. This was vivid, and very creative. It rivaled her own.

"You have magnificent dreams," she said. "This feels so real."

"Thank you," he replied, sounding so much like Daniel.

They were now flying in a bubble. The other dancers spun around them as they floated up into the air. She could see other bubbles of dancers in the distance. There was no gravity, she felt weightless. For all she knew, they could be falling down instead of floating up.

He grinned with perfect white teeth as he said, "This dream is inspired by one of my favorite movies. Only this is so much better than watching it on a screen, don't you think?"

"Amazing." She could sense the weightlessness in her body, smell the wine on Cliff's breath, hear the sophisticated music rebounding off the spherical enclosure. The vibrations from the full orchestral waltz made rainbow pattern ripples all along the bubble enclosure. It was truly amazing.

A thought struck her, maybe she could add something to his dream? She imagined rose petals and they began to fall all around them in every shade of pink and red.

Cliff's forehead scrunched as the petals fell like rain, "Was that from you?"

"Yes." She made miniature bushes of roses start to grow out of the objects floating in their bubble. A pitcher of water soared by with roses spilling out. A chair became rose dryad.

"Stop that, it doesn't fit," he demanded, temperamentally. His blue eyes reminded her of an ocean of icebergs.

The roses disappeared instantly. "It's only a dream, Cliff."

"I can see why my brother is so fascinated with you," he remarked. "Has he told you what he wants with you?"

"No, he merely said that ..." she was about to say 'he said that I was the only one who could stop you' before she thought better of it. "He said that you wanted to kill everyone, is that true? That you killed your own parents."

The bubble broke and they fell. "He lied to you." His voice was harsh and deep. He drifted away from her and his cream-colored tights, tan boots and white frilly jacket melted into rocket legs, black microfiber shorts and a bare muscular torso with a metallic right arm. His rocket thrusters began to emit a bright, roaring light.

Catherine reached out and used rose bush vines to tangle him so that he couldn't get away. He struggled, thorns drawing blood, and asked, "Who are you?"

"Catherine Newton," she replied, simply and haughtily.

For a brief second she could have sworn there was a smirk on his face and then the whole universe exploded in red petals, blinding her and sending her accelerating backwards.

She sat straight up in bed. It took a few seconds for her to get her bearings. The circular cushion, the lion throw, and the man on the floor bundled up with the remaining throws and cushions all went from looking foreign to looking somewhat familiar to being her current reality within a few heartbeats.

Then the dream came back to her, piece by piece. So grand and beautiful. How could she have accidently entered Cliff's dream? That wasn't possible, was it? It started out as her dream, she knew that. How else could he have known what the banquet room looked like? Or, had it not been Tripod's banquet room after all?

She had so many questions. Had Daniel lied to her about his brother? What did Daniel really want with her? If she could enter Cliff's dreams so easily, maybe she should enter Daniel's and ask him why. She laid back down, closed her eyes and tried to control her breathing. A few minutes later she drifted back to sleep.

She was at the wooden, domed arena. The sandy dirt floor was covered in blood and Daniel stood in the center, panting. "Daniel," she said and he turned to assess her.

"I was wondering when you would arrive," he said, going back to his training simulation. Attackers appeared long enough for him to kill them and then they disappeared.

She reached out in her mind and made his sword evaporate and the arena turn to an ocean to wash away all the blood. She then brought her and Daniel back to a red cliff overlooking the town of Desert Grande. One she met him at so many times these last few months.

"You are getting stronger, a few weeks ago you had trouble changing other's dreams," Daniel said and then gazed down the side of the cliff. "I wish you had brought me somewhere else though." His appearance had changed back to the familiar metal plated head, rusty goatee and golden eyes that were typical of his appearance in the dream world.

"Is that how you see yourself?" she said. "Why do you have a metal plate on your head?"

He touched his head, hand coming across the strange object and then sat down on the smooth red rock. "I guess I see myself this way. I believe it is partly how your mind sees me as well. This dimension has many mysteries."

She sat next to him and gently touched the skin near the metal plate. "But why have this on your head? Is your brain okay?"

"No, I've had brain surgery. A special surgery that I helped invent, but never expected to have had performed on me."

"What was the surgery for?" She followed his eyes as they glanced back over the side of the cliff.

"An implant ... for the prosthetics ... it enhances synaptic response while also projecting brainwaves ... it helps run the cybornetics so that they are faster, more reactive."

"What happened to you?" she sat next to him on the cliff, staring down into the valley below.

He looked down and then she could hear a young woman screaming for an instant before the scene changed. They sat across from each other in a hospital office. He was behind a desk that had the name "Dr. Daniel Jahren, Neurology" written on a plaque-stand in the center. Above his head diplomas and awards hung all over the wall.

"Why have you come to see me?" he asked, clasping his black-gloved hands and sitting back in his chair. He wore a doctor's white jacket, but still had on all black underneath and black gloves.

"I saw your brother tonight ... somehow I entered his dream. It was ... amazing ... like nothing I have ever seen," she said, sitting in the guest chair across from him and wearing one of the outfits she normally wore to school. She felt like she was in the principal's office.

"What happened? Did he say anything? Did he tell you where he was?" Daniel leaned forward, grilling her like a detective.

"I ... he ... we danced. I had on this beautiful dress ... there was a bubble ... he asked me what you wanted with me, and ... he said you lied when I said he wanted to kill everyone," she barely got it all out. She tried to stick-to, and remember, the important stuff but she felt like she might be missing something. He made her very nervous when those glowing gold eyes started flashing symbols.

"You didn't tell him anything else? Where we are? Anything?" As he spoke, the room felt smaller and smaller as his eyes got brighter.

"No! Of course not! Please, this is getting intense, Daniel!"

"I am sorry ... I ... I am not as in control as I thought ... I did not mean to scare you."

They were transported to a meadow full of soft grass. They sat on a picnic blanket with a basket full of food and two wine glasses. It was sunny and warm, with a light breeze of oak trees from the nearby forest. "It is not as glamorous as one of your meadows, but I thought you might like this place." He was cheerful and wearing a white dress shirt, half open and billowing out in the breeze like on the cover of a romance novel. The metal plate on his head replaced with wavy locks that hung just below his ears, sometimes flying into his face in the wind. He had normal, human skin and eyes. He poured her a glass of Chardonnay.

"Thank you," she said when she received the wine. "Why would Cliff say you were lying?"

The glass lacked the proper smooth texture, the drink lacked the appropriate dry, sweet taste. She noticed the grass was a bit blurry a few feet away. Daniel wasn't quite as good at making dreamscapes as his brother. She added in the details.

"Because he is manipulative, and he wants to think he is right," he answered. "That the ends excuse the means."

"What are his ends?" She needed to know what would make a man capable of killing his own parents. "What is it that he really wants?"

"I do not care. What he wants to do is pathological."

"Oh." That answer served to only make her more curious.

"You must not seek him out, Catherine. If he shows up again, run. Or better yet, wake up. He is much more powerful than you can imagine, and even I have no idea what he is capable of in this dimension."

"Believe me, it wasn't on purpose ... it just happened. Why is he so powerful here? Does this whole dream thing have to do with why you need me?"

"I do not feel comfortable talking about that here, not when I do not know who could be watching, or listening."

"Oh, but it does have something to do with all of this, right?"

"I ... I cannot say." He skimmed the surroundings, as if expecting his brother to pop out any second. "Promise me you will run or wake-up if you see him again?"

"Sure." She turned her eyes down and focused on drinking her wine. What could Cliff possibly do to her in a dream? It was a ridiculous request.

"Catherine, please ..." Daniel insisted.

She picked up a wedge of cheese and thought about the cheese she'd eaten at dinner and barely tasted because of the trauma of seeing a guy getting beheaded and eaten. An tribute for the winning fighter. The least-appetizing appetizer imaginable. "Oh, that reminds me about your fight tomorrow. At dinner tonight they said the prize fighter might not be a man, I think maybe it is a woman. The fighter wasn't at the banquet."

"Not a man?"

"Yes, I think it might be a woman. Possibly one of Tripod's personal guards."

"We can find out, and test your progress ..."

"We can?"

"Yes." Daniel sat cross-legged with his hands on his knees like a buddha figure and levitated a few inches above the ground. Projecting thoughts of being a wiseman, evidently. Or a wisecrack. "There is more to this dimension than you know. Space, time, gravity ... the rules are ... bendable."

"I have no idea why you keep calling this a dimension ... or what any of that means ..."

"Take my hand," he said, extending his right hand, a hand that was completely human and soft to the touch. The whole world faded away to grey clouds, except for his hand holding hers. It was oddly very comforting, grounding even. "Now you are in control, Catherine." His voice echoed into the hollow epicenter of a storm that began to churn around them. "Try to find the fighter."

Catherine concentrated on the thought of a prize fighter, of Lord Tripod and his world of Chinese warriors and flesh-hungry Komodo dragons.

Tripod came into view, only he had three legs, three arms and three heads. He towered fifty feet tall. The dragons beside him had wings, and breathed fire at the arena of people burning in their seats. Tripod noticed Catherine and Daniel holding hands before him and he sneered, doing a characteristic hand motion that sent the dragons towards them. Catherine thought of a wall of water protecting her and Daniel. The dragons and their fire could not penetrate it. Tripod had a massive axe and slammed it down against their wall of water, so Catherine focused on making the water as hard as steel. The axe shattered into a million pieces.

"Where is your prize fighter?" Daniel challenged the monstrous dwarf.

Tripod chuckled and an underground door opened up, lifting a 20-foot-tall machine from beneath into the arena. The robot began firing bullets from automatic guns at its shoulders. Its hands were spinning blades and its legs were made of a hundreds of knife edges as it crossed the arena towards them in a galloping stride that rapidly closed the distance.

Catherine concentrated on the meadow and picnic from earlier. Her and Daniel were now safely sitting back on the blanket, unscathed. Bullets had gone through both of them, and she'd felt burning, bruising pain and searing flesh. But, now it was all completely gone. She felt fine.

"So, Tripod is going to have me fight a robot." Daniel didn't look too happy about his fate. "There is one more thing we can try. I have never been able to do it ... but I think you might be able to."

"What is it?" she was curious, but her body vibrated ... she was shaken to the core. Some part of her knew whatever he was thinking was too dangerous, and her body objected. "I feel strange. Whatever it is, I don't think I should do it."

"Strange? How? Do you even know what I am about to ask you? This is beyond my understanding, beyond what science has proven that is undoubtedly why I am having so much trouble with it –"

"No!"

"Why do you feel you cannot do it?"

"I don't know, my body just feels ... strange ... like a vibration, a shift ... and I don't like it. If there is such a thing as intuition, I think it's saying not to do whatever you're about to ask."

Catherine was terrible at following her intuition. The uncle that raised her after her dad died made sure she was grounded in reality, not dreams or visions. Nothing about her dreams, or what happened to her dad, or any of the things he'd said in his diary made any sense or helped her in any way. They purely made her life more complicated. From the age of ten she'd pushed her dreams away, and her feelings.

Then Daniel appeared. He came right out of one of her dreams. When he did, it opened up that world for her again. A world she had blocked out, fervently ignored. She hardly remembered how to read her dreams, or her own feelings, anymore. But, this incongruence in her body was like a deep winter in her heart. One thing she did know is that it meant danger.

"What do you know, Catherine?" Daniel held her hand again, adding warmth to the chill that was coming from her core. "What is wrong?"

"Whatever it is you want me to do, we can't do it." Catherine explained, squeezing his hand tighter, drawing as much comfort from him as she could to shake the eerie feeling.

"You are probably right ... my goodness, what if Cliff had heard?" Daniel scanned the surrounding again. "I do not even want to think what could happen if he knew you could ... that he might ... yes, best to leave that unsaid. Good intuition, Catherine."

"Okay." She felt relieved, her body began to warm up in the sunshine. Daniel's hand started to feel hot as it engulfed hers. Wow, his hands were big. He had thick, round-tipped fingers that made hers appear tiny and delicate in their grasp. "Thank, you."

He still held her hand as he asked, "How is *Jordan* treating you? Did he get your medicine? You need to take a vial every six hours, remember."

She blushed red-hot when she realized her outfit changed to the lingerie she was wearing in bed.

Daniel's eyes began to glow amber, he drew his hand away from hers and clenched both fists. "He didn't force you –"

"It isn't what you think! This was all they had for me to wear to bed. Jordan was a perfect gentleman, even sleeping on the floor and letting me have the whole bed to myself."

Okay, maybe not a 'perfect' gentleman. She'd had to ask him to sleep on the floor, sternly. She didn't trust him in her bed. She didn't trust herself with him in her bed. And, she'd reminded him that she had a boyfriend. Jordan wasn't too happy about it.

Man, it had been difficult to say no to him! What she felt for Jordan was pure lust, nothing more. She truly cared about Anthony ... and was confused about what was happening between her and Daniel. She didn't want to hurt Anthony or Daniel ... even if it was her last night on earth ... even if that night would be insanely passionate ...

"Perhaps you should use that good intuition of yours when it comes to men. You have the worst tastes."

"Thanks. What about you?"

"What do you mean?"

"I thought that maybe ... you, umm ... never mind." What had she thought? Did she have feelings for Daniel? Or did she think he had feelings for her? Perhaps she should learn to think before she speaks sometimes.

Daniel inclined his body towards her, and then cupped her face with his thick hands, "Catherine I ..." For a moment it felt like he wanted to kiss her, then he said, " ... do not even know if I will live past tomorrow." He put his hands down and leaned away with slumped shoulders. "The fate of humanity is at stake, and it is all my fault. I have to go." He disappeared, leaving her sitting on the picnic blanket alone and as confused as ever.

Chapter 9

Allegiance in Anarchy

For a man who had never been in a real fight, Daniel had a steep learning curve. He'd spent the last two nights in simulations with multiple attackers sporting swords and axes. All a waste of time. Without Catherine's warning, no question – he would have had little chance of survival. Even now the odds were not in his favor.

He couldn't see much from his position in the champion ring. The teaming pit of sweaty men jostling each other to prove their alpha presence was wearisome, and blocked his view in all directions. Brief glimpses he caught around their foul, crude bodies confirmed Catherine was safely inside Lord Tripod's enclosed spectator box at the opposite end of the arena. He didn't appreciate that Luca had his arm on the back of her chair and was laughing alongside Tripod.

He knew Luca was working out a deal to remove Catherine from both Daniel and Anthony's grasps. It was more than convenient that they happened to be ensnared by a gang Luca used to have dealings with in his Army Intelligence days. The helicopter fuel ran low at the appropriate time, to necessitate landing right in Tripod's territory. Daniel had greatly underestimated Luca's ability to plan, calculate and deceive. And now Daniel may well pay for that mistake with his life.

"Nice tats," one of the burly men in the ring said sardonically, sneering.

Daniel glared at the man, causing him to quickly turn away. Daniel had been forced to wear only the standard black silken pants, exposing the rest of his body. The black streaks of the Quinta virus traversed most of his chest, back and right arm. The virus made his skin look like a tattoo artist attempted a painting by M.C. Escher and ended up with one by Jackson Pollock. The burn scars from the accident that took out his legs and left arm were evident under the black marking and generated the repulsion he'd feared, clear on everyone's grimacing faces. Plus, even though the ring was jam-packed, no one wanted to be within two feet of him. At least he was able to stand in the center of the pit with his arms crossed and feet shoulder width apart, comfortably contemplating his next move without having to deal with some barbarian knocking into him.

The crowd began to chant, demanding a fight. The first few men in the champion ring were corralled. Like yesterday, there would be a series of lesser fights without weapons before any real bloodshed. The goal was to be the last man standing after a flag was thrown down in the center of the arena. There weren't many other rules. Pummeling, biting, and strikes below the belt were all allowed. Then there would be a few gladiator death matches, followed by the main event.

Two men of the original six released were currently standing in the on the battlefield, taking turns trying to punch each other out. Swaying where they stood, neither was able to knock the other down. The crowd began to boo and leer ... not satisfied with the boring exchange of punches.

Five more men were released to try and finish the two dawdlers off. One of the guys came out tripping the others and kicked another one in the face. Unfortunately, the brut behind him hammered him in the back of the head using a powerful strike formed by placing his left hand over his right fist. The brut ended up taking out the rest and winning this particular round.

Apparently, each man had to win a few battles before earning the privilege to enter the final death match that granted freedom and the favor of Lord Tripod. Luca had special privilege because he'd been a former champion. He'd also graciously offered Daniel as a spectacular main event combatant that would draw the biggest crowd he'd ever seen.

The last set of fighters were released to kill one another with their favorite weapon of choice. Daniel was left in the Champion ring alone. He now had a clear view and scanned the dugouts for Sasha and Anthony. Unsurprisingly, he was not able to spot where they were located. He knew Tripod had plans for them.

The warriors on the dirty fighting pit wrestled, stabbed and screamed. One by one they fell and didn't get up. The remaining fighter was the one who'd disparaged Daniel's 'tattoos.' He was led out by two guards with uproarious applause from the crowd. Daniel knew the man's victory was short lived, he would likely die from the gash in his abdomen before receiving the appropriate medical attention.

A group of women came in to perform a slow dance with fans to the beat of drums played by four men in the center. Each man had a different sized drum. The crowd broke out in scattered applause as the women finished their act and left the arena.

Fireworks rang out – flashing lights flying up from pillars around the circular gladiator enclosure. A rumbling that started beneath the pit made the stands shake and also caused the spectators to stand and cheer wildly.

This was far more fanfare than yesterday. A prelude to a fight like never before. A high expectation. Daniel's heart fluttered, and he swallowed the panic rising to choke his throat. This could be the end, but what a way to go out. No, he had to live. He had to! *Focus! Concentrate on winning the fight!*

The guards corralled him into the arena as the center of the pit opened up not even 25 feet in front of him. He gripped a spiked steel shield and a seven foot long metal staff with one foot long blades on each end, bracing himself for what was about to climb out of the depths below.

Like in the dream, a towering monster of a robot slowly rose from the opening in the arena pit. The miniguns on each shoulder, and the hands of spinning blades were the same but the legs had less knives and the entire body was hollower. The hydraulic tubing, Daniel's main target, was evident throughout and not well protected.

The guards ran back inside their enclosure and shut the door right before the shoulders of the robot lit up with bright orange flames shooting out from the rapid fire of the miniguns aimed right at Daniel.

He held his shield in front of his body as he rocketed up and over the machine, drawing fire that went into a screaming crowd. Within a heartbeat an entire section of the arena was fleeing or dead, and part of the ceiling now lay on the dirt floor. He landed on the back of the robot and endeavored to rip off one of the guns while jamming his shield into the feed line for the other one. The struggle took about 3 seconds, but the machine let off hundreds of bullets as it spun to knock Daniel off. Enough bullets to rouse the rest of the spectators to trample each other in an attempt to find the nearest exit.

His left foot was stuck in the monster's back, so he used his staff as leverage to break free and managed to wedge the bladed edge into the back gears that ran the spinning arms, jamming them. He then jumped to the ground 30 feet away from the robot. He fired the remaining bullets feeding the minigun he'd detached, aiming for hydraulic lines. The gushing of amber fluid preceded the machine's last galloping leap toward him, then the robot toppled over – mere inches in front of Daniel's metallic feet.

The arena was mostly empty now, except for the dead who'd been brutally trampled or accidently shot. Now Daniel could add murderer to the gruesome list of things he'd never wanted to become. The sight of the lifeless bodies in the stands would no doubt haunt him forever, along with Amy's screams.

The spectator box had a few cracks, but withstood multiple bullets that did not penetrate. Catherine stood safely enclosed in the box, and had her hands over her mouth in shock. Both Luca and Tripod were on their feet as well, and furious. The party immediately headed towards the dirt pit.

Daniel placed the minigun on the ground and backed up a few feet from it to let them know he was unarmed and willing to comply. Now they knew he had been complying from the beginning. Any other way would have been too much of a risk to Catherine.

"Masterful! Ripping out an 85-pound minigun like it was a toy. I noticed you didn't use your metallic arm for that. There is more to you than simply a few modified appendages and a handsome face. What are you, exactly?" Tripod was on one of his dragons and his entire female bodyguard surrounded him in a formation with weapons drawn.

"Lord Tripod," Daniel said with a bow. "We need your aid in finding something. If you release my party on our quest –"

"Do you dare ask me to release you AND your friends? After destroying my arena along with my prize fighter?"

"Lord Tripod, I –" Luca began but was swiftly cut off by one of Tripod's center hand motions. It swirled to the left, along with an entire flank of armed & cloaked bodyguards to surround Daniel.

"I would like to make a bargain." Tripod made another motion and a set of male guards brought out Sasha and Anthony, both bloodied and bruised. Catherine screamed out when she saw, and Luca held her by the waist and whispered in her ear, stopping her from running towards her ill-fated boyfriend.

"I'm a man of my word, the three of you will be freed tonight. However, I made no such promise for your friends. If you agree to act as my new prize fighter ... your friends' lives will be spared. If not ..." He made a motion, pointing up the middle finger on his center hand and the floor opened up. Inside was 20 or so Komodo dragons, slithering and sliding over each other to try to reach the opening. Forked tongues flicked in and out of their toothy jaws, tasting the particles of blood in the air.

The guards positioned Anthony and Sasha on the edge of the exposed pit.

Luca nodded to Daniel, making a show of encouraging him to agree in front of Catherine. Daniel scowled back at him. They both knew from the beginning how this would end.

Daniel ground his teeth as he replied, "I have no time to be your little toy." Every day he wasted meant many more than one of two lives would be lost. He merely couldn't waist time playing games to entertain Tripod while Cliff launched a virus that would kill millions. How many were likely infected in the two days they'd already wasted? He only hoped Catherine would forgive him for what he had to do.

"That is unfortunate." Tripod pointed two fingers downward on his right hand and then Anthony and Sasha were flung, screaming and kicking, into the pit of dragons. The large, vicious animals were hungry, swiftly latching onto their food and ripping flesh from limb, and limb from body.

Catherine screamed, sounding so much like Amy it broke his heart. “Please, Daniel! Please stop them! Please!” Luca wrestled with her, begging her to remain calm as he judged the distance between them and the armed bodyguard. She broke free of Luca, elbowing him in the face, and ran towards the pit of dragons.

One of the many robed bodyguard unsheathed her sword and followed after her. Before she could slice Catherine in half, Luca managed to kick the woman in the back of the leg, dropping her to the ground. He then stepped on her sword hand, put his knee in her back and wrestled her around, trying to prevent the other hand from reaching for other weapons. Another bodyguard pulled out a throwing knife aimed for Catherine back ...

Daniel put his left arm up and an ionizing laser blast electrified all the cloaked assassins on that side, including the one with the throwing knife out. He grabbed onto one of the spears pointed at him and used it, and the body of the woman holding it, to knock down all the armed bodyguard to his right. Another charged blue light blast from his left hand and Tripod and the women immediately surrounding him fell writhing in the dirt.

Luca skillfully sliced a few of the bodyguards into bloody pieces during the commotion. He now held two swords dripping dark red in his vicious murderer hands and charged towards the warriors still standing.

Catherine clung to the edge of the pit, screaming for someone to help get Anthony out.

Daniel picked up one of the spears and hurled himself onto one of the lizards inside, crushing its back. He used the spear to stab anything that attacked while zapping the rest with the bright blue electric beam. Once the beasts backed up, he took hold of what remained of Sasha and Anthony and leaped into the air. When he landed, he found the woman in black & gold silks that Tripod had called Jasmine held Catherine with a knife to her throat.

"One more move, and she dies," Jasmine threatened. She was ready to slit Catherine's throat in an instant.

All of the lights in the arena abruptly went out, leaving them in pitch black. Daniel immediately switched his vision to projection. Owls circled all around them, hooting and clawing at the eyes of the Chinese warriors recovering from being zapped.

The distraction was enough that Catherine got free of Jasmine's grip and knelt next to Anthony. "Daniel, you're a doctor, help him!"

Daniel ripped pieces of what remained of Anthony's shirt to tie off what was left of his limbs. He handed Luca and Catherine pieces of the cloth and they followed suit. All around them owls, and men wearing green jumpsuits, fought Tripod and his bodyguard.

Lord Tripod's entourage got funneled into the back of the arena, where more of his guard came to join in the fight. The new additions brought guns and electric shields. Apparently not all of Tripod's people used old fashioned weapons. A full-on war raged around them.

"Catherine, here, now," Daniel demanded, drawing her close inside his protective grasp before Luca could reach her and drag her away. He scanned the arena for the nearest exit.

"We can help your friends, come," said an east Asian woman with cropped black hair. She was in her late twenties and wearing a green jumpsuit as well, only she had on a backpack made of electronics, with flashing red LEDs. Her glasses were bulked on each side with what was probably an electronic vision enhancement package. Or a video recording and emitting system. Maybe both.

"Thank you!" Catherine exclaimed, hugging the woman.

Two of the men in green lifted Anthony, and Daniel picked up Sasha.

A few of the men in green began to tie up Luca.

"He is with me," Daniel said, begrudgingly. It would be nice to be rid of the man, but Catherine would not be too happy with what these people would likely do to their prisoner.

"Sorry, my mistake, he was wearing the regalia of the dragon gang." She made a slashing motion and the men untied Luca. An interesting excuse, given they hadn't touched Catherine who was wearing the same type outfit sporting a dragon on the sleeve.

"These two will bleed to death in a matter of minutes –" Daniel insisted.

"Heliker, Dmitriy get the blood, now!" The woman with the electronic backpack yelled. "We have a lot of experience with these types of wounds. My name is Esha, by the way." She pressed a button on the right side-strap of her backpack and the owls stopped their attack and flew towards the opening in the raftered ceiling. "Follow me," she said hastening towards an exit on the opposite end of where the standoff with Lord Tripod was taking place inside the arena.

Two men, each carrying a half-gallon bag of red liquid, punctured the dismembered people being carried. Not even slowing down while they administered the fluid, they hurriedly exited the arena into the daylight sun of LA.

"What blood type is that? You could kill them if you've given them the wrong –"

"It's artificial, meant to only last until we get to base. It will help supply the oxygen needed until then." Esha then directed her troops to go through the maze of a fallen skyscraper overrun by weeds.

Following closely behind at a moderate jog while keeping Sasha as comfortable as he could, Daniel asked, "Is it perfluorocarbon based? How were you able to synthesize it?" He stepped over a rotted office chair, through a cubicle crushed and between questionably stable floor beams.

"I don't know ... I'm not a doctor ... are you?" Esha asked as they exited the other end of the collapsed high-rise. She directed him to enter the tail end of a heavily armed truck, one of three among several SUV's.

The two medics helping him administer first aid to Sasha and Anthony climbed in the truck bed ahead of him. The guys holding Anthony lifted his body inside and went to the front of the truck to drive.

"Yes," Daniel replied, easing Sasha into the back of the truck and then jumping inside.

"Fantastic, Cybersausage will find that quite useful." She slapped the side of the truck and it accelerated forward.

He watched as Luca and Catherine were loaded into the back of an SUV that quickly caught up to his truck.

Securely in the clutches of another gang. This time Daniel had a better feeling. This gang had an appreciation for technology. In particular, the electronically controlled, and metal-clawed, owls were noteworthy.

Daniel felt Sasha's pulse, she was still alive. She'd passed out while they were running. She fared better than Anthony, but her legs would not be salvaged.

One of the two medically trained men, the one Esha had referred to as Heliker, applied a balm to dressings he was carefully switching out with the one's they had already applied. Heliker was about as tall and broad as Anthony, over six foot three and with a body builder's physique.

"What is that?" Daniel pointed at the dressings.

The dark, curly haired, stout man that Esha had referred to as Dmitriy answered, "It will clean the bite and prevent the venom –"

"I thought that the Komodo dragon's mouth was full of bacterial that killed its victims." Daniel admitted he knew little of the creatures, except that most of their prey never survived long after a bite.

"No, the venom is an anticoagulant that will probably cause these two unfortunate souls to bleed-out long before we get to base," Dmitriy explained. Heliker frowned at him and shook his head, busily attempting to save the lives Dmitriy just disparaged.

"So, you're a doctor?" Heliker asked. "What do you think?"

Daniel crawled over to Anthony as steadily as he could while being jostled by the bumpy road and haphazardly moving vehicle. He checked Anthony's pulse and felt his head. The pulse was weak and head warm to the touch. "How close is the base?"

He barely finished his sentence when the vehicle lurched to a stop. Half a dozen men came to the back of the truck to help them out. Daniel hopped down to find that they had arrived at an industrial site. People went in and out of a large factory with a bird symbol on the side. The bird was black and resembled an A, with the bird wings pointing downward. The same symbol each person in green had patched on their sleeve.

They rushed into the building, and packed themselves like sardines inside an industrial elevator that took them downwards. They were then led into an open room with several cots and shelves. Dmitriy took samples of blood from each patient for testing on an Eldoncard to determine blood type. He rifled through the room and came back with IV stands and macro drips. They were well supplied, the room had a refrigerator filled with bags of blood of each type ready for infusion.

"Do you have anything to perform surgery here?" Daniel asked and Heliker hurriedly went searching throughout the room. "Dmitriy, do you have any barbiturates? Morphine? Whiskey? Anything?"

"So, you're a field surgeon? Military?" Dmitriy asked while going to a cabinet to get bags and vials of the requested clear liquids.

"No, I was a neurosurgeon at UCLA medical center before ... the war." Daniel answered carefully but forgot about his own appearance. Dmitriy stopped what he was doing and stared at him, apparently Daniel looking 22 didn't add up with his previous statement and he wondered if Daniel were even human. Daniel hated when people wondered if he were human.

"This is everything we have," Heliker said, wheeling over a cart loaded with saws, scalpels, clamps, and numerous other items no-doubt raided from a nearby hospital.

"They'll need to be cleaned," Daniel said and Heliker ran to find some isopropyl.

Once he had the cleaned equipment, and had directed Dmitriy to administer the necessary sedative, Daniel began working on Anthony.

"You're removing that much?" Heliker said in shock when Daniel began to saw into Anthony's upper thigh.

"Yes, the damaged tissue will prevent adequate blood flow. The sooner we can get the ruined areas removed, the better chance he has of living. Heliker, be ready with those clamps when I ask, okay? Dmitriy, watch that dip and make sure he stays under."

A few hours later and both patients were stabilized. Daniel was starting to feel the lack of coffee over the last few days and sank into an office chair near the wall by the refrigerators.

A man in a wheelchair came into the room. He was tall and lean with a slight smile on his face, hazel eyes and a greying head of well-trimmed, short, brown hair. He had a hefty leather version of the black bird symbol over the chest of his green leather outfit, reminiscent of a super hero costume. Both Dmitriy and Heliker stood straight up and greeted him immediately.

So, this is their leader, Cybersausage. I better not offend him like I did the last gang leader and end up in an even bigger, bloodier mess. Daniel thought as he got up from his seat to show respect, despite the aching all throughout his body.

"Hi, I'm Cybersausage." He reached out to shake hands. "The quasi-leader of this gang, if you could say an anarchist group had a leader anyway. But enough about me, who are you?"

"My name is Daniel. Thank you for your help in saving my ... colleagues. I'm grateful for your aid."

"You're welcome. But, I must admit ... when I heard about a cyborg being captured by the dragon gang, I had to know more. And you're a doctor! What a bonus! Please, tell me how you came about your marvelous prosthetics."

"A co-invention. I have more, in fact." Daniel couldn't help but notice Cybersausage's missing legs and right hand. "I could provide you with what you need ... if you assist me in locating something here in the city of LA."

"What an offer! My goodness, yes ... well, we will need the prosthetics first, of course. You understand."

Daniel gritted his teeth. It would take days to get the supplies from Colorado, days! But, what choice did he have? He needed supplies to get into Susan's lab now that Tripod had taken all of his belongings. And he needed coffee – the family special blend that could only be found in one place ... the same place the prosthetics were located. "Can you get me in and out of the wall tonight?"

"That isn't an easy feat –"

"I have a helicopter. Its parked near the old SouthBay Pavillion, or what's left of it."

"Daniel was it?" Cybersausage reached his hand out to shake his again. "Daniel, you are quickly becoming my new best friend."

Chapter 10

Mother of Lies

"Let me out!" Catherine banged on the locked aluminum door. "I need to see my friends! Please!" She had been escorted into a small apartment hours ago and left there alone. There were no windows, but there was a bed in the center, kitchenette to the right and a full bathroom on the left. It was decorated to be cozy and comfortable, but the lock on the door made it claustrophobic.

She paced back and forth between the kitchen and the entrance and then pummeled on the door again, pleading to be let out for the thousandth time. She was starting to feel weak and lightheaded – she'd left her medicine in the spectator box at the arena.

The door swung open and Daniel walked in, covered in dried blood and still wearing only the black pants from his earlier gladiator match. "I am so relieved you are alright. I had to make sure," he said, reaching out to her.

"Is Anthony okay? Please, Daniel ... please tell me he isn't ... that he ..." She tried, but she couldn't finish the sentence as she backed away from his attempt to embrace her.

"He will live. Sasha is stabilized as well. The leader here, Cybersausage, has agreed to help us."

"I can't believe you let them be hurled into that pit to die. How could you do that?" She balled her fists at her side and thought about doing something she'd probably regret, like break her fist on his face.

"I am sorry ... I ..." he began but then stopped. "No, I am not sorry. Do you realize what is at stake here? How many people could die because we had to save those two today? What are the lives of two in comparison to millions?"

"Daniel, I don't understand. You never explain anything. All I know is that I had to watch a person I care about be brutally mauled – no that doesn't even begin to describe it – eaten alive? Savagely ripped apart?" her voice got louder and shriller as she explained the horror she'd witnessed, "while you stood there and coldly did nothing!" The tears poured down her face but she glared at Daniel as best she could. *What kind of monster are you?* she screamed at him in her head.

"I'm not a monster, Catherine," he said and she shuddered as the words echoed her thoughts. He came towards her but she backed away again. He continued, "You have to understand, every day that Cliff is loose means people will die. All innocent. All just as deserving to live as Sasha and Anthony."

"How? Why?" she asked. He'd mentioned Cliff and a virus before, but she knew very few details, especially nothing that would warrant what happened earlier.

"I told you, he has a virus. Several in fact, that could wipe out everyone on the planet in a manner of months, maybe weeks. I found a way to stop the one he'd planned to use before, but when he woke up a few days ago he took my father's research and fled. I know he will try to duplicate the effects of R.V. 321J-2017, and might even create something worse. We have to stop him."

Catherine studied Daniel – his shoulders drooped, there were dark circles under his pleading eyes. It was hard for her to fathom the decision he'd made earlier. She couldn't relate to the feeling that a threat far off in the distance was more important than people dying right in front of her face. Maybe what he feared was valid, but she merely couldn't feel it. She did sense his loneliness and exhaustion when she gazed into his eyes. He looked like a man who desperately wanted her to believe him. Maybe he wasn't a monster. *Was it a coincidence that he said he wasn't a monster, right as I thought it?*

"It wasn't a coincidence, Catherine, I –"

"Oh my god, what?!?" She held her hands over her mouth and backed away again, this time slamming right into the bed which she fell back onto, landing unexpectantly on her butt.

Daniel glanced in the direction of the open door, where guards stood waiting for him. "I have to go. Cybersausage has offered us aid, but only if I go to the mine and bring him back some prosthetics. I plan to get some for Anthony and Sasha too. This is going to delay us for days," he breathed out heavily, dismayed. " ... but it is the only way. Lets just hope

Cliff is running into as many issues with the viruses as we are getting to Susan's lab. There is so much I want to tell you, that I need to tell you ..." He held his right hand out to touch her shoulder but she shied away and his hand quivered before retracting. "Maybe one day you will understand ... and never have to make the decisions I have ..." He turned and walked towards the door. As he was about to exit he halted briefly and said, "I plan to take a nap on the helicopter tonight. Hopefully I see you in the other dimension." He was gone, the door slammed shut and locked behind him.

So much was running through Catherine's head as she sat on the bed starring at the metal door. Had Daniel read her mind? Could he read everyone's mind? The strong emotions she felt when looking at him, were those *from* him? Was he able to put things in her head? The idea of thoughts being put into her head was infuriating. The lights turned down for a second in the apartment and then went back to normal just as she glanced up. *What was going on?*

It was so annoying that Daniel never explained anything! He'd mentioned the other dimension, or his fancy way of saying the dream world. She had no idea why he kept calling the dream world another 'dimension.' Maybe he would provide some answers there tonight.

She laid down on the bed, and felt her aching body melt into the soft mattress. The lack of medicine and emotional ordeals of the day should make it easy to find sleep ... that is if she could get her mind to stop racing.

It seemed like hours went by before the dead bugs in the glass of the ceiling light above her bed faded away behind sleepy lids finally fluttering shut.

The stars of the night sky fell as she was lifted up into the heavens above. The stars grew numerous until their individual brightness merged into one light and she was left afloat in a white expanse. She focused her thoughts on Daniel Jahren and was brought into his bunker deep in the Colorado mountain. Two figures stood arguing, and she hid behind a shelf so she could listen secretly.

"I think I deserve to know if she is my niece, Daniel," Cliff stated. He had his arms outstretched, palms up and leaned slightly forward. "It would make it awkward if she kissed me. She sure seemed like she wanted to last night." He wore neat slacks and a white, collared shirt. His blonde hair was immaculately trimmed.

His appearance made Catherine think of an office manager at a department store who moonlighted as a male runway model on the weekend. *Who was Cliff talking about? Daniel had a daughter?* She wondered.

"I was buried here as long as you were, how could I have ..." Daniel crooked his head and squinted in Catherine's direction but then quickly faced back to answer Cliff. "Susan married another man, one that she was afraid to tell you about for years." He was dressed in the military outfit they'd left the bunker wearing two days ago. He had his usual rusty, trimmed goatee. His wavy, ruddy-brown hair was the same as it was in real life, messy and long enough to touch his collar, and his head was lacking its typical metal plate from the dream world.

"But she told *you*?" Cliff said with narrowed eyes and furrowed brow.

"Yes, at the rehearsal dinner. She wanted me to know she had moved on before I married Amy."

"How kind of her to do that right before she killed her. Maybe she was lying to you to throw you off of her murderous intent?"

"Are you starting to believe your own lies, brother? Or do you expect me to believe you still? Can you not help but try and manipulate? Fortunately, your head games will not work in here."

"Why is that? I don't understand why I am 'here' ... why you're here ... and why you planned to leave me there," he pointed to one of the cylindrical cases on the floor, "until I rotted away and died. You'd developed an inoculation, why didn't you release me?"

The building shook. Tiny pieces of the ceiling and dust fell and objects on the shelves threatened to fall off. The lights wavered on and off. The two men took no notice, they were in a staring contest, inches from each other. For a second Catherine thought they might start punching each other.

"You want to know why? For the same reason why you can't admit that you murdered our parents. Because you are out of your mind, out of control and yet you think you should control the world and everyone in it."

"I should control the world! It would be better off. I'm destined to control the world. I will, and she," he nodded in the direction of Catherine, who was kneeling behind a shelf. She could barely hear Cliff because he spoke so softly when he said, "is going to help me just like her mother did."

"She? Who?" Daniel glanced towards Catherine's hiding spot and hurriedly back to Cliff. "What do you know? What are you planning?"

Cliff snickered. "Come visit me and see, you know where I am. You'd really appreciate what I've done with the place. Please come, and bring her with you, I'd adore meeting her in person."

"Leave Catherine out of –" Daniel disappeared, likely awoken in real life.

"How rude," Cliff stated, waiting for Daniel to re-appear.

Catherine's heart pounded a thousand beats a minute. *Cliff thought that she would help him? Cliff knew her mother? He'd nodded to her position, had he seen her or was that a general nod?* She held her breath and sat as still as possible. She thought about leaving but she had so many unanswered questions.

"Come out, come out, wherever you are ..." Cliff teased, staring straight at where Catherine had wrongly thought she was concealed.

She took a deep breath, then emerged, slowly ambling past large shelves of supplies and into the middle of the room where Cliff stood patiently waiting beside the row of incubation pods. Astonishingly, her clothes changed to a bright-yellow, ankle-length, chiffon sundress with matching ballerina-style slippers. Her long brunet hair was neatly set to the side in a large, loose braid. An outfit he must want to see her wear because she sure didn't pick it out. It was decades out of style.

"Catherine Newton, we meet again," he bowed. "You're even more beautiful than your mother, you know. Did she ever mention me?"

"No, she died long before I ... how do you know my mother?" She bit her lip, trying not to give away too much while needing to know the truth.

"Dr. Susan Aldean was one of the most brilliant scientists to have ever graced the earth. I was lucky to have known her. You look so much like your mother that I thought you were Susan when I first saw you."

"You're mistaken, my mother was Sarah Newton."

Catherine had a short-lived feeling of relief before Cliff answered, "Am I? Has Daniel not told you?"

"Told me what?" She was starting to think Daniel hadn't told her a lot of things. Cliff's ominous words made her skin prickle in a cold mist that came from nowhere.

"I can see why he would want to keep it from you." He shook his head, let out a deep sigh and sat down on one of the pods. He patted the space next to him, inviting her to sit. She remained standing, and crossed her arms for emphasis.

Cliff shrugged and said, "Your mother killed his fiancé in a desperate act of passion the night before his wedding. She was sentenced to life in prison for murder here in Colorado. She escaped and, for good reason, changed her identity and fled the state."

"That can't be true ... my mother, she isn't a murderer." Even as she said it, she thought about how Daniel had a way of gazing into her eyes with such sadness, like she was a long-lost lover. Maybe she reminded him of the love he'd lost ... or the one who'd taken that love from him.

Cliff bent forward, placed his elbows on his knees and wrung his hands. "I'm sorry to say that she was, in fact, a convicted murderer. Love is peculiar, it makes you do things you never thought you would." He glanced up periodically as he spoke, likely trying to gauge her reaction to his lies.

"You're lying." Catherine had been warned by Daniel that Cliff was a liar, and dangerous. But this information, this was unexpected. It had a ring of truth to it that Catherine had trouble shaking off.

"Ha! I loved your mother, you know, so much that ... I ... I never told *anyone* this ... but I broke her out of prison myself. I never did like Daniel's fiancé Amy anyway, so Susan did me a favor."

"That can't be true, you must be lying." She was trying to call his bluff. But, was having trouble internalizing the information. He was so detailed ... could it be true?

Far too confidently, Cliff asked, "Am I?" He stared at her with intensity, and a tinge of pity. "What has Daniel told you?"

"He said you're the murderer and that he needs my help to stop you from killing everyone with a virus." Catherine had never been good at lying, the honest truth had come out of her mouth before she could stop it. She bit her lip, knowing she'd screwed-up.

"Did he? Now that doesn't make much sense, now does it? Exactly how could *you* help stop a virus?" The way he said 'you' had such derision, like he thought of her as a child or completely incapable for being a threat in any way. It echoed the feelings she had inside about herself.

He shook his head and the scene changed to one of a small room.

Catherine lay on a couch, a pillow behind her head, contemplating how Cliff made a good point – it didn't make sense what Daniel told her. "I don't know what Daniel is thinking or why he needs me."

Cliff sat in an armchair across from her, taking notes on a notepad. "Are you romantically involved with Daniel?"

The question took her by surprise. "What? No! I mean, he's attractive ... I ... its only that he's mostly been in my dreams ... I didn't even know he was real until a few days ago."

"I see. How interesting." Cliff took more notes. "What do you even know about Daniel?"

"Very little, really. I know that his ... I mean *your* family had a research and development facility in Desert Grande, and that you developed revolutionary prosthetics." She turned her head on the pillow to peer at Cliff, wondering why he wore no prosthetics.

"True, true ..." he said, relaxing into a contemplative pose. He tapped the side of his mouth with the pencil in his right hand, eyes far off and considering. Catherine hadn't seen a pencil in years, it was so strange. Everything was digital now. Pencils and notepads like the one he had showed how out of touch with time Cliff was.

Catherine felt drawn into Cliff's contemplation. He crossed his left ankle over his right knee using his left hand. His every action was so specific, controlled, detailed ... the entire room was so real that Catherine had trouble remembering this was a dream.

"Did you know your mother worked with me and Daniel at that very research and development facility you mentioned?"

"No, I ... don't actually know much about her ... she died when I was young. Here in LA."

"I'm sure that was hard for you." He jotted down more notes and held his left hand over his mouth. Then he gazed up and asked, "Why was she in LA?"

"I don't know. My father hardly spoke about what she did. She had a laborator ... Oh god, that is what Daniel wants us to find! We're tying to find my mother's lab? But why?"

"Why indeed." He smiled as he turned the page to write more notes on a blank sheet.

"What are you writing?" It suddenly struck her that she'd revealed exactly what Daniel had told her not to – precisely where they were and what they were doing. But he wasn't writing down anything about LA or a lab. In fact ... he wrote something to do with Idaho.

"Directions. I want you to memorize this and come find me. Daniel is lying to you, and whatever he has planned for you ..." He shook his head with a dreadful expression: chin pushing his lips up in a tight-lipped frown with eyes opened wide. "I'm worried that he may be getting back at you for what your mother did to his fiancé." He tore the paper off and handed it to her.

There was a knock on the door, and Cliff said, "You better get that."

She got up and reached for the wooden door handle. As it opened, a bright light flashed.

Catherine sat bolt upright in her bed, breathing hard and heart pounding. Her body was shaking, and her throat was parched. She climbed out of bed and got a glass of water from the kitchenette. The water from the sink had a metallic taste, and left a soft residue in her mouth and throat; but, it quenched her thirst. She wondered what was in it that made it taste so odd, and then nearly dropped the glass, realizing the water could have radiation contamination.

Wait, why wasn't everyone in protective suits? She hadn't even thought about it since being abducted from the helicopter. Everyone wore normal clothes ... and there were so many people! All of LA was supposed to be decimated and radioactive, wasn't it? No one outwardly showed signs of illness ... she felt fine, a little shook-up from her dream and weak from lack of medicine ... but fine none-the-less.

She went into the bathroom to check her reflection in the mirror above the sink, to see if she looked any different. What she saw was appalling and frightening. Her pink robes, face and neck were all splattered with dried blood. Anthony's blood. Tears welled up in her eyes, and she faced away from the mirror. She needed a shower, and didn't care if it was irradiated and made her skin fall off. She'd rather have no skin then be covered in Anthony's blood.

After scrubbing her body for a half-hour in burning hot water, she wrapped herself in a towel and robotically searched the room for something clean to wear. There were green coveralls, white cotton undergarments and thick woolen socks in a chest of drawers on the other side of the bed. Under the bed were sets of tan combat boots. She found the smallest pair, still too big, and laced them extra tight to make up for the additional space in the toe. After she was dressed, she stared vacantly at the locked metal door.

She'd never felt so emotionally drained in her life and was left with a consuming void. She questioned her own identity. Had she been a high school English teacher? It was like a fading dream ... was it real? What was real? Apparently, dreams were real. What was reality anymore? It all melded together and she felt adrift.

She went into the bathroom, found a comb and began detangling her hair, staring blankly in the mirror. She didn't understand why she was even here in LA. How could she stop a virus? Cliff had an outstanding point. What he'd said made sense, and now she questioned everything Daniel had said.

Why hadn't Daniel told her that he knew her mother? Why would he hide that from her? What kind of person had her mother been? A *murderer*?

In her reflection, she tried to find the resemblance. Growing up, she'd been told she took strongly after her Native American father ... but she saw her mother's delicate French features in her nose, chin and even the lips. All she had were pictures to compare, because she was too young to remember her mother before she died. The pictures in her mind were made from drawings in her father's journal. Except one, a family portrait that she'd kept on her nightstand her whole life–her parents holding her as a baby.

What were Daniel's special plans for her? Was Cliff right? Is that why Daniel wanted her to avoid Cliff, to keep the truth from her? The horrible truth

The door she was staring holes into swung open and a tall, stout man with curly black hair came into the room. "He needs you. Come with me."

"Who needs me?" she hurried to catch up to the man as he marched out the door and through the narrow hallway of apartments.

"The cyborg doctor, he just got back. I'm Dmitriy by the way." The man held out his hand. She shook it in a firm grip and noticed he had spirited, bright-blue eyes, a Jewish nose and a thin-lipped smirk. "Have you had anything to eat yet? You look famished, and boney enough to be seconds from death. I'd better get you something before you pass out and I have to carry your boney butt to triage."

He took a left into a hallway that lead out to a breakroom. He yanked a plastic wrapped sandwich from a rack, and an apple juice bottle from a cold box and handed it to her. "Eat it while we walk, we don't have time to stop."

She was having trouble keeping up with him and attempting to open her apple juice while holding the sandwich. When she managed to get it open, she spilled half of it trying to drink and haul her 'boney butt' through the building. The bread was soggy, and she had no idea what kind of cheese and meat she consumed. She chewed off pieces and swallowed while concentrating mostly on not tripping on the wires, cables, boxes and her own feet as they traversed a factory floor.

They got into the most frightening elevator imaginable. It had fenced sides, a slatted floor, and a large gate that had to be drawn closed before they descended in a jerking motion that very nearly made her fall on her face. She glanced upwards to see chains moving and dared not look down.

When they safely landed, Dmitriy led her through another hallway and into an open room. A room with two patients on gurneys. She promptly ran to Anthony, who lay rigid and was covered in a baby-blue hospital blanket from the neck down.

"Anthony? Anthony, its me, Catherine." His eyes were closed and she couldn't tell if he was breathing. "Is he okay, why isn't he moving?"

"He is under general anesthesia, Catherine. We are prepping him for surgery." Daniel said from behind her.

She was afraid to look behind her, or to even think about what Cliff had told her about Daniel and her mother. "Why do you need me, Daniel?" she said, not moving from Anthony's side.

He held her by the shoulders and tenderly spun her around to meet his golden eyes. "Catherine I ... I think it is imperative that you understand everything about this –" he held up a small black rectangular object in a clear plastic container "k – and what I am about to do with it."

Chapter 11

Cyborg Army is Born

Three times. That's how many times Catherine threw-up bits of sandwich swimming in pink liquid. Not because she was sick, it was because she had to endure watching every gory detail of brain surgery performed not once, but twice. Daniel explained each incision, and then especially detailed the placement of a microchip in the brain near the spinal column. Catherine was not good with gory. Her empathetic nature made her experience having a saw chunk out her skull and rubbery fingers dig in her brain as she watched it happen to Anthony and Sasha. They couldn't feel it because they were knocked out with drugs, but she felt it.

When one of the medics aiding Daniel operate drew back the blanket covering Anthony's body to reveal no arms, no legs ... Catherine fainted. When she came around, she had a cup of red liquid waiting next to the cot she was laying on. She swallowed as much of her medicine as she could while watching Daniel install a socketing device in all four of Anthony's stubs. Daniel then did the same operation on Sasha's two leg stumps. His two medical assistants, Heliker and Dmitriy, followed his every direction like robotic drones.

He brought out an ancient lap-top and opened up software. He had Catherine step through every motion on the keyboard as an application communicated with the microchips and ran a calibration.

When both microchips were validated, he pulled out a syringe of grey liquid and inserted a small amount of it into Anthony's muscles. He did the same with another syringe to Sasha. After a few minutes, black streaks started emanating from the injection sites.

He directed Dmitriy to end the anesthesia and then they all waited patiently for the two patients to awake.

As they waited, taking turns making each other yawn, Catherine realized someone was missing. "Where is Jordan?"

Daniel gulped back a big swing from a dark grey thermos labeled "No NOT Drink" in red letters. The aroma coming out as he drank was reminiscent of coffee, and something else she couldn't quite place. "I don't know," he stated matter-of-factly. He might as well have said, "I don't give a damn."

"Didn't he fly the helicopter to so you could obtain more supplies?" she asked, slightly annoyed with his callous attitude.

"No, one of Cybersausage's men, he had an access code for a closer entrance. It saved us almost two hours, roundtrip," he replied and took another swig of coffee.

"So, you haven't seen him since we arrived yesterday? Why didn't you bring him here?" Her voice became harsher as she spoke. Jordan was probably locked in an apartment and had no idea what was going on or where anyone was. He undoubtedly felt like she did yesterday – frantic and worried.

"If you have not noticed, I have been fairly occupied saving your boyfriend's life for you. I have been far too busy to babysit your 'co-worker' Jordan."

She scoffed, he wasn't usually this abrupt with her. She crossed her arms and scowled at him.

He appeared immediately chagrined, and sighed. "I'm sorry, Catherine. Heliker, Dmitriy ... do either of you know where the other gentleman we arrived with is located? Can one of you go get him?"

The medical assistants looked at each other and mumbled a few things about not knowing what he was talking about, etc ...

Daniel sat up in his seat and his eyes flashed gold. He reached for Catherine's hand and whispered softly, "I think they found out who he was ..." he glanced back at the medical assistants arguing under their breath. " ... and he has been taken to answer for his crimes. I'm sorry."

"I'm sorry!" she practically screeched. "That is all you have to say, 'I'm sorry'?" She threw his hand back at him and stood up. "Jordan helped you, and he saved my life yesterday and you think 'I'm sorry' will somehow fix everything?"

"Wha ... what is going on? Catherine?" Anthony's eyes were open and he attempted to move in an awkward metallic-clanking lurch. "What happened to me?" His voice nearly as shrill as hers had been a few seconds ago.

Daniel was at his side, lightning fast. He stood over him and said simply, "Relax," and Anthony stopped trying to move and began to take deeper breaths. "You have sustained severe injuries to your limbs. We made repairs that you may find suitable. Concentrate on your right arm, can you feel it?" Anthony nodded. "Try to raise your arm." The arm flew up swiftly and would have knocked Daniel out had he not immediately gotten out of the way. "Good." Daniel made a shooing motion and everyone else stepped back and away from Anthony's bedside.

"What is this? What happened to my arm?" Anthony stared in horror at the metallic, silver and black prosthetic. He moved his fingers and bent his wrist. There were many moving parts, all exposed. He reached for Daniel's white jacket and pulled him close, "What have you done to me?"

Catherine thought she saw a small flash in Daniel's eyes right before Anthony suddenly let go and put his arm back down to his side.

"Now I want you to concentrate on your legs, can you feel them?" Another nod from Anthony. "Okay, now I want you to carefully use your arm to help yourself sit up."

Anthony propped himself up, and began examining his left hand, the mirror opposite of his right. He clasped them together and released them. The blanket fell down and his naked body was revealed. He jerked the covering back quickly to hide his genitals. "At least I know those are fine," he said, blushing and peering over at Catherine with a sheepish grin.

"I can get him some shorts, I'll be right back." The medical assistant Daniel had referred to as Heliker dashed out the room.

"These arms, they are so responsive. How is this possible?"

"They are made of a composite titanium blend, but the real reason you have strength now to control them is that I've given you the Quinta virus." Daniel explained.

Anthony stared at his own massive, muscular chest and stomach ... the virus not only caused black, vein-like streaks on his skin, but it swelled his muscles which were huge to begin with.

"How does the Quinta virus work?" Dmitriy asked.

"It turns your cells into a graphene factory, layering muscle tissue with carbon fibers on a nano level. It was designed by my brother Cliff and my father, initially used to counter the effects of Cliff's muscular dystrophy."

"Here you go." Heliker was back and tossed Anthony a pair of green cargo-pant shorts that he slid over his legs and under his butt. They fit pretty lose, but well enough. He'd brought another outfit too, for Sasha.

"Okay, Anthony. Now, I want you to try to stand. I am right here if you need support."

Anthony stood warily, taking small steps at first, then began walking in large strides. "How is this possible? How do these things read my mind? How do they know what I want?"

"You have a neuro-responsive electro-transmitter in your brain."

"A what?" Anthony felt all over his shaved head and stopped in the back where there was a large square bandage that hid a cut. Daniel had applied a pink liquid and the incision had completely sealed, leaving only a red scar. "You put something in my brain?"

"It was necessary –"

"What gave you the right to play God? Brain implants? Viruses? Who do you think you are?" Anthony charged towards Daniel and stopped, hands outstretched, inches from tackling him. Anthony growled and grimaced before putting his hands down, standing up straight, walking over to a cot and laying down.

In practically the same instant that Anthony closed his eyes, Sasha opened her eyes wide and started screaming. Catherine took her hand and tried to calm her down. Daniel came to her side and gave her the same speech he'd given Anthony, starting with the word 'Relax' and ending 3 minutes later with her walking on her new legs, asking about the implants and freaking out. She even ended up ambling over to a cot and laying down as well.

"Start them both on a 40 mg Morphine drip, and add one of these –" he held up a vial of purple liquid, "–in 8 ounces of water when they wake again."

"Are you leaving?" Heliker asked.

"Yes, we need to find the man that came with us, Jordan. We'll knock down every apartment door if we have to." Daniel laid his hand on Catherine's upper arm, and flashed her a small smile.

"You can't do that," Dmitriy objected.

"You won't find him in the apartments," Heliker added.

"Then where is he?" Daniel demanded, eyes flashing gold so brightly that both men took a step back.

"I ... I ... I will take you there myself," Heliker's wide-eyed look of terror seemed so strange on such a tall, muscular man.

Daniel filled a 10-inch square, black bag with purple vials, bandages, and antiseptic clothes and a few other things. "I have a feeling we will need these."

"Why? Why, Daniel? God, what did they do to him?" Catherine trailed him and Heliker as the long-legged men bolted out of triage and headed toward the frightful industrial elevator.

"Catherine, there is a lot that you don't know about *Jordan,*" Daniel explained with his usual distaste at the name 'Jordan.' "He ... he has killed many people."

"That is an understatement! Last time Loco Luca was in LA, he basically leveled our old headquarters with a MK-47 grenade launcher. When people fled he took them out one by one with an M-16 assault rifle. Men, women, children, old people, disabled people, everyone ..." Heliker grimly detailed the mass murder while they descended to the very bottom of the building. He slid the elevator gate open and said, "As you can imagine, Cybersausage has been taking his time."

Catherine didn't want to imagine. She hurriedly tried to keep up with the tall men's strides as they filed into a narrow, dark hallway into a dimly lit room. Heliker must be mistaken, there was no way Jordan could have killed innocent people like that. There must be some kind of mix up. Unless ... was this the gang that killed Maria?

"You can't be in her–!" A guard tried to say but was flung into the wall across the room before he could get out anything more.

Catherine ran into the room and gasped at the sight in front of her.

Jordan was stripped down, wearing only tattered pieces of his burgundy pants. He had sharp metal wire constraining each of his limbs to the four corners of a bed's box-spring. There was no padding, so the coils of the springs were fully exposed against his bare back. Wires were attached to the coils, and led back to a small box with dials on the front that was plugged into the wall electric socket. The room smelled like burnt flesh. Jordan's eyes were black and practically swollen shut and he had gashes and bruises all over his body.

Heliker and Daniel unstrapped Jordan while Catherine searched the room for a sink, glasses or anything she could find to fill with water. She found a mug next to a sink in an adjacent bathroom, rinsed it out and emptied one of the purple vials in the water.

Daniel began administering first aid to the large gashes in Jordan's chest while Catherine held Jordan's face and tried to get him to take sips of the drink.

Jordan reached his hand out to touch her cheek and tried to smile with a swollen, bloodied lip. "You came for me."

"Yes, yes of course." Her throat ached with the tears that wanted to well up, but she held them back to give Jordan a reassuring smile.

"We should bring him to the triage room," Daniel suggested.

"No, Cybersausage will be there by now. It's best to take him to her room, and hope that no one sees us."

"I can help with that," Daniel casually remarked, lifting Jordan up on one side while Heliker lifted his other side.

"You can make us invisible?" Heliker almost whispered, half in awe.

"No, I'm not a parlor magician. I can be persuasive, if I need to be," Daniel admitted.

As they were exiting the torture room Catherine asked, “Is he going to be okay?” referring to the man embedded in the wall.

“Yes, he’s merely knocked out,” Heliker answered. “Nice move by the way, you’re a pretty scary dude. Lawson there weighs almost 200 lbs and you flicked him like a gnat.”

“I ... honestly had no idea that would happen. I guess I do not fully know my own strength.”

They managed to make it up to Catherine’s apartment without running into anyone. They saw a few people further down hallways, or inside open doorways; but, no one turned to look in their direction or deemed to notice the group carrying a bloody man through the facility.

“Catherine, help him get cleaned up and changed. I need to get back to triage and see if I can convince Cybersausage to pardon him.”

“Daniel, there is something I need to tell you ...” Catherine began.

“What is it?” He laid Jordan carefully on the bed and set the bag of medical supplies on the counter.

Heliker stood in the doorway, checking up and down the hallway. “We’ve got to go.”

She held onto Daniel’s arm so he couldn’t leave. “I saw Cliff again, last night in my dreams.” Catherine had thought carefully about what to say next and hoped she wasn’t saying the wrong thing when she said, “I saw you both. He told me about you and my mother.”

“Whatever he told you, it was a lie.” Daniel stated flatly. “We can talk about that later tonight. Right now I have to smooth things over or none of us will be safe, do you understand?”

“Yes,” Catherine released his arm, then peered up at him and said. “Thank you, Daniel. For helping Jordan and Anthony today.”

“Catherine, you know I am doing all of this for you.” He took her by her shoulders and looked her directly in the eyes. “Please give me a chance to explain about your mother. I know you have so many questions and it is never the right time ... its complicated … but, please know that I want to tell you everything."

"We have to head back," Heliker said from the door. "We've been gone too long."

Daniel reached out his right hand and squeezed Catherine's left hand, reminding her of how comforting his hand had been in her dream. He brandished one of his sad smiles before exiting the room.

They'd left the door unlocked, and that made the room far less confining, literally.

"Jordan, how are you doing?" She went to stand by his bedside, trying to focus on his eyes and not the trauma to his body.

"I guess you couldn't wait to get me in your bed again, Catherine." Jordan pushed himself up, groaning.

"That's right, I couldn't help myself," she laughed and then went into the bathroom to get a wet washcloth and a dry towel. She sat next to him, laid the towel beside him on the bed and began cleaning the dried blood off of his body.

He watched her for a few minutes and then said, "You should have left me to die, it would have been less suffering in the long run."

"What do you mea –" she was interrupted with him putting his hand behind her neck and drawing her in tenderly for a soft kiss. As their lips touched, the heat in her body pulsed, and made her vision blur. After he released her tingling lips, she caught her breath but was still stunned. He held her so close she could feel his warm breath on her cheek. "Anthony, I –"

"My name is Jordan." He let go of her and closed his eyes, leaning back against the wall behind the bed and grimacing.

"I know. I was going to say, 'Anthony, I don't want to hurt him.' He has been through so much and … I should break up with him but I don't know how. I care about him … it's just …"

"Why do you want to break up with him?" There was hope in Jordan's eyes that made her heart flutter.

"When we began dating, he was exactly who I was expected to be with. Handsome, hard-working and with a big heart. He even asked me to marry him right before he went to blow-up the mine."

"What did you say?" Jordan had taken the wet washcloth and was wiping the wounds on his left arm and hand clean. Most of the sores likely came from a whip because they were thin and had slight bruising around the cuts.

"I said no. I thought it was over then and a part of me was relieved. Then he went to blow up the mine like a suicidal idiot. But, when I woke from the coma in the hospital he was by my side." She took the cloth back from him and went into the bathroom to clean it again. She looked at herself in the mirror, at her lips still tingling with the memory of Jordan's kiss and thinking about it made her heart flutter again. He was such a good kisser!

"So, you got back together with him?" Jordan said from the bedroom, loud enough for her to hear him. "Because he was in the hospital with you?"

"Not exactly," she yelled back, wringing out the washcloth. She came back in the room and sat next to Jordan on the bed again, handing him the cloth. "I told him I had gone over to your place at night ... then he broke up with me for cheating on him and stormed off before I could finish telling him everything that happened."

Jordan laughed, "What an idiot!"

"I got back to my house the next day, and he was there, watching Sass. I explained to him what happened, that you'd kidnapped me –"

"I was trying to protect you." Jordan interrupted, he still thought that drugging her and tying her to his bed was some kind of favor.

"Yeah, well we didn't exactly say we got back together but I think ... I mean I know he thought we got back together. Things have been happening so fast since then that I haven't had time to tell him it's over. I mean, I care about him but ..." she bit her lip. She knew Jordan thought that he might be the reason she wanted to break up with Anthony. But, the truth was that she'd been thinking about it for months and realized, just like Daniel said, Anthony simply wasn't right for her.

"Just tell him, get it over with quickly. Like a band aid." He slid his hand along her neck and down her collar bone slowly. "Drawing it out can be –" he slid his hand further down and she caught her breath, "torture."

She leaned away before his fingers could make it into her coveralls, and moved his hand back to his own chest. "I have trouble telling him anything. You know I couldn't even tell him about Daniel. I couldn't even bring myself to tell him I'd had dreams about cyborgs –"

"But you told me, why?"

She took the cloth from him and went into the bathroom to rinse it out and warm it up with fresh water. She came back into the room, sat next to him and began cleaning his face. His dark brown eyes followed her the whole time. He stopped her hand and asked again, "Why, Catherine? Why did you tell me?"

"I don't know ... maybe because I thought you were as crazy as I was."

"Not quite as crazy." He grinned. "I am trained to get people to say things to me, you know. So, you were at a slight disadvantage."

"You think you made me tell you?" She squinted her eyes at him, wondering if what he said was true.

"Most of what I do is so ingrained that I don't even know I'm doing it. I was taught to find details about a person and use that to get information. For instance, I can tell you're attracted to me by the way your eyes dilate when you look at me. I know you want to be with me, even if you won't admit that to yourself."

"I see ..." All this talk about reading her mind reminded her of what happened last night with Daniel, and the way he interacted today with Anthony and Sasha was so bizarre.

"What is it?" Jordan's concerned voice broke through her ruminating.

She took the rag into the bathroom to clean it again and collect her thoughts. When she came back in she asked, "Have you noticed anything strange about Daniel?"

"Okay, you're going to have to be more specific, there is a LOT strange about him."

She began cleaning his chest, where most of the damage had been done. There were a couple of areas that Daniel had bandaged in the basement and the dressings were already bled through. "How he can ... how sometimes ... I think he might be able to read my mind."

"What makes you think that?" Jordan had that blank stare that meant he was calculating everything she said carefully.

"Last night I thought the word 'monster' in my head and then he immediately said he wasn't a monster. Then, later when I thought how much of a coincidence that was he immediately said 'its not a coincidence' but then left before explaining more."

"That is –" he began but then she ripped a bandage off and he paused for a breath "–curious. I have had my own suspicions as well. Is there anything else that makes you think he reads minds?"

"Yes. Today he made me watch as he implanted microchips in Sasha and Anthony's brains. He said it runs their prosthetics, and that he has one that runs his prosthetics too. But, I think it does more than that."

"Wait, he implanted a microchip in their brains?" Jordan took hold of her hand.

Catherine nodded and got up to get search through the bag Daniel had left on the counter, looking for the pink liquid he'd used earlier. She placed a thin line of the liquid along a jagged gash down Jordan's ribs that she'd just cleaned. The wound closed immediately. He said, "That burned," like it was a mere observation.

"Yes." She placed a bandage over the delicate pink scar. "And what was even more disturbing was how they reacted to him when they woke up. He said 'Relax' and they instantly relaxed. Anthony charged at him and stopped without him even saying a word, and he went and laid down ... like he was directed somehow."

"That isn't mind reading, Catherine, that is mind control."

Catherine studied him, he wasn't surprised at all by what she'd revealed. "Your chest is clean, now we need to work on your back."

He turned so that he sat on the edge of the bed, back towards her. She gasped when she saw the wounds, then tears fell. The pain he must be going through ... there wasn't an inch that didn't have ripped flesh. He'd definitely been thrashed by a cat o' nine tails or something similar. It must have happened yesterday, because the wounds were crusted with dried blood. Over top of the ripped flesh were spiral burn scars from the electrified box spring. It looked like his back was cooked. She didn't even know where to begin. She just sat there and cried, hand shaking while she held the wet washcloth, unable to touch him.

"That bad, huh?" he remarked, of course he knew how bad it must be ... he'd experienced it.

"I'm so sorry Jordan ... I ..."

"Some people would say I deserved this, some would say I deserved worse." He turned to gaze at her as he said, "I know I don't deserve you," and then he kissed her again. The world went still as he pressed his lips against hers.

"Please Jordan, you need to stop doing that," she practically whispered. She pulled her head back, and turned her face away. He continued kissing her neck and décolletage. Her heart beat faster and she felt like she was being entranced.

"A little sugar helps the medicine go down." He winked and then turned away. "Place the rag at the top to let it soften the dried blood." He flinched and gasped for the first time as she followed his directions. "Do you have any more washcloths?"

Three more washcloths and his back was covered. She poured a purple vial into a cup of water and handed it to him. "Maybe this will help." She made a cup for herself and sat on a chair by the door. She didn't trust sitting next to him anymore-if he hadn't stopped, she sure wouldn't have.

Her thoughts went to the dream she'd had the night before. To what Cliff said and how confused she was about Daniel. "Jordan ..."

"Yes?" The bruising on his face was already beginning to fade and the swelling around his eyes was completely gone.

"Do you even think there is a virus ... that ... that we are even here to try to stop a virus after all?"

"I never did."

Chapter 12

Friends in Low Places

Sleep was a luxury not typically afforded doctors in triage. Besides the brief naps on the helicopter, Daniel hadn't slept in days. The long hours were taking their toll, and reminding him of his interning days at UCLA Medical Center. A lifetime ago.

Cybersausage wanted himself and some of his men retrofitted with 'upgrades' after he saw the remarkable capabilities of Sasha and Anthony. A trade – for Luca's life, and sanctuary for Daniel's entourage during their search for Susan's lab.

Dmitriy and Heliker were barely hanging on, but performing remarkably under the circumstances. Daniel was tempted to give them some of his parent's proprietary coffee blend. But, the risks far outweighed the rewards, and regular coffee would have to suffice. The most he could do was give them a half-hour break every few hours.

He'd sent Sasha and Anthony back to the apartments hours ago, to get food and rest. He also wanted to get them away from the commotion generated by the ornithology-themed anarchists with missing limbs filling-up the triage room.

Daniel had no idea what these people called themselves, and hadn't asked. It didn't matter so long as they kept their end of the bargain. He'd limited the number of gang members allowed into the room, and negotiated from fifteen operations down to five per day over the last two days.

Cybersausage and six of his men lay in cots, all recovering and snoring. Besides that, the room was empty.

Daniel sat back in a chair between the cots, drinking from his thermos and rubbing his temples. He tried to enjoy the silence until Dmitriy and Heliker got back from break or Cybersausage woke up from the anesthesia. He waited, and decompressed his weary mind.

He missed seeing Catherine last night – her beautiful dreams, her delicate grace and sweet smile. She was the light in decades of darkness. He despised leaving her alone with Luca. That man was a barnacle, a leach, a festering lesion. Luca had no idea how much out of his league Catherine was, how special she was. Luca didn't want her to reach her potential, he only wanted her for himself. The lustful things in that man's head made Daniel want to rip him in half.

Cybersausage's eyes fluttered and he began to moan. Daniel stood, aching joints and back cracking as he stretched. Two bounding steps and he was at Cybersausage's side. Foreign thoughts whispered in the far reaches of Daniel's mind: *The weight, there is weight. Heavy. Hand?*

Cybersausage had his right hand up, six inches in front of his face. He laid on his cot, moving his new metallic fingers, squinting. His brow furrowed when he tried to touch his thumb to the tip of his index finger. It took him three tries. Then he tried the next finger to thumb, and the next. He made a fist and released it. Daniel helped him sit up, then removed the blanket to show him his new legs. He didn't have to read his mind to feel the thrill Cybersausage felt moving his legs to the side of the cot, and preparing to stand.

"I will be here to support you," Daniel said, taking hold of Cybersausage under the right arm and lifting him up. The man had lost his legs to meningococcal meningitis as a child. The memory of how to control them was not going to be as strong as many of his gang who'd lost their limbs to Tripod's Komodo dragons or sword-wielding Chinese fighters.

Cybersausage rocked forward and back when his feet landed on the floor. He slipped and grasped onto Daniel's chest so that he didn't fall face first. His hand lingered over his defined muscles a bit longer than necessary, and Daniel blushed at Cybersausage's thoughts. Daniel was flattered; but, it was hard for him to imagine himself as a 'stud muffin,' especially with the scaring and black streaks on his body.

Daniel walked with Cybersausage through the aisle between cots. They reached the far wall and came back again. The movement of leg bending, weight settling, pushing forward and repeat was starting to become a steady rhythm. Cybersausage was focused, concentrating on every step.

"I believe you are catching on," Daniel said, gingerly coming to a stop and ducking under Cybersausage's arm to release him to try on his own. "I will be right here." He stood by his side, reaching out only to steady him when he got a bit too ambitious and lurched forward. "Slow and steady."

Heliker and Dmitriy stumbled in from the cafeteria, each with a cup of coffee and some snacks. Heliker set a plate of pastries down on a counter near the sink. "We thought you might be hungry ... you do eat?" He was serious, they hadn't seen him eat in two days, and he wasn't sure if Daniel was human.

"Yes, thank you." The bitter coffee left Daniel without much of an appetite and he'd been drinking it non-stop to keep his energy up. He wasn't sure about how to handle Heliker and his food offering. Heliker seemed to think Daniel was some kind of super hero or god. Far from both. He decided to eat a pastry to prove his mortality.

Dmitriy chewed on the remains of a raspberry filled donut covered in confectioners' sugar. He had a white mustache as he asked, "Only three more, right?" *Then we can sleep, God I am so damn tired.* Daniel heard Dmitriy's thoughts like a begging echo in his mind.

Now that Cybersausage had a Mod, Daniel would have a much easier time getting what he wanted. But, he had to be subtle.

"That is up to Cybersausage," Daniel focused his mind on impressions of fatigue and knives slipping, images of surgery gone wrong in tired hands, then projected it outwards.

"My goodness, you all look so ..." Cybersausage searched for words, replaying the images in his head. "I think it would be best, for everyone's sake, if you got some rest this afternoon and we began again tomorrow."

Daniel smiled, and said to the tired medics. "You may go." Heliker and Dmitriy nearly fell over in relief. They raced to the exit and jostled each other in the doorway, fighting over who would get through first.

Daniel watched them leave and then turned to Cybersausage and said, “I need to find a place, and I’m not sure of the exact location. Do you know someone who has access to old schematics of LA?” It wasn’t a request, he filled his mind with urgency and let it disseminate into the room. The Mod in Cybersausage’s head made the simple request an undeniable command.

“I have a friend, a hacker, he can find anything. His code name is Snowwolf, and he’s always up for a challenge. Where’s this place you need to find with such ... exigency?” Cybersausage stood a good inch and a half taller than Daniel now, and apparently the new height was making him feel more powerful.

“Anaheim.”

“I see, hummm. Do you realize that was the heart of the initial blast?” Anaheim was the last place Cybersausage wanted to go, a sense of imminent danger radiated out of him like a beacon.

“Yes, I’ve read. I assume you have radiation protection gear.”

“Central doesn’t like to share what I am about to tell you –” Cybersausage bent down and nearly fell as he tried to sit on a cot, but Daniel steadied him. “ – because they don’t want to own that they blocked out so many people from civilization and left them to rot behind a wall.”

“Was there no uranium in the bomb?” Daniel could see clear images from Cybersausage mind of mass devastation, but nothing of radiation.

“No, there was. The blast wasn’t a surface detonation so it didn’t penetrate into the earth, it dissipated into the air, like Hiroshima. The bomb had less than 5 lbs or uranium ... so Anaheim isn’t even very radioactive. But, still, no one goes near the place ... the ‘wildlife’ there has ... I guess you could say ‘evolved’ but I don’t think a 30-pound rat is much of an evolution.”

An image of a giant frothy-mouthed rat flinging itself onto a man in black played in Cybersausage’s mind. Daniel asked, “So, you mean to say we may run into rabid, radioactive rats?”

"Yes, of unusual size." Cybersausage snickered a bit. Daniel caught glimpses of an old movie in his mind, some kind of reference to a princess story. Even though he found it funny, Cybersausage was completely serious about the rats. "Plus, something you may not have read, is that most of Anaheim is submerged from the last earthquake –"

"Submerged?" Daniel inquired and Cybersausage's mind held an image of skyscrapers poking out of the ocean, similar to what Daniel had seen when flying over San Diego.

"Some areas completely, other areas in only a foot or so of water ... these legs, are they rust proof?"

"Titanium and carbon fiber do not corrode."

"Fantastic. I'd like to join you on your search, if you don't mind. Let me introduce you to Snowwolf." Cybersausage held his hand out and Daniel lifted him to his new metal feet. His movement wasn't as fluid as Daniel's but he was no longer rocking and sliding. He'd caught on more rapidly than expected, and learned to take slow, calculating steps. He stepped cautiously onto the elevator grating but then opened his stride down the halls of the same basement Luca had been imprisoned in yesterday.

He knocked three times on a sealed, metal door and a perky male voice inside said, "Come in!"

The room was filled with computers, monitors and projectors. The walls and floor were coated in a white, reflective paint. Not an inch of the room was still, all displaying live feeds of different scenes, presumably places in the city of LA. Even the floor had projections.

Cybersausage opened his arm out motioning for Daniel to enter the room ahead of him. He leaned his head toward a man sitting cross-legged in the middle of the room wearing the same green coveralls as everyone else, except he also had on a pair of intricately designed gloves. "Doctor, meet Snowwolf."

"What's up." The man on the floor remarked, not stopping from what he was doing or turning around. He was a short, chubby fellow in his mid-fifties with a bristling brown beard.

"Snowwolf, I'd like to introduce you to my new friend, Dr. Daniel ... I forget, what was your last name?" Cybersausage said, ushering Daniel to move further into the room than where we was standing back in the doorway trying to take-in all the images.

"Jahren."

The monitor in the front of the room suddenly changed to a picture of Daniel when he was a faculty member UCLA Medical Center. The one to the left showed him receiving the Gustav O. Lienhard Award for Advancement of Health Care from the National Academy of Medicine. Several other monitors displayed various awards in neurolgy from around the globe. A video someone took at the banquet where he accepted the Swartz Prize projected on the floor. He'd never seen himself giving a speech, he was so young, bashful and awkward.

Cybersausage let out a whistle and said, "Man, I knew you weren't just any doctor."

Daniel watched as pieces of his old life played out around him, it was unsettling. One monitor below the first presented the news coverage of the explosion at his family's research facility in Colorado. Another depicted his gravestone in Mesa Heights, in what is now called the city of Desert Grande. Obituaries of his entire family, including his mother, father and brother.

How was Snowwolf pulling this information up? Daniel peered down to see Snowwolf's fingers moving a mile a minute. He had a device similar to the one that the owl woman, Esha, had worn over his face. Daniel guessed he was using enhanced augmented reality glasses and a virtual keyboard.

Then a newspaper wedding announcement caught Daniel's eye. An announcement of his impending nuptials. In the center of the article was a photo of himself holding a beaming, beautiful Amy. They held each other under the cottonwood tree. The tree where they had first met as children. The love between them, the hope in her eyes, the loss ... the utter agony. The devastation hit him like a ton of bricks and he nearly fell to the floor under the weight. Every monitor in the room went black and both of the other men groaned as if in physical pain.

The room was dark but, behind his squeezed-closed lids, Daniel could see the last kiss ... Amy's innocent blue eyes fondly twinkling in the lights of the restaurant balcony where the rehearsal dinner unfolded around them. Her curly blonde hair moved softly across his fingers resting on her exposed back; bared teasingly by the low-cut pink dress she wore so well. Then she laughed, and chided him for being late ...

Tears rolled down his cheeks as the lights came back on in the room. One by one, the screens popped back on ... still reflecting the triumphs and tragedies of Daniel's life.

He hadn't thought about that night in so long. The night he lost the love of his life. Years of depression and then Susan had implanted the new Mod. And with it, the memories fell away. Was it the training in the other dimension that had finally allowed him to unlock those memories? Whatever it was, he never expected that it would still hurt this much, this long after Amy was gone.

Daniel wanted to go back to sleep, to never feel again.

"Your emotions ... they are ... overwhelming. I *feel* them." Cybersausage had his hand on the back of his head, where the Mod was located. So much for Daniel's attempt at being subtle.

"Yeah, Dude, you're like an emotional projector, for real." Snowwolf said. He'd turned himself around to face his new guest and now sat cross-armed as well as cross-legged. His squinting eyes were locked on Daniel.

Daniel towered over Snowwolf, standing still as death, with fists clenched and shoulders tensed upwards. He let the pain wash out of him with the tears that fell.

"Find what you can on a research laboratory in Anaheim, called Newton Dreamworks." Daniel didn't bother to wipe the tears from his face. He put intention and purpose in every word, drilling them in. He had one job to do. He had to stop Cliff.

Snowwolf spun around and began air typing with his gloves. The screens started displaying images of Susan, or Sarah Newton, from her business webpage. There was a pang in his heart when he saw her face. Knowing that she'd moved on with another man helped him get over it quickly though.

She'd done a good job of changing her identity, because Snowwolf wasn't finding anything on her past.

Information on her dream studies and grants showed up. "Why do you care about a dream research lab?" Snowwolf asked.

"Doctor Newton developed something I need. Can we get to it tonight?"

"Wait, what? *Tonight*?" Cybersausage had been leaning against the wall, but stood straight up as he spoke.

"It is located in the north central section of Anaheim, 30 yards northeast of the intersection of SR-57 and SR-91, or the Orange and Riverside Freeways. You're in luck that it isn't completely submerged." There was a live feed video of a six-story building, the kind that held several business offices. All the windows were broken, likely from the nuclear explosion, and the first floor was submerged in sea water nearly half-way up the height of the busted-out entryway. Another monitor showed a building schematic – Newton Dreamworks took up most the third floor.

"Thank you for the detailed information." Daniel announced. "It was nice to meet you, Snowwolf."

"Yeah, right. Next time I want to feel like killing myself again, I'll give you a call."

~ ~ ~

The first place Anthony went when he was released from triage was to find Catherine. The moment he opened her apartment door he half expected her to run to him, jumping into his arms.

But, she wasn't there.

"Is this the right apartment?" he asked the old scarecrow of a woman who'd steered him here. She was pushing 90, and blind in one eye. Maybe she had dementia, maybe it was the wrong room.

"Yes, this is it," she screeched. She leaned forward to peek into the room and brushed Anthony with the hunchback on her hunchback.

He was about to leave and find someone who was more reliable when he noticed something on the floor–a crumpled-up pink robe like the one Catherine wore in the arena. He bolted to it, and examined it to find the dragon symbol on the sleeve. It was covered in blood. *Her blood?* No, last time he saw her she was wearing a green jumpsuit, like everyone else, and was perfectly healthy. He searched the room, finding bloody rags in the sink and bandages in the trash. *Had she been injured since yesterday afternoon?*

"Maybe she's at lunch," said the old hag.

His stomach gurgled at the word 'lunch' and he dipped his chin in acknowledgment of her good idea. He let the lady lead him, ever so sluggishly, to the cafeteria.

The cafeteria was evidently the hub of the building, more people in green filled the room than he's seen throughout the factory and hallways combined. Twenty wooden benches, mostly full of men and women eating and chatting, took up the front half. There was a divider between the front and back of the cafeteria, on one side people took-up trays and formed lines. On the other end of the divider they poured out with stuffed plates.

He scanned the room and spotted Sasha, sitting alone at a long wooden table. She was surrounded by a group of men checking-out her legs. The men laughed, spoke in hushed words, then high fived each other before moving on to their own table a few feet away.

Anthony walked past Sasha, and glared at the men. He headed straight to the kitchen behind the divider to see if Catherine was back there.

The kitchen was a place his mother would love –no one used combinators. It was full of open flame grills, and it smelled wonderful. The line for food was long, and he searched the heads for his girlfriend's long, brunette hair among the throng in green coveralls clamoring for portions to be ladled onto their plates.

Maybe Catherine went back to triage and he'd somehow missed her on the way. His mouth was watering in envy at the grits and shrimp that passed by on another guy's tray. Then his nostrils caught the aroma of seared fish ... was that halibut? Fish always came out rubbery in the combinator.

He was so excited, he snagged a tray and got in line. He thanked the woman behind the service counter and bounded to the tables to sit across from Sasha. The food was everything he'd hoped for and more – the most delicious meal of his life. He'd gotten a flank of seared halibut. Then added field greens covered in almond slivers and fresh strawberries with a light, tangy vinaigrette. He'd finished the plate before even looking up at Sasha. When he finally did, he saw there were tears in her eyes and she held onto her spork like she wanted to stab someone with it.

It was probably the legs thing, from the guys leering around her earlier. She had on the same outfit as Anthony, baggy green cargo shorts and a white tank top with a green jacket that had a black owl in flight on the back. It wasn't exactly alluring, but Sasha could make any outfit look sensual over her voluptuous body. But, how did those men think her legs were attractive? They were metal!

"What's wrong, Sasha?" he asked.

"это пиздец ... did you hear ... what ..." She scowled at the men at the table to the right, which only made them laugh harder. She stabbed a piece of chicken piccata with her spork, over and over.

"No, I didn't hear, but I can guess." Anthony wasn't sure what to do. She was visibly furious, but these men hadn't done anything to her except do some disrespectful trash talk between guys. Yes, they deserved to be put in their place, but Sasha and Anthony were guests and he didn't want to start something that got him in trouble. Especially when he didn't even know where Catherine was. Sasha glared at the men and they jeered, again. He caught one word 'sex-bot' that made him glare at the men too. "Want me to say something?"

She shook her head, then went back to trying to kill her food –tears began to well up in her eyes and the bottom of her chin quivered delicately.

He hated seeing women cry. "I'll be right back." Maybe he could get these guys to stop kidding around and apologize.

When he got to the table, the four men stood up. He still stood 3-4 inches taller than any of them. He rolled up his sleeves and crossed his arms for affect before he spoke a word. The sight of metal should have made them back up, but instead they snickered.

"Hot stuff sent over her plaything?" the shortest man said. He was about as ugly as they come – with a huge, crooked nose and acne box scars on his cheeks.

"Speechless, pretty boy-toy?" said the lanky blue-eyed, caramel-skinned man in braids to the left and behind an Asian, rotund guy eyeing Anthony up and down. The Asian man reminded him of a sumo wrestler.

The forth man stood behind the short wise-guy. He could have been twin brothers with the lanky braided guy, except he had about forty pounds extra on him, pure muscle, and had the most ridiculous, fat-lipped grin.

"That young woman there –" Anthony glanced back towards Sasha, who stared back with a blank wide-eyed look on her face. "–has been through more than any of you can imagine. I think she deserves an apology."

"What, did we hurt your little sex-bot's feelings?" the short one teased. "Why don't you go sit down before we break your toy parts off and beat you with them."

"Oh damn, that's hilarious Leo," the lanky one said, and gave Leo a high five.

"Toy parts?" Anthony couldn't help but laugh uproariously. They must not have gotten word of the exhibition in triage last night. An exhibition that made Anthony feel invincible. "Can a toy do this?" He picked up the six-foot table with one hand and threw it over their heads and across the room. The wood shattered to tiny pieces against the concrete wall. It felt as light as tossing socks in a hamper.

Ten to twenty more men came to stand behind the four jeering fools, none looked as impressed as they should.

Sasha was up, and beside Anthony. "Anthony, please, it isn't worth it. Let's go."

Then one guy, Leo, had the gall to stick his hand out, reaching toward Sasha's rear end. Anthony stopped the hand by grabbing it at the wrist, but accidently held it too hard because it abruptly became a squishy, bloody pulp. Anthony let go and the hand fell backwards on the limp wrist.

Before he could apologize, the lanky guy took a swing at him. He ducked back, afraid to block his arm because he didn't want to accidently rip it off. He saw a metal leg kick up from his left – Sasha's leg. The guy flew back against five men behind him who then fell backwards like bowling pins. She'd nearly kicked his head off! The guy's jaw was smashed and there was blood gushing out of his mouth and nose.

Anthony figured these guys would get the picture with that display, but seeing their friends injured fueled attacks from several men at once. There was pandemonium, blood and screams, while Anthony and Sasha defended themselves from multiple attackers. He focused mostly on trying not to kill anyone.

He heard a crack – something struck the back of his head with excruciating force. The last thing he saw were stars in his blurring vision.

Chapter 13

To the Armory

Sasha stood guard over Anthony's body, daring anyone to make a move. The crowd of thugs began to disperse, defeated men carrying away their fallen comrades. She'd managed not to kill anyone, probably. The cafeteria was a disaster, a few people here and there picked up tables and started sweeping away splintered wood and mopping-up blood. She got the feeling the reason the tables were made of coarse cedar was because this kind of thing happened a lot.

"Nice job," said a bright-eyed, middle-aged woman with a pixie haircut dyed maroon. "I hate those bastards. I especially love what you did to Fred, his jaw will be wired shut for a month. It'll be nice not having to listen to the trash that comes out of that big mouth." She crouched next to Anthony and checked his vitals. "I think your boyfriend will be okay, he'll have a spectacular knot on his noggin though. Man, he's snoring like a wildebeest!"

Sasha crouched next to the woman. "He's not my boyfriend. Is there anywhere in this god-forsaken place that is safe?"

"Yes, you have an apartment, right?" The red-head said it like she was hoping Sasha would say no and she could invite her to her own apartment. "My name's Crissa," she said, holding out a purple-nailed hand with calluses that come from intensive physical labor. She shook hands with intensity and vigor, and held Sasha's hand a bit longer than necessary.

"Yes, but I haven't been there yet. I decided to get something to eat first. I was waiting for him to show me where ..." she stopped speaking when she noticed the old woman who'd come in with Anthony moving towards her at a snail's pace. The lady had remained near the entrance, reading a book, during the commotion.

"Cybersausage told me to help you to your apartment. I can take you there now if you want." The wrinkled and shrunken woman was barely understandable, likely due to the strain of age stretching her vocal chords.

Crissa helped Sasha lift Anthony, with Sasha carrying most of the weight. Still, she was glad for the aide. They ambled through the factory floor and into a lengthy hallway, inches at a time. Sasha anticipated the old woman might die any second. The lady kept shuffling her feet, then stopping, shuffling, stopping, shuffling, stopping ... and if Sasha had hair anymore she would have ripped every strand out in frustration. Anthony's snoring certainly didn't help calm her nerves either.

"Sounds like two gremlins fighting," Crissa said, grimacing at Anthony's gaping maw.

"Gremlins?" Sasha had never heard the term before, but for some reason the image of a small, fury creature with big slit-pupil eyes filled her imagination.

"Savage, pointy-eared beasts. They snarl and growl like this big guy."

"Here," the withered woman declared, standing still in front of a metal door with the number 114 on it. She lethargically crooked and stretched for the handle. She barely twisted the knob, then was unable to apply enough force forward to open the door.

"I've got it," Crissa said, thrusting open the door with her hip. She helped Sasha put Anthony on the bed. "Let me know if you need anything. I'm always happy to help a kick-ass doll like you." She winked and left hurriedly, pushing the old woman through the door in front of her. The swift exist was undoubtedly to get far away from Anthony's snarling snores.

Sasha scanned her surroundings. This apartment must belong to someone else – there were used towels strewn about, dirty rags in the sink, and the trash was full of crimson bandages. Then she spotted clothes on the bathroom floor. Burgundy pants and a pink silk robe – Jordan and Catherine. *Where were they?*

She riffled through the entire apartment, collecting evidence and assessing the situation. Either Catherine or Jordan had been severely injured, but didn't get brought to triage. How peculiar.

In the kitchen she found a tray of cubes in the ice box. A cold compress would help reduce the swelling inside Anthony's skull. The last thing that man needed was brain damage.

There were no clean rags, so she got a pair of folded briefs from the chest of drawers and stuck ice cubes inside. She laid on the bed next to Anthony, gently lifting his bald head and placing the ice behind it and then let his head softly fall back down. With no hair, snoring, and drooling, he was still more attractive than any man she'd ever met. A chiseled god.

She lay next to him, watching his large chest steadily raise and lower. As she waited for him to awake, she wondering how she'd gotten into this mess. Ever since she'd run into this big zadrota, her mind wasn't her own. She'd saved his life the day they met and what did she get in return? Her whole career down the toilet.

She was starting to question her own motives. Had she come forward with the truth to Alluri, would he have listened? She'd told herself he wouldn't have, that his greed would have caused him to turn a blind eye to the murders, the sickness, the risks. He'd probably have tossed her aside too, for knowing the truth. That is what she told herself when she decided to help Anthony; but, was it true?

She took off her jacket, inspecting the dark streaks on her bicep and forearm. The skin felt the same, it was like a tattoo. But it wasn't raised like a fresh tattoo would be. She'd studied the Quinta virus in the lab, but Dr. Steinman was the only one to use it on patients. He'd charged ahead before she was done with her research in Kirishi on the liquid vials she'd gotten less than a week before. Dr. Steinman's heedless human experimentation was one of the reasons she insisted on going to Mesa Heights and investigating his work in person.

Had this Quinta virus driven Dr. Steinman mad? Or was it the combination of viruses and bacteria uncovered in the labs buried within the mine? Would she go mad and start murdering people too, like Dr. Steinman? She shivered at the thought and moved closer to Anthony's warm body.

Would Anthony go mad? No, he was so controlled today. He even looked like he wanted to apologize to those ... those

... there was no word. They thought she was a sexual object, not a person. She could *see* the grotesque things they imagined, so vile. The images were foreign in her mind, and intrusive. Like being witness to her own rape in detail. It made her want to scratch out her eyeballs. Maybe that's what happened to Daniel's eyes – he'd seen too much. The white scars on his lids meant he'd gained his enhanced vision through trauma.

The door flung open, and the very man she'd just been thinking about appeared.

Daniel immediately asked, "Where is Catherine?"

"Catherine, huh? What? Where am I?" Anthony sat up, holding the back of his head and blinking.

"She isn't here. Neither is Jordan," Sasha answered. She stood up as nonchalantly as she could from where she'd been in the bed. Laying so close to Anthony suddenly felt too intimate of a position to be in with Daniel's perceptive gaze on her.

"I thought she was with you." Anthony attempted to fish out the cold compress that fell down the back of his jacket when he'd sat up. He quivered and shook as the briefs emptied ice inside his shirt and onto his bare skin.

Cybersausage came into the room behind Daniel. "Oh my. What happened to you, gorgeous?" he asked Anthony, taking in the scene, likely noticing the blood splatter on both Anthony and Sasha.

"I'll tell you what happened, your guys attacked us in the cafeteria." Anthony glowered at Cybersausage. He managed to put the ice pack back together and pressed it against his head.

"I see. I'm so sorry about that. My gosh, I've had to replace the furniture in there nearly a dozen times this year." He sat down on the chair near the door and crossed his metal legs. He smiled down at the appendages, uncrossed them and then crossed them again before continuing, "It's one of the few places we gather, so it makes for a spectacular stage to show off in front of others. Even if you're showing off how much of a jerk you can be."

"Do you know where Catherine and Luca might be, Cybersausage?" Daniel probed. His quick assessment of the situation indicated he'd realized the blood was not Anthony or Sasha's and they were fine, minus a bump on Anthony's head.

Sasha could almost *feel* his mind working. She sensed his urgency to ... l eave tonight? His golden eyes were suddenly on her, unblinking.

"I honestly don't know. If they aren't here or in the cafeteria, then I can only imagine they may have left. I spread the word not to engage with Luca, so if he decided to leave I suspect that no one would have stopped him."

Daniel's gaze switched back to Cybersausage, and Sasha let out the breath she'd unknowingly been holding. "What do you mean left?" he asked, but she could have sworn she heard, "Find them, now."

"I'll have Esha investigate, she has Watchers all over this area. Her owls can literally find a needle in a haystack."

"Alight. Then we head out, now." Daniel's words were a command, Sasha felt herself walking towards the door, without even questioning why ... or where they were going. Anthony was right behind her.

"We'll need a few more of my men. Oooh and we'll need to visit the armory!" Cybersausage led the way through the chaotic factory floor.

Men were busy overhauling trucks, SUVs, and other vehicles – weaponizing and reinforcing them with steel plates underneath. In one corner of the factory was a paint station, where they were busily applying green camouflage with their group logo on the side of more automobiles.

The armory was on the highest level of the building. When the elevator arrived Cybersausage inputted a code into a door control box, and then put his eyes up to the retinal scanner on the side. The scanner lit-up green and the door clicked. They walked into a room that had to take up the whole upper floor. It was like a grocery store, but exclusively for weapons ... aisle after aisle of guns, bows, knives, grenades, swords, axes ... Each aisle had a large black and white banner with a number on it.

"I'll be downstairs gathering the troops. Take what you need and get a few more for, say four or five more guys? Meet me by the hangar doors we passed in the factory below –the yellow ones. Oh, and don't forget bullets, they're on aisles twelve through twenty. Have fun!" Cybersausge left cheerily marching out the door at almost a skip. That man was far too happy.

"Why do we need weapons? Where are we going?" Anthony asked, he was practically licking his lips at all the weapons.

"We may run into Tripod's gang again, or rats." Daniel said, visually perusing the room. Besides a slight head movement he stood still, will Sasha and Anthony on either side of him.

"Rats?" Sasha had no idea why that was important for Daniel to mention. Rats were no threat. Unless there were thousands of rats, then that could be a problem.

"Yes, supposedly giant ones. Anthony, what weapons would you suggest?" The uncertainty in Daniel's voice felt outlandish and both Sasha and Anthony turned to gawk at him. He didn't know what weapons to choose? There was something *Daniel* didn't know?

"I ... I don't know. I hunt elk, deer, occasionally a turkey ... I've never –"

"Any of these rifles look familiar, Anthony?" Daniel expected a twenty-four-year-old man from a heavily gun-restricted country to know about assault weapons. Anthony could barely handle the hunting rifle he'd brought when they'd high-jacked the helicopter.

"Follow me." Sasha directed the men through the aisles, picking out automatic assault rifles and tossing each man three. Her favorite section was knives –butterflies, stilettos, machetes ..."I suggest you each carry at least one." She picked four for herself.

Then she found the aisle with clothing. "Put on a couple of those vests." She nodded towards the line of hanging Kevlar while she went to rummage through a bin filled with waist bands, straps, and pouches. The straps for her knives anchored nicely through the slats in her new legs. The utility belts she found would hold four magazines each.

"Do I want to know how you know about this stuff, Sasha?" Anthony caught the knife strap she threw at him and slid it through the tubing of his right 'thigh.'

She tossed both men a few utility belts. "Put one of those on your waists."

The men followed her directions and then trailed her as she headed to aisle twelve.

"Sasha, you never answered me." Anthony asked.

"No ... I ... maybe Daniel will explain." She filled up a magazine with 39 mm bullets. The bullets all had the anarchist's logo etched on the side and X's carved-out on the top. She shook her head, "Zadrotas." These fools who'd carved the bullets probably thought the X's made them deadlier, all it did was make them less accurate.

"I am at a loss, I do not know much about you Sasha Mikhailov. You're the research director at Greggo Sands in Kirishi Russia. You have a PhD in Chemical Engineering from Saint-Petersburg University, as well as a bachelor's in Biomedical Engineering." Daniel filled rifle magazines with the 39 mm bullets and loaded them into a pouch strapped to his waist. "Nothing that would suggest a knowledge of firearms."

Anthony stood on the other side of her, doing the same thing as Daniel, but eyeballing her with judgment that she wasn't sure she deserved.

"When I met you Anthony, I had two assignments. One – to find out why the viruses were being leaked out into the local lake in Mesa Heights. Two –to bring back any new findings to my home country."

"You mean report it back to Alluri?" Anthony queried. "So he could sell it and make money off of people losing their lives?" He had some trouble packing the rifle magazine using his new prosthetic hands, he kept crushing the magazine and bullets.

"No, that is not who I, ultimately, report to, Anthony." She watched as the information sank in. It took a minute, he wasn't exactly a speedy thinker. She finished all four of her magazines and began helping him load his bullets before the shock hit him.

"And what will you do with the ... information ... that you now have?" Daniel's glowing eyes met hers and she kept her thoughts on the munitions in her hands ... one, two, three ... she counted the bullets going into the magazine.

"If we make it out of here alive ..." Anthony added. "Is this –" he held out an AK-47, "–l going to help us against the radiation out there? I mean, we're probably all going to die from the exposure we've already had."

Anthony sure was handsome, but he didn't catch on fast. She could at least let him know he wasn't going to die, of radiation anyway, "Your government, what you like to call Central, has been lying to you."

"What? There was never a nuclear explosion?" Anthony was stunned. He actually believed that there wasn't an explosion? He had to have lived through the radioactive dust, even if he was a toddler ... that was hard to forget.

"No, there was. Only the first blast that hit Anaheim was small, and exploded before touching ground. There is hardly any radiation here, or any of the west coast cities that were firmed upon. Antiballistic missiles caught all the ICBM's mid-air. The missiles still caused extensive damage, but the wall was built in fear of an invasion that never happened."

"That explains why there are so many people here ..." Anthony leaned back against the shelf of magazines and crossed his arms, deep in thought.

Daniel added, "I must admit, I am no expert in radiation. Even I thought the area we needed to get into tonight would be dangerously radioactive until Cybersausage told me otherwise. Central hid the information well." His hands were quick! He completed all four of his magazines, sixteen more for Cybersausage's men, and put the last bullet in his second magazine for Anthony in the time it took for her to finish all of hers and half of Anthony's.

Sasha motioned for the men to follow her as she headed to aisle forty, explosives, and attached two SIP grenades to her new utility belt. "I'm sure there is some radiation, the whole world isn't what it used to be and there isn't a place on this planet unaffected by the dust, but we won't die from it ... tonight."

"Well that is a relief! Where are we going, anyway?" Anthony picked a piece of green leaf from his teeth, likely from the salad he engulfed earlier.

"Downstairs." Daniel gave Sasha a stare that made her think he was considering tossing her out the nearest window. She turned away from his mesmerizing gaze to see Anthony's back – he'd loaded up with their supplies and was marching out the door. Her heart started to beat out of her throat as she turned back to Daniel's tractor-beam eyes.

"Please, I thought you knew ..." she said, backing away.

"What are you doing here, Dr. Mikhailov?" he more than asked, the question pounded in her head.

"Your research Dr. Jahren, is amazing." She backed away further, and he followed. "Why would you want to hide it from the world? Reprogramming viruses to aid in red blood cell formation, liver enzyme production, even thickening sinew! These can help so many people. And the prosthetics –"

"Вы избегаете моего вопроса." He pointed out her evasion of the question, in flawless Russian.

"Пожалуйста, не знаю ..." She tried to plead unawareness, but he wasn't buying it. His eyes narrowed and his fists clenched. She figured there was no point in evading further, he might rip the truth out of her. "I found out Dr. Steinman was murdering people, and was going to kill Anthony." Her back touched against the wall and Daniel came closer as she said, "And Anthony has such conviction –"

"It is not his faith that you are interested in, Dr. Mikhailov." Daniel stood less than a foot from her, and she saw pity in his eyes. Was that empathy in reference to her attraction for Anthony?

"I'm only human, please," she begged, not sure of how human Daniel was anymore but hoping he would buy that she was here for Anthony ... which in part, was true.

"I am as human as you are ... what are you planning to do with your Mod?" he asked.

"My what?"

"The microchip implanted in your head. You must have guessed by now that it does more than run the prosthetics you've been using adeptly to back away from me while we have been having an innocent conversation. Innocent if you have nothing to hide."

"I don't know –"

"Don't lie to me." His eyes were mirrors, and she saw gold symbols flashing behind them. Inside her head his words were making a screaming echo. *Don't lie to me, Don't lie to me, Don't lie to me! Are you planning to take your Mod back to Russia?*

"Yes." The Mod is the exact technology RS-13 wanted her to find and bring back from the mine. He top mission priority.

"Yes, what?"

She got the feeling he knew the answer, only that he wanted her to say it aloud. "Yes, I think this 'Mod' is something I would be expected to take back to my home country."

"Do you realize the potential it has if put into the wrong hands?" Daniel crossed his arms, looming over her like a chastising father.

Visions of men attacking and moving against their will filled Sasha's mind. Of men made into slaves to an invisible force.

"Do you think your own government is so much better than ours? That anyone could be trusted with this power?" His question held gravity.

Visions of Russia invading China, and through India, with a cyborg army.

"No." As she said it, she realized the inevitable consequences. The Mods could change ... everything. Who could be trusted?

He breathed a sigh of relief, and adjusted his magazine pouches on his chest strap over the thick Kevlar vest to match how she'd placed hers.

"But, how is it okay for you to possess this technology? Who is to stop you from inflicting your will on anyone? Or everyone?"

"That is not what I want. I never meant for this ... for any of it." Exasperated, he turned away from her and then put his back to the wall beside her. "The Mod you have, it was originally designed to control the prosthetics. That is all. My brother Cliff lost his legs experimenting with microorganisms to make him stronger. A few of those viruses and bacterium your company was able to uncover."

"Amazing work, Dr. Jahren. The way you were able to get the separate strains to enhance each other, to make a synergistic system that harnessed the endocrine system's innate abilities ... truly remarkable."

"My father's, mostly." He explained. "My focus was on neurology, and prosthetics."

"I am grateful." She raised her right leg and lowered it. "Less than 48 hours ago these were flesh and blood, now I walk around as if I've had metal legs my whole life. Simply miraculous technology."

"We designed those prosthetics together, Cliff and I. He wanted something he could use to control his new limbs from his mind. I ... I wanted to help. But, Cliff ... he was able to twist it, turn it into something more. Susan, the one who invented the microchips, she knew ... long before I did. The one she put into my head after ... after Cliff ..." Whatever it was, Daniel couldn't bring himself to say it, a deep tragedy emanated from his every breath. He swallowed hard and cleared his throat. "The Mod I have was made to be more advanced. Susan made it to protect me from him, knowing Cliff was spiraling out of control. She hoped I could stop him ... but I couldn't ... and she suffered greatly for my inadequacy."

His microchip was more advanced, still he feared her taking the one she had to Russia? That didn't add up quite right. "My Mod, it can't do what yours does? I can't put thoughts in people's head and control them like you?"

"Maybe, maybe one day you will, even with the older version of the Mod. Biological organisms tend to evolve, as you know. The human mind is especially good at adapting, and some people are more naturally prone to being able to manipulate the microchip. It took me decades to get to where I am now, and I still don't dare face Cliff, even though his Mod is not as advanced."

"Are you trying to get as far away from him as you can? Why are we here in LA? Where are we going tonight? Does Cliff truly have a virus then? I bet there isn't a virus."

"You know, those steel blue eyes of yours feel like blades when you ask questions in rapid fire like that." He gave her a sideways look and began heading towards the door, picking up the rifles and ammo belts he'd laid down earlier on his way.

She fetched her rifle and hurriedly caught up. "Am I right? Cliff doesn't have a virus? We're here for something else, aren't we?"

"No, no and yes."

"Right." She couldn't help but be intrigued, what more was there?

"You remind me of my father," he said, smiling down at her while he chivalrously held the armory door open. "Insatiably curious, to a fault."

Chapter 14

Escape from LA

The sun was getting real low. Jordan checked the hazy orange horizon for a good place to bunker down for the night. Shadows danced as he ran through the Mojave Desert, northeast of LA in the area north of what used to be Palmdale, CA. Two days of no sleep and he was starting to feel like everything moved around him.

He figured Daniel or Cybersausage's Forsaken would expect him to go south. He'd stolen supplies and a truck without anyone noticing, and removed the tracking device near the driver side rotor and driven off in the middle of the night. He'd managed to get out of LA with no tails. None that he could see anyway. It had all been way too easy, which made him think he might be missing something.

"How ... much ... further?" Catherine asked, bent forward and sucking in air between words. They'd been jogging in the open desert since ditching the truck in a residential neighborhood a few hours ago. Jordan ran ahead and could see only Joshua trees and Creosote bushes for miles in every direction. They would have to camp out in the open, completely exposed.

Out of breath, and lungs burning, Jordan said, "We ... can stop ... here." He took position between a Joshua tree and the only decently sized boulder he'd seen for miles. He figured the six-foot-wide, three-foot-tall, granite rock would provide some cover.

Catherine set her bag down next to the large stone and fell to her knees, gasping for air. "Oh ... thank goodness! I thought ... we would ... never stop."

Jordan set his bag down on the east end of the boulder, then sat next to it. He peered behind them, around the rock, to the southwest for any signs of followers. Nothing. They were alone. He opened his bag and chugged back the cannister of water from inside. He waited until he caught his breath before saying, "Tomorrow we should make the border wall tunnel before noon, it's about 8 miles straight east of here."

"And the tunnel, how long is that? Are you sure its still there?" Catherine crawled over to Jordan. She put her back against the boulder and pulled her bag onto her lap, then closed her eyes. A bark scorpion crept towards her hand along her backpack and Jordan flung it away before she opened her eyes wide and asked, "What was that?"

"We need to create a parameter, use this –" he unloaded a container with a waxy substance inside that smelled like eucalyptus and handed it to her, "– to spread on any rocks, sticks ... anything laying around. Look out for scorpions, they aren't deadly but the sting will make you wish you were dead for the next eight hours."

"How far do I spread this out?" She began smearing the waxy repellant on her bag and the boulder behind her.

"Six feet in every direction," Jordan replied, gathering dried brush to make a fire. The temperature was getting low enough in the high desert for them to start shivering in their sweat-drenched clothes. The bone-dry sand had a way of drawing out moisture, and the evaporating sweat made it feel ten degrees colder.

"I wish we were still in the truck." She started visibly shaking and chattering her teeth.

Jordan hurriedly got the fire started and ushered her next to him. She snuggled up under his arm and he drew a thermal blanket over the two of them, followed by another tan one he'd brought for camouflage. He put a bag between himself and the freezing cold boulder and laid back, pulling her body onto his right side. Once she stopped chattering and shaking, it was pleasant. They stared into the rising flames as darkness descended and the stars came out in a canopy of twinkling lights above.

How long had it been since he'd held someone close like this? Seven years? He'd been alone for so long. He hadn't exactly wanted to let anyone close. To love was to lose, and he wondered how much of his heart he had left to give. Catherine made him feel warm inside and out. He'd forgotten how comforting it felt.

"Thank you," he barely heard Catherine say softly. Her face was right below his chin, and he could feel her breathing on his forearm as he held her snugly.

"For what?"

"Everything."

Jordan kissed her forehead and hugged her closer. He was unsure what to say. Catherine was nothing but trouble. The kind of trouble he couldn't help but get into, apparently. How many times had he been close to death the last few days? Four? But, he also hadn't felt so alive in so long ... A pack of coyotes howling to the east reminded him that they were still not quite safely out of trouble. He tensed, listening to see if the coyotes were getting closer or moving away. Away. He relaxed again.

"How is you back feeling?" Catherine asked, likely thinking his tense movements were from pain and not the threat of a coyote pack descending.

"I can't feel a thing. I have no idea what my back looks like; but, I'm confident its healed. Daniel is quite a miraculous doctor." Not only did his back feel fine, but all the aches and pains in his body from years of fighting were gone as well. It was mind blowing, especially considering he hadn't slept in days.

"How are we going to alert Central when we get to the other side?" Catherine's hand was on his chest, her fingers playing with the hair sticking out the top of his coverall zipper. She yawned, and he could feel her breathing steadying for sleep.

"Inside the tunnel there is a callbox."

"A callbox?" She yawned again. "A callbox sounds ... official."

It made him yawn, and his eyes blurred the brush bbq into a yellow mass. He blinked, eyes fading to more closed than open.

"Won't they find out who you are if you use it? Will you get in trouble?" She tilted her head back, gazing up at him. Her lips were so close to his, her body so warm it radiated her pheromones upward, intoxicating him. He tilted his chin downward compulsively going in for a kiss.

He stopped himself close enough to feel the heat of her lips next to his and drew his chin back. He wanted to kiss her so badly but instead answered, “That is a risk I’m willing to take.” They locked eyes for a few seconds. Then she glanced down at his lips, and bit her lower lip before laying her head back below his chin.

She wasn’t ready to admit her feelings and he wasn’t going to push it. He wanted her to want him and he knew he was still trying to live down the kidnapping incident in her mind. After their last kiss, she’d purposefully kept her distance from him. So, as a show of good faith, he was letting her make the decisions. Even leaving The Forsaken headquarters had been her idea. A great idea it was too, he couldn’t stand the sight of them. He couldn’t wait to rip the green coveralls off and burn them as soon as he found new clothes.

The desert was so quiet that he could hear the rhythm of Catherine’s heart. It was erratic at first, then calmed. Her breathing slowed and she began to faintly snore. The peacefulness lulled Jordan’s eyelids closed and he fell into a deep slumber.

Flashes of images. So quick it was hard to pick out details. Jordan saw Catherine in his arms, then she was Maria, then she was his mother, then a skeleton and the coyotes were gnawing on its bones, dragging them from under the blanket.

He fought back the rabid animals but they grew in size and were now five scorpions with the heads of men. He battled them in Tripod’s arena. He brandished two long swords and sliced the scorpion-men’s abdomens. They gushed yellow ooze that burned to the touch, emitting yellow fumes. The odor of sulfur and seared flesh filled the air. They stung his back with razor blades on their tails, over and over and over.

He tried to stab back with both of his swords, going numb in his arms and then he collapsed face forward in the dirt.

He stood on a boulder and was alone, nothing anywhere except a sandy desert. The sand began to drown him in an ocean of pebbles, Creosote bushes and Joshua trees. He held his breath as his head went under. He figured he would eventually run out of oxygen, but he never did. He opened his mouth to breath and what filled his lungs was surprisingly cool and clean air.

He felt sucked forward by the air, hauled out of his desert sand grave.

He walked up behind Catherine, she was talking to another man. She turned to him and said words he couldn't understand. They stood in the Mojave Desert, near the border wall at the location he'd planned to take her in the morning. The man had laughing bright blue eyes, and looked somewhat familiar. But, before Jordan could place where he'd seen him, Catherine motioned her hand towards Jordan's chest.

He felt flung backwards and the man and Catherine faded to nothing. He floated in blackness, a deep lonely expanse. There was a faint sound, getting louder in the distance. *Whooo.Hoowhooooo.*

Jordan opened his eyes, jolted awake as he heard the sound again. *Whoo. Hoowhooooo.* An owl, circling above. He swiftly and carefully kicked out the flames with the fine sand, so fine it was like dust. He kept his movements small so it didn't draw too much attention or wake Catherine. Then he laid as still as he could.

The horizon began to shift to a lighter blue than the deep purple of pure night. It must be an hour or so before sunrise. He listened for more from the owl. It could be an emissary for The Forsaken or it could just be a natural predator hunting for mice in the bushes.

"Cliff, no! Stop!" Catherine mumbled in her sleep. He gingerly glided the blanket over her head to muffle the noise of her nightmare.

He surveyed the sky. The only thing he could hear was his own blood pounding in his veins. Then a swooshing noise from behind the boulder and a four-foot shadow appeared over their campsite. He tilted his head back to see a great horned owl peering down at him, its head turned sideways while it perched on the stone, mere inches from his face. Its sharp talons were reinforced with steel strips and the top of its head, right between the large pointed ears, had a black box embedded with a red led flashing. Definitely not natural.

"Up, we have to go now!" He shook Catherine awake and began searching through his bag, owl watching the entire time. He pulled out a device that he wasn't sure would help. He'd found it near the bug repellant canister in the supply cabinets at The Forsaken base, and assumed it was for coyotes. But maybe it would work on owls too. He pressed the button on top of the can shaped device and an excruciatingly loud noise was emitted. The bird flew away, directly southwest. He pressed the button to stop the noise before his own eardrums bled, then threw the device into his bag, along with the blankets.

Catherine took her hands off her ears and said, "Maybe a little warning next time?"

"That was a scout, they know our position. We need to haul it to the border wall. Now!"

"Jordan ... ummm ... there is something I need to tell you."

"Tell me while we –"

"No, stop." She took his arm before he could sling his backpack across his back. "We can't go to the border wall, we have to go back."

"What? What do you mean go back, we're almost there!" There was no way in hell he was going back.

"Cliff, he will be there –"

"Cliff? As in Daniel's brother Cliff?"

"Yes." She sat on the boulder, wringing her hands and glancing nervously to the east. Exactly in the direction of the border wall entrance. A direction she should know nothing about.

"Catherine ..." he shook his head and sat next to her, letting his bag drop. "What is it that you need to tell me?"

The sky was getting lighter by the minute, Jordan half expected Cybersausage and his men to pull up any second in off-road vehicles. He waited patiently for her to find the words, she kept opening her mouth to talk, then stopping.

"I have these dreams ... I know I told you about my dreams of cyborgs and you found that article on Daniel and Cliff. Then you did more research and started to freak out about viruses."

"Yes, I clearly remember that." He hadn't 'freaked out,' but he didn't want to argue.

"Okay, its just ... hard ... you know, to know where to start."

"So, you dreamed Cliff was waiting for us at the border?"

"Yes." She answered, quizzically.

"Then we should head north for a while, I know another way." He stood up, lifting Catherine up with him, and began marching north. He had no intention of going back into LA, for any reason.

Catherine followed and, after a few steps, she said, "Wait ... why is it so easy for you to believe in my dreams? Even before Daniel showed up, you knew ... I didn't even know it was real. How? Jordan, how did you know?"

They were not maintaining nearly the pace as yesterday, but they wouldn't need to go far because there was an old military base they could hide out in, until they figured-out the best path. It was less than 5 miles.

"Jordan, you never answered me ... how is it that you believe my dreams are real?"

He slowed down to let her catch up and answered, "We experimented on different interrogation techniques when I was in Army Intelligence. One device we used was able to project images, thoughts from a person, in another room while they were interviewed. We found that if we kept the person in a room, let them fall asleep, we could get even more intel. The images weren't the best, blurry shapes, mismatched colors ... but it was better than nothing. One day we left two people in a room at once. Intermittently the images were exactly the same, at exactly the same time."

They'd crested a hill and the dry lake bed blared white-blue with the imminent sunrise. As Catherine came over the hill, she slid on the fine sand and pebbles and almost landed on her butt before Jordan caught her and then she nearly dragged him down too.

"Sorry!" She clung to his bicep.

"The lake bed silt is slippery. The hardened exterior betrays the moist interior."

She got the hang of it and kept moving, feet crunching the cracked lake bed surface. "So, the two people, they were dreaming of the same thing at once?" she asked after a few minutes of being mesmerized by the strange surface she was treading on. Parts of the white clay sparkled in the dim light.

"Yes. We did the experiment a few more times, with other sets of people and it didn't happen again for a while. Then one day, with a person whose images were the clearest I've ever seen, it happened again ... only for much longer."

The area they traversed was so flat that the horizon rippled in front of them. There were rolling hills in the distance, black against the blue horizon. A giant aircraft hangar, white in front of one of the black hills, was their destination and they were bee-lining straight for it.

"What you're saying is that some people can affect other people's dreams?" Catherine pulled out two of the purple vials, emptied them into a sixteen ounce water bottle, took a few swigs and offered the rest to Jordan.

He drank more than half of what remained in one gulp, then answered, "Yes, and with what I found out about the Jahren's prosthetics being run on brain implants ... and what you told me about him appearing in your dreams and saying he was 'asleep,' it wasn't hard to come to the conclusion that the implants amplified this phenomenon."

"You knew? All along? You knew?" She held his arm, halting him from moving forward. She came around to face him, glaring up at him through squinted eyes.

"I told you from the beginning, don't you remember? I was going to show you the research I'd done. Then you came in with that foolishness about Anthony and his hair-brained idea to blow up the mine ... I had to stop you, to protect you."

"But the viruses ... you said you were trying to protect me from viruses. At your cabin, that's what you said. I definitely remember that."

"I was trying to protect you, and myself, from viruses. There are viruses. Daniel's father, Martin Jahren, used them to create medicine. He played around with some very deadly strains too ... one that wiped out all of the Desert Grande area, several times over, during the last few centuries." He stood there, waiting for her to understand. She just crossed her arms and stood her ground, squinting even more.

"I'm confused ... you agreed with me that there were no viruses not even forty eight hours ago."

"Catherine, of course there are viruses. But, what I agreed with you about is that whatever it is Daniel is searching for in LA, whatever it is he needs *you* for ... it has nothing to do with a virus." He could see a light go on in her eyes, and he took that to mean she understood. "Come on, those owls could be back any second." He glanced backward, no sign of birds, SUVs, anything ... but that didn't mean they weren't on their way.

Catherine began ambling forward, deep in thought. Jordan walked beside her, waiting for the inevitable questions.

"So, Jordan, you're so smart that you figured it all out. Tell me, what does Daniel want with me?"

A few things popped into Jordan's head that he was definitely not going to share with Catherine at that moment. Daniel's eyes literally lit-up every time he looked at her, the guy was completely enamored. But, Jordan knew there was more to it than that. "Catherine ... I ... I dreamed about you last night. You were talking to Cliff, standing at the border wall."

"I didn't think you would ... I mean, you were there for an instant and ... I'm sorry for pushing you out. When you appeared it solidified the area, even the number on the entrance ... you were showing him everything!"

"I was?"

"Yes. He is so powerful in dreams ... he can extract things from the deepest recesses of your mind, control your emotions, play with your thoughts. Daniel warned me, but I ... I can be so stupid sometimes." She started marching forward.

"You are far from stupid, Catherine." He kept pace. "Daniel says many strange things, I like to ignore him too."

They now briskly hiked over a broken-up runway. The tarmac was crumbled to pieces, and Jordan nearly twisted his ankle on a deep crevice. This time Catherine caught him before he fell.

"I don't know what to do ... Cliff wants me to meet him in Idaho. He gave me a piece of paper with an address that is burned in my mind: 1020 S Manitou Ave, Boise, ID. He says that Daniel has been lying to us and Daniel is the one who is trying to take over the world, not Cliff."

They reached the building, and Jordan kicked open a regular door next to the slightly ajar aircraft sized entrance. He couldn't believe what he was hearing from Catherine. How could she believe for an instant what Cliff was saying? Was Cliff *that* persuasive in dreams?

Jordan had never been in this building before, but knew it was stocked with weapons, vehicles, fuel and food in an underground emergency bunker. He simply needed to find a way down, and hoped he remembered to codes right. He'd been given access years ago in case he needed to use it as a hide-away. He scanned the open, empty space through the low light from the sunrise coming in through the ajar hangar door, as well as the busted-up glass above. He reached into his bag for a light band and so did Catherine, they both strapped the bands above their foreheads. He pointed to a stairwell to the far left, "There."

Catherine followed on his heels, leaving small footprints next to his much bigger ones in the almost inch-thick dust on the hangar floor. "What do you think, Jordan?"

They climbed down the stairwell filled with spiderwebs. No one must have been here in over a decade. "I think many things."

"C'mon." She kept directly behind him, avoiding all contact with spiderwebs.

"Fine. I think that Cliff is lying to you, manipulating you. I think deep down you know that."

"Okay, fair enough. What about Daniel and his claim about needing my help to stop a virus?"

"I think that Daniel has special plans for you that you aren't going to like. I think there are viruses, but there is no way a virus could 'enslave' people like Daniel said, so I think he must be lying too."

He found the entrance to the hallway that should lead to the bunker, and put in a code he hoped would work. Red flashing lights. "Dammit." He tried another code and more red flashes. He struggled to think of what the code could be, then he noticed something scratched into the coating on the metal door frame above. "Bunch of morons," he said as he entered the numbers and the door control lit up green.

"Let me get this right ... you believe in people communicating in dreams, you believe in cyborgs that can control your mind, but you stop at viruses that can enslave people? Why would Daniel lie about that?"

She had a point. The man was annoying, but Daniel had been honest about everything else. "It's ... just not what viruses do." Was it possible? That would be like some kind of ... zombie virus. There was a cordyceps fungus that zombified ants, but that was a fungus, not a virus. "It doesn't matter, anyway."

They traversed a fifteen-foot-wide, round-roofed tunnel that had about a 20-degree decline. There was a steel double door on the end, 50 feet down.

"What if you're wrong, Jordan? What if I'm wrong? What if Cliff is going to kill everyone, or enslave them with a virus? What if Daniel's plan is the only thing that can stop him, and he needs me? What if –"

He took her by the shoulders and wanted to shake her but instead said, "Catherine, stop!" He realized that came out too harshly and let go. He turned back to the last door and said, much more gently, "Catherine ... we can 'what-if' all day long and it doesn't change a thing."

She practically glared holes in his face. "And why is that?"

He'd been inputting number combinations into the control box next to the bunker entrance and getting nothing. He made rhymes for each of his codes, translating numbers to letters to spell out something he could use in a rhyme. It was a way for him to commit vast amounts of data to long term memory. Typically, his rhymes had to do with the place they dealt with, and so he knew this one had to rhyme with Muroc. The combination had to have six letters ... he tried squawk, enlock ... was it warlock? No, that was seven letters ...This could take all night! Wait ... was it 'o'clock'? He inputted 7-2-5-7-2-5 and the lock clicked.

He held open the door and said, "Because we are about to alert Central."

Chapter 15

Indomitable Rats

The open-top, amphibious, jeep-like vehicles owned by Cybersausage's gang had no problem conquering the mixed-terrain into Anaheim. They took two, each held four people. An small, but elite group. Those not driving were required to keep watch for threats along the way. The jeeps were otherwise not well protected. In fact, they had nothing to shield from road bombs because the weight of steel plates would be too much for the underwater portion of the voyage.

Daniel sat behind Cybersausage, who controlled drones and communicated with base intel using headgear and a backpack similar to what Esha had worn. He scouted the path ahead. Another man sat in the back with Daniel and had his AK-47 automatic assault rifle drawn and ready over his rolled-down window. The other amphibious vehicle held Sasha, Anthony and two more of Cybersausage's men, each with rifles drawn and ready.

Everyone was tense, this was a hostile area. It was uninhabited due to the higher level of radiation. However, it bordered Tripod's territory, therefore his assassins might take notice and decide the small, vulnerable party was an easy target. So far the trip was eerily quiet, and dead still outside the moving jeeps.

They took a path into Anaheim from the northeast, which had the least damaged streets. They traveled west on what used to be the California 91 Express. They made better time than before the war when there would be stop and go traffic on the road at this hour. The Santa Ana River covered most of the broken-up freeway in a few inches of water. All buildings they passed had broken out windows. Some buildings were completely collapsed with palm trees already growing within the remains.

Every orifice or every structure held a possible sniper in waiting. The seven quadcopter drones were equipped with detonators, and could be used as aerial bombs, if needed.

Cybersausage maintained flawless control, sending drones into buildings and back while he sat in his jeep moving at forty miles an hour.

Daniel experimented with his ocular implants. He had no idea the extent of what Dr. Brooke Dawson, their creator, programmed into them. She was heavily influenced by Cliff. When the cybernetic eyes were first installed, years ago, he realized pretty quickly that the implants were not simply for helping blind patients.

He'd never been in a war campaign, but the menu options for military purposes were impressive. He'd activated option 'campaign mode' from the many possible selections and it was remarkable. He could see an ant crawling on a structure 100 feet away and site the trajectory of his bullet as he aimed his gun.

The most fascinating finding was made before leaving the hangar. He'd noticed he could see the heat signature of people, even behind concrete walls. He knew enough about infrared technology to know its limits–the depth of penetration for infrared was less than half an inch. The heat detection system bandwidth had to be well beyond the usual infrared frequency spectrum to pick up a person behind a wall.

"Scouts report the area is clear ahead," Cybersausage yelled back over the rumble of the engine and the rubber meeting the road. "The water level is about four feet at our destination, tides going out."

That was good news. The only bad news was that they were headed straight into the setting sun. The entire skyline was an orange, hazy blur of low clouds filled with dust kicked up by the strong Santa Ana winds. There would be little light by the time they got to Susan's laboratory.

To make matters worse, Daniel had no idea what he would find there. He was going off of his gut and a few cryptic messages left on his office line when he woke for the first time, three years too late. Messages left by a desperate Susan, who didn't know if anyone survived and didn't want to say too much in case it was Cliff who heard. Daniel deleted the messages years ago, but they played in his head as if she'd spoken to him yesterday.

The first: "I still look for you in my dreams, Daniel. I hope you remember the ants."

The second: "Seattle's rain is tears long forgotten, but a new star is born."

The last: "The fates wove it long ago Daniel, please forgive me. Find me and I will explain, or search for me on a different plane. Goodbye."

From the messages, he knew that she was still alive, and found something in her research on dreams she wanted to share with him. He knew she moved on with the dreamwalker she was dating and had a child in LA.

But, the last message made no sense. The fates? It wasn't like her to believe in anything supernatural, mystical or spiritual. She was a hard-core scientist. He assumed the 'other plane' was the dream dimension, but he never succeeded in finding her there. Maybe she was long dead when he awoke and tried. The thought brought deep sadness. Years of searching for her in vain ... but the searching had lead him to Catherine. She was worth the wait.

The amphibious jeep languidly gargled into deepening water. The spray on the sides from the churning wheels smelled of salt and seaweed.

"We'll be moving at a slower click from here on out." Cybersausage explained.

Daniel glanced over the side and down into the brackish estuary. Who knew what lay beneath the murky depths. Great white sharks that could crawl on land? Hammer heads with two heads? Enlarged rats? After decades of radiation ... anything was possible. A fanged fairy mermaid for all he –

Gunfire rang out, startling Daniel. Anthony. Firing at a 'perceived' threat in the water. Cybersausage sent his drones back to inspect, and as Daniel suspected, there was nothing. However, if any of Tripod's gang was in the area, they now knew they weren't the only ones.

Daniel had to wonder if his imagining of fantastical creatures in the water might have affected Anthony. He needed to be more careful with his thoughts.

The sun no longer appeared in the sky when they reached the industrial complex with the office building that held

Susan's lab. The fading light made monsters of every shadow. The building leaned back at a ten degree angle to the south, and had several massive fissures running through the sidewalls. As high as three feet above the waterline barnacles and seaweed clung to the stained and molded concrete. The wind whipped and whistled through the openings and the only other sound for miles was the lapping of ocean waves and the occasional cry of a seagull.

They moored the jeeps to an old lamp post near the busted-open entrance in the center of the structure. The men affixed lights on the end of their riffles, and waded into the chilly water.

"Jeeze, it's cold enough to turn me into a eunuch!" Cybersausage exclaimed when everything up to his torso penetrated the water. The ebb and flow of the ocean made it difficult to stand steady as he held a wristband above the rippling surface. He pressed a button on the side of the wristband that turned on a 3-D hologram of the building structure from twenty years ago. "The main stairwell, if it's still intact, will be ten yards north once we get inside. It leads right to where we want to go."

The group followed Cybersausage through the wide entrance – a twenty-foot-tall, forty-foot-wide area that used to be made of thick glass. Daniel switched his ocular flashlight mode on when he came inside the unlit building. A few of the men who'd never seen his eyes on full beam said curse words of surprise at the bright light.

"You're welcome." Daniel said, staring straight at the staircase door and dipping his chin for emphasis.

The group took a second to catch on, Sasha following his vision first. They waded through the debris-filled foyer and reached the staircase door. Two of Cybersausage's men took turns throwing their entire body weight at the door, but were unsuccessful. It was either locked or covered in water enough to seal it tight. Then Anthony came around and pushed the door open with such force that it flew off its hinges, busted up the wall, and sent a two-foot wave back to completely drench the entire group.

"Sorry," Anthony said, genuinely chagrined at soaking everyone. However, he had a slight smirk that gave away his feelings about his new strength. He stood next to the door embedded in the wall, head down, apologizing to each person as they walked up the stairs.

Cybersausage splashed Anthony in the face with water and Sasha called him a Zadrota.

"Thanks." Daniel pushed the 'humble' Anthony forward, and up the stairs ahead of him.

Less than thirty seconds later Cybersausage called down from up above, "Umm, guys, we have a problem."

Daniel squeezed past the group piled up on the second set of stairs, close to where the second story floor should be. There were no more stairs for a good ten feet above their heads, and much of the second story level of the building was missing. It was completely unstable. "Is there another stairwell?"

Cybersausage projected the floorplan from his wristband. "Yes, we can try the building's southeast egress." He pointed to where they were and then where the other staircase should be in the hologram. "I'd say ... thirty or so yards south of the main entrance."

The group funneled down the staircase and back into the chilly, dark water. Desks, chairs and other debris floated on the surface with crabs, sea urchin and starfish taking refuge inside the deteriorating remains. A rancid, reddish foam covered the water's surface and was thickest around the objects they pushed out of their way. The putrid smell of rotting flesh grew stronger as they gradually moved south. The carcass of an enormous, furry animal lay between a toppled filing cabinet and a structural beam.

"One of those unusual rodents I was talking about," Cybersausage said, pointing his rifle, and light, at the decomposing corpse of a five-foot-long, two-foot-wide, bloated rat. Its eyes and lower jaw were missing, and it had a crab crawling in its mouth.

One of the men jabbed the corpse with his rifle to push it out of the path to the staircase, only to have the end of his gun sink into the decaying flesh. When he went to pull out his weapon, the body of the rat flipped over to expose its four clawed feet sticking straight up. As the rat rotated in the water, an octopus-like creature that had been clinging to its underbelly leapt onto the face of the man who'd poked at the rodent. The man started firing his gun like a blind lunatic.

Sasha tackled him, pushing his weapon into the water. Before she was able to get the gun from of the man, he'd shot so many bullets into a pillar that the building began to creak and rumble. Whole sections of the ceiling and ducting started to fall.

Chaos ensued. People were struck down with rubble from above and the building shifted in a deafening lurch.

"Hurry, to the exit!" One of the men shouted and headed back the way they'd come.

"No, to the staircase!" Daniel charged forward even though the second floor was collapsing around them. He had to get to Susan's lab, there was no turning back now.

Sasha wrestled with the man with the cephalopod on his face, dipping in and out of the water and dodging ceiling panels. She ripped at the tentacles attached at the man's head and then began stabbing with a four-inch utility knife at the giant squid-shaped grey body.

The group split, some followed Daniel to the stairs, some tried to leave until one of the men screamed, "Something bit my leg!"

"Carl, Ryan –get Marcus, now!" Cybersausage directed men to the one who was now bleeding and shooting into the water.

"There is something in here!" The man called Carl remarked, helping Ryan pull Marcus towards the staircase.

The stairwell door was open and the group made it up into the first flight before the building settled.

Daniel stopped to check Marcus's injuries. Half of his calf was missing, apparently bitten by a creature with sharp, serrated teeth. Likely a shark. Unfortunately, the thermal imaging hadn't helped Daniel see any of the cold-blooded sea creatures or he would have warned everyone.

"Where is Sasha?" Anthony asked, at almost the instant she splashed through the doorway. Splatted blue and red covered her face and body.

"Where's Robert?" Ryan, the cowardly man who'd tried to leave before Marcus got bit, demanded of Sasha.

"Whatever that thing was, it wasn't an octopus. It ate half his face before I managed to rip the thing off. The guy, Robert I'm guessing, he died from shock or venom or something ... I have no idea what, but he isn't moving," she explained, panting and dragging herself onto the staircase and out of the water. She never took her eyes off of where she'd come from, expecting another monster to pop out any second. "I think that thing is still alive."

"We have to go back!" Exclaimed the man Cybersausage had referred to as Carl.

"He's dead, Carl. You heard what Sasha said, Robert is dead. We can gather his remains on the way out after we're done. I'm sorry, we still have to get what we came for or there was no point in any of this." Cybersausage put his hand on Carl's shoulder. Carl leaned back against the wall, crossing his arms ... empty arms. "Where's you weapon? Your gear?"

"I lost the gun when an air duct nearly crushed me and I dove into the water. Then I had to detach my vest when it got stuck between the duct and a pillar and I nearly drowned." Carl was a red-haired, slightly-cubby, young man, no more than twenty-five years old. The way Cybersausage leaned in to speak comforting words in his ear, he might be his lover.

Daniel didn't want to pry. He focused on helping Marcus, creating a tourniquet for his calf and constructing a stabilizing compress so that he would be able to put weight on the leg.

Ryan knelt next to Daniel, flicking some of the reddish foam off of his jacket. "This filth is teaming with who knows what. We'll need to get him back immediately to prevent an infection. We should leave, now." Ryan's dark blue eyes flashed from the bloody leg, to Sasha and back up to Daniel. He was a middle-aged man, with balding, dirty-blond hair and a thick beard to match. He had an old burn scar on his face and neck that turned his beard white in those areas and he was missing most of his right ear.

Daniel gathered from his thoughts that Ryan had extensive experience with missions like this one, and whenever they went this poorly, this quickly, it never ended well. He didn't think any of them would make it out alive. Between Carl and Ryan's attitude and Marcus's injury, the whole group was starting to think it was best to head back already. Daniel hated being manipulative, but he projected thoughts of moving forward, at all costs, and made eye contact with everyone to make sure the message was driven in.

Anthony knelt on the other side of Marcus, facing Ryan, "We have one job to do tonight, and we're doing it."

"He's right, we're not quitters." Sasha added, sitting on the end of the stairs, weapon pointed at the water. Daniel got the impression she wanted that creature to come back, so she could drop a magazine of bullets down its ink-filled throat.

"I've dressed the wound well, an hour or so will make little difference in his condition. Marcus, can you climb? Or would you rather stay on the stairwell?" Daniel kept images of moving up the stairs in his mind, endeavoring to motivate everyone upwards.

"With a little help, I'm sure I can make it." The pain Marcus felt was evident by his clenched teeth as he spoke. He let Ryan and Anthony lift him up. He groaned, but the man was tough and wore a strained smile to show he was not about to let a missing calf stop him. He was as tall and broad as Anthony, with a dark goatee and bald head. He leaned on Anthony, who lifted him up the stairs. Anthony had no trouble carrying the guy, even Sasha could have carried Marcus on her own with the Quinta virus in her muscles.

"Good." Daniel replied, letting everyone move ahead of him so they could use the light from his eyes to see more of the path ahead than the puny light provided by their gunsights.

They made good time ascending for the first few flights, then Cybersausage shouted down, "You're not going to like this."

Daniel moved to the front of the group and inspected the passageway. More stairs missing, just five feet below the third-floor level. Not a problem. He jumped up, easily landing on the broken ledge of the third story.

Cybersausage whistled, then said, "I can't wait to try that," before leaping up next to Daniel. He landed with a hearty laugh, and a heavy thud that caused the building to creak again.

"Watch out!" Daniel hauled Cybersausage away right before the floor beneath him gave out. There was now a six-foot hole where the ledge used to be.

"I *know* you don't expect me to jump up there," Carl said, with major attitude.

Sasha took him by the waist and leapt up, releasing Carl next to a burnt-up couch a few inches from the ledge. "You're welcome," she said, with her usual half-grin.

Carl looked like he was going to puke –staring down from the ledge. Then he took a step back and glared at Sasha.

Daniel heard Anthony's thoughts, he was about to leap with both Marcus and Ryan in tow. Daniel shouted in his head, *one at a time!* That caused Anthony to pause long enough for Daniel to say, "Anthony, maybe you should take Marcus first." He relocated away from the ledge to make room and in his head suggested others do the same.

Sasha and Cybersausage moved back promptly, Cybersausage yanking Carl with him.

Anthony bounded into the air, several feet above where he needed to be, almost hitting the ceiling that was twelve feet high. He let Marcus down by a blackened cubicle, one of many cubicles on the third floor. He was more careful, and more accurate, when he came back with Ryan.

With each landing the building grumbled, and Daniel worried that the third level might fall away like the second one had.

Movement caught the corner of Daniel's eye. Something scurried, claws scratching, as it ran behind the cubicle where Marcus sat on the floor. He could see the heat signature, from the size and shape, he could guess what it was. "There is a rodent behind you."

Marcus pulled his weapon around and aimed. "I don't see a –" Before he could finish his sentence, bullets started to fly at the giant rat in mid-leap. The yellow teeth on the thing had to be four inches long, and they were buried in Marcus's neck, tearing throat tissue apart.

Everyone fired at the monstrous rodent, and it ceased moving after a few seconds. Daniel didn't have to be a doctor to know Marcus wouldn't make it. But, Sasha had her hand on his neck, attempting to stop the bleeding. His eyes were wide in panic and shock, and he gargled on the blood choking him and spilling out of his mouth.

Daniel detected two more heat signatures behind the charred cubicles. He began firing and projected the locations in his mind, hoping others would fire as well. Once those were dead, he found two more on the other side of the stairwell. The other men spread out and eliminated the threats while Sasha tended to Marcus in his death throws.

"This place is infested!" Anthony remarked after the bullets finally stopped.

"I warned you," Cybersausage said. He knelt next to Sasha, who's hands were trembling and covered in blood. He checked Marcus's pulse and shook his head. "This isn't the first time The Forsaken has run into these dirty rats."

Daniel realized that The Forsaken was the name of Cybersausage's anarchist group. It was a fitting name, knowing what the government had done by leaving them behind a seventy-foot, armed wall to rot in radiation poisoning. He felt the betrayal, the abandonment coming from Cybersausage, and even from Carl and Ryan.

"I'm sorry ..." Marcus' blood might as well have been on his own hands, as well as Roberts. Two dead, because of him. "Know that what we are doing here will save millions of lives." Daniel sure hoped so anyway. He allowed waves of gratitude and condolence to emanate to the men who's heads hung low around the body of their fallen friend.

Sasha stood, wiped her hands on her already blood-soaked jacket and began reloading her rifle with a fresh magazine, everyone else followed her example. Daniel read her thoughts ... Marcus was her driver on the way here–they'd chatted. He was a nice guy, with a family. He deserved better. She looked up at Daniel with a bone-chillingly cold expression, he would have thought she felt nothing if he couldn't read her mind.

"We need to find the main office for Newton Dreamworks, it is somewhere on this level. The faster we get to it, the faster we get out of here." Daniel didn't want to waste time, and let the urgency soak into his words.

Cybersausage displayed the hologram again, then marked a spot in the center of the building. A maze of office spaces stood between the stairwell and their destination. He turned and tilted his head toward a narrow hallway. "Through there."

"I think it is best if I lead the way this time." Daniel scanned the cluttered room for thermal signatures, nothing new. "Follow me."

The group kept close, Anthony taking up the rear and walking backwards. He had his gun aimed at any shadow that caught his eye.

They passed a gaping doorway that led into a gloomy office. Daniel paused to thoroughly scan before proceeding forward, ensuring nothing lurked in the office that would attack the people following behind him through the hallway.

Twenty feet past the doorway, the hallway lead into a spacious lobby. The room held a round-cornered reception desk across from chairs in rows facing a tv screen dangling down to the floor. A waiting room for a doctor's office. Most of the furniture was intact, though scorched.

"This is it," Cybersausage moved into the reception booth. "Newton Dreamworks. What are we looking for?"

Ryan and Carl rifled through the lobby, overturning chairs and knocked the dangling tv off the wall.

"I will know it when I see it." Daniel came into the booth with Cybersausage. There was nothing interesting except a row of filing cabinets inside. He opened one, and scanned the contents. "It will not be in here, these are patient records."

"Can you give us a clue?" Sasha stood on the other side of the reception desk, and in her mind she was asking if Daniel even knew what he was looking for.

Daniel hadn't expected this to in-fact be a dream research clinic, he'd thought that the title was a front for Susan's microchip research. Maybe he was wrong all along? No, there had to be more. "We need to find a laboratory."

"We came here for a laboratory?" Anthony leaned on the counter, head bent down to check-out what was inside. "Don't you have a ton of those back home?"

"The laboratory would be somewhere behind those double doors." Cybersausage indicated the slightly ajar, twisted doors on the other side of the reception booth. Then he pushed them open.

The room beyond held a series of glass-enclosed cells to either side of a long aisle. Most of the enclosures were busted open and the beds that were in each cell were burnt and frayed. Shattered fragments of glass were everywhere, and so were rats.

Fangs and claws bounded forward in hissing, furry masses.

Gunfire rang out in deafening tones.

Chapter 16

Susan's Gift

Cybersausage and Daniel dove back to the other side of the reception counter. The bodies of rats began to spill forward, scrambling over each other. Giant, hairy creatures with sharp, buck-toothed fangs and dingy yellow, glowing eyes lay bloodied in a forming pile, and more climbed over.

Sasha drew out a small round object from her utility belt, counted to three, and then tossed the grenade into the mound of bodies growing in the entrance to the other room. The doorway exploded in amber flames. The garlic-like odor of phosphorus filled the air, mixed with burnt fur. The whole building shook. There was a creaking shift followed by a domino-like sound of thuds in the distance that could be heard over the ringing in everyone's ears.

The flash of the flame overloaded Daniel's thermal detection system, it began a reset mode. He could still see better than anyone else in the room. Their vision was completely shot from the bright light. He saw no movement, but did notice a huge hole in the floor in the back of the reception area. Most of the rodent bodies had fallen into the hole.

Cybersausage said something no one could quite make-out because the close-range grenade caused humming in everyone's ears. Cochlear nerve-cell damage that might take minutes, hours or years to heal.

Daniel made a mental demand to each individual in the group. Then he traversed the damaged floor and vaulted over the rat pit into the room beyond. Anthony, Sasha and Cybersausage accepted the thought-projection as a clear, undeniable command and hurriedly filed in behind him. One of the benefits of the Mods in their heads – ability to follow orders without question. Ryan and Carl were suggestable – getting up more slowly and with some confusion. Despite not having a Mod they still carefully followed behind the others along the edge of the pit and into the next room, as requested.

Daniel felt ashamed for using the Mod in this way, but was also starting to understand why Cliff liked the power so much. It made getting what needed to be done much easier, especially in situations like this one.

Daniel's ocular implants finally finished resetting the "campaign mode." He could see the heat coming off of everyone in his party. Thankfully, no more creatures were lurking in the room. They'd either all been killed or fled.

He passed nearly two dozen sleep study cells, treading carefully over the broken glass and gnawed bones strewed about. There were nests of shredded sheets, clothing and mattress stuffing. A human skull buried inside one of the nests made it clear where the bones had come from. Daniel tried to imagine that the people died peacefully in their sleep.

There has to be an office area somewhere! he thought. A door stood at the end of the aisle of bedchambers. This one still intact, but sealed tightly shut. It was locked with a pin combo box on the handle. He heard a thought from Sasha, and moved over to let her at the door.

She motioned for everyone to get back, and proceeded to fire at the lock from a 45-degree angle. The lockbox fell off and she kicked the door open. The whole building creaked again with the impact. Daniel passed her a look, not having to say or think a thing for her to mouth, "Sorry." She stared up at the dust falling from the unsteady building, praying the ceiling wouldn't fall on her head. She wasn't the only one praying.

Daniel led the way into the chamber beyond. The cool, dry air inside smelled like a hospital–like plastic, electronics and rubbing alcohol. The rubber seal around the steel door had kept the odor of seawater and rodent feces at bay and there were no windows to let in the outside elements. The room was filled with monitoring equipment, and computers. Nothing was burnt, mold infested or ripped apart. Aside from a thin layer of dust, the area was surprisingly intact.

"Is this the laboratory you're looking for?" Sasha asked and Daniel shook his head.

It was a laboratory, with spaces set aside for cognitive performance evaluations. But, it wasn't the kind that developed microchips.

Daniel started to worry he'd misunderstood Susan's messages. Or that this was simply a sleep study center. Or her microchip research was somewhere else, in some other city or building. *What if the microchip was in Idaho, and Cliff found it?* The thought made his mouth dry and his heart race.

"This place makes me uneasy," Carl said. He stood next to Cybersausage, who was dusting off an old mainframe computer. An electroencephalogram sat on the counter and Carl picked it up. "What's this?"

"An EEG cap, used for monitoring brain waves." Daniel saw quite a few of them in the large room. Not all the EEGs were the same, some were made with technology he'd never seen. Some were multi-colored caps with only twenty-four leads, while others looked more like a pile of wires. A few had no leads at all, made of flat bands.

"This is a back-up power supply." Ryan knelt down near a two-foot-long, foot-wide black box on the floor. "For the computers." He'd wiped it off with his gloved hand. "Want me to turn it on?"

"Go for it," Cybersausage replied.

When Ryan pressed the button, the room buzzed with computers and monitors coming online. There was a faint smell of burnt electronics, and the monitors flashed brightly in start-up routines, ending on blue login screens. Surprisingly, the overhead lights came on too. Why they'd needed back-up power for the entire lab was puzzling.

Anthony laughed, and everyone turned to stare at him. "Sorry, I half expected these things to crawl around when the power came on." He had an EEG in his hands. Its many cables did look like spider legs, or Medusa's head. Daniel had never thought of them that way, but now Anthony's ridiculous thoughts were in his mind.

"We need to keep moving," Daniel commanded. "This is not what we came here for." He turned and headed further into the building, through a swinging double door. He didn't stop to wait for agreement, he knew he didn't need too. The others followed him into the dark hallway beyond without question.

Every ten feet there was a door on either side of the hallway. More doors. More locks. Each door had a name on a sign below a small glass window. Dr. Mark Stiles. Dr. Laura Marsh. Dr. Rebecca Ellis. Dr. August Stein. Offices. He scanned for Dr. Sarah Newton. A splash of hope jolted his heart. There is was! At the end of the hall. At the center of the building. He nearly ran to it.

Locked, of course. No window either. He didn't want to break in, it seemed disrespectful. Plus, he didn't know how much the precarious supports of the building could take before they came down and crushed everyone inside.

"Daniel, the code could be anything. We have to break in." Sasha knew his thoughts, though he didn't think he was projecting them. He was startled for an instant before realizing she'd merely read his facial expression.

"No, I know her. I can figure this out." He tried the date they met. Her birthday. Her real name. The word 'dream.' Nothing. Each time he turned the handle and the door didn't open he got more frustrated. On the last try he almost broke the handle off. He turned away and took a few calming breaths of stale, dusty air that made him cough.

Everyone stared at him, sharing his aggravation. Carl had his arms crossed and was tapping the ground with his right foot. Anthony squinted at the handle, trying to think of something to put into the combo ... his thoughts were mostly on four letter picnic items –cake, pork, chip, wine, soda. Ridiculous! How could Anthony possibly think tha – wait, could it be *Ants*? It worked! Like in Susan's message, 'remember the ants.' He thought she was referring to the colony of ants that she'd used to explain communal thought. Apparently, it meant her door code.

The wearied, bloodied and messy group ambled into the private room of Dr. Sarah Newton. This was no simple office. Yes, there was a desk, chair, computer, etc ... normal office stuff to the immediate left. But, Daniel's heart almost leapt out of his chest when he saw an electronics clean room in the back of the 800 square foot space. A place no doubt made to make microchips. This was it. If the advanced microchip he'd hoped Susan had made for him was anywhere, it would be here.

It took him two seconds in the clean room to realize it wasn't in there. Processing tanks, microscopes, lead framing ... no parts, no chips. He came out of the clean room disappointed, but then joined the others searching through the office area.

"This one has a back-up too." Ryan didn't ask for permission this time before turning on the back-up power supply near Susan's computer.

Daniel combed over a lab counter to the left of the entrance and glanced back at the buzzing sound as the computer monitor came online. He noticed a picture frame next to the screen on the desk. Susan –smiling, happily holding up her baby. A little girl in a lacey pink dress. Her husband, Darren, stood next to her with his arms encompassing her and the child. Daniel felt loss, he missed Susan. But, he also felt comfort in her evident happiness.

"That's ... that's Catherine's parents!" Anthony exclaimed, snatching the picture up. "I know this picture! Catherine keeps a copy on her bedroom night stand." He went outside of the room, staring at the door sign and back at Daniel. Daniel told him to be quiet in a thought projection and Anthony said no more.

Sasha's eyebrow was raised, but she kept quiet as well. Her mind was racing with questions, and Daniel tried to ignore them all. He needed to focus on finding the microchip amid the room crammed with file cabinets, drawers and shelves stocked full of miscellaneous stuff.

Cybersausage decided to sit on the chair in front of the computer. The monitor had a blue lock screen. "Do you know this password too?"

Daniel knew the operating system security might lock him out after a few tries, so he was careful with his reply. "Try 'Catherine.'"

"Nope." Carl stated the obvious, and Daniel glared at him. "What?" Carl was quite expressive with his pouty lips and screechy voice. Daniel didn't have to read his mind to know that much of Carl's attitude towards him was due to jealousy at Cybersausage's attention.

"Maybe the husband? Or her birthday? Birthdays are common." Sasha suggested.

Daniel gave them the info, but neither was the passcode. He was surprised it didn't lock them out after the third failed attempt, but was also starting to wonder why he was even trying.

"Look, I did not come here to hack into her computer." Daniel turned and continued his search through the room for a microchip. He went to open the closest file cabinet to find that it was jam-packed with folders. Folders bursting with papers. He thumbed through them quickly, hoping to find something on the Mods. One paper caught his eye. It was on a machine that could project dreams, and there was an invoice for its purchase in the same folder.

Cybersausage and Carl were trying different password combinations and laughing. Obviously, having fun playing sleuth. Susan must not have set a lock-out limit.

Sasha, Ryan and Anthony combed through the room, with intent to announce anything unusual they found. Good. At least they knew what was important.

Daniel moved on to a different file cabinet, more papers on equipment and dream research. Nothing on microchips. Another filing cabinet, more papers. More dream stuff. His attention was drawn back to the computer when Carl snickered and said, "Try 'Daniel.' Humm ... okay, Daniel4Ever."

"My goodness, I think it worked." Cybersausage gave Carl a congratulatory smack on the butt that made him squeal in delight. "Good job!" The screen changed from blue to loading Susan's homepage, one completely filled with application and folder icons.

Her personal password, one she used every day, was 'Daniel4Ever'? Daniel was flattered and deeply saddened at the same time. He kept rummaging through the cabinet drawers, trying not to think about what it meant.

"I found something." Anthony held up a locked box, wooden and about a cubic foot. He'd drew it out of a cabinet above the counter to the left of the entrance. "It's weighs more than I would expect."

Sasha crossed the room to take the box from him, and used the screwdriver on the swiss army knife she produced from her pocket to work the hinges loose. After a few minutes of unscrewing, she popped open the lid.

A giant gold nugget sat inside, cushioned by tool foam. There was also a torn-off piece of paper with an address. Daniel recognized his mother's handwriting. Had his mother given Susan the address for a stash of gold instead of Miss Tinny's reservation the night of the lab explosion? Knowing his mother, that is exactly what she'd done. Daniel took the note and put it in his pocket.

"Holy mother of God, that thing must be worth ninety cred!" Ryan, who'd just came from snooping through the clean room said from behind Daniel, Anthony and Sasha. The three were leaning over the counter that held the wooden box and golden treasure. "Is that what we came for?" He had a 6-inch, square computer motherboard in his hand. "I found this too. Back in that enclosure. There was some pretty cool equipment in there." He'd removed it from one of the deposition machines and planned to bring it back with him as a souvenir.

"No, none of this is what we're looking for. Keep searching." Daniel's hope still latched on, there were four more file cabinets he hadn't searched. The whole right wall was covered in equipment cabinets. It could be in any one of them.

"Can you at least tell us what we're looking for?" Ryan asked, eyeing the gold nugget and thinking about who he knew that would kill for it. Thinking he might kill for it.

Daniel sent Sasha a warning and she closed the box and held onto it tight. Ryan licked his lips but knew he had no chance against her.

"You will know it when you see it." Daniel projected thought-images to the group. Visions of a small object, maybe in a box, safe or case. The others spread out, now with clearer purpose.

"Daniel, you might want to see this ..." Cybersausage didn't take his eyes off the computer screen as he spoke. Carl sat in a chair next to him, elbow to elbow.

His thoughts were clear as day in Daniel's head. He'd been trying to crack a protected folder, titled 'Jahren,' that was in another folder, titled 'Archive,' in the 'Research' partition on the main drive. Cybersausage needed to know what it was, his curiosity insatiable.

"We can bring it back to Snowwolf, he can –" Carl began.

"No," Daniel said. "It might be personal." What was it? Daniel was afraid of what might be in that folder. But, he wanted to know ..."Try 'Seattle'." It was the place they were going to run off to, before Cliff took hold of Daniel's mind and twisted his thoughts against Susan. It was a gut feeling, and it was correct.

The folder was had only videos, ten of them to be exact. Cybersausage scrolled down to the oldest one, dated October 26, 2017. Less than a month after the last time he'd seen her. "Should we open them?" he asked.

Daniel hesitated, but then said, "Go ahead."

Susan's voice, the smooth southern French accent, brought back a flood of memories – her floral scent, her clicking heels echoing in the hall as she walked, her passionate kisses. "Daniel, I know you are still alive. Somewhere. Somehow. I can feel it. I know what you did, and I ... I forgive you. You had to lie to me ... it was the only way to stop Cliff. I love you. I will always love you." Her words were a confession, it was as if she was trying to convince herself they were true. Like a private therapy session.

In the next video she talked about her nightmares, one of Daniel still trying to defeat Cliff in an endless battle that destroyed the whole world. She mentioned working on a microchip that would help him, if he were still alive. She ended it with, "Are you still alive, my love?"

So, she did work on a microchip! Daniel knew she would.

The next one, more than two months later, was about how she'd spoken to Miss Tinny. How and why she'd decided to meet Daniel's old Native American nanny after all. How Miss Tinny knew about Cliff's dreams, and how his dreams had scared her. "Miss Tinny says she sees you in her dreams sometimes, it gives me hope." She recited a strange prophecy from her tribal elders that had stuck with her. The prophecy was about a giant spider web, snakes of iron, black rivers and roads that projected images in the sun. The world would end when a blue star fell from the sky. She mentioned seeking out other dream-walkers again, and how she'd reconnected with Darren.

Daniel thought about one of the last things he had told Susan, "Leave, go to your dream-walker, Darren. Forget about this place. Forget about me, it's too late for me." He had said it to protect her from Cliff. It had broken his heart to say those words. But, better his heart was broken than Susan be dead.

"We are finding out so much more than I thought possible. When Darren told me he knew me from his dreams, I thought it was a pick up line." She laughed, as softly and sweetly as he remembered her. Warm brown eyes on a doll faced cropped by dull brown hair and framed in dainty glasses. She was happier. Darren made her happy. "But now, now we can see it. We've captured images. We've taken the best dream-walkers in the world, and the best psychics. With the new equipment, we can see their dreams." That message was four months after the last one and around the time of the invoice for the dream-projection machine from the United Kingdom.

More months went by between the next few videos. She talked about her new life in LA and starting a company. About branching out, and visiting other dream clinics on the cutting edge of understanding human cognizance. They were converging on the idea that the mind could bend space and time –comparing the human brain to a quantum computer going in and out of the quantum realm. There was a lab in Munich working on definable proof.

Nothing more about a microchip or helping Daniel. The videos were becoming more like diary entries. Had she given up the idea to help him? Or was all the dream research relevant? She'd mentioned before that he needed to work on his dreaming skills if he were to have a chance against Cliff. He'd had improvement in becoming a lucid dreamer and that seemed to help him break away from Cliff's control.

"I figured it out. Well, Darren did. I mean his brain did," she laughs again, eyes sparkling with delight. Her skin was radiant, and she was even more beautiful than he'd ever seen her. "I decided to try something new. Much of what we've found has to do with biology, how the brain adapts to technology. So, I did something crazy. I went to Switzerland for gene splicing. Darren would never forgive me if he knew, but the limbic system, it is inherited by the father. He's the most powerful dream-walker I've ever met, I had to use his DNA. He asked me to marry him when he found out I was pregnant, I had to say yes. I hope you understand."

He'd known for years that she had moved on and married Darren, that she'd had his child but ... was Catherine *engineered*? He pushed past Cybersausage and clicked on the next video himself.

"She is growing fast. My little miracle. Her numbers are off the charts, better than I expected. She has so much potential, she is going to change the world. She went into a tantrum and knocked out our entire electrical system. We had to get back up power supplies installed to handle the EMI surges she can generate. I wish you could meet her. I know you will one day. I am just worried it will not be enough. If someone like Cliff gets a Mod, or worse, if Cliff survived. I've been working on a new design, made especially for Catherine. When she's old enough to choose it, of course. If she does, she could save the world."

It all made so much sense. It explained why he was drawn to Catherine. Why her dreams were so powerful. He'd thought at first that it was simply because she was Susan's daughter that he'd found her dreams. He'd known Catherine had many special gifts, but never imagined Susan would have formulated her own daughter!

"What's a Mod?" Carl asked, inches from Daniels face, hot breath ketones filling Daniel's nostrils.

"It's the brain implant that runs the prosthetics," Sasha answered. She had come to watch the videos, as did Ryan and Anthony. All six in the group were crowded so close it was making the air moist and thick with salty, sweaty body heat with a tinge of rancid foam from the lower level.

Daniel thought about commanding them to all go search the hallway, or the other offices. But there was only one more video and Susan had already revealed much more than he had intended for them to know. More than he even knew. The cat was out of the bag, and there was no point putting it back in. His curiosity, and the intrigue of the five people surrounding him, propelled him to click on the last video.

"Darren had a dream about a bomb last night. A nuclear bomb. He said the west coast was not going to survive. War was coming. He begged me to leave LA." She was frantic and scared, eyes red and baggy from lack of sleep. "He took Catherine to Montana, to visit with his brother. I know she will be safe there. I'm so close to being done with the new Mod. Years of research coming to a head. I can't go. My lab is here." She took a deep breath to calm down. Then sat back and rubbed her eyes. "Darren isn't always right ... but if he is ... Daniel, if I'm gone ... my real research, the Mod for Catherine, it will be behind the third filing cabinet ... if I can finish it anyway. I have to go. I don't think there is much time."

Did she finish the Mod? He checked the date of the video, November 3, 2020. Only a few days before the nuclear bomb hit Anaheim. He tried not to think about the bones in the room of rats.

Daniel's first instinct was to go move the third filing cabinet from the entrance in Susan's office. Anthony and Sasha felt the same way, Anthony reaching the cabinet first. He lifted the six-foot by two-foot, metal cabinet filled with papers like it was a tiny trash bin and set it down five feet away. A cut in the drywall. Barely visible. One foot square in size. Sasha used her knife to yank the square loose, it landed on the floor in a flakey white mess.

A box. Simple, three-inch square, half-inch thick, and made of a shiny metal. It sat inside the nook between studs on a make-shift wooden shelf.

Daniel opened it, and smiled. "Time to go."

Chapter 17

Way Down We Go

"Esha tracked them a half hour ago heading to an old military base, northeast of LA." Cybersausage explained, yelling back over the noise of the amphibious jeep barreling down the dilapidated highway. "We have to stop by headquarters first, but we can go straight there afterwards."

It was an unnecessary explanation. Daniel already knew. He had listened to the message when it came in, Cybersausage thoughts as loud in Daniel mind as if Daniel thought them himself. Ever since he heard, he'd been consumed with wondering why Catherine ran off in the first place.

Had Luca kidnapped her again? Was she running away to protect Luca from Cybersausage's Forsaken? What about her dream of Cliff? How much had that affected her? After her dream her thoughts were guarded and she'd trembled when Daniel touched her. He'd tried so hard to re-assure her, but maybe it wasn't enough. He should have told her about her mother. But, he hadn't wanted his feelings for Susan to affect how Catherine felt about him.

"I'm not going anywhere, when I get back I'm taking a hot shower and going straight to sleep!" Carl was clearly audible, even over the road noise, as he complained to Cybersausage. He was driving and kept taking his hands off the wheel as he spoke. Daniel could easily tell he was not used to missions like this, without him saying a word. Unfortunately, Carl said a lot of words to that affect. Most of which Daniel ignored. "You said this would be fun, you never said anything about rats! Rats! Were you trying to get me killed?"

Cybersausage patiently let Carl go off, nodding an apologizing. Though every once and a while he reached over to steady the vehicle when Carl felt that throwing up his hands in protest was more important than driving.

Daniel focused on scanning the area for threats through the cold, damp foggy morning air. What little remained of Robert next to him in the back seat sure wasn't going to help fire on any of Tripod's assassins if they sprang up. Anthony in the vehicle behind him was also ready, gun in window. They had Marcus's corpse in their jeep's back seat, and Sasha held onto her gold nugget prize in the front, with Ryan driving.

They'd made it out of the half-collapsed building into the early morning hours right before dawn – without a single incident. It had been too easy. It made Daniel more nervous they would run into trouble on the way to The Forsaken headquarters.

Everyone was exhausted, most having not slept in twenty-four hours of adrenaline rush after adrenaline rush. Daniel was more exhausted more than anyone. He needed coffee. He hadn't slept in days and hadn't had coffee in 12.52 hrs. Thankfully the heavily cracked and pot-holed freeway kept jolting him awake.

The brisk fog penetrated deep into his bones, driven-in by the speed of the jeep. It also concealed their caravan from any would-be attackers. Cybersausage didn't even bother to deploy his drones. When they'd gotten out of the building, his first recon expedition came back with a white expanse for miles. One of the drones crashed into a building on its way back, unable to see well in the dense fog.

The ocular implants on campaign mode had the best visibility. He'd searched for a fog setting, but there was no protocol for this kind of low visibility. Campaign mode was the best option, given a heat signature would surely be picked-up even in these conditions.

Nothing. No one. The coast was clear of threats. It went counter to the feeling of foreboding that Daniel felt in his gut.

They pulled up to headquarters and a crowd of gang members came out to greet them. The mob was shocked to find that the weary figures climbing out of the vehicles were covered in blood, and wafting the aroma of putrid death soaked in fetid seawater.

Daniel heard Marcus's wife wailing, and couldn't bring himself to turn to look. He reminded himself that Marcus's life was lost in the pursuit of something far bigger. But, in his heart there was nothing but anger. Anger at Cliff. Anger at himself for not being able to stop his brother.

Sasha marched towards the main factory entrance, a forty-foot pair of sliding double doors. Daniel stopped her by grabbing her arm, for which she glared at him through teary eyes that he knew she was ashamed to show. "Its okay to have feelings, Sasha," he said sympathetically. She nodded and wiped her eyes. He heard a thought, *Damn PMS*. Then Sasha turned beat red. Daniel cleared his throat and let go of her arm. "Oh, sorry about that."

Anthony approached and promptly asked, "Have they found Catherine? Is she okay? Did Jordan kidnap her again? You should never have left her alone with that maniac!"

"Yes, we know their exact location. Meet back here in fifteen minutes and we will head out."

~ ~ ~

"Motion sensors were tripped at coordinates 34°54'11.99" N -117°53'0.59" W, less than five miles from the border entrance you asked me to search." The fair haired, freckle-faced Dr. Frank Ferris said through pudgy cheeks huffing for air as he entered the dusty, equipment-filled room. His thick-framed glasses fogged with condensation as he caught his breath.

Ferris had always been the most reliable of Cliff's associates.

"Thank you, Ferris." Cliff answered, coming out from the underside of a surface mount technology solder flow conveyer. The machine had stopped working last night, and he'd had to replace two relays. "Can you do me a favor and go get Dawson and Lobbs? Thanks."

"Yes, do you want us to go with you? Its Daniel, right? What do you think he is up to down there? It's a military base –"

Cliff didn't say a thing. He commanded Ferris to shut up and find the others in his mind. Ferris ran out quicker than he'd come in, white lab coat billowing out behind him.

Cliff had no idea how long Catherine would stay put near the border. But, he did know she was the key to finding Daniel and stopping whatever plan he had.

He switched on the reflow heater, setting solder temperature to 230 degrees Celsius. He checked the conveyer and the program cycle. The machine ran beautifully.

He pulled off his gloves and set them down on a workbench and stared at his hands. A week ago he had a right hand, a right arm. A week ago he had two parents and a brother helping him make his inventions into reality. A week ago was over twenty years ago. It was still hard to wrap his mind around waking up in a post-apocalyptic future. Not just his world but the entire world was changed forever. And not for the better.

This world needed him now more than ever. Russia, China and India were in a cold war dead-lock. Each not-so-secretly amassing weapons of mass destruction again, despite The Nepal Accords. The Americas resources were being plundered to feed their feud. To make it worse, what was left of the entire American and Canadian population didn't even have a clue –safely behind their wall and censored into ignorant bliss.

The stupid wall. What a joke. Still, it made getting to Catherine complicated. He'd planned to meet her on the other side, to lure her out. But she had never made it through and contacted Central like she was supposed to. Now he had to find a way to get past the wall. Go through the underground tunnel? No, too slow. He had a feeling he needed to get there as fast as possible ... which probably meant he would have to go alone. Unless Dawson, Lobbs or Ferris had a better idea.

"Ferris said you wanted to see us?" Dr. Steven Lobbs asked, coming to sit next to Cliff on an office chair by the work counter for the solder reflow chamber.

The facility had stood the test of time well, but the equipment was abandoned decades ago and needed work. Lobbs had been especially useful in getting the microchip manufacturing line running again. He specialized in micro-biomimicry and mostly used that knowledge to create enhancements for the Mod's within the human body. Primarily microelectromechanical devices that harnessed body heat, so he knew all about how to properly make a tiny integrated circuit.

"Yes, where are the other two?" Cliff put his impatience in check, smiling when he wanted to grit his teeth. Lobbs worked best with sugar, not spice. Lobbs was a tall, lean Armenian who was as quick on his feet as he was with his wits. But, like most ivy-league PhD's, Lobbs had an ego that bruised easy and healed slow.

"Ferris is having trouble with Dawson. She's consumed with designing her new toy, the augmented reality interface for those ocular implants she loves. I can't believe she replaced her own eyeballs!" Lobbs shuddered and shoved his hands into the pockets of his white lab coat. "I mean, I believe in my work ... but I'm not about to start replacing body parts." He glanced down at Cliff's legs and quickly glanced away. "Not that having mechanical body parts is a bad ... I ..."

"You what? If you all had legs like mine, we could fly right to the wall together without me having to figure out how to carry you 300 miles." Cliff was proud of his legs, he even demonstrated the hover tech as he spoke. With arms crossed, he smiled smugly down from six feet above Lobbs.

"We're going through the wall? Why?" Dawson's bright green eyes had an unnatural glow, and teal tint. They used to be a nice, natural blue. Her mind raced so fast Cliff had to put in effort to read her thoughts. Her ocular implants were more like two super computers, and she was currently using them to calculate his thrust, distance and energy output. "You won't have enough fuel to make the trip, the solid metal hydride core is rated for only 2 flight hours at maximum output, 170 knots. Even at a lower –"

Cliff interrupter her, "Daniel made alterations while we were in hibernation. He fixed most of the hydrogen storage issues by adding a carbon nanotube scaffold, controlled by a CMR interface, into the lithium nitride solution ... absolutely brilliant." He shook his head, and landed smoothly on the ground. "Its stuff like that, you know? That shows how important it is we get my brother back here, now. We need him."

"Impressive." Dr. Brooke Dawson's words and blank expression were in stark contrast to her thoughts. She never did have the most positive attitude, but had shared far less of her pessimism in words than she stewed on in her head. Her thought, "Like hell Daniel is going to help us, you lunatic," was not appreciated in the least. She knew he heard the thought too. She didn't care.

Cliff didn't want to argue with Dawson about why they needed Daniel. He sent her a mental image of Daniel's ocular implants in use to entice her to want to experiment on him. She smiled, the thought steering her mind to curiosity instead of condemnation.

Brooke Dawson was the most creative and intelligent person he knew, besides his own family members. If it wasn't for her manic-depressive disposition, he would have considered breeding with her. However, even being a tall, stunning, long-legged brunette wasn't enough to compensate for that attitude. Plus, it was clear she was asexual, only passionate about her inventions and not about other humans.

"We're here, Cliff. What's the plan?" Ferris sat in an office chair next to Lobbs, leaning back with his hands clasped behind his head and legs crossed at the feet. Relaxed, and arrogant.

"I would like to know your thoughts on how we will get past the western barrier wall. Daniel is on the other side, and I could use your help to retrieve him."

"There is a military base, not even 40 miles from here, there might be a plane –" Lobbs started to say.

"And who is going to fly a plane? Are you a military pilot, Lobbs?" Dawson was quick to point out the flaw in his plan and he scowled at her. "Anyone else here a military pilot?"

"A base may have a weapon stash we could use to break through the wall." Ferris suggested. "A rocket launcher, or a tank could be useful."

"Its an Air Force base, Ferris. They won't have a tank, though they may have Humvees." Lobbs added. "A Humvee might have a machine gun. Though, it would get us to the wall far slower than the hovercraft we came here on."

"We could dismantle it, attach its weapon to the hovercraft." Ferris had no concept of physics, what he suggested would rip the tiny hover vehicle to pieces on the first shot from a rocket launcher.

Dawson, in a monotone voice said, "I've always wanted to fire a rocket launcher."

Lobbs' idea to raid a military base was ludicrous. If there was anything serviceable left on the base they didn't have time to search for or retrofit it.

"We have adequate weapons, there is nothing we need from a military base." Cliff shared, briefly, with a mental push for them to not ask questions. They had no idea of the extent his family had worked with the government in secret. In fact, very few people knew and most of them were now dead.

"In Colorado." Dawson added. "Why don't you go alone? We all have plenty to do here."

"She's right, Daniel isn't a priority right now." Lobbs had no idea what Daniel was capable of, none of them did.

It was frustrating, but Cliff had to play a delicate tight rope act of what to share and not share with these three in order to keep them working with him. "One thing I know is that Daniel will stop at nothing to ensure what we are doing here is never achieved. He already developed an inoculation for R.V. 321J-2017, forcing us to experiment with new strains. I need to talk to him, to get him to understand the importance of what we're going to accomplish, for humanity."

"And you think you can convince him to help us?" Dawson snickered. "He locked us all in hibernation pods."

Cliff wanted to smack that smirk off of her face, but instead said, "I believe I can persuade him, given enough time." She had no idea the control he had over her and everyone else in the room with a Mod. But, that was the last thing he wanted to explain about. Not when they were so close to executing his plan.

Cliff didn't like it, but he knew Dawson was right, he should probably go to the border alone. It wasn't easy keeping these three convinced, Daniel might ruin that. Dawson in particular questioned him more and more each day.

"Oh, I almost forgot." Ferris sat up in his seat and addressed Cliff. "The strain R.V 376-2040 is working magnificently, even better than you anticipated. Five patients are exhibiting reduced brain function, with abnormal aggression. Quinta was key, as you suspected." Ferris beamed with pride. In his head he thought he was the one who came up with the mix of the two viruses, not Cliff. He sometimes forgot that Cliff could read his mind.

Cliff crossed his arms and raised his eyebrow, looking askance at Ferris. "I'm glad *we* were able to duplicate the needed effects." Ferris sat up and said, 'sorry,' in his head. Cliff continued, "I think it is time we tested a Mod. Dawson, Lobbs – is the surgery room complete?"

"Yesterday." Lobbs replied. Dawson nodded.

"Good. Start with one Mod, and if that works in controlling the virus, do the other four. I'll gather more on my way back from California with Daniel." The three scientists marveled at Cliff's confidence. He ordered them to get to work in his head as he marched out the door.

~ ~ ~

"Catherine? Catherine!" Anthony yelled as he entered the abandoned military aircraft hangar. "It's me, Anthony."

"Don't move!" Esha insisted, crouching down beside Anthony's metal feet. "These are their footprints."

"Where?" Cybersausage kneeled alongside her and she pointed.

Large boots with smaller boots next to them had made impressions in the heavy dust layer on the hangar floor. Cybersausage's eyes and the light on the end of his gun followed a path the pair of boots had taken that ended with half a dozen men shuffling around and completely destroying the evidence.

Cybersausage yelled, "Oh, great job guys! Jeeze. Thanks for obliterating the trail!"

Esha shook her soft-brown haired head and gazed up at Cybersausage with a cunning smile. "At least we know they definitely came in here. These tracks are fresh."

"Yes, but where did they go?" Cybersausage asked. "Can the owls track them in here?"

"They won't like it, I haven't fed them since 0600. But, I can see if they will try," she replied, pressing a button on her vest that caused the rest of the lights on it to go from white to red.

Four owls swooped through the broken windows at the top of the hangar doors. They began meandering between the men.

Esha put on her visor and stood up. She turned in a circle, then back, then circled the other way. “They are having trouble with all the people in the room.”

The birds stopped circling the men on the ground and flew up into the ceiling structural beams and then down hallways on either side of the man opening.

Anthony decided to keep calling Catherine’s name and head deeper into the building towards a staircase full of spiderwebs. Sasha joined him. She was at his side, using her gun light in coordination with his to scope the area.

For some reason, Daniel stood in the middle of the room facing the hangar doors. He had his eyes squeezed tightly closed. Usually he kept them open to help everyone see with those disturbingly bright beams. Daniel’s hands were clenched at his side and he looked like he was mumbling.

Sasha tugged on Anthony’s jacket sleeve, and asked “Do you think there is something going on with Daniel? I almost get the feeling that –”

Sasha wasn’t able to finish her sentence because Anthony’s left hand was on her throat. He had no idea why he would do that! He had a strange urge to squeeze tighter and it took everything he had to stop himself from killing her. The thoughts of crushing her windpipe, or of ripping her throat out, felt foreign and he rejected them as best he could. Yet, he couldn’t let go.

“Anthony, please! What are you doing? Stop!” She was choking as she spoke, barely able to get the words out, her eyes wide in shock. He held her a foot off the ground and had wrenched her gun out of her hands before she could shoot.

“I’m sorry! I don’t know what’s going on,” Anthony explained, unable to move and watching her slowly die in front of him. “I’m so sorry!” Were the prosthetic arms acting on their own? These unholy body parts that had been forced upon him were now enacting their evil will?

She tried to scream for help but couldn’t. She took her knife out and stabbed at his face and torso, arm span unable to reach past his to her targets. Then she started hacking at his mechanical arm and kicking. He swiveled his body and shook her to avoid her metal feet making contact. The movement caught the attention of Cybersausage and his men.

"Hey! What are you doing! Put her down!" shouted one of the men.

"I don't know, I –" Anthony didn't finish his sentence before he started firing his gun at the man. Pulling the trigger and pointing it at another human being without any control over his own body was horrifying. Sasha was still squirming and turning purple in his left hand while he murdered members of The Forsaken with the rifle in his right. He couldn't stop. He had no control. He felt bullets hitting his Kevlar vest –two entered his torso above the protection, one grazed his neck. The blood fell and so did the men, dying all around him. It was so fast, a matter of seconds.

"Anthony, stop!" Daniel yelled and Anthony let go of Sasha and his weapon at the same time. She lay still on the floor.

There was a bright blue flash, the hangar doors were blasted completely away and light spilled into the room. A deafening ring, and the floor shook. Dust and hot wind smacked so hard into Anthony that he fell to the floor.

Anthony lay next to Sasha's body, his head throbbing. He got to his knees and held Sasha's head up, checking for a pulse on the bruised neck. He prayed he hadn't killed her. He felt nothing but the floor rumbling with another explosion.

He glanced up at the opening in the hangar to see more bright explosions, and shielded his eyes. When he looked up again, he saw that where Esha and Cybersausage had been by the hangar doors now lay two piles of ash on the floor.

A shadowy figure came through the entrance. There were more bright flashes that emanated from the man's right arm and ended with people ablaze.

Anthony heaved Sasha's body up and into his arms and then hid behind a large structural beam. He could hardly hear a thing through the ringing in his ears and his vision was impaired by the smoke and upheaval of dust off the floor. The flashes were a lightening storm in the dust, with strikes getting further and further apart.

"Where is she, what have you done with Catherine?" Daniel's desperate voice echoed in the room as the ringing in Anthony's ears faded.

Anthony glanced on the other side of the pillar to see Daniel still standing in the same spot as earlier, dead center of the room and unmoving. A tall figure with legs like rockets similar to Daniel's strode confidently up to him, stopping only two feet from his face.

"Catherine? Now why would I care about her, brother." The man replied. "Tell me ... Tell ME!" he screamed in his face.

Daniel squeezed his eyes shut again, pained and concentrating.

Anthony thought about picking up his gun. That had to be Cliff, the one who wanted to kill everyone with a virus. He gently laid Sasha's body down and slowly crept out to retrieve his weapon. *NO Anthony, get back!* The thought was clear in his head and he hid back behind the pillar. *Guard your thoughts, stay quiet!* Another foreign thought, but the command was so overwhelming that he almost stopped breathing to stay quiet.

"You will tell me everything, eventually." Cliff said. "For now, you have a choice. I can kill your little friend over there, or you can come with me."

Anthony heard a buzzing, like a capacitor charging and the room began to glow white-blue. He had a feeling there was something aimed right at the pillar he was hiding behind.

"Alight, I will go with you," Daniel said and the light and buzzing noise ceased.

In Anthony's mind was one thought "Tell her everything" before he heard the sound of rocket thrusters and saw shadows from two flashes exiting through the hangar opening.

For a few seconds Anthony only heard his blood pulsing near his ears, then there was the faint hoot of an owl in the rafters. He checked Sasha's pulse again, hoping to feel something this time, knowing it was foolish. The blood oozed from his neck wound, down his arm and dripped on her lifeless body, mixing with his tears. He prayed to God for forgiveness as his consciousness faded. His last thoughts were on the fires of hell that would surely consume him for his sins.

Chapter 18

Time to Choose

Catherine put her hand on Anthony's neck, desperately trying and stop the bleeding and hoping that he was still alive. She shook him and begged, "Anthony, please be okay!"

His eyes fluttered open and she said, "Oh, thank God! Anthony, what happened?"

"Are you an angel?" he said, eyes unfocused and blinking closed.

"Stay with me, Anthony. Please!" she cried, right hand filling with blood, left hand slapping Anthony lightly on the cheek to keep him conscious.

"He's lost a lot of blood." Jordan carefully opened up Anthony's vest and the jacket underneath. He examined his chest, finding that the top of Anthony's white t-shirt was now red. He ripped open his shirt, then tore it into pieces and began wadding it up and applying it across Anthony's bullet wounds.

"I can help, I brought an infusion kit that was in the truck." An unknown man wearing the green coveralls of The Forsaken rushed in with one of the same synthetic blood kits they'd used when rescuing Catherine from Tripod's gang. He also brought a first aid kit.

"What happened?" Catherine asked. "Where is everyone?"

"I don't know. We came here searching for you two. I went down that hallway," he nodded towards the one on the far end of the open area. "I heard gunfire. I got back in here in time to see this guy blast the hangar doors, and everyone standing in front of them, into pure ash." He administered the infusion into Anthony and then began searching through the first aid kit he'd brought. "I fired at him but he raised his arm, a blue light came out and I dove behind a column for cover. That's the last thing I remember. I woke up a few minutes ago under a pile of rubble." He replaced Catherine's hand on Anthony's neck with a bandage. Then bandaged the two bullet holes near the collar bone. "We need to get him back to headquarters ASAP."

Jordan and the man lifted Anthony onto their shoulders. The man was the same height as Jordan and as blonde and fair skinned as Jordan was dark. Catherine followed closely behind them, asking, "What did the guy look like? The one that blasted the hangar doors?"

"I saw him for a brief second, through ash and dust ... but I think he had legs like that other guy, the cyborg doctor. Yeah, come to think of it, the guy looked a lot like him."

"Cliff," was all Jordan said, and Catherine knew he was right. He put Anthony onto the pick-up truck bed, then left her alone in the back while he got in the passenger seat with the other man.

"Anthony? Anthony, can you hear me?" she asked and his eyes fluttered open. "You're going to be okay, we're going to get you help now."

"Sasha ... Sasha ... is she ..." he began a choking sob.

Catherine recalled Sasha's hauntingly blank stare when Jordan lifted her limp body from Anthony's lap. "I'm sorry, she didn't make it, Anthony."

"I ... I killed her."

"What? Why would you do that?" She felt his forehead for a fever, he was ice cold. She made eye contact with Jordan, who stared back at her from the cab and she willed the truck to move faster. It was already speeding at a reckless pace, but she felt it lurch forward.

"I couldn't help it ... I ... my arm did it. And those men ... God please forgive me!"

She moved around to get behind Anthony, and held his head to her chest, attempting to cushion him from the jolting of the vehicle. "Your arm killed people?" Catherine thought he must be delusional from lack of blood. He would never hurt someone if he could help it, much less kill someone.

"Do you ... do you think God will forgive me?" he pleaded.

"Of course, he knows you heart, Babe. God knows you would never hurt anyone. You're a good man. You're going to be okay. Hang in there, please."

The entire time it took for them to speed to headquarters on the main freeway Anthony mumbled about forgiveness and prayed. At least she knew he was conscious. Did he truly believe he killed people?

When they arrived, Jordan and the other man lifted Anthony out and rushed him through the factory door. "This guy's pretty light." The man remarked while they were in the gated elevator. He was visibly uncomfortable in the awkward silence of the confined space. Jordan just scowled at him, and Catherine was too worried to think of anything to break the tension.

When they got into the medical triage room, other people finally noticed they had arrived. "Where is Cybersausage? Where is Daniel?" Dmitriy asked, inspecting Anthony's wounds when they laid him on the operation table.

"I saw Cybersausage turn to ash, the same almost happened to me. This guy, another cyborg, came and attacked us. Only Anthony and I survived." The guy from the hangar explained, and then pointed at Jordan and Catherine. "These two came out of wherever they were hiding while I was off getting the infusion kit out of the truck."

"No. No ... that's ... no. And Esha? Where is Esha? Please tell me ..." Heliker asked from where he stood beside Dmitriy, he stopped speaking when the man shook his head.

"He's lost a lot of blood. Heliker ... HELIKER," Dmitriy yelled the name, shocking him out of his stupor. "Anthony is going to die. Fluids. NOW!"

"He's going to die?" Catherine almost screeched.

"Most likely. We will try our best though ..." Dmitriy injected a clear syringe into Anthony's chest. "What about Daniel? The cyborg doctor? Where is he? We could use his help right now."

Everyone looked to the lone survivor, and he stammered before saying, "I didn't see him when I came-to. I don't know. For all I know, he is one of those piles of ash."

"Cliff wouldn't kill his brother." Catherine knew, logically, that if Cliff had wanted Daniel dead, he would have done it a long time ago. Plus, why come all the way out here just to kill him? It didn't make sense.

"Wait, you're saying the other cyborg was Daniel's brother?" Heliker asked, coming back with two bags of fluids –one red, one clear –on an IV stand. "How did he find you?" He glared at Catherine, plainly implicating her in the murders of his friends. Deep down, she felt like it could all be her fault too.

"We knew nothing about what was going on." Jordan defensively answered for Catherine. "We know next to nothing about Cliff, only that he is the only one who could have done this."

"Where were you? Why did you leave headquarters?" asked the man who'd survived in the aircraft hangar. His face was covered in scratches and dirt. He'd gotten a rag from the shelf above the sink. He used the rag to wipe away the dust and blood as he spoke. "What were you doing at that old military base?"

Jordan swiftly responded with, "We didn't exactly feel welcome, after the greeting Cybersausage gave me."

Catherine hadn't thought about what she would say, and was glad Jordan was so quick witted. It had been her idea to leave, fearing Daniel had dubious plans for her. Having been convinced by Cliff there was no virus and that Daniel was lying. Plus, she had wanted to make sure Jordan was safe.

"What's going on in here? Steve, where's Cybersausage?" A big-boned, young red-headed guy with a lisp bounded into the room. "I saw his truck outside."

"He didn't make it." Steve, the lone survivor, replied. "Carl, he –"

"He didn't make it back? Why is he still there, weren't these two who he was looking for?" Carl didn't catch on to what Steve was trying to tell him. "Where's Esha and the rest?"

Steve had his mouth open, searching for how best to give the news before finally saying, "No, Carl. Cybersausage, Esha, Evan, Craig, Marshall ... they're all *dead*."

Carl almost fell to the floor, Jordan caught him and helped him to a cot.

Anthony began to moan, Dmitriy had pliers in his chest and was digging out a bullet. "He needs more morphine."

Heliker reset a digital controller on the IV stand. "If you felt so unwelcome, why are you back now?"

"We heard an explosion, then came out to inspect. We saw Anthony dying and wanted to make sure he got help. We'll be on our way as soon as he's fixed up." Jordan lied. He did it so easily and naturally too.

The truth was they'd seen the group come in on a video monitor outside the building and Catherine had argued with Jordan to let her out to talk to Daniel. After the last dream where Cliff had forced Jordan to show him where she was, she had started to realize Daniel was right about Cliff's manipulative tendencies. She was on her way up from the bunker when gunfire rang out. Jordan rushed to her and begged her to come back down. Within seconds the building was shaking and they ran to brace in a doorway until the explosions stopped.

"So, you don't know, do you?" Carl said, sitting up in his cot. He was flushed and his knuckles were white on his knees. "Daniel never talked to you?"

"Talked to me about what?" she queried.

"About this." Carl went to one of the counters near the far wall, opened a drawer and pulled out a metal box. He handed it to her.

"What is this?" She opened the box to find a microchip, similar to the ones Daniel had installed for everyone who'd received prosthetics.

"A gift, from you mother." He might as well have said, "The reason everyone is dead," from the look he gave her.

"Your mother?" Jordan asked. "You're full of secrets, aren't you, Catherine."

"Where did you get this?" There was blood on both of her shaking hands holding the metal box. Blood that wasn't her own, again. If she'd stayed here, would any of them have died? If she'd listened to Daniel and stayed away from Cliff, would he have found their location?

"Your mother's, Dr. Sarah Newton's, office in Anaheim. She made that for you. So you could help Daniel. At least, that's what she said in a video recording. What does it do?" Carl explained.

"I ... I don't know. My mother died when I was a baby. I barely know Daniel, and he never told me ... I mean, Cliff ... he told me ..." She bit her lip, she didn't want to admit that all of this was her fault. That she was a murderer, like her murderer mother.

"Catherine, what did Cliff tell you? Please, the more we know, the more we can help you." Jordan put his hand on her shoulder and removed the box from her weak grasp, setting it down on a counter.

"In my dreams, Cliff told me he worked with my mom. He said she killed Daniel's fiancé and that Daniel wanted to take revenge on me, that's why he brought me here."

Jordan's grip on her shoulder got tighter, "And you believed him?" She grimaced and he let go. "Cliff lied."

"How do you know?" Catherine asked. "The way Daniel looks at me ... with such agony."

"Because it's obvious Daniel is in love with you." Jordan confessed. "The agony in his eyes is unreciprocated love ... how could you not know?"

"He's ... I ..." Catherine wondered how such a remarkable, intelligent and powerful man could possibly be in love with her. Was Jordan projecting his own feelings onto Daniel?

"And, apparently, he loved your mother too." Carl revealed a removeable micro-disc drive from his pocket. "We brought this back for Snowwolf to decrypt this morning. Her files on dream research. A whole folder full of videos was devoted to Daniel. From his reaction, she meant a lot to him. That guy doesn't hide his feelings well."

"I'm such a fool," she whispered softly. She'd been so blind. She'd been such a fool believing Daniel could hate her for something her mother did. All this time he'd had nothing but love in his heart. Her decision to leave, to turn her back on him, had cost Anthony's life and maybe Daniel's too. Their deaths were on her hands.

A blurry Jordan stood before her with a washcloth to wipe away tears and the blood from her hands. "We're all fools, sometimes." He replied tenderly, and then brought her into his warm body to wrap his comforting arms around her.

"Catherine ..." Anthony's strained voice jolted her out of self-loathing. She came to his bedside and put a hand on his chest, feeling the strained and shallow rise and fall of his breath. "Daniel, he asked me to ... to tell you everything."

Dmitriy shook his head, and took a step back from the gurney. The holes in Anthony's chest were still open and only one bullet lay in a metal bin next to his head.

Catherine's pulse increased in panic and her voice cracked when she asked, "Tell me what? What happened to Daniel?"

"Cliff, he found us ... Daniel had to go with him ... to save me. Catherine, he ... I know what you are ... you're not human."

"What? Not human?" Her first thought was that Anthony was delusional.

Carl explained, "Your mother, she engineered you with your father's DNA."

That struck the delusional assessment out of her head and made her feel faint.

"You were made ... to save the world." Anthony reached up and put his hand in her hair. "I knew ... always knew you were special." His eyes closed and his arm fell limp.

"Anthony," she said, shaking him. His eyes opened again, then he smiled when he focused on her. She had a sinking feeling and frantically said, "I love you, don't leave me!"

"I knew it." He replied, still smiling. His eyes glossed over, and his face relaxed into a blank stare.

Anthony was gone.

"I'm sorry. I couldn't get the other bullets out without doing more damage and I think one punctured the top of his lung." Dmitriy's words were far from consoling. "I'm surprised he lasted as long as he did. I mean, he had all his appendages removed and replaced two days ago and was out running around ..." Dmitriy trailed off when she glared at him.

Heliker finished his thoughts. "Likely the grey injection or that purple concoction Daniel makes you guys drink."

"Grey injection?" Jordan inquired. He stood a few feet behind Catherine, giving her space with Anthony.

Catherine put her fingers over Anthony's eyelids to shut them. He was so handsome and peaceful. Too young and innocent to die like this. She hoped he was already in heaven.

"I think he called it 'Quinta,' it causes black streaks but makes people super strong. Some of the guys who got it have been real edgy and rude though." Heliker explained.

"What guys got it?" Jordan inquired.

"The ones who needed prosthetics. We've only done a handful but Cybersausage had plans for more." Heliker led Jordan to a cabinet of metal body parts, and a drawer of microchips.

"What I don't understand is why Anthony had one of our bullets in his chest." Dmitriy held up a brass object with a squashed, but still distinct, symbol of a bird in flight.

That reminded Catherine of what Anthony said in the truck, maybe he hadn't been delusional then either. "I think Cliff made him kill people. Anthony would never hurt anyone and he said something about his arm killing people, that he'd killed Sasha too."

"Cliff can do that?" Heliker gasped. "Is he even more powerful than his brother?"

"Yes, Daniel was afraid of him," she replied. Silence filled the room.

"The gunfire, before the explosion. That was Anthony?" Steve asked, perplexed.

"I guess so." Catherine needed to know if everything Anthony had said was true. She turned to Carl and asked, "Am I human?"

"Bless him, but that gorgeous man wasn't too bright. Your mother said she did gene splicing in Switzerland. Unless there is more to the story, I'd say you are as human as anyone."

"Gene splicing? For what?" Jordan inquired. He had come to put his hand on the small of her back, haunted eyes searching hers.

She peered up at Jordan, wondering if this was how he felt when Maria died –ripped apart inside, filled with guilt and an ever-increasing rage. Anthony deserved so much more than this, he was a good man. She may not have loved Anthony in the way that he'd wanted, the way he needed. But, she loved him ... and now he was gone. His dreams of being a father were gone. His sisters lost their big brother, and who was going to tell them?

"I don't know. She said something technical I didn't understand about her father's DNA. We can watch the videos if you want. I'll take you to the wolf's den." Carl offered.

Catherine felt out of sync, out of phase with the events unfolding around her. She needed answers. Something that would make her feel like all of this death and suffering had a reason, a purpose. She took one last look at Anthony, her heart aching. "Let's go."

In the basement of the complex, past the room in which they'd tortured Jordan, was a room unlike any other Catherine had ever seen. Images everywhere, each changing every few seconds to another one ... surveillance, news, browsers, profiles. There was nothing else in the room besides screens, computers, server boxes and power chords ... and a small cushion on the floor in the center.

"He must be –" Carl started to say but a furry man, about 5'6" wearing a visor and lighted vest entered and finished his sentence with "–getting coffee."

"Snowwolf," Carl bowed his head slightly towards the bearded, long haired man who patted Carl on the back and responded with, "Carl," and a similar head gesture.

"They want to see what you unlocked, particularly the Jahren-Seattle folder. This is Catherine and ... wait I never did find-out your name?"

"Jordan," he answered for himself, obviously not wanting to share the name Luca.

"I know who you are, who you *both* are." Snowwolf lifted his visor and narrowed his dark-brown eyes at Jordan. Then he pursed his lips and put the visor back on. "Where is Cybersausage? His coms went out an hour ago, it isn't like him. Esha too. All I got was a bright blue power surge and then nothing."

Carl explained with difficulty, "He's ... he's not coming back. Daniel's brother, Cliff, showed up and killed everyone."

"I didn't see that coming ..." Snowwolf sat down hard in the center of the room on the small cushion. He raised his gloved hands and started to type like there was a keyboard in the air. Images of Colorado, of Cliff, of Cliff's prosthetics company surrounded them–360 degrees around, some 3-D. Even details like co-patents with a company in Japan on nano-motors and award ceremonies for the advancements in prosthetics where brought up. Nothing on Catherine's mother.

"We came here to see what was found at Sarah Newton's lab," Catherine stated. The last thing she wanted to do was stare at images of Cliff's face, the man who killed Anthony. The man who'd forced Anthony to murder people against his will –a fate she knew Anthony found worse than death.

"Fine, put it in that one." Snowwolf indicated a computer stand and Carl inserted the half-inch flat memory disc. Files opened. Newton Dreamworks files. "Which video?" He didn't stop for a response. He opened ten videos at once, each on a different screen.

Catherine watched her mother giving heart-breaking confessions to a man she loved, a man she thought might be dead. Daniel. Her mother was so beautiful, and had a French accent of all things. She talked about dream research too, and Catherine understood little. It was hard to follow everything going on at once. Her laugh ... Catherine had her mother's laugh.

"Stop, that one!" She pointed to the screen in the upper left-hand corner of the room. "Replay what she just said."

" ... Darren would never forgive me if he knew, but the limbic system, it is inherited by the father. He's the most powerful dream-walker I've ever met, I had to use his DNA. He asked me to marry him ..."

"Dream-walker DNA? My father was a dream-walker? What does that mean?"

"It is a Native American term ... it means someone like a Shaman ... someone who can go into and manipulate dreams." Jordan continued, "Someone like you, Catherine."

"So, I can stop Cliff by dream-walking? That doesn't make any sense." Catherine looked up at Jordan for an answer, but his eyes were glued to the screens.

She watched her mother explain about designing her own daughter to stop Cliff, or someone like him. She talked about changing the world and then about saving the world. The videos were short, and Snowwolf had them on repeat.

"Stop Cliff?" Snowwolf asked. "Stop him from what?"

"Daniel ... he said Cliff had a virus, and I was the only one who could stop him. It makes no sense."

"Don't you see? Those Mods, the ones apparently your mother created, they do much more than run prosthetics. They can be used to control other people too. I still don't know about stopping a virus, but I have a feeling that the microchip your mother made was specifically for that purpose–to control people. I think Daniel wanted you to put it in ..." Jordan pointed to her head, " ... and use it to control Cliff because he's too weak to kill his own brother."

"Daniel did say he had special plans for me ... still ... do you think I want to put an implant in my brain and go fight a murderous psychopath?"

"I didn't say that. I told you before, let's get out of here. Alert Central like I wanted to, and let them deal with it."

"There probably is a virus," Snowwolf added.

"What do you mean?" Jordan and Catherine asked at the same time.

"Check this out." Images of the Jahren family popped up on the screens. Martin Jahren's numerous patents in oncolytic virotherapy dating back to the 1960's made it clear what Daniel's father specialized in.

"Yeah, that's the least of it. Search retroviruses of southern Colorado." Images of piles of Native Americans and early Dutch colonists dead from a plague filled the room. Jordan then said, "See, dangerous stuff. Why do you think their family moved there?" He stared down at Catherine, obviously trying to remind her why he'd wanted to kidnap her. "But, a virus can't control people and that is what Daniel said."

"Oh yes it can!" Snowwolf brought up images of cats, rats, and ants ... all with viruses causing them to perform odd, and sometimes suicidal, behavior.

"Holy mother of God!" Carl held his hand to his chest. "So, you're saying Cliff has some zombie virus, and is going to unleash it on humanity?"

"And Daniel can't stop him because Cliff has a mind controlling power that is far beyond his own ... I seriously doubt Central is going to do much, just saying. They ain't worth shi –" Snowwolf's opinion of Central was made pretty clear after a few more curses.

Daniel had said the virus Cliff had could kill or enslave millions in days ... there was no time for further debate. He mother's words, "when she's old enough to choose it ... she could save the world," resounded in her head. Anthony had said it too, "you were made to save the world."

"Fine. I'll do it." Catherine wondered how the microchip would affect her, if she would still be herself.

Jordan shook his head, "Please don't do this, Catherine. You don't have to –"

Her mind was made up. "I'm the only one who can stop him."

"Its what you were made for, Catherine." Carl said, "Only, can you do me a favor?"

"What?"

"Kill that son of a bitch."

Chapter 19

Destination Retribution

Voices. Foreign voices. They filled Catherine's head. Voices far away. Voices close. Voices everywhere.

A man in a cafeteria argued with another man, thought of using his spork for something other than eating. Then thought better of it.

A woman working in a lab, her mind racing a million miles an hour as she scanned through 3-D browsers of information.

A man with groggy thoughts stuck in a chamber, unable to move. Taking shallow breaths. Hoping against all odds that he could escape.

A woman under a truck, replacing the oil.

A man walking down a hall.

A woman dreaming.

A man crying.

Voices very close too.

A man calculated the trajectory of tossing someone through a cabinet if the woman he cared about didn't wake up.

A man disinfected tools in a sink. He wished he'd asked the woman he'd had a crush on to go see a movie in the theater room. He'd made her a wooden owl, but never gave it to her. Now she was gone forever.

Another wondered if he'd used the right amount of anesthesia for an operation he'd performed–Dmitriy? Other voices in her head answered 'No.' Some got louder, some asked questions. It was overwhelming.

"Catherine? Did she say my name?" Dmitriy's voice responded, floating somewhere in the pandemonium of voices –somehow nearer than the others.

"I didn't hear anything." Jordan's voice replied.

Their voices were different. Above her, around her in waves that rippled. The other voices remained somewhere else. She tried to shut them all out but some started to scream.

"Ouch, man I have the worst headache all the sudden." Heliker's voice, above and to the right.

"Yeah, me too." Dmitriy replied, to the right as well.

"Me too." Jordan continued, "Like a sudden pressure in my brain." His voice was closest, to her left.

Catherine tried to find her own thoughts in the chaos. So many voices, so many thoughts.

A woman sat shivering on a cold cell floor. A man in a similar cell paced. Then another lay staring blankly at the ceiling. Dozens of people in cells. Make-shift, clear polycarbonate cells. So much rage. Rage and nothing else.

Another man analyzed a map of the main rivers and tributaries in what used to be Idaho. He stopped what he was doing and turned around, feeling like someone was watching him. Then went back to studying his map.

A man shattered the cedar bench in the cafeteria with one fist. One metal fist. He loved his new power. His friends patted him on the back and cheered. He removed a splinter from between his palm. His fingers and palm had hundreds of moving parts.

Catherine tried to reign in her thoughts, to find her center. It felt like a bad dream. Like she was jumping into twenty people's dreams at once. She concentrated on her breathing, on her body. On here. On now. One breath in. One exhale. Again. It was a struggle–the voices interrupted often. She started the exercise over and over until she felt in control of her own mind again, her own voice.

The voices never ceased, but she'd finally found her own. She found who she was, and calmly held onto her identity among the crowd in her head. Her center. Her core.

Relaxed, grounded, she opened her eyes and sat up in the gurney in the triage room of The Forsaken headquarters. She felt the back of her head, only a small patch of hair missing. She'd asked them to be conservative. One of her best features was her long locks, they had taken years to grow out and she didn't feel she could pull off the bald look. She traced a delicate scar in the center of a one-inch shaved square between crown and nape. Then she began braiding her hair. The act helped center her in the room.

"Catherine? How do you feel?" Jordan's voice said but his thoughts were, "Are you different? Are you reading my mind?"

"Yes," was the only reply he needed. She couldn't help it, his thoughts were like her own now. She had trouble distinguishing between the three people in the room–Jordan, Heliker and Dmitriy. Their thoughts were so close to her center, likely due to their physical proximity around her.

"What's it like, what's going on?" Heliker asked as his mind projected images of super heroes and villains, a comic landscape of epic proportions. Not reality. Reality was a bad headache and voices incessantly gnawing at her brain. She showed him reality and he quivered, falling back against the counter–unable to handle the mental cacophony.

Jordan held her hand and vaguely smiled but was so ... calculating. Thinking like a chess player, several moves ahead. Charting scenarios. He hated The Forsaken, wanted them all dead. Part of him wanted her to kill them all. He hated himself for hating everyone so much. He strategically placed his hand on hers to gain her trust, giving her what he thought she wanted. And the way he saw her ... untainted, naïve and desperately needing a savior. It made him feel human again to protect her. Made him forget about his past. He knelt in pain as she tore through his mind, unable to control herself, her curiosity taking the helm.

"Please, stop ..." he begged as she replayed the worst of his transgressions in horrified awe. She ceased only when he squeezed her hand so hard it hurt. He gazed up at her from where he had fallen to his knees. Daniel had been right about Jordan all along. Jordan killed without remorse. Murdered, in cold blood, innocent people. Jordan had known about what Tripod was going to do to Anthony and Sasha. He'd hoped the robot would kill Daniel too and then he would have Catherine to himself. He'd planned the whole thing before they'd even left his cabin.

"Did you want some of the Quinta virus too? Daniel gave it to all of the patients with prosthetics." Dmitriy asked and she delved his memories. She couldn't help it, it was like working her own memory, a reflex. A part of him enjoyed the intimacy of sharing her mind, even the pain as she stumbled with her new abilities. It intrigued him, but also frightened him.

Inept. Bungling. She was causing so much pain to everyone around her. She tried to be calm, to focus on simple things.

"No, that's ... a muscle enhancer." She replied after replaying Daniel's explanation of the virus's effects from memories of her own that rebounded and merged with Dmitriy's.

"Oh, what were you doing? I felt like you were using my brain, like I was the co-pilot." Dmitriy remarked. "Do you think Daniel could do that too? Or anyone else with a microchip?" His thoughts immediately went to wanting one in his own head. To connect, to feel close to others. He felt like no one understood him. He wanted to merge with her again. He enjoyed the pain too, it made him feel alive. All the death around him, he was becoming numb.

"This is far beyond Daniel's capabilities." Jordan stood now, leaning against the counter a few feet from where Catherine still sat on the hospital bed. "When he tried to read my mind, or put a thought in, I could tell. It felt foreign. I could push him out, ignore his wishes. What she just did to me ... was complete and utter control." 'An utter violation,' he said in his mind.

"None of the other people with a Mod, that's what Daniel called it, could do anything special as far as I could tell. In fact, I noticed Daniel controlled people better when they had a Mod." Heliker added, he'd envied the power. But, after what Catherine showed him, he wanted nothing to do with it. He flinched when she looked at him.

"Her Mod is custom ... Catherine, what is it that you feel?" Jordan's mind wondered many things. It was hard to separate out the question he asked aloud, with the many he asked internally. It was also hard to look at him now, and not see the images of the people he had murdered. Those thoughts were burned into her brain as if she had done the acts of violence herself.

She shut her eyes and chose her words carefully, gradually saying, "I ... we ... so many voices ... so many ... images, thoughts, feelings ... I don't ... I don't know who I am anymore." The words rang in her mind, *Who am I?* Other voices tried to answer and she began her breathing exercise again. Centering.

"We can take it out, Catherine. It is obviously causing you pain ..." Heliker genuinely felt sorry for her, and feared what would happened if she ... sneezed? " ... and you keep giving me a headache every time you talk or look at me –"

She almost laughed, almost agreed to go back under the knife. Then recollections came flooding in to remind her of why she'd chosen to get the implant in the first place – recollections of Anthony dying, of the horror on Carl's face when he found out about Cybersausage and on Heliker's face when he found out about Esha. She replayed those thoughts for Heliker and he quickly shut up and changed his mind. "You're right, he has to pay for what he's done."

There was only one thing left to do. She mustered as much courage as she could find before saying, "Heliker, Dmitriy ... pack up. We're taking the helicopter now. Jordan, you're flying." She had tried to make the commands simple, clear ... but the pain her sharp words caused the three men started an unexpected chain reaction. A rush of voices. A rush of thoughts. "Quiet!"

The lights went out in the room and the men around her fell to the ground, holding their skulls. "I'm sorry." She focused on centering again. Breath. Exhale. Feel the air on your skin. Feel the cotton coveralls on your body. Breath. Center.

The men stood and their thoughts began again. *What's happening? Did she do that? What have we done!?! What have we created!!?!*

She focused on her breathing. Then she noticed the calmer she got, the calmer their thoughts got. She began to hold onto the thought this is for a good reason. For a purpose. They were safe, she meant them no harm.

The lights came back on, Heliker had managed to reach a back-up generator in the pitch black room.

Dmitriy, Heliker and Jordan were all scared. Their fear filled her but she let it wash over her instead of trying to stop it. She held onto the courage at her core, and the anger.

Dmitriy and Heliker helped her off the gurney and began packing up Daniel's supplies. She wanted everything out of here. This technology was not something she wanted any evidence of, anywhere.

Jordan said, "I will make sure the helicopter is ready," in his usual voice, with his usual stoic expressing ... but his thoughts betrayed him. He feared her, and wondered the extent of her abilities and if she would ever know how to control them. Wondered if he could ever trust his own mind around her again. He felt powerless, and weak, and he hated that more than anything. He had expected her to be like Daniel –he thought he could block Daniel, and could block Daniel's commands. But this, this was too much power. He couldn't handle it. He couldn't handle her in his head. There was too much he was ashamed of.

In the past she would have wondered at his cold expression. Gone over a hundred 'what ifs' and 'maybes' as she pondered, in circles, his choices. Now, she knew. She knew exactly what was going on ... how all the scenarios he played out in his head went. Those cold, calculated scenarios.

She watched him leave with that familiar, long, confident stride ... knowing Jordan could never feel the same about her again. Knowing that was the last time she would ever see him ... and she let him go.

~ ~ ~

River maps of the local area all showed the same thing–tons of small outlets, nothing major. The Snake and the Boise would be good for distributing to a few of the local settlements. The major systems were the Missouri to the north and the Colorado to the south. Lobbs' idea was brilliant. All the new settlements were off of rivers, the whole continent would be infected in a matter of days.

Dawson barged into the dimly-lit, cramped office without knocking. "Cliff, there is something going on. There is someone in my head, other than you."

"Are you hallucinating? A side effect of working too long on your augmented reality interface, maybe?" Cliff delved her thoughts, unnerved by the coincidence of a brief headache followed a few minutes later by an even stronger one that left him on his knees. He'd thought it was from breathing in all that radioactive dust in LA area earlier, or from not drinking coffee since noon. She'd felt what he'd felt, at the exact same time. "Who do you think it is?"

"I don't know, but I would bet a silver dollar that Daniel knows," she replied. "Where is he?" Her eyes glowed in the dim light.

"He was harder to convince than I anticipated ... I put him in one of the pods."

"I see." Her blank expression, and monotone voice, would never have revealed her thought, "I told you so," with the attitude of a teasing big sister.

Cliff sent her away. Sometimes he wished he couldn't read her mind.

He went back to studying the maps. A hologram of the new cities hovered over a projection of rivers, which sat on a physical map of aquifers. He jotted down the length of time it would take the new virus combination to move through the entire system, covering all city water supplies. Then added the amount of time for symptoms to begin, then the expected survival duration.

He began a human population query on a database within a computer sitting on a stand. The stand sat to the right of the mahogany office desk he was using for mapping inside the small office room. One hundred major cities on the North American continent.

He used a red ink pen to mark the physical aquifer map with the population density numbers. Then did more math on how many people would die versus how many he could control and when.

The figures weren't bad, better than expected. If Central played their part, an estimated 90% would survive. Ten percent was a small sacrifice for the future of unparalleled discovery and prosperity he envisioned for humanity.

If he could get the microchip facility up and running soon, the whole world could participate. An entire globe – united.

Cliff sat back in his chair and smiled. Daniel would see then, he'd be proud. He'd understand.

"What are you planning?" The thought reverberated in his head, unfamiliar and repeating with an excruciating clarity. A shadow hung over the maps and he glanced up to see Catherine Newton, the spitting image of Susan without glasses, standing outside the glass of the office door. She wore green coveralls and had her hair tied into a long braid. She opened the door and asked aloud, "Cliff, what are you planning?" The words echoed in his head, resonating with the thought bounding in his skull.

Cliff rubbed his temples and felt panic rising in his chest. He could think of nothing else but, "What are you planning?" and the pain in his head.

He commanded back, "I can't think. Stop it!" He used every ounce of his will. The pounding thought ceased.

Catherine braced herself on the other side of the mapping table. She had her eyes closed and took deep breaths. Slowly, and gently, she asked, "What are you planning, Cliff?"

"The dissemination of Quinta- R.V 376-2040 through the North America water supply." He said it before he could even think to not. Had she just made him tell her his plan?

"Why? What is that?" Her rapid response caused an ache in his cerebral cortex.

Cliff tried to block his mind to keep her out but couldn't. He went on the offensive – prodding her mind. He pushed thoughts of her sitting and explaining herself to him instead.

She crumpled into the chair opposite his, confused. A win.

"You are out of control, Catherine." Maybe he could convince her to take a valium ...

She squinted and his heartbeat rapidly increased, threatening to pound out of his chest. Unintentionally, he stood up and took the computer and threw it through the wall. Then he crushed the projector in his mechanical right hand and knocked the hologram machine from the ceiling. All without the ability to stop himself. She grinned as she said, "Am I?"

In his dreams she'd been a scared, mousy little thing. Imaginative, yes. Powerful, absolutely not. This was not the same person, it couldn't be.

"Is that how you saw me?" she whispered, eyes glazed, seeing something beyond her vision. Gently she said, "Sit."

Cliff sat so hard he almost broke the chair. His mind tried to work out if she was always like this of if Daniel had something to do with it. He pushed back. He questioned. A brief image of a microchip in a metal box, held by bloody, trembling hands. Before he could make out much more, the image of himself covered in tubes and electronics and sitting in a heavily modified wheelchair breached his imagination.

She spoke slowly, "That is how you are, in dreams. Why?" Her question had compelling force, but he couldn't answer. He had no idea why he appeared that way. Her words had more force as she said, "Crippled, barely alive. Heavily dependent on technology. This is how you see yourself, or how you expect others to see you."

Anger rose in his veins, boiling. "I'm far from dependent on anyone or anything!" He reached for the table. The next thing he knew the door was missing and shattered glass made a trail to where the table was now embedded in a machine on the factory floor across the hall.

Catherine stood aghast, body flush against the side wall of the small office. She hadn't expected his sudden outburst and barely got out of the way in time. She was far from off guard now though. He was unable to move a muscle – caught in a grimace and crouch, with arms flung out.

"You have quite a hot temper, don't you?" She asked, the words echoing in his mind again, causing a migraine of epic proportions. She squeezed her eyes shut and began to breath deeply. Then whispered, "Sit."

They both sat in office chairs, mere feet from each other, separated only by air. He felt her in his mind, digging around. Blundering from his childhood to his last memories of his parents.

"You hate being told what to do, don't you? But had no problem making Anthony kill people?" Her words were flat and delicately placed.

"Anthony?" The question was met with the image of a strappingly handsome young man. A man he'd seen in the aircraft hangar this morning wearing his prosthetics. "His mind was easiest to control, I needed to eliminate all threats."

"So easy for you, to kill."

Her judgement offended him. "It was self-defense. Daniel made me, if he hadn't left ... if he'd come when I'd asked –" Cliffs head abruptly throbbed, he rubbed his temples again.

"You blame Daniel?" Her voice pierced his brain, it was torture talking to her.

Cliff attempted to fight back. He showed her how he'd tried to get Daniel to come out of the building on his own and he refused. He showed her how he'd visited Daniel's dreams, asking him to come to Idaho so he could show him what he was working on. He sent images of what he dreamed the world would be and how Daniel wouldn't help. Images of flying cities, of people never dying. Medical enhancements –no more blind, deaf or impaired. No more hole in the ozone layer, no more global warming threat.

She fought back too. She fired back with images of Anthony dying, bullet wounds in his chest. Images of Anthony laughing with his sisters. Of a fluffy sheep dog licking Anthony's face. Of Anthony holding her, kissing her ... sharing his wishes for the future ... handing her a bouquet of wildflowers he'd picked himself.

"He was your boyfriend? I didn't know." Cliff admitted. He'd thought she was his brother's girlfriend ... it never occurred to him that she had another man in her life. He'd had hopes of seducing Catherine. If she was anything like Susan she would be a great asset. She was younger and more beautiful than Susan too, and the thought of stealing her from his brother made her even more enticing.

"Would it have changed anything, had you known I cared about Anthony?" She spoke gently. She genuinely wanted to know. Her guilt over Anthony's death was palpable. "Would you still have made him murder people against his will?"

"No." Another admission he didn't want to give. Never had another person controlled his mind like this, it felt wrong. Very, very wrong.

"Now you know what it's like."

Was this her way of punishing him? Had she come here to torment him for killing her boyfriend? Or, had she come to find Daniel?

"Where is Daniel?" Again, she didn't have a handle on her mind control. The question hit his brain like an anvil, leaving him unable to speak or even think. "Is he here?" Another anvil.

After a few seconds of suffering, he was able to get out, "You need help, Catherine. I can help you. You don't know what you're doing."

"Cliff! What happened?" Dawson and Ferris stood where the door used to.

Cliff's instinct was to get them to knock Catherine out, bludgeon her to stop the pain in his head. They didn't move, despite his best efforts. Both had wide eyes that darted rapidly between him and Catherine. Ferris began to convulse and Dawson's eyes glowed bright green.

They were caught in a mental vice. However, the distraction was enough for Cliff to gain control of his right hand. He charged the xenon plasma ray in his palm, aimed right at Catherine's troublesome head. The microsecond of buzzing it took to charge was enough warning for her to jump backwards, out of the glass office window and into the factory beyond.

The lights in the factory went out and came back on.

Cliff walked out of the room to finish Catherine off only to find that she was missing. Dawson and Ferris lay outside, faced down on the cement floor. How long ago had it been that he'd aimed the plasma blast at Catherine's face? It felt like seconds ago, but it couldn't have been.

He saw drops of blood leading off to the hallway on the left and took one step before noticing something out of the corner of his eye that made him turn around. People in dark blue smocks, the clothes Ferris had given to all of his 'volunteer' patients. Zombie-like, but moving quickly, they navigated around the machinery in the factory with their eyes focused only on him.

He tried to get them to stop with a mental command, only a few halted and were then trampled by the rest of the throng continuing forward. He held up the plasma ray and Dawson took hold of his arm, unsnapping it from his shoulder socket. The palm still emitted a beam and part of the ceiling and sidewall came down in a searing flash. He took Dawson by the neck and tossed her against the wall, were she lay wilted. He put his arm back on and began zapping the attackers coming to infect or kill him on Catherine's command.

Chapter 20

Love and Agony

Searing, excruciating, unadulterated pain emanated from Catherine's right arm, burnt beyond being able to touch it without even sharper agony. She couldn't see the damage, or find out how much remained because her vision was completely shot – retina singed from gazing into the intense light coming out of Cliff's palm. She'd barely escaped with her life, it all happened so rapidly.

She should have waited, she wasn't ready for this. Her impulse to seek retribution for Anthony's death, and for her own loss of self-identity, caused her to be rash. She'd hacked around Cliff's mind like a lumberjack in weeds. She had no idea what she was doing, and was up against a pro. A steep learning curve, and she'd taken a steep fall. Every ounce of concentration was now on stopping Cliff from killing her, and sending out a cry for help to all the voices nearby.

She had no idea how many voices there were ... dozens, hundreds, thousands. They filled her head as she plead for them to stop Cliff. Some spoke back to her, but she had no time for answers. Some of the closest voices were trapped in cells, and she used the ones that weren't to set the others free to go after Cliff.

Her left hand felt along the hallway wall, searching for a doorway or exit. She knew she needed to get out of firing range, fast. Her tremulous fingertips glided over a slick, chilly thing ... hard –a metal door handle. She nearly tripped on something on the floor inside a dust-filled, stuffy-air room ... the faint scent of bleach indicated it might be a broom closet. She slipped the door quietly closed behind her and collapsed to her knees.

Her mind played images like she was in Snowwolf's den. The visions were through the eyes of the others she had set loose to hunt down her attacker. Horrified, she watched, and felt everything. Cliff slaughtered them all. Burning them to the ground. They didn't even have time to scream. There was an instant feeling of pain like she felt in her arm, and then their voice in her head went silent. They had no chance against him despite the weapons some had taken up. If they hid behind equipment, he hunted them down. He took them out, one by one, ruthlessly.

She was afraid to reach out to Cliff, afraid he might find her if she touched his mind. He could go on the offensive like a viper. Scared to death of being bit by his venomous bite, she tried to touch his mind anyway – he had to be stopped. She couldn't watch anymore people die. His voice was tricky to find, he reacted so instinctively–without thought. Or, he was guarding his thoughts somehow.

She scanned the voices ... one stood out, familiar. A man stuck in a small enclosure, barely conscious, partly under some kind of heavy sedative.

"Daniel?" she asked, and his tremendous relief with the groggy thought, "Catherine!?!" confirmed her suspicion.

He sent images of the room where the pod he was in was located. He was here at the microchip manufacturing facility, in a room down the hallway. Not too far away.

Catherine found two people, near enough to get to Daniel's location, and gave them an urgent command to set him free. She added his location and likeness. They responded, recognizing parts of the factory ... one man even recognized the incubation pod, recognized Dr. Daniel Jahren.

She followed the man's mind, seeing through his eyes, centering on his reality. The view was odd, misshaped at the edges ... oh, he had on glasses. The big blue-green eyes under thick frames reflected in the pod window. He punched in numbers, the destabilization routine would take a half hour – too slow! He pulled out tubes and flipped a latch on the side. Another man in a blue smock reached into the pod and Daniel blinked into the light as he was heaved out.

Daniel's eyes flashed from bright beams to pure red, then to clear white glass. Then finally to white with moving black text ... computer code resetting. He breathed heavy and leaned on both men, swaying with vertigo and quivering.

After his eyes finally settled on his usual semi-normal brown-gold, he took a deep breath and demanded, "What is happening? Where is Cliff?"

Man, he was always so demanding! Wait, who is thinking that?

Catherine re-centered in her own mind, drawing into the feeling of her body inside the cleaning closet. Cold, dank. Searing pain in her right arm. The sudden chaos in her head and pain of her body were all consuming.

Breath. Just breath. Inhale. Exhale.

She heard a loud explosion that jolted her attention outward. Daniel. He'd found Cliff.

She discovered Daniel's mind again, this time he was fully conscious, fully aware. A stark difference. She clung to his control, fleeing the bedlam of her own mind, settling into his being.

"I feel you, I know you're here," he whispered softly to her. His focus was scattered but calm and collected, a balance within his own pandemonium. He felt her, himself and Cliff strongly as he aimed a sonic weapon embedded into his left hand to levitate objects into Cliff's path to block the plasma beams from incinerating people. He spoke to many other voices in his own head, telling them to run for safety. To escape, get as far away as they could.

"Daniel, I'm only trying to defend myself. Your little pet, Catherine, made them attack me!" Cliff dodged a trash bin aimed at his head, and then began heading straight toward us. "She's ... out of control. Did you give her some kind of new Mod?"

Papers flew, pens too. Light objects filled the air. We hid behind a pillar for cover. Cliff was getting closer.

"She's unstable. Can't you feel that? Her pain? Her agony? Let's make it stop!" His will was strong, urging us to seek that annoying Catherine out, to kill her.

Focus. It was all we could do to stop him from taking over. "Catherine, help me, please!" we begged. Cliff got closer, and the closer he got, the stronger his will.

We ran. The large equipment was harder to levitate, it took too long for the resonance to build. Still ... we aimed and hoped. "Catherine, please. Find yourself."

Separating the consciousness was harder than merging. Catherine managed to use her own heart beat to steady herself between the two beings. It was like a metronome to remind her of where her true center was. "Daniel, I don't know what to do."

"I believe in you. You can stop him." He was having difficulty finding things to throw in his brother's path. Cliff was agile. Daniel resorted to physically lifting and flinging objects. Anything he could find.

Cliff attempted to funnel him into a hallway where he would have a clear shot at Daniel's legs so he could stop him from running around and wrecking the factory. Daniel juggernauted through a wall, and knocked down a structural beam. The building began to rumble and shake.

"Stop it! You're destroying everything!" Cliff plunged to the left, barely missing the x-ray inspection module Daniel plucked from the ground and hurled at him. "Damn it! Lobbs and I spent hours rigging that to operate properly!"

Cliff was getting that look, the same one he got as a kid before going into a temperamental rage.

Catherine knew that meant she had to try something, and fast, before Cliff lost his mind and zapped Daniel to ash. She still felt blocked from Cliff's conscious, unable to find or penetrate it. So, in a last-ditch effort, she reached out everywhere and to everyone, yelling "Stop!"

Daniel froze. Cliff froze. She could feel their confusion. She could feel Cliff! Not knowing how long the window of opportunity would last, she demanded, "Take your arm off, put it on the floor." He didn't comply. She knew she would have to merge with his consciousness, he was too powerful at this distance. She settled into his thoughts, moved into his core.

Cliff fought back, trying to reject the control. "Get out of my head!" he screamed. Daniel was there too. He stood a foot away, glaring at us, but he was also in our mind.

"What have you done, Cliff? Why are you at an old microchip factory?" Daniel asked aloud, but also from within. He was masterful, using the question as an intimate suggestion. The request was a whisper on the mind that reflected the words. It tickled the senses of a specific part of the brain. A surgeon's precision.

"We've reformulated. I'm planning a global event." Cliff beamed proudly. Images of people in zombie-like states, clawing at walls with bloodshot eyes and black streaks on their bodies. Then, flashes of microchips implanted in skulls.

"How many will die for your plan? For your ambition?" Daniel's rage smoldered, but the focus was still there. Still razor sharp on the ever-reactive amygdala. "How many have died already?"

"A small percentage, only 534,562," Cliff replied. He added the numbers calculated by the current population to the ones he'd killed in the last few days. Then he added more when Catherine prodded him, reminding him about Anthony and the others at the hangar early this morning. "534,670 ... it would have been less if you had come with me ... if she hadn't sent people to attack me."

"Does that include our Father? Or Mom?" Daniel lost precision on that question, and his voice shook with rage and anguish.

Cliff fought and struggled to break free. Catherine had trouble holding on because of how disturbed she was at his callousness towards the deaths of all of those people. Even his parents he blamed on Daniel. She didn't want to be so intimate with thoughts like those, they felt like they infected her own being.

"If you would have believed in me, listened to me, none of this –" his screams interrupted the blame game he tried so hard to play. Catherine didn't want to hear it and neither did Daniel.

She forced him to see his own actions with his own two hands. Focused his thoughts on his own hand tossing his mother against the edge of a metal table, puncturing her lung with a broken rib. His own hand clasping the grenade between himself and his father, seeing the disappointment in his father's eyes before it exploded. He'd known the Kevlar would protect him and not his father. She made him watch his hand let go of a teenage girl, causing her to fall to her death below as she gazed up at him in fear-infused panic.

"What!?!" Daniel's fury broke the bonds of consciousness between the three of them. "You let her go!" He had his hands on Cliff's shirt in an instant, then pitched him through a wall.

Catherine scarcely held her grasp on Cliff's mind, but managed to kept him from defending himself. Because of her deep bond, she could feel his body slam into the thick cement like it was her own. His left shoulder and back hit like a sledgehammer, knocking the wind from his lungs and practically knocking him out too.

The lights in the factory flickered as energy surged, some of the lights on the factory ceiling erupted like fireworks.

"For so long I wanted to believe you were not pure evil." Daniel strode methodically to where Cliff lay limp on the floor. "Even mother and father ... I conceded were in self-defense." Daniel yanked Cliff by the arm and threw him into another wall.

Cliff squirmed in his mind, prying loose from Catherine's tenuous grip as Daniel approached again for more punishment.

He held Cliff up by the collar of his shirt. He frothed at the mouth in anger as he said, "Amy was an innocent young girl. You ruined her life! And for what? WHAT! TELL ME!!" The doctor's precision was gone, he was engulfed in pure rage.

Catherine's warning, "Watch out!" and a buzzing coming from Cliff's right hand broke through the red Daniel was seeing in time for him to catch Cliff's hand and aim it away. The ceiling melted away in a four-foot-wide hole.

For a few seconds the brothers were deadlocked. Both held the other's weaponized hands at bay. Both bombarded the other's mind. Then Daniel head butted Cliff, knocking him backwards.

Catherine crawled back into Cliff's mind during the weak moment after the head injury, slowly making her way into his core, trying not to be noticed. She didn't know what to do.

Cliff wanted his brother to be proud of him, to help him. That is all he ever wanted. He'd let go of Amy out of pure envy. It was heartbreakingly sad but also troubling because Cliff felt nothing for the girl who's life he ruined.

"Why couldn't you love me as much as you loved that trailer trash slut? You ignored me when she was around." Cliff aimed his weapon at anything that moved, directing plasma hot enough to melt part of Daniel's mechanical leg when he leapt to the right. "You would rather write her letters, and read poems about cats than help me with my crutches. My body was failing me, and so was my brother. I needed you."

Catherine hated being in this monster's head, but she knew she had to stop him, somehow. She concentrated on what made him move, made him-him.

She found something odd. Something like nothing she'd ever felt before, like *feeling* a bright light. Not warm, not cold. It gleamed within him and resonated within her. She realized she had a light as well. Her own light pulsed in time with his. Was this the Mod? Only one way to find out. With all her will, she blocked out his light.

Suddenly fully in her own body, she cried out in pain. The burnt arm throbbed, and a tingling numbness spread up her right side. The cacophony of voices was there to greet her too, a chorus of screeching and bawling in unison with her own.

She heard Daniel's voice in her head beg, "Catherine ... please ... stop!"

She reigned in her thoughts, feelings, bodily hurt. Breathing. Focusing. Trying the way Daniel had in his mind. Segmenting. Scattering the voices in a grid away from her core, but not shutting anyone out. Because when she tried to shut them out they screamed louder.

Calm, collected, Catherine found Daniel. With the delicate, surgeon-like focus she'd learned from briefly being one with his mind, she asked, "Where is Cliff?"

Cliff was being carried in Daniel's arms like a child. Eyes closed, peaceful. "He is in a coma. He has no consciousness, but he is still alive. What did you do?"

Catherine was relieved she hadn't killed him, she never wanted to kill him. She'd hoped she could change him. After being in his head it was hard not to have sympathy for him. However, she also realized she couldn't change him. His thinking was so … corrupt.

Daniel was relieved his brother was alive as well, though he had more mixed feelings. For instance, he felt it was fitting Cliff would suffer a coma, after what he did to Amy.

Daniel walked with Cliff in his arms to the incubation pod. He smoothly laid him inside and set it to a deep sleep. He closed the lid and felt like he was closing a coffin.

"Wasn't Amy your fiancé, Daniel?" Catherine probed, tenderly, not wanting to awaken the rage he'd gone into after seeing her fall. She realized why he didn't like that cliff, the one with the best view of the city of Desert Grand.

"Yes," Daniel answered and let pictures of his childhood sweetheart flow into Catherine's mind. She hadn't died that day on the cliff, she'd gone into a coma.

"My mother, did she … murder Amy?" Catherine played the dream with Cliff to Daniel, so Daniel could see why she'd run away from The Forsaken headquarters. She didn't want to face Daniel, knowing her mother had killed his fiancé. She'd thought the agony in Daniel's eyes was from how she reminded him of her murderous mother. That he'd wanted to take revenge.

Catherine gasped when he sent back scenes of her mother being taken away in handcuffs, of a trial and conviction. All entangled with emotions of profound betrayal.

"I'm so sorry, Daniel," she whispered aloud, sending condoling feelings his way. She wondered if he wanted revenge.

He answered her with more scenes, bits and pieces of clues that Cliff was controlling him during the time of Susan's trial. An odd feeling here and there, even a whole day he couldn't remember. Also, behaviors that were not normal for him, or his parents. Little things that added up. Then he showed how he broke Susan out of prison, even though he still wasn't sure if she'd murdered Amy.

Catherine realized the length and depth of Cliff's manipulation. And the depth of Daniel's love for Susan. There was no vengeance in his heart.

"Where are you?" he gently asked, his mental medical precision back in the request.

"Not far," she replied along with an abridged mental video of her earlier interaction with Cliff and the path her fingers felt along the wall to her hiding place.

He laughed, "You did all of this from a broom closet?" His affection for her made her giddy. A strange response, but it felt natural. He adored her tenacity.

The knob to the cleaning room felt just as cold and slick in Daniel's hand as it had felt in hers. Through his eyes she could see herself, in the fetal position, laying on her left side, on the grimy floor. There wasn't much left of her right arm and her eyes were glazed, staring far off. Her face was pink and her eyebrows were charred. The bottom of her braid that had laid over her right shoulder was missing.

"Dawson, Ferris! Get over here!" he yelled down the hallway and then seized her up and into his arms, careful of her wounds.

There was still a sharp jolt of pain from the movement. She braced her mind and body as best she could but most of the voices in her head felt it. Some moaned.

"I had no idea you would be so potent, Catherine," Daniel winced at the agony seeping from Catherine that went beyond empathy. "I had no idea you could generate pain in others."

"I'm sorry ... I'm trying to control it ... its ..." she gave him a taste of what she felt like inside, what went through her mind. When she'd showed the same thing to Heliker, he'd almost had a mental breakdown. Daniel, however, had no trouble following along, and understood completely. Daniel had an innate ability to grasp many ideas/concepts at once, which made him particularly good at mind control.

He smiled down at her, laying her on a medical bed in one of the clear-walled cell's she'd seen earlier. Ferris and Dawson prepped an IV and gathered surgical supplies. Daniel had been commanding them the entire time he followed her thoughts.

"Why didn't you stop Cliff yourself, Daniel?" She couldn't help but ask, realizing Daniel was highly adept in his mental abilities. He had skills well beyond her own. His precision made her look like a blundering fool.

"Catherine, you are far more powerful than I am and you still had trouble with Cliff." He added scenes to his words. Formulating the entire scene inside the aircraft hangar where Anthony shot people down while choking Sasha –Daniel barely fought Cliff back enough to get Anthony to stop killing everyone.

"I failed completely." He'd been forced to go with Cliff to save Anthony and also in the hopes it would keep Cliff from searching for Catherine. Daniel followed Cliff through the destroyed barrier wall and back to a hovercraft Cliff had parked nearby. As he got into the vehicle, Cliff injected him with a sedative that Daniel hadn't even seen coming.

"I had no chance against him. You did far more today than you know. Maybe you are rough around the edges, but when you have twenty years of sharpening your skills like I do, you will be capable of so much more than you can imagine now. You must have gotten the implant in only hours ago. That reminds me ..." he delved her brain, drawing out the journey she'd been on since he'd last seen her.

Catherine re-lived the last forty-eight hours. Not at all what she wanted to do but she knew Daniel needed to know. Together they felt the heartbreak of Anthony's last breath. The fascination she felt watching her mother. The turmoil that came in waking with the implant. The abandonment as Jordan walked out. Then the courage she mustered to immediately get to the helicopter and to go straight to Cliff.

"You're so brave."

"Brave? I hid in a broom closet, remember," she reminded him. "I should have waited to come here."

"You had lost Anthony, and then *Jordan* ... you were distraught, angry ... I know how you felt." He showed her the night he found out Luca, the murderer who'd killed a man named Jordan just to take his identity, had kidnapped her. Daniel cared so much about her, at the risk of death, or waking up his brother, he'd set an detonation and dug through the rubble for hours to reach her.

"You did that all for me? Why?" She could feel his desperate emotions, his need to protect her at all costs. So much he'd sacrificed, so much he'd risked–all for her.

He wiped the tears from her eyes, and then cupped her chin with his hand. He opened his mind freely to her so she would know everything. She delved and he didn't even brace himself, he let her move through his mind without resistance.

When he made it out of the mine, he'd frantically searched everywhere, only to find her underneath her car and half the hillside. He'd lifted the car and flown her straight to the hospital. The joy Daniel felt when she finally woke up a week later made Catherine smile, it was infectious.

She searched those moments she'd feared she reminded him of the love he'd lost. Where she thought there was loss and sadness over a love long gone, she found something entirely different. Daniel felt tragedy. The tragedy of loving someone, or wanting to kiss and hold someone that did not love him. Someone who he barely dared to hope would, one day, love him back. The moments of agony in his eyes where when he held back the affection he feared would drive her away. He didn't think his shattered heart could handle losing her too.

"We're ready." Dr. Brooke Dawson said in a monotone voice that was in stark contrast to her excitement over getting to put in another set of ocular implants –her favorite invention. She'd made some improvements and couldn't wait to see how they worked on a patient.

Dr. Ferris laid a right arm and socketing interface on a cart and said, "This is one of the ones Cliff brought. He was tinkering with a new design." Ferris wasn't happy about Cliff being put in a pod, he practically worshipped Cliff. It took constant nudging from Daniel to keep Ferris in line.

Catherine's heart skipped a beat when she realized who the implants were for. Eyes. A right arm. She would be a cyborg soon, like Daniel. "Were these the special plans you had for me, all along, Daniel?" In her mind she added, "Turning me into a cyborg like you?"

He brushed her hair back from her face, kissed her cheek softly and then tenderly said, "Not at all."

Right before the anesthesia hit and she went unconscious, she got the image of a beautiful dream. In the dream Daniel held her hand, she smiled into his warm golden eyes while they walked in a field of dewy grass and shimmering wildflowers at twilight.

Epilogue

The snake river wound in front of Dr. Steven Lobbs as he drove over a small bridge. When he'd dumped a container of grey liquid upstream in the water, it floated away on the white crested, fast moving current with no reaction. The water had been clear. That was thirty minutes ago. The harsh noon sunshine made his eyes squint and tear-up, maybe they were playing a trick on him. Was the water really black? He pulled over on the other side of the bridge and trotted down to the riverfront. He placed his hand in the cool steam, his fingers came back black as death.

❄ ❄ ❄

Thank you for reading.

Please review this book. Reviews help others find Absolutely Amazing eBooks and inspire us to keep providing these marvelous tales.

If you would like to be put on our email list to receive updates on new releases, contests, and promotions, please go to AbsolutelyAmazingEbooks.com and sign up.

ABOUT THE AUTHOR

H.A. Burns lives in a rainy Seattle suburb with her fur babies: a Siberian Husky, an orange tabby cat and an equally scruffy husband. She has been an engineer in the aerospace industry ever since proudly graduating with a degree in Materials Science & Engineering from the University of Washington in Seattle, WA. She has been telling stories to entertain her four siblings her whole life and is constantly coming up with book ideas inspired by dreams, advancements in science and technology, and all the interesting people she meets. Being a busy professional engineer, she would jot down the ideas and say "One Day" to turning them into full novels for many years until a debilitating battle with Ulcerative Colitis stripped her of her ability to do anything else. She realized then that it is amazing what you can do with a laptop on a toilet if you put your mind to it and ignore the smell. Literally making the most of a crappy situation, with literature.

ABSOLUTELY AMAZING eBOOKS

AbsolutelyAmazingEbooks.com
or AA-eBooks.com

22080968R00375

Made in the USA
San Bernardino, CA
14 January 2019